THE FAR
PAVILIONS

M.M. KAYE
THE FAR PAVILIONS

VOLUME TWO

ST. MARTIN'S PRESS NEW YORK

Plan of Kabul Residency drawn by
Reginald Piggott

There had been little conversation that night, as all three travellers were tired, and once in bed Ash had slept better than he had for many weeks.

His bed had been put out on a partially screened roof for greater coolness, and awakening in the pearly hot-weather dawn he looked down from the parapet and saw Zarin at his prayers in the garden below. Waiting until these were over, he went down to join him and walk and talk under fruit trees that were full of birds greeting the new day with a clamour of cawing and song. The talk had been mainly of the Regiment, for the subject of Gulkote could keep until Koda Dad was ready to listen, and Zarin had closed the long gap of the past year by bringing Ash up to date on a number of matters that for one reason or another he had not wished to entrust to a bazaar letter-writer. Details concerning his personal life and items of news about various men of Ash's old troop: the possibility of trouble with the Jowaki Afridis over the construction of a cart-road through the Khyber Pass, and the doings of those who had provided an escort for the *Padishah*'s eldest son, the Prince of Wales, when he visited Lahore during the past cold weather.

The Prince, said Zarin, had been so pleased by the bearing and behaviour of the Guides that he had written to his august mother, who had replied by appointing him Honorary Colonel to the Corps, and commanding that in future the Guides should be styled 'The Queen's Own Corps of Guides' and wear on their colours and appointments the Royal Cypher within the Garter (Zarin's translation of this last would have startled the College of Heralds considerably). By the time they had eaten the morning meal the sun was up, and after they had paid their respects to the lady of the house—who received them seated behind an ancient and much broken *chik* through which she could be plainly seen, but which preserved, if only technically, the rules of *purdah*—they were free to seek out Zarin's father.

It was already too hot to be abroad, so the three of them had spent the day in the old, high-ceilinged room that had been allotted to Koda Dad because it was the coolest in the house. Here, protected from the heat by *kus-kus* tatties, and sitting cross-legged on the uncarpeted floor of polished *chunam* that was pleasantly cool to the touch, Ash told for the third time the tale of his journey to Bhithor, this time with few evasions, telling it all from the beginning and leaving nothing out—save only that he had lost his heart to the girl who had once been known to all of them as 'Kairi-Bai'.

Zarin had interrupted the tale with questions and exclamations, but Koda Dad, never a talkative man, had listened in silence, though it was to him rather than to Zarin that Ash spoke. The discovery of Hira Lal's earring had drawn a grunt of surprise from him and the account of Biju Ram's death a grim nod of approval, while a smile had commended Ash's handling of the Rana's attempt at blackmail. But apart from that he had offered no comments, and when at last the tale was ended, he said only: 'It was an ill day for Gulkote when its Rajah's heart was caught by the beauty of an evil and covetous woman, and many paid for his folly with their lives. Yet for all his faults he was a good man, as I know well. I am sad to hear that he is dead, for he was a good friend to me during the many years that I lived in his shadow: thirty-and-three of them . . . for we were both young men when we met. Young and strong. And heedless . . . heedless . . .'

He sighed deeply and fell silent again, and after a moment or two Ash realized, with an odd sensation of panic, that Koda Dad had fallen into the light sleep of old age. It was only then that he noticed for the first time how many physical changes had come about since their last meeting: the thinness of body that the voluminous Pathan dress had partially disguised, and the many new wrinkles that seamed that familiar face; the curiously fragile appearance of the parchment-coloured skin that had once been so brown and leathery, and the fact that under the brave scarlet dye, hair and beard were now snow-white . . . and very scanty.

Ash would have noticed this at once had he not been so taken up with his own affairs, yet now that he had done so the change both shocked and frightened him, bringing home to him as nothing else could have done the shortness of the human span and the terrifying swiftness of Time. It was as though he had come without warning upon one of those mile-stones that long after they are passed, stand out in one's memory as marking the end of a phase—or perhaps a turning point?—and something of this must have shown in his face, for when he looked away and caught Zarin's gaze there was both understanding and compassion in it.

'It comes to all of us, Ashok,' said Zarin quietly: 'He is now well past his seventieth year. There are not many who live as long; and few who have been as contented with their lot. My father has been fortunate in that he has had a full life and a good one; which is surely as much as anyone can ask of God. May we two be granted the like.'

'*Ameen,*' said Ash under his breath. 'But I—I did not realize . . . Has he been ill?'

'Ill? This is not a sickness—unless old age be one. This is no more than the weight of years. And who is to say that he will not see many more of them? But among our people, seventy is accounted a great age.'

Ash knew that to be true. The men of the Border hills lived hard lives, and a tribesman was considered old at forty while his wife was often a grandmother before she was thirty, and Koda Dad had already exceeded the three-score-years-and-ten that had been promised to the descendants of Adam. Of late Ash had begun to think of life as far too long, and to see it in imagination as an endless road stretching away ahead of him and leading nowhere, along which he must walk alone; yet now, abruptly, he saw that it was also cruelly short, and was unreasonably shaken by this commonplace discovery. Zarin, who was still watching him and knew him well enough to follow his train of thought, said consolingly: 'There is still myself, Ashok. And the Regiment also.'

Ash nodded without replying. Yes, there was still Zarin, and the Regiment: and when he was allowed to return to Mardan there would be Wally also, and Koda Dad's village lay only a mile or so beyond the Border and a short march away. Koda Dad, who had suddenly become so old . . . Studying the old Pathan's sleeping face, Ash saw the lines of character that were engraved there as clearly as the lines of time: the kindness and wisdom, the firmness, integrity and humour, written plain. A strong face; and a peaceful one. The face of a man who has experienced much and come to terms with life, accepting the bad with the good and regarding both as no more than a part of living—and of the inscrutable purpose of God.

Reviewing his own achievements by the light of Koda Dad's long and eventful life, it struck Ash with stunning force that they could be summed up as a brief list of sorry failures. He had begun by making an utter fool of himself over Belinda and ended by losing Juli. And in between he had failed George, proved himself to be an intractable and disappointing officer, and—indirectly—caused the death of Ala Yar. For had it not been for his quixotic behaviour in the matter of the carbines, Ala Yar would still be alive and probably, at that moment, gossiping comfortably with Mahdoo on the back verandah of a bungalow in Mardan.

To set against that it could be said that he had saved Jhoti's life, avenged the deaths of Hira Lal and Lalji, and succeeded in rescuing Karidkote's reputation and treasury from disaster. But that was poor compensation for the dismal tale of his previous failures; or for the fact that his brief and passionate love-affair with Juli could only add to her unhappiness in the life to which her own loyalty had doomed her—a life that he did not dare allow himself to think about.

There were few things, in these days, that he cared to look back on; and even less that he could look forward to. But among the former there had always been Koda Dad, a source of wisdom and comfort and a rock to lean upon. Koda Dad and Zarin, Mahdoo and Wally. Only four human beings out of all the teeming millions in the world; yet of immeasurable importance to him. And he was about to lose them. When Koda Dad and Zarin recrossed the Indus and Wally left for Mardan in a month's time, he would be unable to follow them, for they would have entered territory from which he himself was excluded until the Guides agreed to take him back again—which, for all he knew, might not be for years. If so, this could well be the last time he would ever see Koda Dad.

As for Mahdoo, he too was growing old and frail; and if Koda Dad, the immutable, could crumble in this fashion, how much more so could Mahdoo, who did not possess half the old Pathan's stamina and must be at least his equal in age? It did not bear thinking of. Yet he thought of it now, grimly and despairingly, seeing his life as a fragile house—an empty one, since there was no Juli—which once he had planned to cram with treasure. A house supported by four pillars, two of them now almost worn out and in the nature of things unlikely to last very much longer . . . When those two fell, as one day they must, the walls might still stand. But if a third were to fail, his case would be desperate, and if all went, the house would crash to the ground and break apart, exposing its emptiness.

Koda Dad's head nodded and fell forward, and the movement awoke him: 'So now there is a new ruler in Gulkote,' said the old man, continuing the conversation where it had ended when he dozed off. 'That is good. Provided he does not take after his mother. But if

God wills, his father's blood will prove stronger; and if so Gulkote—
Chut! that is no longer the name. I forget the new one, but no matter.
It will always be Gulkote to me and whenever I think of it, it is with
affection; for until the mother of my sons died, my days there were
pleasant ones. A good life . . . Yes, a good life. Ah! here is Ha-
bibah. I did not realize that it was so late.'

When the sun dipped behind the hills and the air began to cool,
Ash and Zarin went out to exercise the horses in the dusty evening
light, and when they returned it was to find that the Begum had invited a number of her brother's old friends and acquaintances to dine
with them, so there had been no further opportunity for private talk
that night. The next day was Sunday, and as Zarin must be back in
Mardan in time to prepare for parade on Monday morning (which in
the hot weather was at 5.30 a.m.), father and son would be leaving
some time after nightfall. The three spent that day as they had spent
the previous one, talking together in Koda Dad's room and resting
during the heat of the afternoon, and towards evening the Begum
sent a servant to tell Zarin that his aunt wished to see him on some
matter connected with the possible purchase of land near Hoti Mardan, and Ash and Koda Dad went up to the roof to catch the cooler
air as the sun went down behind the hills around Attock.

It was the first time they had been alone together, and in an hour
or so Koda Dad would be gone and there was no knowing when they
would meet again. But though Ash would have given a great deal to
be able to ask for advice and comfort as he had done so often in the
past, both as a child in Gulkote and a junior subaltern in Mardan, he
could not bring himself to do so. The problem was too personal and
the wound still too raw, and he shrank from probing either, and
made conversation instead: talking of his coming leave in Kashmir
and the prospects of shooting, in a light, cheerful voice that would
have deceived ninety-nine people out of a hundred but failed entirely
to deceive Koda Dad.

The old Pathan listened and nodded, but did not speak. Then, as
the sky took fire from the setting sun, the first stirring of the evening
breeze carried a faint, high-pitched cry from the distant city. *'La
Ill-ah ha! il ill-ah ho!'*—'There is no God but God!' It was the voice
of the muezzin from the minaret of a mosque in Attock, calling the
Faithful to prayer, and Koda Dad rose to his feet, and unrolling a
small mat that he had carried up to the roof, turned to face Mecca
and began his evening prayers.

Ash looked down from the parapet and saw that several of the household were doing the same in the garden below, and that the aged porter was also at his devotions in the road outside the gate. He watched them for a moment or two as they knelt, bowed their heads to the dust, rose and knelt again, muttering the traditional prayers that were said at this hour; and presently he turned away to face the north-east where, hidden by the heat-haze and the dust and distance, lay the Dur Khaima. But he did not say his own prayer—that ancient Hindu invocation that he had adopted so long ago. He had meant to, but before the words could shape themselves, his mental picture of the goddess of his childhood faded, and he found himself thinking instead of Juli.

He had told her that he would think of her every hour of every day, yet he had tried not to do so; partly because he had not been able to bear it, and also because he had decided that his only hope lay in taking her uncle's advice and putting the past behind him. It had been like barring a door and throwing all his weight against it to keep out a flood that was building up outside, and though it had been impossible to prevent trickles from that flood seeping under the lintel and through cracks in the wood, he had managed somehow to shut out the worst of it. But now, suddenly, the bars snapped and the door gave way, and he was drowning in the same savage tide of love and anguish and loss that had swept over him in Kaka-ji's tent when he realized that he had made his last appeal and lost; and that he would never see Juli again . . .

Koda Dad finished his prayers and turned to see Ash standing by the parapet with his back towards him, facing the 'Pindi road and the eastern horizon where a full moon was drifting slowly up into the sky as the sun sank down in the glowing, dusty, golden West. The rigidity of that back and the spasmodic clenching and unclenching of the lean, nervous hands told Koda Dad almost as much as the determined lightness of Ash's conversation had done, and the old man said quietly:

'What is amiss, Ashok?'

Ash turned quickly—too quickly, for he had not given himself time to control his features, and Koda Dad caught his breath in the involuntary hiss that greets the sight of a fellow-creature in physical agony.

'*Ai, Ai,* child—it cannot be as bad as that,' exclaimed Koda Dad, distressed. 'No, do not lie to me'—his uplifted hand checked Ash's automatic denial—'I have not known you since your seventh year for nothing. Nor have I become so blind that I cannot see what is written on your face, or so deaf that I cannot hear what is in your voice; and I am not yet so old that I cannot remember my own youth. Who is she, my son?'

'*She*—?' Ash stared at him, startled.

Koda Dad said dryly: 'You forget that I have seen you troubled in some such manner before—only then it was calf-love and no more than a boy's foolishness. But now . . . now I think it cuts deeper; for you are no longer a boy. It is Kairi-Bai, is it not?'

Ash caught his breath and his face whitened. 'How did you . . . But you can't . . . I did not—'

He stopped, and Koda Dad shook his head and said: 'No, you did not betray yourself in words. It was those you did not speak that warned me of something amiss. You told of two brides and spoke of the younger one by name, describing her and telling of things that she had said and done. But save when you could not avoid it you did not mention the elder, and when you did, your voice changed and became without feeling and you spoke as though there was a restraint upon you. Yet this was that same Kairi-Bai whom we all knew, and to whom you owed your escape from the Hawa Mahal. Yet you told us almost nothing of her and spoke of her as you would have spoken of a stranger. That told its own tale. That, and the change in you. It could be nothing else. Am I not right?'

Ash smiled crookedly and said: 'You are always right, my father. But it shames me to learn that I can be so transparent and that my face and voice are so easily read.'

'There is no need,' said Koda Dad placidly. 'No one but myself could have done so—and then only because of my long knowledge and affection for you, and because I remember the old days very clearly. I will not press you to tell me anything that you do not wish, but I am troubled for you, my son. It grieves me deeply to see you so unhappy, and if I can be of any help—'

'You have always been that,' said Ash quickly. 'I leaned upon you as a child and I have done so again and again when—when I was a raw recruit. Also I know well that had I taken your advice more often I would have saved myself much sorrow.'

'Tell me,' said Koda Dad. He seated himself cross-legged on the warm stone, prepared to listen, while Ash leaned on the parapet, and looking out across the Begum's garden to where the Indus glowed red-gold in the sunset, told all those things he had left out of his tale on the previous day, omitting only the happenings of one night . . .

When he had finished, Koda Dad sighed and said inconsequentially: 'Her father had great courage and many good qualities, and he ruled his people wisely—but not his own household. There he was both weak and idle, being one who greatly disliked tears and arguments and quarrelling. *Hai mai!*'

He fell silent, brooding on the past, and presently he said: 'Yet he too never broke a promise. If he gave his word, he kept it, as befits a Rajput. Therefore it is only right that Kairi-Bai should do likewise, as from what you have told me I see that she has inherited only the good. This you may see only as your misfortune, yet in time I think you will come to see that it was best for both of you that she had the courage to keep faith, since had she done as you desired (and lived to tell of it, which I think unlikely) you would not have found happiness together.'

Ash turned from his contemplation of the darkening river and said harshly: 'Why do you say that? I would have done anything—everything.'

Once again Koda Dad's sinewy, authoritative hand checked him: 'Do not talk like a child, Ashok. I do not doubt that you would have done all that was in your power to make her happy. But it is not in your power to build a new world; or to turn back time. Only the One God could do that—were it necessary. And it would be very necessary for you! I myself have had little or no experience of your people, but I have sons and kinsmen who know the ways of the Sahib-log; and having ears to hear, I have listened and learned much during the years since I left Gulkote. Now as I do not believe that all I have heard can be lies, you, Ashok, will now listen to me.'

Ash smiled faintly and sketched a mock-humble salute, but Koda Dad frowned him down and said sharply: 'This is not a matter for jest, boy. Once, long ago, in the days when the rule of the Company Bahadur' (he meant the East India Company) 'was young and there were no memsahibs in Hind, the Sahibs took wives from among the women of this land and none spoke against it. But when the Company waxed strong their ships brought out many memsahibs, and the memsahibs frowned upon this practice, openly despising all those who associated with Indian women—above all, those who married them—and showing scorn and contempt towards the children of mixed blood. Seeing this, the people of Hind were angry and they too

set their faces against it, so that now both regard it with equal disfavour. Therefore neither Kairi's people nor yours would have permitted a marriage between you.'

'They could not have stopped us,' declared Ash angrily.

'Maybe not. But they would have tried. And if you had persisted,
and made her your wife, you would have found that few if any mem-
log would have consented to meet her or invite her into their houses,
or allowed their daughters to enter hers; and none would treat her as
an equal—not even her own people, who would do likewise, and
speak ill of her behind her back because she, a king's daughter, must
accept such treatment from many *Angrezi* women whose own parents were far less well-born than hers. They would despise her as the
Rana and his nobles did, because her grandfather was a *feringhi* and
her mother a half-caste; for in this respect, as you will have learned
in Bhithor, her people can be as cruel as yours. It is a failing common to all races, being a matter of instinct that goes deeper than
reason: the distrust of the pure-bred for the half-breed. One cannot
overcome it, and had you brought Kairi-Bai away with you, you
would have discovered these things soon enough—and discovered too
that there would be no refuge for you here; your Regiment would not
have wished to have you back, and other Regiments would not have
been anxious to accept one whom the Guides had rejected.'

'I know,' said Ash tiredly. 'I too had thought of that. But I am not
a poor man, and we should have had each other.'

'*Beshak*. But unless you lived in the wilderness, or made yourselves a new world, you would also have had neighbours—native-
born villagers or townsmen to whom you would have been foreigners. You might well have learned to like their ways and earned
their friendship and acceptance, and in the end been content. But
bardast (tolerance) is a rare flower that grows in few places and
withers too easily. I know that the path you now tread is a hard one,
but I believe it to be the best for you both; and if Kairi-Bai has had
the courage to choose it, have you so much less, that you cannot accept it?'

'I have already done so,' said Ash: and added wryly, 'There was
no choice.'

'None,' agreed Koda Dad. 'Therefore what profit is there in repin-
ing? What is written is written. You should rather give thanks for
that which was good, instead of wasting your time in fruitless regret
for what you cannot have. There are many desirable things in life be-

sides the possession of one woman, or one man: this even you must know. Were it not so, how lonely and desolate a world it would be for the many, the very many, who through ill-luck or by reason of being ill-favoured, or from some other cause, never meet that one? You are more fortunate than you know. And now,' said Koda Dad firmly, 'we will talk of other things. The hour grows late and I have much to tell you before I go.'

Ash had expected him to talk of mutual acquaintances in villages beyond the Border, but he had spoken instead of far-away Kabul, where, so he said, agents and spies of the 'Russ-log' had recently become so numerous that there was a jest in that city that out of every five men to be met with in the streets, one was a servant of the Tsar, two were taking bribes from him and the remaining two lived in hopes of doing so. The Amir, Shere Ali, had scant love for the British, and when Lord Northbrook, the recently retired Governor General, had refused to give him any firm assurance of protection, he had turned instead to Russia, with the result that during the past three years relations between Britain and Afghanistan had deteriorated alarmingly.

'It is to be hoped that the new Lat-Sahib will come to a better understanding with the Amir,' said Koda Dad. 'Otherwise there will surely be another war between the Afghans and the Raj—and the last one should have taught both that neither can look to gain advantage from such a conflict.'

Ash observed with a smile that according to Kairi's uncle, the Rao-Sahib, no one learnt over-much from the mistakes of their parents and even less from those of their grandparents; for the reason that all men, using hindsight, were convinced that they could have done better, and in trying to prove it either ended up making the same mistakes, or new ones that their children and their children's children would criticize in their turn. 'He told me,' said Ash, 'that old men forget, while young ones tend to dismiss events that occurred before they were born as ancient history. Something that happened very long ago and was naturally mismanaged, considering that everyone involved—as can be seen by looking at the survivors—was either a creaking grey-beard or a bald-headed old fool. In other words, their own parents, grandparents, uncles and aunts.'

Koda Dad frowned at the lightness of his tone, and said with a trace of sharpness: 'You may laugh, but it would be as well if all those who like myself can remember that first war against the

Afghans, and all who like you and my son Zarin Khan had yet to be born, would consider that conflict, and what became of it.'

'I have read of it,' returned Ash lightly. 'It does not make a pretty tale.'

'*Pretty!*' snorted Koda Dad. 'No, it was not pretty, and all who engaged in it suffered sorely. Not only Afghans and *Angrezis,* but Sikhs, Jats and Punjabis and the many others who served in the great army that the Raj sent against Shere Ali's father, the Amir Dost Mohammed. That army won a great victory, slaying large numbers of Afghans and occupying Kabul, where they remained for two years and doubtless expected to stay for many more. Yet in the end they were forced to abandon it and to retreat through the mountains— close on seventeen thousand of them, men, women and children, of whom how many think you reached Jalalabad? One!—one only out of all that great company who marched out of Kabul in the year that my son Awal Shah was born. The rest, save for some few whom the Amir's son took into custody, died among the passes, butchered by the tribes who fell upon them like wolves upon a flock of sheep, for they were weakened by cold, it being winter and the snow lying deep. Some four months later my father had occasion to pass that way, and saw their bones lying scattered thick for mile upon mile along the hillsides, as though . . .'

'I too,' said Ash, 'for even after all these years, many are still left. But all that happened very long ago, so why should it disturb you now? What is wrong, Bapu-ji?'

'Many things,' said Koda Dad soberly. 'That tale that I have just told you, for one. It is not so old a tale, since many men still living must have seen what my father saw, and there must also be others, far younger than myself, who took part in that great killing and later told their sons and grandsons of these things.'

'What of it? There is nothing strange in that.'

'No. But why is it that now of a sudden, and after so many years, the tale of the destruction of that army is being told again in every town and village and household throughout Afghanistan and the lands that border upon it? I myself have heard it told a score of times in the past few weeks; and it bodes no good, for the telling of it breeds conceit and over-confidence, encouraging our young men to think scornfully of the Raj and to belittle its power and the strength of its armies. And there is another curious thing: the teller is nearly always a stranger, passing through. A merchant perhaps, or a Powin-dah, or some wandering mendicant; a holy man on pilgrimage or someone on a visit to relatives in another part of the country, who has asked for a night's lodging. These strangers tell the story well, making it live again in the minds of folk who first heard it ten, twenty, thirty years ago, and had almost forgotten it, but who now retell it to each other and become boastful and full of wild talk. I have begun to wonder of late if there is not something behind it. Some plan . . . or some person.'

'Such as Shere Ali, or the Tsar of Russia?' suggested Ash. 'But why? It would not pay Shere Ali to embark on a war with the British.'

'True. But it might please the Russ-log if he should do so, for then he would hasten to ally himself to them so that he might call upon them to aid him. All the Border knows that the Russ-log have already swallowed up much of the territory of the Khans; and were they to gain a firm foothold in Afghanistan, who knows but that they might one day use it as a base for the conquest of Hind? I for one have no desire to see the Russ-log replace the Raj—though to speak truth, child, I would be happy to see the Raj depart from this land and the Government return once again to the hands of those to whom it rightfully belongs: the native-born.'

'Like myself,' observed Ash with a grin.

'*Chut!* You know very well what I mean—to the men of Hind whose land this is and whose forefathers owned the soil, not to foreign conquerers.'

'Such as Barbur the Mogul, and other followers of the Prophet?' asked Ash wickedly. 'Those were also foreigners who conquered the land of the Hindus, so if the Raj goes, it may well be that those whose forefathers owned the soil will next expel all Mussulmans.'

Koda Dad bristled wrathfully, and then, as the truth of the observation struck him, relaxed again and said with a rueful laugh: 'I confess I had overlooked that. Yes indeed. We be foreigners both: twice over, I being a Pathan and you . . . you neither of this country or of *Belait*. But the Mussulmans came here many centuries ago, and Hind has become their homeland—the only one they know. They are grafted onto it too strongly to be separated: wherefore—' He checked, frowning, and said: 'How did we come to be talking of these things? I was speaking of Afghanistan. I am troubled by what is brewing beyond the Border, Ashok, and if it is possible for you to speak a word into the ear of those in authority—'

'Who—*me?*' interrupted Ash, and gave a shout of laughter. 'Bapu-ji, you cannot be serious. Who do you suppose would listen to me?'

'But are there not many Burra-Sahibs in Rawalpindi, Colonel-Sahibs and General-Sahibs to whom you are known, who would listen to you?'

'To a junior officer? And one who could produce no proof?'

'But I *myself* have told you—'

'That certain men are going from village to village in the Border country, telling the tale of something that happened long before I was born. Yes, I know. But what someone else has told me is not proof. I should need more than that if I expected to be believed—much more. Without it they would laugh at me; or more likely give me a sharp reprimand for wasting their valuable time with a pack of bazaar rumours, and suspect me of trying to make myself seem important.'

'But surely,' urged Koda Dad, puzzled, 'your elders in Rawalpindi must hold you in high favour now that you have just completed a difficult mission with honour? Had they not thought well of you, they would never have chosen you for such work in the first place.'

'You are wrong there, my father,' said Ash bitterly. 'They chose me only because it offered a chance to remove me as far as possible from my friends, and from the frontier. And because Hindustani is my mother-tongue and the work required someone who could both speak and understand it with ease. That was all.'

'But now that you are back, having done well—?'

'Now that I am back they must find some other way to get rid of me until such time as my Regiment is willing to receive me again. Until then I am merely a nuisance. No, Bapu-ji, you would do better to ask Awal or Zarin to speak to Battye-Sahib or the Commandant. They would at least be given a hearing, which I should not.'

'What is that I am to say to Battye-Sahib?' asked Zarin's voice from behind them. His feet had made no sound on the stone stairway, for as Fatima Begum did not permit the wearing of shoes in her house, they had not heard him approach.

'*Billah!* I am getting deaf in my old age,' said Koda Dad, annoyed. 'It is as well that I have no enemies, for a babe could stalk me in the open. I did not hear you; and Ashok, who should have done so, was talking so loudly that his ears were full of the sound of his own foolish words.'

Zarin and Ash grinned at each other, and Ash said: 'Alas, Bapu-ji, they were not foolish. I still lie under the disfavour of those in authority, both in Rawalpindi and Mardan, and until I have served my sentence you cannot expect any words of mine to carry weight with them. Besides, they must know these things already. They have spies everywhere; or if they have not, they should have.'

'What is the talk?' asked Zarin, seating himself beside his father. 'What things should already be known?'

'Your father,' said Ash, 'tells me that there is trouble brewing in Afghanistan, and he fears that unless it is nipped in the bud it may lead to an alliance between the Amir and the Russ-log: which in turn would lead to another war.'

'Good! We could do with one,' approved Zarin. 'We have eaten idleness for too long, and it is time we were given a chance to fight again. But if the Sirkar fears that Shere Ali will permit the Russ-log to gain control of Kabul, or the tribes allow them to occupy the country, then they know nothing of the Amir or his people.'

'True . . . that is true,' conceded his father. 'And if this new Lat-Sahib' (he meant Lord Lytton, who had succeeded Lord Northbrook as Viceroy and Governor-General) 'can be prevailed upon to tread carefully, using patience and friendship and much wisdom in his dealings with the problems of the Amir and the people of Afghanistan, then all may yet be well. But should his councillors continue on the present course, I am very sure that the end will be war, and though when I was young I too relished fighting and danger, I find that now I am old I have no wish to see villages burned and crops laid waste, and the bodies of all those who once lived there lying unburied; food for the foxes and the carrion crows.'

'Yet the mullahs tell us that no man dies before his time,' said Zarin gently. 'Our fates are written.'

'It may be,' admitted Koda Dad doubtfully. 'But that is something else that of late I have become less sure of; for how can the mullahs —or even the Prophet himself?—read all the mind of God? There is also another thing—I have still three sons (for I count Ashok here as one), all of them *jawans** who serve in a regiment that will be among the very first to be called upon to fight if there should be another war

---

* Literally young men: but also used colloquially to mean soldiers.

with Afghanistan; and though you will say I am growing womanish, yet I would prefer that they were not cut down in their prime but lived, as I have done, to see their sons grow to manhood and beget many grandsons; and when they die at the last that they should die full of years and contentment . . . as I, their father, will do. Therefore it distresses me to hear the whispers that go up and down the Frontier, and to see the storm clouds gather.'

'Do not fear, Bapu-ji,' consoled Ash, stooping to touch the old man's feet. 'A wind will arise and blow these clouds away, and you can be at ease again—while your three sons bite their nails for idleness, and quarrel with their friends for lack of an enemy to fight.'

'*Thak!*' (let be) snorted Koda Dad, preparing to rise. 'You are as bad as Zarin. You think of war only as a game or as a chance to obtain promotion and honour.'

'And loot,' added Ash with a laugh. 'Do not forget the loot, my father. I spent eight days in Kabul searching for Dilasah Khan, and it is a rich city.'

He reached down a hand to help the old man to his feet, but Koda Dad brushed it aside and rose without assistance, settling his turban and remarking austerely that the young displayed too much levity and not enough respect for their elders. 'Let us go down. It is time that we ate, for I must see my sister and also rest awhile before we start our journey back.'

They ate together in the open courtyard, and afterwards went up to pay their respects to Fatima Begum and to thank her for her hospitality. The old lady kept them gossiping for well over an hour before dismissing them to get what sleep they could before midnight; at which hour a servant awakened them and they rose and dressed, and leaving that hospitable house, rode away together down through Attock to the bridge of boats.

The Indus was a wide expanse of molten silver under the blaze of the full moon, and as ever, the voice of the 'Father of Rivers' filled the night with sound, hissing and chuckling between the tethered boats that jerked and strained against the current, and rising to a sustained thunder downstream where the gorge narrowed. It was not too easy to make oneself heard above the river noises, and none of the three attempted it. There was, in any case, nothing more to be said, and when they dismounted at the bridge head to embrace as sons and brothers in the Border country are accustomed to do on meeting or parting, they did so without words.

Ash helped Koda Dad to remount, and taking one of the old man's hands in both his own, pressed it to his forehead, holding it there for a long moment before he released it and stood back to let the two men ride forward onto the bridge. The horses' hooves rang loud on the tarred planks, like drum beats tapping out a counterpoint to the roar and chuckle of the river. But the sound diminished swiftly, and all too soon it merged with the noise of water and was lost.

The sentry on duty at the bridge yawned largely and lit a cheap bazaar-made cigarette, and Ash's horse, taking exception to the sudden fizz and splutter of the sulphur match and the brief flare of light, threw up its head and began to snort and sidle. But Ash did not move. He waited until the two horsemen reached the far side, and as they breasted the rise of the road, saw the taller of the two lift a hand in farewell and the other check his mount to look back. At that range it was impossible to make out his features, but the moonlight was brilliant enough to show that familiar nod of admonition, and Ash smiled and held up both his hands in a gesture of acceptance. He saw Koda Dad nod again as though satisfied, and the next moment father and son rode on, and Ash watched them grow smaller and smaller until they reached a turn in the Peshawar road and were swallowed up by the shadow of the hillsides.

'You do not go with your friends, then?' asked the sentry idly.

For a moment it seemed as though Ash had not heard the question, and then he turned and said slowly: 'No . . . no, I cannot go with them . . .'

'*Afsos,*' commiserated the sentry with easy sympathy, and yawned again. Ash bade him good-night, and mounting the restive horse, rode back alone to the Begum's house where he was to spend the remainder of the night and the best part of the following day.

The old lady had sent for him next morning and they had talked together for over an hour—or rather the Begum had talked while Ash, separated from her by the split-cane *chik,* had listened, and occasionally answered a question. The rest of the time he had been left very much to himself. For which he was grateful, as it gave him a much needed period of quiet in which to think over what Koda Dad had said on the subject of Anjuli; and when he left the Begum's house shortly after moonrise, he was in better spirits and a more equable frame of mind than he had enjoyed for some considerable time; and with a quieter heart. He did not press his horse, but took the sixty-odd miles at a leisurely pace, and having changed into his own clothes in a convenient cane-brake, arrived back at the rest-house by the Murree road well before the moon was down. The temperature in his room was well over a hundred and the *punkah* did not work, but he had spent the day there, and left on the following morning for the pines and the hill breezes of Murree.

Wally had joined him a day later, and the two had trekked into Kashmir by way of Domel and the Jhelum gorge, and spent a month camping and shooting among the mountains beyond Sopore. During which time Wally had grown a short-lived beard, and Ash an impressive cavalry moustache.

It had been a halcyon interlude, for the weather had been perfect, and there had been endless things to talk about and to discuss. But though Ash, while again omitting any reference to Juli, had told Wally in some detail about his visit to Fatima Begum's house, oddly enough (or perhaps understandably, considering how preoccupied he had been with his personal problems) he had not thought to mention Koda Dad's tale of trouble brewing beyond the Border. It had slipped his mind, for he had, in fact, not paid over-much attention to it: there was always trouble on the Frontier, and the affairs of Afghanistan did not interest him as much as his own.

Half-way through July the weather broke, and after enduring three days of pouring rain and impenetrable mist on a mountain side, the campers beat a hasty retreat to Srinagar, where they pitched their tents in a grove of *chenar* trees near the city, and made arrangements to return by tonga along the cart-road—the prospect of long marches on foot through a continuous downpour being too dismal to contemplate.

After the keen, pine-scented air of the mountains, they found Srinagar unpleasantly warm and humid, the city itself a squalid jumble of ramshackle wooden houses, crammed together and intersected by insanitary alleyways, or narrow canals that smelt like open sewers —and frequently were. But the Dal Lake was ablaze with lotus blossoms and alive with the flashing blue and green and gold of innumerable kingfishers and bee-eaters, and they bathed and lazed, gorged themselves on the cherries, peaches, mulberries and melons for which the valley was famous, and visited Shalimar and Nishat—the enchanting pleasure gardens that the Mogul Emperor, Jehangir, son of the great Akbar, had built on the shores of the Dal.

Yet all too soon, like all pleasant times, the careless, sun-gilt days were over and they were being rattled and jolted along the flat cart-road to Baramullah at the mouth of the valley, and from there into the mountains and the pouring rain; clattering through vast rock gorges and forests of pine and deodar, jogging through the streets of little hill villages, and along tracks that were no more than narrow shelves scraped out of mountainsides that dropped sheer away to where the foam-torn Jhelum River roared in spate three hundred feet below.

They were not sorry to see Murree again, and to be able to sleep in beds that were both dry and comfortable, though Murree too had been swathed in the mist and rain of the monsoon. But as they jogged down the endless turns of the hill road, the clouds thinned and the temperature rose, and long before they reached the level of the plains they were back again in the gruelling heat of the hot weather.

Mahdoo was back from his holiday in his home village of Mansera beyond Abbottabad, and feeling, he said, rested and greatly refreshed. But though he looked much the same, it was clear that the long journey to Bhithor and that headlong return in the worst of the hot weather had left its mark on him, and that he like Koda Dad Khan was beginning to feel his age. He had brought a young relative with him: a good-tempered, gangling youth of sixteen with a deeply pock-marked face, who answered to the name of Kadera and would in time, said Mahdoo, become a good cook: 'For if I am to have a "makey-learn", I prefer to choose my own and not be worried by some *chokra* who cannot be trusted to boil water, let alone prepare a *burra khana!*'

The bungalow smelt stalely of mildew and lamp-oil and overpoweringly of flowers, the *mali* (gardener) having filled every available jar with tight bunches of marigolds and zinnias, and there was a pile of letters on the hall table, mostly mail from Home and addressed to Wally. Two, not in English, were for Ash, and both had been written over six weeks ago and described the ceremonies and festivity that had accompanied the installation of the new Maharajah of Karidkote. One was from Kaka-ji and the other from Mulraj, and both had thanked Ash yet again for his 'services to their Maharajah and the State', and passed on messages from Jhoti, who appeared to be in high feather and wanted to know how soon the Sahib would be able

Three Dog Bakery
727 State St.
Santa Barbara, CA 93101

Reference 3 Dog - 41037
12/01/2002 02:33:30 PM

Clerk: Mariela O

1   Ad152b511c $12.00T
       tUb. Munch bucket-bones, cookies

                   SubTotal $12.00
                        Tax $0.93

                     Total $12.93
                     Cash $20.00

                   CHANGE $7.07

7 Day return with original
bag and receipt. No returns   on
treats-food/chews, or sale items.
<Thank You>

to visit Karidkote. But apart from that reference to his 'services', there had been no mention at all of Bhithor.

'Well, what else did I expect?' thought Ash, folding away the sheets of soft, hand-made paper. As far as Karidkote was concerned that chapter was closed, and there was no point in turning back the pages when there was so much to look forward to. Besides, in India the posts were still slow and uncertain, and the distance between the two states of Karidkote and Bhithor was roughly the same as that which separated London from Vienna or Madrid. It was also unlikely that the Rana, having failed to cheat the late Maharajah, would wish to correspond with his successor or encourage Jhoti's sisters to do so.

That same evening, their first back from leave, Wally had suggested that they drop in at the Club to look up various friends and hear the latest news of the station, but as Ash preferred to stay and talk to Mahdoo, he had gone there alone—to return two hours later with an unexpected guest: Wigram Battye, who was also on his way back from leave.

Lieutenant Battye had been shooting on the borders of Poonch, and Wally, meeting him on the Mall and hearing that he intended to spend a day or two in 'Pindi, had insisted that he would be far more comfortable in their bungalow than at the Club (which was not strictly true) and brought him back in triumph. For though Ash still held first place in Wally's regard, Wigram came a close second, not only because he happened to be a likeable and very popular officer, but because his eldest brother, Quentin—killed in action during the Mutiny—occupied a special niche in Wally's private hall of fame.

Quentin Battye had taken part in that famous march to the Ridge of Delhi when the Guides, at the height of the hot weather, had covered close on six hundred miles in twenty-two days, storming a rebel-held village on the way, and going into action within half an hour of their arrival at the Ridge, despite having marched thirty miles since dawn. The battle had been Quentin's first and last. He had been mortally wounded ('*noble Battye, ever to the fore*' wrote Captain Daly in his diary that evening), and dying a few hours later had muttered with his last breath the words of a famous Roman: '*Dulce et decorum est, pro patria mori.*'

Wally, himself a patriot and a romantic, had been moved by that story and fully approved the sentiment. He too considered that to die for one's country would be a good and splendid thing, and in his eyes

Quentin's brothers, Wigram and Fred, both now serving with the Guides, were tinged with the gold of reflected glory, as well as being what he termed 'cracking good fellows'.

Wigram, for his part, had taken to young Walter Hamilton at their first meeting over a year and a half ago, which was in itself no small tribute to Wally's character and personality, considering that the meeting had been arranged by Ash, whom Wigram regarded as being wild to a fault—not to mention the fact that young Hamilton obviously regarded him as some sort of hero instead of a thoroughly difficult and insubordinate junior officer who, in the opinion of his seniors (and they included Lieutenant Battye), had been more than lucky to escape being cashiered.

In the circumstances, Wigram might have been forgiven if he had decided to steer well clear of Pandy Martyn's protégé. But it had not taken him long to realize that there was nothing slavish in the younger man's attitude towards Ashton, and that his admiration for him did not mean that he would try and emulate his exploits. Walter's head might be in the clouds, but both his feet were firmly on the ground, and he had a mind of his own. 'A good boy,' thought Wigram. 'The kind who will make a first class Frontier officer, and who men will follow anywhere because he will always be out in front . . . like Quentin.' Wigram had made a point of seeing what he could of Ensign Hamilton whenever duty or pleasure brought him to Rawalpindi, and had spoken so warmly of him to the Commandant and the Second-in-Command that it was largely due to his efforts that Walter had been offered a commission in the Corps of Guides.

Ash was not unaware that Wigram, as a dedicated soldier, regarded him with a certain amount of disapproval, and though they were on tolerably good terms, and on the whole got on well together, that it was Walter's company that Wigram enjoyed, and Walter who brought out the best in Quentin's quieter, steadier brother, making him laugh and relax and behave as though he too was a young ensign again.

Watching them now as they joked and talked together, Ash could only be grateful for Wigram's presence, though at any other time he might well have felt a twinge of jealousy at Wally's obvious admiration for the older man, and the fact that they had plainly seen a good deal of each other during the eight months that he had been away, and become fast friends. But he had not been looking forward to these last few days in the bungalow, with the rooms strewn with reminders of Wally's departure and the loneliness that would follow, and Wigram's presence would not only help to make the time pass quicker, but ease the strain of parting from the only real friend he had ever made among men of his own blood.

It would also help Wally, since as Wigram was leaving on the same day they would be riding together, which not only meant that Wally would have a companion on the journey, but that he would arrive in Mardan in the company of one of the most popular officers in the Corps. That alone should guarantee him a flying start, and his own engaging personality, together with the excellent reports that Zarin would have carried back, would do the rest.

Ash had no fears for Wally's future in the Guides: he had been born under a bright star and would one day make a great name for himself. The sort of name that he, Ash, had once imagined himself making.

The bungalow had seemed very quiet after Wally had gone, and there were no more martial hymns from his bathroom of a morning. It also seemed intolerably empty—empty and over-large, and depressingly squalid.

Ash had not noticed until now how dilapidated it had become, or how shoddy were the few bits of furniture they had hired at an exorbitant monthly rate from a contractor in the bazaar. He had thought it comfortable enough before, and despite certain obvious drawbacks, even friendly. But now it appeared sordid and inhospitable, and the smell of mildew and dust and mice that pervaded it was an active offence. The room that had been Wally's study and bedroom already looked as though it had been unoccupied for years, and the only proof that he had ever slept and worked there was a torn scrap of paper that appeared to be part of a laundry list.

Looking about that empty room, Ash was conscious of an uncomfortable conviction that he had lost Wally. They would meet again, and certainly see a good deal of each other in the future once he himself was allowed to return to the Regiment. But time and events would be bound to loosen the close ties of friendship that at present existed between them. Wally would find other and worthier men to admire—Wigram, for one—and because he was bound to be liked and to make friends wherever he went, he would be an immensely popular officer and an asset to the Guides. Ash did not do him the injustice of imagining that he would allow any new friendship to diminish the old one, yet its quality was bound to alter at the will of circumstances and pressures, and what officialdom termed 'the exigencies of the service'.

The morning had been dark and overcast, and now a gust of wind, forerunner of one of the violent monsoon rainstorms that periodically drenched the plains, swept through the deserted room, setting the *chiks* flapping and bringing with it a small cloud of dust and dead neem leaves from the verandah beyond. It sent the crumpled fragment of paper, sole relic of Wally's occupation, bowling across the matting to Ash's feet, and he stooped and picked it up, and smoothing it out saw that it was not a laundry list. The poet had been jotting down rhymes—

Divine. shine. pine. mine. wine? Valentine. en . . .

En—? 'Entwine?' pondered Ash, amused. Or perhaps something more exotic, like 'encarnadine'—? (Wally's verse was apt to be peppered with such words). Ash wondered whom he had been addressing, and if one day he would meet a girl who would not only attract his passing fancy, but capture it and keep it for good. Somehow he could not picture Wally as a sober and settled *pater familias*. As a love-lorn suitor, yes. But a suitor who took good care not to press his suit too hard or allow himself to be taken too seriously, and who preferred to pursue some unobtainable She.

'The fact is,' mused Ash, 'that he enjoys paying court to pretty girls and scribbling poems bewailing their cruelty or praising their eyebrows or ankles or the way they laugh, but that's about as far as it goes, because the thing he is really in love with is glory. Military glory, God help him. Until he gets that out of his system, no girl has a ghost of a chance. Oh well, he's bound to grow out of it one of these days: and out of me too, I suppose.'

He turned the scrap of paper over and discovered on the reverse side part of an exercise in Persian. Wally had evidently been translating a passage from Genesis into that language, and it occurred to Ash that this crumpled fragment of paper provided an accurate sketch of the boy's character, in that it bore evidence of his piety, his attempts to write verse, his light-hearted philandering, and his dogged determination to pass the Higher Standard in Languages with Honours. The translation proved to be a surprisingly good one, and reading the graceful Persian script, Ash realized that Wally must have been studying even harder than he had thought—

. . . set a mark upon Cain, lest any finding him should kill him.

*And Cain went out from the presence of the Lord, and dwelt in the
land of Nod, on the East of Eden . . .*

Ash shivered, and crumpling up the scrap of paper into a ball,
flicked it away as though it had stung him. Despite his upbringing, he
was not overgiven to superstition and a belief in omens. But Koda
Dad had talked of trouble in Afghanistan and been disturbed by the
possibility of another Afghan war, because the Frontier Force Regiments would be the first to become involved; and Ash knew that
among men of the Border country, and thoughout Central Asia, it is
believed that the plain of Kabul is the Land of Cain—that same Nod
that lies to the East of Eden—and that Cain's bones lie buried beneath
a hill to the south of the city of Kabul, which he is said to have
founded.

The link was far fetched, and the fact that Wally had selected that
particular passage for translation could hardly be termed a coincidence, for he had recently been reading the memoirs of the first
Mogul Emperor, Barbur the Tiger, and on learning of that legend,
had obviously been sufficiently interested to look up the story in
Genesis, and later use it as an exercise in translation. There was
nothing in the least remarkable about it, decided Ash, ashamed of
that superstitious shiver. But all the same, he wished that he had not
read the thing; because that part of him that was and always would
be Ashok saw it as an ill-omen, and not all the Western scepticism of
the Pelham-Martyns or those years at an English public school could
wholly succeed in convincing him that this was absurd.

A second gust of wind whisked the little ball of paper under the
flapping *chik* and across the verandah into the dusty waste of the
compound beyond, and the last trace of Wally's occupancy had gone.
And as Ash closed the door against the whirling dust the first drops
of rain splashed down, and in the next moment the day was dark and
full of the roar of falling water.

34

The downpour lasted over the weekend. It laid the dust and lowered the temperature, and flooded out the snakes who lived in holes below the bungalow and among the tree roots, and who now took up residence in the bathrooms and between the flower pots on the verandah —from where they were evicted by the servants to the accompaniment of much shouting and noise.

Unfortunately it had not been possible to evict Captain Lionel Crimpley, who moved into the bungalow on the Monday in place of Wally, for there happened to be a severe shortage of accommodation in Rawalpindi at the time, and if it had not been Crimpley it would have been someone else. Though Ash was of the opinion that almost anyone else would have been preferable.

Lionel Crimpley was a good ten years older than Ash, and he considered that his seniority should have entitled him to better quarters. He deeply resented having to share half a bungalow with a junior officer, and made no secret of the fact—or that he disliked everything about the country in which he had elected to serve, and regarded its inhabitants as inferiors, irrespective of rank or position. He had been genuinely horrified when a few days after his arrival he had heard voices and laughter coming from Ash's room, and on walking in without knocking, discovered the owner enjoying a joke with his cook who, to make matters worse, was actually smoking a hookah.

To give Crimpley his due, he had supposed that Ash must be out and that his servants had taken advantage of his absence to sit around in his chairs and gossip. He had apologized for his intrusion and left, looking inexpressibly shocked, and that evening at the Club had described the disgraceful incident to a like-minded crony, one Major Raikes, whose acquaintance he had made when their respective regiments were stationed at Meerut.

Major Raikes said that he was not at all surprised; there had been some very queer rumours going around concerning young Pandy Martyn. 'If you ask me, there's something deuced fishy about the feller,' pronounced Major Raikes. 'Speaks the lingo a sight too well, for one thing. Mind you, I'm all for bein' able to speak it well enough to carry on out here, but that don't mean one need speak it so well that one could pass for a native provided one was blacked up.'

'Quite so,' agreed Lionel Crimpley, who, though like all Indian Army officers had had to pass the set language examinations, had never added to a meagre vocabulary or outgrown an unmistakably British intonation.

'Any case,' continued Major Raikes, warming to the subject, 'hob-nobbin'' with these people on equal terms don't do us any good as a race. What happened in '57 could happen again if we don't see to it that the natives have a proper respect for us. You ought to speak to young Pandy Martyn, y'know. High time someone did, if he's started getting pally with his *nauker-log* (servants).'

Captain Crimpley had thought the advice good and acted upon it at the first opportunity. And Ash, who had been fortunate enough not to have encountered this particular viewpoint before (the Crimp-ley–Raikes species being a rarity), had begun by being amused, but on discovering, with incredulity, that his mentor was perfectly seri-ous, ended by losing his temper. There had been an unfortunate scene, and Lionel Crimpley, enraged at being addressed in such op-probrious terms—and by an officer junior to him in rank—had com-plained to the Brigade Major, demanding an immediate apology and the offender's head on a platter, and insisting that he, Crimpley, be given other and more suitable quarters, or if that was not possible, that Lieutenant Pelham-Martyn should be expelled from the bunga-low instantly, as he himself refused to remain under the same roof as any insolent, abusive, unlicked cub who smoked and gossiped with the servants, and moreover . . .

There had been a good deal more on this head, and the Brigade Major had not been pleased. He held no brief for Captain Crimpley, or for Captain Crimpley's views, but then neither did he approve of Lieutenant Pelham-Martyn's, for his own were strictly middle-of-the-road and he disliked extremes. In his opinion, the attitudes of both Crimpley and Pelham-Martyn were equally displeasing, and neither could be held blameless. But as no junior officer must be allowed to hurl abusive epithets at one senior to him, whatever the provocation, Ash had received a sharp dressing-down, while Crimpley for his part had been brusquely informed that for the time being both he and Lieutenant Pelham-Martyn would remain where they were, as no al-ternative accommodation could be provided for either of them.

'And serve them right,' thought the Brigade Major, pleased with himself for this judgement of Solomon and unaware how severe a punishment he had inflicted on both offenders.

The best that either could do was to see as little of each other as their cramped quarters permitted, but the next few months had not been pleasant ones, even though the Captain did little more than sleep in the bungalow, and took all his meals in the mess or at the Club. 'Couldn't possibly bring myself to eat or drink with a fellow of that stamp,' confided the Captain, airing his grievances to his friend Major Raikes. 'And if you ask me, our Government is making a great mistake in allowing that sort of outsider to come to this country at all. They ought to recognize the kind and weed 'em out at once.'

'Crimpley,' wrote Ash angrily, describing him in a letter to Wally, 'is precisely the type of supercilious, bone-headed bastard who ought never to be allowed to set foot in this country, for he and his kind can ruin the life-work of a thousand good men by a single fatuous display of rudeness and insularity. Thank God there are only a very few of them. But even one would be too many, and it is depressing to think that our descendants will probably accept the view that dear Lionel was "typical", and that the whole damned lot of us, from Clive onwards, were a bunch of pompous, insular, overbearing and mannerless poops!'

Ash had many acquaintances in the cantonment, but no close friends. He had not needed any while Wally had been there, and now that Wally had gone he did not trouble to make any others among his fellow Club members, largely because he preferred to see as little as possible of Crimpley, who could always be found at the 'Pindi Club out of office hours. Instead, he took to spending much of his free time in the company of men like Kasim Ali or Ranjee Narayan, sons of well-to-do middle-class men who lived with their families in large, rambling houses set in leafy gardens on the outskirts of the city, or in tall flat-roofed ones in the city itself. Merchants, bankers, cultivators and landowners, contractors or dealers in gems. The solid, sober backbone of any city.

Ash found their company much more relaxing and their conversation more to his taste than anything that he could find in social gatherings within the cantonments, for their talk ranged over a much wider field of subjects—theology, philosophy, crops and trade, the problems of local government and administration—and was not confined to horses, station-scandal and military 'shop'; or to the politics and squabbles of democratic nations on the far side of the world.

Yet even here he was not wholly at ease, for though his hosts were unfailingly kind and extended themselves to make him feel at home, he was always conscious of a barrier, carefully disguised, but still there. They liked him. They were genuinely interested in his views. They enjoyed his company and were pleased that he should speak their tongue as well as they themselves did . . . But he was not one of them. He might be a welcome guest, but he was also a *feringhi:* a foreigner and a member of the foreign Raj. Nor was that the only barrier—

Because he was not of their faith or their blood, there were certain things that they did not discuss with him or mention in his presence; and though their young children came and went freely and accepted him without question, he never caught so much as a glimpse of their women-folk. When visiting Ranjee Narayan's house or in the homes of Ranjee's relatives and friends, there was also the barrier of caste, for many of the older generation could not (to quote Captain Crimpley) 'bring themselves to eat or drink with a fellow of that stamp', because their religious beliefs forbade it.

Ash saw nothing odd in this, for he realized that one cannot change immemorial attitudes in a decade or two. But there was no denying that it tended to make social intercourse between the Orthodox and the Outsider a difficult and somewhat delicate business.

There had been talk that cold weather of an important conference to be held in Peshawar between the representatives of Great Britain and the Amir of Afghanistan, on the question of a treaty between the two countries. The political implications of this had been the subject of much discussion in Rawalpindi—and indeed throughout the Northern Punjab—but despite what Koda Dad had told him, Ash had not paid over-much attention to it, mainly because he seldom went to the Club or the mess and so missed a good deal that he might otherwise have heard.

Zarin had managed to visit Rawalpindi once or twice during the autumn, and Wally had actually been able to get a week's leave at Christmas, which he and Ash had spent shooting duck and snipe on the Chenab near Morala. The week had passed very pleasantly, but by contrast the long days that succeeded it seemed even more tedious, though Wally wrote regularly and Zarin at intervals, and once in a while there would be a letter from Kaka-ji that brought news of Karidkote and messages from Jhoti and Mulraj; but no mention of

Anjuli—or of Bhithor. Koda Dad too wrote, though only to say that he was well, and that things were much the same as they had been at the time of their last meeting—which Ash took to be a reminder that the situation he had spoken of last summer still prevailed and showed no signs of improving.

Captain Crimpley, who occasionally caught sight of one of these letters (the post was laid out daily on the hall table), spoke scathingly at the Club about Pandy Martyn's correspondents, and hinted that they should be investigated by Intelligence. But apart from Major Raikes, no one paid any attention to these allegations. The Captain and his crony were not popular with their fellow members, and it is unlikely that they could have done Ash much harm if it had not been for the affair of Mr Adrian Porson, that well-known lecturer and globe-trotter . . .

January and February had come and gone. The days were warm and sunny, and Mr Porson was among the last of these birds-of-passage to appear in Rawalpindi, the genus preferring to be out of the country well before the first of April. He had already spent several months seeing India under the aegis of such exalted personages as Governors, Residents and Members of Council, and was at present staying with the Commissioner of Rawalpindi, *en route* to his final port of call, Peshawar, before returning to Bombay and Home. The object of this tour had been to acquire material for a series of critical lectures on 'Our Eastern Empire', and by now he considered himself to be an authority on the subject, and had chosen to air his views to a group of members at the 'Pindi Club one early March evening.

'The trouble is,' said Mr Porson in a voice trained to carry to the back rows of a hall, 'that as I see it, the only Indians you people out here care to know are either Maharajahs or peasants. You would seem to have no objection to hob-nobbing with a ruling prince and pronouncing him to be quite a "decent sort of chap", but, one asks oneself, how is it that you fail to make friends with Indian men and women of your own class? That, if you will forgive plain speaking, one finds inexcusable, as it indicates a degree of shortsightedness and prejudice, not to say racial snobbery, that must strike any thinking person as offensive in the extreme. Particularly when one compares it with the patronizing indulgence extended to your "faithful old servants" that you speak so highly of—the subservient "Uncle Toms" who wait on you hand and foot and care for all your creature comforts, the—'

It was at this point that Ash, who had dropped in to pay a Club bill and paused to listen to Mr Porson's discourse, was moved to intervene:

'It would be interesting, sir,' observed Ash, in a tone that cut across those rolling periods like acid, 'to know why you should sneer at faithfulness. I had always supposed it to be one of the Christian virtues, but obviously, I was wrong.'

The unexpectedness of the attack took Mr Porson aback, but only momentarily. Recovering himself, he turned to look the interrupter up and down, and then said blandly: 'Not at all. One was merely endeavoring to illustrate a point: that in this country, all you Anglo-Indians obviously get on admirably with your inferiors and enjoy the company of your betters, but make no effort at all to make friends with your equals.'

'May one ask, sir,' inquired Ash with deceptive mildness, 'how many years you have spent in this country?'

'Oh, shut up, Pandy!' muttered an anxious acquaintance, jerking warningly at Ash's coat-sleeve. *'Stash it!'*

Mr Porson, however, remained unruffled, not because he was used to being heckled (the type of audience he was accustomed to lecture to were far too well-bred to interrupt the speaker), but he could recognize a heckler when he saw one, and now he sat back in his chair, smoothed his waistcoat, and placing the tips of his plump fingers together, prepared to deal with this boorish young Anglo-Indian:

'The answer to your question, my dear sir, is "none". One is only a visitor to these shores, and—'

'One's first visit, I presume?' cut in Ash.

Mr Porson frowned, and then, deciding to be tolerant, laughed. 'Quite right. I arrived in Bombay in November, and alas, I leave again by the end of this month; one's time is not one's own, you understand. But then someone like myself, a mere visitor with a fresh eye and an open mind, is, I fancy, better qualified to see flaws in a system, it being a true saying that "The onlooker sees most of the game!"'

'Not in this case,' said Ash shortly. 'The particular flaw you have singled out is one that a great many globe-trotters and temporary visitors have noticed and commented on, but as far as I know, none of these critics has stayed here long enough to practise what they preach. Had they done so, they would very soon have discovered that in nine cases out of ten the boot is on the other foot, for the middle classes in this country—like their counterparts in any other one—are a pretty conservative lot, and it is they more often than the Anglo-Indians who call the tune. I am afraid, sir, that you fall into an error common to superficial observers when you accuse your countrymen of cold-shouldering them. It is not nearly as simple as that, because it's by no means a one-sided affair, you know.'

'If by that you mean what I think you mean,' intervened Major Raikes angrily, 'then, by George, I'd like to say—'

'A moment, please!' said Mr Porson authoritatively, quelling the interruption with a firm gesture of one podgy hand. He turned back to Ash: 'But my dear young man, one is, of course, prepared to believe that many Indians of this class might hesitate to invite into their homes *some* of the British whom one has, oneself, had occasion to meet out here. (One need not particularize, need one? No names, no pack-drill!) But surely it should be the duty of every one of you to do all in your power to break down the barriers and get on close terms with these people? Only by doing so can you come to understand one another's view-point, and help to forge those bonds of loyalty and mutual respect without which our Raj cannot hope to retain its hold on this country.'

This time it was Ash who laughed, and with a genuine amusement that made Mr Porson stiffen angrily. 'You make it sound very easy, sir; and I won't pretend that it isn't possible, because of course it is. But what makes you think that they really wish to make friends with us? Can you give me one good reason, one single one, why they should?'

'Well, after all, we are—' Mr Porson stopped himself just in time, and actually blushed.

'Their conquerors?' said Ash, finishing the sentence for him. 'I see. You feel that as members of a subject race they should be gratified to receive invitations from us, and be only too eager to welcome us into their own homes?'

'Nothing of the sort!' snapped Mr Porson, his empurpled countenance betraying only too clearly that this was precisely what he had thought—though he would certainly have put it in different words. 'I merely intended—What I meant to say was . . . Well, one has to admit that we are in a—in a position to offer a great deal in the way of—of . . . Western culture, for instance. Our literature. Our discoveries in the fields of medicine and science and . . . and so on. You had no right to put words into my mouth, Mr—er . . . ?'

'Pelham-Martyn,' supplied Ash helpfully.

'Oh.' Mr Porson was somewhat taken aback, for he happened to be acquainted with several Pelham-Martyns and had once lunched at Pelham Abbas, where, having monopolized the conversation through two courses, he had received one of Sir Matthew's stinging set-downs. The episode was still green in his memory, and if this outspoken young man should be related to that family—

'If I did you an injustice, sir, I apologize,' said Ash. 'It was a natural assumption, as a great many visitors do seem to hold that view—'

Had he stopped there, the chances are that he would have been back in Mardan that summer, and much that came later would not have happened—or happened differently. But the subject under discussion was one that interested him a great deal, and so he did not leave well alone, '—but it might help you to modify it,' continued Ash, 'if you were to try putting yourself in the other fellow's shoes just for a minute or two.'

'Putting myself . . . ?' Mr Porson was offended. 'In what way, may one ask?'

'Well, look at it this way, sir,' said Ash earnestly. 'Imagine the British Isles as conquered territory, as it was in Roman times, but part of an Indian Empire instead. An Imperial colony, in which Indians hold every post of real authority, with an Indian Governor-General and Council proclaiming and enforcing laws that are completely alien to your way of life and thought, but which make it necessary for you to learn their language if you hope to hold any reasonably well-paid post under them. Indians controlling all the public services, garrisoning your country with their troops and recruiting your countrymen to serve in the ranks of regiments that they themselves would officer, declaring anyone who protested against their authority a dangerous agitator, and putting down any rising with all the force at their command. And don't forget, sir, that the last of those risings would have been less than twenty years ago, when you yourself were already a grown man. You would remember that rising very well, for even if you had not fought in it yourself, you would have known people who had, and who had died in it—or been hanged for complicity, or suspicion of complicity, or merely because they had a white skin, in the reprisals that followed it. Taking all that into account, would you yourself be eager to get on close and friendly terms with your Indian rulers? If so, I can only say that you must be a truly Christian person, and that it has been an honour to meet you. Your servant, sir.'

He bowed, and turning on his heel, walked out without waiting to hear if Mr Porson had anything further to say.

Mr Porson had not. Having never considered the problem from that angle, he was temporarily silenced. But Major Raikes and his friend Captain Crimpley, who had been among those present, had both said a great deal. Neither had any liking for Mr Porson, whose opinions and criticisms on the subject of Anglo-Indians they considered offensive, but Ash's views (and his temerity in expressing them to a stranger old enough to be his father and brought to the Club as a guest) had touched both on the raw.

'Brazen impertinence and sheer bloody bad manners,' fumed Lionel Crimpley. 'Butting into a private conversation and spouting a lot of seditious twaddle to a man he hadn't even been introduced to. And a house-guest of the Commissioner's, too! It was a calculated affront to the entire Club, and the Committee should force that young sweep to apologize or get out.'

'Oh, rats to that,' retorted Major Raikes, dismissing the Committee with an impatient sweep of the hand. 'The Committee can look after itself, and as for that numbskull Porson, he's nothing but a swollen-headed snob. But no officer has a right to say the sort of things that Pelham-Martyn said, or even think them. All that tripe about supposin' the British Isles were garrisoned by Indian troops— putting ideas into their heads, that's what it is, and damned treasonable ideas, too. It's about time someone kicked that young man's backside hard, and the sooner the better.'

Now there can always be found in any military station—as in any town or city anywhere in the world—a smattering of bored and muscular louts who delight in violence and are only too eager to take a hand in 'teaching a lesson' to any individual whose views they do not happen to share. Major Raikes therefore had no difficulty in recruiting half-a-dozen of these simple-minded souls, and two nights later they burst into Ash's bedroom in the small hours to drag him from his bed and beat him insensible. Or at least, that had been the idea.

In the event it had not turned out quite the way they had planned it, for they had neglected to take into account the fact that Ash was a remarkably light sleeper, and had long ago, from stark necessity, learned how to defend himself; and that when it came to fighting he had no respect for Queensberry Rules or any false ideas as to 'sportsmanship'.

They had also, unfortunately, failed to realize that the uproar would arouse the occupants of the servants' quarters as well as the sleeping *chowkidar,* all of whom, imagining that the bungalow was being attacked by a gang of robbers, had seized any weapon they could lay hands on and charged bravely to the assistance of Pelham-Sahib, the *chowkidar* wielding chain and *lathi* with deadly effect, Gul Baz laying about him with an iron bar, while Kulu Ram, Mahdoo and the sweeper had pinned their faiths respectively to a polo-stick, the kitchen poker and a long-handled broom . . .

By the time lights were brought and the mêlée sorted out, both sides had sustained casualties, and Ash was certainly insensible; though not, as intended, from the attentions of Major Raikes and his bravos, but as a result of tripping over a fallen chair in the darkness and knocking himself out on the corner of the dressing-table. The Major himself had received a broken nose and a sprained ankle, and no combatant, with the sole exception of the agile Kulu Ram, had come out of the engagement unmarked.

The affray, though brief, had been far too noisy (and its impressive tally of minor fractures, black eyes, cuts, sprains and bruises, too glaringly visible) to be ignored or glossed over. Questions had been asked in official quarters, and as the answers had been considered unsatisfactory, a searching inquiry had been instituted. This had revealed the shocking fact that native servants had actually taken part in the fracas, attacking and being attacked by British officers. The Authorities had been horrified: 'Can't have this sort of thing going on,' declared the Brigade Commander, who had served with Havelock's forces in Cawnpore and Lucknow during the Mutiny and had never forgotten it. 'Could lead to anything. Anything! We shall have to get rid of that young trouble-maker, and in double-quick time.'

'Which one?' inquired a senior Major, pardonably confused. 'If you mean Pelham-Martyn, I can't see that he can be held responsible for—'

'I know, I know,' snapped the Brigade Commander impatiently. 'I'm not saying that it was his fault. Though it can be argued that he provoked the attack by speaking out of turn at the Club, and being rude to that fellow who is staying with the Commissioner. But there is no denying that, intentionally or otherwise, he is a trouble-maker:

always has been—his own regiment got him transferred to us, and still don't seem to want him back. Besides, it was his *nauker-log* who attacked Raikes and Co., don't forget. They may have had every reason for doing so, and if it *had* turned out to be a raid by a band of dacoits, we'd have said they were loyal fellows for coming to his rescue. But in the circumstances, this isn't at all the sort of tale we want circulating round cantonments or told as a joke in the city, so the sooner we get rid of him the better.'

Major Raikes, his nose and ankle in plaster, had been severely reprimanded for his part in the affair and ordered to take himself off on leave until his injuries were healed. His confederates had been confined to their quarters for a similar period, after receiving a tongue-lashing that they would remember for the rest of their lives. But Ash, who as the victim and not the aggressor might have been expected to escape any share of blame, had been given twenty-four hours in which to pack up his belongings, settle his debts and arrange to leave with his servants and his baggage by road to Jhelum, where they would take the mail-train bound for Delhi and Bombay.

He was to serve on attachment with Roper's Horse, a cavalry regiment stationed at Ahmadabad in Gujerat, nearly four hundred miles north of Bombay—and more than two thousand miles distant by road and rail from Rawalpindi . . .

On the whole, Ash had not been sorry to leave 'Pindi. There were things he would miss: the company of several friends in the city, the foothills that could be reached so easily on horseback, the sight of high mountains clear-cut against the sky, and the hint of woodsmoke and pine-needles that sometimes tinged the air when the wind blew down from the north. On the other hand, it could not be much more than seventy miles to the border of Rajputana, and little more than a hundred as the crow flies from Bhithor; he would be nearer Juli, and even though he could not enter the Rana's territory, that was some small consolation—as was the fact that however unfair he considered his arbitrary expulsion from Rawalpindi, he was not disposed to quarrel with a verdict that rescued him from sharing a bungalow with Lionel Crimpley.

There was also some comfort in the thought that in any case he would not have been able to see either Wally or Zarin for some time to come, as all leave for the Guides had recently been cancelled following rumours that further trouble was to be expected from the

Jowaki Afridis, who apparently objected to some change in plan over the allowance paid to them by the Government in return for keeping the peace.

A letter from Mardan had brought Ash this piece of news only a day after the raid on his bungalow, and the reflection that neither of his friends would be able to visit 'Pindi until the Jowaki matter was resolved had gone a long way towards softening his resentment at being so unjustly bundled off to Ahmadabad. But re-reading that letter from Wally, he had been reminded again of what Koda Dad had said on the roof of Fatima Begum's house at Attock, and was fretted by the thought that if there should be a war, the Guides would certainly be involved in it. The whole Corps would be sent, and some, inevitably, would never come back. But he, Ash, would be out of it all—kicking his heels in a dull and dusty cantonment in far-away Gujerat.

It was a lowering thought, yet on consideration he was unwilling to believe that this business of the Jowaki Afridis would develop into anything serious, or that it was connected in any way with the incidents that Koda Dad had related. The truth was that Koda Dad was getting old, and the old were apt to make much of trifles and take a pessimistic view of the future. There was no reason to take those stories too seriously.

Ash's last day in Rawalpindi had been a busy one. He had arranged the sale of two of his horses and despatched Baj Raj to the care of Wally in Mardan, paid a number of farewell visits to friends in the city, and scribbled several hurried letters to say that he was on his way to Gujerat and would probably be stationed there for at least eighteen months if not longer.

'. . . and if during that time you should chance to be visiting your nieces,' wrote Ash to Kaka-ji, 'may I hope that you will honour me by travelling a little further, so that I may enjoy the felicity of meeting you again? The extra distance would not be too great. No more I think than fifty *koss* as the crow flies, and though it may well be half as much again by road, that is still only four or five days' journey, and I myself would come two thirds of that way to meet you. More if you would permit it, though that, I fear, you would not do . . .'

Kaka-ji would certainly not permit it. Nor did Ash have any real hope that the old man would even consider undertaking another journey to Bhithor. Yet there was always a chance that he might, and if he did he would certainly see and speak to Juli, and though he would not make any mention of her in writing, he could not, surely, refuse to speak of her if he and Ash should meet, when he must know that there were times when Ash would willingly have given an eye or a hand to hear that she was well and not too unhappy—or to have any news of her at all. Even bad news would have been easier to bear than this complete silence.

'I am getting too old for such journeys,' grumbled Mahdoo, stowing his baggage aboard the mail-train on the following night. 'It is time I took my *wazifa* (pension) and settled down to spend my last days in peace and idleness, instead of all this running to and fro across the length and breadth of Hind.'

'Do you mean that, Cha-cha-ji?' asked Ash, startled.

'Why should I say it if I did not?' snapped the old man.

'To punish me, perhaps? But if you do mean it, there is a dâk-*ghari* that leaves here in the morning and you could be in Abbottabad within three days.'

'And what will become of you if I leave?' demanded Mahdoo, rounding on him angrily. 'Will you ask Gul Baz for his advice as you ask for mine? Or take it when it is given, as you have on many occasions taken mine? Besides, I am tied to you by a promise that I gave many years ago to Anderson-Sahib; and also by one that I gave to Ala Yar. By affection, too, which is an even stronger bond . . . but it is true that I grow old and tired and useless, and I have no wish to end my days in the south among idol-worshippers whose hearts are as black as their skins. When my time comes I would choose to die in the north where a man may smell the clean wind that blows off the high snows.'

'That will be as God wills,' said Ash lightly, 'nor am I being sent to Gujerat for a lifetime. It is only for a short while, Cha-cha, and when it is over I will surely be permitted to return to Mardan; and then you shall take as much leave as you wish—or retire, if you must.'

Mahdoo sniffed, and went away to see to the bestowal of his own baggage, muttering to himself and looking unconvinced.

The train was only half-full that night, and Ash had been relieved to find himself the only occupant of a four-berth compartment, and thereby freed from the obligation of making conversation. But as the wheels began to turn and the lights and tumult of the railway station slid slowly past the carriage windows, giving place to darkness, he would have been grateful for a companion, for now that he was alone and idle, the optimism that had sustained him during the past two days suddenly left him, and he was no longer so certain that he would only be required to spend a year or eighteen months in Gujerat. Supposing it was two years—or three . . . or four? Supposing the Guides were to decide that on consideration they were not prepared to take him back at all?—ever!

The train rattled and jolted, and the oil lamp that swayed to every jolt stank abominably and filled the closed carriage with the stench of hot kerosene. Ash rose and turned it out, and lying back in the clamorous darkness, wondered how long it would be before he saw the Khyber again—and had the uncomfortable fancy that he could hear a reply in the voice of the clattering wheels—a harsh, mocking voice that repeated with maddening insistence, 'Never again! Never again! Never again . . .'

The train journey to Bombay seemed far longer than he remembered it to have been on the last occasion that he had come that way, over five years ago. He had been travelling in the opposite direction then, and in the company of Belinda and her mother and the unfortunate George. Five years . . . Was it really only five years? It felt more like twelve—or twenty.

The railways were supposed to have made great strides since then, but Ash could see very little difference. Admittedly, an average speed of fifteen miles an hour was an improvement, but the carriages were just as dusty and uncomfortable, the stops as frequent, and there being still no through-train to Bombay, passengers were compelled to change trains as often as before. As for his carriage companions (for he had not been left in sole possession for long) they could hardly have been less enlivening. But at Bombay, where the mail-train stopped and Ash and his servants and baggage transferred into another one bound for Baroda and Ahmadabad, his luck changed. He found himself sharing a two-berth carriage with a small and inoffensive-looking gentleman whose placid manner and mild blue eyes were belied by red whiskers and a cauliflower-ear, and who introduced himself, in a voice as mild as his eyes, as Bert Stiggins, late of Her Majesty's Navy and now Captain and owner of a small coastal trading ship, the *Morala,* docked at Porbandar on the west coast of Gujerat.

The mildness, however, proved to be deceptive; for just as the train was due to leave, two late arrivals pushed their way into the carriage, asserting loudly that they had reserved it for their own use and that Ash and Mr Stiggins were occupying it illegally. The interlopers were both members of a well-known trading concern, and they had obviously dined far too well before setting out for the station, since they seemed incapable of understanding that the number of the carriage they had reserved did not tally with the one they were attempting to occupy. Either that or they were spoiling for a fight, and if a brawl was what they desired, Ash was more than willing to accommodate them. But he was forestalled.

Mr Stiggins, who had been sitting peacefully on his berth while Ash and the guard attempted to use reason, rose to his feet as one of the intruders kicked the guard's legs from under him, toppling him backwards on to the platform outside, while the other aimed a wild punch at Ash, who had leapt to the guard's assistance.

'You leave this to me, sonny,' advised Mr Stiggins soothingly, and put Ash aside without apparent effort.

Ten seconds later both intruders were lying flat on their backs on the platform, wondering dazedly what had hit them, while Mr Stiggins tossed their belongings after them, apologized on their behalf to the ruffled guard, shut and fastened the carriage door and returned placidly to his seat.

'Well I'll be damned!' gasped Ash, unable to believe his eyes. 'How on earth did you do that?'

Mr Stiggins, who was not even out of breath, looked faintly embarrassed and confessed to having learnt his fighting in the Navy and 'brushed up on it' in bars and other places—notably in Japan. 'Them Japs is up to all sorts o' tricks; and very useful I've found 'em,' said Mr Stiggins. 'They lets the other bloke do all the work and knock 'imself out, so's ter speak. Simple, if you knows the way of it.'

He blew gently on the cracked skin of a knuckle, and glancing out of the window at the still recumbent gladiators, remarked in a tone of concern that 'if them pore young fellers didn't look slippy' they were going to miss the train, as no one among the gaping crowd of bystanders seemed to be interested in carrying them to their carriage. 'Let's 'ope it'll be a lesson to them both to go easy on the likker in future. As the Good Book says, "wine is a mocker, strong drink is ragin'."'

'Are you a teetotaller, Mr Stiggins?' inquired Ash, regarding his small companion with considerable awe.

'Cap'n Stiggins,' corrected that gentleman mildly. 'No, I likes a nip now an' then, but I don't 'old with wallowin' in it. Moderation in all things is me motto. One swaller too many, an' there y'are takin' on all comers an' like as not endin' up in the clink. Or, as it may be, missin' yore train like them pore young drunks are adoin' this very min-ute . . . there, wot did I tell yer?'

The guard, taking his revenge, had blown the whistle, and the train pulled out of Bombay Central Station a mere ten minutes late, leaving behind two would-be passengers who sat holding their heads and groaning amid scattered hand luggage and grinning coolies.

Ash learned a good deal about the little Captain during the re-maining days of the journey, and his admiration for the Captain's fighting powers was soon equalled by his respect for the man himself. Herbert Stiggins, nicknamed 'Red' for reasons not wholly confined to the colour of his hair (he was known up and down the coast as the *'Lal-lerai-wallah'*, the 'Red fighting-fellow'), had parted company with the Navy almost half a century ago while still in his teens, and was at present engaged in the coastal trade, plying mainly between Sind and Gujerat. The *Morala* had recently been damaged in a colli-sion with a dhow running without lights, and her owner explained to Ash that he had been in Bombay to see a lawyer about a claim for damages, and was on his way back.

His conversation was as salty and invigorating as the sea and in-terlarded with frequent quotations from the Bible and the Book of Common Prayer—the only printed works apart from manuals on sailing and navigation that he had ever read—and altogether he proved such an entertaining companion that by the time the train at last pulled into Ahmadabad, the two had become the best of friends.

Ahmadabad, the noble city that Sultan Ahmad Shah built in the first half of the fifteenth century, retained few traces of its legendary beauty and splendour. It was set in flat, featureless surroundings near the banks of the Sabarmati River, and the fertile land was as different from the harsh, lion-coloured Border country as the sowars of Roper's Horse were different, both in appearance and temperament, from the men of the Frontier Force regiments; the Gujeratis being by nature a peace-loving folk whose best-known proverb is 'Make friends with your enemy'.

Their senior officers struck Ash as being surprisingly old and staid, and far more set in their ways than those in his own Regiment; while as for their Commanding Officer, Colonel Pomfret, he might have been Rip Van Winkle in person, complete with ragged white beard and a set of ideas that were at least fifty years out of date.

The cantonment, however, differed little from the scores of similar cantonments scattered across the length and breadth of India: an ancient fort, a dusty sun-baked parade ground, barracks and cavalry lines, a small bazaar and a few European shops and a number of officers' bungalows standing in tree-shaded compounds where parakeets, doves and crows roosted among the branches and little striped squirrels scuffled among the tree roots.

Life there followed a familiar pattern of reveille, stables, musketry and office work, but on the social side Ash made a pleasant discovery: the presence of an old acquaintance from the Peshawar days—no other than Mrs Viccary, whose husband had recently been transferred to Gujerat. The pleasure had been mutual, and Edith Viccary's bungalow soon became a second home to him since she was, as ever, an interested and sympathetic listener, and as the last time he had seen her was prior to Belinda's defection and his own disappearance over the Border into Afghanistan, there was much that he had to tell her.

As far as his work was concerned, he found himself at a grave disadvantage in the matter of language. Once, long ago, he had learned Gujerati from a member of his father's camp; but that was too far back for him to remember it, so now he must start again from the beginning, and like any newcomer, study hard to master it. The fact that he had spoken it as a child may possibly have helped him to make better progress than he would otherwise have done—certainly his fellow officers, unaware of his background (though the nickname of 'Pandy' had followed him), were astonished at the speed with which he picked it up, though their Colonel, who thirty years ago had met Professor Hilary Pelham-Martyn and subsequently read at least one volume of the Professor's monumental work *The Languages and Dialects of the Indian Sub-Continent,* did not think it strange that the son should have inherited his father's linguistic talents. He could only hope that the young man had not also inherited his parent's unorthodox views.

But Ash's behaviour during the first few months of his attachment gave no cause for alarm. He performed his duties in a perfectly satisfactory manner, though without over-much enthusiasm, and was voted a 'dull dog' by the junior officers because he showed even less for cards and convivial evenings in the mess. Though they agreed that this could well be due to the heat, for the hot-weather temperatures were apt to cast a damper on the liveliest of spirits, and once the cold season came round he might prove more gregarious.

In this respect, however, the arrival of the cold weather had made no difference, except that his prowess on the polo field was sufficiently outstanding to permit allowances to be made for his lack of sociability and the fact that he continued to make no effort to take part in the amusements of the station, but whenever possible refused invitations to attend card-parties, picnics and paper-chases, or to act in amateur theatricals.

The ladies of the station, who had begun by taking considerable interest in the newcomer, ended by agreeing with the junior officers that he was either deplorably dull or insufferably conceited—the verdict depending on age and temperament—and in either case, no asset to station society; an opinion that had been reinforced by his shameless conduct in inviting a vulgar individual, apparently the skipper of a cargo-boat, to dine with him at the English Club (Red Stiggins had been on a brief business trip to Ahmadabad and had encountered Ash by chance in the city).

This episode had put an end to any further attempts to entice or dragoon Ash into attending purely social functions, and thereafter he had been left to go his own way and do what he pleased with his spare time, which suited him very well. He spent a large part of the latter in studying, and much of the rest exploring the countryside beyond the city, where the ground was littered with the relics of a great past, now overgrown by creepers and almost forgotten: old tombs and the ruins of temples and water tanks, built of stone that had been quarried in hills many miles to the north.

The great peninsula of Gujerat was for the most part flat and without scenic interest, and because of its abundant rainfall, a lush and fertile land, green with crops, banana groves, mango, orange and lemon trees, palms and cotton. It was a country very dissimilar to the Rajputana that Ash remembered so vividly, yet the low hills that bordered it to the north-east marked the frontiers of the Country of the Kings, and on the far side of them—barely more than a hundred miles as the crow flies—lay Bhithor. Bhithor and Juli . . .

He tried not to think of that, but it was difficult not to do so during the slow, furnace-like months of the hot weather, when the day's work must begin at first-light if it was to be done before the temperatures reached a point that made any form of physical or mental activity almost impossible, and the hours between mid-morning and late afternoon were spent indoors with the shutters closed against the heat and the glare, with nothing to do but keep still—and if possible, sleep.

The majority of citizens, and all the Europeans, seemed to find no difficulty in doing one or the other, but to Ash these hot, idle hours were the worst part of the day . . . too much time—aeons of it—in which to think and remember and regret. Therefore he studied Gujerati in an effort to kill two birds with one stone, and mastered the language at a rate that astonished his munshi and won the admiration of the sowars . . . and was still unable to keep from thinking unprofitable thoughts.

He should have grown used to that by now, for he had been plagued in this fashion for over a year. But somehow it had been easier to accept the situation as irrevocable when hundreds of miles separated him from Juli and there was nothing in his surroundings to remind him of her. Besides, Rawalpindi, even after Wally's departure, had provided some palliatives—half-a-dozen good friends, his horses, and an occasional weekend in Murree from where he could see the Kashmir snows . . . Even the feud with Crimpley and his friend Raikes had had its uses. It had at least served as a distraction, and almost without his knowing it, the pain of loss had begun to ease a little and the gnawing sense of restlessness to decrease, until there had actually been times when he had come through an entire day without thinking of Juli at all.

But here in Ahmadabad that was no longer so and sometimes he wondered if space, as measured in miles, could have an effect on thought. Was it because he was now so much nearer to her in terms of distance that the memory of her was again so vivid and so continuously in his mind? From here Bhithor was only three days' journey away . . . four at most . . . If he were to set out now—'You are not attending, Sahib!' the munshi would reprove him. 'Read me that sentence again—remembering what I told you about the tense.'

Ash would drag his mind back from the past and fix it on the present; and when the lesson ended, cast about for something else, anything else, to keep him occupied until the worst of the day's heat was over and he could go out and ride. But in October, with the end of the hot weather in sight, the outlook became considerably brighter. The cold season was a time of intense military activity, and now, as though to make up for the unavoidable idleness and lethargy of the past months, camps, manoeuvres and training exercises followed one another at speed, while any spare time was taken up by such energetic pastimes as polo, racing and gymkhanas.

Best of all, Ash acquired two things that did more than all the rest to take his mind off his personal problems and compensate him for being banished from the Frontier, and the Guides. A friend, Sarjevan Desai, the son of a local landowner. And a horse named Dagobaz.

Sarjevan, known to his intimates as Sarji, was a great-nephew of the Risaldar-Major—a fierce, wise, grey-whiskered warrior who was by now something of a legend in Roper's Horse, for he had served with it since its inception some forty years ago, joining it as a lad of fifteen in the days when the land was ruled by the East India Company.

The Risaldar-Major was a martinet and a notable horseman, and he appeared to be related to most of the local aristocracy, among them Sarjevan's late father, who had been the son of one of his many sisters. Sarji himself was no military man. He had inherited a large estate, and with it his father's passion for horses, which he bred more for his own pleasure than for profit, refusing to sell to anyone he did not personally know and like.

His great-uncle, having taken a favourable view of the newly joined British officer, had introduced Sarji to Lieutenant Pelham-

Martyn with instructions to see that the Sahib was fitted out with mounts that would not disgrace the good name of the Regiment—or of Gujerat. And fortunately for Ash, the two had taken to each other. They were the same age and their mutual love of horses had cemented an immediate liking that had soon become friendship, with the result that Ash had acquired, for a not unreasonable figure, a stable that was the envy of his fellow officers and that included a pedigree black stallion of Arab descent: Dagobaz, 'The Trickster'.

Since the days when he had been a horse-boy in the stables of Duni Chand of Gulkote, Ash had seen and ridden and later on owned many horses. But never yet had he seen anything to equal this one for beauty, mettle and speed. Even Baj Raj, now in Wally's care in Mardan, paled into insignificance by contrast. Dagobaz was almost three years old when he came into Ash's possession, and at first Sarji had been reluctant to sell him, not because of his spectacular looks and promise, but because the stallion had not been named Dagobaz for nothing. He might have the appearance of perfection, but his character did not match his looks; he possessed a fiery and uncertain temper, together with a dislike of being ridden that no amount of patient training had so far been able to overcome.

'I do not say that he is vicious,' said Sarji, 'or that he cannot be mounted. He can. But unlike the others he has still not outgrown his hatred for the feel of a man upon his back. This you can sense in your bones when you ride him, and it does not make for comfort. He has a will of his own, that horse—a will of iron—and by now even the best of my syces are ready to admit defeat. They say he has a thousand tricks whereby he may rid himself of a rider, and that when one thinks one has learned them all, lo! he has a new one—and there one is again, sprawling in the dust or among the thorn-scrub and faced with another walk home. You are taken in by his beauty; but if you buy him—and I would sell him to no one else—you may well live to regret it. Do not say I have not warned you!'

But Ash had only laughed and bought the black horse for a price that in view of its looks and its pedigree was ridiculous: and never had cause to regret it. Sarji had always been good with horses and was an excellent rider, but being a rich man's son he had not gained his experience the hard way, as Ash had done, by working with them as a child in the lowly capacity of horse-boy.

Ash had made no attempt to ride Dagobaz for at least ten days, but during that time he spent every moment he could spare in the stable or in the enclosed field adjoining it, handling the horse, grooming him, feeding him raw carrots and lumps of *gur* (the crude brown stuff that is extracted from sugar-cane) and talking to him by the hour together. Dagobaz, at first suspicious, soon grew used to him and presently began to make a few tentative overtures of his own until eventually, on hearing Ash's low whistle, he would prick up his ears and answer to it with a soft whinnying, and trot over to greet him.

Rapport having been established, the rest had been comparatively easy: though Ash had suffered a few reverses and had on one occasion found himself faced with a five-mile walk back to the cantonments. Yet in the end even Sarji had to admit that 'The Trickster' had been wrongly named and should now be re-titled 'The Saint'. But Ash had retained the old name, for in some ways it was still applicable. Dagobaz had accepted him as a friend and his master, but showed plainly that he was a 'one-man' horse and that his affection and obedience were reserved for Ash alone. No one else could ride him with impunity, not even his syce, Kulu Ram; though he would grudgingly permit that individual to exercise him on the rare occasions when Ash was unable to do so—giving as much trouble as possible in the process, so that Kulu Ram was driven to declare that he was no horse but a devil in disguise. But with Ash on his back, he behaved like an angel.

He was a big horse by Arab standards, and the length of his stride was phenomenal. Ash discovered that he could, when pressed, outdistance anything else on four legs, including Sarji's pet hunting cheetahs—though the cheetah is reputed to be the swiftest of all animals and can easily run down a buck. He had, in addition, a mouth of velvet, the manners of a prince, and a truly royal temper that discouraged strangers—and syces—from taking liberties with him. But as Sarji had truly said, there was no vice in him, and once Ash had succeeded in winning his heart, he proved to be as docile and affectionate as a kitten and as intelligent as a well-trained gun-dog. So much so, that within two months of his purchase, and notwithstanding his known foibles, Ash had received at least half-a-dozen offers for him, all of them greatly in excess of the sum that he himself had paid—and all of them refused.

There was not, Ash asserted, enough gold in all India to buy Dagobaz. In proof of which he trained the stallion to jump, entered him in a local cross-country race and won it by over fifteen lengths (to the dismay of the bookmakers, who knowing that the horse had never raced before had rashly offered long odds), and for the best part of a month rode him on parade in place of the more experienced charger that he had acquired on his arrival in the station. Dagobaz, though unfamiliar with the drill, had taken it in his stride, and apart from one attempt to keep ahead of the line, had behaved as if he had been trained to it from the beginning.

'There's nothing he can't do!' declared Ash, boasting of his performance to Sarji. 'That horse is human. And a damn' sight cleverer than most humans, at that. I swear he understands every word I say. He uses his head, too. He'd make a wonderful polo-pony, except that I don't need another, so I'd rather keep him just to ride and . . . Did you see the way he took that irrigation channel with the well on the near side of it? Flew it like a bird. By God, he should have been called Pegasus. The Colonel says I can race him in Bombay next cold weather—that is if I'm still here.'

'You expect to go before then?' asked Sarji.

'Not expect,' corrected Ash wryly. 'Only hope. Didn't they tell you I was serving a sentence? I'm on attachment; and as I shall have been here a year in March, there's just a chance that the powers in Rawalpindi may relent and send word that I may go back to my own *rissala.*'

'What powers are those?' inquired Sarji, interested.

'Gods,' said Ash flippantly. 'Tin gods that say unto one "go" and he goeth, and to another "come" and he cometh. I received the first order and perforce obeyed: now I hope for the second.'

'So?' Sarji was puzzled but polite. 'And what of Dagobaz? Will you take him with you when you go?'

'Of course. You don't think I'd part with him, do you? If I couldn't take him any other way, I'd ride him back. But if I'm to be left here to rot for another year, I mean to take him down to Bombay for the races, and the entire Regiment are planning to put their shirts on him.'

'*Shirts?*'

'Money. They are going to bet every rupee they can lay hands on.'

'Ah! I too. I shall go to Bombay with you and I shall back you with a *lakh* of rupees for your first race, and make a fortune!'

'We all will. You and I and your great-uncle the Risaldar-Sahib, and every man in the Regiment. And afterwards Dagobaz will have a silver cup as big as a bucket to drink out of.'

Ash's opinion of the black horse was shared by many; though not by Mahdoo, who refused to see anything admirable in the animal and openly regretted its purchase.

'I believe that you care more for that Child of the Pit than for anyone else,' complained Mahdoo crossly as Ash, returning at dusk after an evening ride, fed Dagobaz with sugar before sending him back to the stables. 'It is not fitting to give one's heart to an animal, who has no soul.'

'Yet Allah made horses for our use,' retorted Ash, laughing. 'Is it not written in the Koran, in the Sura of the War-Steeds . . . *"By the snorting of war-steeds which strike fire with their hooves as they gallop to the raid at dawn, and with a trail of dust split the foe in two: man is ungrateful to his Lord! To this he himself shall bear witness."* Would you have me ungrateful for such gifts as these, Cha-cha?'

'I would have you spend less time talking to a brute-beast, and more on those who have your welfare at heart. Such as Hamilton-Sahib, to whom, as I know well, you have sent only one short letter since the day that you acquired that son of perdition.'

Ash started and had the grace to look guilty: 'Have I not? I did not realize . . . I will write to him now, tonight.'

'First read what he has to say. This came by the morning's dâk, but it seems that you were in too great a hurry to glance at your letters before you went off to that creature's stable. This thick one is, I think, from Hamilton-Sahib; and we also, Gul Baz and I, would like news of him and of our friends in Mardan.'

He proffered a brass salver bearing half-a-dozen letters, and Ash snatched up the bulkiest, and tearing open the envelope, carried it into the lamp-lit bungalow to read it:

'The cavalry have been having a damned dull time of it lately,' wrote Wally, 'but the infantry, lucky devils, have been having no end of larks. I can't remember if I told you about that trouble with the Jowaki Afridis over the Government suddenly deciding to stop bribing them (sorry, I believe I should have said "paying them an allowance". *Wah illah!*) in return for keeping open the road through the Kohat Pass, and offering them an equivalent sum for safeguarding the Khushalgarh road and telegraph line.

'They didn't take to the idea at all, and after a bit they began to make their displeasure felt by plundering and burning villages and attacking escorts and police stations. Then they burned down a bridge on the Khushalgarh road and that seems to have got the Powers-that-Be on the raw—a sort of last straw on their august shoulders. They decided that the Jowaki jokers must be given a sharp rap over the knuckles, and, I regret to say, that was just about all it was. A quick dash into Jowaki territory by three columns, one of them ours—201 bayonets with Campbell in command and Stuart, Hammond, Wigram and Fred in support—burn a village or two and nip back again. *Bus!* (enough). The columns were under arms in vile heat for twenty hours, marched nearly thirty miles and had eleven casualties—our fellows had two men wounded. Short and sweet, and apparently a complete waste of everyone's time, for the Jowakis remain noticeably unimpressed and are still cutting-up with unabated vigour.

'I suppose this means that we shall be having another go at them before long. If so, I hope the Big-Wigs let the cavalry get into the act. I'd like to see a bit of action for a change. Zarin sends his salaams and asks me to tell you that he is afraid his father was right. He says that you will know what he means, and I hope you do because I don't. Let us have some news of you. You haven't answered my last letter yet and it's months since I heard from you. But as no news is good news, I presume you are alive and enjoying yourself. My salaams to Mahdoo and Gul Baz . . .'

'When you write, send ours to him,' said Mahdoo, and added sourly: 'And ask him if he has need of another servant: an old man who was once a good cook.'

The other servants had settled down contentedly enough, for as there was no shortage of accommodation in the Ahmadabad cantonment, Ash had a whole bungalow to himself with a large compound and plenty of servants' quarters: a luxury seldom enjoyed by a junior officer in any military station. Kulu Ram had been pleased to approve of the stables, and Gul Baz, who had left his wife and family in Hoti Mardan, had made himself comfortable by installing a local woman in the hut behind his quarters—a silent and retiring creature who kept herself to herself, cooked and washed and generally attended to the wants of her temporary protector.

Mahdoo, however, was too old for such arrangements; and he hated everything about Gujerat with the possible exception of Ahmadabad's great mosque, where the founder of the city, Sultan Ahmad Shah, lies buried. For the rest, he detested the heat and the humidity, the lush, dripping greenery in the compound, and the rain clouds that during the monsoon had driven in on a wind that smelled of the sea, to empty their contents on the roofs and roads and parade groud of the cantonment until the whole area was awash and it seemed, at times, as though the bungalows were islands floating in a waste of water. The food did not agree with him, and he distrusted the local people, whose language he did not understand and whose ways were not his.

'He is too old to change,' said Gul Baz, excusing Mahdoo's crotchetiness. 'He misses the scents and sounds of the north, and the food and talk and customs of his own people.'

'As you do,' said Ash, and added under his breath: 'and I also.'

'True, Sahib. But then if God is merciful you and I will have many more years to live, and therefore if we spend one or two in this place, what matter? But with Mahdoo-ji it is different, for he knows that for him the years are few.'

'I should not have brought him here,' said Ash remorsefully. 'Yet how could I help it, when he refused to be left behind? I would send him on leave at once if I thought he would stay in his own home until we go north again, but I know he would not, so if we are to spend another hot season in this place it would be better for him to stay here now while it is cool, and leave for the north in the first half of February. That way he will miss the months of greatest heat and the worst of the monsoon; and if we are still here when it is over, I may even be able to send to tell him that he need wait only a little longer and meet us in Mardan. Because by that time I must surely know my fate.'

In this last respect, Ash was to be proved right: though in a way that he had not foreseen.

Throughout that cold-weather season, whenever the Regiment was not in camp or engaged in manoeuvres, Ash would rise with the dawn in order to take Dagobaz out for an early-morning gallop. And on most evenings he would ride out alone or with Sarji to explore the countryside, returning to his bungalow only after dusk had fallen.

There was much to be seen, for Gujerat is not only drenched in history, but is the legendary scene of the chief exploits and death of the god Khrishna, the Indian Apollo. Every hill and stream has its link with some mythological happening, and the land is strewn with the ruins of tombs and temples so ancient that the names of those who built them have long been forgotten. Among the memorials to the dead—the magnificent, pillared domes of the great and the sculptured slabs of humbler men—one curious motif attracted Ash's attention, for it appeared over and over again. A woman's arm, ornamented with intricately carved bracelets and armbands.

'That?' said Sarji in answer to a question. 'Oh, it commemorates a suttee. A widow who burned herself on her husband's funeral pyre. It is a very old custom, one that your Government has forbidden—and rightly, I think. Though there are still those who would not agree with me. Yet I remember my grandfather, who was a learned and enlightened man, telling me that many thinkers, himself among them, believe that this practice arose through the error of a scribe when the laws were first put down in writing, many centuries ago. The original law, they say, laid down that when a man dies his body must be given to the fire and his widow must afterwards 'go within the house' —in other words, live in seclusion for the remainder of her life—but that a scribe, writing this down long after, left out the last two words by mistake, so that it came to be believed that 'go within' meant to go within the fire. Perhaps that is true; and if so it is as well that the Raj has given orders that the practice must cease, for to be burned alive is a cruel death, though many thousands upon thousands of our women have not flinched from it, but considered it an honour.'

'And many more have been forced to endure it against their will, if even half the tales one hears are true,' said Ash grimly.

Sarji shrugged. 'Maybe. But then their lives would have been a burden to them had they lived, so perhaps they were better off dead; and you must not forget that she who becomes suttee becomes holy. Her name is honoured and her very ashes are venerated—look there.' He pointed with his riding whip to where a vivid splash of colour glowed bright against the dark stone and the tangle of greenery.

Someone had draped a garland of fresh marigolds over one of the carved weather-worn arms that bore silent witness to the hideous death of a wife who had dutifully 'completed a life of uninterrupted conjugal devotedness by the act of *saha-gamana*', and accompanied her husband's corpse into the flames. The stone was half hidden by grass and creepers, but someone—another woman, surely?—had decked it with flowers, and though the afternoon was windless and very warm, Ash shivered, and said violently: 'Well if we have done nothing else, at least we can mark up one thing to our credit—that we put a stop to *that* particular horror.'

Sarji shrugged again; which might have meant anything—or nothing—and he began to talk of other matters as they turned their horses and made for the open country.

The two went riding together at least once or twice a week, and often at weekends or holidays they would go on longer trips together, staying away for a night or two, and choosing a route at random. Sometimes to Patri and the shallow waters of the Rann of Kutch, where the air smells of salt and seaweed and the rotting fish-heads that the boatmen fling out on the shore for the gulls to dispose of. Sometimes east towards Baroda, the capital city of His Highness Siraji Rao, the Gaekwar, or south, to the Gulf of Cambay where the great rollers drive in from the Arabian Sea between those two outposts of the Portuguese Empire, Diu Island and Damman—and where, on several occasions, they found the cargo-boat *Morala* at anchor, and went on board to collogue with her owner, Captain Red Stiggins. But only when he was alone did Ash ride northward in the direction of the distant blue ranges that lay between Gujerat and Rajputana.

Sarji was a cheerful and entertaining companion, but when Ash chose to ride towards the hills he did not want companionship, for on these occasions he would make for a lonely, ruin-crowned knoll overlooking the river below Bijapur from where he would gaze at the jagged outline of those ancient hills, and know that Juli had only to look out of a window of the Rung Mahal to see them too . . .

They looked so easy to cross: a low and insubstantial barrier, dusty-gold in the evening light or aquamarine in the shimmering heat-haze of the early afternoon. Yet he had learned that there were few paths through them; and even fewer passes where it was possible for a man to cross on foot, let alone on horseback. The hazards of those mountain passes, and the trackless miles of tiger-jungle that clothed the lower slopes, discouraged would-be travellers to Rajputana from attempting short cuts, and led the majority to turn westward and make a detour by way of Palanpur, or else go south to Bombay, and travel by rail or road through the *ghats*. But as Ash could see no prospect of his ever being able to enter Rajputana again, the difficulty or otherwise of finding a way through those hills was unimportant. Even if there had been a paved highway between Ahmadabad and Bhithor, it would have made no difference, because the Country of the Kings was forbidden territory, and like Moses, he could gaze at the promised land but he must not enter it.

Ash would sit on the knoll for hours, absorbed and motionless—so still that the birds and squirrels and even the shy lizards would often stray within reach of his hand, or a butterfly come to rest on his head. Only when Dagobaz—turned loose to crop among the ruins—became impatient and thrust an anxious nose into his breast, would he awake as though from a deep sleep, and coming stiffly to his feet, mount and ride back across the flat lands to Ahmadabad and the bungalow in cantonments.

On these days he would invariably find Mahdoo waiting for him, squatting unobtrusively in a corner of the verandah from where he could see the front gate while at the same time keeping a watchful eye upon the kitchen and the servants' quarters in case his assistant, young Kadera, should neglect his duties.

Mahdoo was not happy. He was feeling the weight of his years and he was also deeply uneasy on Ash's account. It was not that he had any idea where Ash went, or what he had been doing on these particular occasions. But though his knowledge of geography was slight, his knowledge of Ash was extensive, and once having learned that the borders of Rajputana lay less than a day's ride to the north, his intuition had supplied an answer that alarmed him. Bhithor was not so far beyond that border.

Their proximity to the Rana's kingdom worried Mahdoo a great deal, for though he had never heard so much as a whisper involving Anjuli-Bai, he had realized long ago that something far more serious than the Rana's attempts at blackmail and treachery had occurred there. Something deeply personal to Ash-Sahib that had struck at his happiness and peace of mind, and destroyed both.

Mahdoo was no fool. He was, on the contrary, a shrewd old man who had known and loved Ash for many years, and that combination of shrewdness, knowledge and affection had enabled him to make a fairly accurate guess at the cause of his child's trouble; though he hoped very much that he was mistaken, for if he were not, then the situation was not merely tragic, but profoundly shocking. Despite his many years of service with the Sahib-log and his long sojourn in their country, Mahdoo still held firmly to the opinion that all decent women (particularly young and beautiful ones) should be kept in strict purdah—European ones excepted of course, as their customs were different and they could hardly be blamed for going about unveiled when their men-folk were foolish enough to permit such immodest behaviour.

The ones he had blamed were those who had permitted the Rajkumaries and their women to meet and talk so freely and frequently with Ash-Sahib, who had naturally (or so Mahdoo surmised) ended by falling in love with one of them, which was a terrible thing to have happened. But at least it was over and done with, and before long he would forget this woman as he had forgotten the other one—that yellow-haired miss-sahib from Peshawar. He could hardly fail to do so, thought Mahdoo, when one considered the vast distance that separated Rawalpindi from Bhithor and the unlikelihood of his ever having occasion to enter Rajputana again.

Yet little more than a year later, by some evil chance he was sent south once more—and to Ahmadabad, of all places, so that here they were, once again within range of that sinister, medieval little state from which Mahdoo, for his part, had been so profoundly thankful to escape. Worse still, his child was plainly unhappy and given to strange moods, while he himself was filled with foreboding. Surely Ash-Sahib would not be so foolish as to cross into Rajputana and attempt to enter Bhithor again? Or would he? . . . young men in love were capable of any folly, yet if he were to venture once more into the Rana's territory, this time alone, without the backing of armed men and the authority (or even the permission) of the Government, he might not leave it again alive.

In Mahdoo's opinion, the Rana was not a man to forgive anyone who had got the better of him, let alone someone who had threatened him in the presence of his councillors and courtiers, and nothing would be likely to please him more than to learn that his adversary had returned secretly (and presumably in disguise) without the knowledge or consent of anyone in authority; for then if the Sahib were simply to disappear and never be heard of again, how could anyone bring accusations against the state? It would merely be said that he must have lost his way among the hills and died of thirst or met with an accident, and who would be able to prove that he had so much as set foot in Bhithor, or even intended to do so?

Mahdoo had spent sleepless nights worrying over the possibilities, and though he had never served in any but a bachelor's establishment and had always taken a poor view of memsahibs and their ways, he now began to hope against hope that his child would meet some beautiful young miss-sahib among the British community in Ahmadabad, who would make him forget the unknown girl from Karidkote who had caused him so much sorrow.

But Ash continued to ride out alone and in the direction of the hills at least one day out of every seven, and appeared to prefer Sarji's society, or the Viccarys', to that of any of the available miss-sahibs in the station. Wherefore Mahdoo continued to worry over the possible consequences of those solitary rides and to fear the worst, and when, towards the end of January, Ash told him that he was to take long leave and go to his own village for the duration of the hot weather, the old man had been indignant.

'What?—and leave you to the care of young Kadera, who without my supervision could easily give you food that would upset your stomach? Never! Besides, if I were not here there would be no one to see that you did not commit any number of follies. No, no, child. I will stay.'

'To hear you talk, Cha-cha-ji,' retorted Ash, torn between amusement and irritation, 'anyone would think that I was a feeble-minded child.'

'And they would not be altogether wrong, *mera beta**,' returned Mahdoo tartly, 'for there are times when you behave as one.'

'Do I so? Yet this is not the first time you have taken leave and left me to manage without you, and you never raised a *gurrh-burrh* about it before.'

'Maybe not. But you were in the Punjab then, and among your own kind, not here in Gujerat, which is neither your country nor mine. Besides, I know what I know, and I do not trust you to keep out of trouble when my back is turned.'

But Ash only laughed and said: 'Uncle, if I give you my solemn oath that I will behave as soberly and circumspectly as a virtuous grandmother until you return, will you go? It need only be for a few months; and if before then my luck has changed and I am recalled to Mardan, you can meet me there instead. You know very well that you are in need of a rest and will be all the better for a month or two in the good air of the hills, with your family to cook and care for you and wait on you hand and foot. You need feeding up on good Punjabi food, and bracing with the clean winds of the mountains, after all these warm, heavy airs. *Hai mai,* I wish I could go with you.'

'I too,' said Mahdoo fervently. But he had raised no further objections, for he too hoped that Ash's period of exile would soon be over, and that any time now he would be recalled to his own Regiment. With Hamilton-Sahib and Battye-Sahib to plead his cause and

* my son

press for his return, that day could surely not be too far off, and if so, he, Mahdoo, might never have to return to this pestilential place.

He had left on the tenth of February, accompanied by one of the syces whose home was near Rawalpindi, and Ash had seen him off at the railway station and had stayed on the crowded platform watching the train chug slowly away, a prey to conflicting emotions. He was sorry to see the old man go, and he would miss the pawky advice and the nightly talks that were spiced with gossip and punctuated by the familiar bubble of the hookah. On the other hand there was no deny-ing that it was in some ways a relief to be rid of that anxious surveil-lance for a while. Mahdoo obviously knew or suspected too much, and was beginning to show it too clearly for comfort. A temporary separation would do them both good, and there was no doubt that the old man's health and spirits had suffered from the move to Gujerat and his dislike for the country and its people. All the same . . .

Ash watched the train disappearing in the distance, and long after the last smudge of smoke had thinned and vanished he stood staring after it, remembering the first time he had seen Mahdoo. Mahdoo and Ala Yar and Colonel Anderson, who had taken him under their collective wing and had been good to him when he was a bewildered boy speaking, feeling and thinking of himself as Ashok, and unable to credit that he was in reality an *Angrezi* with a name that he could not even pronounce; or that he was being shipped off to an unknown land to be turned into a 'Sahib' by strangers who, so he was told, were his father's people.

Remembering that day, the faces and forms of those three men were all at once as clear in his mind's eye as though they were there in the flesh and standing with him on the crowded platform: Colonel Anderson and Ala Yar, who were both dead, and Mahdoo, who was still very much alive and whom he had just seen on to the train and waved goodbye to as the Bombay-and-Baroda Mail drew out of the station. Yet there was something wrong with their faces—and sud-denly he realized what it was. He was not seeing Mahdoo as he was now—grey and wrinkled and shrunk to half his former size—but as he had been then, when Colonel Anderson and Ala Yar were alive and all three men had seemed tall and strong and a little larger than life. It was as if Mahdoo had in some way joined them and become part of the past . . . which was, of course, absurd.

Gul Baz, who had accompanied them to the railway station,

coughed discreetly to indicate that time was passing, and Ash awoke from his reverie, and turning away, walked quickly back along the platform and out into the yard to where a tonga waited to take them back to the bungalow.

Book Six

Juli

36

Perhaps it was just as well for Mahdoo that he left when he did, for his anxiety on Ash's account would have been considerably increased had he been present two days later, when an unexpected visitor arrived at Ash's bungalow in cantonments.

The Regiment had been out on a training exercise, and Ash had returned an hour after sunset to find a hired tonga standing among the shadows near the gate, and Gul Baz waiting on the verandah steps to inform him that he had a caller. 'It is the Hakim from Karidkote,' said Gul Baz. 'The Rao-Sahib's Hakim, Gobind Dass. He waits within.'

It was indeed Gobind. But the sudden spasm of terror that had made Ash's heart miss a beat on hearing his name vanished at the sight of his face. This was no bearer of bad tidings sent by Kaka-ji to break the news that Juli was sick or dying, or dead—or even that her husband was ill-treating her. Gobind looked as spruce and calm and as reassuring as ever, and he explained that he was on his way to Bhithor at the earnest request of Shushila-Rani, who had become worried about her husband's health and had no faith in the Rana's personal physician, an elderly gentleman of seventy-eight whose methods, she asserted, were several hundred years out of date.

'And as the Rani herself is at last with child, and must at such a time be saved any unnecessary anxiety,' said Gobind, 'my master the Rao-Sahib felt that it was not possible to refuse her request. Wherefore you see me now on my way to Bhithor. Though I do not know what good I can do—or will be permitted to do, since I cannot believe that the Rana's own hakims will be pleased at a stranger being called in to treat him.'

'Is he seriously ill, then?' asked Ash, with a flicker of hope.

Gobind shrugged and spread out his hands in an expressive gesture. 'Who can say? You know how it is with Shushila-Rani. She is one who will always make the most of every small ache or twinge of discomfort, and it is more than likely that she is doing so now. Nevertheless, I have been sent to see what I can do, and to remain in Bhithor for as long as I am needed.'

Accompanied only by a single servant, a plump, foolish-faced yokel named Munilal, Gobind had travelled to Bombay, from where he had come by way of Baroda and Ahmadabad: 'For the Rao-Sahib, knowing that you have been sent here, insisted that I should come by this way, saying that his nieces the Ranis would be pleased to have news of you, and that you in turn would wish to hear news of your friends in Karidkote. See, here are letters: the Rao-Sahib does not trust the public dâk, and so he entrusted them to me, giving strict orders that I was to put them into your own hand and no other . . . as I have now done.'

There were three letters, for in addition to Kaka-ji, Jhoti and Mulraj had also written; though only briefly, as Gobind, they said, would give him all the news. Neither of their letters contained anything that could not have been read aloud to anyone—Jhoti's being largely concerned with sport and horses, and ending with a frivolous description of the British Resident (whom he seemed to have taken in dislike on the trivial grounds that the man wore pince-nez and looked at him over them) while Mulraj's merely conveyed good wishes and the hope that Ash would see his way to visiting them on his next leave.

Kaka-ji's letter on the other hand was of considerable interest. Reading it, Ash understood why it had been necessary to send it by the hand of someone as trustworthy as Gobind instead of through the public post, and also why it had been essential to send Gobind to Bhithor by way of Ahmadabad.

The first part of the letter merely covered in more detail the ground that Gobind had already sketched in outline: Shushila's urgent plea for a doctor that she could trust, and the necessity of complying with it because of her condition. This was followed by a request that Ash would assist Gobind in the matter of horses and a guide and anything else that might be necessary to ensure his safe arrival in Bhithor, the money to cover all expenses being in Gobind's possession.

Having dealt with these matters, Kaka-ji had gone on to confess that he was anxious about his nieces and that it was for this reason, rather than the one he had initially given, that he had agreed at once to send Gobind to Bhithor.

'They have no one there whom they can trust,' wrote Kaka-ji, 'or that we here can rely upon to send us truthful reports on their well-being, since Shushila cannot write and we have as yet had no word from her half-sister, which is strange. We have reason to believe that the eunuch who writes on their behalf is untrustworthy, for the few letters we receive say nothing except that they are well and happy, yet we have learned that the *dai* Geeta, and no less than two of the waiting-women who accompanied them from Karidkote, all of whom were faithful servants and greatly attached to my nieces, are dead, though no mention of this was made in any letter.

'I doubt very much if we should have learned of it at all had not a trader visiting Bhithor heard the tale and repeated it to another in Ajmer, who in turn told it to a man who by chance has a cousin living here in Karidkote. Thus it came to our ears as no more than a traveller's tale, but the families of the three women heard it, and being greatly disturbed they petitioned Jhoti to inquire of his brother-in-law the Rana if it were true. This he did, and after much delay an answer came back to say that the two waiting-women had died of a fever, while the *dai* had broken her neck falling down a flight of stairs.

'The Rana professed himself astonished to learn that neither the Senior nor the Junior Rani had thought to mention the matter in their letters to their dear brother, and could only suppose that they had not deemed the death of servants to be worthy of being brought to his notice. In which he, the Rana, agreed with them—

'But you and I know,' wrote Kaka-ji, 'that had they been free to write as they pleased, they would not have failed to mention it. Therefore I am sure in my own mind that what the eunuch writes are the words of the Rana or the Rana's minions, though it may well be that I am over-anxious and that all is indeed well with them. Nevertheless I would feel easier if I had some way of knowing beyond doubt that this was so, and now it seems as though the gods have provided one. The Rana was pleased with Gobind, who, as you will remember, cured him of boils when his own hakims had failed to do so; and it is certain that he must have been feeling unwell when he permitted Shushila-Bai to ask that Gobind should come with all speed to Bhithor to heal him.

'It is an answer to prayer, as Gobind will be able to learn how it is with Jhoti's sisters, and I have instructed him to devise some method of passing on any news to you, for as you live beyond the borders of Rajasthan, you can send it on in safety to Karidkote. I would not have troubled you with this had I not known that you too would have reason to be concerned over this matter and would wish to satisfy yourself, even as I do, that all is well. If it is not, you will be able to send word to us; and then Jhoti and his advisers will decide on what action they will take.'

'—if any,' thought Ash grimly. For though the princes still maintained their private armies, 'the State Forces', the enormous distance that separated Karidkote from Bhithor was enough to ensure that no military action could be taken by the one against the other, even supposing that the Government of India would have permitted such a thing, which they most certainly would not. Jhoti's only hope would be to lodge a complaint through the proper channels—in this case, the British Resident—from where it would be passed on to the Political Department, who would send to Ajmer, requesting the Agent-to-the-Governor-General to tell the officer in charge of the particular section of Rajputana that included Bhithor to investigate the complaint, and report on it.

Remembering the dilatoriness and disbelief of the Political Officer, and how impossible it had been to make him think ill of the Rana or take any action that might conceivably be questioned by his superiors in Ajmer, Simla and Calcutta, Ash had little hope that anything useful would come of that. Particularly as there would be no question of the Political Officer (or indeed anyone else) being allowed to see or speak to either of the Rana's wives, who of course kept strict purdah. Any attempt to force such an interview would lead to uproar not only in Bhithor, but throughout India, and the most that would be granted—though even that was unlikely—would be an interview with an unseen woman seated on the far side of a curtain and undoubtedly surrounded by a number of people, all of whom would be in the Rana's pay and would keep a check on every word she said.

Under such conditions the truth was unlikely to be spoken; nor would there be any proof that the speaker was in fact one of the Ranis and not some carefully coached Zenana woman. All things considered, thought Ash, it was a thousand pities that Jhoti should have chosen to take some silly boy's *zid* against the Resident in Karidkote . . .

He looked up from the letter in his hand, and meeting Gobind's quiet gaze, said, 'Do you know what is written here?'

Gobind nodded. 'The Rao-Sahib did me the honour of reading it to me before he sealed it, so that I should realize how necessary it was to guard it with great care and see that it did not fall into the wrong hands.'

'Ah,' said Ash, and reached for the lamp.

Held above the glass chimney, the two sheets of thick Indian-made paper blackened and curled and then burst into flame, and Ash turned them this way and that, watching them burn until at length the flames neared his fingers and he dropped the smouldering fragments to the floor, and putting his foot on them, ground them to powder with a vicious twist of his heel.

'There. That has removed at least one of the Rao-Sahib's causes for anxiety. As for the rest, his fears may be well founded, but they come too late. Had he torn up the marriage contracts no one would have blamed him. But he did not do so, and now the harm is done, for the laws and customs of the land are on the Rana's side—and so too is the Political-Sahib, as we have cause to know.'

'That may be true,' agreed Gobind quietly. 'But you are less than just to the Rao-Sahib. Had you known the late Maharajah, you would have realized that the Rao-Sahib had no choice but to do as he did, and see that the marriages were performed.'

'I know,' admitted Ash with a sharp sigh. 'I am sorry. I should not have spoken like that. I know very well that in the circumstances he could do nothing else. Besides, it is over, and we cannot alter the past.'

'That even the gods cannot do,' agreed Gobind soberly. 'But it is the Rao-Sahib's hope, and mine also, that you and I, Sahib, may perhaps be able to do a little towards shaping the future.'

There had been no more talk that night, for Gobind was very tired. Neither he nor his servant Manilal had ever been on a train before, and the journey having left them dizzy and exhausted, both were still asleep when Ash left to go on parade the following morning. It was not until the day's work was over and afternoon well advanced that he was able to speak to Gobind again, but as he had slept very little during the previous night, he had been able to give a good deal of thought to Kaka-ji's disclosures and—when this became intolerable because of the fears that it aroused in him for Juli's safety —to more mundane matters such as the arrangements that must be made for getting Gobind safely to Bhithor. These he put in hand first thing in the morning, despatching his head syce, Kulu Ram, to choose and bargain for a pair of horses from a local dealer, and sending a message to Sarji, asking if he knew anyone who would act as a guide for two travellers wishing to go to Bhithor and anxious to leave on the following day.

The horses and Sarji's reply had been waiting for him on his return to the bungalow, and both had proved equally satisfactory: Sarji wrote that he was sending his own particular *shikari*, Bukta (a hunter who knew every path, game-track and short-cut through the hills), to guide Ash's friends to Bhithor, while the horses that Kulu Ram had purchased were sturdy and reliable animals, sound in wind and limb and capable, said Kulu Ram, of covering as many *koss* a day as the Hakim-Sahib required of them.

There remained only one other matter to be settled, the most important of all: how to establish some method of communication between Gobind in Bhithor and Ash in Ahmadabad without arousing the suspicions of the Rana.

The two had discussed this for hours, riding side by side along the river bank, ostensibly to try out the newly purchased horses but in reality to ensure against being overheard; and later they had talked together in Ash's bedroom until well after midnight, their voices so low that Gul Baz, who had been stationed on the verandah outside to warn off intruders, was barely able to catch more than a faint murmur of sound.

Time was short and there was much that had to be done. A code of some sort was essential if they were to communicate at all—something simple enough to be memorized and that would arouse no suspicions in the event of a message being intercepted—and when they had worked that out to their satisfaction they had to consider ways and means of getting news out of Bhithor, because if the Rana had anything to hide he would certainly see to it that Gobind was closely watched. That problem, however, would have to be solved by Gobind alone, and then only after he had arrived in Bhithor and was able to assess the situation there and discover how much freedom, if any, he would be allowed. Yet plans must still be made, for even if the majority of them proved on his arrival to be impracticable, one at least might work.

'There is also my servant, Manilal,' said Gobind, 'who on account of his speech and appearance is taken to be a simpleton: a foolish yokel, incapable of guile—which is far from the truth. I think we may well find a use for him.'

By the time the clock struck twelve they had discussed at least a dozen plans, one of which resulted in Gobind setting off at nine o'clock on the following morning in search of a certain European-owned shop in the city, because as he had said, 'If the worst comes to the worst I can always say that I must go to Ahmadabad for more drugs with which to treat His Highness. Is there a good *dewai dukan* (medicine shop) in this city? A foreign one, for choice?'

'There is one in the cantonments: Jobbling & Sons, the Chemists, where all the Sahibs and memsahibs buy their tooth powder and air-lotions and many patent medicines from *Belait*. You should be able to get any *dewai* you want there. But the Rana will never let you return here to fetch anything yourself.'

'Maybe not. But whoever is sent here will have to bring with them a piece of paper on which I will have written down the drugs I require. Therefore tomorrow I will visit this chemist and make inquiries as to what medicines they sell, and also try if I cannot get on good terms with the shopkeeper.'

He had left for Bhithor shortly after mid-day, taking with him an assortment of pills and potions that he had bought earlier on the advice of Mr Pereiras, the Eurasian manager of Jobbling & Sons' Ahmadabad branch, with whom he had soon come to a friendly understanding. Ash had returned from the lines in time to see him off, and the two had conferred briefly on the verandah before Gobind and Manilal, accompanied by Sarji's *shikari,* Bukta, who was to guide them to Bhithor by way of Palanpore and the foothills below Mount Abu, rode away from the bungalow and were lost to view among the flame-trees that lined the long cantonment road.

Ten days later Sarji send word that the *shikari* was back, having led the Hakim and his servant to within a mile of the frontier of Bhithor. The Hakim had rewarded Bukta liberally for his services and sent a verbal message to Pelham-Sahib to the effect that he would pray daily that the Sahib would be blessed by health and good fortune and that all things would go smoothly in the months ahead. A pious hope that needed no decoding.

As the days became hotter, Ash rose earlier and earlier of a morning so that he could take Dagobaz out for an hour or two before the routine of Stables; and now that the seasonal training was over, there was more office work. His evenings were usually taken up with polo practice, for the game that had been a new one on the Frontier when he first joined the Guides had spread like wild-fire, until now even cavalry regiments in the south had taken it up, and Ash, having played it before, was much in demand.

His days were therefore fully occupied, which was a godsend to him; though he did not see it like that, and probably would not have admitted it if he had. But at least it prevented him from thinking too much about what might be happening to Juli, and made him tired enough to sleep at night instead of driving himself to the verge of mental exhaustion by lying awake brooding and worrying about the information in Kaka-ji's letter, and its possible implications. Hard work and violent exercise were an anodyne, and one that he should have been grateful for.

Mahdoo wrote by the hand of a bazaar letter-writer to say that he had arrived safely and was pleased to be back in Mansera once more. He was in good health and hoped that Ash was too, and that Gul Baz was looking after him properly. His entire family (there were now three more great-grandchildren, two of them boys) sent their earnest wishes for his continued health, happiness and prosperity—etc., etc. . . .

Ash replied to this, but did not mention Gobind's visit. And curiously enough, neither did Gul Baz when he wrote as promised to give the old man the latest news of Pelham-Sahib and his household, and to assure Mahdoo that they were all keeping well. Though as far as Gul Baz was concerned his silence on that particular point was purely a matter of instinct, since neither Ash nor Gobind had suggested that it might be wiser not to talk of it. But then he too was worried.

Gul Baz, like Mahdoo, had a healthy distrust of Bhithor, and no wish to see the Sahib involved once again in anything whatever to do with that lawless and sinister state or its unprincipled ruler. Yet this, he feared, was what the Hakim from Karidkote was striving to do—though why, and in what way, was more than he could guess (Gul Baz knew a great deal less about Ash than Mahdoo did, and that wise old man had taken care to keep certain of his suspicions to himself).

The anxiety that Gobind's unheralded arrival had aroused in him should, by rights, have subsided with that gentleman's departure. But it had not done so, for Gul Baz noticed that after that the Sahib took to making many small purchases at an *Angrezi*-owned pharmacy, the same shop, by a coincidence—or was it a coincidence?—that the Hakim had patronized on his last morning, and where, according to the driver of the hired tonga that had taken him there (a chatty individual whom Gul Baz had later questioned), he had spent over half an hour in consultation with the shopkeeper, and eventually bought an assortment of foreign nostrums.

By itself, there was nothing strange in that, it being no secret that the Hakim had been sent for to treat the Rana of Bhithor, whom he had once cured of a painful affliction and who therefore had great faith in his powers. Yet why should the Sahib, whose health was excellent, now take to shopping there as often as three or four times a week, when previously he had always left it to Gul Baz to keep him supplied with soap and tooth powder and such things?

Gul Baz did not like it. But there was nothing he could do about it and no one with whom he cared to discuss it. He could only keep his own counsel and hope against hope that an order would soon come from Mardan, summoning the Sahib back to the Guides and the North-West Frontier, for now he too was eager to be away, and hungry for the sight of his own Border-country and the speech of his own people.

Ash, on the other hand—who only a short while ago had been equally impatient to see the last of Gujerat—was suddenly afraid of having to leave it, because if he were to be recalled to Mardan before Gobind managed to smuggle out some news from Bhithor, he might never know what had happened there, or be able to send on a message to Kaka-ji, or do anything to help.

The very thought was so intolerable that at this juncture he would actually have been relieved to hear that he must serve another five years in Gujerat; or even ten or twenty, for to leave now could mean deserting Juli just when she might need help more than she had ever needed it before, and at a time when her very life might depend on his presence here in Ahmadabad, and his willingness to do anything he could to help her.

He had deserted her twice before: once in Gulkote when she was a child, and again in Bhithor—though that had been sorely against his will. He would not do so a third time. Yet if he was ordered back to Mardan, what then? Would it do any good if he were to write to Wally and Wigram Battye, asking them to use their influence to get his recall postponed if they should hear that it was being considered? But then, having told both of them how much he wanted to get back to the Guides, how did he propose to explain this abrupt *volte face* . . . ? 'I'm sorry I can't tell you why I've changed my mind and would rather not come back to the Corps just now, but you'll just have to take my word for it that it's vitally important that I should be able to remain here for the time being—'

They would think he must be ill or mad, and Wally, at least, would expect to be trusted with the truth. But as the truth could not be told there was no point in writing at all.

Ash fell back on hope. With luck the 'Tin Gods' who had banished him to Gujerat had forgotten about him and would leave him alone. Or better still, Gobind would manage to get in touch with him and tell him that their fears were groundless and that all was well with the Ranis of Bhithor, in which case it would not matter how soon he was recalled to the Guides. The sooner the better in fact, for Wally's last letter had increased his longing to get back almost as much as Kaka-ji's letter had made him wish to stay.

Wally wrote to say that the Guides had been in action again, and that Zarin had been wounded, though not seriously. The letter gave a detailed description of the affray (which involved a gang of Utman Khel tribesmen who two years previously had murdered a number of coolies working on the Swat River canal-works), and sang the praises of its instigator, one Captain Cavagnari, Deputy Commissioner of Peshawar, who having heard that the leader and several members of the gang were living in a village called Sapri some five miles upstream from Fort Abazai and just inside the Utman Khel border, sent a message to the village headman demanding their surrender, together with a large sum of money to furnish pensions for the families of the murdered coolies.

The inhabitants of Sapri, fondly imagining their village to be impregnable, replied offensively, and Captain Cavagnari decided to take them by surprise and laid his plans accordingly. Under the command of Wigram Battye, three officers of the Guides, two hundred and sixty-four sowars of the cavalry and a dozen sepoys of the infantry—the latter mounted on mules—set off one night after dark for Sapri, accompanied by Cavagnari, who had managed to keep the whole operation so secret that two of the officers had actually been playing racquets up to the last moment, and left almost straight from the courts.

The first part of the march had been simple, but eight miles short of their goal the country became so rough that the horses and mules had to be sent to Fort Abazai, while the Guides groped their way forward in the darkness on foot. Sapri, still confident that the intervening wilderness of rocks, precipices and nullahs afforded ample protection against any attack, awoke in the dawn to find itself surrounded and rushed for its arms, but after a brisk spell of fighting during which the murdered coolies were fully avenged, the ring-leaders and nine others who had been implicated in that massacre were taken prisoner.

'Our losses were only seven men wounded,' wrote Wally, 'and Wigram has put up Jaggat Singh and Daffadar Tura Baz for the Order of Merit for "Conspicuous bravery in action". So as you can see, we haven't exactly been living an idle life up here. What about you down there? You know, I hate to say it, but your letters seem to contain a great deal about this pearl among horses that you have acquired, but next to nothing about yourself, and it's you and your doings I want to hear about, and not his. Or does nothing ever happen in Ahmadabad and Roper's Horse-Show? Wigram says to send you his salaams. Zarin ditto. Did you hear about that young ass Rikki Smith of the 75th N.I.? Well you'd hardly credit it, but . . .' The rest of the letter consisted of gossip.

Ash put it away with a sigh. He must write to Zarin, and tell him to take better care of himself in future. It was great to hear from Wally and get all the news and gossip of the Regiment; but it would be better still to be able to talk to him again—and to serve once more with a regiment that was always in action, instead of one that had seen little or none since the days of the Mutiny, and to which he was only temporarily attached as an uninvited guest who had been wished on them by a higher authority, and who might at any moment be recalled to his own Corps; '. . . only not too soon,' prayed Ash: not until he had heard from Gobind . . .

But the days dragged by and no word came out of Bhithor; though it was spring now, and over a year since he had arrived in Ahmadabad 'on temporary attachment' to Roper's Horse. How long was temporary? 'This year, next year, sometime . . . ?' What *was* Gobind doing?

Ash paid yet another visit to Jobbling's the Chemist, where he bought a bottle of liniment for the treatment of a fictitious sprain, and passed the time of day with Mr Pereiras, an inveterate gossip who could be counted upon to mention any item of interest (such as a special order for medicines for a ruling prince) without any prompting.

Mr Pereiras had been as voluble as ever and Ash had learned several things about the ailments of a number of prominent people, though nothing about the Rana of Bhithor. But that same evening, returning late to his bungalow, there on the verandah waited a fat, travel-stained figure: Gobind's personal servant, Manilal, bringing news at last.

'This oaf has been here for two hours,' said Gul Baz indignantly, speaking in Pushtu (Bhithor again!), 'but he refuses to eat or drink until he has spoken with you, though I have told him a score of times that when the Sahib returns it will be to bathe and change and eat his dinner before speaking to anyone. But this man is a fool and will not listen.'

'He is the Hakim's servant, and I will see him now,' said Ash, beckoning Manilal to follow. 'And in private.'

The news from Bhithor was neither good nor bad, a circumstance well illustrated by the fact that Manilal had been allowed to travel to Ahmadabad, but that Gobind had not dared send a letter with him for fear that he would be searched. 'Which was done,' said Manilal with a ghost of a smile, '—very thoroughly.' The message was therefore a verbal one.

The Rana, reported Gobind, was suffering from a combination of boils, indigestion and headaches, due largely to chronic constipation. His physical condition, as was only to be expected considering his mode of life, was poor, but improving—the foreign medicines having proved most efficacious. As for the Ranis, from what he had heard, all was well with them.

The younger and Senior Rani, whose confinement was imminent, was reported to be in good health and eagerly awaiting the birth of her child, whom the soothsayers, astrologers and midwives all confidently predicted would be a son. Already preparations were being made to celebrate this auspicious event in a most lavish manner, and a messenger stood ready to ride with the news to the nearest telegraph office (a distance of many miles) from where it would be sent to Karidkote. But Gobind was somewhat disturbed to learn that this was not, as he had supposed, the Senior Rani's first pregnancy but the third . . .

He was at a loss to know why no hint of the two previous pregnancies had ever reached Karidkote, since one would have expected such a pleasant piece of news to be announced immediately, but the fact remained that she had twice miscarried in the early months. This, he imagined, might well have been due to grief and shock, as the first miscarriage had coincided with the deaths of her two waiting-women, and the second with that of the faithful old *dai,* Geeta: which hardly seemed like a coincidence. But though he still suspected that there was some mystery connected with those deaths, one thing was quite clear: the Senior Rani was neither ill-treated nor unhappy.

Extraordinary as it might seem, the marriage that had begun so ominously for her had, if gossip was to be believed (and he personally was inclined to credit it), turned out to be an unqualified success, the little Rani having taken it into her head to fall wildly in love with her unprepossessing husband, while the Rana, for his part, had found the combination of exquisite beauty and extravagant adoration so refreshing to his jaded palate that he had actually lost interest in his catamites, and to please her had dismissed the two handsome and degenerate young men who had previously been his favourite companions. All of which made good hearing.

The Junior Rani, on the other hand, had been less fortunate. Unlike her sister she had not found favour with the Rana and he had refused to consummate the marriage, declaring openly that he would not deign to father a child by a half-caste. She had been banished to a wing of one of the smaller and seldom-used palaces outside the city, from where, after only a month, she had been recalled at the insistence of the Senior Rani. Later she had again left the Zenana Quarters—this time for the Pearl Palace—only to be recalled once more after some months of separation. Since when she had been permitted to remain in the Rung Mahal, and now lived quietly retired in her own suite of rooms.

Gobind was of the opinion that the Rana probably intended to divorce her, and to send her back to Karidkote as soon as her sister the Senior Rani became less dependent upon her, which could be expected to happen once there were little sons and daughters to occupy Shushila-Bai's attention. But this of course was only conjecture, for the Sahib must realize that it was almost impossible (and indeed extremely dangerous) for anyone in Gobind's position to ask leading questions about the Ranis of Bhithor, or to show too much interest in their welfare and their relations with the Rana. Therefore he could well be mistaken in this, as well as in other matters. But though a wife only in name, at least the Junior Rani appeared to be safe and in good health, and it was to be hoped that the same could soon be said for the Senior Rani.

Gobind trusted that the Sahib would write as soon as possible to Karidkote to set the Rao-Sahib's mind at rest. For the present there would appear to be no cause for anxiety, and but for the fact that the deaths of the *dai* and the waiting-women had been concealed from their relations he, Gobind, would have said that there was nothing wrong in Bhithor, or at least, not so far as the two Ranis were concerned. Nevertheless, he confessed that those deaths continued to trouble him: there was something not quite right about them—something unexplained.

'What does he mean by that?' asked Ash. 'What sort of thing?'

Manilal shrugged and said slowly: 'There are too many stories . . . moreover, no two of them agree, which is a strange thing. Like my master, I too am from Karidkote and therefore a stranger and suspect. I cannot ask too many questions or betray too much interest: I can only listen. But it is not difficult to guide the talk into certain channels without seeming to do so, and sitting among the palace servants or strolling in the bazaars of an evening, I have now and then dropped a little word that like a pebble in a pool has set ripples circling outwards . . . If these women did indeed die of a fever, why should there be any talk? Why should anyone trouble themselves over something that happens so often, and to so many? Yet these three deaths have not been forgotten, and those who speak of it do so in whispers; some saying that the serving-women died from this cause and others from that, but none agreeing except on one point—that no one knows the real cause.'

'What do they say of the third woman, the *dai* Geeta?' asked Ash, who remembered the old lady with gratitude.

'They say it was given out that she fell by accident down a steep flight of stairs, or from a certain window, or from the rooftops of the Queen's Palace—for again the stories are all different. There are those who whisper that she was pushed and others who hold that she was dead before she fell—strangled or poisoned, or killed by a blow on the head, and afterwards flung down from a high place so that it would appear to be an accident. Yet no one has put forward a reason why these things should have been done, or by whom—or upon whose orders. Therefore it may be that they are nothing more than the invention of babblers and scandalmongers who like to pretend to more knowledge than their neighbours. But it is curious . . . Curious that there should still be so much talk when two of the women have been dead for well over a year, and the *dai* for close on one.'

That was all the news from Bhithor, and apart from the death of old Geeta, it was better news than Ash had expected. But Manilal was not too sure that he would be allowed to come to Ahmadabad a second time—

The men who had stopped and searched him had found nothing on him except two empty medicine bottles and some money. But they had questioned him exhaustively as to what messages his master had charged him to deliver, to which he had replied, gabbling parrot-wise: 'I require six more bottles of the medicine that was formerly in the larger bottle and two more of that in the smaller, here is the money in payment.' Adding that he meant also to buy on his own account some chickens, the Rao-Sahib being fond of eggs, and perhaps some melons and a certain kind of sweetmeat, and . . .

When they put a stop to this by twisting his arm and demanding to know what further messages the Hakim had sent, he wept copiously (it was one of his accomplishments) and asked *what* other messages? His master had strictly instructed him to take these bottles to the *dewai dukan* in Ahmadabad, and to say to the shopkeeper: 'I require five bottles of . . .' or was it *three* bottles? . . . there now—they had muddled him with their questions and put it out of his head, and the Hakim would be angry.

In the end they had given up and released him, deciding that he was much too foolish to remember more than one thing at a time. 'Also,' said Manilal thoughtfully, 'I do not think that the Rana any longer distrusts the Hakim-Sahib, whose skill and medicines have afforded him much relief, for when the Hakim-Sahib said that he required a further supply of a certain *Angrezi dewai* and desired that I, knowing the *dewai* shop, should be sent to fetch it, there was no objection; though at first they would have had me buy fifty or a hundred bottles, but the Hakim-Sahib said that long before a fraction of that number had been used, the rest would be bad. Even so, the eight will last a long time, so as my master has done as the Sahib suggested in the matter of pigeons, he has charged me to acquire a pair of birds from the Sahib's friend to take back with me.'

This last referred to one of the many plans that had been discussed during Gobind's short visit. Sarji kept carrier-pigeons, and Ash had suggested that he ask for one or two of the birds for Gobind to take with him to Bhithor.

Gobind had refused to do anything so foolish, pointing out that to do this would merely give rise to the suspicion that he intended to send messages to someone outside the state. But he had agreed that something might be made of the idea, and it had been decided that as soon as he was settled in Bhithor he would show a great interest in birds and collect as many as possible—including pigeons, of which there were always great numbers in any Indian city.

Once the people had become accustomed to the sight of the Hakim from Karidkote feeding parrots and putting up nesting boxes and dovecotes, he would see if it was possible to find some way of smuggling in a pair of Sarji's carrier-pigeons.

Manilal's arrival had now solved that particular problem. And as Gobind, on his part, had established a reputation as a bird-lover, it only remained for Ash to acquire the pigeons; though in view of what he had just heard, it seemed to him unnecessary, as there was no great urgency about sending good news out of Bhithor—that could safely be left to the Rana and the Telegraph Office. But if Gobind thought it wise, Ash was not disposed to argue, and he had acquired the birds that same night, riding over to Sarji's estate by moonlight and returning with two pigeons in a small wire cage.

He had pledged Sarji to secrecy after telling him as little as possible (and even that little was not strictly accurate), and Manilal had left next morning, taking with him half-a-dozen bottles of Potter's Sovereign Specific for the Relief of Indigestion and two of Jobbling & Sons' best castor oil, together with an assortment of fruit and sweetmeats and a large wicker-work basket that appeared, on inspection, to contain live poultry: three hens and a cockerel—the fact that it also contained two pigeons being unnoticeable, owing to a cunningly contrived false bottom and the presence of the clucking fowls.

37

'Anyone would think there were no eggs to be had in Bhithor,' sniffed Gul Baz, watching the Hakim's servant ride away. 'And being a fool, he will certainly have been cheated over the price of those chickens.'

Gul Baz was glad to see the back of Manilal, and afraid that his visit might have the same depressing effect upon the Sahib's spirits that the Hakim's had done. But he need not have worried. Manilal's news had lifted a crushing load off Ash's mind, and his spirits soared. Juli was safe and well—and she had 'not found favour with the Rana'.

The relief that those few words had brought him had been so great that hearing them he had, for a moment, felt light-headed. All the intolerable things he had imagined happening to her—the thought of what she might be called upon to endure, and the ugly pictures that would rise before his mind's eye whenever he could not sleep—none of them were true. She was safe from the Rana; and perhaps Gobind was right and once the child was born, Shu-shu would cease to cling to her sister and the Rana would divorce her and send her back to Karidkote. She would be free. Free to marry again . . .

Lying awake in the dark after returning with the pigeons, he had known that he could wait now; and without impatience, because the future that had looked so bleak and meaningless was suddenly filled with hope, and there was something to live for again.

'Pandy seems to be in pretty high feather these days,' remarked the Senior Subaltern a week later, glancing out of a mess window as Ash ran down the steps, vaulted onto his horse and rode off singing 'Johnnie was a Lancer'. 'What do you suppose has come over him?'

'Whatever it is, it's an improvement,' observed the Adjutant, looking up from a tattered copy of *The Bengal Gazette*. 'He hasn't exactly been a ray of sunshine up to now. Perhaps someone has left him a fortune.'

'He doesn't need one,' put in a married Captain a shade sourly.

'Well, he hasn't been, because as a matter of fact I asked him that,' confessed the first speaker ingenuously.

'And what did he say?' inquired the Adjutant, interested.

'Snubbed me. Said he'd been given something a damn' sight better: a future. Which I imagine was his way of saying "If you ask a silly question you'll get a silly answer"—in other words, "mind your own business".'

'Did he, by Jove?' said the Adjutant looking startled. 'I'm not so sure about that. Sounds to me as though he may have heard something, though I'm blowed if I know how he could have done. We only got it an hour ago, and I know the C.O. hasn't passed it on yet.'

'Passed on what?'

'Well, I suppose there's really no reason why you shouldn't know, now that Pandy obviously does. He's to return to his own regiment. An order to that effect came by this morning's dâk. But I imagine that someone at Military Headquarters in 'Pindi blabbed in advance and one of his friends passed on the good news a week or so ago, which would account for his sudden rise in spirits.'

The Adjutant was mistaken. On the contrary, by the time Ash learned of his impending departure the entire mess and most of the rank and file of Roper's Horse had already heard the news, so that in fact he himself was among the last to hear of it. But as far as he was concerned it could not have come at a better time. A fortnight ago he would have received it with dismay, but now there was no longer any urgent reason for wishing to stay here; and coming at this moment, the news seemed to him an omen that his luck had changed at last.

As if to bear this out, the order for his recall ended with the welcome information that Lieutenant Pelham-Martyn was to take any leave due to him before, and not after, rejoining. This meant that he could take at least three months if he wished, as apart from an occasional weekend and a brief visit to Cutch, he had taken no leave since the summer of '76 when he had trekked to Kashmir with Wally —the two of them having decided to save up their leave against the day when Ash returned to the Frontier, when they could go on another trek together, this time to Spiti and across the high passes into Tibet.

'How soon are you proposing to leave us, Pandy?' inquired the Adjutant as Ash came through the outer office after seeing the Colonel.

'As soon as it's convenient,' said Ash promptly.

'Oh, I fancy it's convenient now. We haven't got much on at the moment, so it will be up to you to decide. And there's no need for you to look so damned pleased about it, either!'

Ash laughed and said: 'Was I looking pleased? I'm sorry. It's not that I'm glad to leave. I've had some good times here, but—Well, you might say I've been serving a sentence for the last four years: "doing a stretch". Now it's over and I can go back to my own regiment and my old friends and to my own part of the world again, and I can't help feeling pleased about it. No reflection on Roper's Horse. They're a fine lot.'

'Don't mention it,' said the Adjutant graciously. 'Though I take it we are not to be compared with the Guides. Ah well, I expect I should feel the same, in your shoes. Strange how absurdly attached one becomes to one's own particular crowd. I suppose you won't be selling that horse of yours?'

'Dagobaz? Not likely!'

'I was afraid not. Well, even if we don't exactly break our hearts over losing you, Pandy, we're going to miss that black devil. He'd have won every race you entered him for, next season; and we'd have cleaned out every bookmaker in the Province. How do you propose to get him to Mardan?'

'Take him up by train. He won't like it, but I can always doss down with him if necessary. He'll have his own syce, anyway.'

'If you'll take my advice,' said the Adjutant, 'you'll nip down and see the station-master this evening. It's not all that easy to reserve a truck, and if you plan to leave fairly soon, you'd better make sure that you can get one. Otherwise you may find yourself being held up for a good deal longer than you expect.'

'Thanks for the tip,' said Ash gratefully, and took himself off then and there to the railway station, where he discovered that the Adjutant had been right. If he meant to travel on the same train as Dagobaz, it did not look as though he would be able to leave Ahmadabad within the next ten or fifteen days. And even that would entail a judicious amount of bribery and corruption.

'Arranging accommodation for quadruped is veree difficult affair and will occupy much time, for it will mean much booking ahead,' explained the Eurasian station-master. 'You see, Mr Martyn, there are too many trains, all of different gauges. Now if I obtain a horse-van for you on thee Bombay-and-Baroda line, this is veree fine. But then that is only small part of your journey, and what, I am asking, will occur when you arrive at Bombay Central and find that none is available on thee G.I.P. railway, to which you will there transfer yourself? Or when you must change again at Aligarh onto thee East

Indian Railway Line, which is again different gauge, and there is likewise no van? I am fearing veree greatly, sir, that you will endure many vexatious delays if you leave hastily and before all these bookings are pukka.'

Ash had hoped to leave within a day or two, but he accepted the station-master's verdict with good grace. There was, he decided, no tearing hurry. The delay would give him more time in which to dispose of the rest of his stable, and allow Wally more time to arrange matters at his end. There was no point in trying to rush things, and anyway, another week or so in Ahmadabad would be no great hardship.

He returned to the bungalow in high spirits, and that night he wrote several letters before he went to bed. A long one to Wally, full of plans for their leave, a brief one to Zarin, sending messages to Koda Dad whom he said he hoped to see again before long, and another to Mahdoo, telling him the good news and urging him to stay where he was until further notice and to be prepared to come to Mardan in two to three months' time—Gul Baz, who would also be going on leave, would come and fetch him when the time was ripe.

'The old one will be pleased,' beamed Gul Baz, collecting the finished letters. 'I will see that Gokal takes these at once to the dâk-*khana* (post office) so that they go out with the morning dâk and there is no delay.'

Wally's telegraphed reply arrived a few days later. It read: *Unable get leave before end May owing unforeseen circumstances can meet you Lahore thirtieth three rousing cheers writing.*

Coming on top of the station-master's gloomy assessment of the time needed to complete travelling arrangements for Dagobaz, this was not as disappointing as it might have been, for at most it meant delaying his departure for a few more weeks—unless he left as soon as possible and made straight for Mardan, from where he could reach Koda Dad's village in a day and put in the extra time there until Wally's leave was due.

The prospect was an alluring one, but on consideration he discarded it—largely because it occurred to him that in view of the reason for his four-year exile from the North-West Frontier Province, it would hardly be diplomatic to celebrate the lifting of the ban by spending the first few days of his leave on the wrong side of the Border. Besides, it would also entail a lot of extra travelling, as Lahore was the obvious starting-point for the trek he had in mind.

On both these counts his reasoning was sound; but the decision proved to be a vital one, though at the time he did not realize this. It was only long afterwards, on looking back, that he recognized how much had hung upon it. Had he chosen to leave for the Punjab at the first possible date, he would not have received Gobind's message, and if he had not had that . . . But in the event he elected to stay and having been given permission to take a month's local leave 'pending departure' in addition to the three he had already put in for, he went off to shoot a lioness in the Gir Forest with Sarji and Sarji's wise, wizened, little *shikari,* Bukta, leaving Gul Baz to deal with packing up the bungalow.

The lioness they were after was a notorious man-eater who for two years had terrorized an area larger than the Isle of Wight, and was reported to have killed more than fifty people. A price had been put on her head and a score of sportsmen and *shikaris* had gone after her, but the man-eater had grown too cunning, and so far the only hunter to lay eyes on her had not lived to tell the tale.

That Ash succeeded where so many had failed was due in part to beginners' luck, but even more to the genius of Bukta, who—so Sarji averred—had more knowledge of *shikar* in his little finger than any other ten *shikaris* between the Gulfs of Kutch and Cambay. In recognition of this, and remembering his services to Gobind and Manilal, Ash had presented the little man with a Lee Enfield rifle, the first that Bukta had ever seen, and on which he had cast covetous eyes.

Bukta's delight in the rifle and its performance more than equalled Ash's satisfaction in bringing down the man-eater, though his pleasure in this success would have been keener if it had not been that on the very day before they were to leave for the forest, one of the pigeons that Manilal had taken with him to Bhithor returned.

Sarji had seen it come homing into the pigeon-loft above the stables, and had sent a servant to Ash's bungalow with a sealed packet containing the scrap of paper that had been fastened to its leg.

The message was a short one: Shushila had given birth to a daughter and mother and child were both well. That was all. But reading it, Ash was conscious of a sudden sinking of his heart. A daughter . . . a daughter instead of the longed-for son . . . Would a girl succeed in filling Shu-shu's heart and mind to the extent that a boy would have done?—enough to make her lose her dependence on Juli and allow her to go?

He tried to console himself with the reflection that, son or daughter, the baby was Shushila's first-born; and if it took after her it would be beautiful, so that once she got over the disappointment at its sex she was bound to love it dearly. Nevertheless a doubt remained: a small, lurking shadow in the back of his mind that spoilt some of his enjoyment in the tense, exciting, frightening days and nights in the Gir Forest that followed.

Returning in triumph to Ahmadabad with the scraped and salted hide of the man-eater, he encountered an *ekka* being driven at a rattling pace in the opposite direction, and was almost past it when he recognized one of the occupants and pulled up to hail him.

'Red!' yelled Ash. 'Hi, Captain Red—belay there.'

The *ekka* came to a stop and Ash ranged alongside, demanding to know what Captain Stiggins was about, where he was off to, and why hadn't he sent word that he would be visiting Ahmadabad?

'Bin seeing an agent. I'm on me way back to Malia. Didn't know I'd be a comin' 'ere until the last minute,' said Captain Stiggins, answering the questions in strict rotation. He added that he had called at Ash's bungalow on the previous day and been told by Gul Baz that the Sahib was away on leave in the Gir Forest, pending his return to the North-West Frontier.

'Then why didn't you wait? He must have told you that I was expected back today, and you know very well that there's always a bed for you any time you want it,' said Ash indignantly.

'Couldn't, son. I gotter get back to the old *Morala*. We're shippin' a cargo o'cotton over to Kutch termorrer. But I was right sorry to 'ear that you were orf up ter the Frontier and that I'd missed seein' you ter say good-bye and good luck.'

'Come on back with me, Red,' urged Ash. 'Surely the cotton can wait? After all, if there was gale or a fog or something like that it would have to, wouldn't it? Dammit, this may be the last time I'll see you!'

'Wouldn't be serprised,' nodded the Captain. 'But that's life, that is. 'Ere today and gorn tomorrer; "Man fleeth as a shadder an' never continueth in one stay". No son; carn't be done, not no 'ow. But I gotter better idea. Seein' as you're on leaf, why don't yer come along o' me for the trip? Land yer back nex' Toosday, cross me 'eart.'

Ash had accepted with alacrity and spent the next few days on board the *Morala* as the guest of the owner, lazing on deck in the shadow of the sails, fishing over the side for shark and barracuda, or listening to tales of the old East India Squadron in the days of John Company's greatness.

It was a peaceful and relaxing interlude, and when the Captain disclosed that the *Morala* would be sailing in a few weeks for the coast of Baluchistan, and suggested that Ash and Gul Baz should come half-way and be put off at Kati on the Indus, from where they could go by river boat up to Attock, he was tempted to agree. But there was Wally to be thought of—and Dagobaz too. The *Morala* had no proper accommodation for a horse, and on the open deck Dagobaz would have had a bad time of it in anything more than a gentle swell. He was obliged to refuse the offer, though he did so with regret, the more so because he realized that he was unlikely to meet Red Stiggins again, and he had enjoyed knowing him.

That was the worst of making friends like Red and Sarji: people who were not 'members of the Club'—that closed society of Anglo-Indians who were moved across the vast map of India from this station to that and back again, on order from Simla or Calcutta or some other Seat of the Mighty, so that in time most of them came to know each other by repute even if they never actually met.

There was always a chance that in the course of his military career he would meet Mrs Viccary or one or other of the officers of Roper's Horse once more. But the odds were against his ever seeing either Sarji or Red again, and the thought depressed him, for in their different ways both had helped to make his stay in Gujerat far more enjoyable than it might otherwise have been: Sarji more than Red, for while Captain Stiggins had been something of a shooting star, flashing briefly into view and disappearing again with equal abruptness, Sarji had been a frequent and valued companion. Gay and talkative or restfully silent to suit the occasion, seldom if ever out of temper, he had been an invaluable ally in times of restlessness and despair, and had provided a means of escape from the restricted life of the cantonment.

'I shall miss Sarji,' thought Ash. 'And Red too.' But there would be Wally waiting for him at Lahore and Zarin in Mardan, with Koda Dad a mere afternoon's ride away across the plain. And old Mahdoo would be in his quarters at Mardan ahead of him, pleased to be on familiar territory once more and waiting to welcome him back. It was a pleasant prospect, and suddenly he could not wait to leave.

But he was never to see Mahdoo again. The letter that he had written telling the old man of his recall to Mardan had arrived too late, for Mahdoo had died in his sleep less than twenty-four hours before it should have reached him, and by the time it was delivered he was already in his grave. His relations, who did not understand the workings of the telegraph, sent the news by dâk to young Kadera, his assistant, and Gul Baz was waiting with it when Ash returned to Ahmadabad.

'It is a great loss to us all,' said Gul Baz. 'He was a good man. But he has fulfilled his years and his reward is sure, since it is written in the Sura of the Merciful "shall the reward of goodness be anything but good?" Therefore do not grieve for him, Sahib.'

But Ash had grieved deeply for Mahdoo, mourning the loss of someone who had been part of his life ever since that far-off day when he had been handed over to the care of Colonel Anderson and sent off on the first stage of the long journey to Bombay and England, a journey that would have been a nightmare had it not been for the presence of Mahdoo and Ala Yar, who had talked to him in his own tongue; and on many occasions during the years that followed given him advice and comfort and support. When he returned to India they had come with him, and when Ala Yar died, Mahdoo had remained at his post. Now he too had gone, and Ash could not bear to think that he would never see that kindly wrinkled face again, or hear the bubble of his hookah in the twilight.

The blow had been all the worse for coming at a time when the future had taken a rosier hue, and on the heels of those exhilarating days in the Gir Forest and that peaceful voyage on the *Morala*. Ash took it hard, and attempted to work off his grief by going for long, solitary rides across country, giving Dagobaz his head and taking banks, irrigation ditches, thorn hedges and sunken roads as they came, and at a reckless speed as though he were striving to out-distance his thoughts and memories. But both kept pace with him, and the restlessness and disquiet that had temporarily left him was back once more.

However fast and far he rode, and however tired he was on his return, he could not sleep; and Gul Baz, coming to wake him with the morning mug of tea, would find him standing on the verandah, staring out across the acre of trees and dusty grass that passed for a garden. And would know from his haggard face and the lines about his eyes that the night had again been a white one.

'It is not right that you should grieve in this manner,' chided Gul Baz disapprovingly, 'for it is written in the Book that "all who live on earth are doomed to die". Therefore to mourn thus is to question the wisdom of God, who of His goodness permitted Mahdoo-ji to live to a peaceful and honourable old age, and decreed both the hour and the manner of his death. Put aside your sorrow and be thankful that so many good years upon this earth were granted to one who is now in Paradise. Moreover, very soon now you will be back in Mardan and among friends again, and all this will be behind you. I will go again to the railway station and inquire if the carriages have been arranged for yet. All is packed and ready here, and we can leave within a day.'

'I'll go myself,' said Ash. And he had ridden down to the station and received the welcome news that the reservations he had asked for had been made at last—but for the following Thursday, which meant that he would have to spend the best part of another week in Ahmadabad.

The thought of sitting around among the packed and corded luggage that stood ready in the bungalow was dispiriting, and he decided that he would ride over to Sarji's house and ask if he could stay there for part of the time. But he was saved the trouble, for on returning to his bungalow he found Sarji himself waiting for him on the verandah, comfortably ensconced in one of the long wicker chairs.

'I have something for you,' said Sarji, lifting a languid hand. 'The second pigeon came back this morning, and as I had business in the city I thought I would play *chupprassi* (peon) and bring you the message myself.'

Ash snatched the small scrap of paper from him, and unrolling it, read the first lines with a sudden lift of the heart. *'The Rana is ill of a fatal sickness and will not live for more than a handful of days'*, wrote Gobind. *'This has become clear to all . . .'*

'Dying!' thought Ash, and smiled without knowing it—a wide, grim, glittering smile that showed his clenched teeth—'he may be dead already. She will be a widow—she'll be free.' He felt no sympathy for the Rana. Or for Shu-shu, who if gossip could be believed had fallen in love with the man, because he could only think of what this would mean for Juli and himself: Juli widowed, and free . . .

He steadied himself and read on; and all at once the day was no longer hot or the sunlight bright, and there was a constriction about his heart.

'. . . *and I have now learned that when he dies his wives will be-*

*come suttee, being burned with him according to the custom. This is
already spoken of, for his people follow the old laws and pay no
heed to those of the Raj, and unless you can prevent it, it will surely
be done. I will strive to keep him alive for as long as possible. But it
will not be long. Therefore warn those in authority that they must act
swiftly. Manilal will leave for Ahmadabad within the hour. Send
more pigeons and . . .'*

The lines of minute writing blurred and wavered before Ash's eyes
and he could no longer focus them. He turned blindly away and
groping for the back of the nearest chair, gripped it as though to
steady himself and spoke in a breathless whisper: 'No—it's not possible! They couldn't do it!'

The words were barely audible, but the horror in them was unmistakable and it shocked Sarji out of his lounging attitude. He said
sharply: 'It is bad news, then? What is it? What is not possible?'

'Saha-gamana,' whispered Ash without turning. 'Suttee . . . The
Rana is dying, and when he dies they mean to see that his wives are
burnt with him. I must see the Commissioner—the Colonel—I
must . . .'

'Ah, *chut!*' said Sarji impatiently. 'Do not distress yourself, my
friend. They will not do it. It is against the law.'

Ash jerked round to glare at him. 'You do not know Bhithor!'—his
voice had shot up, and Gul Baz, appearing in a doorway with a tray
of refreshments, froze at the sound of that hated word—'or the
Rana. Or—' He broke off and, turning, leapt down the verandah
steps shouting for Kulu Ram to bring Dagobaz back.

A moment later he was again in the saddle and galloping down the
drive like a maniac, raising a cloud of dust and grit and leaving Sarji,
Gul Baz and Kulu Ram to stare after him in open-mouthed dismay.

38

'I can only suppose that you have taken leave of your senses,' said Colonel Pomfret austerely. 'No, of course I cannot send any of my men into Bhithor. Such an action would be quite out of order; nor, I may say, would I do so if it were not. Matters of this nature are best left to the civil authorities or the police, and not to the army; though I would advise you against bursting in on anyone else in this unceremonious manner with some wild rumour that no one in their right minds would take seriously. I cannot understand what you are doing here, anyway. I thought you were on leave and off shooting somewhere.'

Two white patches showed on Ash's lean cheeks, but he managed to keep his voice under control and said briefly: 'I was, sir.'

'Then you had better go back there. No point in hanging about cantonments doing nothing. Haven't they been able to arrange your reservations on the trains yet?'

'Yes, sir. They're for next Thursday. But—'

'Hmm. Wouldn't have given you leave if I'd known that you'd be staying here at a loose end for all this time. Well, if you've said all you want to say, you will oblige me by leaving. I have work to do. Good-day.'

Ash withdrew, and disregarding the Colonel's advice, called on the Commissioner; only to find that the Commissioner shared Colonel Pomfret's views—particularly on the subject of junior officers who demanded to see him towards mid-day and on being told that the hour was inconvenient, and they should either come later in the day or earlier on the following one, burst into his presence with some cock-and-bull story and a demand that he, the Commissioner, should take immediate action on it.

'Poppycock!' snorted the Commissioner. 'I don't believe a word of it: and if you knew these people as well as I do, you wouldn't either. It don't do to believe more than a fraction of what they tell you, as most of 'em will always tell a lie rather than speak the truth, and trying to find out what really happened is like drawing eye-teeth or hunting for that proverbial needle in a haystack. This friend of yours —Guptar or Gobind or whatever his name is—is either pulling your leg or else he's too gullible by half. I can assure you that no one nowadays would dare to be party to such a thing as you suggest, and it's easy to see that your credulous friend has been the victim of a hoax. And you too, I fancy! Well, let me remind you that this is 1878 and that the law against suttee has been in force for over forty years. It is not likely to be flouted now.'

'But you don't know Bhithor!' cried Ash, as he had to both Sarji and Colonel Pomfret. 'Bhithor doesn't belong to this century, let alone this half of it. I don't believe they have taken in that there is such a thing as the British Raj, or if they have, that it has anything whatever to do with them.'

'Gammon,' snapped the Commissioner, annoyed (he lunched at noon and it was already past that), 'you exaggerate. It is obvious that—'

'But you haven't *been* there,' interrupted Ash.

'What has that to say to anything? Bhithor is neither in my Province nor under my jurisdiction, so even were I inclined to place any credence in this ridiculous tale, which I fear I am not, I could still do nothing to help you. Your informant would have been better advised to approach the Political Officer responsible for that section of Rajputana—that is, if he really believes his own story, which I doubt.'

'But sir, I have told you that he cannot get any message out of Bhithor,' persisted Ash desperately. 'There is no telegraph or post office, and though they may allow his servant to come here to buy medicines and drugs, they would never permit him to go anywhere else. If you would only send a telegram to the Political Agent—'

'I shall do no such thing,' said the Commissioner testily, and rose to his feet to show that the interview was at an end. 'It has never been the policy of my Department to interfere with the administration of other provinces or to instruct those in charge of them, who are, believe me, more than able to deal competently with their own affairs.'

Ash said slowly: 'Then . . . you will not do anything?'

'It is not a question of "will not", but "cannot". And now, if you will excuse me—'

Ash ignored the request and stayed where he was, arguing, pleading and explaining for a further five minutes. But to no avail, for the Commissioner had merely lost his temper, and having informed him tersely that he was meddling in matters that he did not understand (and that were, in any case, no concern of his) had ended by ordering him to leave immediately or be forcibly removed by the guard.

Ash left, realizing that he had wasted the best part of two hours and that if he had had his wits about him he would have sent off a telegram before attempting to talk to anyone.

The Telegraph Office was closed to the public during the time of the mid-day meal and afternoon siesta, but he routed out an indignant clerk and induced him to send off four urgent telegrams: one to Kaka-ji, another to Jhoti, the third to that same Political Officer who had been so unhelpful in the matter of the Rana's chicanery over the marriage contracts, and finally (in case that obstinate official proved to be as useless now as he had been on that occasion) a fourth to the Honourable the Agent to the Governor-General, Rajputana—familiarly known as the A.G.G.—in Ajmer: an afterthought that was to prove disastrous, though it had seemed an excellent idea at the time. But then Ash had no idea who the present incumbent was, and had not taken the trouble to find out.

It had not been at all easy to cajole the Eurasian telegraph clerk into transmitting these telegrams. The contents of all four had alarmed him, and he had protested strongly against 'such high matters' being sent in clear. Messages of this kind ought, in his opinion, to be sent in code or not at all. 'I am telling you, sir, that telegrams, they are not secret things. By no means. They are getting sent on from one *tar-khana* to another, and veree many cheeky fellows are seeing them by the way—peons and such-like too—and they will be chitter-chattering about them to one and all.'

'Good,' said Ash shortly, 'I'm delighted to hear it. The more talk the better.'

'But sir—!' wailed the clerk, 'there will be much unfortunate gossip and scandal. And what if this Rana-Sahib should not after all die, and you are finding yourself in loads of trouble for misrepresentation and libels and such things? And me too, because I am sending out these accusations? I may be blamed for this and get into hot waters, and if I am losing my job—'

It had taken fifteen minutes and fifty rupees to overcome the clerk's scruples, and the telegrams had been sent. After which Ash had gone to the bungalow of Mr Pettigrew, District Superintendent of Police, in the hope (a faint one by now) that the police might prove more helpful than the military or the civil arm.

Mr Pettigrew had certainly been less sceptical than either Colonel Pomfret or the Commissioner, but he too had pointed out that this was a matter for the authorities in Rajputana, adding that they probably knew a good deal more about what went on there than Lieutenant Pelham-Martyn would seem to think. However he had at least promised to send a personal telegram to a colleague in Ajmer—one Carnaby, who was a personal friend of his.

'Nothing official, you understand,' said Pettigrew. 'One doesn't want to stick one's neck out and sound like a meddling nosey-parker. And to be honest, I can't say that I take this pigeon-post message of yours all that seriously. You'll probably find it's all a hum. On the other hand, it's just possible that there might be something in it, so there's no harm in dropping a hint to Tim Carnaby—just to be on the safe side. He's not the type of fellow who prefers to let sleeping dogs lie, and he'll certainly see that it's looked into. I'll get a wire sent off to him at once, and you can be sure that if anything needs to be done he'll do it.'

Ash thanked him with a good deal of fervour and rode away feeling much easier in his mind. After the agonizing frustration of the morning, it was reassuring to find someone who did not dismiss Gobind's warning as pure nonsense, and was actually prepared to do something about it—even though that something was no more than an unofficial hint to a personal friend.

But as matters turned out he might have saved himself the visit, for the D.S.P.'s efforts on his behalf came to nothing. The friend had gone on leave three days before the telegram was dispatched, and owing to Pettigrew's anxiety to avoid any suggestion of interfering with another man's work, the information it contained had been presented in such casual and chatty terms that it failed to convey any suggestion of urgency. The officer deputizing for the absent Tim Carnaby had, in consequence, not thought it worthwhile to send it on and had thrust it into a drawer with other letters that he could read on his return.

The effects of Ash's own telegrams had been equally abortive. Jhoti, with Kaka-ji's approval, had sent one of his own to the A.G.G. Rajputana, on receipt of which the A.G.G. had in turn wired the British Resident in Karidkote, whose reply had been non-committal. It was, he said, well known that the Rana's health was not of the best, but this was the first anyone in Karidkote had heard that he might be dying, and he had reason to believe that the source of this information was not entirely trustworthy. Anything emanating from that particular quarter should be treated with reserve, as the officer in question not only appeared to have too much influence over the young Maharajah, but was by reputation both eccentric and undisciplined.

Unfortunately, these observations had arrived in Ajmer only hours before a letter from the Political Officer; and taken together the two communications had effectively destroyed Ash's credibility—and with it any chance that his warnings would be taken seriously. For by an unkind quirk of fate the newly appointed Agent to the Governor-General, who had taken office only a few weeks previously, happened to be that same Ambrose Podmore-Smyth—now Sir Ambrose —who six years earlier had married Belinda Harlowe. And what with Belinda and her father and the gossips of the Peshawar Club, everything he had heard of young Pelham-Martyn had inspired him with a dislike for his wife's former suitor that time had done nothing to eradicate.

Sir Ambrose strongly disapproved of Englishmen who 'went native', and his wife's garbled account of her ex-admirer's early history (it was perhaps fortunate that Belinda could not recall the name of the state in which Ash had lived—and very little else either) had scandalized her husband. No wonder the fellow lacked steadiness and a proper sense of moral values, and had brought disgrace upon his race and his regiment by absconding into tribal territory with a handful of dismissed sepoys. One could only hope that he would meet a speedy and merciful death there and no more would be heard of him.

Sir Ambrose had been unpleasantly surprised to find that a telegram from Ahmadabad, sent in clear and containing startling allegations, was from someone signing himself Pelham-Martyn. He could not believe it was the same Pelham-Martyn, but as the name was an uncommon one it might be worthwhile to check, and he had directed his Personal Assistant to do so immediately; and also to see that a copy of the telegram was sent to the Political Officer whose area included Bhithor, inviting his comments. After which, conscious of having done all that could be expected of him, he had retired to his wife's drawing-room for a pre-tiffin drink, where he happened to mention the odd coincidence of that name from the past.

'You mean *Ashton?*' cried Belinda (a Belinda, alas, whom Ash would barely have recognized). 'Then he did get back safely after all! Well I must say, I never thought he would. Nor did anyone else. Papa said it was good riddance of bad rubbish. But I don't think Ashton was bad, only rather wild. Just fancy his turning up again.'

'He has not "turned up",' said Sir Ambrose tartly. 'There is no reason to believe it's the same fellow. Might be a relative: though I doubt it. Probably no connection at all, and we shall find—'

'Oh fiddlesticks!' interrupted his wife. 'Of course it's Ashton—it's so like him. He was always getting mixed up with things that were none of his business; and with natives, too. Now here he is doing it again. It must be him. It couldn't be anyone else. I wonder what on earth he's doing in this part of the world? Do you suppose he's still . . .' She broke off, and leaning back in her chair, surveyed her lord and master with a dissatisfied eye.

Time and the climate of India had not been kind to Sir Ambrose. They had changed him from a portly, self-satisfied man into an obese, bald and insufferably pompous one, and Belinda, studying that purple countenance with its fringe of grey whiskers and plethora of chins, caught herself wondering if it had been worth it. She was Lady Podmore-Smyth, the wife of a tolerably rich and important man, and mother of two healthy children (both girls, which was not her fault though Ambrose seemed to think otherwise) and yet she was not happy.

Life as a Resident's lady had not been nearly as amusing as she had imagined: she missed the gaiety of a military station in British India, disliked the whole tedious and painful business of child-bearing, found her husband dull and existence in a native state boring beyond words. 'I wonder,' mused Belinda aloud, 'what he looks like now? He used to be very handsome . . . and so madly in love with me.'

She preened herself complacently, sublimely unaware that the years had been even more unkind to her than they had to her elderly husband, and that she was no longer the slim slip of a girl who had once been the belle of Peshawar, but a stout matron with faded blond hair, an acid tongue and a discontented expression. 'Of course, that was why he did it—ran away from his regiment I mean. I've always known that he did it because of me and that he went in search of death; or to forget. Poor Ashton . . . I have often thought that if only I had been a little kinder—'

'Rubbish,' snorted Sir Ambrose. 'If you have given so much as one moment's thought to him from that day to this, I confess I should be exceedingly surprised. As for his being madly in love with you . . . Now, now, Belinda, there's no need to make a scene about it; I'm sorry I mentioned the fellow. I should have known better . . . I am *not* shouting—!'

He stamped out of the room in a fury, banging the door behind him, and was not best pleased when his Personal Assistant's inquiries disclosed that the author of that impertinent telegram was indeed none other than the Ashton Pelham-Martyn who had once aspired to his wife's hand and subsequently caused a great deal of talk by behaving in a manner that could only be described as unbalanced. Nor was his temper improved when later on the Political Officer's reply to his request for comments on the contents of the telegram arrived.

Ash's chickens were coming home to roost with a vengeance, for Major Spiller, the Political Officer (who had never forgiven what he had taken to be a rude and insufferably high-handed letter, sent from Bhithor over two years ago), began by saying that he himself had received a similar telegram from the same source, and went on to comment at length—and forcibly.

He had already, wrote Spiller, had some experience of Captain, now Lieutenant, Pelham-Martyn in the past, and considered him to be an officious trouble-maker bent on creating a scandal and causing dissention. A few years ago the fellow had done his utmost to disrupt relations between the Government of India and the State of Bhithor (which until then had always been cordial in the extreme) and had it not been for his, Spiller's, firmness, he might well have succeeded in doing so. Now, once again, for reasons best known to himself, he was endeavouring to stir up trouble. However, as no reliance could be placed on anything he said, Major Spiller for one intended to treat these wild allegations with the contempt they deserved: particularly in view of the fact that those whose business it was to know what went on in Bhithor had assured him that the Rana's illness was no more than a slight recurrence of the malarial fever with which he had been plagued at intervals during the past few years, and there was not the least danger of his succumbing to it. The whole thing was a mare's nest, and it might be as well if Lieutenant Pelham-Martyn was given a sufficiently strong reprimand to discourage him from any further meddling in matters that were no concern of his; and it was inexcusable that . . .

Sir Ambrose had not bothered to read further, since the writer's opinion merely confirmed his own: Belinda had been right and that insufferable young blackguard was at his old tricks again. Sir Ambrose threw the entire correspondence into the waste-paper basket, and having dictated a soothing reply to His Highness the Maharajah of Karidkote, assuring him that there was no need for anxiety, sent a frosty letter to Army Headquarters, complaining of Lieutenant Pelham-Martyn's 'subversive activities' and suggesting that it might be as well if his present interests and past history were investigated with a view to his being deported as an Undesirable British Subject.

At about the same time as his telegram (together with Jhoti's, and the Resident's and the Political Officer's comments) was being consigned to the Honourable the Agent to the Governor-General's waste-paper basket, Ash was greeting a tired and dusty traveller who had arrived that morning from Bhithor.

Manilal had set out for Ahmadabad less than twenty minutes after Gobind had released the second pigeon. But while the pigeon had covered the distance in a few hours, Manilal had taken the best part of a week, for his horse had strained a tendon and thereafter he had been forced to go slowly, the roads being rutted by cart-wheels and deep in dust, which did not make for easy going at the best of times.

'What news?' demanded Ash, running down the steps as the tired man dismounted under the shadow of the porch. Ash had ridden out three days running in the hope of intercepting Manilal, and had become increasingly anxious when there had been no sign of him, or any reply from the District Superintendent of Police's friend in Ajmer (he had not been so sanguine as to imagine that his own telegrams would be answered). To tempt Fate, he had stayed indoors that morning, and towards noon Fate had rewarded him by sending Gobind's servant to the bungalow.

'Very little,' croaked Manilal, whose throat was dry with dust: 'except that he was still alive when I left. But who knows what may have happened since? Has the Sahib warned the Government and Karidkote of what is toward?'

'Assuredly, within a few hours of that pigeon reaching home. I have done all I could.'

'That is good news,' said Manilal hoarsely. 'Have I your leave, Sahib, to eat and drink and perhaps rest a little before I talk further? I have not slept since the horse injured himself shying in terror at a tiger that crossed our path.'

He slept for the rest of the day and reappeared after sundown, still heavy-eyed, to squat on the verandah and tell Ash all that Gobind had not been able to send by pigeon-post. Apparently the palace physicians still said that the Rana would recover, insisting that he was only suffering an unusually severe attack of malarial fever to which he had been subject for many years. But in Gobind's view this was no mere fever, but a sickness of the body for which there was no cure, and the most that could be done was to administer drugs to relieve the pain—and hope to delay the end until the Government sent someone in authority to see to it that when he died it would mean one death only, and not three.

Gobind had apparently managed, by devious means, to establish contact with the Junior Rani through a serving-woman whose relatives were susceptible to bribery, and who was herself said to be much attached to Kairi-Bai. In this way several messages had been smuggled into the Zenana Quarters, and one or two had even been answered, though the replies had been short and uncommunicative, and told Gobind nothing beyond the fact that the Junior Rani and her sister were well—which should have satisfied him, but failed to do so because there was something about those letters that made him uneasy—perhaps the very fact that they were too cautious. Was Nimi, the serving-woman, not to be trusted, and did Kairi-Bai know or suspect this? But if that were so it could only mean that there was something that must be concealed . . . unless he was being needlessly suspicious.

Then the baby had been born, and on the following morning Gobind had received a letter from Kairi-Bai that was not in answer to one of his own. It had been a frantic plea for help, not for herself, but for Shushila-Rani, who was in a serious condition and must have attention at once—if possible, a European nurse from the nearest *Angrezi* hospital. It was a matter of the utmost urgency and Gobind must send for one immediately and in secret, before it was too late.

There had been a withered *dakh* flower enclosed in the letter, which is the sign for danger; and seeing it Gobind had been seized with the terrifying suspicion that the Senior Rani, having failed to produce an heir, was perhaps being poisoned—as rumour said the previous one had been—

'Yet what could the Hakim-Sahib do?' asked Manilal with a shrug. 'It was not possible for him to do as Kairi-Bai desired. And even if he had been able to send such a message out of Bhithor, the Rana would never have permitted any foreign woman, doctor or not, to force her way into the Zenana and examine his wife. Not unless such a one came with a strong escort of soldiers, guns and police-Sahibs, or unless he himself could be persuaded to send for one.'

Gobind had courageously tried the latter course, but the Rana would not hear of it and was angered that such a suggestion should even have been put to him. He despised all foreigners as barbarians and would, if he had his way, have refused to allow any of them to set foot in his state, let alone have any personal contact with him. Had not he, alone among all his neighbouring princes, refused to appear at any of the durbars arranged by the Raj to announce that the Queen of England had been declared *Kaiser-i-Hind* (empress of India), excusing himself on the grounds that he had fallen ill and was unfortunately unable to travel?

The suggestion that he of all people should now invite an *Angrezi* woman to come and poke her nose in his wife's affairs was offensive. Besides, what could a foreign woman possibly know of Hindu medicine and the arts of healing? There was nothing wrong with the Rani that rest and proper care would not put right, and if the Hakim doubted it he was at liberty to question the *dai* who had presided at the birth.

Gobind had taken advantage of this unexpected offer, and been favourably impressed by the midwife; though she had been strangely uncommunicative on the subject of her predecessor, old Geeta from Karidkote, and when questioned about the dead woman had muttered that she knew nothing—nothing at all—and hastily changed the subject. Apart from that, she struck him as a sensible woman with a sound knowledge of midwifery.

The *dai* had assured him that contrary to all expectations, the birth had proved an easy one. There had been no complications and the Rani was in good health. Her disappointment at the infant's sex had affected her spirits, but that was understandable as she had set her heart on having a son, and the astrologers and soothsayers, not to mention her own women, had foolishly bolstered her hopes by assuring her that the coming child would be a boy. However, she would get over that before long, and if the gods were kind the next one, or the one after that, would be a son. There was plenty of time for she was young—and also far stronger than her frail appearance suggested.

The *dai* had given Gobind a good deal of technical information on the subject of the Rani's physical condition following her delivery, and left him feeling reassured as to her health and no longer so uneasy as to her safety, since he did not believe that the woman was lying. He came to the conclusion that Kairi-Bai must have heard those ugly whispers about the death of the Rana's previous wife, and was in consequence afraid that now her sister too had borne a daughter she might be removed in the same way. This was highly unlikely, if only for the reason that Shushila-Bai was an exceptionally beautiful woman whom the Rana loved, while her predecessor, from all reports, had been plain, fat and stupid, and wholly lacking in charm.

Gobind had sent a reassuring note to the Junior Rani, but had received no answer; and a week later the baby had died.

There had been a rumour in the palace that the *dai* too was dead, though some said that she had only been dismissed following a dispute with the Rani's half-sister, who had accused her of failing to take proper care of the child. It was also said that the Rana, angered by the Junior Rani's interference, had given orders that she was to keep to her own rooms and neither see nor speak to her sister until further notice: an edict that Gobind feared would cause even more distress to the Senior Rani than the Junior one . . . if it were true.

But then a great many of the palace rumours were not. The Rung Mahal, said Manilal, stank of evil and bred rumours as a midden breeds flies, being crammed with idle courtiers, place-seekers and hangers-on, in addition to hordes of servants, none of whom had enough to do and therefore relieved their boredom by engaging in feuds and generally making mischief. 'They sit about and chew *pan* and talk scandal—when they are not asleep,' said Manilal scornfully. 'And most of their talk is lies, for each one wishes to make out that he is privy to more than the others, and invents a tale to draw attention to himself and gain importance; and if the tale is a scandalous one, so much the better, virtue being too often very dull.'

Nevertheless the rumours had disturbed Gobind and he had done his best to discover if there was any truth in them, but however much the Rana's people might gossip among themselves about the affairs of the Zenana, they were at pains to avoid that subject when talking to the men from Karidkote, and the most that Gobind learned was that no one could be blamed for the baby's death. It had been an undersized and sickly little creature whose hold on life had been precarious from the start, and the Senior Rani was prostrated with grief at its loss, having become very fond of it once she recovered from her disappointment that it was a daughter instead of a son.

About the Junior Rani and the *dai* there had been no further information, and Gobind could only hope that if it were true that Kairi-Bai had again been parted from her sister, the Rana would soon rescind the order for the sake of the bereaved mother—unless of course, he had lost interest in her and was using this method of punishing both women: the one for interfering and the other for having failed to give him a son. That was more than possible.

'But surely this serving-woman or her family could have given you or your master news of the Junior Rani? And of the *dai* too?' said Ash.

Manilal shook his head and explained that although the woman Nimi had acted as a go-between in the matter of the letters, it had at no time been possible to have any speech with her, the Hakim-Sahib's only contact with her being through her parents who accepted payment on her behalf, and to whom he gave his letters and received the occasional reply. But either they knew nothing of what went on in the Zenana, or considered it safer to pretend that they did not.

'They profess to being ignorant,' said Manilal, 'and we have learned nothing from them beyond that they have this daughter Nimi, who they say is devoted to her mistress the Junior Rani, but who is certainly rapacious, for she demands more and more money for each letter that she takes in or out of the Women's Quarters.'

Ash said: 'If you have only their word for that, it may be that she does what she does for love, and knows nothing of the sums they extort in her name.'

'Let us hope so,' said Manilal earnestly, 'for many risks are cheerfully undertaken for love. But those who take them only for payment may turn traitor if another is willing to pay more, and if it becomes known that the Hakim-Sahib is corresponding in secret with the Junior Rani, then I think all our lives will be endangered: not only his, but hers too—and mine also, together with the woman's relatives. As for the woman herself, her life would not be worth so much as a grain of corn.'

Manilal shivered involuntarily and his teeth made a little chattering sound. They had, he told Ash, learned nothing more when the Rana fell seriously ill, and before very long it became plain to all that the illness could be mortal.

'Only then did we learn by a chance whisper overheard in the palace—and later through the open talk in the city and certain unseemly jests in the bazaars—that if he died his wives would burn with him; for save for his father, the old Rana, who died of the cholera, no ruler of Bhithor has ever gone to the pyre alone—and for him it was only because there had been no wives to become suttee as they too, and his favourite concubine also, had already taken the disease and died of it. But it seems that when his predecessor died, in the year that Mahadaji Sindia retook Delhi, fourteen women—wives and concubines—followed him into the flames; and before that never less than three or four and often more than a score. Now the wits say that this time there will be only two, there being no concubines but only catamites.'

Ash's mouth twisted in a tight-lipped grimace of disgust, and Manil said: 'Yes, it is an ugly jest. Though well deserved. But what matters is that even the jesters take for granted that the Ranis will become suttee, as do all in Bhithor. It is, they say, the custom; though the common folk no longer observe it, and only a very few of the noble families have done so during the life-time of the present Rana. Yet the people still consider it incumbent upon the royal house to respect the old laws, for the honour of Bhithor and all who dwell there—particularly those who do *not* keep them. For when the Rana's wives become suttees they will stand, as it were, as a symbol and a substitute for all those widows who have shrunk from doing so, or been prevented from it by their relatives.'

'In fact,' said Ash savagely, and in English, 'it is still expedient that one man should die for the people. In this case, two women.' He saw that Manil was looking startled, and reverted to the vernacular: 'Well, they are not going to die, so Bhithor will just have to do without its scapegoats and burnt offerings. When do you return?'

'As soon as I can procure more pigeons and another six bottles of useless medicines from the *dewai dukan*. Also a fresh horse, for my own will not be fit to ride for some days yet and I dare not delay my return. I have lost too much time already. Can the Sahib perhaps help in the matter of a horse?'

'Surely. You may leave that to me. The pigeons and medicines also. What you need is rest, and you had best get as much of that as you can while you have the chance. Give me the empty bottles. Gul Baz shall fetch what you require as soon as the shop opens tomorrow morning.'

Manil handed them over, retired to his charpoy and was asleep again within minutes: a deep, refreshing sleep from which he did not awake until the sun was up and the crows, doves and parrots were quarrelling over the spilt grain by the stables, while the well-wheel squeaked in descant to the clatter of cooking pots and all the familiar sounds of an Indian morning. But by that time Ash had already been gone two hours, leaving a message telling Manilal to procure such things as he needed and meet him at Sarji's house.

The message had been delivered by Gul Baz, in a voice laden with disapproval, together with half-a-dozen bottles of patent medicines from Jobbling & Sons, the Chemists. Manilal made his way to the bazaar, where he bought a large wicker basket, a quantity of food and fresh fruit, and three chickens. The basket, like the one he had previously taken into Bhithor, had a false bottom. But this time it had not been used, for Ash had made other plans: ones that did not include carrier-pigeons.

Unlike Manilal, Ash had stayed awake for most of the night. There had been a great many things to think about, but his mind had discarded the larger issues and fastened instead on a comparatively trivial one: Manilal's curious use of an old and unkind nickname, *Kairi*. Who could have been unkind enough to see that even someone like Manilal, mixing with the other servants in the Rung Mahal and listening to their gossip, and to the talk in the bazaars, could use it automatically when speaking of her? It was a small thing. But as a straw in the wind shows the direction in which the wind is blowing, it was a clear indication of the contempt in which Juli was held by her husband's people, and—more disturbingly—that only someone from Karidkote could have been responsible for repeating that cruel nickname and encouraging its use in the Zenana, from where it would have spread to the rest of the palace.

Half-a-dozen of their own women had remained with Juli and Shu-shu, and Ash could only hope that the one responsible was among the three who were now dead (though he could not believe it was Geeta), because if not, there was a traitor among those closest to the Ranis: a female counterpart to Nandu's spy, Biju Ram, unsuspected by her young mistresses because she came from Karidkote, and currying favour with the Rana by denigrating the wife he so despised. It was an unpleasant thought, and also a frightening one because it meant that even if the Rana lived or the Raj sent troops to enforce the law against widow-burning, Juli and her sister might still be exposed to more dangers than Gobind suspected.

Ash did not doubt that the Government of India would see to it that if the Rana died there would be no suttee. But if the Rana lived they might not be able to protect Juli from punishment (or Gobind and Manilal either, should he find out about those smuggled letters) for that would be a purely domestic matter. Even if all three were to die or simply disappear, it was doubtful if the authorities would ever hear about it. And if they did, and asked questions, they would not ask soon enough; for in a country of vast distances and poor communications these things took time, and once the trail was cold, any explanation, such as a sudden fever, or the bland statement that the Hakim and his servant had left the state and were presumably on their way back to Karidkote, would have to be accepted, for there would be no evidence. And no way of proving anything . . .

Ash shivered involuntarily, as Manilal had done, and thought in panic: 'I must go myself. I can't sit here and do nothing while Juli . . . Manilal was right: the Rung Mahal stinks of evil and anything could happen there. Besides if Gobind can get letters to her, so can I . . . not from here, but I could from there . . . I could warn her to be on her guard because one of the Karidkote women may be disloyal, and ask about the *dai* and what really is happening. She wouldn't run away with me before, but she may feel differently now, and if so I'll find a way of getting her out—and if she still won't, at least I can satisfy myself that the police and the Political Department are taking steps to see that if that animal dies, no one is going to try to force his widows onto the pyre.'

It would have to be force with Shu-shu. They'd have to drag her to the burning ground, or tie her up and carry her, and Ash imagined that she would probably die of fright long before they got her there. Juli had told him once that Shu-shu had always been terrified at the very idea of suttee, and that it was for this reason she had not wanted to get married, because her mother . . . 'I hope,' thought Ash viciously, 'that there is a special hell for people like Janoo-Rani.'

When Gul Baz brought in the tea at dawn, he found the Sahib already up and dressed, and engaged in packing the small *bistra*—a leather-bound strip of canvas that he took with him on night exercises rolled up and strapped to the back of the saddle. Yet a glance was enough to show that he was not planning on being away for a mere night and a day. On the contrary he was, he said, going on a journey that might keep him away for anything up to a month, though on the other hand he could be back again in a matter of eight or ten days—his plans were uncertain.

There was nothing unusual about this, except that always before any packing that had to be done was left to Gul Baz, and there was generally far more of it than could be contained in that small roll of canvas: several changes of clothing, for a start. But this time Gul Baz saw that the Sahib meant to travel light, and was taking only a cake of soap, a razor and single country-made blanket in addition to his service revolver and fifty rounds. There were also four small and disproportionately heavy cardboard boxes, each containing fifty rounds of rifle ammunition.

Recognizing these, Gul Baz had allowed himself to hope that the Sahib was only going on another trip to the Gir Forest—though why he should take the revolver and need such a vast amount of ammunition . . .

The hope died as Ash went over to the dressing-table, and unlocking a drawer, took out and pocketed a small pistol and a handful of rounds (items that he could certainly have no use for on any shooting expedition) and a tin cash-box that he emptied onto the table, remarking that it was a stroke of luck that Haddon-Sahib should have decided to pay cash for the two polo-ponies, as it would save him a trip to the bank. He began to sort it into separate piles of gold, silver and notes, counting under his breath, and did not look up when Gul Baz said heavily, and not as a question: 'The Sahib goes to Bhithor, then.'

'Yes,' said Ash '—though that is for your ear alone . . . three fifty, four hundred, four fifty-nine, five . . . six—'

'I knew it,' exclaimed Gul Baz bitterly. 'This was what Mahdoo-ji was always afraid of; and on the day that I saw that hakim from Karidkote drive up to this bungalow I knew that the old one had been right to be afraid. Do not go, Sahib, I beg of you. No good can come of meddling in the affairs of that ill-omened place.'

Ash shrugged and went on counting, and presently Gul Baz said: 'Then if you must, at least let me go with you. And Kulu Ram also.'

Ash looked up to smile and shake his head. 'I would if I could. But it would not be safe—you might be recognized.'

'And what of yourself?' retorted Gul Baz angrily. 'Do you suppose they will have forgotten you so soon, when you gave them such good cause to remember you?'

'Ah, but this time I shall not be going to Bhithor as a Sahib. I shall go in the guise of a boxwallah; or a traveller on pilgrimage to the temples at Mount Abu. Or perhaps a hakim from Bombay . . . yes, I think a hakim might be best, as that will give me an excuse to meet a fellow doctor, Gobind Dass. And you can be sure that no one will know me—though some might know you, and more would know Kulu Ram, who often rode with me to the city. Besides, I shall not be going alone. I shall have Manilal with me.'

'That fat fool!' said Gul Baz with a scornful sniff.

Ash laughed and said: 'Fat he may be, but fool he is not: of that I can assure you. If he chooses to let people think him one, it is for a good reason, and believe me, I shall be safe in his hands. Now let me see, where was I?—Seven hundred . . . seven eighty . . . eight . . . nine hundred . . . one sixty-two—' He finished counting the money, and having stowed away a large part of it in the pockets of his riding coat, returned the rest to the cash-box and handed it to Gul Baz, who received it in grim silence.

'Well, there you are, Gul Baz. That should be more than enough to cover the wages and expenses of the household until I return.'

'And what if you do not?' demanded Gul Baz stonily.

'I have left two letters which you will find in the small top drawer of my desk. If after six weeks I have not returned and you have received no word from me, give them to Pettigrew-Sahib of the police. He will act upon them and see that you and the others do not suffer any hardship. But you need not worry: I shall come back. Now as to the Hakim's servant, when he wakes tell him that when he is ready to leave, to come to the Sirdar Sarjevan Desai's house near the village of Janapat, where I will meet him. Also to take the bay mare in place of his own horse that is lame. Tell Kulu Ram to see to it, and—no, I had better tell him myself.'

'He will not be pleased,' said Gul Baz.

'Maybe not. But it is necessary. Do not let us quarrel, Gul Baz. This is something that I must do. It is laid upon me.'

Gul Baz sighed and said half to himself: 'What is written, is written,' and did not argue any more. He went off to tell Kulu Ram that the Sahib required saddle-bags, and to bring Dagobaz round to the porch in a quarter of an hour's time; and having done that, fetched fresh tea—the original mug by now being cold. But when he would have brought the sporting rifle, Ash shook his head and said that he did not need it—'For I do not think a hakim would own such a weapon.'

'Then why take the bullets?'

'Because these I shall need. They are of the same calibre as those that the *pultons* use; and over the years many Government rifles have found their way into other hands, so I can safely take the other.' He had taken the cavalry carbine, and, as an after-thought, his shot-gun and fifty cartridges.

Gul Baz dismantled the shot-gun and stowed it in the *bistra,* and when all was ready, carried the heavy canvas roll out to the porch. And as he watched Ash mount Dagobaz and ride away in the crystal-clear light of dawn, he wondered what Mahdoo would have done if he had been there.

Would Mahdoo perhaps have been able to turn the Sahib from his course? Gul Baz thought it highly unlikely. Yet for the first time he was glad that the old man was no longer alive so that he, Gul Baz, was spared from having to explain how it had come about that he had stood by and seen Pelham-Sahib riding away to certain death: and been unable to do anything to prevent it.

39

Ash's first call had been at the house of the District Superintendent of Police, whom he had found lightly clad in a dressing-gown and slippers, eating *chota-hazri* on his verandah. The sun was still below the horizon, but Mr Pettigrew, a hospitable soul, did not seem to mind receiving a caller at such an early hour. He waved aside Ash's apologies and sent for another cup and plate and more coffee.

'Nonsense, my dear chap. Of course you can stay for a few minutes. What's the hurry? Have a slice of papaya—or what about a mango? No, I'm afraid I still haven't had a word from old Tim. Can't think what he's playing at. I thought I was bound to get an answer to that telegram. But I expect he's too busy. However, you needn't worry, he's not the sort of chap who'd stick it in a drawer and forget it. In fact, he probably went off to Bhithor to see that there's no hanky-panky. Have some more coffee?'

'No thanks,' said Ash, rising. 'I must go. There are one or two things I have to do.' He hesitated for a moment, and then added: 'I'm going off into the country for a few days' shooting.'

'Lucky beggar,' said Mr Pettigrew enviously. 'Wish I was. But then I don't get my leave until August. Well, good hunting.'

Ash had no better luck at the Telegraph Office. The clerk on duty said that there were no telegrams for him, and assured him yet again that if any had been received they would have been sent immediately to his bungalow. 'This I am telling you before, Mr Pelham. We are never losing or mislaying such things. That I can promise. If your correspondents have unfortunately not sent reply, can I help it? Should they do so you shall receive same within a flash.'

The clerk was obviously ruffled, and Ash apologized and left. He was not particularly worried by the absence of any replies. He realized that as there was not much that could be safely said, the most he could expect would be a bare acknowledgement. But he had hoped for that, if only because experience had taught him that even urgent messages can, on occasion, be pigeon-holed through error or idleness —it being a matter of history that the frantic telegram from Delhi, warning of the outbreak of the Great Mutiny, had been handed during a dinner-party to a high official who had put it in his pocket unread, and forgotten all about it until next day; by which time it was far too late for him to do anything about it.

In the present circumstances, Ash would have welcomed any form of acknowledgement, however curt, for the sake of his own peace of mind. But as Mr Pettigrew had pointed out, it did not follow that because he had received none, no action was being taken, but on the contrary probably showed that it was being taken, and that there was no time to spare for sending unnecessary messages.

Sarji's land lay some twenty-odd miles to the north of Ahmadabad, on the west bank of the Sabarmutti, and the morning was far advanced before Ash reached his friend's house. The servants, who knew him well, informed him that their master had been up since dawn overseeing the accouchement of a valuable brood mare, and had only recently returned. The Sirdar was at the moment breaking his fast, but if the Sahib would have the goodness to wait? Dagobaz, whose black satin coat was now sandy-grey and rough with dust, allowed himself to be led away by one of Sarji's grooms while Ash, after being given water to wash with, was politely ushered through a swaying bead curtain into a side room, and served with food and drink.

He was not invited to share Sarji's meal, and did not expect to be. For though Sarji was broad-minded, and capable when in camp or away from his home of relaxing a great many rules, here on his own ground and under the eye of his family priest it was a different matter. Among his own people a greater strictness was expected, and as his caste forbade him from sitting down to eat with one who ranked as an outcaste, his *Angrezi* friend must eat alone—and from cups and dishes that were kept solely for his own use.

Sarji was a close friend, but the rules of caste were strict and not to be lightly broken, but Ash could never avoid a pang that was part hurt and part surprise whenever he encountered those rules in action. The fact that he understood them far better than the vast majority of his fellow *feringhis* never diminished that automatic sense of shock at being made to feel a pariah—someone with whom even a close friend could not sit down to eat and drink without risking ostracism, because that simple, human act defiled the doer, and until the defilement was cleansed no one would willingly associate with him.

Drinking iced sherbet and eating vegetable curry, *kachoris* and *kela halwa* in that cool, ground-floor room in Sarji's house, Ash wondered if the family priest was aware that Sarji had often broken this particular taboo when they were out together. Somehow, he doubted it. When the dishes had been removed and he was alone again, he lit a cigarette and sat blowing smoke-rings at the ceiling and thinking.

He was remembering something that Sarji's *shikari* Bukta, who had guided Gobind and Manilal to Bhithor, had told him one day when they were out shooting, when he, Ash, had been speaking of that journey. Bukta had mentioned the existence of another and shorter way into the valley of Bhithor: a secret way that avoided the forts and the frontier posts and came out a mere *koss* from the city itself, and that he had been shown many years ago by a friend, a Bhithori, who claimed to have discovered it and had used it for the purpose of smuggling stolen goods in and out of the Rana's territory.

'Horses, mostly,' Bukta had said with a reminiscent grin. 'One could safely ask a good price in Gujerat or Baroda for a horse that had been stolen in Bhithor, as its owner would never think to look for it here because no one else (or so my friend said) knew of this path. In those days, being young, I had little respect for the law and would often help him—with much profit to myself. But he died, and I became respectable. Yet though it is now many years since I followed his secret path, it is still clear in my mind, and I know that I could find my way along it as easily as though I had only used it yesterday. I did not speak of it to the Hakim-Sahib, as it would have been neither wise nor fitting for him to arrive by such a road.'

Ten minutes later, when his host appeared in the doorway, Ash was so deep in thought that he did not even hear the clash of the bead curtain.

Sarji came in with apologies for keeping his guest waiting, but something in Ash's face checked the polite phrases that were on his tongue, and he said sharply: *'Kia hogia, bhai?'*

Ash looked up, startled, and coming to his feet said: 'Nothing has happened—as yet. But it is necessary that I go to Bhithor, and I have come to ask for your help because I cannot go as I am. I must go in disguise—and as quickly as possible. I need a guide who knows the secret ways through the jungles and across the hills. Will you lend me your *shikari,* Bukta?'

'Of course,' Sarji said promptly. 'When do we start?'

'We? Oh no, Sarji! This is not a shooting trip. This is serious.'

'I know that. The look on your face told me so as soon as I came in. Besides, if you cannot enter Bhithor except in disguise, then it can only mean that it is dangerous for you to go there at all. Very dangerous.'

Ash shrugged impatiently and did not answer, and Sarji said thoughtfully: 'I never asked you any questions about Bhithor, because it seemed to me that you did not wish to speak of it. But ever since you asked me to send Bukta to guide some hakim who wished to go there—and later, over the matter of the pigeons—I admit I have often wondered. You do not have to tell me anything you do not wish, but if you go into danger, then I will go with you; two swords being better than one. Or do you perhaps not trust me to keep a still tongue?'

Ash said irritably: 'Don't talk nonsense, Sarji. You know it is not that. It is only . . . well, this is something that concerns no one but myself and . . . and it is not a thing that I would wish to speak of to anyone. But you have already been of great help to me; and now again you are willing to help, and without question. I am more than grateful for that, and it is only fair that you should have some explanation of . . . of what is toward.'

'Do not tell me anything you would rather not,' said Sarji quickly. 'It will make no difference.'

'I wonder? Perhaps not. But then again it is just possible that it might, so I think it may be better for you to know what errand I go on before you decide whether to help me or not, since it touches upon a custom that your people have honoured for many centuries. Can anyone overhear us?'

Sarji's eyebrows lifted, but he said briefly: 'Not if we walk outside among the trees.' He led the way into a garden where roses, jasmine and canna lilies wilted in the heat, and here, safely out of earshot of any loitering servant, listened to the tale of the two princesses of Karidkote whom a young British officer had been detailed to escort to their wedding in Bhithor; of the tribulation and treachery they had encountered on arrival, and the terrible fate that threatened them now.

The story was incomplete and to some extent inaccurate. Ash saw no reason to mention his previous connection with the State of Karidkote, and as he had no intention of disclosing his own involvement with the elder princess, he could not give his main reason for returning to Bhithor, only the secondary one—his need to assure himself that steps were being taken to guard against the Rana's wives becoming suttees, if and when the Rana died; which was something that

Sarji, as a Hindu, might feel disinclined to interfere with, for it was a custom hallowed by centuries of use, and one that even now would probably be regarded as a meritorious act by his priests and the great majority of his people.

Apart from these omissions the tale he told was accurate, and included an account of his abortive interviews with Colonel Pomfret, the Commissioner and the Superintendent of Police, and of the telegrams that had been sent and not answered:

'So you see why I have to go myself,' said Ash in conclusion. 'I cannot just sit here and hope for the best when I know only too well how slowly and cautiously the Raj can act at times; and how reluctant it has become to interfere in the affairs of the princes. The officials of the Raj require proof and they will not move without it. But in a case like this the proof will be a handful of ashes and charred bones, and nothing they can do then will undo what has been done, for even they cannot bring the dead back to life . . . Once the pyre has been lit it will be too late to do anything, except gaol a handful of people and levy a fine upon the state—and make excuses for themselves for not acting sooner, which will not help those poor girls . . .

'Sarji, *I* brought those two to Bhithor. You may say that I had no choice, but that doesn't make me feel any better about it, and if they are burned alive I shall have it on my conscience to the end of my life. That's no reason, though, why you should get involved in this, and if you feel you would rather have nothing to do with it—I mean . . . as a Hindu—'

'*Chut!*' said Sarji. 'I am no bigot to desire the return of a cruel custom that was outlawed before I was born. Times change, my friend; and men change with them—even Hindus. Do your Christians in *Belait* still burn witches, or fellow-Christians who do not agree as to the manner in which they shall worship the same God? I have heard that this was once your custom, but not that it is still so.'

'Of course not. But—'

'But you think we of this country are incapable of any similar progress? That is not so—though there are many things that we do not see in the same light as your people do. I myself would not have any widow burn herself unless she desired it above all things, loving her husband so greatly that she could not endure to live without him and so chose of her own free will to follow him. That, I confess, I would not prevent, since unlike your people, I do not consider that I have a right to decide that a man or a woman may not take their own life if they choose to do so. Perhaps this is because life is less important to us than it is to you, who being Christians have only the one life on this earth, whereas we have many. We die and are re-born again a hundred thousand or a thousand thousand times; or it may be many more. Who knows? Therefore what matter if we choose to shorten one of these lives by our own desire?'

Ash said: 'But suicide is a crime.'

'To your people. Not to mine. And this is still my country, and not yours. As my life is also mine. But to contrive the death of another is murder, which I do not condone; and because I have seen and spoken with the Hakim from Karidkote, I am ready to believe him if he says that the Ranis of Bhithor stand in danger of being forced to the pyre against their will, for I judged him to be a good man, and no liar. Therefore I will do all that I can to help you and him, and the Ranis also. You have only to tell me what you need.'

Manilal, arriving at mid-day, was met by the *shikari* Bukta, and taken into the presence of the master of the house and a man whom he did not immediately recognize: which was understandable. Sarji and Bukta had taken great pains with Ash's disguise, and walnut juice when properly applied is an admirable dye, though it does not last over-long. Ash had also shaved off his moustache, and it would never have occurred to anyone that this was not a compatriot of Sar-jevar's. A sober, middle-class Indian, with a parent or ancestor who hailed from the hills where men are fairer of skin than in hotter parts of the country, and whose dress proclaimed him a professional man in good standing. A vakil (lawyer), perhaps, or a hakim, from some-where like Baroda or Bombay.

Manilal, that stolid and imperturbable person, was for once be-trayed into a startled gasp, and stood open-mouthed, staring at Ash as though he could not believe his eyes. '*Ai-yah!*' breathed Manilal, awed, 'it is wonderful. And yet . . . yet it is only a matter of clothes and a razor. But what is the meaning of this, Sahib?'

'Ashok,' corrected Ash with a grin. 'In this garb I have another name, and am no longer a Sahib.'

'What does the—what does Ashok mean to do?' inquired Manilal.

Ash told him, and Manilal listened, looking doubtful, and when he had finished, said cautiously that it might serve, but that the Sahib—Ashok—must take into account that the Bhithoris were a surly and suspicious folk, apt to suspect any stranger of being a spy. More especially in the present circumstances. 'They have no liking for strangers at the best of times,' said Manilal, 'and should their Rana die, they would think nothing of slitting all our throats if they thought that we stood in the way of anything that they desired.'

'Such as a *tamarsha*,' said Ash, spitting out the word as though it were a bad taste in his mouth. 'What you mean is that they are looking forward to the enjoyable spectacle of two high-born and beautiful young women walking unveiled to the burning ground, and being burned alive there before their eyes.'

'That is true,' agreed Manilal quietly. 'To look on the face of a queen, and to watch her die, is something that few will see more than once in a lifetime; so to many it will indeed seem a great *tamarsha*. But to others—maybe to all—it will be a holy occasion: one that bestows merit on everyone who is present. Therefore on both counts the people of Bhithor will be enraged if any should attempt to prevent it, and only a strong force of well-armed soldiers or police of the Raj will be able to restrain them. But one man, or two or three, can do nothing. Except lose their lives needlessly.'

'I know,' said Ash soberly. 'And I have already thought deeply. I go because I must. It is laid on me. But there is no reason for anyone to go with me, and my friend the Sirdar here knows that.'

'He also knows,' put in Sarji, 'that anyone riding such a horse as Dagobaz would not be travelling alone without a servant or a syce. I can act the part of one or other; or if need be, both.'

Ash laughed and said: 'You see how it is? The Sirdar comes of his own free will and I cannot prevent him. Any more than you can prevent me. As for Bukta, he goes only to show us the secret paths into Bhithor, so that we may go swiftly and not lose ourselves among the hills, or be stopped and questioned and perhaps turned back by those who guard the known ways. Once our road ahead is clear, there will be no need to take him further and he can return here in safety. You of course must go back to Bhithor by the same road that you came by, and be seen to return openly. It would not do for you to return secretly.'

'And you?' asked Manilal, still doubtful. 'When you have reached the city, what will you do then?'

'That is in the lap of the gods. How can I know until I see what the situation is and have talked to the Hakim-Sahib, and learned what measures the Sirkar has taken.'

'If they have taken any,' muttered Manilal sceptically.

'Indeed so. Which is why I go. I must discover if they have done so; and if they have not, take what steps I can to see that they do.'

Manilal shrugged and capitulated. But he warned Ash to be very careful about approaching Gobind; his master had never been *persona grata* with the palace circle in Bhithor, and the Rana's councillors and courtiers had been hostile to him from the first.

'The Hakim-Sahib has many enemies,' said Manilal. 'Some hate him because he is from Karidkote, and some because he is more skilled in the arts of healing than they—while others hate him because he, a stranger, has the ear of the Rana. Me they dislike because I am his servant. But fortunately they also look upon me as a simpleton, which means that we can meet any day as strangers, and by chance, in the main bazaar or the Street of the Coppersmiths, where there are always crowds.'

For the next quarter-of-an-hour they had discussed their plans in some detail, before Manilal left, riding one of Sarji's country-bred hacks in place of Ash's bay, which was thought too showy an animal for a hakim's servant to have acquired. He would take longer to reach Bhithor than the two who meant to go there by way of a smugglers' route across the hills, but he did not think that the difference would be more than a few days: two or three at most.

In fact, it was nearer five. For no one in all Gujerat had a better knowledge of the trails through the jungles and hills than Bukta, whose father, having fled to Gujerat as a youth (according to Bukta he had killed a powerful man of his own country, somewhere in Central India), had taught his son to hunt and track almost as soon as he could walk.

Bukta had made them wait a full half hour so that Manilal should get well ahead, yet still managed to bring them to the fringes of the jungle by the time the sun had set. Despite the difficulties of the terrain, they had actually covered close on fifty miles in less than six hours, in the course of which they had crossed the Hathmati by ferry-boat, and Sarji declared that at this rate they would be in Bhithor tomorrow. But Bukta shook his head, saying that although up to now the going had been easy (which was not how Ash would have described it) once among the jungle-clad foothills they would find it increasingly difficult, and much of the trail could only be taken at a foot's pace.

They made camp near a stream, and being tired, slept soundly, taking it in turn to keep watch, as there were both tiger and leopard in these jungles and Bukta feared for the horses. Sarji, who had taken the last watch of the night, woke them at first light, and by mid-morning they were free of the jungle and among the bare slopes of the hills, where, as Bukta had predicted, they could only cover a few miles an hour, moving in single file.

Ash had brought a compass with him, but even with this to aid him he realized that left to himself among these hills he would have become hopelessly lost within a matter of minutes. The spurs and ridges ran this way and that in an aimless, featureless maze. But Bukta appeared to see and recognize landmarks that were invisible to his companions and he pressed ahead unhesitatingly, riding where the ground permitted, and where it did not, plodding forward on foot, leading his pony along narrow rock ledges or across precipitous slopes of shale or slippery, sun-bleached grass.

Once they halted for an hour by a spring among a wilderness of rocks, and later, as the afternoon drew towards evening and the folds and gullies filled with shadow, they descended a hair-raising cliff and came upon a little wooded valley, less than half-a-mile long, they lay like some lost oasis among the harsh, treeless hills. Here another spring debouched from the rocks above to send a thin silver waterfall tumbling down into a deep pool that was fringed with grass and rushes and shaded by trees—a surprising sight in that barren land, and a most welcome one, for the day had been very hot and the horses were parched with thirst.

There were many animal tracks leading down to the pool and marking the damp verges, but no sign that it had been recently visited by men; which seemed to relieve Bukta, though he must have realized hours ago that for many seasons neither men nor horses could have used the trail he had been following all day, since had they done so they would have left unmistakable traces—horse droppings and the ashes of old fires.

There was nothing of that description to be seen now, and only after digging down among the roots of a certain old and twisted wild fig tree did Bukta unearth a few blackened stones, and announce with a grunt of satisfaction that this was where he and his smuggling friend used to light their cooking fire. 'I was a young man then and neither of you can have been born, as that was many years ago. But it is clear to me that none save wild creatures have come to this place for a long time; which is as well, for I can light a fire here in safety.'

They spent the night there, keeping the fire alight as a protection against the wild creatures that Bukta had spoken of, and were away again before the sun gilded the crests of the hills. That day was a repetition of the previous one; except that as there had been places where it was possible for the horses to trot, they had made better time, so that when evening came Ash had been all for pressing on. But Bukta had been adamant, pointing out that they were all tired, and tired men were prone to make mistakes—and weary horses apt to stumble. Also that the miles that lay ahead of them were among the most difficult, and to attempt them by night would be courting disaster, for he could easily miss the path.

The prospect of being lost in that trackless sea of hills was one he, Bukta, did not fancy; and besides, had not the Hakim's servant told them that it was the custom in Bhithor to close the city gates an hour after sunset? If that were so, there was nothing to be gained by pressing forward, and in his opinion they would be well advised to time their arrival for dusk on the following day, when men and cattle and flocks of goats would be streaming homeward from the fields and the grazing grounds that surrounded the city, and they would be unremarked among the crowds.

'He is right, you know,' said Sarji. 'In the evening, when the cooking fires are lit and the air is full of smoke and dust, the light is poorer—and men less inclined to curiosity, their thoughts being fixed on rest and food.'

Ash had reluctantly agreed, and they found a cave among the rocks on a high ridge, and having turned the horses loose to graze, ate a cold meal for fear that a fire might attract attention, and spent the night there, going forward again only when the sun was up.

There was still no sign of a path to follow, and as far as Ash could see, not so much as a goat-track marked the bare hillsides where the scanty grass of winter was already turning brown and brittle with the approach of the hot weather. But Bukta led the way as confidently as ever, and the others followed: today for the most part on foot across steep slopes where they and their horses slithered on the brittle grass or picked their way among broken rocks, riding only occasionally in single file along some narrow ravine between sheer hillsides.

There were no springs here, and they were parched with thirst by the time they crossed a high ridge at mid-afternoon and looking down, saw below them, in a rocky hollow, a small pool of water that glittered in the slanting sunlight like a jewel in a setting of brass. It was shaded by a solitary and incongruous palm that had somehow managed to find a foothold among the rocks, and must have been fed by a spring, for the water was unexpectedly cool. To the dry-throated men and thirsty horses it tasted like nectar, and when they had drunk their fill, Bukta allowed them half an hour's rest before they scrambled up the far slope, and reaching the top of another ridge, once again moved downwards.

An hour later they reached the floor of a narrow canyon that wound and twisted between the folds of the hills like the track of some giant snake, and for the first time that day they rode forward at a brisk pace on level ground. It was a welcome change but it did not last long, for after less than a mile the canyon ended abruptly in what appeared to be an impassable barrier: the debris of some ancient landslide that blocked it with a forty-foot wall of boulders and scree.

Ash and Sarji pulled up and stared at the obstruction in dismay, imagining that Bukta had taken a wrong turning and that they would have to go back. But the *shikari* dismounted, and beckoning them to do the same, walked forward leading his horse; and following doubtfully behind him they rounded a boulder the size of a small house, passed between two more, and entered a narrow crevice some twenty feet in length, where the saddle flaps brushed the rock on either side.

Like the canyon, this too appeared to come to a dead end. But Bukta turned sharply to the left, and after a further ten or twelve paces, right again—and suddenly Ash found himself out in the open, and facing the self-same stretch of valley where the Karidkote camp had been pitched two long years ago.

There was little to show where that great sea of tents and carts had once stood. All that remained of it were the dilapidated ruins of the stout, thatched-roofed sheds that Mulraj had had built to shelter the horses and elephants from the fierce glare of the sun; and of these only a handful were still standing, for sun, rain and wind, and the depredations of white ants, had combined to bring them down.

Bukta heard Ash gasp, and turned to him grinning. 'Did I not say that the road here was well hidden? No one who did not know it would dream that there was a way through those rocks, or think of searching for one.'

Ash glanced behind him and saw nothing but tumbled boulders and the steep flank of a hill, and realized that he himself must have looked out at this spot at least a hundred times, and ridden past it on numerous occasions, without ever suspecting that there was a way through those rocks and back into the folds of the hills behind them. He turned to study the place carefully so that he would recognize it again in case of need, noting such landmarks as a triple-fanged ridge on the hillcrest above, with a patch of shale in the shape of an arrowhead lying immediately below it.

The shale should be easy to see from a long way off, as it was several shades lighter than the hillside, while the tip of the arrow pointed directly downwards to the spot where he now stood. And nearer at hand, a mere dozen yards away, stood a twelve-foot-high boulder, liberally streaked with bird droppings and flaunting a tall tuft of grass that had sprouted from some crevice on the summit. He would recognize that boulder again, thought Ash, for combined with those parallel white streaks, the grass gave it the appearance of a plumed helmet, and he took careful note of its position in relation to the rocks that concealed the entrance to the canyon.

The old *shikari,* watching him, nodded in approval. 'The Sahib does well to mark this place carefully,' said Bukta, 'for it is not easy to find again from this side. Well, there lies your way to the city. You had better leave me fifty rounds—and the shot-gun and cartridges also. It will cause talk if you carry more than one weapon apiece. I will remain here until such time as you return.'

'That may be much longer than you think,' observed Ash grimly.

Bukta waved a negligent hand. 'No matter. There is both water and grazing here, and having food and the Sahib's shot-gun—not forgetting the beautiful new *Angrezi* rifle that the Sahib gave me, and my own old one also—I shall neither go hungry nor fear attack, so can wait a long time. Besides, it is in my mind that you may wish to leave in haste and by this same road, it being the only one that is not guarded, and I do not think you would find your way back to Gujerat without me.'

'That much is certain,' agreed Sarji with a curt laugh. 'Stay then, and wait for us. For I too think that we may need to leave in haste.'

The city being no more than a few miles distant and the sun still well above the horizon, they returned to the canyon and rested in the shade until the light mellowed and the shadow of the hills at their back crept forward and engulfed the valley, leaving only the opposite range warm gold against an evening sky. Only then did they rise, and whistling up the horses, led them back through the narrow passage between the rocks, mounted, and having bade goodbye to Bukta, rode out across the valley towards the dusty, beaten track along which Ash had ridden so often in the days when he and Kaka-ji and Mulraj had gone again and again to argue with the Diwan and the Rana's councillors over the disputed marriage contracts of the brides from Karidkote.

The valley had not changed, nor had the forts that overlooked it, nor the frowning walls and flat, jostling rooftops of Bhithor that blocked its far end and masked the great lake and the wide, enclosed amphitheatre of plain beyond. Nothing had changed: except himself, thought Ash wryly. In appearance, at least, he bore no resemblance to the young British officer who had ridden along this same track on a blazing spring morning, bound for the Rung Mahal and his first sight of the unpleasant despot who was to become Anjuli's husband.

He had been wearing the elaborately frogged ceremonial full-dress of his Corps, a sword had clanked at his hip and spurs jingled on his boot heels and an escort of twenty armed men had ridden behind him. While today he rode with only one companion, a man like himself, an unremarkable, middle-class Indian, clean-shaven and soberly clad, well mounted as befitted a traveller on a long journey, and armed, as a precaution against dacoits and other chance-met malefactors, with a rusty second-hand carbine of a type that was officially restricted to the army, but could be acquired—at a price—in almost any thieves-market from Cape Comorin to the Khyber.

Ash had taken pains to give that serviceable weapon the outward appearance of neglect, an effect that was purely illusory and in no degree altered its performance, and Dagobaz too had suffered a similar transformation; Bukta having insisted on altering his coat with touches of bleach and an application of reddish-brown dye before they started out, on the grounds that someone might recognize the horse, if not its rider, and it was better that both be disguised so that if any accident befell them they could not be easily traced.

In addition to this the black stallion's once gleaming coat was rough with dust, while the expensive English saddle had been changed for a shabby though stoutly-made one, normally used by one of Sarji's peons, so that his whole appearance, like that of his rider, was now undistinguished enough to escape notice. For though anyone with an eye for horseflesh could not fail to recognize his quality, the average passer-by would not have spared him a second glance; and as Sarji had predicted, such citizens as were to be met with at that hour had other things on their minds, for by now the sun was almost down, and those who had worked in the fields all day were coming home. The air was full of dust and the low, blue haze of smoke, and there was a rich smell of cattle and goats and of cooking pots simmering over innumerable fires.

The ancient bronze lamp that hung under the arch of the Elephant Gate was already being lit, and two of the three guards, their muskets laid aside, were squatting on the stone plinth by the guard-room door, intent on a game of chance and completely oblivious of the noise and the jostling throng of men and animals. The third was engaged in a wordy warfare with a carter whose off-wheel had become jammed against the gate-post, and no one challenged the two tired and dusty riders who had joined the hurrying stream of the home-ward-bound.

Few if any even noticed them, and those who did were not sufficiently interested to take a second look, for it is only in small villages that men are familiar with the names and faces of every member of their community, and Bhithor was a city of close on thirty thousand inhabitants—of which at least a tenth were attached in one capacity or another to the court, and since these lived within the precincts of the royal palace, many were not personally known to a large number of the citizens, particularly to those who lived in the poorer quarters of the town.

Ash had good reason to know every turn and twist of the streets that lay between the *Hathi Pol* and the Rung Mahal, having ridden that way far too often to have forgotten it, but he knew very little of the rest of the city and must rely on the information that Manilal had given him. There was no inn or any public *serai* where a traveller could put up for a night, as Bhithor lay well off the beaten track and few travellers, it seemed, cared to visit the place: nor were they welcome.

The ease with which Ash and Sarji had entered the city was counterbalanced by the difficulty they experienced in finding a place to lodge, and night had fallen before they managed to rent a room over a charcoal-seller's shop, with permission to stable their horses in a rickety shed that occupied a corner of the yard below.

The charcoal-seller was old and infirm, and like most Bhithoris, distrusted all strangers on principle. But he was also avaricious, and though his sight and hearing were bad, both were still good enough to enable him to catch the gleam of silver and the chink of coins. He

asked no questions, but after some haggling agreed to take them in
for a sum that was, in the circumstances, not too excessive, and
raised no objection to their staying as long as they chose, providing
that they paid for each day in advance.

This being settled and the first day's rent paid over to him, he took
no further interest in them, and fortunately for his lodgers, the
members of his household were to prove equally incurious. These
consisted of three women (a humble, silent wife, an equally silent
mother-in-law and an ancient servant) and his only son, a simple-
minded youth who helped in the shop, and was apparently dumb, for
neither Ash nor Sarji ever heard him speak.

All in all, they had good reason to be grateful to the anonymous Samaritan who had chanced to hear them being refused lodging in another house and advised them to try this one, for they could not have
been better suited. Their landlord did not trouble to ask where they
came from or what business had brought them to Bhithor, and
plainly did not care. Also—which was equally plain and far more
important—neither he nor his family were addicted to gossiping with
their neighbours.

'Surely the gods were with us when they brought us to this place,'
said Sarji, who had anticipated having to answer a great many
searching questions. 'These folk are not friendly, but they do not
seem to me as bad as the Hakim's servant made out that all Bhithoris were. They are at least harmless.'

'As long as we pay them,' observed Ash dryly. 'But do not make
the mistake of thinking that because they are old and blind and
wholly uninterested in us, they are typical of the inhabitants of this
city. They are not; and you would do well to remember that and be
always upon your guard when you go abroad. We cannot afford to
attract attention.'

During the next few days, except for an hour each morning and
evening when they exercised the horses, they spent their time strolling about the city, looking and listening and gleaning what information they could from the talk in the bazaars and wine shops. To
those who asked, they gave the tale that had been agreed upon: that
they were members of a party travelling to Mount Abu, who had become separated from their companions, and in endeavouring to overtake them had lost their way among the hills. Faced with the prospect of dying with thirst, they had been overjoyed at finding
themselves in such a salubrious and hospitable spot as this, and in-

tended to remain here for a few days in order to recover from their ordeal and rest their horses.

The story apparently sounded feasible, for it had been accepted without question. But if this was a weight off Ash's mind, it was the only one, because those who heard the tale had all made the same comment: that he would have to resign himself to staying longer than a few days, as only a week ago an edict had gone out forbidding anyone to leave the state until further notice—this by order of the Diwan and the council, acting on behalf of the Rana, who was 'temporarily indisposed'. 'So it may be many days before you will be free to continue your journey to Mount Abu; perhaps a month; or even more . . .'

'But why?' Ash had asked, disquieted by this news. 'For what reason?'

The answer had invariably been either a shrug, or the classic reply of those who accept every dictate of Government or fate as something beyond comprehension: 'Who knows?' But one man, who had been listening while a vendor of fruit served Ash with a seer of loquats and gave him this familiar answer, had been more outspoken.

According to this citizen, the reason was perfectly obvious to anyone but a donkey. The Diwan (and everyone else in Bhithor) knew that the Rana was dying, and had no wish for the news to reach the ears of some officious *feringhi*, who might think it necessary to stir up trouble with the authorities and start interfering with matters of purely domestic interest. Therefore the Diwan had very properly 'barred the gates of the state', to ensure that no spy in the service of the Government of India, or any idle chatterer either, should carry lying tales and evil talk to the Sahib-log in Ajmer—or to anyone else for that matter. 'For what we choose to do, or what we choose not to do, is our affair; and we in Bhithor do not brook interference from foreigners.'

So that was it: the Diwan was making certain that the only news leaving Bhithor would be such as he and his fellow-councillors approved, and that it would be carried by his own men and no one else. Ash wondered if Manilal would be denied entry, and if so, how he, Ash, was going to contact Gobind. But this was a minor worry compared with the fact that there was as yet no sign of any detachment of police or soldiery from British India, or the least indication that the Government intended to interest itself in the affairs of Bhithor.

Past experience had led Ash to talk slightingly of the Political

Agencys' 'see-no-evil, hear-no-evil' attitude towards the independent states of Rajputana, and their kid-glove handling of the princes. But knowing that the great majority of Political Officers did invaluable work and were not as he had chosen to describe them, he had never really believed that in the present instance those concerned would not act with speed and firmness once they were aware of what was in the wind. And as both he and Mr Pettigrew of the police had taken steps to see that they should be made aware of it, he had arrived in Bhithor expecting to find a strong detachment of troops or police quartered in the city; or at the very least, that Spiller, the Political Officer, was occupying one of the royal guest-houses in the Ram Bagh.

The last thing he had expected to find was that no officer representing the authority of the Raj had arrived in Bhithor—or, as far as he could discover, intended to arrive. And now that the 'gates of the state' had been closed and he and Sarji, like Gobind, were shut off from the outside world, it was going to be very difficult, if not impossible, to get any word out to the British authorities—except by means of Bukta's road, which would be a slow and circuitous route to Ajmer, and might well take too long to be of any use. Because the hot season was already here, and should the Rana die he would be cremated within a matter of hours—and Juli and Shushila with him.

'I don't understand it,' said Ash, pacing to and fro in the room above the shop like a caged wolf. 'One telegram might have gone astray, but surely not all *four*—! It's not possible. Kaka-ji or Jhoti are bound to have done something. They at least know what these people here are capable of—and so does Mulraj. They must have warned Simla. In fact they probably wired the Viceroy direct, and the A.G.G. Rajputana, too. Yet no one seems to have moved a finger. I can't understand it. I cannot!'

'Be calm, my friend,' urged Sarji. 'Who knows but that the Sirkar has already posted agents here in disguise?'

'What good would that do?' demanded Ash angrily. 'What do you suppose two or three spies—or six or a dozen—could do against all Bhithor? What is needed here is some senior Sahib from the Political Department or the police, with at least two companies of troops, or a strong detachment of police—Sikhs for choice. But there is no sign that the Government of India means to move in the matter, and now that the frontier has been closed, its spies—if any were sent here,

which I doubt—cannot get out. And you and I can do nothing.
Nothing!'

'Except pray that the gods, and your friend the Hakim, will pro-
long the life of the Rana until such time as the Burra-Sahibs in Simla
and Ajmer choose to bestir themselves and make inquiries as to what
goes on in Bhithor,' observed Sarji unhelpfully.

He removed himself, leaving Ash to his pacing, and went down to
see to the horses; and that done, sauntered through the bazaars again
in search of news and in the hope of seeing a fat, foolish-seeming
face among the drifting crowds. But there was still no sign of Manilal, and Sarji returned to the little room above the charcoal-vendor's
shop in low spirits, convinced that the Hakim's servant must have
met with some accident or else been stopped by the frontier guards
and refused permission to re-enter the state; in which case the Sahib
—Ashok—would undoubtedly go to the Hakim's house and demand
to see him, thereby attracting to himself the attention of the Hakim's
enemies—all those jealous physicians whose noses he had put out of
joint and the many courtiers, councillors and priests who strongly
resented the favour shown by their Rana to this interloper from the
north.

Sarji had been in Bhithor for five days, but two had been more
than enough to convince him that Ash's account of its ruler and his
people had not been exaggerated; and that night, for the first time, it
occurred to him that this masquerade on which he had embarked so
light-heartedly was likely to prove a far more dangerous affair than
he had imagined, and that if that fat and cunning man Manilal failed
to return to Bhithor, the odds on his own chances of leaving it alive
were too small to be worth betting on.

Lying awake in the hot darkness and listening to Ash's quiet
breathing and the reverberating snores of the dumb youth in the
shop below, Sarji shivered and wished fervently that he was back in
his own safe and pleasant house among the lush green fields and banana groves near Janapat. Life was good, and he had no wish to die,
particularly at the hands of these medieval-minded Bhithoris. He
heard a horse snort and stamp and a hoof thud against the wooden
side of the shed as Dagobaz or his own Moti Raj lashed out angrily at
some foraging rat or mongoose, and the sounds reminded him that
there was still a way of escape open to them: Bukta's road. That at
least was neither closed nor guarded, and tomorrow, if the fat ser-

vant again failed to put in an appearance, he, Sarji, would put his foot down.

He would have a straight talk with Ashok, and make him see that in the circumstances it was futile to invite suspicion and discovery by remaining any longer in Bhithor, and that their wisest course would be to leave by the way they had come and make for Ajmer by way of Deesa and Sirohi. True, this would take time, as it involved a considerable detour. But once there Ashok, in his own guise, would be able to see and speak to senior representatives of the Political Department and the police, explain the situation and inform them (if they did not already know it) that Bhithor had sealed itself off from the outside world and was now virtually a fortress.

Sarji distrusted the telegraph and all new-fangled means of communication, and was not in the least surprised that his friend's wires had evoked no response. A letter delivered by a trustworthy peon was, in his opinion, far more reliable. And better still was a face-to-face talk, for that way there could be no mistakes.

But as it happened there was no need for them to go to Ajmer, for Manilal was already in Bhithor. He had arrived late that evening, just as the gates were closing. And on the following morning he went to the bazaar to make some small purchases, where he fell into conversation with two visitors to the city: a tall, lean-faced man from Baroda and a small-boned Gujerati, who were debating the rival merits of mangoes and papayas with the owner of a fruit shop.

40

Gobind had not been pleased to see the Sahib.

The doctor from Karidkote had hoped against hope that when Manilal returned it would be with news that help was on the way, and during the past week he had looked to see the Political Officer or some senior Police-Sahib ride up to the Elephant Gate with a strong contingent of armed men at their back. Instead, he learned that Pelham-Sahib, having sent off several urgent telegrams that had not been answered, had insisted against all advice on coming to Bhithor himself, and was presumably at that moment somewhere in the city, disguised, and accompanied by a Gujerati friend posing as his servant.

Gobind's dismay at official lethargy was only equalled by his alarm at this disclosure, and though he seldom lost his temper, he did so now—for which he could be forgiven, as he had been living under considerable strain and Ash's presence only increased it. Gobind could not see that any good purpose could be served by the Sahib coming to Bhithor at this juncture unless he had been able to do so openly, and with the full backing of the Government. It was a piece of suicidal folly, for apart from the fact that he could do no good, if he were to be recognized he would certainly be killed; and not one of his own people would ever know what had happened to him, since according to Manilal he had left without telling anyone of his intentions.

The whole venture, in Gobind's opinion, was foolhardy to the point of madness, and could only add a further hazard to a situation that was already fraught with more dangers than he cared to contemplate. He could not understand it. Until now he had regarded Pelham-Sahib as a man of sense, and would have expected him to make straight for Ajmer to discover for himself why his telegraphed warnings had not been answered, and what action had been taken or decided upon—not dress up as a Hindu and come play-acting to Bhithor, as though it were possible for one man to turn several thousand from their purpose.

'He must leave at once,' declared Gobind, turning on Manilal. 'His presence here endangers us all: you and I and those few remaining waiting-women from Karidkote as well as the Ranis, whose peril is great enough already without this folly. If either he or his friend should be unmasked there is no one here who would not believe that we sent for him, and they will see to it that not one of us leaves Bhithor alive. He can do nothing here but much harm. You should have told him so, and done everything in your power to turn him from this madness.'

'I did what I could,' protested Manilal, 'but his heart was set on it and he would not listen to me.'

'He will listen to me,' said Gobind grimly. 'You shall bring him here tomorrow. But think carefully how you go about it, for as you know, we walk on egg-shells and cannot afford to draw attention to him or suspicion on ourselves.'

Manilal had been careful. The following morning, within an hour of his meeting Ash and Sarji at a fruit-stall, half the bazaar had learned from him that the man from Baroda had studied Ayurvedic medicine in the sacred city of Kashi (Benares) and had hopes of becoming a practitioner in that ancient science. So no one thought it strange that such a person should desire to meet and talk with a hakim of a different school, it being known that professional men of opposing views delighted in argument and discussion. He had taken special pains to see that anyone he suspected of spying on his master heard the tale, and in order to avoid any suggestion of secrecy, arranged that the visitor should call openly on the Hakim-Sahib—and in daylight.

This last had not been too easy, as shortly before the hour set for the visit, Gobind had been summoned to the palace, from where he had not returned until the late afternoon, tired and dispirited, and in no mood to receive guests, particularly one on whom he had pinned so many hopes, only to be disappointed.

He greeted Ash unsmilingly, accepted without comment his explanation as to why he had thought it necessary to come to Bhithor, and when he had finished, said in a colourless voice: 'I had hoped that you would be able to summon help, and when none came I feared that a hawk must have slain the last pigeon before it won home, and that my servant here had either been stopped at the frontier and held on some trumped-up charge, or had met with an accident and failed to reach you. But it did not enter my mind that you could have dispatched warnings to the Sahib-log in Ajmer and to His Highness of Karidkote and my master the Rao-Sahib, and received no help from any quarter. It is beyond my understanding.'

'And mine,' confessed Ash bitterly.

'If you ask me,' said Sarji, who had accompanied Ash to the interview, 'the clerk who accepted those telegrams was a rogue, and must have kept the money himself instead of sending on your messages. It would not be the first time that such a thing has happened, and—'

'Oh, what does it matter what happened to them?' interrupted Ash impatiently. 'Something did, and that's the important thing. The point is, what do we do now?'

'Leave at once for Ajmer,' said Sarji promptly, repeating the solution he had arrived at during the watches of the night and already urged upon Ash. 'And when we get there, demand to see the Agent-General-Sahib himself, and the police Sahibs too, and tell them—'

This time it was Gobind who cut him short. 'It is too late for that,' said Gobind curtly.

'Because the frontiers are closed? But there is another way out of Bhithor. The way that we came in by. That is still open, for none here know of it.'

'So my servant Manilal told me. But even if you could leave by any road you chose, it would still be too late. Because the Rana will die tonight.'

He heard Ash catch his breath in a gasp that was harshly audible in the stillness that followed, and turning to look at him, saw the blood drain from his face and realized with a sharp sense of incredulity that the Sahib was afraid, desperately afraid. And in the next moment, and with as much certainty as though it had been shouted aloud, he knew why—

So this was the reason for the Sahib's presence in Bhithor. Not mere foolishness and bravado, or an egotistical belief that no 'black man' would dare lay hands on a member of the conquering race, and that one *Angrezi* should be able to over-awe the Diwan and the council and put the fear of the Raj into the local inhabitants. No—the Sahib had come because he could not help it. Because he had to come. Manilal had spoken no more than the truth when he had said 'his heart was set on it'.

It was a complication that Gobind would never have dreamed of, and the discovery appalled him as much as it had appalled Kaka-ji and Mahdoo, and for the same reasons. 'A casteless man . . . a foreigner . . . a Christian,' thought Gobind, shocked to the depths of his orthodox soul. This was what came of relaxing the rules of purdah and permitting young maidens to meet and talk freely with a strange man, Sahib or no. And when the man was young and well-looking and the maidens beautiful, what else could one expect? It should never have been allowed; and he blamed the Rao-Sahib and Mulraj and young Jhoti, and everyone else whose duty it had been to see to the safety and welfare of the future Ranis. Unpora-Bai most of all.

But he knew that such thoughts were futile. What was done was done; and in any case, there was no reason to suppose that the Sahib's feelings had been reciprocated, as in all probability the one to whom he had lost his heart had remained wholly unaware of it. Gobind could only hope so. But this sudden insight into the Sahib's motives did nothing to improve his own disquiet. It merely added to his anxiety, since who could tell what folly a man in love might be capable of committing?

For a space there was silence in the room, and even Sarji seemed unwilling to break it. Gobind watched the blood come slowly back to the Sahib's face and knew what he would say before he said it . . .

'I must see the Diwan myself,' said Ash at last. 'That is our only chance.'

'It will not serve,' said Gobind curtly. 'That much I can tell you now. If you think differently, then you do not know him, nor have you any understanding of the temper and disposition of his fellow councillors or the people of this city.'

'Maybe. But I can at least warn him that if he permits the Ranis to burn, he and his fellow councillors will be held responsible, and that the Raj will send a Political-Sahib and a regiment from Ajmer to arrest him and to take over the state and make it a part of British India.'

'He will not believe you,' said Gobind quietly. 'And he will be right: for even to so small and remote a place as this there has come talk of unrest in the north and of the *pultons* gathering for war. This you too must have heard as your own *pulton* will surely be among them, and having heard you must also know that the Raj will not move in this matter once it is done and cannot be undone. They will have no desire to stir up a hornets' nest in Rajasthan at a time when they have such grave matters as Afghanistan on their minds. And consider, Sahib: news of the suttee may not reach the ears of those in authority for many days—even weeks—and when it does, it will be too late to do more than send Spiller-Sahib to speak to the Diwan and council and perhaps impose a fine. But necks are not broken by hard words, and a fine can be paid from the Treasury or by means of a tax upon the people. Neither the Diwan nor his purse will suffer.'

'There is also another thing,' put in Sarji, addressing Ash. 'Unless he is a fool he will know very well that you did not come here as an accredited spokesman of your Raj, for had you done so you would not have entered Bhithor secretly. Like a thief, and in disguise.'

'That is so,' confirmed Gobind. 'And as the Diwan is not a fool, you will neither turn him from his purpose nor save the Ranis from the fire. You will only throw away your life to no purpose—and ours with it, for you and your friend have come openly to this house, which is watched, and once your identity is known, all our heads will fall to ensure that there is no one left to carry tales of your fate. Even those who gave you lodging will not be spared in case they might have noticed more than they should during the past few days, and be tempted to speak of it.'

Ash might have argued some of Gobind's previous statements, but he was forced to recognize the truth of this one; and to be silenced by it. Had it only been a question of risking his own life in an attempt to save Juli's, he would have done so gladly and without a second's thought. But he had no right to sacrifice the lives of eight other people (for the charcoal-seller and his wife would not be the only ones in that house to have their throats cut; all five would die for the crime of having rented him a room to lodge in).

He sat staring blindly out at the view beyond the window where the low sunlight glowed rose-red on the outer walls of the Rung Mahal, his mind desperately engaged with wild plans for rescuing Juli, each one more hazardous and impractical than the last . . .

If only he could find some way of getting into the palace he could shoot down the Zenana guard, and having barred the door behind him, snatch Juli from among her women and lower her over the walls on a rope and follow himself while the enemy battered on the door; and then . . . No, that was patently impossible—it would entail tying up a score of screaming women who if left at liberty would unbar the door the instant his back was turned. He would have to have help—

Between them, he and Sarji could muster five weapons, while Gobind and Manilal could surely contrive to get possession of a musket or two. Then if Gobind was right about the Rana, it should be possible, under cover of the confusion that would reign in the palace

that night, for five determined men to force their way into the Zenana Quarters and liberate two women, as everyone who could would
be in or near the dying man's room, and few would have any attention to spare for the women. Vigilance was bound to be relaxed, and
it might even be possible to enter the palace in the wake of Gobind,
who would be admitted without question and—

Why, of course—that was how they could do it! Gobind must in-
troduce him as a fellow-physician, a well-known practitioner of
Ayurvedic medicine whose opinion could be valuable in this crisis.
Sarji could pass as his assistant while Manilal, being the Hakim's servant carrying drugs, was unlikely to be questioned, and having
gained admission to the palace the worst would be over, as from
there they could probably bluff their way to the door of the Zenana
without recourse to violence, and once inside, the rest should be comparatively simple. With the Rana dead or dying, screams and lamen-
tation from the Women's Quarters would cause no remark, and there
would be an ample supply of sheets and saris that could be used to
gag and tie up the more troublesome women and knot into ropes by
which the Ranis and their rescuers could descend to the dry ditch
below the outer wall, from where they could escape while the city
slept. It was a hare-brained scheme, but it might work: and anything, however desperate, was better than leaving Juli to her fate.
But if it failed . . .

'I should have made straight for Ajmer,' thought Ash. 'I could
have made them listen to me. I ought to have realized that this could
happen . . . that telegrams might go astray or be read and pigeon-
holed by some underling who didn't realize . . . I should never have
. . . Juli, oh God, *Juli!* My dear love . . . It can't happen . . .
there must be some way, something I can do. I cannot stand aside
and let her die . . .'

He did not realize that he had spoken those last few words aloud
until Sarji said: 'Her? Do you think then that it is planned that only
one will follow her husband's body to the burning ground, and the
other be permitted to live?'

The blind look left Ash's eyes and two spots of colour showed
darkly on his cheeks. He said confusedly: 'No, I didn't mean . . . I
suppose they will both go. But we must not let it come to that. I have
been thinking—'

He propounded his plan and the two men listened to it: Gobind
impassively and the more volatile Sarji occasionally nodding ap-

proval and sometimes shaking his head. When he finished it was Sarji who spoke first: 'It could succeed. But to win free of the palace would not be enough, as the city gates are closed and barred at nightfall. We should still be trapped, for even if we tied up every woman in the Zenana so that the alarm would not be given until after dawn, we could not ride out unseen and unremarked.'

Ash said: 'We would have to leave the horses outside the walls, and as for getting out of the city, we can do that in the same way as we shall get out of the palace—over the wall with ropes; and if all goes well we should join Bukta and be out of the valley before the sky begins to lighten. I know it will be difficult and dangerous. I know there will be a great many risks and that things may go wrong. But it is a chance.'

'It is not one that we can afford to take,' said Gobind flatly.

'But—'

'No, Sahib. Let me speak. Perhaps I should have told you earlier that I can no longer return to the Rung Mahal. When I left today, it was for the last time.'

According to Gobind, the Rana's councillors had been urging him to adopt an heir ever since it was learned that the Senior Rani's child was another daughter, and when he had fallen ill they had redoubled their pleas, but to no avail. He would not believe that his sickness was mortal: he would recover and sire other children, sons who would grow up to be strong men—they would see. Meanwhile, as he had no near relations apart from a pair of sickly daughters (who had failed to give him grandsons and whose husbands he despised) he refused to jeopardize the future of his line by adopting some other man's brat. His mind was made up.

Nothing that anyone could say had changed that . . . until this morning. Today, some time during the small hours, he had recognized at last that he was dying; and appalled by the prospect of descending to that hell called *Pât*, to which men who have no son to light their pyre are doomed, he had agreed to adopt an heir—though not, as had been feared, a child from the family of the Diwan, or one or other of his current favourites.

His choice had fallen instead upon the youngest grandchild of a distant relative on his mother's side—that same semi-royal relative who had been sent to greet the brides from Karidkote on their arrival in Bhithor. The boy had been sent for in haste and such ceremonies as were necessary had been rushed through, because though the choice might be a disappointment to many, even those who had cherished hopes on behalf of their own sons preferred that it should be an unimportant six-year-old rather than the child of some rival. The Rana, in fact, had remained shrewd to the end; but the effort involved had drained the last of his strength, and the affair being concluded he had collapsed and passed into a coma.

'He no longer knows me,' said Gobind. 'Or anyone else. Wherefore his priests and his own physicians, who have always deeply resented me, have seized their opportunity and had me expelled from his sickroom. They have also prevailed upon the Diwan, who has no love for Karidkote, to forbid me to set foot again in the palace. Believe me, they will see to it that I do not return, so you cannot use me as a cover for any attempt to enter the Rung Mahal yourself. And if you think to shoot your way in you are mad; kings are not permitted to die alone and in peace, and tonight there will be more guards and many more wakeful people in the palace than ever before, since all now know that the Rana is dying. Every passage-way and courtyard will be thronged with men who wait to hear that he has drawn his last breath, and because there is much of value in the palace, the Diwan has ordered extra guards on every door of every room—fearing, so it is said, that various trifles such as jade vases and ornaments made of gold and ivory might vanish before he himself has had time to abstract them. That last may be only slander, but I can tell you that any attempt to enter the palace by force of arms will fail.'

Ash said nothing but his face spoke for him, and Gobind said gently: 'Sahib, I am not so wedded to my life that I would hesitate to risk losing it if I thought that there was even the smallest chance that your plan would succeed. It is because I know there is not that I would restrain you from it. And also because if it fails, as it must, the very ones whom you hoped to save may be suspected of complicity in the plot and condemned to an even worse death than the fire. Whereas if you wait and do nothing rash, it is possible that even at the eleventh hour the Sirkar may move to prevent the burning— Yes, yes, Sahib! I know that it does not appear likely. But how do we know that they too have not laid their plans? We cannot be sure, and if we throw away our lives needlessly—killing many in that fight, as we should do, and further endangering the Ranis—it may well prove we have, as they say, "lost Delhi for the sake of a fish".'

'He is right,' affirmed Sarji abruptly. 'If he can no longer enter the palace there is no hope of our being admitted, and to attempt to force our way in would be madness. I may be foolish, but I am not mad—nor, I hope, are you.'

Ash's mouth twitched in a parody of a smile, and he said: 'Not yet, but—but I still cannot bring myself to believe that there is nothing I can do, and that I must resign myself to seeing . . .'

He stopped with a shudder and fell silent again, and Gobind, observing him with a professional eye, decided that madness might not be so very far off. The Sahib, it was plain, had endured much during the past week or two, and the accumulated effects of strain, fear and anxiety—and a stubborn refusal to despair contending with the gradual death of hope—had stretched his nerves almost to breaking point. In his present mood he was a danger to them all, and the next thing he would suggest was sure to be some wild scheme for snatching the Ranis as they walked through the crowds on their way to the burning ground, relying on surprise, and hoping to escape under cover of the uproar and confusion that such an act would create among a milling and unmanageable mass of sightseers.

Gobind himself had, in fact, already given some thought to this particular line of action; but on consideration he had been forced to reject it, realizing that the crowd itself would wreck any such enterprise, for the people of Bhithor would be worked up to a high pitch of excitement and anticipation, and the threat of being robbed of the spectacle they had gathered to see would turn them in an instant into a raving mob. They would tear the impious intruders to pieces, and there would be no hope of escaping from them. Gobind knew this even if the Sahib did not, and he could only hope that he would be able to convince him that any such attempt would be worse than useless. But he was not called upon to do so, though he had been right in supposing that Ash was bound to think of it.

Ash had done so; but only to come to the same conclusion as Gobind. He too was aware that a crowd keyed to a high pitch of excitement can be more dangerous than a wounded leopard or a charging elephant—and that a mob is hydra-headed. If there was a way of saving Juli, it was not that one.

He rose to his feet stiffly, as though it was an effort to move, and said in a flat, formal voice: 'There does not seem to be anything else to say. If either you or Manilal can think of any plan that might succeed, I would be grateful if you would let me know. I will do the same for you. We still have a few more hours of daylight and the whole of the coming night in which to think of one, and if the Rana's hold on life is stronger than you suppose, we may even have another day and another night as well; who knows?'

'Only the gods,' said Gobind soberly. 'Let us pray to them that tomorrow the Sirkar will send us a regiment, or at least a Political-Sahib from Ajmer. If you will take my advice, Sahib, you will try to sleep tonight. A tired man is apt to make errors of judgement and you may have need of all your wits and your strength. Be assured that I will send Manilal to you if there is any news, or if I should see any way out of this tangle.'

He bowed gravely above his lifted hands, palms pressed together, and Manilal saw them out and barred the door behind them.

'Where are you going?' demanded Sarji suspiciously, as Ash turned left into an alleyway that led in the opposite direction to the quarter of the town where they lodged.

'To the Suttee Gate. I must see the way that they will come, and the road they will take. I would have done so before if I had not been so sure that the Sirkar would step in before it was too late.'

The alleyway skirted that side of the Rung Mahal where the Ze-nana Quarter lay, and presently they came to a narrow gateway cut through the thickness of the palace wall. It was an unobtrusive gate, barely wide enough to take two people walking abreast, and decorated with a curious formal pattern that on closer inspection proved to be made up of the prints of innumerable slender hands, the hands of queens and concubines who down the long centuries had walked through that gate on their way to the fire and to sanctification.

Ash had seen and noted it on his previous visit to Bhithor, and now he did no more than glance at it as they passed. His interest was not in the gate but the route that the procession would take from there to the pyre. The burning-ground lay some distance from the city, and as the city gates would be closed within an hour of sundown there was no time to waste, and he hurried Sarji forward, taking note as they went of every turn and twist and alleyway between the Suttee Gate of the Rung Mahal and the *Mori* Gate, which was the nearest of the city gates.

Ten minutes saw them out in the open country and walking along a dusty road that led straight as an arrow towards the hills. There were no houses here, and no cover, but there was a good deal of traffic on the road, mostly pedestrian and all of it moving towards the city. Presently Ash said: 'There should be a path leading off to the right somewhere here. I used to ride across this bit of country, but I never actually visited the memorial *chattris* and the burning-ground. I did not think then that . . .' He left the sentence unfinished to stop a herd-boy who was driving his cattle back to the city, and inquire the way to the burning-ground.

'You mean Govidan? Are you strangers that you do not know where the burning-ground of the Ranas lies?' asked the boy, staring. 'It is over there—where the *chattris* are. You can see them above the trees. The path is no more than a stone's throw ahead of you. Are you holy men, or do you go to make arrangements for the Rana's burning? Ah, that will be a great *tamarsha*. But he is not dead yet, for when he dies the gongs will beat, and my father says they can be heard as far as the Ram Bagh, so that all . . .'

Ash thrust an anna into the boy's hand and left him, and a few minutes later they came to the spot where a side path led right-handed out of the main road towards the lake. The path, like the road, was deep in dust, but here there were no cartwheel tracks and few traces of cattle or goats. But a party of horsemen had obviously ridden down it and returned again fairly recently, for the least breath of wind would have smoothed away those hoof-prints.

'They came to select a site for the funeral pyre,' said Sarji.

Ash nodded without speaking, his gaze on the dark patch of greenery ahead. Behind him the evening was full of sounds: the bleating of goats and the lowing of cattle, the shrill cries of herd-boys and the soft cooing of doves, the clamorous call of a partridge and from somewhere on the road the squeak and squeal of cart-wheels rumbling homeward to the city. Comfortable, everyday sounds; pleasantly familiar and very different from the deafening babble of the peering, jostling, wailing crowd that would gather here only too soon, jammed together shoulder to shoulder and pressing in on either side of this same dusty path that he was walking along now . . .

If he rode here he would have to leave Dagobaz tethered somewhere well beyond the crowds, for apart from the multitudes who would flock here to watch the cremation, thousands more would accompany the bier and its escort, milling about it and moving slowly forward in a rolling tide of humanity, resistless and terrifying. Visualizing the scene, Ash realized that the only advantage to be gained from it would be anonymity. No one was going to pay the least attention to him if he joined that crowd. He would merely be one of them, another onlooker, unremarkable and unremarked—provided he came on foot. A mounted man would be far too conspicuous; and in any case, Dagobaz was unused to such crowds and there was no knowing how he would react to one.

'It would not be possible,' muttered Sarji, whose mind had evidently been moving on similar lines. 'Had this place only been on the other side of the city, there might have been a chance. But we could never get away from here even if we could cut our way through the crowd at our backs, since those hills there hem us in on one side and the lake on the other, while over there—' he jerked his chin to the eastward '—there is no way out, so we should have to ride back towards the city and everyone here would know it.'

'Yes, I realized that.'

'Then why are we here?' There was more than a trace of uneasiness in Sarji's voice.

'Because I wanted to see the place for myself before I made up my mind. I thought perhaps that there might turn out to be some . . . some feature of it that could be turned to advantage, or that might suggest something to me. There may yet be. If there is not, we shall be no worse off.'

The hoof-prints stopped within the fringe of a dense grove of trees, and it was easy to see where the riders had dismounted and left their horses before entering the grove on foot. Ash and Sarji, following the same path between avenues of tree-trunks and out into the open again, found themselves in a large clearing in the centre of what appeared to be a deserted city: a city of palaces or temples, set among the trees.

There were buildings everywhere. Memorial *chattris*. Vast, empty, symbolic tombs, built of the local sandstone and intricately and beautifully carved, some of them three and four storeys high so that their airy, domed pavilions, screened in pierced stone and piled one upon the other in the manner of a fantastic house of cards, stood well above the tree-tops.

Each *chattri* commemorated a Rana of Bhithor, and had been raised on the spot where his body had been burned. And each, in the manner of a temple, had been built to surround or face on to a large tank, so that any who came to pray could perform the proper ablutions. It did not appear that many did so, for the water in the tanks was mostly green and stagnant and full of weeds and mud fish, and many of the *chattris* were half ruined. Pigeons, parrots and owls had built nests in crevices between the stones and among the weathered carvings that decorated pediments, archways and domes, a troop of monkeys pranced along the walls and the trees were full of birds quarrelling with each other as they came home to roost. But apart from the birds and monkeys and a solitary priest who was saying his prayers while standing waist-deep in one of the tanks, the place appeared to be deserted, and Ash surveyed it with the eye of a General planning a battle.

That open space over there was the obvious site for a new pyre, and to judge from the many footprints that patterned the dust at that particular spot, it had been inspected during the past day by a large number of people who had walked all over and around it, stood talking together for a considerable time, and gone away without visiting any other part of the grove. These marks were proof that this was where the next Rana would be cremated and where in time his *chattri* would be built, and there was also enough space here for several thousand onlookers as well as the protagonists—and an excellent field of fire for anyone standing above the crowd, say on the terrace of a near-by *chattri* . . .

Sarji touched his friend's arm and spoke in a whisper that had been forced on him by the brooding atmosphere of the place: 'Look —they have hung *chiks* up there. What do you suppose that is for?'

Ash's gaze followed the direction of Sarji's pointing hand, and saw that one storey of the nearest *chattri* had indeed been enclosed with split-cane *chiks* that hung between each pair of pillars, thus turning the top-but-one pavilion on the near side into a small room.

'Probably for some of the purdah women who want to watch. The Diwan's wife and daughters—people like that. They'll get an excellent view from there,' said Ash, and turned away quickly, nauseated by the thought that not only the ignorant and humbly-born women, but pampered, aristocratic ones would be equally eager to watch two members of their own sex burned alive—and think themselves blessed by being present.

He made a circuit of the grove, walking between the crowded *chattris* and the silent tanks that mirrored walls and terraces and domes that had been built before the days of Clive and Warren Hastings; and by the time he returned to the central clearing it was deep in shadow.

'Let us get away,' urged Sarji with a shiver. 'This is an ill-omened spot, and the sun is almost down. I would not be caught near this place when night falls for all the gold in the Rana's treasury. Have you seen all that you wish to see?'

'Yes,' said Ash. 'All and more. We can go now.'

He did not speak again during the walk back to the *Mori* Gate, and for once Sarji too showed no desire to talk. The sight of that silent, tree-enclosed city of tombs had shaken him more than he cared to own, and once again he found himself wishing that he had never become involved in this affair. Admittedly, Ashok had acknowledged that any last-minute attempt at a rescue from the grove was out of the question, but Sarji had an uneasy conviction that he had something else in mind—some scheme that he intended to carry out alone and without asking advice or assistance from anyone. Well, if he must, he must. There was little one could do to prevent him. But it was bound to end in disaster, and as the Hakim had pointed out, failure would inevitably end in death for all of them. How long, wondered Sarji, would Bukta wait before realizing that his master and the Sahib would never return . . . ?

There were many more people than usual in the city that night, for by now the news that the Rana was dying had reached every village and hamlet in the state, and his subjects were flocking into the capital in order to witness his obsequies, and to look upon the suttees and acquire merit by being present at their sanctification. The talk in the streets was all of the approaching ceremonies, every temple was crowded, and by nightfall the square in front of the palace was overflowing with townsfolk and peasants who gaped at the main gate of the Rung Mahal while they waited for news.

Even the charcoal-seller and his silent wife seemed to have caught some of the excitement, for they greeted the return of their lodgers with unexpected loquacity and a hail of questions. Where had they been and what had they seen and heard? Was it true that they had visited the Rana's foreign physician, a hakim from Karidkote, and if so had he told them anything new?

Did they know that when a Rana of Bhithor died, the great bronze gongs that hung in a gate-tower on the walls of the Rung Mahal were beaten so that all might know of his passing? Should the gongs sound by night, the twin forts that guarded the city would light beacon fires on hearing them; thus signalling the news to every hamlet and village in Bhithor, while in the city itself the outer gates would instantly be thrown open so that the ruler's spirit might pass out—choosing by which it would leave, east or west, north or south.

'And also in order that any who wish to take up positions on the road along which the bier will be carried can do so,' said the charcoal-seller. Adding that it was a wise precaution, as otherwise people who wished to be in the forefront of the crowd would gather near the gates in great numbers before dawn, causing considerable confusion and probably trampling women and children and elderly persons to death in the rush to be first through the gates when the bars were lifted.

'For myself,' said the charcoal-seller, 'I mean to go to the Suttee Gate and stand in the ditch below the wall. From there one should see well, and I would advise you to do the same, because you will be looking upwards instead of trying to peer over the heads of taller men who may block your view. Ah, it will be a sight worth seeing. It is not often that one has the chance to see a Rani unveiled, and this one is said to be a very queen of beauty. Though the other, her sister whom they call Kairi-Bai, is clumsy and ill-favoured; or so I have heard.'

'Yes indeed,' said Ash, mechanically filling the pause but with his mind so clearly elsewhere that Sarji looked at him sharply and the charcoal-seller, taking offence, turned his back on him and began to shout angrily at the idiot boy. The noise served to rouse Ash from his abstraction, and he inquired abruptly if anyone had left a message for him. But no message had come from Gobind: nor was there any sign that the Government of India intended to exert its authority and enforce its laws.

'There is still time,' consoled Sarji as they left the yard after seeing to their horses and he preceded Ash up the narrow staircase, carrying a lighted lamp and the key. 'The Rana is not dead yet, and for all we know, a *pulton* may arrive here this very night. And if that old fool speaks truth and the gongs have sounded, they will find the gates open.'

'Yes,' said Ash thoughtfully. 'That is going to make it a lot easier.'

Sarji looked back at him with a grin, taking the remark for sarcasm, but Ash's face was serious and intent as though he were concentrating deeply, and there was a look in his eyes that Sarji did not like—an odd, fixed look that boded no good. What had he decided to do? wondered Sarji in sudden panic. Surely he did not *still* believe that the Sirkar would send a regiment to Bhithor? What had the gates got to do with it? *What* was going to be easier?—and for whom? Sarji stumbled on the top step and took an unconscionable time fitting the key into the clumsy iron padlock because his hands were shaking.

The small room was stiflingly hot and reeking of charcoal fumes and the odours of cooking that had drifted up from below in the course of the day, and Ash unbarred the single window and flung it wide to let in the night air, and leaning out over the sill, sniffed the familiar smell of horses. The yard below was in darkness and he could not make out Dagobaz's black shape among the shadows, but Moti Raj's grey coat showed up as a pale blur, and he could hear Dagobaz stamp and snort, disturbed by a rat or the mosquitoes, and angry at being denied his evening exercise.

'Those two will be as glad to get out of this place as I shall,' observed Sarji, groping in a saddle-bag for matches. '*Phew!* it is as hot as a potter's kiln and it stinks of bad *ghee* and stale cabbage—and worse things.'

Ash turned away from the window and said: 'Cheer up. If the Hakim-Sahib is right, this will be the last night you will have to spend here, and by this time tomorrow you will be twenty *koss* away and asleep under the stars, with old Bukta to keep watch.'

'And you?' said Sarji. He had found the matches and lit a second oil lamp, and now he held it up so that the light shone on Ash's face. 'Where will you be?'

'I? Oh, I shall be asleep too. What else?' said Ash, and laughed. He had not laughed like that—or at all—for many days, and it took Sarji aback, for it appeared completely unforced. A gay, relaxed sound; and a reassuring one.

'I'm glad you can still laugh,' observed Sarji. 'Though I do not know why you should do so. The gods know there is little enough to laugh at.'

'If you really want to know,' said Ash, 'I laugh because I have given up. I have "thrown in the towel", as my countrymen say. I admit myself defeated, and it's a relief to know where I stand and to see the future with a clear eye. They say drowning is quite pleasant once you stop struggling, and that is what I have done. To change the subject, have we anything to eat here? I'm starving.'

'I too,' laughed Sarji, his attention instantly diverted by the thought of food—they had not eaten since morning, and then only sparsely; anxiety is not conducive to good appetite and both men had passed a restless night. 'There should be a chuppatti or two and some *pekoras*. That is, if the rats have not got them.'

The rats had not, but the ants had shown more enterprise. What little was left went out of the window, and as Ash refused to patronize one of the eating-houses in the city on the grounds that all would be grossly overcrowded that night and he did not feel equal to waiting for hours on the chance of getting a vacant place, Sarji went off to buy what they needed from a food stall, leaving with a lighter heart and in better spirits than he would have thought possible half an hour ago.

He was relieved beyond measure that his friend should at last come to his senses and see the futility of trying to battle against impossible odds. For to Sarji, Ash's sudden return to normality, and the fact that he could laugh again—and feel hungry—proved that he had indeed made up his mind and was no longer tortured by indecision or torn this way and that between fear and hope and doubts. Now they need not even stay until the Rana died, for as they could not prevent what would follow, there was no point in their remaining in Bhithor one moment longer than necessary.

They would leave at dawn as soon as the gates were open, and Ashok would have no reason to blame himself. He had done all he could and it was not his fault that he could not achieve the impossible. If there was blame let it rest on the shoulders of the Government, who had been warned and refused to take action; and on the Diwan and his fellow-councillors, together with the priests and people of Bhithor, who intended to turn the clock back and practise the old customs of an age that was already over. This time tomorrow he and Ashok and Bukta—and perhaps the Hakim and his servant too— would be safe among the hills. And if they made good time and moved by night (for now there would be a moon to help them) another two days should see them across the border and back once more in Gujerat.

'I will make a thank-offering to my temple in gratitude for my safe return: the price, in silver, of the best horse in my stud,' vowed Sarji. 'And once I am free of this ill-omened place I will never again set foot in it—or in Rajasthan either if I can help it.'

He brought hot food from a cook-shop. Steaming rice and fire-hot vegetable curry, *dal, pekoras,* and half-a-dozen freshly made chuppattis. And from a sweet-stall in another part of the bazaar, *halwasharin* made in the Persian manner with honey and nuts, and an anna's worth of crisp, sticky *jellabies.*

It had been a slow business, for as Ash had predicted, the bazaars were crowded; and though many of the farmers and village-folk who had flocked to the city had thriftily brought their own provisions with them, others had not, and the food shops and stalls were besieged by hungry customers. But it was done at last, and Sarji extracted himself from the press and walked back heavily laden, nibbling *jellabies* and humming the refrain of a song composed by one of Ahmadabad's best-known courtesans.

He was still singing as he mounted the rickety stairs and flung open the door of the rented room. But at the sight of Ash the song stopped short and the singer's eyebrows rose in surprise.

Ash was sitting cross-legged in front of a make-shift desk formed by Dagobaz's saddle, and he was writing a letter—the last of several it seemed, for at least five neatly folded squares of paper lay on the floor beside him. He was using ink and a reed pen that he must have borrowed from the shop below, and writing on pages torn from a cheap loose-leaf notebook; and there would have been nothing surprising about it, except that he was writing in English.

'Who is that for?' demanded Sarji, coming to peer over Ash's shoulder. 'If it is for some Sahib in Ajmer, you will not find a messenger to take it. Not at this hour, or for the next few days either. Have you forgotten that no one may leave the state?'

'No,' said Ash, continuing to write. He finished the letter, and having run his eye over it and made one or two minor corrections, signed his name at the bottom of the paper and handed the pen to Sarji. 'Will you write your name there, below mine? Your full name. It is only to show that you are a witness that I myself wrote this letter, and that this is my signature.'

Sarji stared at him for a moment under frowning brows, and then squatted down and added his name to the paper, the neat, stylized script in strange contrast to the careless Western scrawl above it. He blew on the wet ink to dry it, and returning the letter said: 'Now tell me what all this is about?'

'Later. Let us eat first and talk afterwards. What kept you? You must have been away for hours, and my stomach is as empty as a dry gourd.'

They ate in companionable silence, and when they had finished, Ash strewed the remains of his meal on the window-sill for the crows and sparrows to dispose of in the morning; but when Sarji would have followed suit, he said quickly: 'No, don't do that. No need to waste good food. Wrap it up and put it away in one of the saddle-bags. You may have need of it, for if the crowds are as thick tomorrow as they were tonight, you may find it difficult to buy more before you leave, and it is certain that Bukta will have none to spare by now.'

Sarji stood rigid, his hand still outstretched and his startled gaze asking the question that he could not force his tongue to utter. But Ash answered it as though it had been spoken aloud: 'No, I shall not be coming with you. There is something I have to do here.'

'But—but you said . . .'

'That I had given up. So I have. I have had to give up all hope of rescuing her. It cannot be done. I can see that now. But I can at least save her from being burned alive.'

'*Her?*' repeated Sarji, as he had done earlier that day in Gobind's house when Ash had unconsciously used the singular instead of the plural. But he had not used it so now: he had used it deliberately, because there was no longer any point in concealment. The time for that had gone—together with the need to keep silent.

'Her,' said Ash softly. 'Anjuli-Bai, the Junior Rani.'

'*No,*' breathed Sarji, the barely audible syllable as eloquent of horror as though he had screamed it.

Ash did not misunderstand him, and his smile was rueful and a little bitter. 'That shocks you, doesn't it? But they have a saying in *Belait* that "a cat may look at a king"; and even a casteless *Angrezi* can lose his head and his heart to a princess of Hind, and be unable to regain them. I'm sorry, Sarji. If I had known that it would end like this I would have told you before. But then I never dreamed that it would or could end like this, and so I only told you part of the truth. What I did not tell you, or anyone, was that I had come to love one of the brides whom I had been charged to bring to Bhithor . . . to love her beyond reason. There is no blame on her, for she could not have prevented it. I saw her married to the Rana . . . and came away, leaving my heart in her keeping. That was more than two years ago; but it is hers still—and always will be. Now you know why I had to come here: and also why I cannot leave.'

Sarji released his breath in a long sigh and put a hand on Ash's arm, gripping it. 'Forgive me, my friend. I did not mean to insult you. Or her. I know well that hearts are not like hired servants who can be bidden to do what we desire of them. They stay or go as they will, and we can neither hold nor prevent them. The gods know that I have lost and regained mine a dozen times. For which I have cause to be grateful, for my father lost his once only: to my mother. After she died he was never more than the shell of a man. He would have felt for you. But he could no more prevent my mother's death than you can prevent the Rani's.'

'I know that. But I can and will save her from death by fire,' said Ash with shut teeth.

'How?' Sarji's fingers tightened on his arm and shook it angrily. 'It is not possible, and you know it. If you mean to break into the palace—'

'I don't. I mean to reach the burning-ground ahead of the crowd and take up a position on the terrace of that *chattri:* the one over-looking the spot where they will build the pyre. From there I shall be able to see over the heads of the crowd below, and if by the time the women reach the clearing there has been no intervention by the Sirkar, and I know that the end is near, I shall do the only thing I can for her . . . put a bullet through her heart. I am too good a shot to miss at that range, and it will be a quick death and far more mer-ciful than the fire. She will not even know that she has been hit.'

'You are mad!' whispered Sarji, his face grey with shock. 'Mad.' He snatched his hand away and his voice rose: 'Do you think that those nearest you will not know who has fired the shot? They will tear you in pieces.'

'My body, perhaps. But what will that matter? There are six bul-lets in a revolver, of which I shall only need two: the second will be for myself. Once I have fired it I shall neither know nor care what the mob does to me, and if, as you say, they tear me to pieces, it will be the best thing that could possibly happen, because then no one will ever be able to say who I was or where I came from—or even if I was a man. So we must hope that they will do so. All the same, you would be advised to leave as early as you can: you and the Hakim-Sahib and Manilal . . .

'I have written to the Hakim, telling him that you will meet them at the spot where the road crosses the stream and there are two palm trees and a wayside shrine. Manilal will know it well. They must leave the city by the *Mori* Gate, to make it appear that they mean to attend the cremation; and once in the open country they should be able to separate themselves from the crowd without being observed, and make their way to the valley. I'll deliver that letter myself before I leave. There will be too many people in the square for the watchers to keep tally of everyone who passes the Hakim-Sahib's door.'

'And the other letters?' asked Sarji slowly, glancing at the pile on the floor.

'Those I hope you will take back with you and post at the dâk-khana in Ahmadabad.' Ash picked them up and handed them over one by one: 'This is the one that you put your name to: it is my Will and I have addressed it to a lawyer in *Belait*. And this, which is also in *Angrezi*, is for a Captain-Sahib in my Regiment in Mardan. These two are for an old man, a Pathan, who has been as a father to me, and for his son who has been my friend for many years. And this—No, this one too I will deliver myself to the Hakim-Sahib to take to Karidkote, as it is for the Ranis' uncle. This last is for my bearer, Gul Baz. Will you see that he gets it? And that he and the other servants get back safely to their homes?'

Sarji nodded wordlessly, and having scanned the letters carefully, stowed them away under his shirt without making any further effort to argue or plead.

Ash said: 'There is one other thing you can do for me—as a great favour. I would give much not to ask it of you, for it will mean delaying your departure, and delay could be dangerous. But I can't see any other way, because unless I am to risk getting caught up in the crowds and finding myself in the thick of the press from where I may not even be able to see her, I must reach the burning-ground ahead of the rest, which means that I cannot go on foot. But if it's true that the city gates will be thrown open if the gongs sound to-night to signal the Rana's death, when we hear them I have only to saddle Dagobaz and ride for the nearest gate, and from there in my own time to the *chattris*. The sooner I go the less likely I am to be stopped by the crowds, but it would be wiser for you to come later and with less haste, and . . . if you will give me an hour's start I will leave Dagobaz at the edge of the grove, on the side furthest from the city and behind the ruined *chattri* with the triple dome—the crowds will not reach as far back as that, and you should find him easily enough. Will you take him with you Sarji, for my sake? I would not ask it of you except that I could not bear to abandon him in such a place as this. Will you do that for me?'

'You do not need to ask,' said Sarji brusquely.

'Thank you. You are a true friend. And now, as there may be much to do tomorrow, let us take the Hakim-Sahib's advice, and sleep.'

'Can you do so?' asked Sarji curiously.

'Why not? I have not slept well for many nights because my mind would not let me rest. But now that all the problems are settled and the way ahead is clear, there is nothing to keep me awake. Besides, if Gobind is right about the Rana, I shall need a clear eye and a steady hand tomorrow.'

He rose to his feet, yawned and stretched, and crossing to the window looked out at the night sky and wondered what Juli was doing, and if she was thinking of him. Probably not, since by now Shushila must be half mad with terror, and Juli would have no thought to spare for anyone or anything else. Not for her lover or her old uncle, or for the mountains and deodar forests of Gulkote. Least of all for herself, even though she faced the same fate as Shu-shu. It had always been this way, and would be to the last. Dear Juli . . . dear, loving, faithful Kairi-Bai. He found it difficult to realize that tomorrow or the next day he would actually see her again. Only very briefly, and then—

Would the crash of his revolver herald darkness and nothingness? Or afterwards would they meet again, and be together for ever and ever? Was there a life after death? He had never been sure, though all his close friends seemed to be certain enough. Their faith was firm, and he envied them that. Wally, Zarin, Mahdoo and Koda Dad, Kaka-ji and Sarjevar might differ as to what form it would take, but they did not doubt that there was one. Well, he would soon know if they were right . . .

Wally was a believer. He believed in God and in the immortality of the soul, 'the resurrection of the body, and life in the world to come'. And also in such old-fashioned deities as duty and courage, loyalty, patriotism and 'the Regiment'; for which reason—quite apart from the fact that there was no time now to write a lengthy letter—it had been impossible to tell him the truth.

To have written to him at all was probably a mistake, thought Ash. It might have been kinder, in the long run, if he had merely dropped out of Wally's life without a word or a sign, and let him think what he liked. But the thought of Wally waiting and wondering, hoping against hope that one day his friend and hero would return, was not to be borne; and besides, there was another consideration—the fact that Wally (and only Wally) could be counted upon to do everything in his power to have his friend's disappearance investigated, which would ensure that the burning of the Rana's widows would not be kept secret, as Bhithor would wish . . .

True, Gobind would know what had happened; and so would Kaka-ji and Jhoti and some others. But Ash did not believe that Karidkote would take the matter up officially once the thing was done. The Ranis' family were, after all, devout Hindus, and it was difficult to expect them to regard a suttee in the same light as it appeared to foreigners. They would certainly have done what they could to prevent it, but having failed, they would see no profit in raising a scandal, particularly when in their heart of hearts they—and the majority of their co-religionists—must still regard the act in question as a meritorious one.

As for Koda Dad and Zarin, they too would keep silent, on the grounds that what Ashok chose to do was his own affair. And though the Guides and the military authorities in Peshawar and Rawalpindi would of course make inquiries, his past history would tell against him, since it would be argued that he had done this sort of thing before—disappeared for the best part of two years and been presumed dead—so that when he failed to report back to his Regiment he would once again be listed as 'Absent Without Leave', and after a time his name would be struck from the records and he would be written off as *Missing, believed dead.*

But Wally could be trusted to go on hoping and to badger senior army officers, importune officials of the Government, and write letters to *The Times of India* and *The Pioneer,* until someone would eventually have to take notice of the affair. And though it was unlikely that the true facts of Lieutenant Pelham-Martyn's disappearance would ever emerge, at least there would be no more suttees in Bhithor.

Ash watched the moonlight creep up the side of a house that backed on to the yard, and remembered a night among the ruins of Taxila, when he had talked for hours, telling Wally the incredible tale of his childhood, as he had never been able to tell it to anyone else except Mrs Viccary. It was strange to think that of all his friends, Wally should be the only one who could not be told the truth now. With the others, it was different: for one thing, they had no built-in prejudice against a man taking his own life. They did not regard that as a sin, as Christians were taught to do. Nor did they hold that a man was master of his fate.

But to Wally—a practising Christian, and a dedicated soldier in love with his regiment—suicide would seem unforgivable: a sin not only against God, but the Guides, because at this particular time, when 'wars and rumours of wars' were the talk of the North-West Frontier, it would be regarded as a form of cowardice comparable with 'Desertion in the face of the enemy'. For if hostilities on a scale of the first conflict with Afghanistan broke out the Guides were going to need the services of every officer and every man, and since cowardice and 'letting the side down' were the two cardinal sins in Wally's lexicon, he would undoubtedly think that the needs of Queen and Country should take precedence over any purely personal attachment, however deep, and that if Ash was set on dying, then the proper and honourable course would have been for him to hurry back to Mardan and take up his duties, and hope to be killed in battle, leading his men.

But then Wally had never known Anjuli-Bai, Princess of Karidkote and Rani of Bhithor, so the letter addressed to him was, in consequence, a very brief one and would allow him to suppose (if or when he should hear that Ash was dead) that he had died at the hands of a mob, following an unsuccessful attempt to prevent the burning of a widow. That way he would still be able to think of his friend as a hero—and keep his illusions.

'He'll grow out of them one day,' thought Ash. 'And no one else will talk: certainly not the Bhithoris. The Bhithoris will lie and evade and pervert the truth until even those who were there and saw it all won't be quite sure what happened—if anything. In the end it will probably be given out that the Ranis died of typhoid fever, and the authorities may even pretend to believe it in order to save their faces and avoid having to take any action.'

As for him, no one but a handful of his friends would ever know or care what had become of him . . . 'This time tomorrow, it may all be over,' thought Ash; and was surprised to find that he could face the prospect with so little emotion. He had always imagined that the phrase about the 'condemned man eating a hearty breakfast' had been meant as a grim joke, but now he realized that it was probably true, for once one gave up all hope, a curious peace took its place. One accepted the inevitable, and ceased struggling. He had been hagridden for days by fear and hope and the need to make plans that had invariably proved impossible to carry out, and now that all that was ended he could only feel a sense of exhausted relief, as though he had been freed from a burden that had become too heavy to carry.

The stars were growing pale as the moonlight brightened, and now the line of hills beyond the city was no longer a vague shadow against the indigo of the night sky, but sharp-edged with silver as though they were covered in snow; and for a magical moment it seemed to Ash as though he saw the Dur Khaima itself, transported to this hot and arid corner of Rajputana to bestow a last blessing on a some-time worshipper. He picked up a handful of the crumbs that he had strewn on the window-sill, and let them fall again, murmuring the old prayer . . . *O, Lord, forgive . . . Thou art everywhere, but I worship thee here . . .*

The years had gone so fast . . . so fast. But it had been a good life, and he had much to be thankful for; and so many memories to take with him—wherever it was that one went. If it were true, as some said, that when men died their spirits returned to the place that they had loved best during their lifetime, then he, Ash, would awake to find himself among the mountains, perhaps at long last in that very valley that Sita had described so often that he could almost believe that he had seen it. The valley in which they would build themselves a hut out of deodar logs, and where they would plant cherry trees and grow corn and chillies and lemons, and keep a goat. And allow Kairi-Bai to come with them . . .

The thought brought him the first comfort he had found that day, and when he turned from the window and lay down, fully dressed on the string bed, he was smiling.

41

Gobind had been right: the Rana did not live through the night. He died in the dark hour before dawn, and not long afterwards the stillness was shattered by the boom of the great bronze gongs that have announced the death of every ruler of Bhithor since Bika Rae, the first Rana, founded the city.

The sound shuddered through the hot darkness and reverberated among the surrounding hills like a roll of thunder, the echoes passing it on and on down the valley and out across the quiet lake. It woke the sleeping city and sent flocks of roosting crows wheeling and cawing above the rooftops, and brought Ash from his bed, instantly awake and alert.

The little room was still breathlessly hot, for the night wind had died. The moon too had gone, hidden by the hills and leaving the room in such darkness that it took Ash a minute or two to find and light the lamp. But once that was done the rest was easy, and five minutes later he was down in the yard with Sarji and saddling Dagobaz.

There had been no need for silence or caution. The night was filled with the deep-throated booming of the gongs, and by now lamps were being relit in every house and the crowds who had slept in the open were awake and vocal.

Dagobaz did not care for the gongs. His ears were laid flat back and his nostrils flared as though, like the horses in the Old Testament who cried 'Ha Ha!' among the trumpets, he could smell *the battle afar off, the thunder of the Captains, and the shouting*. He had flung up his head and whinnied when he heard Ash's step, and for once stood quietly without backing or sidling, or playing any of his usual tricks.

'This is the first time I have known him to behave so well,' said Sarji. 'He is one who likes to show that he has a will of his own and does not wear a saddle from meekness—or choice. You would almost think that he knows there is serious work afoot.'

'Of course he does. He knows everything, don't you, my son?'

Dagobaz bowed his head to nuzzle Ash's shoulder as though in affectionate agreement, and Ash rubbed his cheek against the velvet nose and said with a catch in his voice: 'Be good to him, Sarji. Don't let him . . .' He broke off abruptly, aware of a constriction in his throat, and for the next few minutes busied himself with the remaining straps. When he spoke again his voice was curt and unemotional:

'There, that's done. I've left you the carbine, Sarji. I shan't need it, but you and the others may, so you must take it with you. You know what to do, don't you? There's no need to go over it again. We have been good friends, you and I, and I'm sorry that I let you get involved in this affair and brought you into danger—and that it had to end like this. I should never have let you come, but then I'd hoped that . . . Oh well, it doesn't matter now. But be careful, Sarji—be very careful. For if anything were to happen to you—'

'It won't,' said Sarji quickly. 'Do not worry, I will be careful, I promise you. Here, you had better take my whip. It may come in useful to clear a way through the crowds. You have the revolver?'

'Yes, open the yard door for me, will you? Goodbye, Sarji. Good luck . . . and thank you.'

They embraced as brothers do, and then Sarji went ahead with the lamp, and unbarring the door, held it open while Ash led Dagobaz out onto the street. 'It will be light soon,' said Sarji, holding the stirrup while Ash mounted. 'The stars are already pale and the dawn is not far off. I wish . . .'

He broke off with a sharp sigh, and Ash leant from the saddle to grip his shoulder for a brief moment, then touching Dagobaz with his heel, he rode away without looking back.

It had not proved as easy as he had thought to reach Gobind's house, for the eerie clamour seemed to have drawn half the population of Bhithor to the Rung Mahal, and not only the square in front of the palace but every street and alleyway leading to it was packed to suffocation. But somehow he had managed to force a way through, using Sarji's whip mercilessly on the surrounding heads and shoulders, and urging Dagobaz onward a foot at a time while the crowd shouted and cursed and gave way before him.

The door of Gobind's house was barred, and anyone deputed to keep watch on it must have been swept up and carried along with the crowd minutes ago, as Ash himself would have been had he not come on horseback. But being mounted gave him another advantage, for by standing up in his stirrups he could just reach a first-floor window that had been left open because of the heat of the night. There was no light in the room behind it—or, as far as he could see, in any part of the house. But when he hammered on the lattice with the butt of the whip, Manilal's round, pale face appeared in the opening.

'What is it? Who is it?'

Ash thrust the two letters at him by way of reply, and without speaking wrenched Dagobaz round and began to force his way back down the street against the moving torrent of people. Ten minutes later he was clear of them and riding hard through dark and almost deserted alleyways towards the *Mori* Gate. Here there were lights again: oil lamps, lanterns and cressets. And more people, though not too many; one or two guards and night-watchmen, and a few small groups of country folk from outlying villages, who had evidently been camping out under the great archway and were now busy preparing an early meal before setting off to join the crowds about the palace.

The glare from the cressets and the wavering gleam of half-a-dozen little cow-dung fires made the sandstone walls glow like burnished copper, and by contrast the landscape that lay beyond the gateway appeared as a square of blackness—for the charcoal-seller had not lied about the opening of the gates: they stood wide and unguarded, so that the spirit of the dead ruler might pass through if it so wished . . .

Legend had it that the gate most favoured on these occasions was the *Thakur* Gate, because of its proximity to the city temple. But until now no one, not even the priests, had ever claimed to see a spirit pass. Tonight, however, all those who had the good fortune to be near the *Mori* Gate were to declare that they had actually seen this happen: that the Rana himself, clad all in gold and mounted on a coal-black horse whose hooves made no sound, had swept past them as silently and swiftly as a sudden gust of wind, and vanished into thin air.

The gold, of course, was pure invention. But then it must be remembered that the spectators were simple folk and saw only what they expected to see. To them, a Rana would naturally be splendidly dressed. It is also possible that a combination of torch-light and the glow from those small cooking fires, falling on Ash's light-brown clothing (and aided by the haze of smoke), could have lent it a fleeting illusion of splendour. But for the rest, the clatter of Dagobaz's hooves had been drowned by the mourning of the gongs, and in order to avoid any risk of being stopped, Ash had taken him through the gateway at full gallop, where once beyond the range of the firelight and the flares, horse and rider had instantly been lost to view.

All unaware that he had destroyed one legend and created another that would be told and re-told for as long as superstition survived or men believed in ghosts, Ash rode away from the city along the dust-laden north road.

For a moment or two the transition from light to darkness made the countryside seem an inky waste and the grey ribbon of the road barely visible for more than a few yards ahead. Then his eyes adjusted to the change and he realized that the dawn was already at hand and the near hills sharply distinct against a brightening sky in which the stars no longer blazed and glittered, but showed as pale as the petals of faded jasmine blossoms.

The little wind that is the forerunner of morning had begun to breathe across the fields, rustling the standing crops and lending an illusion of coolness to the air, and already it was possible to make out objects twenty and thirty yards distant: a boulder, a shrub, a *kikar* tree or a feathery tuft of pampas grass; and further off still, a herd of black-buck trotting sedately away across the plain after a night spent foraging in the cultivated land, and the lean grey shape of a wolf loping steadily towards the hills.

Dagobaz had always revelled in early morning gallops over open country, and of late he had spent too many hours shut up in a shed in the charcoal-seller's yard. In addition to which that frightening and inexplicable booming had set every nerve in his body on edge, and even out here he could still hear it, fainter now, for the breeze was carrying it away down the valley, but still all too audible. He redoubled his efforts to escape it, and as they were now beyond the crop-lands, swerved from the road and took to the rougher ground, his rider making no effort to restrain him.

The wolf glanced over its shoulder and broke into a canter, imagining itself pursued, while further to the left the black-buck herd took fright and went bounding away across the shadowy plain. And for a brief space Ash forgot what lay ahead and was suddenly caught by the familiar intoxication of speed and of being at one with his horse. A tremendous, all-possessing excitement that seemed to hold him rigid, his hands motionless on the reins, his thighs clamped to the saddle. What did it matter if he died today or tomorrow? He had lived. He was alive now—joyously and intensely alive—and if this was the last morning he would ever see, what better way to spend it?

The black stallion's body and his own were one, and his blood sang in rhythm with the pounding hooves as the air fled past them and the ground flowed away beneath them as smoothly as a river. The sound of the gongs dwindled away until it was no louder than the sough of wind under a door, and ahead a water channel cut a wide dark furrow across the plain. Dagobaz took it in his stride and raced on towards a wicked barrier of thorn bushes. Gathering himself together he rose to it smoothly, cleared it with ease, and landing on the far side as lightly as a bird was off again without a check.

Quails, partridges and an occasional sandgrouse whirred up and scattered before him, and a young cobra, rudely disturbed, reared up hissing from the grass and struck out furiously at the flying hooves. But Dagobaz ignored them all and swept on, nostrils wide and mane and tail streaming out on the wind, racing to meet the morning . . .

'You beauty,' crooned Ash, 'you wonder!' He began to sing at the top of his voice, swaying in the saddle in time to the tune and the swift, effortless stride of the horse:

'Thou wast their rock, their fortress and their might!
Thou, Lord, their Captain in the well fought fight.
Thou, in the darkness drear, their one true light—
Alleluia . . . ! Alleluia . . . !'

He laughed aloud, realizing that he had without thinking been singing one of the rousing hymns that he had so often heard Wally sing in his bath of an early morning—and on many other occasions when they had ridden together galloping neck and neck across the plains around Rawalpindi—it being one of Wally's favourite descriptions of a particularly fine day that it was 'A day for singing hymns on'. But the laugh froze in his throat, for suddenly he heard a far-away voice, faint but clearly audible above the pounding hoofbeats, chanting in answer to him: 'Al-le-lu-ia!'

For a moment his heart stopped and he tried to check Dagobaz, because he thought it was Wally. Yet even as he pulled on the rein he realized that what he had heard was only the echo of his own voice thrown back at him from the far hillsides. The discovery sobered him a little; there were villages among those hills, and realizing that if he could hear that sound so clearly there might be others who had done so too, he sang no more. Yet some of the exhilaration that had caused him to do so remained, and instead of feeling sad or apprehensive he was conscious of a curious sense of excitement: the taut, ice-cold excitement of a soldier on the eve of a battle.

By the time Dagobaz slowed down they were far beyond the dark grove of Govidan, and all about them the great amphitheatre in its circle of hills lay bathed in a pearl-pale light that cast no shadows. The quiet stretch of the lake mirrored a sky that was already yellow with the dawn; and as the light brightened and partridges and peacocks awoke and began to call, the gongs in the city stopped beating, and Ash turned back towards the burning-ground.

He rode slowly now, drinking in the beauty of the early morning, the sight and the sound and the scent of it, like a man parched with thirst and slaking it with spring-water. Few people would have found much to admire in such scenery, and to the majority of Europeans the flat, featureless plain and the circle of barren hills would have appeared ugly and daunting. But though Ash had every reason to dislike Bhithor, the dawn sky and the cool pale light slowly flooding the land, the clamour of partridges and peacocks and the scent of dust and smoke and *kikar* blossoms were an integral part of the world that he had loved and was leaving, and he savoured them with a new sense of awareness and a deep feeling of gratitude for benefits received.

He rode with a slack rein, and Dagobaz, having worked off his suppressed energy, was content to keep to a walk for a time. There was no need to hurry, as it was unlikely that the Rana's body would arrive at the burning-ground much before mid-day. For though the funeral would take place as soon as possible because of the heat, the procession would take time to organize, and there were bound to be endless delays. On the other hand the crowds would get there early in order to secure good places, and already there were signs of activity in the grove. Pin-points of brightness, barely visible in the fast-growing light, betokened cow-dung fires, and gossamer veils of smoke crept out from among the tree-trunks, creating an illusion that the place was an island surrounded by shallow water.

As he came nearer Ash could glimpse the saffron-clad figures of priests moving to and fro, and looking towards the city he saw that there were horsemen on the road, riding at a gallop to judge by the dust cloud that rose up behind them and partly obscured the groups of pedestrians that followed in their wake. Presently the twin forts that crowned the hills to the left and right of the city caught the first rays of the sun and flamed red-gold against the cool aquamarine of the sky, and now from every corner of the plain pale smudges of dust told of parties of people converging on the burning-ground in carts and dhoolies, on horseback or on foot. It was clearly time to get to the grove, and obedient to the pressure of Ash's knee, Dagobaz quickened his pace.

Once among the trees on the eastern fringe of the grove, Ash dismounted and led his horse towards the ruins of an ancient *chattri* surmounted by a triple dome. There were several tunnel-like passages in the massive plinth, some of them leading directly to a central tank that was open to the sky, while others sloped sharply upward and had once contained stairways that led up to the broad terrace overlooking it. The stairs had fallen long ago, and nowadays no one visited the ruined *chattri,* but one of the passages was still in good repair, and as a temporary stable would be far cooler and more comfortable than the charcoal-seller's shed.

Ash tethered Dagobaz to a fallen block of masonry and fetched water from the tank in a canvas bucket that he had brought with him. He had also brought grain and a small bundle of *bhoosa* in a saddle-bag, for he knew that Sarji might not be able to collect the horse for another hour or two, and that after that there would be no stopping until they were clear of the valley and far along the trail through the hills. So it was necessary to supply Dagobaz with food and water now.

The water was green and stagnant, but that wild gallop across the dusty plain had made Dagobaz thirsty and he drank it gratefully. When he had finished, Ash fetched a second bucket-full and wedged it carefully between two blocks of sandstone so that it would not collapse. Dagobaz smelt it but did not drink, and ignoring the *bhoosa,* dropped a wet affectionate nose onto his master's shoulder, nuzzling him as though he sensed that there was something wrong.

'You'll be all right with Sarji,' consoled Ash huskily. 'He'll take care of you . . . you'll be all right.' He put an arm about the black head and gave it a brief, hard hug, and then pushing it aside, turned on his heel and walked out of the shadowed archway into the brightness of the sunrise.

The fringes of the grove were still deserted, but near the centre the sound of bird-song gave place to the voices of men. Where the trees stopped behind the *chattris* that faced the open sweep of the burning-ground, groups of people could be seen hurrying to and fro: enterprising vendors of food and drink busily setting up their stalls under the shade of the branches, and already serving a handful of early customers. But as yet there did not appear to be many spectators, and although there were a score of priests and officials and a number of men in the uniform of the palace guard in the clearing, none showed any interest in Ash, since all were far too busy supervising the construction of the pyre and talking among themselves.

The *chattri* nearest to them was a larger and more elaborately decorated version of the far older one where he had left Dagobaz, being built in the form of a hollow square surrounding a vast tank. But here the stairways in the thickness of the outer wall were in excellent repair, and Ash climbed one, and reaching the broad stone terrace without being molested, took up a position in the angle between the outer parapet and the wall of a small pavilion that flanked a much larger central one consisting of three tiers of diminishing width, each tier composed of graceful pillared arches with the final one topped by a number of hump-backed domes.

Similar though smaller structures adorned the other three sides of the square, and below them, from the level of the terrace and facing inward, wide, shallow stone steps led down to the water's edge. The *chattri* had been built to face eastward into the sunrise and the clustered trees, but directly behind it lay the open ground, and today the western pavilions looked down onto a hastily constructed brick platform not thirty yards from the foot of the terrace wall, where half-a-dozen priests were constructing a pyre from logs of cedar and sandalwood strewn with aromatic spices.

The newly risen sun striped the ground with brilliant bars of light and long blue shadows, but as it moved up the sky the shadows shrank and changed their shapes and the dawn wind died; and suddenly the freshness was gone from the morning and the day was breathlessly hot. 'There will be a breeze soon,' thought Ash. But today there was no breeze. The leaves hung limp and still and the dust lay unstirred, and behind him the green, glassy surface of the tank mirrored every detail of the *chattri* so clearly that had he moved to the back of the terrace he would not have needed to look up to where the purdah-screens formed a make-shift room out of the second storey, because it lay there in the water.

For the present it appeared to be untenanted; there was no flicker of movement from behind the split-cane *chiks* that faced towards the burning-ground, but by now there were many more people in the grove: a number of early arrivals from near-by villages, several ash-smeared Sadhus and a further influx of minor officials, puffed up with their own importance and issuing orders to the men who had brought the logs and to those whose task it would be to hold back the crowds and keep a way clear for the funeral procession.

It was as well for Ash that he had taken up his stand when he did, for before long what had begun as a trickle increased to a flood as the thousands from the city poured into the grove, turning the wide, dusty space and the long, narrow aisles between the trees into a sea of humanity that stretched back on either side of the road by which they had come.

Above this, men clustered as thick as swarming bees on the walls and terraces, the stairways, pavilions and rooftops of the surrounding *chattris,* and soon every branch of the nearer trees bore its load of determined spectators. The voice of that multitude was a corporate sound—a deep and deafening one that rose and fell like the purr of some giant cat. And still the wind did not blow . . .

The dust that fumed up under the restless feet of the crowd hung in the air like the smoke trails of the early morning fires, and with every passing minute the heat increased as the sun blazed down on the stone-built *chattris* and glittered blindingly on the quiet surface of the tanks. But the crowd were impervious to these discomforts. They were used to dust and heat and cramped conditions, and it was not often that they had the opportunity to witness such a notable ceremony as the one that would be enacted here today. If it involved a certain amount of discomfort, well, that was a small price to pay for something that all who were privileged to be present would talk of for years to come, and describe to generations yet unborn. For even here, in this remote corner of Rajasthan, there were few who were not becoming uneasily aware that in the India beyond their borders the old ways were changing and old customs dying out, and that if the Raj had its way, this might be the last suttee that anyone in Bhithor would ever see.

Ash, from his vantage point on the terrace, was equally unaffected by the dust and din and the soaring temperature. He would probably not have noticed if it had suddenly begun to rain or snow, for all his faculties were concentrated upon keeping calm and relaxed. It was essential that his eye should be clear and his hand steady because there would be no second chance; and remembering what Kaka-ji had told him about the benefits of meditation, he fixed his gaze on a crack in the top of the parapet and counted his heartbeats, breathing slowly and evenly and forcing himself to think of nothing.

The crowd pressed upon him from the left, but his back was against the wall of the pavilion, and the space between his knees and the edge of the parapet was too narrow to allow room for even the smallest child to squeeze in front of him. So far, this side of the terrace was still in shadow, and the stone at his back still retained some of the coolness of the previous night. Ash relaxed against it and felt curiously peaceful; and very sleepy, which was hardly surprising considering how poorly he had slept ever since Manilal's arrival in Ahmadabad, though in the present circumstances, with the prospect of eternal sleep a mere hour or so away, it seemed a little ridiculous.

Ridiculous or not, he must actually have dozed off; for aroused by the sudden impact of a solid body and a sharp pain in his left foot, he opened his eyes to find that the sun was directly overhead and the crowd was no longer facing away from him, but had turned and were staring up at the *chattri*.

On the terrace itself half-a-dozen helmeted members of the Rana's palace guard were laying about them with their staves in an attempt to clear the way to the stairway leading to the second storey, and as the crowd surged back before them, the stout gentleman on Ash's left had been forced to give ground and had jerked him into wakefulness by stepping on his toes.

'Your pardon,' gasped the stout one, recovering himself and struggling to remain upright. He appeared to be in imminent danger of falling backwards over the parapet to land on the heads of the citizens twenty feet below, and Ash put out a hand to steady him, and inquired what was happening.

'It is some high-born women who have arrived to see the burning,' explained the stranger breathlessly, replacing his turban which had fallen off in the struggle. 'Doubtless the family of the Diwan. Or perhaps that of the heir? They will watch from above—from behind the *chiks* up there. Though the boy himself will walk in the procession and set light to the pyre. They say that his mother . . .'

The man talked on and on, gossiping, speculating and commenting, and Ash nodded now and then, but after a time he ceased to listen. His mouth was dry and he wished he had thought to bring his water-bottle with him instead of leaving it strapped to Dagobaz's saddle. But one of the many things that he had learned during those years in Afghanistan, when he had been masquerading as a Pathan and had to keep the Moslem fast of Ramadan, was how to endure thirst. And as Ramadan lasts a month (during which time no food or water may be taken between dawn and sunset) when it falls in the hot weather it can be no mean test of endurance.

Juli too must be thirsty, thought Ash. It would be another torment to add to those she must suffer on that long, last walk in the dust and the sun between the peering, jostling crowds. And she must be so tired . . . so very tired . . . It was difficult to believe that soon he would actually see her again in the flesh: the real Juli, instead of the one he had only seen in his imagination for the past two years. Her sweet grave eyes and tender mouth; the wide tranquil brow and the faint hollows at her temples and below her cheek bones that he always longed to kiss. His heart turned over at the thought, and it seemed to him that to see her again, if only for a moment, was worth dying for . . .

He wondered what the time was. To judge by the sun it must be well past mid-day, so it could not be long now before the Rana's body was carried out of the Rung Mahal to begin its last, slow-paced journey from the city. And behind it would come Juli . . . Juli and Shushila, Ranis of Bhithor . . .

They would be dressed in all their wedding finery: Juli in yellow and gold and Shu-shu in scarlet. But this time their spangled saris would not be pulled forward over their faces, but thrown back, so that everyone could see them. The suttees. The holy ones . . .

Ash knew that in the past many widows had been given drugs in order that they should not shrink from their duty or make any attempt to avoid their fate, but he did not believe that Juli would go drugged to her death; though she could be trusted to see that Shushu did, and he could only hope that the drugs would be strong ones —potent enough to numb Shushila's senses and shut out reality, while still enabling her to walk. For they would be expected to walk. That was the custom.

He shut his eyes against the glaring sunlight, but found this time that he could no longer shut out thought. Pictures formed behind his closed eye-lids as though he were seeing lantern-slides flashed on a screen: Juli in her yellow and gold wedding-dress with her black hair rippling unbraided to her knees, supporting the dazed, ruby-decked figure of her little sister . . . The two of them moving out from the shadows of the Queen's Palace into the blazing afternoon, walking towards the Suttee Gate and pausing there to dip their hands into a bowl of red dye before pressing them against the stone sides of the archway, where the imprint of their palms and fingers would join those of many former queens of Bhithor who had in their turn passed through that cruel gate on their way to death.

Well, at least it would bear no more prints, thought Ash. And perhaps some time in the next century, fifty, sixty or a hundred years hence, when even such dark corners as this would probably have been tamed and become respectable and law-abiding—and dull—parties of earnest globe-trotters would come to stare at the archway and be told the tale of the Last Suttee. The very last in Bhithor. And of how an unknown madman . . .

Ash had not noticed when the gossiping voice at his elbow ceased, or when the deafening babble of the crowd began to die away until even the hucksters and the children stopped shouting and stood quiet to listen. It was the unexpected silence that broke his waking dream. The watchers had seen puffs of white smoke and bright flashes from the forts that overlooked the city, and now that silence had fallen, they could hear the boom of cannon. The forts were firing a salute as the dead Rana left his capital city for the last time.

A man in the crowd cried shrilly, 'Hark! They come,' and Ash heard a far-off sound, harsh, ululating and indescribably mournful— the screech of conch-shells blown by the Brahmins who walked at the head of the funeral cortège. As he listened there came another sound, equally far away, but as unmistakable: a great roar as thousands of voices greeted the appearance of the suttees with shouts of 'Khaman Kher! Khaman Kher!'—'Well done!'

The crowded terraces and the close-packed masses below stirred and swayed like a field of corn when a gust of wind blows over it, and the babble broke out again, less noisily than before, but so fraught with anticipation that the very air of the hot afternoon seemed to vibrate to the tension that gripped the waiting crowds.

The hum of voices drowned those distant sounds, making it impossible to hear them or to judge how long it would be before the cortège reached the grove. Half an hour, perhaps? The distance by road between the *Mori* Gate and the grove was less than a mile and a half, though the sound of the conches had not to travel so far, it being considerably less as the crow flies. But then Ash had no way of knowing how far the procession had come already. The trees and the *chattris,* the dust and the heat-haze made it impossible to see the road, and it might be nearer than he supposed.

The only thing that he could be sure of was that it would come very slowly, because of the crowds who would press forward to throw garlands upon the bier and make obeisance to the dead man's widows, struggling to touch the hems of their saris as they passed, begging for their prayers and stooping to kiss the ground they had trodden on . . . Yes, it would be a slow business. And even when the cortège reached the burning-ground there would still be plenty of time, for he had taken the trouble to learn all that he could of the rites that would be performed.

Tradition dictated that a suttee should wear her wedding-dress and also deck herself with her finest jewels; but not that it was necessary for her to take such valuable things into the flames. One must, after all, be practical. This meant that Juli would first strip off all her glittering ornaments. The rings, bracelets, earrings, pins and anklets, the necklaces and brooches that had been part of her dowry—all must be removed. After which she must wash her hands in Ganges water and walk three times round the pyre before she mounted it. There would be no need for haste and he would be able to choose his moment.

Only half an hour more . . . perhaps less. Yet all at once it seemed an eternity and he could not wait to have it over and be done with it. To be done with everything—!

And then, without warning, the incredible thing happened:

Someone clutched his arm, and supposing it to be his talkative neighbour he turned impatiently on him, and saw that the garrulous gentleman had been elbowed out of his place by one of the palace servants, and that it was this man who had hold of his arm. In the same moment it flashed across his mind that his purpose must have been discovered, and instinctively he tried to jerk free, but could not because of the wall at his back, and because the grip on his arm had tightened. Before he could move again, a familiar voice spoke urgently from behind the concealing folds of muslin that covered the lower part of the man's face: 'It is I, Ashok. Come with me. Hurry.'

'*Sarji!* What are you doing here? I told you—'

'Be quiet,' muttered Sarji, glancing apprehensively over his shoulder. 'Do not talk. Only follow me.'

'No.' Ash tore at the clutching fingers and said in a furious undertone: 'If you think you can stop me, you are wasting your time. . . . Nothing and no one is going to stop me now. I meant every word I said, and I'm going to go through with it, so—'

'But you cannot; she is here. *Here*—with the Hakim.'

'Who is? If this is a trick to get me away . . .' he stopped short because Sarji had thrust something into his hand. Something thin and small and hard. A broken sliver of mother-of-pearl carved in the semblance of a fish . . .

Ash stared down at it, dazed and disbelieving. And Sarji seized the opportunity to draw him away and drag him, unresisting, through the close-packed crowd that gave them right of way only because of the dress that Sarji wore: the famous saffron, scarlet and orange of a palace servant.

Behind the mass of spectators, a number of soldiers of the State Forces were keeping a path clear between the side exit from the terrace and the stairway leading up to the screened second storey of the central pavilion. But they too recognized the palace colours and let the two men through.

Sarji turned right, and without relaxing his grip on Ash's arm, made for a flight of stairs that plunged downward into shadow and ended at ground level in a short tunnel similar to that in which Dagobaz had been tethered. Only privileged spectators had been permitted to use this route, and there was no one on the stairs, the guards being outside the entrance—those below watching for the cortège and those on the terrace holding back the public. Half-way down there was a break in one wall where a low doorway led into a narrow, dog-leg passage that presumably came out by the central tank, and there was no one here either, for the same reason. Sarji plunged into it, and releasing Ash, loosened the wide end of the muslin turban that had been swathed across his face, and leant against the wall, breathing fast and unsteadily as though he had been running.

'*Wah!*' gasped Sarji, mopping the sweat from his face. 'That was easier than I expected. Let us hope the rest will be.' He stooped and picked up a bundle that lay on the floor. 'Here, put these on quickly. You too must be one of the *nauker-log* from the Rung Mahal, and there is no time to waste.'

The bundle consisted of clothing similar to his own, and while Ash put them on, Sarji gave him a brief account of what had occurred, speaking in a disjointed and barely audible whisper.

He had, he said, been preparing to leave when Manilal arrived at the charcoal-seller's shop with news that upset all their plans. It seemed that the Senior Rani, realizing that she must die, had determined to use the considerable power and influence that she still possessed to save her half-sister Anjuli-Bai from sharing the same fate. This she had done.

On the previous night she had arranged to have her sister taken secretly from the Rung Mahal to a house outside the city, asking only that Anjuli-Bai should witness the final ceremonies; to which end a screened enclosure would be prepared for her use and she would be taken there on the day of the funeral by a picked band of guards and servants, all of whom had been selected because of their known loyalty to the Senior Rani. Word of all this had been brought that very morning by the serving-woman who had often acted as a go-between, and the Hakim had instantly sent Manilal to fetch the Sahib—only to find that the Sahib had already gone.

'So we went back on foot to the Hakim's house,' said Sarji, 'and it was he who devised all this. He even had the clothing in readiness, because, he said, it occurred to him many moons ago that one day he might have to escape from Bhithor—and how better to do this than in the guise of one of the palace servants, who go everywhere without question? So he caused Manilal to buy cloth in the bazaar and to make two sets for their use, in case of need. And later, thinking that he might be able to take one or both of the Ranis with him, two more; and then a fifth and sixth, in case there should be more from Karidkote who would go. We put on those clothes and came here, no one preventing us and—are you ready? Good. See that the end of the turban does not slip down and betray you. Now follow me—and pray to your God that we are not questioned.'

They had not been. The affair had been absurdly easy, for the beauty of Gobind's scheme lay in the fact that the Rung Mahal and the various other royal palaces of Bhithor swarmed with servants; many more than could possibly have been necessary, and certainly too many for any one of them to know more than a third of the others by sight even when they were not on duty and able to leave their faces uncovered. Also on this occasion there was too much of interest going on for the guards on the terrace to notice that two men wearing the dress of royal servants had come up the stairs where only one had gone down.

After the semi-darkness of the passage below, the glare was so intense that Ash had to screw up his eyes against the sunlight as he followed Sarji into the lower storey of the main pavilion, where half-a-dozen members of the Rana's personal bodyguard had been posted to see that the public did not enter. But these too took no interest in a pair of palace servants, and Sarji walked boldly past them and up a curving stairway that led to the second storey, where purdah screens hung between the open archways.

Ash, a pace behind him, could hear him muttering beneath his breath, and realized that he was praying—presumably in thankfulness. Then they had reached the top and Sarji was holding aside a heavy curtain and motioning him to enter.

42

The make-shift room was cooler than might have been expected.

It was also very dark, for all but one of the split-cane *chiks* that enclosed it were lined with a coarse, brick-red cloth embroidered in black and yellow and sewn with little circles of looking-glass after the fashion of Rajputana. The single exception hung between the two centre pillars facing the burning-ground, its fragile slats letting in the only light and providing an excellent view to anyone looking out, while preventing anyone outside from seeing in.

The shadowy enclosure was roughly fifteen foot square and it appeared to be full of people, some of whom were seated. But Ash saw only one. A slim figure standing a little apart from the rest in an attitude that was curiously rigid, and that suggested, starkly, a captive wild animal immobilized by terror.

Juli . . .

He had not really believed it until then. Even after those hasty explanations, and though he held the proof in his hand, he had not been sure that it was not some trick on the part of Sarji and Gobind to lure him away and keep him prisoner until it was all over and too late for him to intervene.

She was standing in front of the unlined *chik,* so that at first he only saw her as a dark figure outlined against the oblong of light: a faceless figure dressed like the others in the garments of a palace servant. Because of those clothes, a stranger entering the room would have taken her for a man. Yet Ash had known her instantly. He would, he thought, have known her even if he had been blind, because the tie between them was stronger than sight and went deeper than externals.

He pulled away the folds of orange and red muslin that had been wrapped about his face, and they looked at each other across the width of that shadowed room. But though Ash had put aside the loose end of his turban, Anjuli did not follow his example, and her face remained hidden except for her eyes.

The beautiful, gold-flecked eyes that he remembered so well were still beautiful—they could never be anything else. But as his own became accustomed to the subdued light he realized that there was neither gladness nor welcome in them, but such a look as might have belonged to the child Kay in Hans Andersen's fairy-story *The Snow Queen,* whose heart had been pierced by a sliver of glass: a blank, frozen look that appalled him.

He started forward to go to her, but was prevented by someone who moved quickly between them and laid a restraining hand on his arm: Gobind, unfamiliar in the same disguise as Juli wore, but with his face uncovered.

'Ashok,' said Gobind. He had not raised his voice, but both tone and touch conveyed a warning so vividly that Ash checked, remembering just in time that except for Sarji, and Juli herself, no one present knew that there was anything between the widowed Rani and himself—and must not know it; especially at this juncture, since there was not one of them who would not be as shocked by it as Sarji or Kaka-ji had been, and the situation was dangerous enough already without his making it worse by alienating his allies.

He forced his gaze from Anjuli though it was an effort to do so, and looked instead at Gobind, who permitted himself to draw a deep breath of relief—he had feared that the Sahib was about to shame the Rani and embarrass them all by some open demonstration of feeling. That danger at least had been averted, and he withdrew his hand and said: 'I thank the gods that you have come; there is much to do, and these here will need watching. The woman most of all, for she would scream if she could, and there are a score of guards within hearing— in the pavilion above us, as well as below.'

'What woman?' said Ash, who had seen only one.

Gobind gestured with a slim hand and for the first time Ash became aware of the others in the curtained room. There were seven of them, not counting Manilal, and only one of these was a woman— presumably a waiting-woman of Juli's. The obese, slug-like man whose pallid cheeks and numerous chins were as smooth as a baby's could only be one of the Zenana eunuchs, and for the rest, two from their dress were palace servants, another two troopers of the State Forces, and one a member of the Rana's bodyguard. All of them were seated on the floor, and all had been gagged and trussed up like fowls—except the last, who was dead. He had been stabbed through the left eye, and the handle of the stiletto-like knife that had been driven into his brain still protruded from the wound.

Gobind's work, thought Ash. No one else would have known how to strike with such deadly accuracy, and it was the only vulnerable spot. The surcoat of chain-mail and the heavy leather helmet with its deep fringe of linked metal would have deflected any attack on the wearer's head, throat or body. There had been only one chance . . .

'Yes,' said Gobind, answering the unspoken question. 'We could not stun him with a blow on the head as we had done with the others, so it was necessary to kill him. Besides, he spoke through the curtain to the eunuch, not knowing that we had the creature safely tied, and from what he said, it became plain that there are those who mean to see that Anjuli-Bai is punished for escaping the fire and thereby failing to do her duty as a Rani of Bhithor. She is not to be allowed to return to Karidkote or retire to one of the smaller palaces, but will go back to the Women's Quarters of the Rung Mahal, where she will spend the rest of her life. And lest she should find that life too pleasant, it has been arranged that as soon as her sister, the Senior Rani, is dead and can no longer intervene to save her, her eyes are to be put out.'

Ash caught his breath in a choking gasp as though the air had been driven from his lungs, and Gobind said grimly: 'Yes, you may well stare. But that is what was planned. The brazier is out there in readiness, and the irons too; and once the pyre was well alight the thing would have been done—here, in this place and by those two, the eunuch and that carrion who lies there with my knife in his brain, the woman and these others helping. When I think of it I am sorry that I did not kill them all.'

'That can be remedied,' said Ash between his teeth. He was shaken by a cold, killing rage that made him long to get his hands on the fat eunuch's throat, and the woman's too, and choke the life out of them—they and the four others, bound and helpless as they were—because of the inhuman thing they had planned to do to Juli. But Gobind's quiet, commanding voice cut through the murderous fog that filled his brain, and brought him back to sanity.

'Let them be,' said Gobind. 'They are only tools. Those who ordered or bribed them to do this thing will be walking in the funeral procession and beyond the reach of our vengeance. It is not justice to kill the slave who does as he is bid, while the master he obeys goes free. Besides, we have no time for vengeance. If we are to leave here alive we shall need that man's gear, and one of the servants' also. Manilal and I will see to that if you and your friend will watch the prisoners.'

He did not wait for an answer, but turned away and began to remove the dead man's accoutrements, starting with the padded leather helmet that was as yet comparatively free from blood, for he had been careful not to withdraw the knife and the wound had bled very little.

Ash allowed himself a brief glance at Juli, but she was still gazing out at the burning-ground and the waiting multitudes; and with her back towards him she was once again only a dark figure silhouetted against the light. He looked away again, and taking out his revolver, stood guard over the prisoners while Sarji watched the entrance and Gobind and Manilal worked swiftly and methodically, unfastening buckles and stripping off the surcoat, which for all their care was not a silent process.

The chain-mail clashed and clinked against the marble floor and jingled as they handled it, and the noise it made seemed very loud in that constricted space. But the surrounding curtains shut it in, and the sound of the enormous crowd outside was more than enough to cover anything less than a scream—or a shot; it would take a considerable commotion to cover that last, and Ash was well aware that the revolver was useless, for if he fired it the guards and servants on the floors above and below them would come running.

Fortunately the captives did not appear to realize this. The mere sight of it had proved enough to make them stop straining at their bonds and sit very still, their eyes above the clumsy gags white-rimmed with terror and staring fixedly at the unfamiliar weapon in his hand.

Gobind and Manilal finished disrobing the corpse and began to help Sarji remove his palace livery and replace it with the dead man's. 'It is fortunate that you are of a size in the matter of height,' observed Gobind, slipping the chain surcoat over his head, 'though I could wish you were stouter, for that thing there was more heavily built than you. Well, it cannot be helped, and luckily those outside will be too interested in the funeral ceremonies to notice small details.'

'—we hope,' amended Sarji with a curt laugh. 'But what if they do?'

'If they do, we die,' said Gobind unemotionally. 'But I think that we shall live. Now let us see to these—' he turned his attention to the bound captives and looked them over critically.

The woman's dark-skinned face was green with fear and the eunuch's pallid one twitched and trembled uncontrollably. Neither expected any mercy (and with good reason, since they themselves would have shown none to the widowed Rani), and having seen their fellow-torturer killed, they probably imagined that the manner of it—the swift upward stab through the eye—had been in retaliation for the injury he himself had intended to inflict on the Junior Rani, and that they, as his partners in guilt, would be dealt with in the same way.

They could well have been had it not been for Gobind—and for something that Manilal found hidden among the woman's clothing—for neither Sarji nor Ash would have had the least compunction in putting an end to them by that or any other method, if their continued existence in any way threatened Anjuli's safety, or their own. Both were in agreement with Manilal, who said flatly: 'We had best kill them all: it is no more than they deserve, and no more than they would do to us if they stood in our place. Let us kill them now and thus make certain that they cannot raise an alarm.'

But Gobind had been trained to save life and not to take it, and he would not agree. He had killed the helmeted guard because there had been no other way of silencing him; it had been necessary and he did not regret it. But to kill the others in cold blood would serve no useful purpose (provided that they were secured so that they could not summon help) and would only rank as murder. At this point Manilal, stooping to tighten the woman's bonds, had discovered that she had something hard and bulky hidden in a fold of cloth wrapped about her waist, and removing it, found it to be a necklace of raw gold set with pearls and carved emeralds: a thing of such magnificence that no waiting-woman could possibly have come by it honestly.

Manilal handed it to Gobind with the comment that the she-devil was clearly also a thief, but the woman shook her head in frantic denial, and Gobind said shortly that it was more likely to be a bribe. 'Look at her'—she had cringed in her bonds and was staring at him as though hypnotized—'this was blood-money, paid in advance for the foul work she had agreed to do. *Pah!*'

He dropped the necklace as though it had been a poisonous snake, and Ash stooped quickly and picked it up. Neither Gobind nor Manilal could possibly have recognized that fabulous jewel, but Ash had seen it twice before: once when the more valuable items listed in the dowries of the brides from Karidkote had been checked in his presence, and again when Anjuli had worn it at the formal departure from the Pearl Palace. He said harshly: 'There should be two bracelets also. See if the eunuch has them. Quickly.'

The eunuch had not (they were found on the two palace servants) but he had something else that Ash had no difficulty in recognizing: a collar of table-cut diamonds fringed with pearls.

He stood looking at it with unseeing eyes. So the vultures were already dividing the spoils!—the Rana had only died last night, but Juli's enemies had wasted no time in seizing her personal possessions, and had actually used some of her own jewels to bribe her would-be torturers. The irony of that would appeal to someone like the Diwan, who had once hoped to retain her dowry while at the same time repudiating her bridal contract and having her returned in disgrace to Karidkote. And from his knowledge of the man and his devious mind, Ash did not believe for a moment that the Diwan would pay such lavish bribes in return for something that he could order to be done for nothing.

It was far more likely that the choice of those jewels had been deliberate, for once the appalling deed had been done, the Diwan would be able to deny all knowledge of it and have the woman and her accomplices arrested. Then, when the jewels were found on them, they could be accused of having blinded the Rani so that she would not discover that they had been stealing her belongings, and they would be condemned to death and garotted. After which he would have nothing to fear, and with his cat's-paws dead, could safely take back the jewels. 'A neat, Machiavellian piece of treachery in fact,' thought Ash cynically.

He looked down at the gagged and bound creatures that only a minute ago he had wanted to murder, and thought: 'No. It's not fair.' And with that old, familiar protest of his childhood, a large part of his rage against them died. They were vile and venial, but Gobind was right; it was not fair to take revenge upon a mere instrument while the hand and brain that guided it escaped scot-free.

He bent above the eunuch and the man's eyes bulged with terror, expecting that the end had come; but Ash had only wanted a piece of muslin. He ripped it from the man's clothes, and knotting the jewels in it, stowed them away in the bosom of his robe, and said curtly: 'It is time we went. But we had better see to it first that these vermin do not raise an alarm too soon. There is nothing to stop them rolling over to the curtains and wriggling out from underneath them the moment we have gone. They should be tied together and then lashed to one of those pillars. Have you any more rope?'

'No, we have used all that we brought with us,' said Gobind. 'But there is plenty of cloth.'

He stooped for Sarji's discarded turban, and using that and the turbans of the prisoners, who were already gagged with their waist-cloths, they lashed the six side by side in a circle with their backs to one of the central pillars, and bound them to it in a cocoon of vividly coloured muslin.

'There. That should keep them safe enough,' said Ash, tying a final reef-knot and jerking it tight. 'And now for God's sake, let us go. We've wasted too much time already, and the sooner we get out of here the better.'

No one stirred. The bound woman was breathing noisily with an odd bubbling sound, and a wandering breath of wind shook the curtains and set the scraps of looking-glass that decorated them glinting and winking like watching eyes. Down below on the terrace and the burning-ground, the waiting crowds were comparatively silent as they listened to the distant tumult that accompanied the approaching cortège. But in the curtained enclosure no one moved.

'Well, come on,' said Ash, the curtness of his voice betraying the extent of his inner tensions. 'We cannot afford to wait. The head of the procession will be here any moment now and raising enough noise to cover any moaning these creatures in here will make. Besides, we must be well clear of the valley before dark, and the later we leave the sooner someone is going to come in here and find the Rani gone. We must go at once.'

But still no one moved, and he glanced quickly from one face to the next, and was baffled by the mixture of exasperation, embarrassment and unease that he saw there: and the fact that they were not looking at him, but at Anjuli. He turned swiftly to follow the direction of their gaze, and saw that her back was still towards them and that she too had not moved. She could not have avoided hearing those last words he had spoken, for he had not lowered his voice. Yet she had not even turned her head.

He said sharply: 'What is it? What is the matter?'

His question had been addressed to Anjuli rather than to the three men, but it was Sarji who answered it:

'The Rani-Sahiba will not leave,' said Sarji, exasperated. 'We had decided that if our plan succeeded, the Hakim-Sahib and Manilal would take her away as soon as she had donned the disguise, leaving me to find you and follow after them. That would have been best for us all, and at first she agreed to it. But then suddenly she said she must wait and see her sister become suttee, and that she would not leave before then. See if you can make her change her mind. We cannot—though the gods know we have tried hard enough.'

Anger blazed up in Ash, and heedless of the watching eyes, he strode across the room, and grasping Anjuli's shoulders, jerked her round to face him:

'Is this true?'

The harshness in his voice was only a small measure of the fury that possessed him, and when she did not answer he shook her savagely: *'Answer me!'*

'She . . . Shushila . . . does not understand,' whispered Anjuli, her eyes still frozen with horror. 'She does not realize what . . . what it will be like. And when she does—'

'Shushila!' Ash spat out the name as though it were an obscenity. 'Always Shushila—and selfish to the end. I suppose she made you promise to do this? She would! Oh, I know she saved you from burning with her, but if she'd really wanted to repay you for all you have done for her, she could have saved you from reprisals at the hands of the Diwan by having you smuggled out of the state, instead of begging you to come here and watch her die.'

'You don't understand,' whispered Anjuli numbly.

'Oh, yes I do. That's where you are wrong. I understand only too well. You are still hypnotized by that selfish, hysterical little egotist, and you are perfectly prepared to jeopardize your chances of escaping from Bhithor and a horrible form of mutilation—and risk all our lives into the bargain, Gobind's, Sarji's, Manilal's and my own, just so that you can carry out your darling little sister's last wishes and watch her commit suicide. Well, I don't care what she made you promise. You are not keeping it. You are going to leave now if I have to carry you.'

His rage was real; yet even as he spoke, a part of his brain was saying, 'This is Juli, whom I love more than anything else in the world, and who I was afraid I should never see again. She is here at last—and all I can do is to be angry with her . . .' It didn't make sense. But then nor did his threat to carry her, for if anything were to draw attention to them, that would. He could not do it, and she would have to walk; and to go with them willingly. There was no other way. But if she would not . . . ?

The funeral cortège must be very near by now. The discordant braying of the conches and the shouts of *'Khaman Kher!'* and *'Hari-bol!'* were growing louder every minute, and already isolated voices in the crowd below had begun to take up the cries.

Anjuli turned her head to listen, and the movement was so slow and vague that Ash recognized suddenly that in her present state of shock, his anger had not reached her. He drew a long breath and steadied himself, and his hands on her shoulders relaxed to tenderness. He said gently, coaxing her as though she were a child: 'Don't you see, dear, as long as Shu-shu thinks you are here, watching her and praying for her, she will be satisfied. Listen to me, Juli. She will never know that you are not, for though you and I can see out through this *chik,* no one out there can see us, so you cannot even signal to her. And if you called out to her, she could not possibly hear you.'

'Yes, I know. But . . .'

'Juli, all you can do is to hurt yourself cruelly by watching a sight that may haunt you for the rest of your life; and that is not going to help her.'

'Yes, I know . . . but you could. *You* could help her.'

'I? No, dear. There is nothing that I or any of us can do for her now. I'm sorry Juli, but that is the truth and you must face it.'

'It isn't. It isn't true.' Anjuli's hands came up to his wrists, and her eyes were no longer frozen but wide and imploring, and at last he saw her face, for the turban-end had become loose when he shook her, and now it fell down about her throat.

The change in that face was like a knife in Ash's heart, because it was terribly altered—more so than he could have dreamed possible. The flesh had wasted from it leaving it thin and drawn and desperate, and as drained of colour as though she had spent the last two years penned up in a dungeon where no gleam of light ever penetrated. There were lines and deep hollows in it that had not been there before, and the dark shadows that circled her eyes owed nothing to the artful use of *kohl* or antimony, but told of fear and intolerable strain; and tears—an ocean of tears . . .

There were tears in her eyes now, and in her breathless, pleading voice, and Ash would have given anything in the world to take her in his arms and kiss them away. But he knew that he must not.

'I *would* have left,' sobbed Anjuli. 'I would have gone at once with your friends, for I could not bear to see what I had been brought here to see, and had they not come I would have shut my eyes and ears to it. But then they—the Hakim-Sahib and your friend—told me why you were not with them, and what you had meant to do for me so that I should not burn to death but die quickly and without pain. You can do that for her.'

Ash took a quick step back and would have snatched his hands away, but now it was Anjuli who held him by the wrists and would not let him go.

'Please—*please,* Ashok! It is not much to ask—only that you will do for her what you would have done for me. She could never endure pain, and when . . . when the flames . . . I cannot bear to think of it. You can save her from that, and then I will go with you gladly—gladly.'

Her voice broke on the word and Ash said huskily: 'You don't know what you are asking. It isn't as easy as that. It would have been different with you, because—because I had meant to go with you; and Sarji and Gobind and Manilal would all have got safely away, for they would have been a long way from here when our time came. But now it would mean that we would all be here; and if the shot were heard and anyone saw where it had come from, we should all die a far worse death than Shushila's.'

'But it will not be heard. Not above all that noise outside. And who will be looking this way? No one—no one, I tell you. Do this for me. On my knees, I beg of you—'

She let go his wrists, and before he could prevent it she was at his feet with the orange and scarlet turban that she wore touching the ground. Ash bent quickly and pulled her upright, and Sarji, from behind them, said tersely: 'Let her have her way. We cannot carry her, so if she will not come with us unless you do as she asks, you have no choice.'

'None,' agreed Ash. 'Very well, since I must, I will do it. But only if you four will go now. I will follow later, when it is done, and meet you in the valley.'

'*No!*' There was pure panic in Anjuli's voice, and she brushed past him and addressed Gobind, who averted his eyes from her unveiled face: 'Hakim-Sahib, tell him that he must not stay here alone—it is madness. There would be no one to watch for other men who may come up here, or help to overpower them as you three did to these others. Tell him we must stay together.'

Gobind was silent for a moment. Then he nodded, though with obvious reluctance, and said to Ash: 'I fear that the Rani-Sahiba is right. We must stay together, for one man alone, looking out through the *chik* into the sunlight and choosing his moment, could not guard his back or listen for steps on the stair at the same time.'

Sarji and Manilal murmured agreement, and Ash shrugged and capitulated. It was, after all, the least he could do for poor little Shu-shu, whom he had brought from her home in the north to this remote and medieval backwater among the arid hills and scorching sands of Rajputana, and handed over to an evil and dissolute husband whose unlamented end had proved to be her death-warrant. And perhaps the least that Juli too could do for her, because although it was only Shu-shu's hysterical refusal to be parted from her half-sister that had brought her to this pass, at the end the little Rani had done what she could to make amends. But for her intervention, Juli would even now be out there in the dust and the glare, walking behind her husband's bier towards the moment when a bullet from her lover's re-volver would give her a swift and merciful death: and if he had been prepared to do that for Juli, it was not fair to refuse the same mercy to her little sister . . . Yet the very idea of doing so appalled him.

Because he loved Juli—because he loved her more than life and because she was so much a part of him that without her life would have no meaning—he could have shot her without a tremor, and never felt that her blood was upon his head; but to put a bullet through Shushila's head was a very different matter, because pity, however strong, did not provide the terrible incentive that love had done. And then, too, his own life would not be involved. The next bullet would not be for himself, and that alone would make him feel like a murderer—or at best, an executioner, which was absurd when he knew that Juli would have faced the flames with far less terror and endured the pain with more fortitude than poor Shu-shu would ever do, and yet he had resolved to save her from that agony . . . and was now sickened by the thought of doing the same for Shu-shu.

Sarji broke in on the confusion of his thoughts by remarking in a matter-of-fact voice that the range would be greater from up here than it had been from the edge of the terrace below, and that as Ash would be aiming downwards, and from at least twelve to fifteen feet higher, it was not going to be easy. He might have been discussing a difficult shot from a *machan* on one of their hunting trips in the Gir Forest, and strangely enough it seemed to take some of the horror out of this supremely horrible situation. For he was talking sense.

If the thing must be done, it must be done well; and at the last possible moment, so that it might be thought that Shushila, having taken her place on the pyre, had fainted. To bungle it would be a disaster, not only for Shushila, but for them all; because though there was every chance that the crack of a single shot would be lost in the noise of the crowd, a second or third could not fail to attract attention, or to pin-point the spot from where it had been fired.

'Do you think you can do it?' asked Sarji, coming to stand beside him.

'I must. I can't afford not to. Have you a knife?'

'You mean for the *chik*. No, but I can cut you a gap in it with this thing—' Sarji set to work with the short spear that all members of the Rana's bodyguard carried, and sliced a small oblong out of the split cane. 'There. That should serve. I do not think the cane would deflect a shot, but it might; and there is no need to take chances.'

He watched Ash take out the service revolver and sight along the barrel, and said in an undertone: 'It is all of forty paces. I have never handled one of those things. Will it reach as far?'

'Yes. But I don't know how accurately. It was never intended for such distances, and I—' He swung round abruptly: 'It's no good, Sarji. I daren't risk it from here. I shall have to get closer. Listen, if I go down there again, will you and the others— Yes, that's it. Why didn't we think of it before? We will all leave now, at once, and when we reach the terrace you three can go on ahead with the Rani-Sahiba, and I will get back to my place near the parapet and—'

Sarji cut brusquely across the sentence: 'You could not get there. The crowds are too thick. It was all I could do to get to you before; and even wearing this livery they would never make room for you now. Besides, it is too late. Listen—they come.'

The conches sounded again. But now the mournful and discordant bray was deafeningly loud, while the roar that followed it came from the crowd lining the last short stretch of pathway that lay within the grove itself. In another minute or so the funeral cortège would be here, and there was no longer time to make for the terrace and try to force a way to the front of the close-packed and half-hysterical multitude that thronged it. It was too late for that.

The crowds on the ground below were swaying backwards and forwards as a flood-tide surges between the supports of a pier, pushing, jostling, craning to see over the heads of those in front, or striving to dodge the indiscriminate blows of men who laid about them with *lathis* in order to keep a way clear for the slow-moving procession. And now the advance guard were emerging from the tree shadows into the golden blaze of the afternoon sun, a phalanx of shaven-headed Brahmins from the city's temples, clad in white loincloths, with ropes of *tulsi* beads adorning their naked chests and the trident mark that is the fork of Vishnu splashed upon their foreheads.

The leaders blew on conches while the rear rank whirled strips of brass bells above the heads of those who walked between, and behind these came a motley company of other holy men, a score or more of them: saints, sadhus and ascetics, jangling bells and chanting; naked and ash-smeared or soberly dressed in flowing robes of saffron or orange, dull red or white; some with their heads shaved and others whose matted hair and beards, having never been cut, reached half-way to their knees. As wild a crew as Ash had ever seen, they had gathered here like kites who can see death from a great distance away, converging together from every corner of the State to attend the suttee. Behind them came the bier, borne high above the crowd and rocking and dipping to the pace of its bearers like a boat on a choppy sea.

The body that it bore was swathed in white and heaped about with garlands, and Ash was astonished to see how small it looked. The Rana had not been a big man, but then he had always been magnificently dressed and glittering with jewels, and always the centre of a subservient court; all of which had tended to make him seem a good deal larger than he was. But the spare, white-shrouded corpse on the bier looked no larger than an under-nourished child of ten. An insignificant object; and a very lonely one, for it was not the focus of the crowd's attention. They had not come here to see a dead man, but a still living woman. And now at last she was here, walking behind the bier; and at the sight of her, pandemonium broke loose, until even the solid fabric of the *chattri* seemed to tremble at the impact of that roar of sound.

Ash had not seen her at first. His gaze had been fixed on the shrunken thing that had once been his enemy. But a movement near him made him turn his head and he saw that Anjuli had come to stand beside him, and that she was staring through the *chik* with an expression of shrinking horror, as though she could not bear to look and yet could not keep herself from looking. And following the direction of that agonized gaze, he saw Shushila. Not the Shushila he had expected to see—bowed, weeping and half-crazed by terror, but a queen . . . a Rani of Bhithor.

Had he been asked, Ash would have insisted that Shu-shu would never be able to walk to the burning-ground unassisted, and that if she walked at all and did not have to be brought in a litter, it would only be because she had been stupefied by drugs and then half dragged and half carried there. But the small, brilliant figure walking behind the Rana's bier was not only alone, but walking upright and unfaltering; and there was pride and dignity in every line of her slender body.

Her small head was erect and the little unshod feet that had never before stepped on anything harsher than Persian carpets and cool polished marble trod slowly and steadily, marking the burning dust with small neat footprints that the adoring crowds behind her pressed forward to obliterate with kisses.

She was dressed as Ash had seen her at the marriage ceremony, in the scarlet and gold wedding dress, and decked with the same jewels as she had worn that day. Pigeon's-blood rubies circled her throat and wrists, glowed on her forehead and her fingers, and swung from her ears. There were rubies too on the chinking golden anklets, and the hard sunlight glittered on the gold embroidery of the full-skirted Rajputani dress and flashed on the little jewelled bodice. But this time she wore no sari, and her long hair was unbound as though for her bridal night. It rippled about her in a silky black curtain that was more beautiful than any sari made by man, and Ash could not drag his gaze from her, though his body cringed from that tragic sight.

She seemed wholly unconscious of the jostling crowds who applauded her, calling on her to bless them and struggling to touch the hem of her skirt as she passed, or of the sea of eyes that stared avidly at her unveiled face. Ash saw that her lips were moving in the age-old invocation that accompanies the last journey of the dead: *Ram, Ram . . . Ram, Ram . . . Ram, Ram . . .*

He said aloud and incredulously: 'You were wrong. She is not afraid.'

The clamour from below almost drowned his words, but Anjuli heard them, and imagining that they had been addressed to her instead of to himself, she said: 'Not yet. It is still only a game to her. No, not a game—I don't mean that. But something that is only happening in her mind. A part she is playing.'

'You mean she is drugged? I don't believe it.'

'Not in the way you mean, but with emotion—and desperation and shock. And—and perhaps . . . triumph . . .'

'*Triumph!*' thought Ash. Yes. The whole parade smacked more of a triumphal progress than a funeral. A procession in honour of a goddess who has deigned to show herself, for this time only, to accept the homage of her shouting, exultant and adoring worshippers. He remembered then that Shushila's mother, in the days before her beauty captured the heart of a Rajah, had been one of a troupe of entertainers: men and women whose livelihood depended upon their ability to capture the attention and applause of an audience—as her daughter was doing now. Shushila, Goddess of Bhithor, beautiful as the dawn and glittering with gold and jewels. Yes, it was a triumph. And even if she was only playing a part, at least she was playing it superbly.

'Well done!' whispered Ash, in a heart-felt endorsement of all those outside who were hailing her with the same words. 'Oh, well done—!'

Beside him, Anjuli too was murmuring to herself, repeating the same invocation as Shushila: '*Ram, Ram—Ram, Ram . . .*' It was only a breath of sound and barely audible in that tumult, but it distracted Ash's attention, and though he knew that the prayer was not for the dead man but for her sister, he told her sharply to be quiet.

His mind was once again in a turmoil and torn with doubts. For watching the unfaltering advance of that graceful scarlet and gold figure, it seemed to him that he had no right to play providence. It would have been excusable if she had been dragged here weeping and terrified, or dazed with drugs. But not when she showed no sign of fear.

She must know by now what lay ahead; and if so, either the stories that Gobind had heard were true and she had come to love the dead man—and loving him, preferred to die cradling his body in her arms rather than live without him—or else, having steeled herself to it, she was glorying in the manner of her death and the prospect of sainthood and veneration. In either case, what right had he to interfere? Besides, her agony would be very quickly over; he had watched the pyre being built and seen the priests heap cotton between the logs and pour oils and clarified butter on it, and had thought even then that once it was lit the smoke alone would probably suffocate poor little Shu-shu before a flame touched her.

'I can't do it,' decided Ash. 'And even if I do, it won't be all that much quicker: Juli ought to know that . . . Oh, God, why don't they hurry up. Why can't they get it over, instead of dragging it out like this.'

His whole being was suddenly flooded with hatred for everyone out there: the presiding priests, the excited onlookers, the mourners in the funeral procession and even the dead man and Shushila herself. Shushila most of all, because—

No, that was not fair, thought Ash; she couldn't help being herself. This was the way she was made, and she could not help battening upon Juli any more than Juli could keep from allowing herself to be battened upon. People were what they were, and they did not change. Yet despite all her selfishness and egotism, at the last Shushu had spared a thought for her sister, and instead of insisting on her support to the end, had let her go—at what cost to herself, no one would ever know. He must not let himself forget that again . . .

The red haze of rage that had momentarily blinded him cleared away, and he saw that Shushila had moved on, and that where she had been there was another small, lonely figure. But this time it was a child: a boy of about five or six years old, walking alone a little way behind her. 'The heir, I suppose,' thought Ash, grateful for something else to think about. 'No, not the heir—the new Rana, of course. Poor little beggar. He looks done up.'

The child was stumbling with weariness and plainly bewildered by the strangeness of his surroundings and his sudden elevation in rank, a rank that was clearly shown by the fact that he walked directly behind the widowed Rani and several paces ahead of the hundred or so men who followed—the nobles, councillors and chiefs of Bhithor who brought up the end of the procession. Prominent among these was the Diwan, who carried a lighted torch that had been lit at the sacred flame in the city temple.

By now the noise had risen to a crescendo as those nearest to her fought to touch the Rani and beg her blessing, and others took up the cry of *Hari-bol* or *Khaman Kher,* or shrieked with pain as the guards rained blows upon them, forcing them back. 'At least the shot will not be heard,' observed Sarji. 'There is that to be thankful for. How much longer do you mean to wait?'

Ash made no reply, and presently Sarji muttered in an undertone that now would have been the time to leave—if they had any sense left in their thick heads. He had not intended his words to carry, but the end of the sentence was startlingly audible; for the crowds outside had suddenly fallen silent, and all at once it was possible to hear the hard breathing of the gagged prisoners and the cooing of doves from somewhere overhead under the eaves of the dome.

The cortège had reached the pyre and the bier was placed on it. And now Shushila began to divest herself of her jewels, taking them off one by one and handing them to the child, who gave them in turn to the Diwan. She stripped them off quickly, almost gaily, as though they were no more than withered flowers or valueless trinkets of which she had tired and was impatient to be rid of, and the silence was so complete that all could hear the clink of them as the new Rana received them and the late Rana's Prime Minister stowed them away in an embroidered bag.

Even Ash in the curtained enclosure heard it, and wondered incuriously if the Diwan would ever relinquish them. Probably not; though they had come from Karidkote, and being part of Shushila's dowry should have been returned there. But he thought it unlikely that either Shu-shu's relatives or the new Rana would ever see them again once the Diwan had got his hands on them.

When all her ornaments had been removed except for a necklace of sacred *tulsi* seeds, Shushila held out her slender ringless hands to a priest, who poured Ganges water over them. The water sparkled in the low sunlight as she shook the bright drops from her fingers, and the assembled priests began to intone in chorus . . .

To the sound of that chanting, she began to walk round the pyre, circling it three times as once, on her wedding day and wearing this same dress, she had circled the sacred fire, tied by her veil to the shrunken thing that now lay waiting for her on a bridal bed of cedar-logs and spices.

The hymn ended and once again the only sound in the grove was the cooing of doves: that soft monotonous sound that together with the throb of a tom-tom and the creak of a well-wheel is the voice of India. The silent crowds stood motionless, and none stirred as the suttee mounted the pyre and seated herself in the lotus posture. She arranged the wide folds of her scarlet dress so as to show it to its best advantage, and then gently lifted the dead man's head onto her lap, settling it with infinite care, as though he were asleep and she did not wish to wake him.

'*Now*,' breathed Anjuli in a whisper that broke in a sob—'Do it now . . . *quickly*, before—before she starts to be afraid.'

'Don't be a fool!' The retort cracked like a whip in the quiet room.

'It would make as much noise as a cannon and bring them all down on us like hornets. Besides—'

He had meant to say 'I'm not going to fire', but he did not do so. There was no point in making things worse for Juli than they were already. But the way in which Shu-shu had cradled that awful head in her lap had made up his mind for him at last, and he had no intention of firing. Juli took too much upon herself: she forgot that her half-sister was no longer a sickly infant or a frail and highly strung little girl who must be protected and cosseted—or that she herself was no longer responsible for her. Shu-shu was a grown woman who knew what she was doing. She was also a wife and a queen—and proving that she could behave as one. This time, for good or ill, she should be allowed to make her own decision.

The crowd outside was still silent, but now a priest began to swing a heavy temple bell that had been carried out from the city, and its harsh notes reverberated through the grove and awoke echoes from the walls and domes of the many *chattris*. One of the Brahmins was sprinkling the dead man and his widow with water brought from the sacred river Ganges—'Mother Gunga'—while others poured more *ghee* and scented oil upon the logs of cedar and sandalwood and over the feet of the Rana.

But Shushila did not move. She sat composed and still, looking down at the grey, skull-like face on her lap. A graven image in scarlet and gold: remote, passionless and strangely unreal. The Diwan took the torch again and gave it into the trembling hands of the boy-Rana, who seemed about to burst into tears. It wavered dangerously in the child's grasp, being over heavy for such small hands to hold, and one of the Brahmins came to his assistance and helped to support it.

The brightness of that flame was a sharp reminder that evening was already drawing near. Only a short time ago it had been almost invisible in the glaring sunlight, but now the sun was no longer fierce enough to dim that plume of light. The shadows had begun to lengthen and the day that had once seemed as though it would never end would soon be over—and with it, Shushila's short life.

She had lost father and mother, and the brother who, for his own ends, had given her in marriage to a man who lived so far away that it had taken months and not weeks to reach her new home. She had been a wife and a queen, had miscarried two children and borne a third who had lived only a few days; and now she had been widowed, and must die . . . 'She is only sixteen—' thought Ash. 'It isn't fair. It isn't *fair!*'

He could hear Sarji's quickened breathing and the thump of his own heart-beats, and though Anjuli was not touching him he knew, without knowing how he knew, that she was shivering violently as though she was very cold or stricken with fever. He thought suddenly that provided he fired a shot she would not know if the bullet had done its work or not, and that he had only to aim over the heads of the crowd. If it comforted Juli to think that her sister had been spared the flames, then all he needed to do was pull the trigger—

But the trees on the far side of the clearing were full of men and boys who clung like monkeys to the boughs, while every *chattri* within range swarmed with spectators, and even a spent bullet or a ricochet could cause death. It would have to be the pyre itself; that was the only safe target. He lifted the revolver and steadied the barrel on the crook of his left arm, and said curtly and without turning his head: 'We leave as soon as I have fired. Are you ready to go?'

'We men are,' said Gobind very softly. 'And if the Rani-Sahiba—'

He hesitated, and Ash finished the sentence for him: '—will cover her face, it will save time. Besides, she has already seen more than enough of this and there is no need for her to stand staring any longer.'

He spoke with deliberate harshness in the hope that Juli would be forced to busy herself rewinding the free end of her turban across her face and so miss the last act of the tragedy. But she made no move to cover her face or turn away. She stayed as though rooted to the spot: wide-eyed, shivering and unable to stir hand or foot, and seemingly unaware that he had spoken.

All of forty paces, Sarji had said. It did not look as far as that, for now that there was no movement in the vast crowd the dust had settled; and with the sun-glare no longer dazzling his sight, the faces of the chief actors in the tragedy could be seen as clearly as though they were only twenty feet away instead of thirty-five to forty paces.

The little Rana was crying. Tears poured down the pallid, childish features that were crumpled with fear and bewilderment and sheer physical exhaustion, and if the Brahmin beside him had not held his small hands firmly about the torch, he would have dropped it. The Brahmin was evidently exhorting him in an undertone, while the Diwan looked scornful and the nobles exchanged glances that varied according to their temperaments—and the degree of their disappointment over the selection of the next ruler. And then Shushila looked up . . . and suddenly her face changed.

Perhaps it was the brightness of the torch, or the sound of it as the flames streamed up on the still air, that woke her from the dream-world in which she had been moving. Her head came up sharply and Ash could see her eyes widen until they looked enormous in her small, pale face. She stared about her, no longer calmly, but with the terrified gaze of a hunted animal, and he could tell the exact moment when reality broke through illusion and she realized, fully, what that flaming brand signalled . . .

The boy's hands, guided by the Brahmin's, lowered the torch until it touched the pyre near the feet of the dead man. Bright flowers of fire sprang up from the wood and blossomed in orange and green and violet, and the new Rana having performed his duty to the old one—his father by adoption—the priest took the brand from him and went quickly to the other end of the pyre and touched it to the logs at the suttee's back. A brilliant tongue of flame shot skyward, and si-multaneously the crowd found its voice and once again roared its homage and approval. But the goddess of their worship thrust aside the head on her lap, and now, suddenly, she was on her feet, staring at those flames and screaming—screaming . . .

The sound of those screams cut through the clamour as the shriek of violin strings cuts through the full tempest of drums and wind-in-struments and brass. It drew a gasping echo from Anjuli, and Ash lifted his aim and fired.

The screams stopped short and the slender scarlet and gold figure stretched out one hand gropingly as though searching for support, and then crumpled at the knees and pitched forward across the corpse at her feet. And as she fell the Brahmin flung the torch on the pyre, and flames gushed up from the oil-drenched wood and threw a shimmering veil of heat and smoke between the watchers and the recumbent figure of the girl who now wore a glittering wedding-dress of fire.

The crash of the shot had sounded appallingly loud in that small confined space, and Ash thrust the revolver into the breast of his robe and turning, said savagely: 'Well, what are you waiting for? Get on—go on Sarji—you first.' Anjuli still seemed dazed, and he pulled the cloth roughly across her nose and mouth and made sure that it was secure, and having adjusted his own, caught her by the shoulders and said: 'Listen to me, Juli—and stop looking like that. You've done all you can for Shushila. She's gone. She has escaped; and if we hope to, we must stop thinking of her and think of ourselves. We come first now. All of us. Do you understand?'

Anjuli nodded dumbly.

'Good. Then turn around and go with Gobind, and don't look back. I shall be behind you. *Walk—!*'

He turned her about and pushed her ahead of him towards the heavy purdah that Manilal was holding open for them, and she followed Sarji through it and down the marble stairway that led to the terrace and the crowds below.

43

He was riding headlong across a stony plain between low, barren hills, and there was a girl on the crupper behind him who clung to him and urged him to ride faster—faster. A girl whose long, unbound hair streamed out on the wind like a black silk flag, so that when he glanced back he could not see the riders who pursued them, but only hear the thunder of following hoofbeats that became louder and nearer . . .

Ash awoke, sweating with terror, to find that the sound of galloping horses was only the desperate beating of his own heart.

The nightmare was a familiar one. But the awakening was not, because this time he was not in his own bed, but lying on hard ground in a dark patch of shadow thrown by a boulder. Below him a belt of scree fell steeply away down a gully that was bright with moonlight, and on either hand the bare hillsides swept upwards to shoulder a sky like a sheet of tarnished steel.

For a moment or two he could not remember how he came to be there, or why. Then memory returned in a scalding flood and he sat up and stared into the shadows. Yes, she was still there; a pale huddled shape lying in a hollow that Bukta had scraped out for her between two boulders and lined with his horse-blanket. At least they had brought her this far in safety, and when Bukta returned—if he returned—

Ash's thoughts checked sickeningly, balking like a horse that suddenly recognizes the dangers of a fence and refuses to face it; for the position of the moon told him that it was long past midnight, and by rights Bukta should have arrived back at least two hours ago.

He stood up cautiously, moving with extreme care to avoid making any noise that might disturb Anjuli, and peered over the boulder; but nothing moved on the bare hillside, and the only sound that he could hear was made by the night wind whispering through the dry grass and between the tumbled rocks. He could not believe that he had slept so soundly that he would not have heard the noise of returning footsteps, yet even if he had, there would still be the horses . . .

But there were no horses on that empty expanse of hillside, and no sign of Bukta, or of anyone else; though far away, in the sky above the valley, a red pulsating glow told of camp fires, and by in-ference, the presence of a large force bivouacked there for the night and only waiting for dawn before taking up the trail.

Ash rested his arms on the boulder, and staring out across the grey folds of the moon-washed hills towards that distant brightness, coldly calculated his own and Juli's chances of survival in an almost waterless region where there were no recognizable paths or land-marks; or none that he himself could recognize, even though he had come that way barely a week ago. Yet if Bukta did not return he would have to find the path back through this trackless maze of ridges himself, and by way of the few places where there had been springs in the parched wilderness—and later on through the many miles of jungle-clad foothills that lay across the northern borders of Gujerat.

It had been no easy road before, but now . . . Once again the train of Ash's thought jarred to a halt and he dropped his head on his folded arms, shutting out the moonlight. But he could not shut out the memory of all that had happened, and now he saw it again, printed searingly behind his closed eyelids . . .

They had walked out of the screened enclosure, Sarji leading, and down the narrow stairway to the terrace where the crowd—spectators and sentries alike—craned to watch the suttee's last moments, and swept by emotion, prayed, shouted or wept as the flames shot up-wards and the pyre became a blazing, blinding pyramid of fire. No one present had spared a glance for the small party of four palace at-tendants led by a helmeted member of the Rana's bodyguard. They had left the *chattri* unhindered and unremarked, and within minutes had reached the shelter of the older and more ruined buildings.

Dagobaz had been standing with his ears pricked, listening; and despite the roar and crackle of the fire and the cries of the crowd he must have heard Ash's step and recognized it, for he whinnied in greeting before he saw him. There were four other horses tethered to a tree near by, one of which was Sarji's own Moti Raj and another the hack he had lent Manilal for the return journey to Bhithor. The third belonged to Gobind, as did the fourth, which he had acquired with one other some weeks earlier, in the hope that it might be possi-ble to rescue both the Ranis.

'I bought one for each of them,' explained Gobind in an aside to Ash as he adjusted the girths, 'but this is the better of the two, so I have left the other behind, which is no loss—we cannot cumber ourselves with spare horses. If the Rani-Sahiba will be pleased to mount—?'

They rode out of the grove and circled back across the dusty plain towards the entrance of the valley, where the walled city stood like a vast block of sandstone in the centre of the valley mouth. The sun had not yet sunk behind the hills, and because here their route lay west they rode directly towards it. Its glare dazzled the eyes of both riders and horses and the heat rose in waves from the stony ground and beat against them—and Ash had forgotten about that nameless merchant of Bhithor who had been a great traveller, and had brought back from foreign parts the secret of how men could speak to each other over great distances with the aid of small shields of polished silver.

Even if he had remembered it would not have helped much—except that he might have been warned. As it was, riding into the eye of the setting sun and half blinded by its glare, he did not see the brief flicker from a high roof-top in the city, or the one from the walls of the right-hand fort, that could be translated as 'Message understood'. And Sarji, who did see them, supposed them to be only sunlight flashing on a window-pane or the burnished barrel of a cannon.

Neither of them was ever to know how their escape came to be discovered so soon, though the explanation was very simple, and proved that Manilal's advice on the score of killing their prisoners had been sound. A gag, however efficient, does not prevent a man—or a woman—from making a certain amount of noise, and when six people combine to moan in chorus, the noise they produce is not inconsiderable. The captives were unable to move but they could moan, and they did so to such good purpose that before long one of the guards below, on his way up to the top storey of the *chattri* from where he hoped to obtain a better view, stopped to listen as he passed the curtained entrance, and supposing the sound to come from the Junior Rani, could not resist twitching it very slightly aside and putting his eye to the crack.

Within minutes all six were free and pouring out a wild tale of murder, assault and abduction. And shortly afterwards a score of soldiers set off in pursuit, guided by the long, betraying cloud of dust that Ash and his companions had raised as they rode away, and that showed like a white streak across the face of the plain. The chances of overtaking the runaways were slight, for they had too good a start and should have got clean away. But as luck would have it, one of the bodyguards had been provided with a signalling shield and charged with keeping in touch with the city and the forts in order to report the safe arrival of the funeral cortège. He now made use of it to flash a warning to both that said, in effect—*Enemy. Five. On horseback. Intercept.*

The signal was seen and acknowledged, and though the hilltop forts could do little, the city took immediate action. There were no more than a handful of troops within its confines that day, the majority having been called on to keep a clear pathway for the funeral procession or sent to control the crowds at the burning-ground. But the few who had remained on guard at the palace were hastily rounded up and dispatched at full gallop to the *Hathi Pol,* the Elephant Gate, with instructions to cut off a party of five horsemen who were presumed to be making for the border.

But for a zealous gunner in the right-hand fort, they would have done so, as by now the fugitives were riding through the gap between the hillside and the northern wall of the city, and were as yet barely level with the *Mori* Gate. Having not seen the signals, or realized that their escape had been discovered, they were not pressing their horses overmuch, for fields of grain and stubble, criss-crossed by irrigation channels, are hardly the safest places to take at a gallop. Besides, the valley with its hard, sun-baked ground lay ahead, and once there, with the city behind them, they would be able to go more quickly.

The sudden appearance of a party of yelling horsemen, who having left by the Elephant Gate were not only well ahead of them but riding at a tangent with the obvious intention of cutting them off before they could reach the valley, was a shattering blow; as was the simultaneous spatter of shots from somewhere away to the right. Yet even then, for a brief moment it seemed to all of them that they must be mistaken and that it was not possible that the shouting men could have any interest in them or the shots be aimed at them, for there had not been time . . . But the moment passed and suddenly they knew without a shadow of doubt—as the fox knows when he hears the hounds give tongue—that the hunt was up and that they were the quarry.

It was too late to turn back; and there was no point in doing so, since by now there would be other men on their heels striving to overtake them. There was nothing for it but to go forward, and reacting as one, they set spurs to their horses and made for the narrowing gap that the men from the city were racing to close.

Whether they would have reached it in time is doubtful. But it was at this point that Fate, in the form of a gunner in the fort, intervened on their behalf.

The garrison of the fort had seen the sun-signals, and had been manning the walls and excitedly watching the approach of the five fugitives and the progress of the pursuit. Their eyrie on the hilltop gave them an advantage that the five did not possess, because from here they could not only see the quarry, but the pursuers who galloped far behind them following their trail, as well as the handful of armed men who had suddenly debouched from the *Hathi Pol* and were now riding to head them off.

The latter had been visible to the garrison from the moment they left the city. But though the fort provided an excellent grandstand from which to view the drama, the antiquated matchlocks and jezails with which the garrisons opened fire on the fugitives were almost useless at that range, while the dust and the dancing, shimmering heat-haze did not make for good marksmanship. Their shots did not take effect, and looking down from the heights it seemed to them that the runaways were in danger of winning the race and breaking through into the valley.

The great bronze cannons had already been fired once that day, but as by tradition they would be fired again to welcome the new Rana back to his city, they were primed and ready. An eager gunner leapt to load one and busied himself lighting a taper while his crew, following his lead, helped to train the monster ahead of the galloping target. The port-fire was applied to the touch-hole and the flash and roar of the explosion was as impressive as ever. But in the excitement of the moment the speed of the riders below had been miscalculated, and the cannon ball missed the fugitives and landed full in the path of the on-coming soldiers from the city.

No one was seriously hurt, but the sudden and totally unexpected fountain of dust, dirt and debris that exploded a bare yard or two ahead, showering them with stones and clods of earth, panicked the already over-excited horses, who instantly reared and bolted. Several of the riders were thrown, and by the time the others had got their mounts under control the quarry had escaped through the gap and were riding like the wind down the long, straight stretch of the valley.

It had been an incredible ride. Terrifying, nerve-racking and at the same time so wildly exhilarating that, if it had not been for Juli, Ash would actually have enjoyed it. Sarji had certainly done so: he had laughed and sung and urged Moti Raj to greater efforts with cries of encouragement and extravagant endearments. Dagobaz too had been in his element, and had he been given his head he would have outdistanced his companions and left them far behind in the first half-mile. But there was Juli to be thought of, and Ash's hands were firm on the reins and he held back, glancing over his shoulder every few seconds to see that she was safe.

The wind had whipped the folds of muslin away from her face and Ash saw that it was set and intent: a pale mask in which only the eyes were alive. She was handling her horse in a manner that would have done credit to her Cossack grandfather, and Ash felt a sudden rush of gratitude towards that old free-booter—and to her father, the old Rajah, who in the face of Janoo-Rani's opposition had insisted that his daughter Kairi-Bai should be taught to ride: 'God bless him, wherever he has gone,' thought Ash fervently.

Gobind too was a good horseman. But Manilal was no more than an adequate one, and the pace was clearly beginning to tell on him; yet he hung on grimly and had the sense to leave everything else to his horse. As for the pursuit, from what little they could see of it through the dust that fumed up in their own wake, it was still in a state of disarray and too far behind to pose a serious threat.

They had avoided the beaten track with its potholes and cart ruts, and kept well to one side of it—the left side, since it was on this side that the entrance to Bukta's road lay—and they had covered more than two thirds of the distance when Anjuli's horse put its foot in a rat hole and came down heavily, pitching her over its head to land spread-eagled in the dust.

The fall had knocked the breath out of her body and she lay still, fighting for air, while her horse struggled to its feet and stood with drooping head and labouring sides. Manilal, who had been following behind, tugged wildly on his near rein to avoid riding over her, and missing her by inches, was carried helplessly onwards, completely out of control and reduced to clinging to the arch of his saddle. But the other three pulled up and circled back.

Ash flung himself off Dagobaz and snatched Juli into his arms; and for a dreadful, heart-stopping moment he thought that she was dead, because she did not move. But one look was enough to reassure him, and he whirled round, holding her, and saw that the hunters were still on their trail, and getting dangerously near.

Gobind too was looking back. He had not dismounted, but was holding Dagobaz's reins as well as Moti Raj's, while Sarji examined the injured horse, and he did not speak—there was no need to for they were all aware of the danger. Sarji said breathlessly: 'The off-fore is badly strained. Dagobaz will have to carry two. Give me the Rani and get back in the saddle. Be quick.'

Ash obeyed, and though Juli was still dazed by her fall she was getting her breath back and she had not lost her wits. When Sarji tossed her up onto the crupper she put her arms about Ash's waist and held on, and they were away again, racing after Manilal who was by now far ahead of them; Gobind and Sarji a length behind to left and right, riding wide of them to avoid being choked by their dust.

The additional weight made no difference at all to Dagobaz, who swept on with the effortless speed of a hawk. But the delay had been fatal, for it had not only reduced their lead to a mere matter of a few hundred yards, but had served to break the headlong impetus of the other two horses, so that now Gobind must use both whip and spur while Sarji rode crouched like a jockey, far forward on Moti Raj's straining neck, and singing no more.

Ash heard the crack of a shot and saw the dust spurt as a musket-ball ploughed into the ground ahead and well to one side, and realized that one of the pursuers had fired at them, and that he should have foreseen this when he took Juli up behind him. He ought to have put her in front, so that his body would have protected her from any aspiring marksmen, but it was too late to do anything about it now; they could not stop, and in any case, the risk of a shot taking effect was minimal, for a muzzle-loading jezail is an unhandy weapon when fired from the back of a galloping horse—and impossible to reload under those conditions.

There was unlikely to be another shot, but that one, though well off target, showed that the pursuit must be gaining on them; and also reminded him that he carried a revolver. Knowing that Dagobaz would answer to the least pressure of his leg, he fumbled in the breast of his robes and guiding Dagobaz by knee, swerved to avoid the dust-cloud behind him, and telling Anjuli to hold close, turned in the saddle and fired at a man on a rangy, country-bred grey who was leading the field by several lengths.

There was no luck about the shot: Koda Dad Khan had been too good a teacher for that, and Ash did not watch to see if it took effect. He looked to his front again, hearing the fall and the hoarse yells of rage from behind, and Sarji's exultant shout as the riderless grey careered past them.

Ahead of them loomed the triple-fanged ridge with the wide, arrow-shaped fall of shale immediately below it: a pale landmark that pin-pointed the position of a tall grass-plumed, white-streaked rock near which—please God!—Bukta the *shikari* would still be waiting for them. Bukta with a spare shot-gun and two boxes of cartridges, and another fifty rounds of rifle ammunition.

If only they could increase their lead and reach the passage through the rockfall with even a minute to spare, they would be able to hold off any number of pursuers, and inflict such damage in the process that by the time darkness fell the survivors would be unlikely to follow them into the hills. But the shouts and the thunder of pursuing hooves were becoming nearer and louder . . . and of a sudden, uncannily familiar, until with a violent sensation of shock and incredulity Ash realized that this was the dream . . .

It had all happened before. Many times. Only this time he was not dreaming. This time he was awake and it was real—the flat, stony plain, the low hills, the sound of pursuing hoof-beats on hard ground and the girl on the crupper who had once been Belinda—except that even then her hair had been black.

The nightmare had come true at last, and as if to prove it, Juli began urging him to go faster—faster. But when he turned, revolver in hand, he found that he could not fire, because she had lost her turban when she fell, and now her loosened hair streamed out behind her like a black silk flag on the wind and made it impossible for him to see the men who galloped behind him.

This was far worse than any of the dreams had been, because he knew that he would not awake from it to find himself sweating with fear, but safe. And he had no idea how it would end. He could only urge Dagobaz to greater speed and pray that they would reach the haven among the rocks in time.

The sun vanished with the abruptness of a snuffed candle as they rode into the shadow of the high ridges; and now they were nearing their goal. Half a mile to go . . . a quarter . . . four hundred yards . . . The white streaks of bird-droppings showed clearly against the purple hillside, and there was someone standing near the grass-crowned rock: a man with a rifle. Bukta, his dun-coloured *shikari*'s clothing almost invisible among the shadows. So he had not gone. He had waited for them; and now he was here and sighting along the barrel of his beloved Lee-Enfield.

Ash had seen Bukta hit a tree-rat at fifty paces and bring down a galloping leopard at twice that range in thick grass; and with the light in his favour and the pursuing soldiery ignorant of his presence, he should be able to pick off at least one of them before they realized their danger, and thereby sow enough confusion among the rest to enable their quarry to reach cover.

There was barely two hundred yards to go now, and Ash found himself laughing exultantly as he waited for the flash: but it did not come—and suddenly he realized that it would not, because he and Sarji and Gobind were in the line of fire, and together they masked the enemy so effectively that the old *shikari* did not dare risk a shot.

They had all forgotten Manilal. The fat man had been carried past the rocks where Bukta waited, but his horse was tiring and he managed to turn it in a wide arc that brought him round facing the way they had come, though from much further out in the valley. Galloping back from this direction, Manilal was able to see what was happening and to size up the situation a good deal more clearly than any of the other actors in the drama.

The passage through the rockfall had been described to him and, always a quick thinker, he realized that his companions would never reach it with enough time in hand, and that the *shikari* could not help them, for he must hold his fire until they were past him—by which time it would be too late. Manilal did not wear spurs, but he still had a whip that he had prudently carried on a loop round his wrist, and now he used it mercilessly, keeping his horse at full gallop and making not for the rocks, but for the bunched and yelling pack from the city.

Ash saw him sweep past and heard the crash and the confusion as he drove full tilt into the pursuers. But there was no time to turn round and see what had happened. There was only time to pull up and leap to the ground, to catch Anjuli as she tumbled off, and grasping her wrist, to pull Dagobaz after them while Sarji and Gobind flung themselves from their horses and followed, and Bukta fired and re-loaded and fired again . . .

The shadowed canyon behind the wall of rock and scree seemed a very peaceful spot after the heat and dust and frenzy of that wild ride. Bukta had been camping there for the past week, and his few belongings, together with the shot-gun and cartridges and the two boxes of ammunition, were neatly laid out on a ledge, and conveniently within reach. His pony, its forefeet hobbled, country-fashion, with a loop of cloth to prevent it straying, was placidly grazing on the dying grass, and the place looked curiously homelike. A haven of peace and safety enclosed by the cliffs of the steeply sloping hillsides, and only to be reached by a passage that was so narrow that a single man armed with a stout sword, let alone a revolver, could have held it against an army . . .

Or so Ash had once thought. But faced now with the reality, he was less sanguine, for there was a limit to the time they could hold out. A limit set by their supply of ammunition and water. There might be enough of the first, but the latter would not last over-long in this dry, torrid heat—especially when there were horses to be considered. Bukta had presumably watered his pony and drunk his fill at the stream in the valley, but that source was now closed to them, and the nearest supply—the little pool among the rocks with its solitary palm-tree—was over an hour's journey away. Other than that they had only the contents of their water-bottles, which might tide them over for a time, but do little for their horses. And it was now several hours since Dagobaz had last drunk; and longer still since he himself had done so.

Ash was suddenly conscious again of his own thirst, which until now had been no more than a minor discomfort when compared with the mental emotions of that eventful day. But he knew that he did not dare slake it for fear that he would not be able to stop himself from draining every drop from the bottle; and they might all be in worse need of its contents soon, and he must endure a little longer. By nightfall there would be dew and then it would not be so bad, but two things were clear: they could not afford to stay here, for without water the quiet canyon could soon cease to be a place of refuge and become a trap; and the sooner they left the better, because once darkness fell even Bukta would find it next to impossible to follow that barely visible track that led back through the hills, dipping and climbing and crossing seemingly impossible slopes and precipitous rock-strewn ridges.

Yet as soon as they left there would be nothing to prevent their pursuers from pouring through the gap and taking up the trail again.

Unless someone stayed behind and held them off until the others . . .

Ash looked quickly at the narrow cleft through which they had just come, and then back at Anjuli, who had dropped to the ground when he released her, and was sitting with closed eyes, her head thrown back against the wall of the canyon. Her dishevelled hair was grey with dust and he saw that there was a snow-white streak in it, like a wide bar of silver laid across the darkness. Her face was so drawn with exhaustion that a stranger would have been forgiven for thinking her an old woman, and it did not seem possible that she was not yet twenty-one.

Ash wished that he could have let her rest there a little longer. She looked as though she needed it—as they all did, horses as well as riders—and though the air in the canyon was stiflingly hot with the accumulated heat of the blazing day, at least the shadows lent it an illusion of coolness, and the tired horses had already begun to nibble at the sun-dried grass. But there was no help for it: they would have to press on, for despite the steep hillsides on either hand and the great wall of rock and scree that lay between them and the valley, they could still hear the muffled crack of Bukta's rifle and the answering spatter of shots that told them that their pursuers had halted and were returning his fire.

Ash's own carbine was still strapped to Sarji's saddle, and he took it down and re-loaded it, and reaching for the boxes of ammunition, stowed them in one of the saddle-bags and said curtly: 'Sarji, you and Gobind must go on ahead with the Rani while I take over from Bukta and hold this rabble off. He will have to go with you because he's the only one who knows the way; and—' He stopped and looked round: 'Where is Manilal? What happened to him?'

But neither Sarji nor Gobind could tell him. There had been no time to look back, or to do anything but urge on the flagging horses; and once they were among the rocks they could no longer see what was happening in the valley. 'But Bukta will have seen that he came to no harm,' said Sarji confidently. 'He never misses, and there will soon be many dead men out there. Hark to him!—he is firing as fast as he can load. If we three go back and help him we should be able to kill them all.'

Ash said sharply: 'No, Sarji. You must leave this to me. We came here to save the Rani, and her safety comes first. We cannot afford to take risks with her life, and though there may be only a handful of

men out there now, there will soon be more coming up behind them
from the burning-ground. Besides, once it is dark none of us will be
able to move, so just do as I say and don't argue—we haven't time.
Gobind, see that the Rani-Sahiba is ready to leave as soon as Bukta
and Manilal get here. She'll have to ride behind one of you, so if
there is any doubt about the other horses being able to take a double
load, Sarji must ride Dagobaz and leave one of the others for me.
Throw me over that shot-gun; I may as well take that too: and the
cartridges— Thanks, Sarji. I'll be back as soon as it's safe to go on.
Don't stop unless you have to. You won't be safe until you're well
beyond the border.'

He shouldered the two guns, picked up the laden saddle-bag,
and without looking at Anjuli went quickly away.

The narrow cut that wound between the rocks was very quiet and
deeply shadowed, for the light was already draining from the thin
sliver of sky that showed high overhead, and it occurred to Ash that
long before the sun was down it would be dark in there: too dark to
see, which might be to his advantage, as anyone unfamiliar with the
passage would probably be held up by the first sharp turn, imagining
that it was a dead-end, whereas he would be able to grope his way
back without much difficulty . . . that was, if he came back.

'No. Not if, when,' thought Ash soberly, for he had remembered
something: a voice from the past saying, *'The Sahib-log do not understand that Truth should be used sparingly, and they call us liars
because when we of this country are asked questions by strangers,
we prefer to lie first and then consider whether the truth would have
served us better.'* And another more recent one that said, 'It don't do
to believe more than a fraction of what these people tell you, for
most of 'em will always tell a lie rather than speak the truth, and trying to find out what really happened is like drawing eye-teeth or
hunting for that proverbial needle in a haystack.'

He would have to come back. There was no 'if' about it, for were
the others to return to Gujerat without him there was no knowing
what trouble they might find themselves involved in, because their
story could so easily be disbelieved (or at best dismissed as the exaggerated out-pourings of a hysterical widow, her uncle's hakim and
his servant, and a local breeder of horses, none of whom could speak
a word of English). Officialdom, as he had good reason to know, was
never very easy to convince; and if there was one thing he could be
certain of it was that everyone in Bhithor, from the Diwan to the

lowliest palace servant, could be counted upon to lie like a trooper in order to conceal the truth. It was even possible that his friends might end up being suspected of murdering him for the sake of his shot-gun and rifle, should he fail to return.

For a moment Ash was almost tempted to go back. But he did not do so. Sarji had many friends in Gujerat and his family was not without influence in the province, while Juli was a princess in her own right, and both she and Gobind would have the support of her brother Jhoti, who was Maharajah of Karidkote. It was the height of absurdity to imagine that they would not be able to manage without him.

He found Bukta strategically ensconced between two large boulders, with his front protected by a flat-topped rock on which he had rested the barrel of his rifle. There were gaps in his cartridge belt and spent cases on the ground about him; and out in the valley a number of frightened horses galloped to and fro with empty saddles and trailing reins, their late riders lying still among the stones and dust, in proof of Sarji's statement that Bukta did not miss. But though the opposition had been drastically reduced it had not been eliminated, and those who survived had taken cover and were returning Bukta's fire.

Their antique weapons could not compare in the matter of range and accuracy with the Lee-Enfield, but they had the advantage of numbers. They could fire four or five shots to every one of Bukta's, and the fusillade that spattered around him filled the air with flying chips of rock, spurts of dust and showers of small stones, and made it too dangerous for him to venture into the open. He could retreat in safety, but that was all; and though the enemy were in no better case, they had time on their side, and reinforcements on the way.

Bukta glanced briefly at Ash and said: 'Go back, Sahib. You can do no good here. You and the others must go quickly into the hills. It is your only chance. We cannot hope to stand against an army, and there are many coming—look there.'

But Ash had already seen. It was indeed an army that was spurring towards them down the valley. The low sunlight glinted on lances, tulwars and jezails, and judging by the size of the dust-cloud that whirled up behind the advancing horde, half the forces of the state had been sent to recapture the widowed Rani and her rescuers. They were still a long way off, but they would be here all too soon.

A bullet smacked into the rock within inches of Ash's head and he ducked to avoid the shower of splinters and said curtly: 'We cannot go without a guide. You know that, Bukta. I will stay here in your place while you get the others away. Now go quickly.'

Bukta did not waste time arguing. He wriggled out backwards, and standing up in the lee of a boulder, slapped the dust from his clothes, and said briefly: 'Do not let anyone get too close, Sahib. Keep them at a distance and fire as often as you can so that they will be unable to tell how many of us are here among the rocks. When it is dark, come away, and if I can I will come back and meet you.'

'You will have to bring one of the horses, for if Manilal is hurt—'

'He is dead,' said Bukta shortly, '—and but for him, all of you would be too, for those dogs were so close on your heels that you could not have dismounted without being overtaken; and I could not fire. But the Hakim's servant rode into them and brought down the leading riders, and fell himself, and as he lay on the ground one coming up behind him smote his head from his body. May he be reborn a prince and a warrior. I will come back for you after moonrise. If not . . .' He shrugged and went away, and Ash lay down behind the flat-topped rock and surveyed the battle-ground, rifle and shot-gun at the ready.

The reinforcements, though much closer now, were still out of range. But one of the original posse, finding that a full two minutes had gone by without a shot being fired by the marksman among the rocks, took this to mean that he must either be dead or had run out of ammunition, and sustained by this belief was incautious enough to show himself. Ash's carbine cracked and the man jerked upright as though pulled by an unseen wire and fell back dead. After that his remaining comrades were careful to keep their heads well down while continuing to fire wildly in the general direction of the rockfall, which allowed Ash to give his full attention to the oncoming horsemen.

The cavalry carbine was accurate up to three hundred yards, though beyond that its effects were more a matter of luck than skill. But remembering Bukta's advice, Ash began to fire into the brown at extreme range, and with deadly effect, for a target provided by upwards of fifty men riding ten to fifteen abreast, and bunched together in a solid phalanx, is one that is almost impossible to miss.

Even at that distance the first shot told, and though it was difficult to see if it was man or a horse that had been hit, the formation disintegrated as if by magic, and a dust-cloud spread out to cover the mêlée as some riders reined in hard and those behind crashed into them, while others swerved out of harm's way and milled around in the smother.

Ash added to the confusion by continuing to fire, and he was reloading for the sixth time when a hand touched his shoulder and he spun round, his heart in his mouth. 'Sarji! Oh God, you frightened me. What the hell do you think you're doing? Didn't I tell you—' He stopped in mid-sentence for behind Sarji stood Gobind.

Another fusillade of shots whined overhead but he did not heed them: 'What is it? What has happened?'

'Nothing,' said Sarji, reaching out to take the carbine from him. 'It is only that we have decided that you must be the one to go on ahead with the Rani-Sahiba, for if there should . . . if things go wrong, you, being a Sahib, can speak better for her and for us all to your countrymen, and obtain justice from the Government. It is three to one, Ashok, for Bukta too agrees that it is wiser so. He will go with you and see that you travel in safety. Now leave us and go; they are waiting for you and will not start until you come.'

'But Gobind cannot use a rifle,' began Ash. 'He—'

'I can load them,' said Gobind, 'and with two rifles your friend will be able to fire quicker than you could do, so that perhaps those out there will come to believe that there are more of us than they thought, and be less bold in consequence. Do not waste time, Sahib, but go swiftly and get the Rani-Sahiba to safety. You need not fear for us, as it will be dark soon, and until then we can hold this place against all Bhithor. Take this with you'—he thrust a small packet into Ash's hand—'and now go.'

Ash looked from one face to the other, and what he saw there made him realize the futility of argument. Besides, they were right, because it was what he had thought himself. He could probably do more for Juli than they could. He said: 'Be careful.'

'We will,' said Sarji. Their hands met in a hard grip and they smiled at each other, the same fleeting tight-lipped smile. Gobind nodded in dismissal and Ash turned obediently and left them.

There was another burst of musketry from the invisible enemy and he heard the rifle crash in reply, and broke into a run . . .

The narrow slit between the rocks had been easier to negotiate now that he was no longer burdened by firearms and ammunition, and at the far side of it Bukta and Anjuli stood waiting for him. He had only to mount Dagobaz and pull Juli up behind him and canter away down the shadowed canyon in the wake of Bukta's little cat-footed pony.

The sound of firing faded and presently all they could hear was the beat of their horses' hooves, the creak and jingle of saddles and bridles, and the croon of the evening breeze blowing through the dry grasses on the hillside. And it was only as they began to climb that he remembered the packet that Gobind had given him, and taking it out, saw that it was the letters he had written last night. All of them. And realized the significance of that. But by then it was too late to turn back, even if he could have done so.

They climbed steadily until the valley lay well below them and hidden from sight by a sea of grassy spurs and high ridges, where the air was no longer tainted by dust and the wind blew cooler. But Bukta showed no sign of halting and pressed on swiftly, leading them forward and upward along paths that to Ash's eyes appeared almost invisible, and across long slopes of shale where they must dismount and lead the horses, whose hooves slipped and slithered among the loose stones.

The sun set in a blaze of gold and amber, and suddenly the sky was green and the corn-coloured hills were blue and indigo and violet—and there below them, cupped in its rocky hollow and half hidden by its solitary palm tree, the lonely pool glinted in the last of the light.

Bukta had led them unerringly to the sole small spot in all those barren hills where they could slake their thirst and gain the energy to press on. But for one of them it was to prove the end of the road . . .

Dagobaz could not have seen the water, for Ash had been leading him. But he must have smelt it, and he too was parched with thirst—and very tired. Bukta's pony, who was familiar with rough country and had not lacked rest or water that day, went down the steep and stony slope as lightly as a cat. But Dagobaz, made incautious by thirst, had been less sure-footed. He had plunged forward eagerly, taking his tired owner unawares, and before Ash could do anything to check him he was sliding helplessly downwards, struggling to keep his footing in a welter of dry earth and loose stones, dragging Ash with him and falling at last among the rocks at the water's edge.

Anjuli had managed to jump to safety and Ash had suffered no more than a few minor cuts and bruises. But Dagobaz could not get on his feet; his right fore-leg had snapped and there was nothing that anyone could do for him.

Had this happened in the plains it might have been possible to have him conveyed to Sarji's farm, where he could have been treated by an experienced veterinary surgeon; and though he would always have been lame and could never have been ridden again, he could at least have spent the rest of his life in honourable retirement among the shade trees in the pastures. But here there was no hope for him.

At first Ash had refused to believe it. And when he did, it was as though everything that had happened that day—the long hours of waiting on the terrace of the *chattri,* the killing of Shushila, the headlong flight down the valley and the death of Manilal—had been building up to this moment, bit by bit, until the accumulated weight had become intolerable. Now it crashed down upon him, beating him to his knees beside the fallen horse, and he took the dusty, sweatstreaked head into his arms and hiding his face against it, wept as he had only done once before in all his life—on the morning that Sita had died.

There is no knowing how long he would have remained there, for he had lost all consciousness of time. But at last a hand gripped his shoulder and Bukta's voice said sternly: 'Enough, Sahib! It grows dark, and we must leave this place while we can still see to do so, for it is overlooked on every side, and should we be caught here we should be trapped without hope of escape. We cannot stop until we reach higher ground, where we shall be safer.'

Ash rose unsteadily, and stood for a moment or two with closed eyes, striving for control. Then he stooped to remove bit and headband and loosen the girth so that Dagobaz might be more comfortable. Untying the water-bottle from its fastening, he emptied the luke-warm contents on the ground and taking it to the pool, refilled it with cool water.

He had forgotten his own needs, but he knew that Dagobaz had been lured to disaster by thirst, and that at least should be assuaged. The black horse was dazed and in pain, and very weary, but he took the water gratefully, and when the flask was empty, Ash handed it over his shoulder to be refilled without looking round or realizing that it was not Bukta but Anjuli who stood beside him and filled it again and again.

Bukta was keeping an anxious eye on the fast-fading light, and when he saw that Dagobaz would take no more, he came forward and said: 'Leave this to me, Sahib. He will feel nothing, I promise you. Put the Rani-Sahiba on my pony and go on a little way.'

Ash turned his head and said harshly: 'There is no need. If I can shoot a young woman I knew well, I can surely do the same for my horse.'

He took out the revolver, but Bukta stretched out a hand for it and said gravely: 'No, Sahib. It is better that I should do this.'

Ash stared back at him for a long moment, and then he sighed deeply and said: 'Yes, you are right. But you will have to do it while I am here, for if I go away he will try to get up and follow me.'

Bukta nodded, and Ash relinquished the revolver and knelt to gentle Dagobaz's weary head and whisper loving words in his ear. Dagobaz nuzzled him and whickered softly in reply, and when the shot came he jerked once. And that was all.

'Come,' said Bukta shortly. 'It is time we left. Do we take the saddle and bridle?'

'No. Leave them.' Ash got to his feet as slowly and stiffly as though he had been an old, old man, and reeling to the pool, sank down by the edge to plunge his face into the water and gulp it down in great mouthfuls like a parched animal, drenching his head and neck and washing away the dust and the tears and the dear, familiar smell of Dagobaz. His thirst quenched he arose, dripping, and shook the water out of his hair and eyes. Anjuli was already seated on the pony, and Bukta turned without a word and set off up the steep hillside in the gathering dusk.

Ash's foot touched something and he looked down and saw the empty water-bottle—and would have left it, because after this he would never be able to drink from it again without remembering all the fleetness and beauty and strength that had once been Dagobaz. But there would be no more water until they reached the spring among the trees, and that was many miles distant. Juli would be thirsty before then. He picked up the bottle and refilled it, and slinging it over his shoulder, followed after the others without looking back to where Dagobaz slept his last sleep among the shadows.

By the time they reached the ridge the stars were out, but Bukta hurried them on and only stopped at last when Anjuli fell asleep in the saddle and would have toppled out of it if they had not happened to be on a level stretch of ground. Even then he had insisted that they camp for the night among a number of large boulders that formed a rough circle in the centre of a wide fall of shale, though it had not been a particularly comfortable spot or one that was easy to reach.

'But you will be able to sleep in safety here,' said Bukta, 'and with no need to keep watch, for not even a snake could approach without setting these stones aslide and rousing you with the clatter.'

He had coaxed the pony across the treacherous, shifting surface, and having tethered it on a grassy slope on the far side of the shale, returned to clear away the larger stones and loose debris from between the boulders to make a sleeping place for Anjuli. That being done, he had produced food for them all: chuppattis that he had cooked himself that morning, and *pekoras* and cold rice and *huldoo* that Sarji had purchased in the city and hurriedly transferred to Bukta's saddle-bags when it was decided that he and Gobind would stay behind to act as rearguard.

Neither Ash nor Anjuli had eaten anything that day, but both were bone-weary and too exhausted by mental and physical stress to have any desire for food. But Bukta had forced them to eat, saying angrily that they would need all their strength if they hoped to make good progress on the morrow, and that to starve themselves would be the height of folly as it would only weaken them and thereby assist their enemies: 'Also you will sleep all the better for a little food, and awake refreshed.'

So they had eaten what they could, and afterwards Anjuli had curled up on the saddle-blanket that Bukta had spread for her, and fallen asleep almost immediately. The old *shikari* had grunted approval, and having urged the Sahib to follow her example, had turned to go away. 'Do you go back for them now?' asked Ash in an undertone.

'What else? It was arranged between us that they would await me near the top of the nullah, and that I would set out as soon as I had placed the Rani-Sahiba and yourself in this spot, which is as safe a one as any in these hills.'

'You are going on foot?' asked Ash, remembering that the pony was tethered on the far side of the shale.

Bukta nodded. 'I shall go quicker on foot. If I rode I would have to wait until the moon was up, as it is still too dark for riding. But the moon will not rise for another hour, by which time I hope to be within eye-shot of the nullah. Moreover a man cannot lead two horses in these hills, and it may be that either the Sirdar-Sahib or the Hakim has suffered a wound or is overwearied, and if so I can lead while they remain in the saddle. All being well, we should be back before midnight, and on our way again by first light. So sleep while you can, Sahib.'

He shouldered his rifle and went away, walking gingerly across the shale that clattered and slid under his hard, bare feet. The stone-noises stopped when he reached the grass, and a moment later the grey starlight had swallowed him up and the night was quiet again, and nothing moved in it but the wind and the pony cropping the sun-dried grass of the hillside.

Ash had never felt less like sleeping, but he knew that Bukta was right and that it was only sensible to get what rest he could, so he lay down among the great boulders and closing his eyes tried to relax his tense muscles, and to make his mind a blank because there was so much that he could not bear to think of: Shushila and Manilal. And now Dagobaz— But he must have been wearier than he knew, for sleep overtook him before he was aware of it; and when the familiar nightmare came on him and he awoke sweating with terror, the moon was high up in the sky and the hills were awash with silver.

Juli was still asleep, and after a time Ash abandoned his fruitless survey of the empty hillside, and turning to look at her, experienced none of the emotions that he would have expected the sight and the nearness to her to arouse in him.

She was here beside him, freed at last from her bondage to a hateful husband and an adored sister, and he should by rights have been light-headed with joy and triumph. Instead it was as though all feeling and emotion had drained out of him, and he could only look at her dispassionately and think 'poor Juli'—and feel sorry for her because she must have suffered so much. But then he was sorry for himself too. For having had to kill little Shu-shu, and for his part in bringing about the deaths of Manilal and Dagobaz, whose mortal remains would soon be mangled and made hideous by jackals and vultures and other eaters of carrion.

If only he could have buried them—! Or burned them, as Shushila had burned, so that their bodies like hers could have become clean ash instead of tattered flesh and reddened bones . . .

Absurdly, it was this thought that hurt most. It seemed in some way a final betrayal that the headless body of fat, faithful, heroic Manilal should be left lying out in the valley, a prey to the corruption and the kites; and that all the strength and grace that had been

Dagobaz should be torn in pieces by jackals and carrion crows. Not that Dagobaz would care. But Manilal . . .

If Fate had permitted Manilal to return to his home in Karidkote and to live out his life there in peace, he too, when he died, would have been taken to the burning-grounds. And afterwards his ashes would have been cast into a mountain stream that would carry them down to the Chenab River, and from there to the Indus—and so at last to the sea. It was not right that his corpse should be left to rot in the open like that of an ownerless dog.

As for Dagobaz— But he would not think of Dagobaz. There was no point in looking back. What was written, was written. The thing to do was to look forward and make plans for the future. Tomorrow . . . tomorrow they would reach that small green oasis among the barren hills and camp there for the night. And the next day they would be among the jungle-clad foothills, and after that it would not be too long before they reached a made road; though the return journey would be slower, for they could not all ride now that Dagobaz . . .

What *was* Bukta doing? The moon had not yet risen when he left, but now it was sinking again, and the breeze that blows steadily between sunset and the small hours was already dwindling down towards the lull that lies between night and morning and ends only with the rising of the dawn wind. He should have been back hours ago. Unless . . . A cold, unpleasant thought slid into Ash's mind and made his skin crawl.

Supposing Bukta had met with an accident on his way to the canyon . . . ? Supposing he had missed his footing in the dark and slipped and fallen—as Dagobaz had done? He might even now be lying stunned and helpless at the foot of some precipitous slope, or creeping painfully on hands and knees up a stony ridge with his ankle broken. Almost anything could have happened to him in these treacherous hills, and as the others would not dare to start without him, they would still be somewhere in the canyon, waiting for him. But how long would they wait?

That faint pulsating glow in the sky above the valley showed that their enemies were still camped there in force, so they would have to leave before the dawn broke, because as soon as it was light enough someone was going to discover that the entrance into the canyon was no longer guarded, and within minutes a hundred men would be on their trail again. If Bukta had met with an accident . . .

'I ought to go and look for him,' thought Ash. 'If he is hurt, I can always come back for the pony and put him up on it. And after all, I've been over that ground twice now, so there is no reason why I should lose my way.'

But he turned to look at Anjuli again, and knew that he must not go. He could not leave her here alone, for if anything happened to him—if he missed his footing on a steep path or lost his way among the hills, and if Bukta were never to come back—what would become of her? How long would she be able to keep alive if she was left to fend for herself among this maze of parched and desolate hills?

She did not even know in which direction Gujerat lay, and could easily wander back into the valley, where she would be captured and almost certainly killed. He could not take the risk of leaving her. He would have to stay and possess his soul in patience, and pray that Bukta and the others would appear before morning.

The hours that followed had seemed interminable. The shadows lengthened as the moon moved down the sky, and when the breeze died the night became so still that he could hear the sound of Juli's soft breathing and from somewhere very far away the faint, faint howl of a jackal pack; but though he strained his ears to catch the click of hooves on hard ground or the murmur of men's voices, he heard no other sounds. The silence had remained unbroken until at last the dawn wind began to blow, softly at first, and then gathering strength as it swept across the hills, flattening the grass and displacing small stones that went clattering down the gully.

It drove the night before it as a housewife drives dust with her broom, and as the moon paled and the stars vanished, the dawn broke in a flood of yellow light along the eastern horizon—and Ash saw a small dark figure appear on the crest of the ridge, to be briefly silhouetted against that saffron sky before it moved downwards, slowly and tiredly towards the gully.

He ran out to meet it, stumbling across the shale and calling out, light-headed with relief and careless of how much noise he made; and it was only when he was half-way up the grassy slope that he stopped, and a cold hand seemed to close about his heart. For he realized that there was still only one figure. Bukta was alone; and as he came nearer Ash saw that his clothes were no longer dust-coloured but hideously dappled with great dark stains.

'They were both dead'—Bukta's voice was flat with exhaustion and he dropped down wearily and without apology, hunkering on the grass like a tired old crow. But the dried blood on his coat was not his own, for he had, he said, arrived only after it was all over.

'It was clear that some of those sons of dogs had climbed up into the hills, and coming down from behind had taken them by surprise. There had been a fight in the nullah and their horses too were dead— and I think very many of their enemies must also have died, for the ground between the rocks and in the nullah was red with blood, and there were many spent cartridges—so many that I doubt if they left so much as one unfired. But by the time I came, the Bhithori dogs had taken away their own dead and wounded. It must have taken many men to carry them back to the city, as only four men had been left behind to keep watch by the entrance to the nullah . . .'

A flicker of a smile showed briefly on Bukta's brown, nut-cracker face, and he said grimly: 'Those four I slew with my knife. One after the other, and without noise; for the fools slept, thinking themselves secure—and why not? They had slain three of us five and must have thought that the other two, one of whom was a woman, would be flying for their lives and far away among the hills. I knew that I should have come away then. But how could I leave the bodies of my master the Sirdar-Sahib, and the Hakim and his servant, lying there unburned at the mercy of wild beasts? That I could not do, and therefore I carried them out one by one to a disused shed that stands near the bank of the stream, making four journeys, for I could not carry Manilal's head and body at one time . . .

'When at last I had brought them all, I pulled down the old, dry thatch and made a great pile of it, and placing the bodies upon it, each a little apart, strewed them with powder from my cartridges, and then cut down the roof-poles and supports so that these fell in-wards. When all was done I fetched water from the stream and said the proper prayers, and taking flint and tinder, set fire to it and came away, leaving it burning . . .'

His voice died on a sigh, and Ash thought numbly, 'Yes. I saw it. I thought it was camp fires. I didn't know—' It appalled him to think that he had actually seen that pulsating glow and had not known that it was Sarji burning . . . Sarji and Gobind and Manilal . . .

Bukta said tiredly: 'It burned very fiercely, the wood being old and dry. And it is my hope that when it has burned out the wind will carry the ashes of the Sirdar-Sahib and the others into the stream which is hard by, and thus by favour of the gods will they be taken onward to the sea.'

He glanced up at Ash's stricken face and added gently: 'Do not look like that, Sahib. To us who worship the gods, death is a very little thing: a brief halt only on a long journey during which birth and death are succeeded by re-birth, and again death; and thus on and on, until at last we achieve Nirvana. Therefore why grieve that these three have completed another stage on that journey, and may even now be embarking on the next?'

Ash did not speak and the old man sighed again; he had been greatly attached to Sarjevar. He was also very tired. The night's work had involved enough gruelling labour to have exhausted many a younger man, and he would have liked to stay where he was and rest awhile, but that was not possible.

Had all gone well he and his companions would by now have been many miles away and no longer in fear of pursuit. But things had gone ill, and to make matters worse he had killed the sleeping sentries and removed and burned the bodies of Sarjevar and the two others, and by doing so, ensured that before long the chase would be taken up again—though probably not before sunrise.

The flames of the pyre he had kindled would have been clearly visible in the city, but he did not think that anyone would have been sent to investigate, since it would be thought that the men who had been left on guard had set fire to the abandoned shed for sport, or to scare away jackals and other night-prowlers who would have been attracted by the scent of blood.

But with the dawn it was certain that many men would come, this time bringing experienced trackers, so that they might be able to follow the trail of the Rani and her surviving rescuers into the hills; which would have done them little good had all gone well, as he had fully expected to be far on the way by this time—too far to fear pursuit. As it was, when the enemy returned in strength they would find the four who had been left on guard lying dead, and the bodies of the three strangers gone; and would know by this that their quarry could not be far off.

Bukta struggled to his feet and said hoarsely: 'Come, Sahib, we are wasting time. There is far to go and great need of haste; and from now on you and I must both go on foot, for there is only the one pony.'

Ash had still not spoken, and now he turned without a word and together they went back down the hillside in the growing light.

44

In the end it had been Bukta and not Anjuli who had ridden the pony.

Anjuli had been aroused by the noise of Ash's tumultuous departure, and when the two men returned they found her awake and waiting. Her eyes widened at the sight of the *shikari*'s blood-stained clothing and she looked at Ash's haggard face and drew her own conclusions. The little colour that a night's sleep had brought to her cheeks drained away and left her looking paler and even more drawn, but she asked no questions, and would have fetched food for them if Bukta had not refused to let them wait. They could, he said, eat later in the day, but now they must leave at once and press on with all the speed they could muster, for there would be men on their trail.

He shouldered the saddle-bags, and Anjuli followed him across the shale to where the pony was grazing placidly on the far slope. But when it had been saddled and Ash told her to mount, she refused to do so, saying that anyone could see that the *shikari* was exhausted, and if speed was essential they would make better time if he rode; she herself was well rested and could easily walk.

Bukta had not bothered to argue. He was too tired and too anxious to waste time over something that was, after all, only sensible. He had merely nodded and said that they must watch to see that he did not fall asleep, for if he should do so, the pony, being surefooted, would choose its own path and might lead them badly astray. The Rani-Sahiba must walk beside him so that she could hold onto a stirrup-leather on the upward slopes.

Ash, who was still numbed by grief, had agreed, though he was less anxious than Bukta. He thought their lead was sufficiently great and did not see how their pursuers could overtake them when they did not even know the road and so must move slowly, searching the ground for signs that would show them which way the quarry had gone.

But Bukta knew that a woman who had spent the last few years penned up in strict purdah, and an elderly *shikari* who for the moment at least was physically exhausted, would never be able to match the speed of angry men who were rested and well fed and burning for revenge. He was also well aware that as soon as the sun rose and the kites came for Dagobaz the men on their trail would see the birds dropping down out of the sky, and so be led to a spot that was no great distance from the gully in which his companions had spent the night.

Therefore he hurried them on, and only when the full heat of the morning was beating down on them, and Anjuli showed signs of flagging, did he pause to change places with her, declaring himself sufficiently rested to go forward on foot. But he would not let them stop, except for a short time at mid-day when they ate a frugal meal in the shade of an overhanging rock and he slept for a space.

That brief cat-nap ended, he urged them on again, plodding steadily forward, and turning whenever they crossed a ridge to look back and search for signs of pursuit. But nothing moved except the landscape, which appeared to quiver in the dancing heat, and in the brassy sky behind them a handful of dark specks that wheeled round and round and told their own tale. The kites and vultures had been driven from their meal by the arrival of men—probably a good many men—and were circling overhead waiting for the intruders to leave.

'They have found the pool,' muttered Bukta, 'and now they will know that we have only one horse between the three of us and must keep to a foot's pace. Let us hope they will take their time drinking the water and quarrelling over who shall have your saddle and bridle.'

Perhaps they had done so. At all events, they did not succeed in coming within eye-shot of the fugitives, and by the time the sun was low in the sky and the parched hillsides were once again streaked with violet shadows, it had become clear that they would not do so now. So clear that when at last, and by starlight, they came to Bukta's old camping ground in the little tree-filled valley, he felt secure enough to light a fire in order to cook chuppattis and discourage any prowling leopard from approaching. And also to wash his blood-stained clothing and spread it out to dry.

They had all three been too exhausted to sleep well that night, and Bukta and Ash had taken it in turns to keep watch, for there were pug-marks in the damp earth at the water's edge and they could not risk losing the pony. By first light they were on the move again and, except that there was less sense of urgency and they did not pause so often to look behind them, the day was a repetition of the one before; though even hotter and more tiring. They rested only when

Bukta permitted it, with the result that nightfall found them footsore, weary and parched with thirst, but among the foothills.

The old *shikari* had slept soundly that night, and so also had Anjuli, worn out by the strain of a long, hot day in the saddle. But though Ash too was very tired, he had slept only fitfully and once again his sleep had been troubled by dreams, not of pursuit or of Dagobaz, but of Shushila. The same dream, endlessly repeated, from which he awoke shuddering: only to dream it again as soon as consciousness slipped from him . . .

Each time he slept, Shushila appeared before him dressed in her bridal array of scarlet and gold, and implored him with tears not to kill her, but he would not listen and raising the revolver he pressed the trigger and saw the lovely, pleading face dissolve in blood. And woke again . . .

'But what else could I have done?' thought Ash angrily. Wasn't it enough that he should have to bear the responsibility for Sarji's death, without being haunted by the reproachful ghost of Shushila, whose end he had merely hastened as Bukta had hastened Dagobaz's? But then Shushila was not an animal: she was a human being, who had decided of her own free will to face death by fire and thereby achieve holiness; and he, Ash, had taken it upon himself to cheat her of that.

He had done more—he had interfered in something that was a matter of faith and a very personal thing; and he could not even be sure that Shushila's convictions were wrong, for did not the Christian calendar contain the names of many men and women who had been burned at the stake for their beliefs, and acclaimed as saints and martyrs?

'If I couldn't save her, I should not have interfered,' thought Ash. But as he had done so and could not undo it, he decided that he must put it out of his mind for ever; and turning over, he fell asleep again—only to meet once more a girl who wrung her hands and wept, and begged him to spare her. It had been a wretched night.

By sunrise next morning they were across the border, and three days later Ash and Bukta were back in Sarji's house, from where they had set out in such haste less than three weeks ago. But Anjuli had not been with them, for on their last night of the jungle Bukta had proffered some advice, waiting until she was asleep before doing so, and speaking very softly to avoid waking her.

He had, he said, been thinking of the future, and he had come to the conclusion that it would be better if they did not disclose the identity of Rani-Sahiba. She would get no sympathy, for not only did many people secretly approve of the old customs and would have every wife become suttee when her man died, but even those who did not tended to look upon a young widow as an ill-omened creature and little better than a slave.

Nor did he believe it advisable to tell anyone the true story of the Sirdar Sarjevar's death. It would be better for all if the Sirdar's family and friends were kept in ignorance of what had happened in Bhithor, as his identity (together with their own) could not have been known there; and in Bukta's opinion it had much better remain unknown, since there was no denying that they had all three entered Bhithor secretly with the intention of spiriting away the late Rana's wives; or that once there they had killed a member of the royal bodyguard, assaulted, gagged and bound a number of palace servants, and having abducted the Junior Rani, had opened fire on the local soldiery (who were very properly attempting to prevent their escape) and succeeded in killing a great many of them . . .

'I do not know your mind,' said Bukta, 'but for my part, I have no wish to be hailed before a Magistrate-Sahib and required to make answer to such charges, and maybe spend the rest of my days in gaol —if I am not hanged for the killings. We know that the Bhithoris would lie and lie, and that even if they were not believed, the Sahibs would still say that we had no right to take the law into our own hands and slay those sons of swine. For that we should receive punishment, and though yours might be no more than hard words from your elders, I am very sure that mine would be gaol; and also that if ever I were released, the Bhithoris would see to it that I did not live to enjoy my freedom for more than a day—which is yet another thing to be thought of, Sahib: we have blackened their faces by putting such an insult upon them, and they will neither forget it nor forgive, and if they were to learn the names of those concerned—'

'They know the Hakim-Sahib's,' said Ash curtly. 'And Manilal's.'

'True. But those two were both from Karidkote, and therefore it will be supposed that their accomplices were also from that state. The Bhithoris can have no reason to think otherwise, for they will never connect you, an officer-Sahib of a *rissala* in Ahmadabad, with the escape of one of the widows of the late Rana. Nor will they try and revenge themselves upon the Rani's people, who are too powerful—and too far away. But you and I are neither: and nor is the

Rani-Sahiba until such time as she is safely back in her own state, which may not be for many weeks if there are to be police inquiries. The law moves slowly, and once let it become known that she is in Gujerat and will be required to give evidence on our behalf and her own, her life will not be worth an anna's purchase. Or yours or mine either. If you think awhile, Sahib, you will know that what I say is true.'

'Yes . . . Yes, I know,' said Ash slowly. The British authorities were going to take a very poor view of the whole affair—even though they bore a large part of the responsibility for it, having failed to take any action of their own—because the fact remained that a large number of men had died, and it was not as if the band of amateur knight-errants could claim to have saved the Ranis from death; Ash himself had actually hastened Shushila's, while Anjuli, by her sister's contrivance, would in any case have escaped being burned on the Rana's pyre. (She would have been blinded instead—but would any-one believe that story when all Bhithor would deny it flatly?)

The Diwan and his fellow-ministers would also claim, with some justification, that the Senior Rani had insisted on her right to immo-late herself on her husband's pyre, and that no one had been able to dissuade her; or to put a stop to it either, as she had the support of the common people who would have brooked no interference from officials or guards. All of which would sound very plausible—far more so than Ash's own story. In the end the court would inflict a fine on Bhithor, which would inevitably be paid by increasing the taxes on the peasantry; and as the new Rana was too young to be held responsible, the Political Department would lecture the Diwan and his accomplices on the evils of breaking the law and the dire consequences that would follow any further misdemeanours, and probably recommend that a detachment of British-Indian troops be quartered on the state for a short period to make a show of strength. And that, as far as Bhithor was concerned, would be that.

But what of Lieutenant Pelham-Martyn and Bukta, *shikari*? How would they come out of the affair? And Juli . . . what would be-come of her if everything became known? When it was learned that she had escaped from Bhithor in the guise of a male servant, with a band of men who were not even related to her and in whose com-pany she had subsequently spent several days and nights, would it be said that she was a brave young woman and much to be pitied? or a shameless one who, careless of rank and reputation, had eloped with a Sahib?—the very Sahib who three years ago had escorted her and her sister to their wedding! Because it would not be long before that too was discovered; and when it was, heads would be shaken and tongues would wag, and before long it would be believed by all that the Sahib and the Rani had been lovers for many years.

Juli's name would become a 'hissing and an abomination' throughout half India, as even if there had been no grain of truth in it, the tale would have sounded plausible. How else to explain Lieutenant Pelham-Martyn's excessive display of anxiety on behalf of the Ranis? . . . his interviews with his Commanding Officer, the Commissioner and the District Inspector of Police? the telegrams he had dispatched on his own responsibility to several important officials, and his subsequent action in journeying to Bhithor in disguise, abducting the Junior Rani and firing on those who had attempted to prevent him?

The fact that there was actually a great deal of truth in it meant that he would have to watch his words and lie about his motives, and make certain that his lies carried conviction. Even then . . .

'I must have been mad,' thought Ash, remembering how he had meant to come back to Ahmadabad and so shock the authorities with the tale of Shu-shu's death and Juli's wrongs that they would be galvanized into taking punitive action against Bhithor and assuming the reins of government until such time as the new Rana came of age.

'Well?' asked Bukta.

'You are right,' said Ash heavily, 'we cannot tell the truth. We shall have to tell lies instead. And they will have to be good ones. Tomorrow I will speak with the Rani-Sahiba and persuade her to agree. While as for our story, we have only to say that you and I and your master the Sirdar went into the jungles to shoot, as we have often done before, and that adventuring beyond the foothills, he and his horse fell from a steep path and were killed; as was my horse also —I myself receiving only bruises. We can also say with truth that it being impossible to bring his body back, we burned it near a stream that will carry his ashes to the sea.'

'And the Rani-Sahiba? How do we explain her?'

Ash thought for a minute or two and then said that she would have to pretend to be the wife of his bearer, Gul Baz; or better still a widowed daughter. 'Tomorrow when we are free of the jungle and can buy food, you must find us a place where the Rani-Sahiba and myself can lie hid while you take the pony and ride to cantonments to fetch Gul Baz—and also a bourka such as Moslem women wear, which will be an excellent disguise for her as it hides all. He and I will decide together on a tale to tell, and when you come for us the Rani-Sahiba can return with him to my bungalow while you and I go to the Sirdar-Sahib's house with our news.'

'And afterwards?'

'That lies with the Rani. But she loved her sister, the suttee, very dearly; and if she should agree to keep silent her sister's death will go unavenged and the Diwan and those others will escape punishment. Therefore for her sister's sake she may prefer to speak out and take the consequences.'

Bukta shrugged and observed philosophically that no one could predict what a woman would do or fail to do, and they must hope that this one would be reasonable, as however dearly she loved her sister she could not undo what had been done, and her sister was dead. 'Let us sleep on it, Sahib. It may be that in the morning you will think differently. Though I trust not, for we both know that the truth is too dangerous to be told.'

Ash had not thought differently in the morning. The cost of this venture had already been appallingly high: it had taken the lives of Sarji, Gobind and Manilal (not to mention Dagobaz and Sarji's beloved Moti Raj), and any number of Bhithoris. And that was too high a price to pay for saving Juli's life if she must lose her reputation and become a byword among Indians and British alike, while Bukta ended his days in gaol and he himself was cashiered and deported. However strongly she might feel about Shushila's fate, she must be brought to see reason.

Ash foresaw difficulties and prepared his arguments accordingly; but they were not needed. Surprisingly, Anjuli had offered no opposition and had consented without demur to everything that had been suggested, even to wearing a bourka and masquerading as a Mohammedan woman, though Ash had pointed out that this could entail spending more than one night in the servants' quarters behind his bungalow, and pretending to be a relative of his bearer's. 'What does that matter?' returned Anjuli indifferently. 'One place is as good as another—and I myself have already been a servant in all but name . . .'

Her agreement brought considerable relief to Bukta, who had expected a good deal of opposition to the suggestion that she should pose as a relative of Gul Baz's—both on the score of caste and her royal blood—and he confided to Ash that the Rani-Sahiba was not only a brave woman, but a clear-headed one; which was much rarer.

Stopping on the outskirts of the first small town they came to, he bade the two to keep hidden while he went ahead on the pony to purchase food and more suitable clothing for them (the garments in which they had left Bhithor being far too conspicuous in Gujerat) and they had continued their journey in the sober dress of the hard-working local villagers—Anjuli still in male attire, as Ash had considered this safer. He had also taken the precaution of burning every shred of those gaudy palace uniforms, for he did not believe in taking chances.

In the late afternoon Bukta brought them by circuitous ways to a ruined tomb that stood among thickets of thorn trees and pampas grass in a desolate stretch of uncultivated land. No paths ran near it and not many people could have known of its existence, since it lay far from the beaten track and there were no villages within several miles. Part of the dome had fallen in many years ago, but the shell of the building remained standing and the tomb-chamber below still contained a pool of brackish water, the remnants of flooding from the rains of the last monsoon. Dust, twigs and fallen feathers littered the ground, but it was cool and dark under the arches, and Bukta swept a space clear, and cutting armfuls of dry grass, strewed it on the paving stones and covered it with the saddle-blanket to make a bed for Anjuli.

He would, he said, be as quick as he could, but it was unlikely that he would return much before sundown on the following day, and if he were later than that they were not to worry—and taking the tired pony he led it away through the tangled thickets and the tall grass. Ash accompanied him as far as the open ground and watched him mount and ride off into the dusty evening sunlight towards Ahmadabad, and only when he could see him no more did he turn and walk slowly back to the ruined tomb.

The thickets that hid it were alive with birds that had spent the heat of the day resting in the shade, while overhead, flights of parrots streamed out from the ruin, making for the distant river. The pigeons, following their example, wheeled up and up before setting off in the same direction, and a peacock woke from its afternoon siesta and paraded up and down between the tall clumps of grass.

But there was no movement from inside the tomb, and finding it empty, Ash suffered a crippling moment of panic, until a movement above him made him look up and he saw that Anjuli had not run away: there was a stairway in the thickness of the wall, and she had climbed it and was standing high above him, outlined against the sky and gazing out across the tree-tops to where the hills rose up along the northern horizon; and something in her face told him that she was not thinking of the country on the far side of them or of the beloved little sister who had died there, but of other hills—the true Hills, the high Himalayas with their vast forests and glittering snow peaks thrusting up into the diamond air of the north.

He had made no noise, but she turned quickly and looked down at him, and once again he was made sharply aware of the toll that Bhithor had taken from her . . .

The girl that he had known and loved and whose picture he had carried in his heart for three long years had gone, and in her place was a stranger. A thin, haggard woman with great haunted eyes and a startling streak of whiteness in her black hair, who looked as though she had endured torture and famine and suffered a long term of imprisonment, shut away from the sunlight and fresh air. There was something else too: something less definable. A curious sense of loss. A deadness. Adversity and sorrow had not broken Anjuli, but they had numbed her.

Ash too was aware of a deadening of his senses. He loved her still: she was Juli, and he could no more stop loving her than he could stop breathing. But now, as they looked at each other, he was not seeing her face only, but the faces of three men: Sarji and Gobind and Manilal, who had lost their lives so that he and she could escape together. The tragedy of those deaths was an open wound in his mind, and for the moment love seemed a trivial thing in comparison with the cruel sacrifice that had been exacted from his friends.

He found the stairway in the wall, and climbing it, joined her on the flat strip of roof that circled the ruined dome. Below them the thorn trees and thickets and the tall grass that had grown up around the tomb were full of shadows and the tomb itself was very dark, but up here the evening sun was bright among the tree-tops and the countryside basked in the dusty golden light of an Indian evening. Out on the plain every stick and stone and blade of grass threw a long blue shadow on the ground, and soon the parrots and the pigeons would be returning to their nests and dusk would sweep down, bringing the stars and another night. And tomorrow—tomorrow or the next day—Bukta would return; and after that the lying would begin . . .

Anjuli had returned to her silent contemplation of the hills along the far horizon, and when at length Ash reached out and touched her, she flinched and took a swift step backward, putting up her hands as though to fend him off. His hand dropped and his brows drew together as he stared at her, frowning, and said harshly: 'What did you think I meant to do? You can't think that I would harm you. Or . . . or is it that you no longer love me? No, don't turn away.' He reached out again and caught her wrists in a grasp that she could not break. 'Look at me, Juli! Now tell me the truth. Is it that you've stopped loving me?'

'I have tried to,' whispered Anjuli bleakly. 'But . . . but it seems—that I cannot help myself . . .' There was such despair in her voice that she might have been admitting to some physical disability like blindness, an affliction that could neither be cured nor ignored and that she must learn to accept and to live with. But Ash was not chilled by it for her mood matched his own.

He knew that though their love for each other had endured and would always endure, it had been temporarily submerged by a smothering weight of guilt and horror, and that until they had struggled free and could breathe again they had no desire for any active demonstration of it. That would return. But for the moment they were both in some way strangers to each other, because it was not only Anjuli who had changed. So much water had flowed under the bridges since they parted that even if they had met again under far happier circumstances it would have been surprising if they had found themselves able to pick up the threads again at the point where they had been cut off. But time was on their side—all the time in the world. They had come through the worst and were together again . . . the rest could wait.

He raised Anjuli's wrists and dropped a light kiss on each, and releasing her said: 'That's all I wanted to know; and now that I know it I know too that as long as we are together nothing can really harm us again. You must believe that. Once you are my wife—'

'Your *wife*—?'

'What else? You can't think that I would lose you a second time.'

'They will never permit you to marry me,' said Anjuli with tired conviction.

'The Bhithoris? They won't dare open their mouths!'

'No, your people; and mine also, who will be of the same mind.'

'You mean they will try and prevent it. But it's no business of theirs. This is our affair: yours and mine. Besides, didn't your own grandfather marry a princess of Hind, though he was a foreigner and not of her faith?'

Anjuli sighed and shook her head again. 'True. But that was in the days before your Raj had come to its full power. There was still a Mogul on the throne in Delhi and Ranjit-Singh held sway over the Punjab; and my grandfather was a great war-lord who took my grandmother as the spoils of war without asking any man's leave, having defeated the army of my grandmother's father in battle. I have been told that she went willingly, for they loved each other greatly. But the times have changed and that could not happen now.'

'It's going to happen now, Heart's-dearest. There is no one who can forbid you to marry me. You're no longer a maid and therefore a chattel to be disposed of to the best advantage. Nor can anyone forbid me to marry you.'

But Anjuli remained unconvinced. She could see no possibility of any marriage, based on religion, between two persons of widely differing faiths; and in their own case, no reason for it either. Or for any legal tie, as for her part she was more than content to spend the rest of her life with Ashok for love's sake, and no ceremony involving words spoken by a priest or magistrate, complete with documents in proof that it had taken place, would ever make any difference to that. She had already taken part in one such ceremony, yet it had not made her a wife in any sense except a purely legal one: a chattel of the Rana's—a despised chattel on whom, after those ceremonies, he had never again deigned to lay eyes. Had it not been for Ashok she would still be a maiden, and he was already the husband of her body as well as of her heart and spirit . . . his to do as he liked with. So what need had they for empty phrases that to one or other of them would mean nothing? or scraps of paper that she herself could not read? Besides—

She turned from him to watch the setting sun that was painting the tree-tops below her bright gold, and said in an undertone as though she were speaking to herself rather than to him: 'They had a name for me in Bhithor. They called me . . . "the half-caste".'

Ash made a small involuntary movement, and she glanced back at him over her shoulder and said without surprise: 'Yes, I should have known that you would hear that too,' and turning her head away again said softly: 'Even the *Nautch*-girl never called me that. She did not dare while my father lived, and when he died, and she taunted me with it, Nandu turned on her. I suppose because it touched his pride, he being my half-brother, and therefore he would not have it spoken of. But in Bhithor it was thrown in my teeth daily, and the priests would not permit me to enter the temple of Lakshmi that is in the gardens of the Queen's House, where the wives and women-folk of the Rana worship . . .'

Her voice died out on a whisper, and Ash said gently: 'You don't have to trouble yourself about such things any longer, Larla. Put them away and forget them. All that is over and done with.'

'Yes, it is over and done with; and being a half-caste there is no need for me to trouble myself as to what my people or my priests will do or say, since it seems that I have neither the one nor the other. Therefore from now on I will be a half-caste, and a woman of no family, from nowhere . . . one whose only god is her husband.'

'Her *wedded* husband,' persisted Ash obstinately.

Anjuli turned to look at him, her face dark against the sunset. 'It may be . . . if you truly desire it, and if . . . But until you have seen those who are in authority over you and spoken with your priests, you cannot know if it is possible, so let us talk no more of it now. The sun is almost gone and I must go down and prepare food for us while it is still light enough to see.'

She slipped past him and went down the dark stairway, and Ash let her go without making any attempt to stop her. Instead he went to stand by the parapet, and leaning his arms on it, looked out towards the hills, as she had done, and reviewed all the difficulties that lay ahead.

45

'I shall have to be careful,' thought Ash. 'Very careful.'

Last night after Bukta had left him he had contemplated flight. Juli and he must leave Gujerat at once, and on no account must he return to Ahmadabad. They could board the Bombay train at some small wayside station, and long before the Diwan's men could pick up their trail they would have left Central India and the Punjab behind them, crossed the Indus and be safely back in Mardan.

It had seemed the obvious thing to do. But then that was the trouble: it was too obvious. It was what he would be expected to do, and therefore he could not do it. He would have to be a lot cleverer than that—and pray that whatever decision he came to was the right one, for if it were not, neither Juli nor he would live long enough to regret it.

He had still not made up his mind when Anjuli called him down to eat. She had made a small fire in the corner of the tomb, and before it went out, Ash burned the packet of letters that he had written in the room above the charcoal-seller's shop in Bhithor, and that Sarji and Gobind had known they dared not keep, because had the Bhithoris found them they would have been evidence that would have betrayed him. He watched them shrivel and turn black, and later, when Anjuli was asleep, he went noiselessly out into the starlight to sit on a fallen block of stone near the entrance of the tomb, to think and plan . . .

He did not doubt that Bhithor and its Diwan would require vengeance for the lives of those who had died—and a lingering death for the widowed Rani, who would be blamed for everything. The hunt would be called against her, and it would not be abandoned until the hunters became convinced that she and her two remaining rescuers had lost their way among the trackless hills and died of thirst and starvation. Only then would Juli be safe. Juli and Bukta. And incidentally, he himself.

He had allowed Bukta to suppose that the Bhithoris would have no reason to connect an officer-Sahib from a cavalry regiment in Ahmadabad with the disappearance of one of the late Rana's widows. But that was not so, since was it not a Captain-Sahib, one Pelham-Martyn of the Guides, who had escorted the Ranis to their wedding and outwitted the Rana and his councillors in the matter of the bride-price and dowries? And had not an officer of the same name recently warned certain British officials in Ahmadabad that if and when the Rana died his widows would burn?—and sent off several strongly worded telegrams to that effect?

Besides, as it was already known in Bhithor that the Hakim-Sahib had arrived there by way of Ahmadabad, and that his servant Manilal had subsequently visited that city on two separate occasions in order to purchase medicines, the Bhithoris would certainly not neglect to send spies there in search of the missing Rani. In fact it was only too likely to be among the first places they would think of; and once there, decided Ash grimly, they would find abundant evidence that he had interested himself in the widows, and almost certainly discover that both Gobind and Manilal had stayed at his bungalow. That last would be the vital link, and unless he was much mistaken, from there it would be only a short step to murder: his own as well as Juli's. And probably Bukta's too.

The odds were frightening, because the one thing he could be certain of was that Bhithor would move quickly. The Diwan could not afford to be dilatory, and search parties would already be hurrying to cover every possible escape route to Karidkote, while others would soon be on their way to Gujerat. Yet after careful consideration Ash came to the conclusion that the best thing he could do—in fact the only thing—was to return to his bungalow and brazen it out.

Juli would have to go on ahead with Gul Baz, while he followed a few days later with Bukta, arriving as though from the direction of Kathiawar in the southern half of the peninsula, instead of from the northern districts that bordered on Rajputana—and with a different lie to account for Sarji's death and the loss of the horses.

They must say that they had changed their plans and gone south together, and that Sarji and the horses had been drowned while crossing a tidal river, the bodies being swept out to sea and lost in the waters of the Gulf of Kutch. His own grief at the loss of his friend (genuine enough, God knew), not to mention the loss of a much-valued horse, would more than account for his showing no further interest in the fate of the Ranis of Bhithor.

He still had a good deal of leave at his disposal: those weeks that he had planned to spend with Wally on trek through the high country beyond the Rotang Pass. The trek would have to be cancelled, for he must spend the next week or so idling about cantonments, disposing of unwanted property and making leisurely arrangements for the homeward journey to Mardan, in order to demonstrate to any who might be interested that he had nothing to hide and was in no particular hurry to leave the station.

The presence of an additional woman in the servants' quarters was unlikely to arouse much interest (even if it were noticed) for who would expect to find a high-born lady, daughter of a Maharajah and widow of a Rana of Bhithor, agreeing to live in seclusion among the Sahib's Mohammedan servants, in the guise of his bearer's wife? Such a thing would be unthinkable, and even those Bhithoris who had termed her 'the half-caste' would not credit it. They would probably watch him for several days, taking careful notes of his behaviour and his every move, and in the end they would come to the conclusion that he could have taken no part in the escape, but had lost interest in the Ranis after sending off those telegrams, and did not intend to do anything more on their behalf. They would return to Bhithor and report as much to the Diwan, who would turn his attention elsewhere. And Juli would be safe.

It was a pity about that trek; Wally was going to be disappointed. But he would understand that it could not be helped, and they could always go another year. There was plenty of time . . .

His mind made up, Ash lay down across the entrance to the tomb so that no human or animal could pass in without waking him, and was asleep before the moon rose. But though tonight his sleep was untroubled by dreams, it was not so with Anjuli, for three times that night she cried out in the grip of a nightmare.

On the first occasion Ash, jerked into consciousness by that choking scream, scrambled up to find that the tomb was filled with a cold radiance. The moon had risen while he slept and was shining in through the broken dome, and by its light he could see Anjuli crouching against the far wall with her arms across her face, as though to blot out some intolerable sight. She was moaning, 'No! No, Shu-shu, no . . . !' and he caught her in his arms and held her close, rocking her shuddering body and murmuring endearments and comfort, until at last the terror left her and for the first time in all those desperate, terrible days, she broke down and wept.

The storm of tears ceased at last, and it seemed to have washed away some of her tension, for presently she relaxed and lay still, and after a time he realized that she had fallen asleep again. Moving very gently so as not to wake her he lay down, still holding her, listening to her shallow breathing and appalled by her thinness.

Had they starved her? . . . from what he knew of the Rana and the Diwan, he would not put it past them, and his mind blackened with rage at the thought as he tightened his arms about the skeletal form that had once been so smooth and firm and sweetly slender, and whose every lovely line and curve his hands and lips had explored with such heart-stopping delight.

Less than an hour later she began to toss and turn, and once more started up, screaming Shu-shu's name. And again, shortly before dawn when the tomb was dark because the moon no longer shone into it, the nightmare trapped her for the third time that night, and she woke in the black darkness and struggled frantically against his restraining arms as though she imagined herself to be in the grip of an enemy come to drag her to a pyre—or towards a brazier where a fire-iron glowed white-hot among the coals.

It had taken longer to quieten her after that last awakening, and as she clung to him, shuddering with the aftermath of terror and begging him to hold her—hold her—the physical desire that had once been a living flame between them, and that Ash had thought lost, blazed up in him so fiercely that he would at that moment have sacrificed their hope of safety to be able to take possession of her body and obtain comfort and release for his own—and with it a temporary forgetfulness of all the problems that pressed upon him.

But there was no answering urge in the wasted body in his arms, and he knew that if he were to take her now it would be by force, for she would recoil from him; and also that if he were to give way to his own desires and to succeed in awakening a like response in her, their situation would be a great deal worse than it was already, because once the barriers were down it would be next to impossible for them to keep apart during the following days. Neither of them would be capable of it, yet if suspicion was to be disarmed it was essential that Juli should spend the next week or ten days in one of the servants' quarters behind his bungalow, and that he himself should go nowhere near her. If he were seen to do so it could be fatal for them both, and this way was better. There would be plenty of time for love-making once they were married and the nightmares were over.

Anjuli fell asleep at last, and presently Ash too slept, and did not wake until she stirred in his arms and drew away from him, aroused by the joyous chorus of parrots, pigeons, doves and weaver-birds greeting the dawn. When the sun was up, and after they had eaten, he told her of the plans he had made during the previous night, and she listened to him, raising no objection and seeming willing enough to fall in with any decisions that he might choose to make: but apart from this they talked very little. Anjuli was still suffering from shock and exhaustion, and for both of them that long day in the ruined tomb had been haunted by the thought of Shushila. Neither of them had been able to put her out of their minds; and though Ash had done his best to do so, the thought of her had returned to him so persistently that he was almost tempted to believe that her uneasy little ghost had followed them there, and was watching them from the shadows of the *kikar* trees.

In the late afternoon Bukta returned accompanied by Gul Baz and two spare horses, and though Anjuli had been awake and heard their voices, she had remained on the roof and let the three men talk together. Bukta had approved of the new plan, for he and Gul Baz had discussed the matter at length, and come to a similar conclusion: 'But I have said that this tale of a wife or a widowed daughter will not serve,' said Gul Baz. 'I have a better plan—'

He had: and what was more, he had already taken steps to put it into operation. After discussing the matter with Bukta they had, he said, decided that the only thing to do was to substitute the Rani-Sahiba for the shy, silent woman whom he had installed more than a year ago in the hut behind his own quarter—and who had in any case been expecting to leave in the near future, since she was aware that the Sahib and his servants were about to return to the North-West Frontier Province, and had always known that the irregular but useful arrangement she had made with the Sahib's bearer would automatically cease when he went back to his own country. As that day was almost here it was only a question of terminating it a little earlier than expected; and this Gul Baz had done.

When he left the bungalow early that morning he had gone in a hired tonga, and taken the woman with him, having let it be known that she wished to visit her mother in her home village, and that they would be returning late. In fact, she would not be returning at all. It would be the Rani-Sahiba who would come back with him, though his fellow-servants would not know that there had been any substitution—one woman in a bourka being very like another. As for the other one, the Sahib need not fear: she had been well paid and there would be no danger from that quarter, for apart from being a close-mouthed woman, there was no chance of her returning to the cantonment area, or even the city, until well after they themselves were back in Mardan.

'But tonight when we return it will be seen that she has come back with me as I said, so if any stranger should come asking questions he will learn nothing, there being nothing to tell. I have here a bourka for the Rani-Sahiba, old but clean. It belonged to that other one and I took it from her, saying it was too worn and mended, and that I would buy her a new one in the bazaar; which I did. Also by good fortune she is a tall woman, for the *shikari* tells me that the Rani-Sahiba is also tall. We shall return after dark, and no one will notice any difference; and once installed in the hut the Rani-Sahiba will be safe, for I shall say she is suffering from some slight sickness and must keep to her bed. There will be no need for her to speak to anyone, or even be seen.'

Ash said: 'And what happens when the time comes for us to leave Gujerat?'

'We have thought of that too,' said Bukta. 'There will be no difficulty. Your servant has only to say that his woman wishes to visit a relative in the Punjab and that he has agreed to take her with him as far as Delhi—or Lahore, if you prefer, it makes no matter. He will arrange all that. He has a head upon his shoulders, has that Pathan. Moreover the woman is known to have lived under his protection for close on a year, while the Rani-Sahiba has only been missing for a handful of days. Now, as to our own return—'

Some twenty minutes later a party of four horsemen could have been seen riding swiftly across the croplands towards the dusty main highway that runs between Khed Brahma and Ahmadabad, and on reaching it they broke into a gallop, heading south.

Twilight overtook them when they were still many miles from the city of Ahmad Shah. But they pressed on through the dusk, and later in the starlight; and when at last they came within sight of the twinkling lights of the cantonment, the moon was rising. They drew rein near a clump of trees and Ash lifted Juli down from the saddle. They did not speak, for they had already said everything that was necessary; and besides all four were anxious and more than a little weary. Gul Baz handed over his horse to Bukta and salaamed to Ash, and followed by Anjuli, who walked a pace behind him as befitted a woman, he went away in the moonlight towards a village on the outskirts of the cantonments where he could hire a tonga to take them back to the bungalow.

Five days later Ash returned to Ahmadabad, riding one of Sarji's horses and attended by one of the syces from Sarji's stables.

The syce had been entertained by Kulu Ram and others before taking the horse back with him later that day, and before he left he told his hosts, with a wealth of detail, the story of the death of his master, who had been tragically drowned while attempting to swim his horse across one of the many tidal rivers that ran into the Gulf of Kutch, and of how the Sahib's horse had also been drowned, and the Sahib himself only saved by a miracle. The tale had lost nothing in the telling, and Gul Baz had been able to report later that it had obviously not occurred to the teller—or to anyone else—to doubt it.

'So that is another ditch safely crossed,' said Gul Baz. 'As for the other matter, that too was passed over in safety. No one has thought to question the identity of the one who returned here with me. Nor will they, for she keeps to her room, feigning poor health; which I think is in part true, for during her second night here she cried out in her sleep so loudly that I awoke and ran out to her hut, fearing that she had been discovered and was being abducted. But she said that it was only a dream and that—' He broke off, seeing Ash's expression, and said: 'Has this happened before, then?'

'Yes. I should have thought of it, and warned you,' said Ash, angry with himself for the omission. He himself had not been troubled by any further dreams of Shushila, but she continued to weigh on his conscience: her small, reproachful face was still apt to rise up before him at unexpected moments, and if this was so with him, how much worse must it be for Juli, who had loved her?

He asked if any of the other servants had been awakened, but Gul Baz did not think so. 'For as you know, my quarter and the one that was Mahdoo-ji's stand apart from the others, and the hut in which the Rani-Sahiba lies is close behind it and thus well shielded from those that are occupied by the other servants. But on the next day I purchased opium and made a draught for her to take after sundown, since when she has slept soundly and made no further outcries in the night—which is as well, for the *shikari* spoke truth when he said that the Sahib might be spied upon.'

According to Gul Baz, on the previous day several strangers had come to the bungalow, one asking for work, another purporting to be a vendor of drugs and simples, and a third inquiring after an errant wife, who, so he said, was believed to have run off with the servant of some Sahib. This last one, on hearing that Pelham-Sahib had left for a shooting trip in Kathiawar earlier in the month and had not yet returned, had asked many questions . . .

'All of which,' said Gul Baz, 'we answered. Sympathizing with him in his distress and telling him many things: though none, I fear, that were of help to him. As for the seller of drugs and such-like, by good fortune he was here again today when the Sahib returned, and he stayed to listen to all that the syce had to tell. Afterwards he packed up his wares and went away, saying that he had many other customers to attend to and could waste no more time here. I do not think he will return, for he has seen for himself that the Sahib came back alone, and learned from that syce, whose tongue wagged as freely as an old woman's, that no third person accompanied the Sahib and the *shikari* when they brought the sad news of the drowning in Kathiawar to the family of the Sirdar Sarjevar Desai.'

'There will be others,' observed Ash pessimistically. 'I do not believe that the Diwan's spies will be satisfied so easily.'

Gul Baz shrugged and said that in his opinion they would very soon tire of hanging about the compound to exchange gossip with people who had nothing of the least interest to disclose, and of shadowing the Sahib round cantonments only to find him engaged in such unsuspicious and mundane matters as social calls and farewell parties, and the tedious but necessary arrangements that must be made with railway officials and booking clerks regarding his return journey to Mardan.

'You have only to go to-and-fro daily,' said Gul Baz, 'letting it be seen that you have nothing to conceal and are in no haste to be gone, and the watchers will soon weary of the game. Another week or ten days should suffice, and after that it will be safe enough for us to shake the dust of this ill-omened place from our shoes and board the rail-*ghari* for Bombay. And may the All Merciful ordain,' he added fervently, 'that we never have reason to return here.'

Ash nodded absently, for his thoughts were on Juli, who must spend a further eight or ten days cooped up in the hot and stifling little hut, not daring to show herself for even a short breath of air, or to sleep at night without the aid of opium. But he had taken Gul Baz's advice, and had seen to it that every minute of the succeeding days should find him openly employed in some leisurely and innocuous activity, because the fact that someone, or more probably several people, were interested was soon clear to him. For though he was careful not to look over his shoulder to see if he was being followed, he realized that even if he had not been warned he would still have been aware that he was under constant surveillance. It was purely a matter of instinct, the same instinct that tells the jungle creatures that they are being stalked by a tiger, or that can warn a man waking in darkness and silence that there is an intruder in his room.

Ash had experienced that feeling before, and recognizing it (with him it took the form of a coldness between his shoulder-blades and a prickling of the hairs at the back of his neck, coupled with an intense and uncomfortable alertness) he had his bed moved up to the flat roof of the bungalow, where anyone who so desired could keep an eye on him and see for themselves that he did not leave it to engage in any surreptitious meetings by night.

The tale of Sarjevar's untimely death and the loss of the peerless Dagobaz had spread through the cantonment, and Ash received a good deal of sympathy from the officers and sowars of Roper's Horse and various members of the British community. And also from the dead man's great-uncle, the Risaldar-Major, who was touched by the Sahib's grief for his lost friend and urged him not to blame himself—which was not in Ash's power, as he knew very well that he was to blame, because he could so easily have refused to let Sarji go with him to Bhithor.

The fact that Sarji's family and friends believed that cock-and-bull story that he and Bukta had invented, and repeated it as the truth to all who called to commiserate, was of great service to Ash, as it conveyed the impression that they had known all along that the two had been shooting in an area that was a great deal further to the south of Ahmadabad than the border of Rajasthan was to the north. And this, taken in conjunction with Ash's behaviour and the absence of any evidence that the late Rana's widow was in Gujerat (or even that she was still alive), evidently succeeded in convincing the Diwan's spies that they were on the wrong track, for by the end of the week Gul Baz was able to report that the bungalow was no longer being watched.

That night there had been no skulking figure among the shadows, and next morning when Ash went riding he did not have to be told that he was not being followed or spied upon, for he could feel it in his bones. All the same he took no chances, but was careful to behave as though the danger still existed; and only when a further three days and nights passed without sign of a watcher did he feel able to relax and breath freely again—and began to think of the future.

Now that he was no longer under surveillance, there was no reason to linger in Ahmadabad a moment longer than necessary. But it was not possible to leave immediately, because two of the three dates proffered by the station master on which he could guarantee accommodation on the train to Bombay with a through booking to Delhi and Lahore had already been lost. The remaining one entailed a further delay of several days, but now Ash closed with it and told Gul Baz to see to all the necessary arrangements for the move, he himself having other things to occupy him.

Despite the anxieties that bedevilled the tense days that followed upon his return to cantonments, the need to engage in trivial pursuits had proved a blessing, for together with the long hours of enforced idleness and the longer nights it had provided him with ample time in which to sort out the problems of the future. Yet the major one still remained unsolved: what to do about Juli?

It had all seemed so simple once; if only she were free he could marry her. Well she was free now, free from both the Rana and Shushila, and there should have been nothing to prevent him doing so. But the trouble lay in the fact that the gap between day-dreaming about remote possibilities and dealing with the reality was so wide as to be almost unbridgeable . . .

The same could be said of his feeling for the Corps of Guides, for at one stage of the unforgettable journey with the bridal camp he had actually considered deserting—leaving India, with Juli, to take refuge in another country and never see Mardan or Wally or Zarin again. It astonished him now that even in the first fever of his passion for Juli he could ever have contemplated such a thing: except that he had been in disgrace at the time, banished from the Regiment and the Frontier, and with no idea how long his exile would last—or any certainty that some future Commandant would not decide that it would be better not to have him back at all. But things were different now . . . he had been recalled to Mardan to take up the duties he had abandoned when he joined the hunt for Dilasah Khan and the stolen carbines, and there was no question of his refusing to return. The ties that bound him to the Guides stretched too far back into the past and were too strong to be easily broken; and even for Juli's sake he would not—could not—bring himself to sever them and lose both Wally and Zarin. Nor was there any point in doing so, when even if he could persuade someone to marry him to Juli, he would never be able to claim her openly as his wife.

'The problem is this—' explained Ash, discussing the matter with Mrs Viccary, who, besides being the only person in Gujerat whom he felt able to tell the story to, could be trusted not to let it go any further and to listen to it without being swayed by any prejudice on the score of Juli's ancestry or his own.

It was not advice that he needed (being well aware that if it ran contrary to his own wishes he would not take it) but someone to talk to. Someone sensible and sympathetic who loved India as he did and with whom he could discuss this whole situation, and by doing so get it straightened out in his own mind. And Mrs Viccary had not failed him: she had neither blamed nor praised, or been shocked by his desire to marry a Hindu widow, or by Anjuli's view that no legal marriage was necessary.

'You see,' said Ash, 'once it was known that we were married she wouldn't be safe.'

'Or you either,' observed Edith Viccary. 'People would talk, and news travels fast in this country.'

That of course was the point; and Ash was inexpressibly grateful to her for seeing it at once instead of bringing up all the more obvious arguments against such a marriage—beginning with the fact that, until he reached the age of thirty or the rank of Major, he could not marry without the consent of his Commanding Officer (which in the circumstances he would certainly not get) and going on to point out that in a regiment such as the Guides, which recruited Mussulmans, Sikhs, Hindus and Gurkhas, a British officer who married a Hindu widow would be anathema. By doing so he would sow dissension among the men under his command, offending not only the caste Hindus, but probably the Sikhs as well, causing the Mussulmans to despise him for thinking so little of his own religion, and Sikhs, Mussulmans and Gurkhas together to suspect him of favouring his wife's co-religionists whenever he was called upon to judge between a Hindu and a man of another faith, or to recommend one or other for promotion. The Guides would ask him to leave, and no other Indian Army regiment would accept him for the same reasons.

Ash knew all about that; and so did Mrs Viccary. But none of it was worth worrying about for the simple reason that even if he could arrange to marry Juli, to do so openly would be tantamount to signing her death warrant—together with his own—since such a marriage, once made public, was bound to cause a great deal of talk and speculation and scandal. And in a country such as India where not only regiments but members of the Civil Service, medical officers, policemen, clergymen, men in trade and numerous other Britishers, all accompanied by large numbers of Indian servants, were moved about from one end of the country to another at short notice, a story of this kind would be gossiped over in the Clubs of every military station from Peshawar to Trivandrum, and in every bazaar where the servants of the 'Sahib-log' gathered to talk over the doings of the *Angrezis* and retail the gossip of the station they had just left. And the Indian grape-vine was the swiftest and most efficient in the world . . .

It would not be long before Bhithor came to hear that the same Guides officer who had escorted the late Rana's wives to their wedding (and been stationed in Gujerat at the time of the Rana's death and the disappearance of one of his widows) had subsequently married a Hindu widow. The Diwan would add two and two together, and coming up with the correct total, would send someone to investigate; after which it would only be a matter of time—probably only a very short time—before Juli died. For Bhithor would require vengeance for their own dead—all those who had died (and there must have been many of them) in the fight to defend the entrance to Bukta's secret road—as well as for the insult that had been put upon them by the abduction of their late Rana's widow.

'It would have to be kept secret,' said Ash.

'Then you still mean to marry her? Even though you tell me that she herself can see no reason for it?'

But Ash was nothing if not obstinate. 'What else? Do you think I want her as a mistress . . . a concubine? I want to know that she's my wife, even though I can't acknowledge her as such. It's—it's something I *have* to do. I can't explain . . .'

'You don't have to,' said Edith Viccary. 'If I were in your place I'd feel the same. Of course you must marry her. But it isn't going to be easy.'

The difficulty, she explained, was that marriage being a Sacrament of the Church, no clergyman would consent to employ it to unite a Christian to a Hindu, unless it could be proved that the latter had undergone a genuine conversion. 'God is not mocked, you know,' added Mrs Viccary softly.

'I didn't mean to mock. But then I never think of Him as being an Englishman—or a Jew or an Indian or any other nationality that we've invented for ourselves. Nor do I believe that He thinks of us like that. But I did realize, as soon as I began to think about it, that the Church wouldn't marry us, any more than Juli's priests would, even if I dared risk asking them, which I don't. But I thought perhaps a magistrate—?'

Edith Viccary shook her head decidedly. She knew the local British magistrate a good deal better than Ash did, and Mr Chadwick, she assured him, was the last person to consent to such a thing. He could also be trusted to report Ash's request for a marriage license to the Commissioner, who apart from being equally horrified would ask a great many awkward questions. And once inquiries were set on foot, the fat would be well and truly in the fire.

'Yes,' said Ash bitterly. 'We can't risk that.'

There seemed to be no way out. It was inconceivable—fatuous and unjust and totally unfair—that two grown people who only wanted to marry each other should not be permitted to do so, when their marriage would harm no one. It was a purely personal matter, and if people could get married at sea without the aid of magistrates and licences, like that couple on the *Canterbury Castle,* there should be some equally simple method by which those on land could do the same, and he—

'By God, that's it!' cried Ash explosively, leaping to his feet. 'Red Stiggins—the *Morala.* Why on earth didn't I think of that before?'

Red had said something about sailing for Karachi 'in a few weeks' time' and had invited him to come along for the voyage. And if the *Morala* had not left yet . . .

Pausing only to bestow a fervent hug on the bewildered Mrs Viccary, he ran from her drawing-room, shouting for Kulu Ram to fetch his horse, and ten minutes later anyone happening to be abroad at that hottest hour of the day would have seen a Sahib riding hell-for-leather down the glaring cantonment road towards the city.

The shrewd Gujerati who looked after Captain Stiggins's business interests in the peninsula had a small office in a street near the Daripur Gate, and he had been enjoying his customary afternoon's siesta when the Sahib burst in on him, demanding to know if the *Morala* had already set sail for Karachi, and if not, when she would be leaving and from where. And this time Ash's luck was in, for the *Morala* had not yet sailed, though she would be doing so very shortly —in the next day or two if all went well, and certainly not later than the end of the week. The ship was at Cambay at the head of the Gulf, and if the Sahib wished to send a message—?

The Sahib did, and was grateful for the offer as he had no time to spare for writing letters. 'Tell him that I accept his invitation and to expect me tomorrow; and that whatever he does, he is not to sail without me.'

There was a great deal to be done and not much time in which to do it, for the port of Cambay was all of sixty miles from Ahmadabad, and Ash rode back to his bungalow at the same breakneck speed at which he had left Mrs Viccary's.

46

Captain Stiggins scratched the copper-coloured stubble on his chin with a horny thumb and stared thoughtfully at Ash for a full two minutes, pondering the matter. Then he said slowly: 'Well now . . . I can't say as I'm pre-cisely the same kind of animal as one of them gilded skippers of a steam packet—no more'n the old *Morala* is a fancy passenger ship. Still, I'm the master of this 'ere craft, and so I don't see as 'ow that shouldn't give me the right to do anything a cove in a frock-coat and brass buttons can do aboard one of them swanky great P & O boats.'

'Then you'll do it, Red?'

'Well, son, I ain't never done such a thing before, so I can't say as I'll go bail for its bein' legal. But I reckon that's yore 'eadache, not mine. And seein' as we're pals, I'm willin' to chance me arm and splice yer . . . now, now—'old yore 'orses, son. I've said as I'll do it as a favour—but I ain't a goin' to do it 'ere and now. Not for you nor no one will I go pretendin' that this 'ere duck-pond is an ocean, so you'll just 'ave to wait until we're standin' well clear o' the land and a good 'arf way between 'ere and Chahbar, see? That's goin' to make it look a sight better in the log-book; and it seems to me, young feller, that yore goin' to need to do everything you can t' make this caper o' yores look ship-shape and above board. Them's my terms, son. Take 'em or leave 'em.'

'Where the hell is Chahbar? I thought you were bound for Karachi.'

'So I am—on the way back. But there's bin a change of plan. I reckon you bin too busy with yore own affairs to notice that there's bin a famine around for nigh on three years now—particular in the south. That's why I'm shippin' a cargo o' cotton to Chahbar, which is way up on the coast of Mekran, and bringin' back a load o' grain. It's a longish haul, but on the way back I could put you ashore any place you fancy. Are you on?'

Ash had hoped to get married with the least possible delay, but he could see the sense of Captain Stiggins's argument, and in any case he had no option but to agree to his terms. It was decided that the ceremony had best be postponed until such time as Sind and the mouth of the Indus lay well astern and the *Morala* was headed north to-

wards Ras Jewan. In the meantime, Red gallantly placed his own cabin at Anjuli's disposal and moved in with his mate, one McNulty, for the duration of the voyage, though in the event all three men (and everyone else on board for that matter) elected to sleep on deck, and only Anjuli kept to her cabin.

The *Morala* only boasted four cabins, and though Red's was certainly the best of these it was far from large and at that season of the year was stiflingly hot. But Anjuli spent the first part of the voyage in it, because she proved to be a poor sailor, and succumbed to a bad attack of sea-sickness that lasted for several days, by which time they had crossed the Tropic of Cancer, and were sailing through a sea that was stained with the silt brought down by the Indus and its four great fellow-rivers of the Punjab.

Gul Baz, who had insisted on accompanying Ash, had also been most vilely ill, but it was not long before he acquired his sea-legs and was up and about again. Anjuli, on the other hand, made a slow recovery. She spent the greater part of the day sleeping, for she was still plagued by bad dreams, and as she found these less frightening by day she stayed awake at night and kept two oil lamps burning from dusk to dawn, despite the fact that they greatly increased the heat in the cramped little cabin.

Ash had nursed her and waited upon her, and he too took to sleeping by day so that he could sit up with her for at least part of the night. But even when she had recovered from her sea-sickness he found that she was still disinclined to talk, and that any reference to Bhithor or the immediate past, however oblique, would make her stiffen into rigidity and bring back that disturbing frozen look to her eyes. He therefore confined himself to speaking only of his own doings and his plans for their joint future, though he suspected that half the time she did not hear what he was saying because she was listening to other voices.

He had confirmed this on several occasions by breaking off in mid-sentence, only to find that she was unaware that he had stopped speaking. Asked what she was thinking of, she would look troubled and say, 'Nothing' . . . until one evening, when that question had broken into her silent brooding so abruptly that she had been startled into an unguarded reply, and answered 'Shushila.'

It was hardly reasonable of Ash to hope that she would by now have stopped tormenting herself with thoughts of Shushila when he himself was unable to do so. But he had got up without a word and left the cabin, and half an hour later it had been Gul Baz and not Ash who had knocked on her door bringing the evening meal, for Ash had been otherwise occupied.

He had taken his problems to Captain Stiggins, and fortified by the Captain's ferocious brandy, was engaged in pouring the whole story into that gentleman's sympathetic ear. 'The trouble is that her sister has always come first with her—right from the beginning,' explained Ash bitterly. 'I used to believe that I was the only one she really loved, and that it was only affection and a strong sense of duty that made her stay with Shu-shu. But it seems I was wrong. I tried to make her run away with me before, you know, but she wouldn't do it because of Shu-shu . . . God! how I came to hate the very sound of that name.'

'Jealous, were you,' nodded Red.

'Of course I was. Wouldn't you have been, in my place? Dammit Red, I was in love with her. I still am. I always will be. And but for that sister of hers—!'

'Well, now that the pore girl's dead, you've no call to be jealous of her any more 'av you?' put in Red soothingly.

'Oh, yes I have, because even now—in fact now more than ever—she's coming between us. I tell you, Red, she might just as well be here on this ship, battening upon what little strength Juli has left, and weeping and whining for sympathy and attention like she used to do. There are times when I'm even ready to believe that there are such things as ghosts, and that hers has followed us here and is doing its damnedest to take Juli away from me.'

'Don't be daft!' snapped the Captain crossly. 'I never 'eard such poppycock. Ghosts indeed!—whatever next?' He pushed the bottle over to Ash and said: 'Better 'av another good swig o' that, son. Won't do you no 'arm to get good n' bosky for a change an' drown yore sorrows, for it sounds to me as though you bin battenin' down yore 'atches too 'ard of late. It'll do you good to open 'em up and let some of the bad air out. It ain't sense to go a bottlin' things up until you gets jealous of a pore lass wots dead and gorn. T'ain't 'ealthy.'

'It's not that,' said Ash, re-filling his glass with an unsteady hand. 'You don't understand, Red. It's because now that she's dead I'm afraid . . . I'm afraid—' His teeth chattered against the rim of the glass as he gulped the raw spirit.

'Afraid o' wot?' demanded Red, frowning. 'That yore Juli won't forget 'er sister? Wot's so bad about that? If she did you'd likely begin to think she was an 'ard 'earted piece, and that's the truth. You just give the pore girl a bit o' time, and you'll find you ain't got nothin' to be afraid of, for she's bound to stop grievin' one day.'

Ash drained his glass and reached for the bottle again, observing impatiently that of course she would; and of course he didn't expect her to forget her sister. It was not that he was afraid of.

'Wot then?'

'That she won't be able to forget that it was I who killed Shushila.'

'You *wot!*' exclaimed Red, startled.

'Didn't I tell you that? I shot her,' said Ash.

He explained how this had come about, and when he had finished Red breathed heavily for a few moments, and downed a further generous helping of brandy before replying. But his verdict when it came brought little comfort: 'It's 'ard to know wot else you could 'ave done,' declared Captain Stiggins thoughtfully. 'But I see wot you mean. At the time like, all she'd be thinkin' of would be 'ow she could save 'er little sister from the pain of bein' roasted alive. But now that it's all over she's maybe blamin' 'erself for not letting the lass 'ave her own way—and you for playin' 'angman, so to speak.'

'Yes. That's what I'm afraid of. She seemed so set on it at the time. She *begged* me to do it. But now . . . now I don't believe she could have been in her right mind. She was half mad with grief, and thinking back I'm not sure I was quite sane myself. Perhaps none of us were . . . but it was far worse for her, because Shu-shu meant more to her than anyone else in the world and she couldn't bear the thought of what she must suffer. She wanted me to shoot her before the flames reached her, and I did. I shouldn't have done it and I've wished ever since that I hadn't, because I cheated her out of sainthood. And now I'm afraid that Juli has begun to find that she can't look at me without remembering that it was I who killed her darling Shu-shu.'

'Bollocks!' retorted Red inelegantly.

'Oh, I don't mean that she blames me for doing it. She knows damned well I only did it for her, and that if it had been up to me I wouldn't have dreamed of risking all our lives by hanging around waiting to shoot the wretched girl. But however clearly she may see that with her head, she knows in her heart that I didn't give a damn about Shu-shu—and that makes a difference.'

'Yes, I can see that,' said Red reflectively. 'If you'd 'ad a fondness

for the lass and done it for that reason—for love as you might say—it
wouldn't 'ave mattered s'much . . . you shootin' 'er.'

'That's it. But then I wasn't fond of her. You'll say because I was
jealous of her, but it was more than that: I resented the hold she had
over Juli, and now I think Juli is probably remembering that, and
adding it to the rest and finding that in spite of herself it has changed
her feelings for me. One can't really blame her, for though I still don't
see what else I could have done, I've never stopped regretting that I
shot that damned girl—and if I can feel like that, why shouldn't Juli
feel equally mixed up about it? Oh, God, what a mess it all is! Let's
open another bottle, Red—I'm going to take your advice and get
drunk.'

They had both got drunk: Red rather less so than Ash, by reason
of having a harder head. And either the advice had been good, or
else the dictum that confession is good for the soul had proved to be
sound, because afterwards Ash certainly felt more relaxed and less
apprehensive about the future, though he did not again make the
mistake of asking Anjuli what she was thinking of. She was still painfully thin; and very pallid, which Ash put down to the airless heat of
Red's cabin. He was sure that once they were married and he could
coax her out onto the open deck and into the fresh air, her health
was bound to improve, and with it her state of mind.

They had been married two hours after the shores of Sind faded
from sight and the *Morala*'s bows were ploughing towards Ras
Jewan and Chahbar. The ceremony had taken place at 2.30 in the
afternoon, in the cramped little saloon, the witnesses being the Mate,
Angus McNulty (who hailed from Dundee and admitted cautiously
that he "might be a Presbyterian"), and an old friend of Red's, one
Hyem Ephraim, an elderly Jew from Cutch who had business interests in Persia and had arranged to sail with Captain Stiggins to
Chahbar. Red himself claimed to be a 'free thinker'—whatever that
meant—but he had dignified the occasion by wearing his best suit and
speaking in a voice of such portentous gravity that Gul Baz, who had
watched the brief ceremony from the doorway, had been convinced
that the *Morala*'s Captain must, in private life, be a particularly wise
and holy *guru*.

Gul Baz, a pious Mohammedan, had been full of misgivings. But
he had not voiced them, for it was too late for that. It had been too
late from the day that the Hakim from Karidkote and his fat servant,
Manilal, had driven up to the Sahib's bungalow in a hired tonga and

he, Gul Baz, had failed to send them away. This Hindu widow was not at all the sort of wife that he had expected his Sahib to choose, and he did not approve of mixed marriages any more than Koda Dad Khan—or Mr Chadwick. Nor did he look forward to explaining to Koda Dad and his sons how this had come about, or the part that he himself had played in it; though how he could have refused his assistance, or prevented his Sahib from leaving for Bhithor in the first place, he did not know. Nevertheless, today he put up his own private prayers for the safety, well-being and future happiness of the bridegroom and his chosen bride, and petitioned the All-Wise to grant them long life and many strong sons.

Anjuli, once a devout Hindu, had not prayed for several years, having come to believe either that the gods did not exist, or that for reasons of their own—possibly because of the foreign blood in her veins—they had turned their faces from her. She did not pray now, and she wore the bourka in place of a wedding dress, which struck no one there as strange, since Western brides traditionally wore white and went veiled to the altar, while in the East a widow's weeds are not black but white.

Ash had cut a slit at one side of the tent-like garment so that he could take her hand, and as all else was hidden by the bourka, that small, square hand was all that the wedding guests saw of the bride. Yet strangely enough each one of them, on that evidence alone, was immediately convinced that Lieutenant Pelham-Martyn's bride was a woman of rare beauty and charm. They were also convinced that she spoke and understood English, for Ash had taught her the few words she must say, and when the time came she spoke them in a low clear voice that copied his intonation so exactly that anyone who did not know her story might well have supposed that the cheap cotton bourka disguised some well-bred Victorian miss.

Ash had not thought to buy a ring in Ahmadabad, and as he did not wear a signet ring, he had removed part of his watch-chain and joined it into a slender circle of gold links. It was this that he now put on Anjuli's finger: *'With this ring, I thee wed . . .'* The brief ceremony that made her his wife had taken less than ten minutes, and when it was over she had returned to her cabin, leaving him to drink the wine that Red had provided, and accept congratulations and good wishes.

The day had been uncomfortably hot, and even with the sea wind blowing, the temperature in the saloon was over ninety degrees; but it would drop towards evening, and when darkness fell the poop deck would be a cool and pleasant place to spend the first night of the honeymoon—always provided that Juli would consent to leave her cabin.

Ash hoped that it would not be too difficult to persuade her, for he had no intention of sweltering in it himself. It was high time that Juli stopped brooding over the death of Shushila and began to look forward instead of back, and to realize that there was nothing to be gained by continuing to mourn. Mourning could not bring the dead back to life, and it was not as though she had anything to reproach herself for. She had done everything she could for Shu-shu, and she should take comfort from that and have the courage to put the black years and the beloved ghost of her little sister behind her.

As a first step, he had asked Red to give them the use of the poop deck above his cabin, and that good-natured man had not only agreed to do this, but had also arranged for the deck to be screened off with canvas for greater privacy, and provided with a small awning that would afford shade by day and protection from the dew by night.

Ash had expected the bride to put up a certain amount of opposition to his plans for her emancipation, and been prepared to coax and persuade her into acceptance. But that had not been necessary. Anjuli had agreed to spend the greater part of her days on deck rather than in the cabin. But with a listlessness that conveyed such a total lack of interest that he had had the sudden and startled impression that her thoughts were elsewhere, and that the coming night— their first as man and wife—held no special significance for her, but was merely another night; so what did it matter whether she spent it on deck with him or by herself in the cabin? For a terrible moment he had actually been afraid that she would, if given the choice, prefer the latter, and he had not dared ask her for fear of what she might say.

His confidence in his ability to make her forget the past and be happy again evaporated, and he found himself wondering if she still had any love for him at all, or if the events of the past few years had worn it away as the wind and water will wear away an apparently solid rock. All at once he did not know, and terrified by the doubt he turned from her and stumbled out of the cabin, to spend the remainder of the afternoon alone on the poop deck, watching the slow-moving shadows of the sails and dreading the coming night because of the possibility that Juli might reject him—or submit to him without love, which would be far worse.

Towards sundown the breeze had freshened a little, tempering the salty heat of the day. And as the sea darkened and the sky turned from green to amethyst and then to indigo, the foam under the cut-water began to glimmer with phosphorus, and the stretched canvas showed iron-grey against a brilliant expanse of stars. Gul Baz, wooden-faced, brought a tray of food to the poop deck and later spread a wide, padded *resai* on the planks below the awning, added a few pillows, and observed in a voice devoid of all expression that the Rani-Sahiba—the Memsahib, he should have said—had already eaten, and had the Sahib any further orders?

The Sahib had none; and Gul Baz, having served coffee in a brass cup, went away taking the almost untouched tray with him. The ship's bell sounded the watch, and from somewhere below and amidships Red, who had been celebrating with the Mate and old Ephraim, bellowed up a convivial good-night to which McNulty added something that Ash did not catch, but that appeared to amuse his companions. The sound of their laughter faded and not long afterwards the murmur of voices from the after-deck where the lascars gathered of an evening also ceased, and the night was silent except for the swish of the sea and the monotonous creak and croon of timber and hemp and taut canvas.

Ash sat listening to those sounds for a long time, reluctant to move because he still did not know how his wife would greet him, and he dreaded a rebuff. Today had seen the fulfilment of a dream, and this night should have been the crowning moment of his life. Yet here he sat, racked with doubts and tormented by indecision—and afraid as he had never been afraid before, because if Juli were to turn from him it meant the end of everything. The final and permanent triumph of Shushila.

As he hesitated, putting off the moment of decision, he suddenly remembered Wally declaiming lines written two centuries earlier by one of his many heroes, James Graham, Marquis of Montrose—'*He either fears his fate too much, Or his deserts are small, That puts it not unto the touch, To win or lose it all . . .*'

Ash smiled wryly, and lifting a hand in a gesture of acknowledgement said aloud, as though his friend were actually present: 'All right. I'll go down. But I'm afraid my deserts are minimal.'

The little cabin was brightly lit, and after the cool freshness of the night air unbearably hot and strongly tainted with the smell of lamp oil. Anjuli was standing by the open port-hole looking out across the shimmering beauty of the phosphorescent sea, and she had not heard the latch lift. Something in her pose—in the tilt of her head and the line of the long black plait of hair—reminded him so strongly of the child Kairi-Bai that almost without knowing it, he spoke to her by that name, whispering it very softly: 'Kairi—'

Anjuli whipped round to face the door, and for the flash of a second there was a look in her eyes that could not be mistaken. It was gone immediately: but not before Ash had seen it and recognized it for what it was—stark terror. The same look that he had once seen in the eyes of Dilasah Khan, thief, traitor and sometime trooper of the Guides, when they had cornered him at last in a cleft of the hills above Spin Khab. And in Biju Ram's on a moonlight night three years ago, and more recently in the terrified gaze of six bound and gagged wretches in the *chattri* at Bhithor.

To see it now in Anjuli's was like receiving a sudden and savage attack from a totally unexpected quarter, and the impact of it made his heart miss a beat and drained the blood from his face.

Anjuli's own face was grey with shock and she said with stiff lips: 'Why did you call me that! You have never . . .' Her voice failed her and she put her hands to her throat as though there was a constriction there that prevented her breathing.

'I suppose—because you reminded me of her,' said Ash slowly. 'I'm sorry. I should have remembered that you did not like me calling you by that name. I didn't think.'

Anjuli shook her head, and said disjointedly: 'No. No, it was not that . . . I don't mind . . . It was only . . . You spoke so softly, and I thought . . . I thought it was . . .'

She faltered to a stop, and Ash said: 'Who did you think it was?'

'Shushila,' whispered Anjuli.

The rustling, swishing water beyond the port-hole seemed to take up the lilting syllables of that name and repeat it over and over again, *Shushila, Shushila, Shushila*— And without warning, rage exploded in Ash, and he slammed the door shut behind him and crossing the cabin in two strides, gripped his wife's shoulders and shook her with a violence that forced the breath from her lungs.

'You will not,' said Ash, speaking between clenched teeth, 'say that name to me again. Now or ever! Do you understand? I'm sick and tired of it. While she was alive I had to stand aside and see you sacrifice yourself and our whole future for her sake, and now that she's dead it seems that you are just as determined to wreck the rest of our lives by brooding and moping and moaning over her memory. She's dead, but you still refuse to face that. You won't let her go, will you?'

He pushed Anjuli away with a savage thrust that sent her reeling against the wall for support, and said gratingly: 'Well, from now on you're going to let the poor girl rest in peace, instead of encouraging her to haunt you. You're my wife now, and I'm damned if I'm going to share you with Shu-shu. I'm not having two women in my bed, even if one of them is a ghost, so you can make up your mind here and now; myself or Shushila. You can't have us both. And if Shu-shu is still so much more important to you than I am, or you blame me for killing her, then you had better go back to your brother Jhoti and forget that you ever knew me, let alone married me.'

Anjuli was staring at him as though she could not believe what she had heard, and when she could command her voice she said with a gasp: 'So that is what you thought!'—and began to laugh: high-pitched and hysterical laughter that shook her emaciated body as violently as Ash's hands had done, and that went on and on . . . until Ash became frightened by it and slapped her across the face with an open palm, and she stopped, shuddering and gasping for breath.

'I'm sorry,' said Ash curtly. 'I shouldn't have done that. But I won't have you behaving in the way she did, as well as making her into a sainted idol.'

'You fool,' breathed Anjuli. 'You *fool!*'

She leaned towards him and her eyes were no longer blank and frozen, but bright with scorn. 'Did you speak to no one in Bhithor? You should have done so, and learned the truth; for I cannot believe that it was not common talk in the bazaars. Even if it were not, then the Hakim-Sahib should have known—or at least suspected. And yet *you*—you thought I was grieving for her!'

'For whom, then?' asked Ash harshly.

'For myself, if anyone. For my blindness and folly in not seeing what I should have seen many years ago; and my conceit in thinking that I was indispensable to her. You do not know what it has been like . . . no one can know. When Geeta died there was no one left whom I could trust . . . no one. There were times when I thought that I should go mad from fear, and others when I tried to kill myself and was prevented—because she did not want me to die—that would have been too easy. You warned me once that she was the *Nautch-*girl's daughter and that I must never forget it. But I would not listen to you. I would not believe . . .'

Her voice failed her and Ash took her hands and drew her towards the nearest chair and pushing her down in it, fetched a cup of water. He stood over her while she drank it, and then sat down opposite her on the edge of the bunk and said quietly: 'I never thought of that. It looks as though we have been at cross-purposes. You had better tell me about it, Larla.'

47

It was a long and ugly story, and listening to it Ash was no longer surprised that the widow whom he had snatched from Bhithor bore so little resemblance to the bride he had escorted there barely two years previously.

For he had been right about Shushila. She had indeed proved herself to be a true daughter of Janoo-Rani—the one-time *Nautch*-girl who had never let anything stand in the way of her own desires, or had the least compunction in eliminating anyone she considered to be a stumbling block in her path.

Anjuli told it as though she had known Shushila's mind from the beginning, though that was not so. 'You must understand,' she said, 'that I did not discover this until almost the end. And even then there were many things that only became clear to me after we had escaped from Bhithor and I was lying hidden in the hut behind your bungalow, where I had nothing to do but sit alone and think—and remember. I believe that I know it all now, so if I tell the tale as though I knew Shushila's thoughts and words as well as those of other people with whom I had little or no contact, I am not pretending to a knowledge that I cannot have had. And I did in some sort know them, for few things can be kept secret in the Women's Quarters where there are always a score of watching eyes and listening ears, and too many wagging tongues.

'Geeta and my two serving-women, and a Bhithori servant-girl who also wished me well, told me all that they heard. And so also did that evil creature whom you left bound and gagged in the *chattri*, for she delighted in tale-bearing and would repeat to me anything that she hoped would hurt me. But I could not bring myself to think ill of Shushila . . . I could not. I believed that she was ignorant of the things that were done in her name, and was sure that they were done by order of the Rana, without her knowledge or consent. I believed that those who wished me well and tried to warn me were mistaken, and that those who wished me ill only told me these things in the hope of wounding me; so I closed my eyes and ears against both. But in the end . . . in the end I had to believe. Because it was Shushila herself—my own sister—who told me.

'Concerning the Rana, there too I should have known what might happen, for I had seen it happen before: only then it had been our brother, Nandu. I told you about that, I think. Nandu treated her harshly, and everyone thought she would hate him for it. Instead she became devoted to him, so much so that sometimes I felt a little hurt by her devotion, and was ashamed of myself for feeling so. Yet it taught me nothing. When she fell in love with that evil, perverted and disease-ridden man who was her husband, I could not understand it, though for her sake I was more than happy that it should be so, and being blind to what might follow, I was truly grateful to the gods for permitting her to find happiness in a marriage that she had fought to avoid and dreaded so greatly.'

Ash said: 'I can believe anything of your half-sister, but not that she loved the Rana. She was probably only play-acting.'

'No. You do not understand. Shushila knew nothing of men and therefore was no judge of one. How could she be, when except for her father and her brothers Nandu and Jhoti, and her uncle, whom she saw only rarely, the only ones to frequent the Women's Quarters were the eunuchs, both of them old and fat? She knew only that it is the sacred duty of a woman to submit herself in all things to her husband, to worship him as a god and to obey his commands, to bear him many children and, lest he should turn to light women, to please him in his bed. In this last, as I know, Janoo-Rani arranged for her to receive instruction by a famous courtesan, so that she should not disappoint her husband when the time came for her to marry. It may be that this aroused in her a hunger that I did not suspect, or else she had been born with that hunger, and kept it hidden from me. Whichever way, it was there . . .

'I would not have believed that such a man as the Rana, who preferred young men and boys to women, could have satisfied it. Yet he must have done so, for from the night that he first lay with her she was his—heart and mind and body. And though I did not know it, from that same night she hated me, because I too was his wife, and the eunuchs who wished to make trouble between us had whispered to her that the Rana admired tall women because they were more like men, and had spoken favourably of me. There was no truth in this, but it aroused her jealousy; and even though he treated me like an outcaste whose touch is defilement, and would neither speak to me nor see me, she became afraid (as I too was afraid) that one day he might come to think differently and have me brought to his bed—

if only to wound her, or because he had drunk too much, or was crazed with *bhang* (hashish).'

That first year had been the worst, for though Anjuli had expected little happiness for herself in her new life, it had never occurred to her that Shushila would turn against her. She tried to convince herself that this was only a passing phase that would end when Shu-shu's first passionate adoration of her husband waned and she discovered, as she must, that the god of her idolatry was a middle-aged libertine, rotted by vice and capable of behaviour that in a less exalted personage would be regarded as unacceptable even by criminals.

But then Anjuli had never really understood Shushila. She was not analytical, and she had quite simply loved Shu-shu from the day that she first took the wailing little girl into her arms and was given charge of the child because its mother was disgusted with it for being a daughter and did not wish to be troubled with it. And to Anjuli love was not something to be loaned and taken back again, or proffered in the hope of reward. It was a gift—a part of one's heart, freely bestowed, and with it as a matter of course went loyalty; the two were indivisible.

She had never been blind to Shushila's faults. But she put the larger part of these down to the spoiling and silliness of the Zenana women, and the remainder to the little girl's nervous temperament and unstable health, and therefore did not hold Shu-shu to blame for them; or realize that in them lay the seeds of darker things that could one day come to flower.

The unbalanced passion that the Rana had so unexpectedly aroused in his youthful bride had set those seeds sprouting, and now they grew at a frightening pace, turning almost overnight into monstrous growths, as certain weeds and toadstools will do in the first downpour of the monsoon rains. In the face of this new and absorbing passion, all the love and care and sympathy that Anjuli had lavished upon her little half-sister for years went for nothing, swept away on an ugly tide of jealousy.

The Rana, and all those who had supported him in his endeavours to avoid taking 'the half-caste' to wife, and who now—together with the Zenana women, the eunuchs and the palace servants—resented her elevation to the rank of Rani and were jealous of her influence over the senior wife, combined to humiliate her, until between them Anjuli's life became a misery.

An order was given that in future 'Kairi-Bai' must keep to her rooms and not be permitted to enter those of the Senior Rani unless expressly summoned; the rooms in question being two small, dark and windowless cells, with doors opening out onto an inner court-yard less than ten foot square and surrounded by high walls. Her jewels had been taken from her, together with the greater part of her trousseau, the shimmering saris of silk and gauze being replaced by cheap stuff such as only poor women wear.

It seemed that no weapon was too petty to use against the girl whom Shushila had insisted on bringing with her to Bhithor—and whose only crime was that she too was a wife of the Rana. Anjuli must also be hidden from his gaze, and such looks as she possessed (little enough in the general opinion, but then there was no account-ing for men's tastes) must be spoiled by near starvation to a point where she would appear to be a gaunt and elderly woman. Her title was never to be used, and for fear that faithful old Geeta and her own two serving-women from Karidkote might show her too much consideration and loyalty, they were taken from her and she was given instead one Promila Devi, that same hard-faced creature whom Ash had seen bound and gagged in the *chattri*.

Promila's role had resembled that of gaoler and spy rather than servant, and it was she who had reported that the two serving-women and the *dai* Geeta were still paying surreptitious visits to 'the half-caste' and smuggling extra food to her. All three had been soundly whipped, and after that even loyal old Geeta had not dared approach Anjuli's apartments again. Then Shushila had become pregnant, and for a time her joy and triumph were so great that she became again the Shu-shu of the old days, demanding her half-sister's attendance whenever she felt tired or out of sorts, and behav-ing as if there had never been any break in their relationship. But it did not last . . .

A few weeks later her pregnancy ended, following a violent attack of colic brought on by eating too many mangoes. 'She was always greedy over mangoes,' explained Anjuli. 'My father had them sent up from the plains each year, picked while still green and packed in great *kiltas* among straw, and Shu-shu could never wait until they ripened properly; afterwards she would have terrible pains in her stomach and cry and scream and blame something else—bad *ghee,* or under-cooked rice. Never the mangoes.'

Now once again Shushila had gorged on her favourite fruit, and by doing so lost her longed-for child. She must have known that the fault was her own, but she could not bear to face it, and because this time the results of greed had been far worse than any passing stomach-ache, she did not put the blame on bad or poorly cooked food, but persuaded herself that some jealous person had tried to poison her. And who else, whispered her Bhithori women—fearful that suspicion might alight on one of them—than the co-wife, Kairi-Bai?

'But by good fortune, I had had no chance to touch her food or drink at that time,' said Anjuli, 'as Shu-shu and her ladies had gone to spend three days at the Pearl Palace on the lake-side, and I had not been asked to go with her. Nor had Geeta, so it was not possible to accuse us. But the two who had been my serving-maids were not so fortunate, for they had been of the party and had helped to pick and wash the mangoes, which came from a grove in the palace grounds. Also both of them were from Karidkote, having come to Bhithor in my service, wherefore the Bhithori women, perhaps fearing that the Rana would blame them for allowing his wife to eat unripe mangoes at such a time, and hoping to deflect his anger, banded together to accuse the foreigners.'

Shushila had been frantic with pain and grief and disappointment, and in her frenzy she had listened to the traducers and had the two women poisoned. 'This, Promila told me,' said Anjuli. 'Though it was given out that they had died of a fever, and I strove to believe it was true; I *made* myself believe it. It was so much easier for me to believe that Promila was lying than that Shu-shu could do such a terrible thing.'

Anjuli herself had been banished to one of the smaller houses in the royal park where she had lived in virtual imprisonment, deprived of all comforts and compelled to cook her own scanty food, while the story had been spread about that she had insisted on remaining there for fear of contracting the fever from which her women had died.

By the late autumn, Shushila was again pregnant. But this time her triumph was marred by her fear of losing a second child, for the early stages of this second pregnancy were accompanied by headaches and morning-sickness, and she felt queasy and frightened—and much in need of comfort, which her husband was incapable of supplying. The Rana's strange penchant for his beautiful wife had still not burned out, but he had never had any patience with ill-health in others, and preferred to keep away when Shushila was not feeling well, and this had added another terror to her fear of losing the child: the terror that she might also lose his favour. Tormented by sickness and anxiety, she turned as she had always done to her half-sister, and Anjuli was brought back to the city palace and once again expected to take up her role of comforter and protector as though nothing had happened.

She had done her best, for she still believed that it was the Rana who was responsible for everything that had happened to her, and that even if Shushila was not entirely ignorant of it, she would not dare to take her older sister's part too openly for fear that it might enrage him and merely drive him into acting even more harshly in future. Geeta too was back in favour once more, her recent disgrace apparently forgotten. But the old lady had not appreciated the favour shown her; she had not forgotten the accusations of attempted poisoning that had followed the disastrous outcome of the mango-colic, and as her long experience as a *dai* warned her that Shushila-Bai's new pregnancy was likely to be a short one, she was in deadly terror of being commanded to prescribe a remedy to cure the Rani's headaches or relieve the racking bouts of sickness. When, inevitably, the command came, she took what precautions she could to protect both herself and Anjuli.

'She told me that I must pretend to be gravely displeased with her,' said Anjuli, 'and to let it be known that I would not speak to her or have any dealings with her, so that afterwards no one could say that we had plotted together. She warned me also that I must never touch anything that my sister was given to eat or drink, and I obeyed her, for by this time I too had learned to be afraid.'

For her own protection, Geeta refused to make use of any herbs or drugs from her own store of medicaments, but demanded fresh ones and saw to it that these were pounded and prepared by other women; and always in full view of the Zenana. But it did her no good.

As she had foreseen, there was a second miscarriage. And as before, Shushila raved and wept and cast about for someone to blame, while the Bhithori women, looking for a scapegoat, talked of poison and the Evil-eye. But though they would probably have liked to accuse 'the half-caste' and thereby curry favour with the Rana by giving him an excuse to be rid of her, Geeta and Anjuli had played their part too well for that. Their enmity had been accepted as truth and sniggered over too often for any *volte face* to be possible now. Therefore only Geeta was blamed.

Despite all her precautions, the old *dai* had been accused of causing this second miscarriage by the use of the potions she had prescribed, and that night she had been killed by Promila Devi and one of the eunuchs, and her frail body taken up to a rooftop overlooking one of the flagged courtyards and thrown down so it would appear that she had fallen to her death by accident. 'Though this I did not learn until much later,' said Anjuli. 'At the time, I heard only that she had fallen, and that it was an accident. And I believed it, for even Promila said so . . .'

On the following morning 'the half-caste' had been sent away again: ostensibly at her own request. She was told that 'permission had been granted for her to retire for a time to the Pearl Palace', and she had in fact been taken there—but to what amounted to solitary confinement in a single underground room.

'I was there for almost a year,' whispered Anjuli, 'and in all that time I only saw two persons: the woman Promila, who was my gaoler, and a *mehtarani* (female sweeper and disposer of filth) who was forbidden to speak to me. Nor did I see the sunlight or the sky, or have enough to eat. I was always hungry—so hungry that I would eat every crumb of the food that was given me, even when it was so rancid and foul that it made me ill. And for all those months I was forced to wear the same clothes that I had been wearing when I was taken from the Zenana, because I was given no others; and no water in which I might wash the ones I wore, which became ragged, and stank . . . as did my hair also, and my whole body. Only when the rains broke was I able to clean myself a little, for then the gutters overflowed and flooded the courtyards, and the water came into my cell and lay inches deep on the floor, so that I was able to bathe in it. But when the rains ended it dried up; and—and the winter was very cold . . .'

She shivered violently, as though she were still cold, and Ash heard her teeth chatter.

By the beginning of February, Anjuli had lost all count of time; and now at last she began to give up hope, and for the first time to have doubts about Shushila and to wonder if her half-sister had forgotten her or preferred not to know what had become of her. Surely she could have done something to help? But then there was bad blood in Shu-shu: her mother had contrived the deaths of her own husband and a co-wife, his fourth bride, while her brother Nandu had been guilty of matricide. Was it possible that Shushila too was capable of evil? Anjuli could not bring herself to believe it, for after all Jhoti too was the *Nautch*-girl's child; though it was true that he favoured his father. Yet the doubts persisted, creeping back to torment her however hard she strove to drive them away . . .

No news from the outside world ever penetrated to her cell, for Promila Devi seldom spoke to her, and the *mehtarani* never. She was therefore unaware that her half-sister had again conceived, or that this time there was every hope of a happy conclusion: there had been no recurrence of the headaches and sickness, and when the child quickened the Zenana confidently predicted a safe delivery, while priests and soothsayers hastened to assure the Rana that all the omens pointed to a son. Nor did Promila make any mention of the Rana's illness and the failure of his doctors to effect a cure, or that the Senior Rani had sent for her uncle's Hakim, Gobind Dass, to treat him.

It was only when Anjuli was suddenly brought back to her rooms in the city palace that she learned these things, and wondered if she did not owe her release to Gobind's imminent arrival rather than to any change of heart on the part of the Rana. Her uncle's personal physician would certainly be charged to inquire as to the health and welfare of both Ranis, and to send news of them to Karidkote; so it would obviously look better if the Junior Rani was known to be in the Women's Quarters of the Rung Mahal with her sister, rather than alone in the Pearl Palace.

Whatever the reason she had come back again to the city palace, where she had been given clean clothes to wear and proper food to eat. But she was still not permitted to leave her own room except to walk in the small enclosed courtyard that faced it—a paved space no bigger than a fair-sized carpet and walled in by the backs of other buildings. But after the long months of semi-darkness in the Pearl Palace, it had seemed almost like Paradise to her, particularly as she saw far less of Promila, for she had been given a second serving-maid, a young and unskilled village-girl, afflicted with a hare-lip and so painfully shy that she conveyed the impression of being half-witted. Anjuli would try and coax her to talk, but Nimi never had much to say for herself, and when Promila was present she would tiptoe around like a terrified mouse, dumb with fear and unable to do more than nod or shake her head when spoken to.

Apart from Promila, Nimi and the inevitable *mehtarani,* no other woman ever entered the little courtyard, but Anjuli could hear their shrill voices and laughter on the far side of the surrounding walls, or, of an evening, from the rooftops where they gathered to gossip and enjoy the evening air. It was through listening to them that she learned of the Rana's illness and the arrival of her uncle's Hakim, Gobind Dass, and was seized by a wild hope that he might somehow be able to arrange for her escape.

If she could only manage to speak to him, or to smuggle out a letter to him explaining her predicament, surely he would not refuse to help her? Even if he could do nothing himself he could appeal on her behalf to Jhoti and Kaka-ji, who had always been fond of her and would demand that she be sent back to Karidkote. Or perhaps he could get in touch with Ashok, who could be counted upon to rescue her even if Promila Devi were to be replaced by ten dragons and the entire palace guard.

But try as she would, she could think of no way of getting in touch with Gobind; and she knew that he for his part would never be permitted to cross the threshold of the Zenana however high he might rise in the Rana's esteem; not even if Shushila were dying. Nevertheless she refused to despair; as long as he was in Bhithor there was hope—someday, somehow, by some means, she would be able to make contact with him. Then one warm evening, when the lamps had just been lit and the courtyard was a well of darkness, it seemed that her faith was to be justified for Nimi, bringing in the evening meal, had brought also a letter from the Hakim . . .

It was, as she learned later, the second that he had written to her. But the first had not reached her, for on his arrival in Bhithor Gobind had sent two letters: one to each Rani, with enclosures from Kaka-ji and their brother the Maharajah. He had sent them openly by the hand of the head eunuch, and both had been taken to Shushila, who had read them and torn them up, and returned a verbal reply that purported to come from both Ranis.

This third letter, addressed to Anjuli, had also been handed to Shushila, and as its contents were innocuous (it asked only for an assurance that both sisters were well) it occurred to her that it might be a good move to let Kairi read it and answer it herself. If the answer contained nothing unsuitable, then it would satisfy the Hakim and keep him from making further inquiries: and if it did, it could be used as proof that Kairi-Bai was a traitress who was plotting to stir up trouble between Bhithor and Karidkote, and attempting to blacken the names of her husband and her half-sister.

The letter had been carefully re-sealed and given to the foolish servant girl Nimi, with instructions to hand it to her mistress after dark and to say only that she had received it from a stranger who had stopped her as she was returning from a visit to the bazaar, and promised her much money if she would hand it to the Junior Rani when no one else was present and bring back an answer when she next went out into the city. The girl had been made to repeat the story until she had it by heart, and warned not to add anything to it— or to answer any questions that her mistress might put to her, on pain of having her tongue torn out. On the other hand, if she did as she was told she would be suitably rewarded . . .

The horrifying threat, coupled by the promise of a reward, should have been more than enough to ensure obedience. But though Nimi might be ignorant and timid, she was not devoid of commonsense and she happened to possess more character than the plotters gave her credit for. Anjuli-Bai had been kind to her (which was something that no one else, not even her parents, had ever been before) so not for worlds would Nimi harm her—and that harm was intended she was sure. Why else would she have been commanded to relate this foolish tale of a stranger, and threatened with torture if she failed to do so? She would deliver the letter, but she would also tell her mistress exactly how she had come by it, and what she had been told to say—leaving it to Anjuli-Bai in her wisdom to decide what to do about it.

That last had not been easy. Anjuli feared a trap and could not be sure who was setting it: was Nimi playing her false, or was the girl's story true? If it was, it confirmed those doubts she had about Shushila, and meant that Shushila had indeed turned against her . . . It was still hard to believe that, yet harder to believe that Nimi was lying, and if she was not . . . ? Perhaps it would be better to play safe and do nothing at all. Yet on consideration, Anjuli realized that if Nimi had not warned her, she would have been only too ready to believe that the letter had reached her in the way described, and would have answered it. Therefore she could be reasonably certain that if she did nothing, Nimi would be suspected of putting her on her guard, and probably tortured into confessing as much.

Paper and pen having been procured, Anjuli had composed a courteous and colourless reply, thanking the Hakim for his inquiry and assuring him that to the best of her knowledge her sister the Senior Rani was in good health, and she herself was well. Nimi had duly delivered the note to Shushila, who had read it and sent it on to

Gobind; and the next time Nimi visited her parents she had dropped the suggestion that if one of them could devise a method of approaching the doctor from Karidkote in secret, there might be much money to be made by using her as a go-between—an idea that had not been her own, but Anjuli's. The bait had been snapped up, and thereafter Nimi had carried other letters from Gobind to the Junior Rani, and Anjuli had replied to them—though still with extreme caution, for she could not be sure that Nimi was not watched, or that this might not be another and more devious trap.

But Shushila was unaware of the correspondence. Having seen her half-sister's reply to the first letter, she had apparently come to the conclusion that imprisonment and harsh treatment had reduced Kairi to such a state of cowed subjection that there was nothing to be feared from her, and now Anjuli was informed that provided she did not enter the Senior Rani's apartments or the gardens, there was no reason why she should not go freely about the Women's Quarters again if she chose to do so.

As the time of the confinement approached, the Zenana women became infected by a heady mixture of anxiety and excitement, and the tension mounted daily until even Anjuli, a disregarded spectator, was disturbed by it and began to fear what its effect must be on her highly strung sister. But to everyone's astonishment, Shushila alone remained immune from the mass emotion. Her spirits had never been higher, and far from giving way to nerves—as anyone acquainted with her would have expected—she continued to glow with health and beauty, and apparently had no qualms. Only Anjuli, learning of this from the chatter of the women, suspected that the reason for it could be traced to those two miscarriages, both of which had occurred so early that they could not in fact be termed 'miscarriages' at all.

She thought it probable (and in this she was right) that Shu-shu had been encouraged to believe—or had persuaded herself to believe? —that the comparatively mild discomforts she had suffered then were all that she need expect now, and that neither the new *dai* nor any of her women had summoned up the courage to undeceive her. It was when the labour pains began that the real trouble would start—and this time there would be no Geeta to help her, and no loving half-sister to cling to for comfort and support.

Shushila's pains had begun shortly before ten o'clock on a warm spring night. And all through the following day, and for part of the next night, her agonized screams rang through the Zenana Quarter and echoed eerily along the colonnades surrounding the gardens. At some time during that interminable day one of her women, grey-faced from fear and lack of sleep, had come running to Anjuli and gasped out that she must come at once—the Rani-Sahiba was calling for her.

There had been nothing for it but to obey. Though Anjuli was under no illusion as to why Shushila should suddenly wish to see her: Shu-shu was in pain and very frightened, and it was the pain and fear that had impelled her to send for the one person who had never failed her and whom she knew, instinctively, would not fail her now. Nor was Anjuli ignorant of the risks she ran in entering her sister's apartments at such a time. If anything went wrong someone would be blamed for it, and it would not be the gods or natural causes, or any of the Bhithoris: it would be pinned on her. This time it would be Kairi-Bai, 'the half-caste', who from spite or jealousy or a desire to be revenged for the way in which she had been treated, had put the Evil-eye on the child or on its mother, and would be made to pay for it.

Yet even knowing that—and had it been possible to refuse to go to Shushila which it was not—she would still have gone. Only someone deaf or stony-hearted could have remained unmoved by those harrowing screams, and Anjuli was neither. She had hurried to Shushila's side, and for the remainder of that agonizing labour it was to her hands that Shushila had clung; dragging at them until they were sore and bleeding and imploring her to call Geeta to stop the pains . . . poor Geeta who had supposedly broken her neck in a fall, over a year ago.

The new *dai* who had replaced Geeta was a capable and experienced woman, but she lacked her predecessor's skill with drugs. Moreover she had never before been required to deal with a patient who not only made no attempt to help herself, but did everything in her power to prevent anyone else from doing so.

The Senior Rani flung herself from side to side, shrieking and screaming with ear-splitting abandon and clawing wildly at the faces of those who strove to restrain her, and had it not been for the timely arrival of her half-sister she would, in the *dai*'s opinion, have ended by doing herself a serious injury or going out of her mind. But the despised co-wife had succeeded where everyone else had failed, for though the screams continued they were less frequent, and presently the frantic girl was striving to bear down as the pains waxed and to relax when they waned, and the *dai* breathed again and began to hope that all might yet be well.

The day ebbed into evening and once again it was night; but few in the Women's Quarters were able to sleep, while those in the birth-chamber were unable even to snatch a mouthful of food. By now Shushila was exhausted, and her throat so sore and swollen that she could no longer scream but only lie still and moan. But she continued to cling to Anjuli's hands as though to a life-line, and Anjuli, aching with weariness, still bent above her, encouraging her, coaxing her to swallow spoonfuls of milk in which strengthening herbs had been brewed, or to sip a little spiced wine; soothing, petting and cajoling her as she had done so often in the past.

'. . . and for a while—for a short while,' said Anjuli, telling the story of that frenetic night, 'it was as though she was a child again and we were friends once more, as in the old days; though even then I knew in my heart that this was not so, and that it would never be so again . . .'

Apart from Shushila's uninhibited and hysterical behaviour, there had been no major complications, and when at long last, just after midnight, the child was born, it came into the world very easily: a strong, healthy infant who bawled lustily and beat the air with tiny waving fists. But the *dai*'s face paled as she lifted it, and the women who had pressed forward eagerly to witness the great moment drew back and were silent. For the child was not the longed-for son that the soothsayers had so confidently promised, but a daughter.

'I saw Shushila's face when they told her,' said Anjuli, 'and I was afraid. Afraid as I have never been before: for myself . . . and for the babe also. For it was as though the dead had come back to life and it was Janoo-Rani who lay there: Janoo-Rani in one of her white rages, as cold and as deadly as a king cobra. I had never seen the resemblance before. But I saw it then. And I knew in that moment that no one in the room was safe. Myself least of all . . . Shushila would strike out like a tigress who has been robbed of its cubs—as she had struck twice before (yes, that too I knew now) when she had been disappointed of a child. But this time it would be worse: this time her rage and disappointment would be ten times greater, because she had carried this child for its full time and been assured that it must be a son, and having endured agony beyond anything she had ever dreamed of to give it birth, it was a daughter.'

Anjuli shuddered again and her voice sank to a whisper. 'When they would have given the babe to her, she stared at it with hatred, and though she was hoarse from screaming and so weak that she could barely whisper, she summoned up breath to say: "An enemy has done this. It is not mine. Take it away—and kill it!" Then she turned her face from it and would not look at it again, though it was her own child, her first-born: bone of her bone and flesh of her flesh. I could not have believed that anyone . . . that any woman . . . But the *dai* said that it was often so with those who had endured a hard labour and were disappointed of a son. They would speak wildly, but it meant nothing; and when they were rested and had held their infants in their arms they came to love them tenderly. But—but I knew my sister better than the *dai* did, and was even more afraid. It was then I think that I came near to hating her . . . yet how can one hate a child, even a cruel one?—and children can be far crueller than their elders because they do not truly understand—they only feel, and strike out, and do not see the end; and Shu-shu herself was little more than one. But I feared her . . . I feared her . . .'

The exhausted *dai* had given Shushila a strong sleeping draught, and as soon as it had taken effect the other women had crept away to spread the dire news to the waiting Zenana, while a trembling and reluctant eunuch had left to inform the sick Rana that he had become the father of yet another daughter. Anjuli had stayed for a while to allow the *dai* to get some rest, and had returned to her own rooms before Shushila awakened; and it was then that she had written that letter to Gobind, imploring his help for Shushila, and begging him to use his influence with the Rana to see if a nurse, an *Angrezi* one, could be sent for immediately to take charge of the mother and child. 'I thought that if perhaps one of them could be brought to Bhithor, she might be able to cure Shushila of her hate and her rages, which were in some way a sickness, and to persuade her that no one was to blame for the sex of the child; least of all the child itself.'

Gobind had received that letter, but no European woman had been summoned to Bhithor; and in any case, admitted Anjuli, there would not have been time. The Zenana was full of rumours and those that came to her ears confirmed her worst fears: Shushila had not repeated her wild outburst against the child, but she still refused to see it, explaining her refusal by saying that the infant was so frail and sickly that it could not possibly live for more than a few days at most, and she dared not face further pain and grief by becoming deeply attached to a child that must shortly be reft from her.

But at least a dozen women had been present when the child was born, and all had seen it and heard its first cries. Nevertheless, the rumour that it was a frail and sickly infant who was not expected to live was repeated so often that even those who had good reason to know otherwise began to believe it; and soon there were few in Bhithor who had not heard that the poor Rani, having been disappointed of a son, must now suffer the added grief of losing her daughter.

'I do not know how it died,' said Anjuli. 'Perhaps they let it starve to death. Though being a strong child that might have taken too long, so they may have chosen a quicker way . . . I can only hope so. But no matter whose hand did the work, it was done by Shushila's orders. And then—then the day after the child's body was carried to the burning-ground, three more of her women and the *dai* also fell ill and were taken away from the Zenana in *dhoolis*—for fear, it was said, that the sickness might spread. Later it was rumoured that all four died, though that may not have been true. At least they did not return again to the Women's Quarters; and when it became known that the ailing Rana had suffered a relapse, they were forgotten in all the turmoil and anxiety that followed, because at such a time who could trouble themselves to inquire what had happened to a few unimportant Zenana women?'

Shushila, who had recovered very quickly from her ordeal, flatly refused to believe that her husband's illness could not be cured. Her faith in her uncle's Hakim remained unshaken and she insisted that the relapse was no more than a temporary set-back, and that another month would see the Rana on his feet again and completely recovered: it was unthinkable that this should not be so. In the meantime she turned her attention to repairing the ravages of pregnancy and parturition, and regaining the slenderness that had previously delighted him, so that when he was well again he would think her as beautiful as ever—and have no eyes and no thoughts for anyone else.

Not until the very end could she be brought to believe that he was dying, and when finally she was forced to believe it, she tried to go to him so that she might hold him in her arms and shield him with her own body from this enemy that threatened him. She would fight Death itself for his sake—and she had fought with teeth and nails against those who had prevented her from running to his bedside.

Her fury and despair had been so terrible to see that her women had fled from her and hidden themselves in the furthest and darkest rooms of the Zenana, while the eunuchs listening outside her door shook their heads and muttered that she was deranged and should be put under restraint. But when the first frenzy of grief had spent itself she shut herself away in her apartment to pray, refusing to eat or drink or to allow anyone to approach her.

It must have been during this time that she made up her mind to die a suttee, and also what she intended to do about her half-sister. For when the news was brought to her that her husband was dead, her plans had been made. She had apparently sent at once for the Diwan, and speaking to him in the presence of the chief eunuch and the woman Promila Devi (who had been at pains to describe that interview to Anjuli) had informed him that she intended to die on her husband's pyre.

She would follow the bier on foot, but she would go alone. 'The half-caste' could not be permitted to defile the Rana's ashes by burning with him, for being no true wife it was not fitting that she should share the honour of becoming suttee. Other arrangements would be made for her . . .

Even the Diwan must have shuddered as he listened to those arrangements, but he had not opposed them, possibly because his failure to have 'the half-caste's' marriage contract repudiated and the woman herself sent back dowerless to her home still rankled, and that if he thought of her at all it was with enmity and resentment, and anger at his own defeat. At all events he had agreed to everything that the Senior Rani had decreed, before hurrying away to consult with the priests and his fellow councillors as to the funeral arrangements. When he had gone, Shushila sent for her half-sister.

Anjuli had not seen her sister since the night of the child's birth, or had any message from her. And when the summons came she imagined that she had been called because Shu-shu was frantic with grief and terror, and desperately in need of support. She did not believe that there would be any talk of suttee, for Ashok had told her that the Raj did not permit the burning of widows and that there was now a law forbidding it. So there was no need for Shushila to fear that she would be forced to die on her husband's pyre. 'But this time I did not go to her willingly,' said Anjuli.

Until recently she had been able to believe, or had made herself believe, that Shushila was innocent of much that had been imputed to her; but now she knew better—not only with her head but in her heart. Yet she could not refuse the summons. She had expected to find the new-made widow weeping and distraught, her hair and clothing torn and her women wailing about her. But there had been no sound from the Senior Rani's apartments, and when she entered there was only one person there: a small erect figure that for a moment she did not even recognize . . .

'I would not have believed that she could look like that. Ugly, and evil—and *cruel*. Cruel beyond words. Even Janoo-Rani had never looked like that, for Janoo had been beautiful and this woman was not. Nor did it seem possible that she could ever have been beautiful —or young. She looked at me with a face of stone and asked me how I dared come into her presence showing no signs of grief. For in this too I had sinned: it was intolerable to her that I should escape the agony of grief that was tearing at her own heart . . .

'She said . . . she told me . . . she told me everything: how she had hated me from the moment she fell in love with her husband, because I too was his wife and she could not endure the thought of it; that she had had me starved and imprisoned to make me pay for that crime, and also in order that I might look old and ugly so that if by chance the Rana should remember my existence, he would turn from me in disgust: that she had ordered the killing of my two serving-maids, and of old Geeta . . . She threw it all in my face as though each word was a blow, and as though it eased her own pain to see me suffer—and how could I *not* suffer? When—when she had finished she told me that she had resolved to become suttee, and that the last thing I would ever see would be the flames uniting her body with her husband's, because she had given orders that when I had seen it my eyes were to be put out with hot irons, and afterwards—afterwards I would be taken back to the Zenana to spend the rest of my life in darkness—as a drudge.

'I—I tried to reason with her. To plead with her. I went on my knees to her and begged her in the name of all that lay between us— the years . . . the tie of blood and the affection we had had for each other in the past, the love—but at that she laughed, and summoning the eunuchs, had me dragged away . . .'

Her voice failed on the last word, and in the silence that followed Ash became aware once more of the sound of the sea and all the many small ship noises; and that the cabin smelled strongly of hot lamp oil and the fried *puris* that had been served with the evening meal and that there was still a lingering odour of stale cigar-smoke to remind him that this had been Red's cabin for many years. But up on the deck it would be cool and the stars were once again familiar ones, for the skies of the south had been left behind—and with them Bhithor and its harsh stony hills, and all that had happened there.

It was over—finished. *Khutam hogia!* Shushila was dead, and all that remained to show that she had ever lived was the print of her small hand on the Suttee Gate of the Rung Mahal. Sarji, Gobind and Manilal had gone; and Dagobaz too . . . They were all part of the past, and though he would not forget them, it would be best not to think of them too often until enough time had passed to allow him to do so calmly, and without pain.

He drew a long slow breath, and reaching out, took Anjuli's hands in his and said gently: 'Why didn't you tell me all this before, Larla?'

'I could not. It was . . . it was as though my heart and mind had been so bruised that I could not endure any more emotion. I only wanted to be quiet; and not to have to answer questions and to put it all into words. I had loved her for so long, and I-had thought that she —that she was fond of me. Even when I thought that I hated her, I found that I could not forget what she had once meant to me . . . how sweet she had been as a child. And then—then when I saw her walk to the pyre, and knew what would happen when she realized what she had done and that there was no escape, I—I could not bear to have her suffer so terrible a death. *I could not!* Yet if I had only gone when you wished, perhaps all those others would not have died. Their blood was on my head and I could not bear it—or bear to hear my own voice relating things that—that even now I can hardly believe can really have happened. I wanted to hide it all away . . . to bury it and pretend that it could not be true. But it would not stay buried.'

'It will now, my Heart,' said Ash, and pulled her up into his arms. 'Oh, my love, I have been so afraid. So terribly afraid. You do not know! All this time I have thought that you were grieving for her, and that you had found out that I could not replace her because she had taken all your love and there was none left for me. I thought I had lost you—'

His voice broke, and suddenly Anjuli's arms were tight about his neck and she was crying, 'No, no, no—it was not so: I have always loved you—always, always. More than anyone in the world—' And then the tears came.

But this time Ash knew that they were healing tears, washing away some of the horror and bitterness and guilt from her bruised heart, and easing the terrible tension that had held her in a vice-like grip for so long. When at last they were spent, he lifted her head and kissed her, and presently they went out together into the cool, star-spangled darkness, and for that night at least, forgot the past and the future and everything and everyone but each other.

48

Ten days later, on a still and pearly morning before sunrise, the *Morala* dropped anchor off Keti on the delta of the Indus, and landed three passengers: a burly Pathan, a slim, clean-shaven man whose dress and bearing proclaimed him to be a citizen of Afghanistan, and a woman in a bourka who was presumably the wife of one or other of them.

The Afghan dress had been acquired on the previous day by Gul Baz, in the course of a brief stop at Karachi where the *Morala* had unloaded a small consignment of dressed hides and dried fruit, taken on, with the grain, a week earlier at Chahbar. It was Red who had suggested its purchase, for Sind was a harsh land, much of it sparsely inhabited, and its people were not noted for hospitality towards strangers: 'But they're leary of Afghans, an' as from wot you've tole me, you can pass yoreself orf as one any day of the week, I'd advise you to do it now. It'll be a sight safer.'

So Ash had gone over the side wearing Afghan dress, and whether it was due to this, or merely a matter of luck, the long journey from the coast of Sind to Attock had been accomplished in safety, if not in comfort.

A *dundhi,* a flat-bottomed river boat normally used for carrying cargo, hired on their behalf through the agency of one of Red's many friends in the coastal-trading business, had taken them up the Indus, initially under sail (during those hours when the tide was in their favour) and later, if the wind failed, by means of a tow rope. Teams of coolies had pulled the clumsy craft forward from village to village, a fresh team taking over each evening while the previous one turned homeward, each man clutching the few small coins that were doled out for his day's labour by the owner of the boat, the *manji,* who with his two sons formed the permanent crew.

In this wise they travelled slowly up the enormous mile-wide river. Past Jerak and Naidarabad and Rohri, to Mithankote where the waters of four of the five great rivers of the Punjab, the Sutlej, Ravi, Chenab and Jhelum, channelled by the Chenab, join the Indus on their way to the sea—and on northward past Dera Ghazi Khan, with the mountains of Baluchistan and Zohb rising up along the western horizon and the flat, burning plains of the Sind Sagar Doab stretching away eastward, to the junction of the Luni River below Dera Ismail Khan. From where, on a night of brilliant moonlight, they saw the crest of the Takht-i-Suliman, a far point of silver, high above the foothills of Baluchistan, and Anjuli had wept tears of joy at seeing snow again.

At first, irked by inactivity, Ash and his bride would leave the boat and walk for part of the way. But by now the hot weather was upon them, and even in the cool of the morning, or towards sunset, the heat turned the bourka into a stifling tent. Then Ash had managed to buy two horses, and after that they rode each day, ranging far afield so that the bourka could be thrown back, and returning to the boat at mid-day to rest in the shade of the small shelter constructed out of planks and matting that did duty for a cabin.

Ash had wished to buy a third horse for Gul Baz. But Gul Baz had no desire to go riding around the countryside. He thoroughly approved of this leisurely method of travelling and enjoyed spending his days sitting in lordly ease under an awning in the bows, though he would ride one of the horses and take the other on a leading rein whenever the Sahib and the Rani-Sahiba decided to travel on the boat.

Time moved slowly on the river, but for Ash and Anjuli it could not move slowly enough, and if they could have had their way the journey would never have ended. The discomforts (and there were many) counted for nothing compared to the delight of being together and free to talk and laugh and make love without fear.

The food might be plain and ill-cooked, but Anjuli, who had known starvation, found no fault with it. And after sleeping for more than a year on the dank stone floor of an underground cellar, what did it matter that the single string bed provided by the *manji* should prove to be so densely populated by bugs that Ashok had thrown it overboard, and thereafter they had slept on the floor with only a thin *resai* (quilt) between them and the rough planks?

As for their tiny, ramshackle cabin with its Noah's Ark roof and matting walls, it might be exceedingly hot and far from comfortable; but then her room in the Women's Quarters of the Rung Mahal had been far hotter, for no breeze ever reached it, while here the matting could be rolled up at will—and there outside lay the river and the white sandbanks, with beyond them the wide, sun-scorched, empty spaces that stretched away and away until they were lost in the heat-haze or made magical by moonlight. To one who had lived penned

up in a small windowless room in the Rung Mahal and endured
months of solitary confinement in a dark cellar, this alone was a
never-failing source of wonder.

For Ash it was enough to see his wife lose her skeletal thinness
and regain much of the beauty and health and serenity that the years
in Bhithor had taken from her. Though this had not happened overnight: that would have been too much to expect. The road back to
normality had been a slow one; almost as slow as their present
progress up the 'Father of Rivers'. But the telling of the true story of
those years had been the first step, and those long, peaceful days on
the *Morala*—the hours of talk and the hours of companionable silence, the shared laughter and the wonderful star-splashed nights
when they made love and fell asleep to the music of the waves and
sea winds—had all helped to heal the cruel wounds that Shushila and
Bhithor had inflicted. Ash watched his wife come alive again and was
happier and more deeply content than he would have believed possible.

The Father of Rivers ran deep and wide: so wide that it often
seemed more like an inland sea than a river, and there were days
when the heat-haze or blowing sand made it impossible to see the far
bank—or either bank, if the boat was under sail. Much of the countryside was barren and desolate, but palm trees, oleanders, tamarind
and tamarisk grew by the river, and even where there were no towns
or villages, there was always life to be seen.

Myriads of birds preyed on the swarms of *chilwa* and other small
fish who teemed in the shallows. Mud-turtles and *ghariyal*—the long-
snouted, fish-eating alligators of the Indian river—basked on the
sandbanks, and sometimes a porpoise could be seen leaping and
turning in deep water, or a great salmon-like *mahseer,* its silver-pink
sides flashing in the sun. In the late evening, when the river ran gold
and the hills of Baluchistan seemed to move nearer across the shadowed plains, flight after flight of wild duck, geese, pelicans and
paddy-birds would pass overhead, while parties of nomads with their
goats and camels would straggle past on their way to new camping
grounds. And at dusk the deer and antelope, and creatures such as
pig and jackal and porcupine, would come down to drink.

Sometimes they saw bands of horsemen far out across the plain,
galloping furiously towards a horizon that was hidden by dust. And
on the river itself there were always other boats: country-boats laden
with fodder or grain, wood, sugar-cane or vegetables, and others

crammed with woolly, bleating cargoes of sheep or goats; ferry-boats plying their trade and fishermen paying out their nets or setting fish-traps; and during the earlier days, an occasional river steamer huffing and puffing its way upstream under a cloud of black smoke, or sweeping past with the current on its way to the coast.

Lessons in English and Pushtu, begun on the *Morala,* became part of the daily routine, and Anjuli proved to be an apt pupil. She made rapid progress, astonishing Ash by the quickness and accuracy with which she assimilated words and phrases and mastered the compli-cated rules of grammar, and he realized that she must always have had a good brain but until now had lacked the opportunity to use it—women in purdah not being expected to interest themselves in any-thing but domestic matters. But now that she had escaped from the almost exclusively feminine world of the Zenana, her intelligence leapt to meet the challenge, and by the time the Kurram hills and the Salt Ranges of Kundian came into sight, she could express herself in her husband's language with a fluency that did credit to her instruc-tor: and even more to her own powers of concentration.

Realizing that they would reach Kala Bagh almost a month before his leave was up, Ash had planned to tie up the boat at some pleas-ant spot and spend the time exploring the countryside on horseback rather than returning to Mardan before he need do so. But with the Salt Range closing in to hem the river between high banks and shut out the breeze, even the nights were no longer cool, while the days had become so hot that the cliffs of rock salt and the blinding white sand by the water's edge, the ground underfoot and even the planks of the boat felt as though they had come fresh-baked from a furnace.

In these conditions, the sooner he got Juli under a proper roof and into a house where there were solid walls and wide verandahs to shut out the cruel heat, and *punkahs* and *kus-kus* tatties to cool the air, the better. And it was then that he remembered Zarin's aunt, Fatima Begum, and the quiet house that stood back from the Attock road, protected by high walls and a garden full of fruit trees. He could leave Juli there in safety, and though it meant that he would have to take the Begum into his confidence, he felt sure that the old lady could be relied upon to keep the matter secret, and also to think of some story that would satisfy the curiosity of her household and pre-vent her servants from talking.

He would get Zarin to arrange it; and that same evening Gul Baz set off on Ash's horse to ride with all speed to Mardan, charged with delivering a verbal message to Zarin and a letter to Hamilton-Sahib, after which he would rejoin the party at Attock. The distance across country was probably no more than seventy *koss,* so two days should be enough to bring him to Mardan, and a night's ride would cover the rest. But it had taken the best part of a week for Ash and Juli to complete the last part of the journey to Attock, for above Kala Bagh the Indus, that for hundreds of miles divides its waters into two, three and sometimes four separate streams—each one larger than an English river—narrows into a single one where a boat must fight its way up against the full force of the current. So that even though the wind had favoured them it was not until six days later, and well after midnight, that they came within reach of Attock. And once again, as on his last visit there, Ash came to Fatima Begum's house by moonlight: only this time he did not come alone.

The path that led up to it was inches deep in dust, but either the horse's bridle chinked or else a nail in Ash's *chuppli* clicked against a pebble, for before he reached the gate it creaked open, and a man moved forward to greet him: '*Stare-mah-sheh!*' said Zarin. 'I told Gul Baz that you would not face that last mile through the gorges.'

'*Khwah-mah-sheh?*' replied Ash, returning the conventional greeting. 'You were right. My courage failed at the sound of the water and the sight of those whirlpools, and I preferred to come dry-shod across the hills.'

He dropped the reins and turned to help Anjuli down from the saddle, and though he knew that she was exhausted by the heat and the hours of riding at a walk along precipitous ways after a long day in the stifling shelter on the boat, he did not attempt to support her, since in the East a respectable woman, when visiting abroad, is an anonymous figure to whom no attention should be paid, and Ash knew that in a country where most people sleep out of doors in the hot weather, the night is apt to be full of eyes. For the same reason he made no introductions, but turned away to take the horse's bridle and follow Zarin through the gate, leaving Anjuli to bring up the rear in the time-honoured fashion that prevails throughout Islam.

The household had evidently retired to bed, but a faint light gleamed in the inner courtyard where Fatima Begum's most trusted attendant, an elderly close-mouthed woman, had been waiting, lantern in hand, to whisk Anjuli away to an upper room. When they had gone, the two men turned to take stock of each other by the light of an oil lamp that had been left burning in a niche by the door; and both thought sharply, and with a curious feeling of loss, how greatly the other had changed since their last meeting in that same house . . .

It was barely two years, yet there were grey hairs in Zarin's beard that had not been there before. And new lines too—one a long, puckered scar that ran from his temple to the corner of his mouth, barely missing his right eye: the mark of a slashing stroke from a tulwar, received, among other wounds, during the attack on Sipri. He had been promoted to Risaldar after that action, and bore in addition to the scar the indefinable stamp that authority and responsibility give to those upon whom they fall.

In Ash the change was less obvious, and possibly someone less well acquainted with him would have missed it, but to Zarin it was striking. His face no longer wore the strained, restless, reckless look that Zarin had found so disturbing at their last meeting, and though it was thinner than ever, the eyes under the black brows were quiet and contented. 'He has found happiness,' thought Zarin with foreboding. 'This alters everything.'

They looked long and searchingly at each other, and a stranger seeing them would have said that they were saying farewell rather than greeting each other after a long absence—and in a sense would have been right, for both were realizing a little sadly, that someone they had once known had gone for ever. Then Ash smiled, and the brief moment of regret vanished. They embraced in the old manner, and Zarin took down the lamp and led the way to a room where cold food had been set ready, and they ate and talked. And talked . . .

Ash learned that Koda Dad had not been too well of late, but that Zarin had sent him word of Ash's arrival and was sure that if he felt well enough to travel he would set out for Attock immediately. Hamilton-Sahib had been away on leave, and Gul Baz was not (as Ash had supposed) waiting on the river bank for the boat, but somewhere in the vicinity of Abbottabad where he had gone in search of the Sahib, who was reported to be on his way back from the Kangan Valley.

'He said you had given him a letter for Hamilton-Sahib and told him to give it into the Sahib's own hand,' said Zarin. 'So, finding him gone, he took it upon himself to go to Abbottabad. He must have met with some delay on the road. Or perhaps Hamilton-Sahib has not yet reached there and Gul Baz has gone on a little way, knowing that I would be here to meet you. I have sent the gatekeeper to watch for the boat and see that your gear is brought up.'

There had been a good deal of regimental and Frontier gossip to catch up on, for Ash had received no news since Wally's last letter, which had been written nearly three months ago, and Zarin had also talked at length of the prospects of war with Afghanistan. But Ash did not touch upon his own doings, or make any mention of Anjuli; and Zarin was careful to ask no questions. That subject could wait until such time as Ashok felt able to discuss it, which would probably be after a good night's rest—something he was unlikely to have had in the raging heat of the Indus gorges.

Ash had indeed slept well that night, and during the following day he had told the whole story of the past months, from the time of Gobind and Manilal's sudden appearance in Ahmadabad to the day when Anjuli had become his wife in a brief ceremony on board the *Morala,* together with a short sketch of the events of three years ago that had led up to it: first to Zarin and later, of necessity, to Fatima Begum, both of whom had been deeply interested.

Zarin had, to some extent, been forewarned; Gul Baz having told him that the woman for whom the Sahib requested Fatima Begum's hospitality was a high-born Hindu widow who he had brought with him from the south, and with whom he had been through some sort of ceremony that purported to make them man and wife (though as this had resembled no form of *Shadi* that Gul Baz had ever heard of, there being no priest and the whole affair lasting less than five minutes, it need not be taken seriously). But it had naturally not occurred to Zarin that the widow in question was a woman he himself knew, or rather one whom he had known, long ago, as the *Feringhi*-Rani's daughter, little Kairi-Bai.

The news that Ashok regarded himself as married to her saddened him, for Zarin had hoped to see his friend contract a suitable marriage to some girl of his own race who would solve his problem of identity, and breed strong sons to follow their father into the Guides and be ideal officers, as they could not fail to inherit his love and understanding of India and its peoples. Yet if he remained faithful to Kairi-Bai this would never come about, since his children would be both illegitimate and half-caste (Zarin too did not consider that the shipboard ceremony described by Gul Baz could be binding), and as such, unsuited to enter the Corps.

On the other hand it was a relief to know that despite his insistence that the ceremony was legal and Kairi-Bai his lawfully wedded wife, Ashok intended to keep the marriage a close secret and install the bride in some discreet little house in Hoti Mardan, where provided he was careful he would be able to visit her without anyone in the cantonment being aware of it. His reasons for acting in this sensible manner obviously did not include any doubts as to the validity of his marriage, but were entirely due to his fears for his so-called wife's safety—fears that Zarin, remembering Janoo-Rani and all that he had been told about Bhithor, considered to be justified. Yet whatever the reasons, he could only be grateful that they had been strong enough to prevent Ashok from wrecking his career by producing the ex-Rani in Mardan and demanding that the Corps accept her as his wife, for if there was one thing that he, Zarin, was sure of, it was that not one of them, from the Commandant-Sahib down to the newest-joined recruit, would have done so. And knowing Ashok as he did, he was inclined to feel grateful to the Diwan of Bhithor and his fellow assassins.

Fatima Begum, being a relic of an earlier age, saw nothing out of the way in the Sahib's desire to keep an Indian girl in some quiet little *Bibi-gurh* (women's house) near his place of work, and said as much to her nephew. Such arrangements, said the Begum, were far from uncommon and would bring no discredit upon the Sahib: when had anyone thought the less of any man for keeping a mistress? She dismissed the tale of a marriage with an impatient wave of the hand, for she had been talking to Anjuli, to whom she had taken a strong fancy, and Anjuli herself, despite all Ashok's assurances, had never been able to believe that anything as devoid of ritual and as quickly over as that strange ceremony on board the *Morala* could possibly be binding in law.

Zarin's aunt had insisted that Anjuli and her husband should spend the remainder of the Sahib's leave as her guests, and told her nephew that she herself would see to it that a suitable house was found for the ex-Rani within easy reach of Mardan; one in which she could live quietly and find no difficulty in keeping her true identity a secret, for no virtuous housewife, declared the Begum, would think of prying into the antecedents of a courtesan; and as she would not be setting up in competition with others in that trade, she would be able to live in safety and seclusion.

This last observation had not been repeated to Ash, who had gratefully accepted the offer. He had not been looking forward to spending the next few weeks scouring the countryside in search of a secluded hideaway for Juli, in a temperature that frequently reached a hundred and fifteen degrees at mid-day, and the Begum's house was large, cool and comfortable—and safe.

On the following day, as there was still no sign of either Koda Dad or Gul Baz, Ash set off for Hasan Abdal, hoping to meet Wally on the Abbottabad road. The house was still in darkness when he arose and left his drowsy wife and went very quietly downstairs, but early as it was, Zarin was up and waiting for him in the courtyard, since he too had to be away before first light. Their roads lay in different directions, for Zarin was returning to Mardan, but he had had Juli's mare saddled for Ash, and the two men mounted in silence, and rode out of the gate as the stars began to pale and from somewhere behind them in the Begum's garden a cock crowed—to be answered by another in the town, and that one by a third in the fort by the river, until presently a dozen cocks were crowing.

The air was still cool, but there was no freshness in it, and already it held more than a hint of the coming day's heat, for the stillness was undisturbed by even a breath of wind, and below the town the veil of mist on the river lay motionless above the swirling water that flowed past the walls of Akbar's fort. The riders drew rein at the junction between the lane and the high road, and for a moment or two sat listening, hoping to hear the distant clop of hoof-beats that might herald the arrival of Koda Dad Khan or Gul Baz. But the long white road lay empty, and except for the cocks and the river there was no sound.

'We shall meet them on the road,' said Zarin, answering the unspoken thoughts of both. 'How soon do you expect to be in Mardan?'

'In three weeks' time. So if your father has not already set out, send word to him to stay in his house, and say that I will come to see him as soon as I can.'

'I will do that. But it may be that I will meet him on the way, and if so he will be waiting here for you in my aunt's house when you return. Well, we must be on our way. *Pa makhe da kha,* Ashok.'

'*Ameen sera,* Zarin Khan.'

They touched hands briefly and parted. And two hours later, as the sun rose, Ash passed through Hasan Abdal, and leaving the 'Pindi road, turned left on to the one that leads to the hills and Abbottabad.

Wally had been eating breakfast under a clump of trees by the roadside near the bank of a small stream that crossed it a mile or so above the town, and he had not at first recognized the lean, travel-stained Afridi who pulled up at sight of him and dismounted among the freckled shadows of the acacias.

Book Seven

My Brother Jonathan

49

'I suppose it was because I wasn't expecting you,' explained Wally, plying his friend with stewed tea, hard-boiled eggs and chuppattis. 'Your letter said to meet you at Attock so I expected to find you there all togged up in one of Rankin's best sun-proof suitings, not jogging along in the dust wearing fancy-dress. I always knew you were able to do it, but I hadn't realized that you could even take me in, and I still don't know how it's done, because your face hasn't altered—or not much—and it can't be just the clothes. Yet until you spoke I took you for just another tribesman. How the divil an all do you do the trick?'

'There's no trick about it,' said Ash, gulping hot tea. 'Or if there is it probably lies in being able to think yourself into the mind and skin of whoever you are pretending to be, until you become that person; which isn't difficult for someone like me, who for most of his formative years imagined himself to be a native of this country. Anyway, most people only see what they expect to see, and if they spot a fellow in a tweed-suit and a deer-stalker they automatically think "Englishman", while one in a *shulwa* and turban, with a flower behind his ear and a *kaisora* hanging from his wrist, must of course be an Afridi. It's as simple as that.'

By now the sun was high and the heat already so fierce that it would have been cruelty to take the tired horses any further; for Wally too had been in the saddle since first light, having camped the previous night near Haripur. He had hired a tonga to bring his bearer and his gear down from Abbottabad, and Gul Baz—who had ridden far and fast in the last few days—had been only too pleased to finish the journey in this vehicle while the Sahib took over the horse.

Unlike Wally, Gul Baz had recognized Ash while he was still a good way off, and had instantly made an excuse to remove Wally's bearer Pir Baksh and the tonga driver to a spot further up the road, from where they would be unable to witness the meeting between the Sahib and his friend, which could not fail to arouse the tonga-wallah's curiosity.

In Gul Baz's opinion too many people already knew that Pelham-Sahib could pass as a frontier tribesman. The story of the pursuit of Dilasah Khan had leaked out and been told and re-told with countless additions and embroideries in every bazaar from Peshawar to Rawalpindi, and Gul Baz did not want to hear it revived again. He therefore kept his two companions engaged in talk until Wally called to him by name, when he hurried over to receive his orders and returned saying that the Sahib had met with an acquaintance—an Afridi horse-dealer—and that as the day was too hot for riding he would stay and talk with the man and take the road later. Meanwhile he desired that the servants would go on ahead in the tonga to Attock dâk-bungalow, where they would engage a room and order a meal for him and wait until he arrived: they need not hurry, as he himself did not intend to set out until late in the afternoon.

'Which means that they'll probably spend the next few hours resting at Hasan Abdal, and arrive in Attock only just ahead of us,' said Wally, watching the tonga rattle past and disappear round a bend in the road, before turning back to resume his interrupted conversation with the pseudo-horse-dealer.

They had not seen each other for almost two years, but in spite of all that had happened during that time it was as though they had parted only yesterday and were continuing a conversation that had been temporarily interrupted. The rapport between them remained unchanged and they might almost have been back in their shared quarter in 'Pindi, talking over the day's work; for Ash had refused to launch into any explanations until he had first heard all Wally's news, partly because he wanted to establish the old footing before he told his own, but largely because he knew that once it was told, neither of them were likely to talk of anything else.

So Wally had talked, and Ash had listened and laughed as he was brought up to date on a dozen matters, regimental, social and general. He learned that the Guides were in 'tremendous shape', the Commandant and the other officers the 'best of fellows', and Wigram Battye (recently promoted to Captain) in particular an 'absolute corker'. In fact the words 'Wigram says' appeared with such frequency that Ash was conscious of a fleeting twinge of jealousy, and a regret for the old days when he himself possessed the major share of Wally's admiration—together with the tallest pedestal in his private pantheon. But those days were gone, and Wally had adquired other gods and made other friends; which was not surprising in someone so eminently likeable.

He was talking now with enormous enthusiasm of the Deputy Commissioner of Peshawar—that same Major Cavagnari who had in-

stigated and planned the operation against the Utman Khel tribes-
men in which Zarin had been wounded, and a later one against
Sharkot where Wally had experienced his first taste of active service.
It was immediately clear that the personality and talents of this oddly
named man had made a deep impression on the impressionable
Wally.

'Faith, it's the jewel of a fellow he is, Ash. A real out-and-outer.
His father was a French count who was an aide-de-camp or a military attaché or something of the sort to one of Bonaparte's brothers,
and he speaks Pushtu like a native and knows more about the tribes
than anyone else on the Frontier. And would you believe it, he's actually a kinsman of mine? We're both related to the Lawrences, because Lord John's wife is my mother's sister-in-law, and mother was a
Blacker, and one of the Blackers had a daughter who married a
Frenchman—an officer in the Cuirassiers—and their daughter married
Major Cavagnari's father. Which makes us vaguely related.'

' "Vaguely" sounds right,' murmured Ash satirically. 'Holy Saint
Patrick, what a mixture!'

'Be damned to you for a benighted Sassenach,' retored Wally,
unruffled; and went on to describe the many excellences of his latest
hero while Ash lay back and listened, watching the speaker's face
and thanking heaven that Wally at least had not changed—except in
one respect: the tale of his doings during the past two years did not
include the mention of a single girl's name.

The Guides and matters military obviously filled his thoughts to
the exclusion of all else, and the gay, careless and largely one-sided
love affairs of the 'Pindi days that had inspired so much bad verse
were apparently a thing of the past. If Wally wrote poems now,
thought Ash, they would not be addressed to some damsel's blue
eyes, but would probably be concerned with such abstract subjects as
Patriotism or Immortality. And the next time he fell in love it would
be for ever: he would marry the girl and settle down and raise a
family.

But that would not be for a long while yet. Because it was plain
that at present he was in love with the Guides and with the romance
of Empire—the warring tribesmen and the wild Khyber hills, the
swift night marches and the sudden dawn attack on some fortified
stronghold across the Border, and the discipline and comradeship of
life in a Corps that had never known what it was like to live on a
peace-time footing, but had always been ready to march at a mo-

ment's notice should trouble flare up on that perennially inflammable Frontier.

Wally did not ask what Ash had been doing with himself during his term of attachment to Roper's Horse; the routine activities of a regiment stationed in some peaceful spot such as Ahmadabad being of little interest to either of them; and as Ash had written reasonably often (and most of his letters had contained some reference to the dullness of army life in the peaceful peninsula) Wally concentrated on the more enlivening topic of the Frontier in general and the Guides in particular. Only when that subject had been covered fairly exhaustively did he demand to know why Ash was masquerading in this outfit, and what had possessed him to waste a valuable leave sweating up the Indus on a *dundhi* instead of going on trek as they had planned, or even coming fishing in the Kangan Valley?

'I asked Gul Baz what you'd been up to,' said Wally, 'but all he would say was that "doubtless the Sahib had good reasons for his actions and would explain them to me himself". Well, it's waiting for an explanation I am, ye spalpeen, and if you're wishful to be forgiven, it had better be a good one.'

'It's a long story,' Ash warned him.

'We've got all day,' returned Wally comfortably, and, rolling his coat into a ball to make a pillow, he lay down in the shade and prepared to listen. 'Carry on, Sergeant-Major. You have our ear.'

The story as told to Wally had taken rather longer to tell than the one Zarin had heard on the previous day, for Zarin had known Kairi-Bai and so did not need to be told anything of her background or people, or her childish attachment to the boy, Ashok. But when Ash had first told Wally of his youth in Gulkote he had not thought to mention Kairi-Bai, and later he had purposely concealed the fact that the State of Karidkote, whose princesses he had been charged with escorting to Bhithor, was the same place under a different name. So there was more that had to be told now; and after the first two minutes Wally was no longer lying lazily on his back, but sitting bolt upright, wide-eyed and open-mouthed.

Zarin had listened to that tale without any noticeable change of expression, but it was not so with Wally; he had never been adept at concealing his emotions, and now his handsome, mobile face betrayed his thoughts as clearly as though they had been written there in capital letters; and reading them Ash realized that he had been wrong in thinking that Wally had not changed.

The old Wally would have been enthralled by it and his sympathies would all have been with Ash and the sad little Princess of Gulkote who, like the heroine of a fairy-tale, had suffered much at the hands of a wicked step-mother and a jealous half-sister. But the present Wally had acquired new loyalties and put away many childish things. He had also, as Ash had surmised, fallen in love with the Guides.

The Guides were now his own Corps and an integral part of him, and he genuinely believed that the members of his own squadron were the pick of the Indian Army, and men such as Wigram Battye and Risaldar-Major Prem Singh the salt of the earth. He had been in action with them: learned in their company the terror and the fierce delight of battle, and seen men die—not just any men, the anonymous ones mentioned in brief official reports ('Our casualties were two dead and five wounded'), but men he had known and cracked jokes with, and whose names and faces and problems were familiar to him.

He would no more dream of riding rough-shod over their customs and convictions, or doing anything that might bring the Regiment in which he and they had the honour to serve into disrepute, than he would consider pilfering from the mess funds or cheating at cards. Nor, in the first flush of his love-affair with the Guides and the Frontier, could he conceive of any worse fate than to be expelled from both. Yet if Ash had really married a Hindu widow, this was exactly what he was heading for—with whip and spur.

'Well?' asked Ash when he had finished and Wally had still not spoken. 'Aren't you even going to wish me happy?'

Wally flushed like a girl and said quickly: 'Of course I do. It's only . . .' He did not seem to know how to end the sentence, and abandoned it.

'That I have taken your breath away?' said Ash with an edge on his voice.

'Well, what did you expect?' asked Wally defensively. 'You must admit it's a bit of a facer. After all, I had no idea that those girls you were taking to Bhithor had anything to do with Gulkote, because you never said a word about that, and so I never imagined . . . Well, how could I? Of course I hope you'll be happy; you know that. But . . . but you're still well short of thirty and you know very well that you're not supposed to marry before then without the consent of the Commandant, and—'

'But I have married,' said Ash gently. 'I *am* married, Wally. No one can alter that now. But you needn't worry; I'm not giving up the Guides. Did you really think I would?'

'But once they know—' began Wally.

'They won't know,' said Ash, and explained why.

'Thank God for that!' sighed Wally devoutly when he had finished. 'How dare you frighten the daylights out of me?'

'You're as bad as Zarin. He doesn't give himself away like you, but I could see that even though he knew Juli when she was a little girl, the fact that I had married her shocked him, because she is a Hindu. But I must admit I thought you'd be less prejudiced.'

'What, *me*? An Irishman?' Wally gave a short and mirthless laugh. 'Why, a cousin of mine once wanted to marry a fellow who happened to be a Catholic, and you've no idea the row that blew up over that. The Protestants all went into hysterics about Anti-Christ and the Scarlet Woman of Rome, while the other lot called Mary a heretic and told Michael that if he married her he'd be excommunicated and everlastingly damned, because she wasn't prepared to turn papist herself and wouldn't sign an undertaking that any children she bore should be brought up as Catholics. Yet these were all adult and presumably intelligent people, and every one of them regarded themselves as Christians. Don't talk to me of prejudice! We're all riddled with it, whatever the colour of our skins; and if you haven't found that out yet, faith, I'm thinking you must have been born with blinkers.'

'No, just without that particular form of prejudice,' said Ash thoughtfully. 'And it's too late for me to acquire it now.'

Wally laughed and observed that Ash did not know how lucky he was; and after an appreciable pause, said a little uncertainly and with an unaccustomed hint of diffidence in his voice: 'Could you . . . can you tell me about her? What is she like?—I don't mean what does she look like, I mean what is it you see in her?'

'Integrity. And tolerance—*bardat,* which Koda Dad once told me was a "rare flower". Juli doesn't make harsh judgements, she tries to understand, and make allowances.'

'What else? There must be something else.'

'Of course—though I should have thought that by itself would have been enough for most people. She is . . .' Ash hesitated, searching for words that would describe what Anjuli meant to him, and then said slowly: 'She is the other half of me. Without her, I am not complete. I don't know why this should be, I only know it is so; and that there is nothing I can't tell her, or talk to her about. She can ride like a Valkyrie and she has all the courage in the world, yet at the same time she is like—like a quiet and beautiful room where one can take refuge from noise and storms and ugliness, and sit back and feel peaceful and happy and completely content: a room that will always be there and always the same . . . Does that sound very dull to you? It doesn't to me. But then I don't want constant change and variety and stimulation in a wife; I can get plenty of that in everyday life and see it happening all around me. I want love and companionship, and I've found that in Juli. She is loving and loyal and courageous. And she is my peace and rest. Does that tell you what you want to know?'

'Yes,' said Wally, and smiled at him. 'I'd like to meet her.'

'So you shall. This evening, I hope.'

Wally had been sitting with his legs drawn up and his hands clasped about them, and now he dropped his chin on his knees, and staring ahead of him at the sun-glare on the white dust of the road and the back-drop of the foothills that lay shimmering in the heat, said contentedly: 'You don't know how much I've been looking forward to you coming back to us. And so have a lot of others; the men still talk about you, and they are always asking for news of you and when you'll be coming back. They have a name for you—they call you "Pelham-Dulkhan"—did you know that? and when we are out on an exercise or on manoeuvres, they tell tales about your doings in Afghanistan round the camp fires at night. I've heard them at it . . . . and now you really are coming back at last—I can't believe it . . . !' He drew a long, slow breath and let it out as slowly.

'Is it kissing the Blarney Stone you've been?' jeered Ash, grinning at him. 'Stop spreading on the butter and talk sense for a change. Tell me about this Afghan business.'

Wally returned the grin, and putting personal matters aside, talked instead, and with considerable knowledge and acumen, of the problem posed by Afghanistan—a subject which at that time was much on the minds of men who served in the Peshawar Field Force.

Ash had been out of touch with Frontier matters for many months, and very little of this had so far penetrated to Gujerat, where men had less reason to trouble themselves over the doings of the Amir of a wild and inaccessible country far and far to the north, beyond the Khyber hills and the mountains of the Safed Koh. But now he was reminded again of what Koda Dad had said to him at their last meeting—and Zarin only yesterday—and as he listened to Wally, he felt as though he had been living in a different world . . .

*   *   *

During the past few years the Amir of Afghanistan, Shere Ali, had found himself in the unenviable position of the 'corn between the upper and the lower millstones'—the simile was his own; the northern and uppermost one being Russia and the lower Great Britain, both of whom had designs on his country.

The latter had already annexed the Punjab and the Border-land beyond the Indus, while the former had swallowed the ancient principalities of Tashkent, Bokara, Kohkund and Kiva. Now Russian armies were massing on the northern frontiers of Afghanistan, and a new Viceroy, Lord Lytton, who combined obstinacy and a lofty ignorance of Afghanistan with a determination to extend the bounds of Empire to the greater glory of his country (and possibly of himself?) had been instructed by Her Majesty's Government to lose no time in sending an Envoy to Afghanistan charged with the task of overcoming the Amir's 'apparent reluctance' to the establishment of British Agencies within his dominions.

That the Amir might not wish to establish anything of the sort, or receive any foreign envoy, apparently did not occur to anyone; or if it did, was dismissed as unimportant. Lord Lytton was to impress upon the Amir that 'Her Majesty's Government must have for their own agents undisputed access to its (Afghanistan's) frontier positions', together with 'adequate means of confidentially conferring with the Amir upon all matters as to which the proposed declaration would recognize a community of interests'. They must also be entitled to 'expect becoming attention to their friendly councils', while the Amir himself 'must be made to understand that subject to all allowances for the condition of the country and the character of its population, territories ultimately dependent upon British Power for their defence must not be closed to those of the Queen's officers, or subjects, who may be duly authorized to enter them by the British Government'.

In return for accepting these humiliating terms, Shere Ali would be given advice from British officers as to how he could improve his military resources, together with the promise of British aid against any unprovoked attack by a foreign power, and (if the Viceroy* thought fit) a subsidy.

* Before India was taken over from the East India Company by the Crown, the title was Governor-General. The last of these and the first Viceroy was Sir John Lawrence.

Lord Lytton was wholly convinced that only by bringing Afghanistan under British influence, and thereby turning that turbulent country into a buffer-state, could the advance of Russia be checked and the safety of India assured. And when the Amir proved reluctant to accept a British Mission in his capital of Kabul, the Viceroy warned him that if he refused he would be alienating a friendly power who could pour an army into his country 'before a single Russian soldier could reach Kabul'—a threat that merely reinforced Shere Ali's suspicions that the British intended to take over his country and extend their borders to the far side of the Hindu Kush.

The Russians too were pressing the Amir to accept a mission of their own, and both powers offered to sign a treaty with him which included a promise to come to his assistance if the other should attack him. But Shere Ali complained, with some truth, that if he were to ally himself with either power, his people would certainly object to foreign soldiers marching into their country, whatever the pretext, as they had never at any time been kindly disposed towards interlopers.

He could have added, with even more truth, that they were a fanatically independent people, much addicted to intrigue, treachery and murder, and that among their other national traits was an intolerance of rulers (or, if it came to that, of any form of authority whatsoever, other than their own desires). The Viceroy's insistence therefore put the Amir in a very awkward position, and he took the only course he could think of. He temporized, hoping that if he could only spin out the negotiations for long enough, something might turn up to save him from the indignity of being forced to accept and protect a permanent British Mission in Kabul, which could not fail to earn him the contempt of his proud and turbulent subjects.

But the more Shere Ali prevaricated, the more determined the Viceroy became to force a British Mission upon him. Lord Lytton saw Afghanistan as an uncivilized backwater inhabited by savages, and that their ruler should have the impertinence to object to a powerful nation such as Great Britain establishing a Mission in his barbarous country was not only insulting, but laughable.

Shere Ali's Prime Minister, Nur Mohammed, travelled to Peshawar to put his master's case, and though sick and ageing and bitterly resentful of the cruel pressures that were being put upon his Amir, no man could have done more. But all to no avail. The new Viceroy had not hesitated to wriggle out of any promises and obligations entered into during negotiations with his predecessor, while at the same time accusing the Amir of failing to keep to the letter of his own undertakings. And when Nur Mohammed would not give way, the Viceroy's spokesman, Sir Neville Chamberlain, turned on him in a rage, and the Amir's insulted Prime Minister and long-time friend left the Conference Chamber in despair, knowing that his arguments and pleadings had failed and there was nothing left to keep alive for.

The British negotiators had chosen to believe that his illness was merely another excuse to gain time. But Nur had been a dying man when he arrived in Peshawar; and when he died there the rumour spread throughout Afghanistan that the *feringhis* had poisoned him. The Amir sent word to say that he was sending a new Envoy to replace him, but the Viceroy ordered that the negotiations be discontinued for lack of any common ground of agreement, and the new Envoy was sent back, while Lord Lytton turned his attention to subverting the Border tribes with a view to bringing about the collapse of Shere Ali by less open means.

Some of this Ash already knew, for the Peshawar Conference had been in session before he had left for Gujerat, and the issues that had been discussed there had been known and hotly debated in every British mess, Club and bungalow throughout the northern Punjab and the Frontier provinces, in addition to the streets and shops of cities, towns and villages—the British taking the view that the Amir was a typically treacherous Afghan, who was intriguing with the Russians and planning to sign a treaty of alliance with the Tsar that would permit free passage through the Khyber Pass to his armies, while Indian opinion held that the British Raj, in typically treacherous fashion, was plotting to overthrow the Amir and add Afghanistan to the Empire.

But once Ash had left the Punjab behind him, he had found that men talked less of the 'Russian menace' than of their own affairs; while from the time he reached Bombay and boarded the slow train that chugged and puffed along the palm-fringed coast towards Surat and Baroda, he had hardly ever heard it mentioned, let alone seriously discussed—despite the fact that the two leading English-language newspapers wrote an occasional leader on the subject, criticizing the Government for its failure to take action, or attacking 'alarmists' who talked of war.

Insulated by distance and the slower pace of life in Gujerat, Ash had soon lost interest in the political wrangling between the High Gods in Simla and the unhappy ruler of the Land of Cain, and it had come as something of a shock to him to discover from Zarin that here in the north men took the matter seriously, and spoke openly of a second Afghan war:

'But I don't suppose it will come to that,' said Wally, not without a tinge of regret. 'Once the Amir and his advisors realize that the Raj is not prepared to take "No" for an answer, they'll give in gracefully and let us send a Mission to Kabul, and that'll be the end of it. Pity, really— No, I don't mean that of course. But it would have been a terrific experience, fighting one's way through those passes. I'd like to be in a real battle.'

'You will be,' said Ash dryly. 'Even if there isn't an all-out war, the tribes are bound to start some sort of trouble before long, because if there's one thing they really enjoy, it's taking a slap at the Raj. It's their favourite sport—like bull-fighting is to the Spaniards. We being the bull. A peaceful existence bores them, and if there happens to be a shortage of blood-feuds, or some fiery mullah starts calling for a *Jehad* (holy war), they sharpen up their tulwars and shoulder their muskets, and *Olé!*—they're off again.'

Wally laughed, and then his face sobered again and he said thoughtfully: 'Wigram says that if the Amir does agree to let a British Mission go to Kabul they'll take an escort with them, and he thinks that as Cavagnari is almost certain to be a member of it, the chances are that he'll see to it that the escort is drawn from the Guides. I wonder who they'll send? Faith, what wouldn't I be giving to be one of them. Just think of it—Kabul! Wouldn't you give anything to go there?'

'No,' Ash's tone was still dry. 'Once was enough.'

'Once . . . ? Oh, of course, you've been there before. What didn't you like about it?'

'A lot of things. It's attractive enough in its way; especially in the spring when the almond trees are in bloom and the mountains all around still white with snow. But the streets and bazaars are dirty and the houses tumble-down and shoddy, and it wasn't called the "Land of Cain" for nothing! You get the feeling that savagery is near the surface, and could break through at any moment like lava from a dormant volcano and that the line drawn between good-will and bloody violence is thinner there than anywhere else in the world. Not that Kabul belongs to the modern world any more than Bhithor does —in fact they have a lot in common: they both live in the past and are hostile to change and to strangers, while the majority of their citizens not only look like cut-throats, but can behave as such if they happen to take a dislike to you.'

Ash added that in his opinion, it was perhaps not so strange that a city reputedly founded by the world's first murderer should have a reputation for treachery and violence; or that its rulers should have been faithful to the tradition of Cain, and indulged in murder and fratricide. The past history of the Amirs being one long tale of bloodshed: fathers killing their sons, sons plotting against their fathers and each other, and uncles disposing of their nephews. 'It's a grisly tale, and if it's true that ghosts are the unquiet spirits of people who died terrible deaths—and that there are such things as ghosts— then Kabul must be full of them. It's a haunted place, and I hope I never see it again.'

'Well, you will if there's war,' observed Wally, 'because the Guides will be in it so they will.'

'True—*if* there is a war. But speaking for myself . . .' the sentence ended in a yawn, and Ash settled himself back in a crotch among the tree roots and closed his eyes against the glaring day, and presently, feeling relaxed and peaceful because he and Wally were together again, he fell asleep.

Wally sat watching him for a long time, seeing the changes that he had missed to begin with, and other things that he had never bothered to notice before: the vulnerability of that thin, reckless face, the sensitive mouth that accorded so ill with the firm obstinate chin, and the purposeful line of the black eyebrows that were at odds with a brow and temples that would have better befitted a poet or a dreamer than a soldier. It was a face at war with itself, beautifully modelled and yet somehow lacking cohesion. And it seemed to Wally that, in spite of the deep unyouthful lines that scored it and the faint scar of that old wound, the sleeper, in some ways, had not really grown up. He still saw things as wrong or right, good or bad, and fair or unfair—as children did, before they learned better. He still thought that he could do something to alter them . . .

All at once Wally felt deeply sorry for his friend, who thought that because a thing was 'unfair' it was wrong and ought to be changed, and who, being unable to look at any problem either from a strictly European or a wholly Asiatic standpoint, was deprived of the comforting armour of national prejudice and left with no defence against the regional bigotries of East and West.

Ash, like his father Hilary, was a civilized and liberal-minded man with an interested and inquiring mind. But unlike Hilary, he had never grasped that the average mind is neither liberal or inquiring, but is in the main intolerant of any attitudes except its own firmly entrenched ones. He had his own gods, but they were neither Christian nor pagan. And he was not and never had been the dashing, romantic and wholly admirable hero of Wally's early imaginings, but was as fallible as the next man—and because of his unorthodox beginnings, possibly more prone to error than most. But he was still Ash, and no one, not even Wigram, could ever take his place in Wally's affections. A hoopoe flew down and began to probe for insects in the hard-packed earth, and Wally watched it idly for a moment or two before following Ash's example and drifting off into sleep.

By the time they awoke the sun was well down and the countryside around them full of shadows. Ash fetched water from the stream, and with this and the food that Gul Baz had left them they made a frugal meal, deciding as they ate that Wally should spend the night at Attock dâk-bungalow after visiting Fatima Begum's house to meet Anjuli, and return to Mardan in the morning.

They had arrived at the house in the dusty amethyst twilight, where the gatekeeper received them incuriously and in answer to Ash's question said no, Koda Dad Khan had not come—doubtless his son, the Risaldar-Sahib, had been able to prevent his father from setting out. He took charge of the horses while Ash sent a message to the Begum, asking her permission to allow his friend, Hamilton-Sahib, to enter her house and meet his wife.

Had Anjuli been a Muslim the suggestion might well have drawn a shocked refusal from the Begum, who by now regarded herself as standing *in loco parentis* to the girl. But as Anjuli was neither a Muslim or a maiden, and her so-called husband not only a Christian but a foreigner, the proper rules could not be expected to apply, and if Pelham-Sahib was prepared to let his men friends hob-nob with his bride, it was no concern of the Begum's. She therefore sent a servant to conduct the two men to Anjuli's room and to tell Ash that if they desired to eat together, the evening meal would be served in a few minutes' time.

The lamps had not yet been lit, but the *kus-kus* tatties had been rolled up and the high, white-washed room was palely luminous with the last of the daylight and the first glimmer of a full moon that was rising above the low, dun-coloured hills beyond Attock.

Anjuli had been standing by an open window, looking down onto the garden where birds were flocking home to roost among the fruit trees while bats flitted out from a score of dark hidden crannies to greet the night. She had not heard the footsteps on the stairs, for the sound had been lost in the chatter of quarrelling birds, and only when the door opened did she turn.

Seeing Ash, but not the man who stood in the shadows behind him, she ran to him and threw her arms around his neck. And that was how Wally had first seen her. A tall, slender girl running towards him with outstretched arms, and with such a blaze of love in her face that for a moment it seemed to him that a light shone on it. She had taken his breath away—and his heart with it.

Afterwards, sitting alone in the moonlight on the verandah of the dâk-bungalow, he found that he had no clear recollection of what she looked like. Only that she was the most beautiful creature he had ever seen—a princess out of a fairy-tale, fashioned from ivory and gold and jet. But then he had never before seen a well-born Indian woman, and knew nothing of the wealth of grace and loveliness that is hidden away behind the purdah screens and jealously guarded from the gaze of all strangers.

Few foreigners were privileged to see or know these women; and those few tended to be the wives of senior British officials, whose views on the charms of 'native women' were apt to be lukewarm, or at best, tinged with condescension. So that when Ash had tried to describe his wife, Wally had made due allowance for a man in love and supposed, indulgently, that the bride might be tolerably good looking—as were one or two of the more expensive courtesans of Ash's acquaintance, whom Wally had met in those early, carefree days in Rawalpindi: brown-skinned women who painted their eyes with *kohl,* chewed *pan* and stained the palms of their slender hands with henna; and whose supple, small-boned bodies smelled of musk and sandalwood and exuded an almost visible aura of sexuality.

Nothing that he had so far seen of India had prepared him for the sight of Anjuli. He had expected a little, dark-complexioned woman, not a long-limbed goddess—Venus Aphrodite—whose skin was paler than ripe wheat, and whose beautiful black-lashed eyes were the colour of peat-water on the moors of Kerry.

Strangely, she did not suggest the East to him, but rather the North, and gazing at her, he had been reminded of snow and pine trees and the cool fresh wind that blows in the high mountains . . .

and of a line in a new book of poems recently sent to him by a dot-ing Aunt—*'And dark and true and tender is the North . . .'* Dark and true and tender;—yes, that was Anjuli. All the heroines of fic-tion had come true in her—she was Eve, she was Juliet, she was Helen . . . ! *'She walks in beauty like the night, of cloudless climes and starry skies. And all that's best of dark and light meet in her as-pect and her eyes,'* declaimed Wally, drunk with unreasoning hap-piness.

He no longer blamed Ash for marrying in haste, for he could imagine himself doing exactly the same thing if he had had the luck to be in Ash's place. There could not be many women in the world like Anjuli, and having found one it would have been madness to lose her for the sake of a career. And yet . . . Wally sighed, and some of the euphoria of the last few hours left him. No, he would probably not have done it—not if he had been given enough time to realize what it might mean in terms of the future, because the Guides had come to count so much to him. Besides, he had cherished dreams of military glory for as long as he could remember; it was something he had grown up with and by now it was too much a part of him to be rooted out and replaced by love for a woman—even such a one as he had seen that night and lost his heart to.

All at once he was filled with gratitude towards Ash and Anjuli: and to God, Who had been good enough to allow him to meet the one woman in the world, and yet put her beyond his reach; so that by losing his heart to her he was saved for ever (or at least, for a long time to come) from falling in love with some lesser star and get-ting married and domesticated and losing his taste for adventure and with it, inevitably, some part of his enthusiasm for his profession and devotion to the men of his own Regiment.

Now that Ash was about to rejoin the Guides, life would be per-fect, and the only cloud in Wally's sky was the fact that there were still three weeks to run before Ash returned to duty. The thought of having to wait another twenty-one days after waiting so long was suddenly unendurable—yet it would have to be endured; and at least there was work and Wigram (who was now Adjutant and a Captain) to help him through it and make the time pass quickly. He had asked Ash if he could tell Wigram about Anjuli, and been pleased though not surprised when Ash had agreed. Everyone liked Wigram, and there was no denying that it would be a relief to be able to tell him about Ash's adventures and his romantic, secret marriage, particularly now that he himself had met the bride and so felt qualified to speak in the couple's defence and persuade Wigram to take a lenient view of the whole affair . . .

Wally rose from the verandah chair, and having searched for something to throw at a pi-dog that sat yelping monotonously by the compound gate, discharged a well-aimed flower-pot and went in to bed humming 'Fight the good fight with all thy might'. Which, in the circumstances, was a healthy sign, for it showed that he was returning to normal after the stresses and strains of that emotional day.

The sun was still well below the horizon when Wally crossed the Indus and took the Peshawar road on the following morning, leaving his bearer Pir Baksh to follow in a tonga with the luggage, and an hour later he breakfasted at the Nowshera dâk-bungalow while his horse rested, before crossing the Kabul River and pressing on towards Risalpur. Mardan was an oasis of shade in a parched land. The fort and the parade-ground, the lines and the familiar back-drop of the Yusafzai hills quivered and swayed in the dancing heat, and far out on the plain towards Jamalgarhi an occasional dust-devil arose to whirl like a spinning-top and die again. But in the cantonment not a leaf stirred, and the dust of the hot weather lay like hoar frost on every stick and stone and blade of grass, reducing greens and browns to a single tint—the colour that Sir Henry Lawrence had chosen for the uniforms of his newly raised Corps of Guides in the days before the Great Mutiny, and that had come to be known as *khaki*.

Wally had gone straight to Wigram's quarters, but Wigram was not there; he had been attending some minor conference in Peshawar, and was not expected back until after sundown. He had, however, returned in time to dine in mess, and later walked back with Wally to the latter's rooms, where he had remained until long after midnight, listening to the saga of Ash and Anjuli-Bai.

The tale had obviously interested him deeply, though the marriage ceremony on board the *Morala* had drawn an angry exclamation and a black frown, and after that he had listened to the rest tight-lipped and with a furrowed brow. But he had made no comments, and at the end of it remarked thoughtfully that he remembered the Commandant saying, at the time when the question of a Court Martial was being discussed following the return of the carbines, that Ashton Pelham-Martyn was not only an insubordinate young hot-head, but an adult enfant-terrible whose penchant for acting on the spur of the moment made him capable of doing any damned silly thing without pausing to think what it could lead to in the long run; yet it had to be remembered that these were the very defects that often proved invaluable in time of war, particularly when accompanied, as in Ashton's case, with considerable courage.

'I think he was right,' said Wigram slowly. 'And if there should be a war, which I pray God there will not be, we may need those defects—and the courage that goes with them.'

He lay back in his chair and was silent for a long time, chewing on the butt of a cheroot that had gone out long ago, and staring abstractedly at the ceiling; and when he spoke again it was to ask a question: 'Do I understand that Ashton intends to spend the remainder of his leave at Attock?'

'Yes,' confirmed Wally. 'He and his wife have been invited to stay with Risaldar Zarin Khan's aunt—she owns that big house in a walled garden that stands back from the 'Pindi road on the far side of the town.'

'*Hmm.* I should like to go over one day and meet the bride. It would—' his gaze fell on the clock and he came hurriedly to his feet: 'Good gracious, is that the right time? I'd no idea it was so late. High time I got my beauty sleep. Good-night, Wally.'

He left to walk back to his own quarters, but not, as it happened, to sleep. Instead, having exchanged his mess dress for the loose cotton trousers that were the customary night-wear at that time of year, he came out onto the verandah, and subsiding into a long-sleeve chair, gave himself up to thought.

50

Captain Battye gazed out unseeingly at the hot moonlight and the black shadows, and thought of his youngest brother, Fred . . . of Fred and Wally and Ashton Pelham-Martyn, Hammond and Hughes and Campbell, Colonel Jenkins the Commandant, Risaldars Prem Singh and Mahmud Khan, Wordi-Major Duni Chand and Sowar Dowlat Ram and a hundred others . . . officers, non-commissioned officers and men of the Guides; their faces passing before him as though on review. If there should be another Afghan war, how many of them would be alive by the time it was over?

He knew that even now, after all these years, the bleached bones of General Elphinstone's demoralized army still littered the defiles where they had been trapped during the retreat from Kabul, and slaughtered like sheep by the vengeful tribesmen. This time it might be Fred's bones that were left there; or Wally's skull that would go trundling before the blast when the wind howled through those haunted passes. Fred and Wally, the forgotten debris of another useless, pointless Afghan war . . .

The first had been fought well before either of those two were born, and though the Afghans had not forgotten it, the British seldom mentioned it—those who remembered it preferring to pretend they did not; which was hardly surprising, as it was an unedifying tale.

In the early years of the century, when 'John Company' ruled half India, a mediocre youth named Shah Shuja had fallen heir to the throne of Afghanistan. Having lost it after a reign that was brief even by the violent standards of that country, he fled to India where he was granted asylum by the Government and settled down to a peaceful existence as a private citizen, while following his departure, his erstwhile subjects indulged in a period of riot and anarchy that came to an abrupt end when a strong and able man, one Dost Mohammed of the Barakzi clan, brought order out of chaos and eventually made himself Amir.

Unfortunately, the Government of India distrusted men of ability. They suspected that the Dost would be difficult to manipulate and might even, if they were not careful, decide to ally himself with Russia; and discussing this possibility in the rarefied atmosphere of

Simla, the Governor-General, Lord Auckland, and his favoured advisers came to the conclusion that it might be a good idea to get rid of the Dost (who had done them no harm and his country much good) and replace him with the now elderly ex-Amir Shah Shuja; their argument being that this aged nonentity, if bound to his British champions by ties of gratitude and self-interest, could not fail to become a biddable tool who would willingly sign any treaty they cared to dictate.

But though the war that Lord Auckland forced upon Afghanistan had ended in total disaster for the British, the majority of those who had helped to launch it did very well for themselves, since to mark the initial victory, medals, titles and honours had been showered upon them—none of which could be taken away. But the dead who rotted in the passes received no decorations: and within two years Dost Mohammed Khan was once again Amir of Afghanistan.

The *waste,* thought Wigram, the injustice and stupidity and the cruel, senseless waste. And all to no purpose, because now once again, after a lapse of almost forty years, it seemed that a handful of men in Simla were planning to force another Amir—the youngest son of that same Dost Mohammed—to accept a permanent British Mission in Kabul. Worse still, there had actually been a time when the Amir would have been only too willing to accommodate them. Five years ago, dismayed by threats of rebellion and the growing power of Russia, Shere Ali had made overtures to the then Viceroy, Lord Northbrook, and asked for an assurance of protection against any aggressor; but his request had been refused. Embittered by this rejection, he had decided to turn instead to Russia (who had shown a flattering eagerness to discuss treaties of friendship and alliance with him); yet now these same *Angrezis,* who had rebuffed him when he asked for help, were actually demanding, as a right, that he should welcome a British Envoy to his capital and cease 'intriguing' with the Tsar.

'If I were in his shoes, I'd see 'em damned first,' thought Wigram, and realized that there was no profit in thinking like that. This was how wars came about.

All those years ago Lord Auckland and his friends had sent thousands of people to their deaths on the mere supposition that Shere Ali's father might consider an alliance with Russia. Was Lord Lytton now about to do the same, and with no more proof than before, basing his decisions on suspicion, gossip and rumour, and the garbled accounts of paid spies?

In the course of the past few years Wigram had seen a good deal of Wally's kinsman the Deputy Commissioner of Peshawar, Major Louis Cavagnari; and until recently his opinion of the D.C. had been almost as high as Wally's. Pierre Louis Napoleon Cavagnari was a curious person to be found occupying such a position, for as Wally had related, his father had been a French count who had served under the great Napoleon, become Military Secretary to Jérôme Bonaparte, King of Westphalia, and married an Irish lady, Elizabeth, daughter of Dean Stewart Blacker of Carrickblacker (though despite his Gallic names the Deputy Commissioner, having been brought up in Ireland, had always regarded himself as British, and preferred his friends to call him 'Louis' because it seemed to him the least foreign of his three given names).

For twenty years he had served with distinction in India's Border lands, seeing service in no less than seven Frontier campaigns, and acquiring an enviable reputation for being able to manage the turbulent tribesmen, whose various dialects he spoke with idiomatic fluency. And though as far as appearance went, the tall, bearded figure might easily have been taken for a professor rather than a man of action, those who knew him declared him to be courageous to a fault. No one had ever accused him of lack of spirit, and he combined a dynamic personality with many excellent qualities; though in common with the majority of his fellow men, these last were offset by some that were less admirable: in his case egotism and personal ambition, a quick temper and a fatal tendency to see things as he wished them to be rather than as they actually were.

Wigram Battye had only recently become aware of these failings. But then he had also had the advantage of seeing Cavagnari in action. The success of the affair at Sipri with its swift night march and surprise attack had been entirely due to the D.C.'s imaginative planning and attention to detail, and that, with several other similar incidents, had given Wigram the greatest possible respect for the man's qualities. Nevertheless, of late he had come to feel less admiring and more critical; and, it must be owned, more than a little apprehensive, for the Deputy Commissioner was a professed supporter of the 'Forward Policy', whose advocates considered that the only way to protect the Indian Empire from the 'Russian menace' was to turn Afghanistan into a British protectorate and plant the Union Jack on the far side of the Hindu Kush.

As this was also the Viceroy's view (and Lord Lytton was known to have a great regard for Major Cavagnari and to take his advice on Frontier matters in preference to that of older and more cautious men), it was not surprising that Wigram Battye should feel uneasy at hearing the D.C. declare—as he had recently heard him do at a dinner party in Peshawar—'If Russia gets a foothold in Afghanistan she will take over that country as she has taken over almost all the old, proud kingdoms of Central Asia; and once she has done that the road through the Khyber will be open and there will be nothing to prevent her marching her armies down to attack and take Peshawar and the Punjab, as Barbur the Tiger did three hundred years ago. I have no quarrel with the Afghan people: my quarrel is solely with their Amir, who, by intriguing with the Tsar, is playing with a fire that unless we can prevent it will destroy his own country, and from there burn its way southward until it has consumed all India . . .'

Cavagnari's use of the first person singular was characteristic of the man and in a different context Wigram would probably have thought nothing of it: but used in this one it dismayed him. His own interest in the dispute between the Government of India and the Amir was entirely non-political, his concern being mainly with the military consequences of a possible war with Afghanistan and the part that his own Corps would be called upon to play in it. He was, after all, a professional soldier. But he also possessed a conscience, and his fear was that the Forward Policy clique intended to embroil the Raj in a second Afghan war without any real justification for doing so—and without fully realizing the enormous difficulties that would face an invading army.

Of the two, it was the former that worried him most, for having always held the view that the Afghan war of '39 had been morally indefensible as well as totally unnecessary, it horrified him to discover that once again History seemed about to repeat itself, and in his opinion it was the plain duty of all honourable men to try to prevent it doing so; the crying need, as Wigram saw it, being for accurate and unedited information as to the true intentions of the Amir Shere Ali and his people.

If it could be proved that Shere Ali was intriguing with the Tsar and about to sign a treaty that would grant Russia military posts and a firm footing in his country, then the Forward Policy men were right and the sooner Britain stepped in to prevent it the better—the prospect of a Russian-controlled Afghanistan with Russian armies stationed along the north-west frontiers of India being unthinkable. But then *was* it true? Wigram had an uneasy feeling that men like Cavagnari and Lord Lytton and other Forward Policy fire-eaters were being deluded by information supplied by Afghan spies who, knowing full well what these particular Sahibs hoped to hear, repeated only what would please, and suppressed anything else—a quirk probably due to a respect for good manners and a desire to please, rather than any deliberate intent to mislead.

Cavagnari of all people would know this, and—or so Wigram hoped—make allowances for it. But would the Viceroy and his councillors realize that the reports of such spies, faithfully forwarded to Simla by the Deputy Commissioner of Peshawar, might be one-sided and fail to give the full picture? that spies, after all, were paid, and might consider themselves to be earning their pay by telling only such news as they had reason to believe would be welcome? It was this thought that had been preying on Wigram's mind of late, and Wally's talk of Ashton had given him an idea . . .

Ashton had spent almost two years in Afghanistan and probably made a number of friends there, certainly in the village of his adoptive father Koda Dad Khan, while it was well known in Mardan that Risaldar Zarin Khan was by no means the only Pathan in the Guides who regarded him almost as a blood-brother. Now supposing Ashton could persuade his friends to organize some form of intelligence service aimed at collecting reliable information which they would pass on to him, and which he in turn could pass on to the Commandant or to Wigram himself, to give to Cavagnari—who whatever his personal views could be counted upon to report it to Simla. Ashton's friends could surely be counted on to tell 'Pelham-Dulkhan' the truth (because they knew that he did not think as the 'Sahib-log' thought) and Ashton himself trusted to repeat what they told him verbatim, without editing it to fit any theories of his own or anyone else's. It was at least an idea, and it might work: and at this juncture, thought Wigram, *anything* was worth trying.

Impelled by a driving sense of urgency and of time running out, he had tried it at the first opportunity, riding over to Attock with Wally at the weekend, and for reasons of secrecy arriving after dark and putting up at the dâk-bungalow with a story that they intended to do some shooting on the following day. Though as things turned out, his idea had produced a result that Wigram had certainly not expected.

Wally's syce had been sent off to the Begum's house with a note for Ash, and the reply had been handed to them as they sat at supper. An hour later the two had left the dâk-bungalow to walk in the hot starlight along the 'Pindi road, and presently, turning off it down a dusty side path, they came to a gate in a high wall where they found an Afridi waiting for them with a lantern; and Wigram—who had not previously seen Ash dressed in this fashion—did not immediately realize who it was.

Captain Battye had given a good deal of thought to the arguments he intended to use and the points he meant to make, and was confident that he had thought of everything. But he had given no thought at all to Juli Pelham-Martyn, born Anjuli-Bai, Princess of Gulkote, for he considered the marriage both ill-judged and distasteful, and had no desire to meet the ex-widow. Ash however had led his guests through the shadowy garden to a small two-storied pavilion, a *barra durri* that stood in a clearing among the fruit trees, and taking them up a short flight of stairs to the screened upper room, said: 'Juli, this is another friend of mine from the Regiment. My wife, Wigram—' and Wigram had found himself shaking hands in the English fashion with a girl in white, and thinking as Wally had done—though without any of Wally's emotion—that she was the loveliest thing he had ever seen.

He saw her exchange a brief glance with Ash, and though he had never been a particularly imaginative man, it seemed to him, as it had once seemed to Kaka-ji, that an invisible current leapt between them, linking them together so that they did not need to touch each other or speak or even smile in order to prove that two people can at times be truly one. He could see too what Walter had meant when he said that she was 'restful'. But somehow he had not expected her to be so young—or to look so vulnerable. This slender young thing in the white *shulwa* appeared to him to be little more than a child, and he thought confusedly that it was the term 'widow' that had misled him: no widow should be as young as this, and he felt as though the ground had been abruptly cut from beneath his feet; though he would have been at a loss to explain why this should be so. But the fact remained that the sight of her had been enough to upset a number of preconceived notions, and all at once he was unsure of himself, and, as a result, of the suggestion he had come here to make.

Was he perhaps being foolishly naïve in expecting Cavagnari, or anyone else for that matter, to abandon their policies and opinions merely on the basis of information from unofficial sources, supposing that information did not agree with their own? Was he, Wigram, taking too much on himself, being conceited enough to imagine that men like Cavagnari and the Viceroy, not to mention a host of bigwigs in Simla, did not know what they were about and needed help and advice from interfering know-nothing amateurs? Yet . . . He became aware that Ash had asked him a question, and replying at random saw by the quizzical lift of a black eyebrow that his answer had betrayed his inattention.

Wigram flushed and apologized in some confusion, and turning to his hostess said: 'I'm sorry, Mrs Pelham; I'm afraid I have not been attending. It was rude of me, and I hope you will forgive my bad manners. You see . . . I came here to put a—a proposition to your husband, and I have been thinking of that instead of listening.'

Anjuli studied him gravely, then she gave a little nod and said politely: 'I understand. You mean you would like to speak to my husband alone.'

'Only if you permit.'

She gave him a brief enchanting smile, and rising, placed her palms together, and then remembering that Ashok had told her that this was not the *Angrezi* way, laughed and held out her hand and said in her careful English: 'Good-night . . . Captain Battye.'

Wigram took her hand in his and unexpectedly bowed over it in a gesture that was as foreign to him as a handshake was to her, and that surprised him almost more than it surprised Ash and Wally. But it had been an instinctive tribute—and also in some way an unspoken apology for the things he had thought about her. Straightening up and looking into the eyes that were almost on a level with his own, he saw that Wally had been right when he said that there were gold flecks in them—unless it was only the reflections from the pierced bronze lamp that hung from the ceiling and sprinkled the little pavilion with stars. But he did not have time to find out, for Anjuli drew her hand away and offered it to Wally before she turned and left them, and watching her retreat into the shadows he had the odd fancy that she was taking the light with her.

All the same, he was relieved to see her go, because her presence would have precluded straight talking, and he had neither the time nor the inclination to defer to feminine sensibilities. As the sound of her footsteps receded on the stair he heard Wally give a little sigh, and presently Ash said: 'Well?'

'She is very beautiful,' said Wigram slowly. 'And very . . . young.'

'Twenty-one,' supplied Ash laconically. 'But I didn't mean "What do you think of her?" I meant what is this proposition you mentioned?'

'Yes, come on now, out with it,' urged Wally. 'It's dying of curiosity I've been. What have you got up your sleeve?'

Wigram grinned but said a shade defensively that now it came to the point he was not so sure that he wanted to say anything: 'The fact is, I'm afraid you may laugh.'

But Ash had not laughed. He knew a good deal about the late Afghan war, and while in Gujerat had re-read Sir John Kaye's book on the subject and been as infuriated by the futility, injustice and tragedy of that bungled attempt at extending the power of the East India Company as his father, Hilary, had been over thirty years earlier.

That such a thing could happen again had seemed so impossible that even after Koda Dad had warned him of it he could not believe that anyone with any sense could consider it, largely because, like most Frontier Force soldiers, he was under no illusions as to the fighting capabilities of the Border tribesmen or the ruggedness of the country in which they lived; and knew only too well the appalling problems posed by supply and transport (quite apart from the actual fighting) that must confront any modern army attempting to advance through a hostile land where every hill-top and ravine, each rock and stone and fold in the ground, could hide an enemy marksman. A land moreover where the soil was so unproductive that at the best of times there was barely enough food for the local inhabitants, and therefore no hope of being able to feed large numbers of invading troops and an even larger number of camp-followers off the country; or of grazing the host of horses, mules and other transport animals that must accompany them. Besides, surely the Generals, if not the civilians in Simla, must have learned the lesson of the previous Afghan war?

Yet listening to Wigram he realized that the lesson, if learned, had been forgotten, and that those who were planning a repeat performance of that sorry tragedy would be at pains to see that it remained so—directing the limelight instead onto the fur-hatted figure of the Russian villain lurking in the wings. 'Yet if it's true that Shere Ali is planning to let in the Russians,' thought Ash, as Wigram had done, 'England will have to step in, because once the Russians get their hands on anything they never let go, and it would be India next.'

The thought of India added to the ever-increasing territories of the Tsar—its towns and villages under the control of Ispravniks and Starostas, Russian Governors in every Province and Russian regiments quartered in every cantonment from Peshawar to Cape Comorin, their guns commanding the great sea ports of Karachi, Bombay, Madras and Calcutta—was enough to make him shudder. But then he knew Afghanistan even better than men like Cavagnari did, and that knowledge inclined him to be sceptical of the fears expressed by the Deputy Commissioner and his fellow war-mongers.

'I remember reading somewhere,' observed Ash meditatively, 'that Henry I of France said of Spain that if you invaded it with a large force you would be destroyed by starvation, while if you invaded it with a small one you would be overwhelmed by a hostile people. Well, you could say the same of Afghanistan. It's an appalling country to invade, and unless the Russians think that they can walk in unchallenged, with the consent of the population as well as the Amir, I can't believe they'd try it—any more than I am prepared to believe that Cavagnari knows much about the Afghans if he thinks for one moment that the Amir's so-called "subjects" will ever tamely submit to having Russian garrisons quartered all over their country. They may be a murderous lot of ruffians with an unenviable reputation for treachery and ruthlessness, but no one has ever denied their courage; or been able to make them do anything they don't like doing. And they don't like being dictated to or ruled by foreigners—any foreigners! Which is why, in my opinion, this whole Russian scare is probably nothing but a turnip lantern.'

'Exactly,' agreed Wigram. 'That's precisely what I'm afraid of. But though I hope I'm wrong, I can't help wondering if—if the Forward Policy fanatics know quite well that it's more than likely that Russia is merely putting out a feeler—testing the temperature of the water so to speak—but are so dead set on this scheme of turning Afghanistan into a buffer-state in order to protect India that they are using this Russian business as a stalking horse to cover their real objective. Though of course if it's true that the Amir is really thinking of signing a treaty with the Tsar—' the sentence remained unfinished, because at this point he had been interrupted by Wally, who refused to believe that his latest hero could possibly be mistaken on a matter of such vital importance, or wrong about anything that concerned the tribal territories of Afghanistan as a whole. Cavagnari, insisted Wally, knew more about that country and its peoples than anyone else in India—any European at all events. Everyone knew that!

Wigram remarked dryly that he expected a great many people had said as much of Macnaghten in '38, though that hadn't prevented him from being murdered by the Afghans three years later, after being largely responsible for attempting to foist Shah Shuja on the throne, and almost wholly responsible for allowing large numbers of British women and children and their down-country servants to join the Occupation Forces in Kabul and be massacred in the Kurd Kabul passes together with the retreating army. As Wally had also studied that disastrous campaign, he was temporarily silenced, and confined himself to listening to Ash and Wigram discussing the possibility of being able to discover what was actually going on in Kabul and whether the Russian threat was real or only a turnip lantern being used by the Forward Policy bloc to frighten the electorate into supporting another war of aggression.

'But supposing we could get the information?' said Ash some ten minutes later. 'We'd have no guarantee that it would be accepted if it turned out to contradict what they want to believe.'

'None,' confirmed Wigram; 'except that if by "they" you mean Cavagnari, he would never suppress it. That's one thing I *am* sure about. He has his own spies of course, as we have always had ours— after all, it was in our original charter that we should employ "men capable of collecting trustworthy intelligence beyond as well as within our borders", and as Deputy Commissioner of Peshawar, Cavagnari probably employs a good many of the same. But I'll go bail that anything of a political nature that they send him—anything to do with Shere Ali's relations with Russia for instance—is sent on at once to Simla, as anything we ourselves could tell him in that line would be too, regardless of whether it contradicted his own theories or not. In any case, one has to try. One can't sit back with folded hands and watch a shipload of passengers heading towards a hidden reef without making any attempt to light a flare or send up a rocket or do anything at all to try and warn them, even if it's only to yell or blow a whistle!'

'No,' agreed Ash slowly. 'One has to do something—even when the chances are that it will prove useless.'

'Yes, that's it. That's how I feel,' sighed Wigram, enormously relieved. He leaned back in his chair, and grinning at Ash said: 'I remember when you first joined us we used to rib you over a habit you had of saying that this or that was "unfair"—it was a favourite word of yours in those days. Well, speaking for myself, I've no objection to fighting a war: it's my trade. But I'd prefer to think that I was fighting in a just one; or at the very least, one that could not have been avoided. And I believe that this one can be. It's not too late.'

Ash remained silent, and Wigram saw that although his gaze appeared to be fixed on the dark oblong of the doorway through which his wife had left, his eyes had the blind unfocused look of one whose thoughts have travelled many miles, or perhaps years away. And indeed Ash was remembering the past and hearing once again as he had in Lalji's audience chamber in Gulkote and in the *chattri* at Bhithor, a long-dead voice exhorting a four-year-old boy not to forget that injustice was the worst sin in the world and must be fought wherever it was found . . . 'even when you know that you cannot win'.

Wigram, who did not know Ash nearly as well as Wally did, noticed only the abstraction. But Wally saw something in the still face that frightened him: an underlying suggestion of desolation and the bleak look of a man who is being forced to make an unpalatable decision. And as he watched, the prescience that is so often a part of the Irish heritage stirred in him, bringing a premonition of disaster that was so strong that instinctively he flung up a hand as though to ward it off . . . and in the same moment heard Ash say quietly: 'I shall have to go myself.'

Wigram had argued with him: they had both argued with him. But in the end they had agreed that he was right. An officer of the Guides would be more likely to be believed than any Afghan who, apart from being paid for services rendered, might well have a personal or tribal antipathy towards the central government in Kabul and so be tempted to twist or be selective with information collected on the far side of the Border. Besides, what was needed now was no longer a matter of which disaffected tribe or local mullah was planning a raid into British India or inciting the Faithful to murder a few infidels, but whether an Amir of Afghanistan was engaged in plotting with the Russians, and if so, how far had he committed himself? Was he indeed preparing to welcome a Russian Mission to Kabul and sign a treaty of alliance with the Tsar, and were his people prepared to support him in this?

Reliable information on these points would be of the greatest possible value to the negotiators in Simla and Peshawar and to Her Majesty's Ministers in London, because such knowledge could mean all the difference between peace and war—which is to say life and death for thousands of human beings. And as Ash pointed out, there was nothing in the Guides' charter to bar an officer from 'collecting trustworthy intelligence beyond as well as within our borders'. 'Anyway, I've lived in the country and I know my way around there, so it isn't as if I shall be in any real danger,' said Ash.

'Gammon!' retorted Wally angrily. 'Don't talk as though we were a pair of sap-heads. You weren't alone last time, but this time you will be; which means that if ever you're tired or ill or wounded and make a slip, there'll be no one to cover it up for you. You'll be a lone stranger, and as such, an object of suspicion. Faith, it's sick you make me—both of you. But I wish to God I could be going with you and that's the truth. When do you mean to leave?'

'As soon as Wigram can fix it with the Commandant. I can't go without his permission, and for all we know he may not give it.'

'He will,' said Wigram. 'He's been just as worried about this business as I have—and half the Frontier Force too, for that matter. We're the ones who'll have to do the fighting if that gilded crew in Simla gets hold of the wrong end of the stick and proceeds to stir up a hornets' nest with it. He may take a bit of persuading, but I think you'll find that he'll see it as a good idea and a possible life-line. And Cavagnari will jump at it. It's just the sort of thing that will appeal to him no end.'

Wigram had been right on both counts.

The Commandant had been talked round, and the Deputy Commissioner had shown considerable enthusiasm for the idea. He had a love of the dramatic, and Ash's story as related to him by Captain Battye enthralled him: 'But if he is to work for me I must see him before he goes, since it will be better if he reports direct to me through the only one of my agents whom I allow to come into Peshawar rather than to one of your men, who will be expected to take any message to you or your Commandant first, leaving one of you to bring it to me. That won't do: the less people involved in this the better—especially for his own safety, as I hope you will explain to him, and to your Commandant. A divided authority always leads to muddle, and as the type of information required will be of no use at regimental level, I prefer that the young man should work exclusively for me. And by the way if, as I understand, he is at present still on leave, I would suggest that he is not permitted to return to Mardan. It would look odd for him to come back to duty for a few days only to leave again.'

'Yes, sir. That has already been thought of. He will be leaving from Attock: it was his own idea.'

'And a very sensible one,' approved Cavagnari. 'Please arrange for him to meet me before he goes.'

Wigram saw no point in telling him that when Ash had volunteered to go into Afghanistan as a spy he had made two conditions, one of which might well have prevented him from going at all. He had insisted that he must be allowed to discuss the whole project with Koda Dad, and that if the old man did not approve, then it would have to be abandoned. The other condition had been that the Guides must promise to look after Anjuli and see to it that she received her rights as his lawful wife in the event of his failing to return.

The latter had been agreed, but when Wigram had expressed doubts about the wisdom of allowing any outside person to learn of Ash's activities, Ash had retorted that he would in any case be telling Zarin, and that he would trust Zarin's father with his life. 'I've known him since I was about six, and I value his opinion more than anyone else's. If he thinks I can do any good then I'll go; but you have to remember that he's a Pathan, and as such a citizen of Afghanistan, so he may take a poor view of spies—even those whose intentions are to prevent a war: I don't know. But I must talk to him first before I decide.'

Wigram had shrugged and said: 'Be it on your own head. It's your life. What do you think his verdict will be?'

'Oh, I should say the chances are that he'll agree with you, as Zarin will too. I admit I haven't much hope that he won't. In fact I'm probably wasting my time as well as his, but I have to make certain.'

'. . . and to receive his blessing,' murmured Wigram in an undervoice. He had spoken a thought aloud without knowing it and the words had been barely audible, but Ash had caught them and said quickly and in a tone of surprise: 'Yes. How did you know?'

Wigram had looked embarrassed and said awkwardly: 'It may sound absurd in this day and age, but my father gave me his before I sailed for India, and I've often found it a comfort to remember that. I suppose it harks back to the Old Testament, when a patriarch's blessing really meant something.'

'"And Esau said . . . bless me, even me also, O my father,"' quoted Wally, speaking for the first time in a long while. 'I hope you'll get it, Ash: for all our sakes.'

Wigram had risen briskly to his feet and said that it was high time they left, adding that he hoped Ash would not be too long over seeing Zarin's father, as he personally had a strong feeling that there might be very little time to spare, and that what they had was running out far too quickly. 'If the Commandant agrees, how soon do you think you could start?'

'That depends on Koda Dad; and on Cavagnari. I shall try and see Koda Dad tomorrow or the next day. Are you two going back to Mardan tonight?'

'We weren't, but we can.'

'When you do, will you take a message from me to Zarin. Tell him that I have to see his father as soon as possible and ask him to let me know if he thinks the old man would be well enough to receive me— I gather he's been ill of late. If so, when and where; but that I'd rather not be seen in his village if it can be avoided. He needn't send word here. Tell him I'll be at the banyan tree near the first milestone outside Nowshera by sunset tomorrow, and that I'll wait there until he comes. He may be on duty, but I expect you can arrange for him to get away.'

But no one was ever to know what Koda Dad would have advised, for he was dead. He had died at about the same hour as Wally and Wigram Battye, on their way to Attock, rode away from Mardan; and because the weather at that season is always cruelly hot he had been buried before nightfall, so that by the time Ash reached the banyan tree on the Nowshera road where Zarin waited for him with the news, Koda Dad Khan, one-time Master of Horse in the little principality of Gulkote, had lain a full twenty-four hours in his grave.

Two days later the Deputy Commissioner of Peshawar and Captain Battye of the Guides Cavalry rode out together, ostensibly to look for possible camp sites in the open country to the south-east of Peshawar.

They went unescorted, and at a time of day when all sensible folk are taking a siesta and the land appears to be deserted. Nevertheless in the course of their ride they met and conversed with another horseman, a lone Afridi whom they found resting in the shade of a tall outcrop of rock, and who might almost have been waiting for them.

To begin with, Cavagnari had done most of the talking, while Ash had confined himself to insisting that he would only agree to collect and send back information provided it was clearly understood that he would report the truth as he found it, even if it should turn out to be a view of the question that the officials in Simla did not wish to hear. 'If I cannot do that, then there is no point in my going,' said Ash. To which Cavagnari had replied with a shade of acidity that naturally he would be expected to keep an open mind, that went without saying; adding that the Commandant, with permission from the appropriate authority, had assigned Lieutenant Pelham-Martyn to act as his, Cavagnari's, personal intelligence officer for a period of six months, irrespective of whether war was declared during that time or not, while giving Cavagnari the right to terminate the arrangement at any moment if he thought fit. 'In which case you would of course return immediately to regimental duty. With a brevet if you wish; you will certainly have earned it and "the labourer is worthy of his hire".'

Ash made a face of disgust and remarked tartly that he had not volunteered for this job in the expectation of reward, and that he had thought that the whole point was having a spy who wasn't getting paid for it. His services were not for hire, and what he was doing could be regarded as repayment—repayment for benefits received, as the Guides had been very good to him and he had done little to repay them.

'You will have a chance to do so now,' observed Cavagnari with an approving nod, and moved on to a discussion of other matters. There were many of these—including the question of arranging for funds to be made available not only to Ash in Afghanistan but to Juli in Attock, together with the various details that would have to be worked out if the story that Lieutenant Pelham-Martyn had been sent off on a 'Course' somewhere down south on the eve of his returning to Mardan was to be believed. The meeting had lasted for some considerable time, and only when the shadows began to lengthen did the two Englishmen turn back to Peshawar, while the Afridi trotted eastward on his gaunt scissor-hocked pony, heading for Attock.

Ash had crossed the Rubicon and now it only remained to tell Anjuli; which was something he had put off doing as long as he could, just in case it should not be necessary—there being always the possibility that Cavagnari, or perhaps the Commandant, would change his mind at the last moment and cancel the venture as too dangerous or impractical; as there had once been the chance that Koda Dad would disapprove.

Telling her had been the hardest thing of all. Even harder than he had thought, for she had implored him to take her with him, insisting that her place was by his side now—doubly so if he were going into danger, because in addition to being able to cook and care for him, her presence would serve to deflect suspicion from him, since who could possibly expect to find a spy accompanied by his wife? The very idea was absurd and would therefore serve to protect him. 'And I would learn to shoot,' pleaded Anjuli. 'You have only to teach me.'

'But you cannot speak enough Pushtu, my Heart.'

'I will learn—I will learn! I promise you I will learn.'

'There is no time, Heart's-dearest, for I must go at once; and if I took you with me and you were unable to speak freely with the women-folk of the country, they would begin to ask questions, and that could be very dangerous—both for our safety and for the work that I have to do. You know that I would take you with me if I could, but I cannot, Larla; and it is only for six months. I will leave Gul Baz here, and you will be safe in the care of the Begum; and—and I will be far safer alone.'

It was in the end this last statement that persuaded her, because she knew in her heart that it was true, and knowing it she pleaded no longer but said only: 'Then I will send my heart with you—it is already in your keeping. Bring it back to me soon, and in safety.'

Ash had assured her that she need have no fears for him. But though he could make light of the danger in words, his body betrayed him: his love-making that night had been different from other nights in that it conveyed a disturbing sense of desperation . . . almost as though he were trying to make the very most of every moment for fear that there would be no tomorrow. So might a man lie with his love on the eve of some hazardous venture: a great battle, or a long and dangerous journey from which he might never return . . .

On the following night when all the household were safely asleep and the moon had not yet risen, Ash slipped quietly out by the back gate of Fatima Begum's garden and set his face towards the hills. And less than twelve hours later he was across the Border and had vanished into Afghanistan: dropping out of sight as completely as a pebble that falls into a deep pool.

51

That summer of 1878, the famine that had taken such a terrible toll in the south crept northward into the Punjab. For once again, for the third year in succession, the monsoon had failed; and when at last the rain fell it was not in the steady downpour that the thirsty land needed, but in fitful and capricious gusts that did little more than turn the surface dust to mud, leaving the earth beneath still iron-hard.

There were other things, apart from the failure of the crops and the fear of war, that made this an evil year, for dissension and disease were rife.

In Hardwar, where the sacred River Ganges enters the plains and vast numbers of pilgrims from all parts of India gather to bathe in its hallowed waters, cholera had struck during the annual festival and thousands died within a matter of hours. The news that Russia had attacked Turkey, and of her victories in the field, had encouraged a number of Indian journalists (always impressed by success and military might) to fill columns in the vernacular press with a spate of inflammatory words in praise of the victors, and when the Government took no notice they became bolder and began to advocate that India join forces with Russia for the overthrow of the Raj, and to urge their countrymen to assassinate British officers. At which point the Government decided that such stuff endangered the 'safety of the state' and passed the Vernacular Press Act, designed to curb the mischief-making proclivities of news-sheets that were not printed in English. But the Act caused as much disaffection as the rabble-rousing articles and incitements to murder had done; and rumour took the place of the printed word.

There were a great many rumours in circulation that year and few were encouraging, except possibly to those who favoured a war with Afghanistan. Some told of Russian armies advancing on the Oxus River in numbers that grew as the tale was passed from mouth to mouth. An army of fifty thousand . . . of sixty thousand. No, eighty thousand . . .

'I have been reliably informed,' wrote Major Cavagnari in a letter to Simla, 'that the Russian force at present advancing on the Oxus consists of a total of fifteen thousand four hundred men, divided into three columns: two of which are seventeen hundred strong, and one of twelve thousand. Also that a Russian Mission, consisting of General Stolietoff and six other officers with an escort of twenty-two Cossacks, left Tashkent late in May in advance of the troops. It is believed that the Amir's family and friends, who fear that the Russo-Turkish affair may lead to hostilities between Russia and Great Britain, have been putting pressure on the Amir to choose between these two rival powers, but that His Highness cannot make up his mind and remains undecided. I must add that in the opinion of my informant (whose views, I would stress, are strictly personal), the Amir would much prefer to avoid declaring for either side, being convinced that his country should strive to remain independent of both. I have given the Government Agent in Peshawar a confidential letter which will be forwarded to you. It was sent to me by the same hand, and purports to be an exact copy of the terms laid down by a Russian Native Envoy who visited Kabul late last year. I cannot, of course, vouch for its accuracy, nor would it be advisable for me to disclose the source of my information. But I can assure you that I have every reason to believe that it is reliable.'

The document referred to was duly forwarded to Simla, and proved to be of considerable interest, the terms stating, among other things, that the Amir should permit the location of Russian Agents at Kabul and other places within his territories; that Russian troops should be quartered at 'four suitable places' on the borders of Afghanistan; and that the Russian Government should be permitted to construct roads and set up telegraph wires linking Samarkand with Kabul and Kabul with Herat and Kandahar. Also that the Afghan Government should establish agents in the capitals of Russia and Tashkent, and permit the passage of Russian troops through their territory, 'if it became desirable that the Russian Government should send an expedition to wage war on India'.

In return the Amir was assured that Russia would regard his enemies as theirs, in no way interfere in the administration and internal affairs of his country, and 'allow the continuance of Afghanistan to the representatives, successors and heirs of the Amir in perpetuity'.

Major Cavagnari had admitted somewhat grudgingly that the unnamed person who had obtained that copy and smuggled it out of Afghanistan had been at pains to point out that though, to the best of his belief, the original document was genuine and that these terms had in fact been drawn up, there was no evidence to suggest that the

Amir had either seen them or would have considered accepting them if he had; while on the other hand there was ample evidence that His Highness was much alarmed by the advance of Russian troops towards his borders, and greatly angered by the news that a Russian Mission was on its way, uninvited, to Kabul.

'There are times,' observed Major Cavagnari tartly to Captain Battye, who was in Peshawar for talks on Divisional Training and had asked for news of Ash, 'when I begin to wonder whose side your friend is on. Ours or the Amir's.'

Wigram smiled a little lop-sidedly and said with a hint of remonstrance: 'I wouldn't say it was a question of sides, sir. If you ask me, I should say rather that he can't help seeing both sides of a question, while the majority of us tend to see only one—our own. Besides, he's always had an obsession about being fair: you could almost call it a bee in his bonnet. If he thought there was something to be said for the Amir, it simply wouldn't occur to him not to say it. We did warn you about that, sir.'

'I know, I know. But I could wish he would not say it so often,' snapped the Deputy Commissioner. 'Fairness is all very well, but one must not forget that what he has to say in defence of the Amir can only be based on hearsay, and what I require is information, not personal theories. In any case his opinions do not square with the facts, since we know that General Stolietoff's Mission is on its way to Kabul, and I myself do not believe for one moment that it is going there uninvited. The Russian Government would never have allowed it to set out unless they had every reason to believe that it would be welcomed in Kabul, for they would not risk a rebuff: and that, to my mind, makes it crystal clear that Shere Ali has been intriguing with them.'

'Then you don't believe,' ventured Wigram, 'that Ashton—'

'Akbar,' corrected Major Cavagnari sharply. 'I consider it essential to avoid mentioning him by any other name even in the course of a private conversation. It is safer.'

'Of course, sir—that Akbar is right in thinking the Amir is anything but pleased by the news that the Mission is on its way?'

'That is something that your—that Akbar cannot possibly know for certain. And to be plain with you, I am beginning to find the tone of his reports disturbing. They display an increasing tendency to put the Amir's viewpoint rather than our own, and there are times when I am not entirely sure that he is . . . let us say, *sound*.'

Wigram said stiffly: 'I assure you there is not the least danger of his turning traitor, if that is what you mean sir.'

'No, *no!*' disclaimed Major Cavagnari testily: 'I meant no such thing. You take me up too quickly. But I must confess that in spite of your warning, I had supposed that as an Englishman he would be able to recognize the Amir's double-dealing for what it is, instead of making excuses for the man—which is what he is doing. He sends me information, some of it of considerable interest, and then confuses the issue with a piece of special pleading on behalf of the Amir, with whose problems he would appear to be too much in sympathy. But there is a simple solution to those problems: let Shere Ali ally himself with Great Britain and cease trafficking with Russia. It is his refusal to do the first and his persistence in the second that is causing the present tension, and I cannot agree with the view put forward by —by Akbar, that he would lose face with his subjects if he acceded to our request, and might even be deposed. Once he has openly declared in favour of an alliance with us, there would be no further danger of Russian aggression, as they would know that any move against Afghanistan would mean war with Great Britain. And with that danger removed, their troops would go home and the situation would return to normal.'

'Except,' remarked Wigram reflectively, 'that there would be a British Mission and British officers in Kabul, instead of Russian ones.'

The Deputy Commissioner's eyebrows twitched together in a frown and he favoured Captain Battye with a long, suspicious stare, and then inquired abruptly if he had been receiving communications from his friend.

'From Ash—Akbar? No,' said Wigram. 'I wasn't quoting. I've heard nothing about him until now, and I did not know if you had. In fact I wasn't even sure he was alive. That's why I called in to ask if you had any news of him, and it's a relief to me to learn that you have. But I'm sorry that he is not proving to be as useful as you had hoped.'

'He is useful. In some ways, exceedingly useful. But he would be even more so if he would confine himself to what is actually happening in Kabul, instead of indulging in what one can only regard as thought-reading. The matter of greatest concern is the whereabouts of this Russian Mission. Has it reached the borders of Afghanistan yet, and will it be refused entry into the country? Or will the Amir throw aside deception, and show himself in his true colours by receiving it at Kabul and thereby declaring himself to be our enemy? Time will show. But we know from several sources that Stolietoff and his Mission must be nearing the end of their journey, and if your friend should send word that they have been welcomed, we shall know where we stand. And so will he, I trust. It should at least open his eyes and show him the folly of attempting to find excuses for Shere Ali's behaviour.'

Time had shown even more quickly than Major Cavagnari had expected, for that very night he had received a brief message to say that the Russian Mission had entered Afghanistan and been accorded a public reception in Kabul. That was all. But the die had been cast, and from that moment a second Afghan war became inevitable.

Details had followed later. The Mission, it appeared, had been welcomed with all honour by the Amir. Elephants had been sent out to meet them, and mounted on these and attended by Afghan ministers and nobles, Stolietoff and his officers had ridden in state through the town of Kabul to the Bala Hissar, the ancient citadel that includes the royal palace of the rulers of Afghanistan, where the Amir Shere Ali and his court had waited to greet them. They had been housed in the Residency, which lies within the Bala Hissar, and accorded a strong guard: and ten days later a splendid military review had been held in their honour. But Louis Cavagnari's confident assertion that his 'unsound' spy would be unable to find any further excuses for Shere Ali proved incorrect.

'Akbar' had found several. He had even suggested that in the circumstances it was to Shere Ali's credit that he had stood out against Russian pressure as long as he had, while as for that review, it had, in his opinion, almost certainly been held less from a desire to do the self-invited visitors honour than as a covert warning—a visual demonstration of the military strength that Afghanistan could bring against any would-be aggressor . . .

'It is believed in Kabul,' wrote Akbar, 'that the Amir has not only come to no arrangement with the Russian Envoy, but is at the moment only playing for time until he sees what action the British Government will take to counter this move. You will undoubtedly hear reports that he has spoken with great bitterness of the way in which he has been treated by Her Majesty's Government; but I have not heard it suggested that he has any intention of yielding to a new friend what he has refused to an old ally, and I would emphasize yet again, and most strongly, that everything I have seen and heard, both in Kabul and elsewhere in Afghanistan, confirms my belief that Shere Ali is neither pro-Russian nor pro-British, but merely an Afghan who is striving to preserve the independence of his country against heavy odds—to name only two, a revolt by the Herati Ghilzais and the fact that his exiled nephew Abdur Rahman, now living under Russian protection, is widely believed to be willing to accede to any terms that his hosts may choose to demand, in return for his uncle's throne.'

But no amount of 'special pleading' could offset the shock and anger of the Viceroy and his advisers on hearing the news that a Russian Envoy had been received by the Amir, and welcomed with all honour, after Great Britain herself had been refused permission to send a similar mission to Kabul. This was an affront that no patriotic Englishman could be expected to stomach, and urgent letters were dispatched to London, pressing for permission to demand that the perfidious Shere Ali should consent to receive a British Mission in Kabul without any further shilly-shallying.

Faced with the irrefutable fact that a Russian Envoy had indeed been received by the Amir, the Foreign Secretary had given his consent, and the Viceroy had immediately set about selecting members for the Mission. The Commander-in-Chief of the Madras Army, General Sir Neville Chamberlain, was chosen to lead it, with two officers—one of them Major Louis Cavagnari—appointed to accompany him for 'political duties'. The party would include a Military Secretary and two aides-de-camp, and Lieutenant Colonel Jenkins was given command of the escort, drawn from his own Regiment and consisting of Major Stewart, Captain Battye, a hundred sabres of the Cavalry and fifty bayonets of the Infantry of the Queen's Own Corps of Guides.

The Mission was to set out for Kabul in September, but meanwhile a native emissary would leave immediately armed with a letter from the Viceroy to the Amir, advising him of the British Envoy's arrival and demanding that arrangements should be made for the safe passage of the Mission through His Highness's territory.

To emphasize the Government's displeasure, the emissary selected for this delicate task was a gentleman who some fourteen years earlier, before the days of Viceroys, had been appointed by the then Governor-General, Lord Lawrence, as Native Envoy to Kabul, and later been summarily recalled for abusing his position by intriguing against Shere Ali himself.

Not surprisingly, this choice of messenger did nothing to make the Amir feel more kindly disposed towards the British; while to make matters worse, Shere Ali was in ill-health and prostrated with grief at the sudden death of his favourite son, the beloved Mir Jan, whom he had chosen to succeed him. The emissary failed to make any headway, and by mid-September was writing to warn the Government that the Amir was in a bad humour, but that his ministers were still hopeful that a satisfactory solution might be achieved, and that he himself was convinced that further discussions were possible— provided the British Mission would delay its departure.

He need not have stressed that last, for travel was slow and Sir Neville Chamberlain, the Envoy Elect, had not yet arrived in Peshawar. When he eventually did so, it was to find that although the Amir had still not come to any decision, Major Cavagnari, anticipating a possible refusal, had already begun negotiating with the Maliks (headmen) of the Khyber tribes for a free passage for the Mission through their several territories. His discussions, unlike those in Kabul, were going well, and agreement had almost been reached when the Governor of the Khyber fortress of Ali Masjid, one Faiz Mohammed, came to hear of them and sent peremptory orders to the Maliks that they were to return immediately to their villages.

The Khyber tribes being titular subjects of the Amir, and their territories—the lands between Peshawar and Ali Masjid—part of Afghanistan, there was only one way to keep them from obeying this command: undertake to pay them the yearly subsidy that they had hitherto received from the Amir, and which would be cut off if they defied Faiz Mohammed's order.

But no one knew better than Major Cavagnari that any such action on the part of the Government would be regarded as an indefensible attempt to detach the tribes from their allegiance to the Amir, and that such hostile behaviour would only serve to convince Shere Ali that the British Mission, far from being 'friendly and peaceful', was in fact the spearhead of an invading army. He therefore abandoned his talks and referred the matter to the Viceroy; who agreed that until the Amir decided for or against the Mission, any private bargaining with the tribes might provide him with legitimate grounds for complaint, but suggested forcing matters to a crisis by sending a letter to Governor Faiz Mohammed, informing him that the Mission intended to set out for Kabul at once, and asking whether he was prepared to grant it safe passage through the Khyber Pass. Should the answer be unfavourable, then Sir Neville Chamberlain was to make a settlement with the Khyber tribes and advance on Ali Masjid . . .

The letter had been dispatched, and Faiz Mohammed had sent a polite reply, pointing out that there was no need to ask his permission, as provided the Amir had given his consent to the Mission proceeding to Kabul, they could do so in safety. On the other hand, if His Highness withheld his consent and they came without it, the garrison of Ali Masjid would be forced to oppose their advance; therefore he would suggest that the Mission delayed its departure and remained in Peshawar until the Amir's decision was known.

But the Envoy, like the Viceroy, had grown impatient of continued procrastination, and come to believe that the British had a right to send a Mission to Afghanistan and that the Amir had no right to refuse them. He sent a telegram to Simla announcing that the Mission was leaving Peshawar for Jamrud, at the limits of British-held territory, and that from there Major Cavagnari, with Colonel Jenkins of the Guides and one or two others, would go forward to Ali Masjid to test the Afghan reaction. If Faiz Mohammed refused to allow them to pass, this could be regarded as a hostile act and equivalent to being fired upon, and the Mission could then return to Peshawar without the disgrace of being turned back.

Cavagnari and his party, which in addition to Colonel Jenkins included Wigram Battye, half-a-dozen men of the Guides and some of the Khyber Maliks, duly left for Ali Masjid where the Governor, true to his promise, duly turned them back; informing Major Cavagnari that considering he had come without permission, after trying to suborn certain subjects of the Amir into giving him passage through His Highness's territories—thereby setting Afridi against Afridi—he could take it as a kindness on account of remembered friendship that he, Faiz Mohammed, had not opened fire on him for the deeds that his Government had done. 'After which,' said Wigram, describing the incident to Wally, 'he shook hands with us and we remounted and rode back to Jamrud with our tails between our legs: or that was what it felt like.'

Wally whistled expressively and Wigram nodded and said: 'No, not an experience I would like to repeat. For let's face it, the fellow was right. That was what was so galling. Our Government has not come out of this affair very well, and I cannot help thinking that if I had been an Afridi I'd have felt exactly as Faiz Mohammed did—and I only hope I'd have behaved as well. Yet I'm willing to lay you odds that because he stuck to his guns and refused to allow the Mission free passage through the pass except with his Amir's permission, it will now be claimed that Afghanistan has put an intolerable affront upon Her Majesty's Government and insulted the entire British Nation, so that we now have no recourse but to declare war.'

'Do you really think so?' demanded Wally a little breathlessly. He came to his feet like a released spring and began to walk about the room as though he could not keep still. 'Somehow it doesn't seem possible. I mean . . . well, one has got used to minor skirmishes, but war—a real war—and an unjust one. It's unthinkable: it can't be allowed to happen. Surely Ash . . .' he swung round on his heel and looked at Wigram. 'Have you heard any news of him?'

'Only that he is still in touch with Cavagnari, which means that he's all right so far.'

Wally sighed and said restlessly: 'He did warn me that he wouldn't be able to let us know how things were going with him, because it would be too risky; and that his wife and Zarin had both agreed to this. He said we three were the only ones who knew—apart from you and Cavagnari and the Commandant of course—and that even the fellow who acts as a link between him and Cavagnari, and who is one of Cavagnari's own men, wasn't to be told who he was . . . that he wasn't an Afghan, I mean. But that Cavagnari would probably let you know that he was keeping in touch, because it had been your idea in the first place.'

'Well, he has let me know, and he is in touch. So you can stop worrying about Ashton.'

'Can I tell his wife?'

'Will you be seeing her?' Wigram sounded surprised and not altogether pleased.

'No. I promised Ash I'd keep an eye on her, but we decided that it would be better if I didn't call at the house. The old Begum doesn't approve; thinks it might cause too much talk, and she's probably right. But I can always send a message by Zarin, as no one would think twice about him visiting his aunt's house when he's been doing it for years. I'd like her to know that Ash is all right. It must be very hard on her . . . not knowing.'

'Very,' agreed Wigram. 'Yes, of course you can let her know. I didn't realize she was still in Attock.'

'He couldn't take her with him, so he left her with the Begum. She used to know Zarin Khan and his father when she was a little girl, so I suppose she feels safe with Zarin's aunt. I gather she's learning how to handle firearms and speak Pushtu in case Ash should be able to send for her. I wish . . .'

His voice ran out abruptly, leaving the sentence unfinished, and after a moment or two Wigram said curiously: 'What is it you wish, Walter?'

Wally's unfocused gaze became alert again and he shook his head quickly in a movement that was very close to a shudder, and said lightly: 'That you would give up traipsing about with the Great and return to the bosom of your own Regiment. Mardan doesn't seem the same, what with you and Stewart and the Commandant off up the Khyber playing nurse-maid to this Mission we hear so much about. However, after this fiasco at Ali Masjid, I presume you'll all find yourselves out of a job.'

Wally presumed right. A report on the set-back at Ali Masjid had been telegraphed to the Viceroy, who replied by disbanding the Mission.

Lord Lytton had got what he wanted: proof. Proof that 'the Russian Menace' was no turnip lantern, but a grim reality with an Envoy already established in Kabul and an army advancing towards the Hindu Kush. Proof that Shere Ali was a treacherous intriguer, who having spurned the hand of friendship extended by Britain had clasped that of the Muscovite, and might even now be signing a treaty that would permit the establishment of Russian-garrisoned outposts along the very borders of India, and allow Russian troops free passage through the Passes. With General Stolietoff and his suite installed in the Bala Hissar itself, anything was possible. And if more were needed to drive home the necessity for immediate action, it had been provided by the public insult offered to Her Majesty's Envoy Sir Neville Chamberlain and a peaceful British Mission, who had not only been refused permission to enter the Amir's territory, but threatened with force should they attempt to do so. Such treatment was not to be borne, and Lord Lytton for one did not intend to bear it.

As an immediate answer to the rebuff at Ali Masjid, the Guides Corps from Mardan were sent to Jamrud, an ancient Sikh fortress that marked the limits of British-held territory; and two days after the short-lived Mission had been disbanded, orders went out for a strong force to be assembled at Multan for the purpose of crossing the Afghan border and threatening Kandahar, and for other regiments to concentrate on the outpost of Thal, where the Kurram River divided the district of Kohat from Afghan territory. A Sikh regiment and a Mountain Battery were brought from Kohat to strengthen the Peshawar garrison, and Major Cavagnari (who could see little future in attempting to re-open negotiations with the Maliks of the Khyber tribes) came up with a new and revolutionary scheme for bringing them over to the British side without wasting time in laborious talks and endless bargaining . . .

Asiatics were known to be inordinately impressed by success—and, conversely, to take a scornful view of losers—and as there could be no denying that the British Power had not shown to advantage in the recent confrontation at Ali Masjid, something ought to be done to wipe out that disgrace and earn the admiration of the tribesmen. And what could be better, suggested Louis Cavagnari, than to assault and capture, in a surprise attack, the very fortress whose Governor and garrison had dared to deny a British Mission passage through the Khyber? That should not only serve to teach the Afghans a lesson, but show them what the Raj could do if it chose to exert itself.

The Viceroy was delighted with this scheme, and ignoring the advice of his Commander-in-Chief and Sir Neville Chamberlain—who protested that the risks far outnumbered any advantages that might be gained—he gave the project his blessing. General Ross, in command at Peshawar, who had also protested, was curtly informed that Ali Masjid must and would be taken. The plan of action involved a swift night march, similar to the one Cavagnari had used so successfully against the Utman Khel tribesmen, followed by a surprise attack at dawn by a force consisting of the Guides and the 1st Sikhs under Colonel Jenkins, supported by 1,000 native and British troops drawn from the Peshawar garrison and supplied with three heavy guns.

As the success of the operation would depend on speed and secrecy, the greatest care must be taken that no hint of the impending attack should be allowed to leak out; and once the fortress was taken, the troops were to be withdrawn, for the Government of India had no intention of holding Ali Masjid, or leaving a garrison there.

Their object was not conquest, but merely to demonstrate, by a swift and brilliant feat of arms, that the Raj could not be insulted with impunity, and what its troops were capable of.

'I don't believe it!' gasped the Commanding Officer of the 1st Sikhs when informed of this by Colonel Jenkins in the privacy of the latter's bungalow. 'Are you trying to tell me that we're expected to march our fellows into Afghanistan to attack and capture a fort like Ali Masjid, and if we get it—which I'm not too sure we shall—to about-turn and march meekly back to Peshawar again, leaving the Afghans to cut up our dead and re-occupy the fort the moment our backs are turned? Why, it's crazy! They can't *all* have gone mad in Simla.'

'I know, I know,' sighed Colonel Jenkins tiredly. 'But crazy or not, we're going to have to do what we're told. "Ours not to reason why, ours but to do and die." '

'But . . . but my bearer always knows where the Regiment is being posted long before I do, and in a place like Peshawar, with the city crawling with Pathans, I wouldn't be surprised if they're on to this already and busy sending word to Faiz Mohammed and his levies to prepare a warm welcome for us. "Surprise" my foot! They'll be ready and waiting for us, and it'll be a miracle if we come out of this without being so badly scorched that the game won't have been worth the candle. Do you suppose the General's gone off his rocker?'

'It's not his idea,' said Colonel Jenkins. 'This is one of Cavagnari's brainwaves. He sees it as a quicker and better method of influencing the Khyber Tribes in our favour than trying to buy them over one by one—stun 'em with awe and admiration for our dash and bravery, and dazzle them with a hurricane one-inning victory. He's convinced the Viceroy that it'll work, so perhaps it sounds better on paper.'

'Then all I can say is that it's a pity it can't be fought on paper!' observed the Commanding Officer of the 1st Sikhs savagely. To which Colonel Jenkins offered no comment, for he too was appalled by the scheme and could only hope that someone—anyone—would be able to bring the Viceroy and the Deputy Commissioner of Peshawar to their senses before it was too late.

Fortunately, his hope was justified. The Military Member of the Viceroy's Council, learning of it only after the order to act upon it had already been given, declared in forthright language that in his opinion the absurdity of abandoning Ali Masjid after capturing it was only equalled by the folly of taking it: a protest that might have been ignored had it not been for the timely arrival in Simla of a telegram bringing news that Ali Masjid had been strongly reinforced by Afghan troops and artillery.

In the light of this piece of information the Viceroy had no option but to cancel the project, and Louis Cavagnari, baulked of his cherished plan to dazzle the Khyber Tribes with a brilliant *coup-de-main* that would make them decide to throw in their lot with the British, turned once more, with tireless patience, to the slow and often exasperating task of striving to attain the same end by words instead of deeds; negotiating with their Maliks, one by one.

Few men could have done it better, but the cajolery, argument and bribery involved took time. Too much time. And he was vividly aware of how little there might be left.

52

The conviction that time was running out was shared by many men that autumn. Not least by that one-time Commandant of the Corps of Guides, Sam Browne—the same who had discussed the boy Ashton's future with Zarin's elder brother, Awal Shah, so many years ago, and decided to send William Ashton's nephew to England in the care of Colonel Anderson.

Sam Browne, now Lieutenant-General Sir 'Sam' and newly appointed to the command of the First Division of the Peshawar Valley Field Force, had not been among those who approved Louis Cavagnari's sensational scheme for the capture of Ali Masjid. But he realized that if war were declared the fortress would have to be taken: not as a flamboyant gesture designed to impress the tribes, but as a matter of stark military necessity. Furthermore, it would have to be attacked within hours rather than days of the declaration, because Ali Masjid was the key to the Khyber Pass, and until it was taken the road to Kabul would remain barred.

In these circumstances it shocked the General to discover how little was known of the country through which his troops might soon have to advance—and this despite the fact that a British Army had marched that way before, and on retreating, suffered one of the most appalling disasters to befall an invading army since Napoleon's *Grande Armée* melted away on the agonizing retreat from Moscow.

'This is ridiculous. I must have maps,' said General Sam. 'We can't go barging bald-headed into those hills without knowing a damn' thing about them. Do you mean to tell me there *are* no maps? None at *all?*'

'Apparently not, sir; only a few rough sketches, and I understand none of those are very accurate,' said the Adjutant-General, adding in extenuation: 'The tribes don't take kindly to strangers wandering around their territories with compasses and theodolites, so you see—'

'No I don't,' snapped the one-armed General. 'But Major Cavagnari tells me that he has already come to an agreement with two of the tribes, and is in hopes of persuading a third—the Mohmands—to allow us free passage through their territory. That being so, it should be possible to send a few men to spy out the land for us. You'd better see to it, will you.'

The Adjutant-General had seen to it, and that same evening two men, Captain Stewart of the Guides and a Mr Scott of the Survey Department, had set out from Peshawar to reconnoitre the Border country and collect what information they could as to the strength and disposition of Faiz Mohammed Khan's forces. They had been absent for the best part of two weeks, and a few days after their return Louis Cavagnari had suggested that it would be a good idea if he were to accompany them on a second reconnaissance to confirm their results: 'And I think it might be as well, sir, if one or two of the officers who were with me during my interview with the Governor of Ali Masjid went with us. They already know something of the country, and a second visit should help to fix a good many important details in their minds; it seems to me that an accurate knowledge of the terrain may shortly be of incalculable value to us all.'

'You are right, there,' agreed the General grimly. 'The more we know about the place the better. Take whom you like.'

Which explains why a few days later dawn found Colonel Jenkins and Wigram Battye scrambling up a steep and almost invisible goat-track on the wrong side of the Border, in the wake of Captain Stewart, Mr Scott and the Deputy Commissioner of Peshawar . . .

The five men had left Jamrud in the chill pre-dawn darkness, and as unobtrusively as possible. Their horses and two sowars of the Guides Cavalry had been waiting for them outside the main gate of the fort, and the small party had mounted and ridden quietly away in the darkness. The moon was down and the stars were already fading, but in the east the sky was beginning to pale, and there was just enough light for the riders to be able to take their horses at a cautious trot across the stretch of plain that lay between Jamrud and the hills; though not enough—or so Major Cavagnari hoped—to make them visible to any watcher on those hillsides. Once safely across the open ground and among the foothills they had dismounted, and leaving their horses in charge of the sowars, gone forward on foot.

It had been a long and arduous climb, and the darkness had not helped. But as the sky overhead was beginning to lighten, they reached the summit of a five-hundred-foot ridge where Scott, who had been leading, stopped at last, panting and breathless. When he was able to command his voice he spoke in a whisper, as though he were afraid that even on this remote and silent hilltop there might be other listeners: 'I think, sir,' he said addressing Major Cavagnari, 'that this is the place you meant.'

Cavagnari nodded and said equally softly: 'Yes. We will wait here,' and his four companions, who were hot and tired and dripping with sweat, subsided thankfully on the ground and stared about them.

They were looking out across tribal territory: the secret and jealously guarded lands of men who recognized no law other than their own desires, and whose forebears have for centuries swept down from these hills like wolf packs to rob and lay waste the villages on the plains whenever the fancy took them: tribesmen who, though titular subjects of the Amir, have always had to be paid to keep the peace and to hold the passes against the enemies of Afghanistan—or, alternatively, bribed to let those enemies through.

Even with the aid of binoculars the light was still not strong enough to allow the five men on the hill-top to detect much detail in the shadowy, treeless maze of ridges and ravines that lay below them, or to pick out Ali Masjid from the hills that surrounded it. But the higher ranges were beginning to catch the first glimmer of dawn and to stand out clearly against the paling sky.

There was frost on the higher hills, and behind them, very far away, Wigram could see the gleam of snow and the white soaring peak of Sikaram, queen of the Safed Koh. It would be winter soon, he thought; the nights would be bitterly cold, and once the snow began to fall the northern passes would be blocked. He wouldn't have said, himself, it was a good time to start a war in a country like Afghanistan . . .

Glancing round at his companions he noticed for the first time that though Stewart, Scott and Colonel Jenkins were all lying at full length among the rocks, elbows propped on the ground as they raked the hills and ridges with their binoculars, Cavagnari alone had remained standing, and unlike the others, showed no interest in the scene ahead. His tall figure, outlined against the sky, conveyed a curious impression of tension, and his head was cocked a little on one side as though he was listening for something; and instinctively, Wigram too began to listen, straining his ears to pick out some unexpected sound in the dawn silence.

At first he could hear nothing but the hiss and whisper of the autumn wind through the rocks and the yellowing grasses, but presently he heard another sound: a faint click of metal on stone, followed by the unmistakable rattle of a displaced pebble rolling away down the hillside. Apparently Cavagnari had heard it too, and Wigram realized suddenly that this was something that the older man had been ex-pecting; for though he made no movement the tension seemed to leave him.

Someone was climbing up towards them from the opposite side of the ridge, and now the others were aware of it too. Colonel Jenkins had dropped his binoculars and there was a revolver in his hand, while Scott and Stewart were on their knees and reaching for their own weapons; but Cavagnari checked them with an imperative ges-ture, and they waited, all five of them, making no sound and holding their breath to listen, while dawn broke over the plains below and the far snows flushed pink in the first glow of the new day.

The unseen climber was obviously an experienced hillman, for considering the difficulties of the terrain he was making excellent progress up the precipitous slope, and as though to prove what little effect the altitude and strenuous exercise had upon him, he began to hum the *Zakmi dil,* which is an old song that all Pathans know. Not loudly, but hissing it through his teeth—for Asiatics do not whistle.

The tune was no more than a thread of sound, but in that dawn stillness it was clearly audible, and hearing it Cavagnari gave a sharp sigh of relief and motioning to his companions to stay where they were, walked quickly forward and down the hillside. The melody broke off and a moment later they heard him give the Pathan greet-ing, *'Stare-mah-sheh,'* and receive the conventional reply, and rising to their feet, looked downward and saw him in conversation with a lean, bearded tribesman who was armed with an antiquated match-lock and girt about with a bandolier stuffed full of brass-topped bullets.

It was not possible to hear what the two were saying, for after that first greeting their voices dropped to a murmur, but it was clear that Cavagnari was asking questions and the Pathan replying to them at some length; and presently, as the light strengthened, the man pointed in the direction of Ali Masjid, accompanying the gesture with an upward jerk of the head, and Cavagnari nodded, and turn-ing, came back to the ridge, the stranger following behind him.

'One of my men,' explained Cavagnari briefly. 'He says that we ought to keep down and stay out of sight, as Ali Masjid is held in force. Also that there is a picket not more than two miles away, and that as soon as the sun is up we shall be able to see it for ourselves.'

The Pathan ducked his head in salute to the Sahib-log, and at a word from Cavagnari, withdrew down the back of the ridge to the shelter of a tumble of rocks some twenty to thirty feet below, where he squatted down to wait, while above him the five men flattened themselves among the stones and took up their binoculars again as the featureless, pasteboard outlines of the hills took on shape and dimension and the morning mists shredded away.

The sky above them was no longer pearl-grey but cerulean, and from somewhere out of sight a partridge began to call. Then of a sudden the grass was streaked with long blue shadows, and four miles away as the crow flies, something glinted brightly in the blaze of the rising sun; pinpointing an insignificant hill-top that until then had been indistinguishable among a hundred others.

'Guns,' breathed Colonel Jenkins. 'Yes, that's Ali Masjid all right, and as your Pathan friend says, it's been well and truly re-inforced. Just look at those breastworks.'

The fort, now suddenly visible, crowned a conical hill that barely showed above a stony ridge that was scored with lines of newly built breastworks which the binoculars showed to be well defended. There was also a cavalry encampment at the foot of the ridge, and presently a small body of horsemen emerged from among the tents, and riding up to the Shagai plateau, made their way across it to a little tower near the Mackeson road: presumably the picket that the Pathan had spoken of.

'Time we went, I think,' decided Major Cavagnari, putting away his binoculars. 'Those fellows have got eyes like hawks, and we don't want to be spotted. Come on.'

They found the Pathan still squatting, frontier-fashion, among the rocks, his jezail across his knees, and Cavagnari motioned the others to go on ahead and went over to exchange a last word with him: but catching up with them a few minutes later as they hurried forward down the grassy hillside towards the safety of the plains and their own side of the border, he checked suddenly and called to Wigram, who stopped and turned:

'Yes, sir?'

'I'm sorry, but I forgot something—' Cavagnari produced a handful of silver and a packet of cheap country-made cigarettes and thrust it at Wigram. 'Be a good fellow and take this up to that man up there, will you? I usually give him a few rupees and some of these things, and I don't want him turning up in Jamrud to demand his baksheesh, and being recognized. We won't wait for you—' He turned and hurried on downward as Wigram started back up the steep slope.

The chill had gone out of the morning and now the sun was hot on Wigram's shoulders and there were butterflies on the hillside: familiar, English-looking butterflies. Fritillaries, brimstones, meadow-browns and tiny common blues that reminded him of summer holidays long ago, when he and Quentin had been boys and gone butterfly-hunting in the fields and lanes of Home. There were birds too, twittering among the grasses, and when a shred of shadow flicked over him he looked up and saw a lammergeyer very high in the blue, soaring majestically above the tumbled ridges of the Khyber.

Now that the sun was up, walking back up the hillside was warmer work than it had been in the chill starlight before dawn, and as he plodded forward, sweat soaked his shirt and ran down into his eyes. He brushed the drops away irritably and wondered if Cavagnari's Pathan would still be there, and if not, what he was supposed to do about it. But a faint sound drifted down to him: the ghost of a melody—*Zakmi dil,* that traditional love-song of a land where homosexuality has always been an accepted part of life . . . *'There's a boy across the river with a bottom like a peach, but alas, I cannot swim . . .'*

The familiar tune was half hummed, half sung, but as the climber drew nearer it changed to something even more familiar, and in that setting, startlingly unexpected: *'D'ye ken John Peel with his coat so gay—'*

Wigram stopped dead, staring upward at the bearded figure squatting in the shade of the rocks. 'Well I'm damned—!' He broke into a run and arrived panting. 'Ashton—you young devil. I didn't recognize you . . . I had no idea . . . Why the deuce didn't you say something? Why—'

Ash had risen to his feet to grasp the outstretched hand. 'Because your friend Cavagnari didn't want the others to know. He wasn't going to let you know either if I hadn't insisted. But I said I had to speak to you, so he agreed to send you back. Sit down, and don't talk too loudly—it's astonishing how far a sound can carry in these hills.'

Wigram subsided cross-legged on the ground, and Ash said: 'Now tell me the news. Have you heard anything of my wife? Is she all right? I haven't dared try to get in touch with her in case . . . And how are Wally and Zarin?—and the Corps and . . . Oh, everything: I've been starving for news!'

Wigram was able to reassure him about Anjuli, one of the Begum's servants having ridden over to Jamrud only three days earlier, bringing a message to Zarin from his Aunt Fatima to say that all under her roof were well and in good heart, and that she hoped the same could be said of him—and also of his friends. As this last was clearly an oblique inquiry as to whether there was any news of Ash, Zarin had sent back a reply saying that no one need have anxiety on that score; he and his friends were in excellent health.

'That was because I'd told him you were getting messages through to Cavagnari, so you were obviously still alive and presumably safe and well,' said Wigram, and went on to talk of Wally and what the Guides were doing, and to describe the war-like preparations that were creating chaos throughout the North-Western territories. Men and guns hurriedly transferred from one command to reinforce another; additional regiments rushed up from down-country to fill the gaps; supply trains pouring into the terminus of the North-Western Railway at Jhelum, blocking the platforms and jamming every siding with truck-loads of dead and dying transport mules and other pack animals abandoned by their native drivers. Not to mention the piles of foodstuffs, clothing and ammunition that the under-staffed Commissariat were totally incapable of coping with . . .

'It's like something out of Dante's Inferno,' said Wigram, 'and the only people who are really enjoying it are the *budmarshes* from every village for miles around, who are having the time of their lives looting the stuff. And to make bad worse, most of the troops from down-country have been sent up wearing tropical kit, so unless something can be done about that pretty quickly, half of them are going to die of pneumonia.'

Ash observed sardonically that it sounded like a typical Staff rumpus, and that if it was like this now, God only knew what it would be like if there really was a war.

'Oh, I expect we shall muddle through all right,' said Wigram tolerantly.

'Why,' demanded Ash, exasperated, 'is it necessary to "muddle through"? Anyone would think that it was "bad form" to plan ahead and— What are you laughing about?'

'You,' grinned Wigram, 'squatting there on your hunkers, the dead-spit of a home-grown Khyber bandit, and spouting about "bad form". You must admit it has its humorous side.'

Ash laughed and apologized, and Wigram said: 'I suppose it's that beard that changes you so completely. I'd absolutely no idea it was you. Anyway, I thought you were in Kabul.'

'I was. But I wanted to see Cavagnari myself instead of writing or sending a verbal message through the usual channels. I thought that if I could talk to him I might be able to persuade him to see things differently; but I was wrong. In fact all I've done is to make him think that I'm growing far too biased in favour of the Amir, and in grave danger of becoming "unreliable". By which I presume he means turning traitor.'

'Been losing your temper again, Ashton?' inquired Wigram with a faint smile. 'Because you're talking poppycock, you know. Of course he doesn't think anything of the sort. Or if he does, it means you've gone out of your way to give him that impression. What have you been saying to upset him?'

'The truth,' said Ash bleakly. 'And I might just as well have saved my breath and stayed in Kabul, for he does not want to believe it. I'm beginning to think that none of them do—the fellows in Simla, I mean.'

'What won't they believe?'

'That there is no danger whatever of the Amir allowing the Russians to build roads and establish military bases in his country, and that even if he were mad enough to agree to it, his people would not and it is they who count. I've told Cavagnari again and again that the Afghans do not want to take sides with either of us: Russia or the Raj— Yes, yes, I know what you're going to say: he said it too . . . "But the Amir welcomed the Russian Mission to Kabul." Well, what if he did? What the hell else could he do—bearing in mind that there was a Russian army across the Oxus and advancing on his borders, half his territories were in revolt, and news of Russian victories in Turkey was spreading across Asia like wildfire? He did his damnedest to put Stolietoff and his lot off, and then tried to delay their arrival; but when it became clear that they were coming anyway, he did the only thing he could do short of shooting them all and taking the consequences: he put a good face on it and gave them a public welcome. That's all there was to it. He didn't want them any more than he wants us, and the Viceroy knows it—or if he doesn't, his intelligence service must be the worst in the world!'

'You must admit that it didn't look too good from this end,' observed Wigram judicially, 'after all, the Amir had refused to receive a British Mission.'

'And why not? We prate about our "rights" in Afghanistan and our "right" to have a Mission in Kabul, but who the hell gave us these "rights"? It isn't our country and it has never been a threat to us—except as a possible ally of Russia's and a base for a Russian attack on India, and everyone knows by now that any danger of that, if it ever existed, ended with the recent signing of the Berlin Treaty. So it's sheer flaming nonsense to pretend that we have anything to fear from Afghanistan herself. The whole thing can almost certainly be settled peaceably; it's not too late for that. There is still time. But it seems that we prefer to consider ourselves seriously threatened and to pretend that we have leaned over backwards to conciliate the Amir, but that our patience is now exhausted. Good God, Wigram, do our blasted Big-wigs *want* a second Afghan war?'

Wigram shrugged his shoulders and said: 'Why ask me? I'm only a poor bloody cavalry officer who does what he's told and goes where he's sent. I'm not in the confidence of the great, so my opinion isn't worth much; but from what I hear, the answer is "Yes"—they do want a war.'

'That's what I thought. Imperialism has gone to their heads and they want to see more and more of the map painted pink, and to go down in the history books as great men; Pro-Consuls and modern Alexanders. *Pah!*—it makes me sick.'

Wigram said: 'You mustn't blame Cavagnari. I heard him tell Faiz Mohammed at Ali Masjid that he was only a servant of the Government, who did what he was told. And that's as true of him as it is of me.'

'Perhaps. But men like him, men who really do know something about the Khyber tribes and can talk to them in their own dialects, should be advising the Viceroy and his fellow fire-eaters to hold their horses, instead of urging them to charge. Which is what he would seem to be doing. Oh well, I've done my best; but it was a mistake to think that anyone could ever make him believe anything that he does not want to believe.'

'It was worth trying,' said Wigram defensively.

'I suppose so,' conceded Ash with a sigh. 'You know, I didn't mean to unload my bile on you. I only meant to ask you about my wife, and about Wally and Zarin and the rest, and to ask you to see that Zarin lets my wife know that you have seen me and talked to me and that I'm all right . . . and so on. I didn't mean to get side-tracked into this other nonsense, but I suppose it's been weighing on my mind too much.'

'I'm not surprised,' said Wigram with feeling. 'It's been weighing on mine too. And if it comes to that, so have you! I've found myself lying awake at night wondering if I did right in interfering and get-ting you involved in all this, and if I wouldn't have done a lot better to keep my mouth shut and avoid having your death on my con-science.'

'I didn't know you had one,' mocked Ash, grinning. 'You don't have to worry, Wigram: I can look after myself. But I admit I shall be infernally glad when this is over.'

'Me too!' agreed Wigram with ungrammatical fervour. 'In fact I'll have a word with the Commandant, and see if he can't ask for you to be recalled.'

Ash's grin faded and he said ruefully: 'No, Wigram, don't tempt me. I walked into this with my eyes open, and you know as well as I do that I must go on with it as long as there is a ghost of a chance that even at this eleventh hour reason may prevail: because Afghan-istan is no country to fight a war in—and an impossible one to hold if you win. And anyway, I object, on principle, to injustice.'

' "It isn't fair" in fact,' murmured Wigram provocatively.

Ash laughed and acknowledged the hit with a raised palm, but remained unrepentant: 'You're right. It isn't fair. And if war is de-clared, it will be an unjust and unjustifiable war, and I do not believe that God will be on our side. Well, it's been good to see you Wigram. Will you see that my wife gets this'—he handed over a folded and sealed piece of paper—'and give my love to Wally and Zarin and tell them that their Uncle Akbar has their interests at heart. And if you have any influence with Cavagnari, try to persuade him that I am neither a liar nor a renegade, and that to the best of my knowledge everything I have told him is strictly true.'

'I'll try,' said Wigram. 'Goodbye—and good luck.'

He rose to his feet and went away down the hillside, and reaching the plain in safety, mounted his waiting horse and rode swiftly back to Jamrud in the bright mid-morning sunlight.

Later that day he had talked with Major Cavagnari about Ash. But the conversation had been brief and inconclusive, and Wigram was left with the impression that he would have done better to leave well alone.

Neither man was, at the time, aware that much of Ash's views were shared by no less a person than Her Majesty's Prime Minister, Lord Beaconsfield—Victoria's beloved 'Dizzy'—who in the course of a speech delivered at the Lord Mayor's Banquet at London's Guildhall had expressed them to a nicety: though he had been careful to avoid naming names . . .

'One would suppose, from all we hear,' Dizzy had said, 'that our Indian Empire is on the eve of being invaded, and that we are about to enter into a struggle with some powerful and unknown foe. In the first place, my Lord Mayor, Her Majesty's Government are by no means apprehensive of any invasion of India by our North-West Frontier. The base of operations of any possible foe is so remote, the communications are so difficult, the aspect of the country is so forbidding, that we do not believe under these circumstances that any invasion of our North-West Frontier is practicable.'

But though the invention of the telegraph had made it possible to send news from one end of India to the other with miraculous speed, communication with England was still painfully slow, so no one in India was aware of these sentiments. Nor would the planners in Simla or the busy Generals in Peshawar and Quetta and Kohat have paid much attention to them if they had known, for though Cavagnari's scheme of capturing Ali Masjid had been abandoned, its ultimate effects had proved catastrophic. The formidable number of the reinforcements that Faiz Mohammed had, as a result, hastily gathered for its defence had seriously alarmed the Viceroy's military advisers, who decided that the presence of so large a force within sight of the Frontier was a danger to India and must be countered by a similar mobilization of troops on the British side of the Border.

Once again couriers from India carried letters to Kabul. Letters that accused the Amir of being *activated by motives inimical to the British Government'* in receiving the Russian Mission, and demanding a *'full and suitable apology'* for the hostile action of the Governor of Ali Masjid in refusing passage to a British one. And once again it was stressed that friendly relations between the two countries depended on the Amir's acceptance of a permanent British Mission in his capital:

'Unless these conditions are accepted, fully and plainly by you,' wrote Lord Lytton, *'and your acceptance received by me not later*

than the 20th November, I shall be compelled to consider your intentions as hostile, and to treat you as a declared enemy of the British Government.'

But the luckless Shere Ali, who had once described himself as being like 'an earthen pipkin between two iron pots' (and who by this time had come to detest the British and distrust their motives), could not decide on how to treat this ultimatum. Instead he hesitated and wavered, wringing his hands and railing against fate, and hoping that if he took no action the crisis might somehow dissolve, as previous ones had done. For after all, the Russians had left Kabul and Stolietoff was now actually writing to him to recommend that he make peace with the British—Stolietoff, whose insistence on thrusting his way into Afghanistan, uninvited, had caused all this trouble in the first place. It was too much!

In Simla the Viceroy's Private Secretary, Colonel Colley, who was as eager for war as his lord and master, was writing: *'Our principal anxiety now is lest the Amir should send an apology, or the Home Government interfere.'*

Colonel Colley need not have been anxious. The twentieth day of November came and went, and there was still no word from the Amir. And on the twenty-first, declaring that he had no quarrel with the Afghan people but only with their ruler, Lord Lytton ordered his Generals to advance. A British Army marched into Afghanistan, and the Second Afghan War had begun.

53

The December weather had been unusually mild, but with the arrival of the New Year the temperature had begun to fall, and there came a day when Ash was aroused in the small hours of the morning by the furtive touch of soft, cold fingers on his cheeks and his closed eyelids.

He had been dreaming again, and in his dream he had been lying half-asleep by the side of a rushing stream in a valley among the mountains. Sita's valley. It was spring and there were pear trees in blossom, and a breeze blowing through the branches loosened the petals and sent them floating down to rest upon his face.

The cool touch of those falling petals and the rushing sound of the stream combined to wake him, and he opened his eyes and realized that he must have slept for a long time, and that while he did so the wind had arisen: and it was snowing.

He had been afraid of this the previous evening. But there had been no wind then, and having lit a small fire in the back of a narrow cave among the rocks, he had cooked himself a meal, and when darkness fell, rolled himself in his blanket and gone to sleep, warmed and comforted by the glow of the firelight. The wind must have arisen some hours later, and now it moaned among the hills and drove a flurry of enormous snowflakes into the cave.

The flakes had settled on Ash's face and beard and he brushed them away, and rising stiffly shook the snow from the folds of his blanket before rewrapping it about his head and shoulders above the sheepskin poshteen that he had worn day and night for the past week or so. The poshteen smelt rankly of smoke and rancid oil, unwashed wool and unwashed humanity, but Ash was grateful for its warmth as the cave was bitterly cold, and would become colder still. Besides, he had become inured to evil smells and did not let such things trouble him.

Peering out into the whirling greyness, he realized that dawn could not be far off, and he turned and groped his way to the back of the cave to light another fire with the aid of a tinder box, using the last of a small supply of charcoal he carried with him, and some spare brushwood that he had taken the precaution of collecting the previous evening. It was not much, but it would serve to heat enough water for a bowl of tea that would warm his stomach and help to bring the circulation back to his numbed feet and cold fingers; and he still had the best part of two chuppattis.

He watched the grass flare up and catch the sticks of wood, and when the charcoal began to glow, placed his brass water-bowl on top of it and sat back to wait while it boiled; and while he waited, thought of all that had happened during the last weeks of the old year and the first few weeks of the new, and wondered how soon he would be permitted to throw his hand in and go back to Mardan; and to Juli.

Lord Lytton's war against Shere Ali (the Viceroy had made a great point of insisting that he had no quarrel with the Amir's subjects) had got off to a good start, despite a series of distressing blunders due to faulty planning. These mishaps, however, had not prevented the fall of Ali Masjid within two days of the outbreak of hostilities, with a loss to the victors of a mere fifteen killed and thirty-four wounded; or, a few days later, the occupation of Dakka and the subsequent occupation of Jalalabad. New Year's Day had seen the British firmly in possession of these three strongpoints, and there had been similar successes on other fronts, notably the occupation by the Kurram Field Force, under the command of Major-General Sir Frederick Roberts, of the Afghan forts in the Kurram Valley.

But something else had occurred in the New Year. Something that had seemed to Ash of such enormous importance that once again he had decided that he must talk directly to Major Cavagnari, who having accompanied the victorious army in the capacity of Political Officer, was at that time in Jalalabad, where he had addressed the durbar held by Sir Sam Browne on the first day of the New Year and endeavoured to explain, to the few Afghan chiefs who had attended it, the reasons for the British Government's declaration of war and its peaceful intentions towards the tribes.

Ash did not think that he would have much difficulty in arranging a meeting with Cavagnari once he reached Jalalabad, for by now the local inhabitants would have realized that they stood in no danger of being massacred by the invading infidels, and would have flocked back to their homes, intent upon selling goods to the troops at greatly inflated prices. The town would therefore once again be swarming with Afridis, and one more would not be remarked.

But he had not allowed for snow, and now he wondered if he

would be able to get to Jalalabad at all, because if the present storm continued for long it could obliterate all the tracks and landmarks that he needed to guide him—if it had not done so already. The thought was a grim one and he held out his hands to the fire with a shiver that was not wholly due to the cold. But his luck was in, for the snow had stopped falling by the time it was light enough for him to start, and towards noon he fell in with a small party of Powindahs making for Jalalabad, and in their company reached the outskirts of that walled city a full hour before sunset.

The business of getting in touch with Major Cavagnari had proved reasonably easy, and late that night he had been met by arrangement, at a spot outside the walls, by a shadowy figure wearing a poshteen and further protected from the freezing night by a dun-coloured shawl; the latter worn wrapped about head and shoulders without entirely concealing a cavalry turban beneath. After Ash had identified himself and answered a few whispered questions, he was taken past the sentries on the gate and along a series of narrow unlit alleyways between the blank walls of houses, to a small and unobtrusive door where a second muffled figure awaited him. A minute later he was being ushered into a lamp-lit room where the ex-Deputy Commissioner of Peshawar, now Political Officer to the Peshawar Valley Field Force, was working late on the piles of reports that littered his desk.

The news that Ash brought was both startling and tragic, though its tragic side escaped Major Cavagnari, who had never had any sympathy with Shere Ali.

The Amir, on learning that his reply to Lord Lytton's ultimatum had arrived too late and that his country was being invaded and his fortresses falling like ripe nuts in a gale, had lost his head and decided to throw himself on the mercy of the Tsar.

The mounting pressure of events had already forced him to acknowledge his eldest son, Yakoub Khan (whom he had kept under house-arrest for many years, and still hated), as his heir and co-ruler in open council, but it had been a bitter and humiliating experience for him, and the only way in which he could avoid the painful embarrassment of having to share his councils with an unfilial son, while his heart still bled for the death of a dearly loved one, was to remove from Kabul. This he had done, explaining that he intended to journey to St Petersburg to lay his case before the Emperor Alexander, and demand justice and the protection of all right-thinking

European Powers against the encroachments of Great Britain . . .

'Yes, I know all this,' said Major Cavagnari patiently, adding with a tinge of rebuke that Ash must not think he was the sole source of information as regards affairs in Kabul. 'We heard of the Amir's intentions. In fact he himself wrote to inform the British Government of the step he was taking, and challenged them to establish their case and explain their intentions to a Congress to be held in St Petersburg. I presume he got the idea of this from the Congress of Berlin, where our differences with Russia were discussed and resolved. I was later informed that he left Kabul on the twenty-second of December for an unknown destination.'

'Mazar-i-Sharif, in his province of Turkestan,' supplied Ash. 'He arrived there on New Year's Day.'

'Indeed? Well, I expect we shall soon receive official confirmation of this.'

'I'm sure you will. But in the circumstances I thought you should know about it as soon as possible, because of course this will make all the difference.'

'In what way?' inquired Cavagnari, still patiently. 'We already knew him to be hand-in-glove with the Russians, and this merely proves that we were right.'

Ash stared. 'But sir— Don't you see, he's no longer of any importance? He's finished himself as far as his people are concerned, because after this he can never return to Kabul or sit on the throne of Afghanistan again. If he'd stayed and stood firm, he would have become the rallying point of every infidel-hating Afghan in his Kingdom—which means ninety-nine and a half per cent of the population —but instead he chose to turn tail and run away, leaving Yakoub Khan to hold the candle. I do assure you, sir, he's finished; bust, smashed, *klas-shu!* But that's not why I came here, for it is no longer of any importance. I came to tell you that he will never reach St Petersburg, because he is dying.'

'*Dying?* Are you sure?' demanded Cavagnari sharply.

'Yes, sir. Those who are closest to him are already saying that he knows this himself and is hastening his death by refusing food and medicines. They say that he is a broken man. Heart-broken by grief at the death of the son he doted upon and the humiliation of having to acknowledge as his heir the one he detested: and also by the intolerable pressures brought to bear on him by Russia and ourselves. He has nothing left to live for, and no one believes that he will ever leave Turkestan—or would get very far if he tried to, as the Russians would certainly turn him back. Now that they have officially shaken hands with us, Afghanistan has obviously become a bit of an embarrassment to them, and I imagine they'd prefer to forget about the place . . . until the next time, of course. I have also heard on good authority that Shere Ali has written to General Kaufman asking him to intercede on his behalf with the Tsar, and that Kaufman has written back urging him not to leave his kingdom and advising him to make terms with the British. So he must know by now that there is no help to be expected from Russia, and that in leaving Kabul he has made a fatal and irreparable mistake. One cannot help feeling sorry for him; but at least it means that the war can now be ended and our troops sent back to India.'

'Back to India?' Cavagnari's brows snapped together. 'I don't understand you.'

'But surely, sir . . . Didn't the Viceroy's proclamation say that we had no quarrel with the Afghan people, but only with Shere Ali? Well, Shere Ali has gone. He's left Kabul, and you of all men, because you understand these people, must know that he will never be allowed to go back again—Yakoub Khan will see to that! Besides, as I've told you, he's a dying man and any day now you are going to hear that he is dead. But whether he lives or dies, he doesn't count any more. So who are we fighting?'

Cavagnari did not answer, and after a moment Ash spoke heatedly into the silence:

'Look, sir, if it's true that we have no quarrel with his people, then I'd like to know what the hell we are still doing here, weeks after he threw up the sponge and did a bunk? I'd like to know what our excuse is now for invading their homes and annexing their territories, and when they resist (which shouldn't surprise us), shooting them down and burning their villages and fields so that their women and children and the old and feeble are left without food and shelter—and in midwinter, too. Because that is what we are doing, and if Lord Lytton meant what he said about having no quarrel with the Afghan people, he should stop this war now, at once; for there is no longer any reason for going on with it.'

'You forget,' said Major Cavagnari coldly, 'that as Shere Ali appointed his son Yakoub Khan co-ruler, Yakoub will now be acting as Regent. Therefore the country still has a ruler.'

'But not an *Amir!*'—it was almost a cry of pain. 'How can we pretend that we have any quarrel with Yakoub, when he has been held prisoner for years and his release has been urged again and again by a number of our own officials? Surely, now that he is virtually ruler of Afghanistan, it should at least be possible to call a truce until we see how he means to behave? It couldn't do us any harm, and it would save a great many lives. But if we are going to press on with this war without even waiting to see what he will do, we shall throw away any chance of turning him into a friend, and merely ensure that he too, like the father he hated, becomes our enemy. Or is that what we want? Is it?'

Once again, Cavagnari did not answer, and Ash repeated the question again, his voice rising dangerously. 'Is that what you *really* want?—you and the Viceroy and the rest of His Excellency's advisers? Is this whole blood-stained business just an excuse to take over Afghanistan and add it to the Empire—and to hell with its people, with whom we say we have no quarrel? Is it? *Is it?* Because if so—'

'You forget yourself, Lieutenant Pelham-Martyn,' interrupted Cavagnari icily.

'Syed Akbar,' corrected Ash with acidity.

Cavagnari ignored the correction and swept on: 'And I must ask you not to shout. If you cannot control yourself you had better leave before you are overheard. We are not in British India now, but in Jalalabad, which is full of spies. I would also point out that it is neither your place nor mine to criticize the orders we are given, or to question matters of policy that lie outside the scope of our knowledge. Our duty is to do what we are told, and if you are incapable of this, then you are of no further use to me or to the Government I have the honour to serve, and I feel that you would do better to sever your relations with us now.'

Ash sighed deeply and relaxed. He felt as though a weight had been lifted off his shoulders: a dragging weight of responsibility that like Sinbad's Old Man of the Sea had been growing steadily heavier and more irksome to carry. Though he had the sense to realize that this was largely his own fault for being conceited enough to imagine that the information he had been at such pains to collect would be considered sufficiently important to affect the decisions of the Viceroy's council, and to weigh the scales of power in favour of peace instead of war. He should have known better.

His usefulness—if any—had lain only in the fact that his messages served to confirm or contradict the accuracy of tales sent in by native spies who were prone to exaggerate, or suspected of being over-credulous. As a check on such stories his own efforts had probably been of use, but apart from that they had counted for very little; and made no difference at all to the Viceroy's decisions—or to anyone else's. The vital issue of Peace or War must already have been decided upon before ever he himself volunteered to serve as a spy, and it would not have been altered except on direct orders from London, or the complete and absolute submission of Shere Ali to the demands of the Viceroy and the Government of India.

'I needn't have bothered,' thought Ash. 'Here have I been thinking of myself as the White Hope of Asia, and imagining that thousands of lives could depend on what I could find out and what use I made of it, and all the time I've been no more than just one more informer spying for the Raj—and not even drawing extra pay and allowances for it!'

The humour of it suddenly struck him and he laughed for the first time in many weeks, and then seeing the startled distaste on Cavagnari's face, apologized:

'I'm sorry, sir. I didn't mean to offend you. It's only that . . . I've been taking myself so seriously of late. Seeing myself as a sort of *deus ex machina* with the fate of my friends and the nation—two nations—depending upon me. You are right to get rid of me. I'm not cut out for this sort of work, and I should have had more sense than to let myself be talked into it in the first place.'

He had not expected the older man to understand how he had felt, but Louis Cavagnari was only English by adoption. The blood in his veins was French and Irish, and he too was a romantic—seeing History not only as the story of times past, but as something in the making. Something that he himself could play a part in . . . Perhaps a great part . . .

His expression softened and he said: 'There is no need to talk like that. You have been a great help. Much of the information that you have sent us has proved valuable, so you must not think that your efforts have been wasted. Or that I am not deeply grateful to you for all that you have done, and all that you have attempted to do. No one is more aware than I am of the grave risks you have run and the dangers you have cheerfully faced; and of the sacrifices you have made. In fact once this campaign is over, I shall have no hesitation in recommending that you be awarded a decoration for bravery.'

'Rats!' observed Ash inelegantly. 'I do beg you will do no such thing, sir. I hate to disillusion you, but for someone like myself there has been precious little danger, for I have never felt very different from the people I have met and talked to while I have been here. I haven't had to—to shed a skin, if you know what I mean, or grow another one. That has made it easy for me. That, and the fact that the country has been so disturbed with levies being rushed from point to point, that a stranger in one of the tribal districts no longer stands out like a sore thumb. So you see I have never really felt afraid for myself. I don't think anyone quite understands that; but it has made a great difference. The only thing I have been afraid of, and that weighed on my mind, has been my responsibility, as I saw it, for preventing a disastrous mistake: another— Oh, well, you know all about that, so there's no point in going into it again.'

'None,' agreed Cavagnari briefly. 'On that subject we must agree to differ. But I repeat, I am sincerely grateful to you. I mean that. I am also sorry that our ways have to part. I shall of course pass on to the proper authorities the news you have just brought me regarding Shere Ali's arrival at Mazar-i-Sharif and the state of his health, and also your personal view of the situation. It may make some difference; I don't know. But the conduct of this war is not in my hands. If it were . . . But that is neither here nor there. This is goodbye then. I presume you will be returning to Mardan? If it would be of any help, I could arrange for you to travel back to Peshawar with one of our convoys.'

'Thank you, sir, but I think it would be better if I found my own way back. Besides, I'm not sure yet when I shall be leaving. That will be up to my Commanding Officer.'

Cavagnari gave him a sharp, suspicious look but refrained from comment and the two men shook hands and parted. The Political Officer turning back immediately to his desk and the work that demanded his attention, while his erstwhile agent was shown out into the street by the confidential servant who had admitted him, and who now locked and barred the door behind him.

After the heated office the night air felt piercingly cold, and the man who on Cavagnari's orders had brought Ash into the fortified town, and been instructed to wait and see him safely out again, had taken shelter from the wind in the doorway of the opposite house, so that for a moment Ash was afraid he had gone, and spoke anxiously into the windy darkness:

'Zarin?'

'I am here,' said Zarin, coming forward. 'You have been a long time talking to the Sahib and I am perished with cold. Did your news please him?'

'Not particularly. He already knew half of it, and will hear the rest within a day or two. But we cannot talk here.'

'No,' agreed Zarin. He led the way through the unlighted streets, moving as swiftly and silently as a cat, and presently stopped beside a low, mud-brick building below the outer wall. Ash heard an iron key grate in a lock, and then he was being shown into a small room lit by a single *chirag* and the red glow from a charcoal brazier that filled the cramped space with a welcome warmth.

'Your quarters?' asked Ash, squatting on his heels and spreading out his hands to the glowing coals.

'No. I have borrowed it from one of the nightwatchmen who is on duty at this time. He will not be back before dawn, so we shall be safe for some hours; and there is much that I wish to hear. Do you know that it is close on seven months since I last saw you? That is more than half a year—and in all that time I have heard nothing. Not one word: save only that Wigram-Sahib had seen and spoken to you on the crest of Sarkai Hill early in November, and that you had asked him to see that a letter went by a safe hand to Attock.'

Zarin had carried that letter himself, and was able to report that Anjuli was in good health and much beloved by all the household, and that she had been studying Pushtu with such diligence that she could already speak it fluently. Also that both she and his aunt prayed daily for Ash's safety and his early return—as did Gul Baz and all in the Begum's house. 'There. Now that I have told you what you most wish to know, you can eat with a quieter mind. Here are chuppattis and *jal frazi* that I have kept hot for you. You do not look to me as though you have fed well of late; if at all—you are as lean as an alley-cat.'

'So would you be if you had come on horseback and by camel, and on foot over the Lataband, from Charikar beyond Kabul in little more than five days,' retorted Ash, falling upon the food. 'It is not a journey to be undertaken in winter, and as it was necessary to come quickly, I have eaten and slept in the saddle so that I need not waste the nights.'

He reached for a tin mug filled with strong tea and liberally sweetened with *gur,* and drank thirstily, and Zarin, watching him, said: 'Is it permitted to ask what news you carried?'

'Why not? I came to tell Cavagnari-Sahib something that he already knew. That the Amir Shere Ali has left Kabul, intending to travel to Russia in order to lay his case before the Tsar. And also, which he did not know, that the Amir is now in Mazar-i-Sharif and will never live to cross the Oxus, let alone reach St Petersburg, for he is a dying man, and therefore his son, Yakoub Khan, is already Amir of Afghanistan in all but name.'

Zarin nodded assent. 'Yes. The first part was already known; the news of Shere Ali's flight was brought to Jalalabad by one of our pensioners, Nakshband Khan, who was once a Risaldar of the Guides Cavalry and now lives in Kabul.'

'I know. I too have been living in Kabul. I obtained work there as a scribe—in the Bala Hissar itself—and it was I who asked him to carry that news to Cavagnari-Sahib.'

'*Wah-illah!* I might have known. But if that is so, why come here yourself in such haste?'

'I came because I hoped to make it clear that this flight of the Amir's means that he can no longer claim to rule Afghanistan, and that this is the end of the road for him, and therefore, if there is any justice, an end to the war also, which the Viceroy-Sahib insisted was against the Amir only. I hoped that this would mean that the fighting could now cease, but it seems not. The war will continue because the Lat-Sahib and the Jung-i-lat-Sahib and other like-minded men wish it to continue. As for me, I am a free man again. Cavagnari-Sahib having told me that he no longer needs my services.'

'So? That is indeed good news!'

'Perhaps. I do not know, for there are two words about that. Zarin —is it possible for me to speak to Hamilton-Sahib without anyone knowing?'

'Not unless you can arrange to stay in Jalalabad until he returns, and I do not know when that will be; he and some others of our *rissala* have accompanied an expedition against the Bazai clan of the Mohmands. They left only yesterday and may not be back for several days.'

'And Battye-Sahib? Has he gone with them? Him I must see.'

'No, he is here. But it will not be easy for you to see him without anyone coming to hear of it, because he has recently been made a Major-Sahib and given command of the *rissala;* and that being so he has much work to do and is seldom alone—unlike Cavagnari-Sahib, who has many visitors who come to see him by stealth and at strange hours of the night. But I will see what can be arranged.'

The news of Wigram's promotion was a surprise to Ash, who did not know that Colonel Jenkins had been given command of a newly formed Brigade consisting of the 4th Mountain Battery, the Guides Infantry and the 1st Sikhs, and he said: 'Tell me what has been happening here. I know almost nothing of what our armies have done, because where I have been the talk has always been of the other side, and I have heard only that the Amir's forces inflicted great casualties on the British before withdrawing from their positions, with small loss to themselves, in order to lure the invaders further from their base-camps and make it easier for small parties of raiders to cut their supply lines. They also speak of the Peiwar Kotal as though it was a great victory for the Afghans, and it was not until yesterday that I learned by chance that this was not so, and that it was stormed and held by our troops. Tell me what you yourself know or have heard at first hand.'

Zarin knew a good deal, and during the hour that followed Ash learned much that he had not known before; though some of it he had suspected. The Guides, being part of the Peshawar Valley Field Force, had not been involved in the battle for the Peiwar Kotal; but a kinsman of Zarin's had taken part in both attacks, and having been wounded and spent a week or two in hospital, was sent home on sick-leave. Zarin had bumped into him in Dakka and been given an account of the action, and according to the wounded man, General Roberts, commander of the Kurram Valley Field Force, had been deceived by the false reports of Turi spies, employed by the Afghans, into thinking that the enemy were retreating in disorder and the heights of the Peiwar Kotal could be taken without a fight. His troops set out in force from the Kurram Forts, only to find at the end of the long march, when all were tired and cold and hungry, that the Afghans were ready and waiting for them, strongly entrenched and in great numbers.

'It was learned afterwards, so my cousin told me,' said Zarin, 'that the enemy's strength had been greatly increased by the arrival of four regiments and six guns from Kabul, so that they numbered close on five thousand men with seventeen guns. Moreover they fought, he said, with great valour and fury, repulsing us again and again and inflicting such heavy losses that it took our army close on two days to capture the Peiwar Kotal. Wherefore the victory when it came proved a most costly one, both in blood and the materials of war.'

Even making allowances for the boastful talk he had heard in Kabul and Charikar, Ash had suspected that all was not going too well for the forces of the Raj; and most of what Zarin told him confirmed this. The victorious advance upon Kabul appeared to have ground to a halt for lack of transport, while the troops encamped in Jalalabad and the Kurram were suffering from sicknesses brought on by the severe cold—the hardest hit being the British regiments and those from down-country, who were unaccustomed to such freezing temperatures. There was also a chronic shortage of pack-animals, and so little fodder in the Khyber that for weeks past the chief Commissariat Officer had been complaining that unless he could send his camels back to the plains for a fortnight's grazing, he would need new ones in the spring to replace the thousands that would be dead, and whose rotting carcasses were bound to breed a pestilence.

Similar complaints, said Zarin, had come from the Kurram front; and also from Kandahar, where that part of General Stewart's army that had occupied Khelat-i-Ghilzai had been forced to fall back and were now encamped. The other part, which had been advancing on Herat, had been brought to a stop on the Helmand—as had General Sam Browne in Jalalabad. Zarin had been told by the men of a new draft that had arrived a few days ago that at Dadar, Jacobabad and Quetta there was the same crippling lack of transport, and that the desert and the passes were strewn with dead camels and abandoned stores . . .

'Were I a superstitious man,' said Zarin, 'which, by the mercy of the All-Merciful, I am not, I would say that this year is an ill-omened one, and that we have entered it under an evil star, not only here in Afghanistan, but eastward also. For there is news that throughout Oudh and the Punjab and the North-West Provinces the winter rains have again failed, and thousands are dying of famine. Had you heard this?'

Ash shook his head and said that he had not; but that what he did know was that here in Afghanistan the entire population were confident of victory, and that Shere Ali had issued a Royal *Firman* in which he spoke of the defeats and casualties suffered by the invaders and the victories gained by his own 'lion-devouring warriors', who in fighting the armies of the Raj displayed such bravery that of those who died, not one of them went to Paradise until he had slain at least three of the enemy. Both sides always spoke like that in time of war: it was only to be expected. Yet because of the nature of the country and the lack of communication between tribes—and because they had not yet suffered a major defeat—there was no Afghan who was not convinced that their forces could easily prevent an advance on Kabul . . .

'They must know well that we have captured Ali Masjid and the Peiwar Kotal,' put in Zarin grimly.

'True. But the men who fought against us there have given such a one-sided account of the fighting, boasting of the losses they inflicted upon us and minimizing their own, that it is not surprising that those who hear their talk still look for another Afghan victory such as their fathers won close on fifty years ago, when they destroyed an entire British Army in the space of a few days. They have never forgotten that tale—as your father himself warned me—and today it is repeated everywhere: even the youngest children know it. Yet I have found no one who remembers or has even heard of General Sale-Sahib's successful defence of this town of Jalalabad; or of Pollack-Sahib's victorious march through the Khyber Pass and his destruction of the Great Bazaar in Kabul. Those are matters that they choose to forget or have never been told of; and in this I think lies our greatest danger, for as long as they remain confident that they can defeat us with ease they will make no terms with us—because they think they have us trapped and can destroy us whenever they choose.'

Zarin gave a short laugh and said: 'Let them try it! They will soon find out that they are mistaken.'

Ash did not reply, for after some of the things that Zarin had told him that night he was not so sure that he was right about this, since how could an invading army move without transport? or hold a captured fortress unless it could keep a garrison armed and fed? Carts had to be drawn and such things as food, ammunition, tents and medical supplies had to be carried by pack animals—who must also be fed. Nor did men who were cold and sick and hungry win battles, and in Ash's opinion Lord Lytton would be well advised to seize the chance that Shere Ali's flight had provided, and call a halt now. To do so would not only prove that he had spoken the truth when he said that this war was against Shere Ali alone, and not against the people of Afghanistan, but if he did it at once, while the British still held Ali Masjid and the Peiwar Kotal and such cities as this one (and could be seen to control the Khyber and the Kurram), it should be possible to come to some equitable agreement with Yakoub Khan when his father died—which would be any day now. This could well lead to a just and lasting peace between the Raj and Afghanistan. But if the war continued, Ash could see only one end to it: another massacre.

Zarin, who had been watching him, may have read his thoughts, for he said philosophically: 'What will be, will be. The matter is not in our hands. Now tell me of your own doings—'

Ash told him, and Zarin brewed more tea and sat sipping it as he listened; and when the tale was ended he said: 'You have more than earned your freedom from Cavagnari-Sahib's service. What do you mean to do now? Shall you join the *rissala* here, or set out for Attock in the morning? After this, they will surely give you leave.'

'That will be for the Commandant-Sahib to decide. See if you can arrange for me to see him tomorrow: not in the camp, for that would be unwise. The river bank will be best; I could walk there in the evening. Can I spend the night here?'

'Assuredly. I will tell the nightwatchman, who is a friend of mine. And as regarding the Commandant-Sahib, I will do what I can.'

Zarin gathered up the dishes and withdrew, and Ash settled down contentedly to sleep, warmed not only by the fire but by the comfortable conviction that all his troubles were over, and that tomorrow or the next day he would be given permission to return to Attock to see Juli and enjoy a few days of well-earned leave, before arriving in Mardan as though he was returning from this mythical course in Poona.

There is little doubt that had he been able to see Wigram that night, or even very early next morning, Ash would have carried out this programme. But here Fate in the form of Major General Sir Sam Browne, v.c., stepped in. The General had invited Cavagnari to take *chota hazri* with him that morning in order that they might discuss a few matters in private, prior to an official conference that would be taking place in the afternoon. And it was in the final moments of this informal talk that Cavagnari, recalling that the General had once been Commandant of the Guides and might therefore be interested, spoke of Ashton Pelham-Martyn and his recent role as an intelligence agent operating from inside Afghanistan.

The General had been more than interested, and having asked a great many questions, remarked that he remembered the boy's arrival in Mardan very well, and that, by Jove, that had been a rum affair . . . curious to think that a lot of fellows who had been there, like Jenkins and Campbell and Battye for instance, had only been junior lieutenants at the time . . .

He relapsed into silence, and Major Cavagnari, taking this to be a hint, made his escape—he had a busy morning ahead of him and must find time to write to Major Campbell (who was officiating as Commandant of the Corps of Guides in the temporary absence of Colonel Jenkins), informing him that he had dispensed with Lieutenant Pelham-Martyn's services, and that as far as he was concerned, the Lieutenant was now free to return to his regimental duties. But even as he was writing this, Colonel Jenkins's replacement was reading another note: one that had been scribbled by Sam Browne and sent off by a galloper within a few minutes of Cavagnari's departure, requesting Major Campbell's presence at the General's quarters at the earliest possible moment.

Campbell had ridden over immediately, wondering what fateful plans were in the wind, and been startled to discover that the General wanted to talk to him about Ash. 'I gather he's here in Jalalabad, and that Cavagnari has given him the sack and seems to think that he will now report at once for duty with the Regiment. Well, I'm sorry to disappoint him, but I have other ideas—'

The General's ideas would probably not have pleased Major Cavagnari had he heard them, for they ran counter to his own views on the reliability of Lieutenant Pelham-Martyn's information. But then, as Sam Browne pointed out, he himself was not interested in the purely political angle but only in the military one—in which sphere he considered that someone like young Pelham-Martyn would be invaluable.

'Cavagnari considers him to have become so pro-Afghan that his bias in their favour made his information suspect, if not actually unreliable. Well, I have my doubts about that. But the point is that the kind of information that we of the Peshawar Valley Field Force require has nothing whatever to do with politics, and provided you can assure me that Pelham-Martyn has not turned traitor, then he is precisely what I have been looking for—someone who can send us early and accurate information as to the existence and whereabouts of hostile bands of tribesmen; their numbers and movements and how well or poorly they are armed, and so on. In a country like this that kind of knowledge is worth more than an extra army corps, and the long and the short of it is that I'm asking you to see to it that this fellow carries on in his present role: only on our behalf instead of for the political Johnnies.'

Chips Campbell, who until now had known nothing whatever about Ashton's work or whereabouts and supposed him to be in Poona, had agreed to the General's request, though expressing the opinion that it 'seemed rather hard luck on the poor chap'.

'You can put the blame on me,' said General Sam. 'Tell him that you are acting on my orders: which is perfectly true. Anyway, until Jenkins returns you are his Commanding Officer, and I'm yours; and there's a war on. Now listen . . .'

Ash had taken the news stoically. It had been a bitter blow, but there was nothing he could do about it. He was a serving officer and he had volunteered for this work, so he listened impassively while Wigram, who had been deputed by Campbell to meet him as though by chance on the river bank in the course of an evening ride, gave him a number of detailed instructions as to the type of information that the General required, the best methods of relaying it, and various other relevant matters . . .

'I can't tell you how sorry I am about this,' said Wigram in conclusion. 'I tried to talk Chips into standing up to General Sam, but he says it would be a waste of time, and I suppose he's right. Oh, and by the way, the General thinks you should leave Jalalabad as soon as possible, and he suggests you continue to use Kabul as your base because sooner or later we shall have to take the place—unless the Afghans call *"Pax!"* before then of course.'

Ash nodded, and that night Zarin, who had arranged the meeting, met him at the same spot outside the walls where they had met on the previous night, and after a brief talk, watched him walk away into the darkness with the slouching, loose-limbed stride of the hillman. And on the following day Wally and his handful of sowars had returned to Jalalabad. But by then Ash was almost twenty miles away among the hills beyond Gandamak.

That had been in January, before the blizzards began and the passes were blocked with snow. Towards the end of the month, a letter that Ash had given to Zarin before he left Jalalabad arrived by devious means at Fatima Begum's house in Attock, and three days later Anjuli set out for Kabul.

Those few days had been fraught ones. Both the Begum and Gul Baz had been horrified at the idea of her even considering such a journey; particularly at that season of the year—and in time of war, too!—it was not to be thought of. And certainly not permitted, as a lone woman travelling through such wild country would be bound to be set upon by *budmarshes,* murderers and robbers. 'But I shall not be alone,' said Anjuli. 'I shall have Gul Baz to protect me.'

Gul Baz had declared that he would have nothing to do with such a mad scheme, and that Pelham-Sahib would have his head if he agreed to it—and rightly so. Whereupon Anjuli announced that in that case she would go alone.

Had she raved and wept they might have felt more capable of dealing with the situation, but she had been perfectly calm. She had neither raised her voice nor indulged in hysterics, but merely said that her place was at her husband's side, and that though she had agreed to a separation that might last for half a year, the prospect of yet another six months—perhaps even more than that—was more than she could face. Besides, now that she could speak Pushtu and pass as an Afghan woman, she would no longer be either a danger or a hindrance to him, while as for any danger to herself, what had she to be afraid of in Afghanistan compared with what she must always be afraid of in India? Here she could never be sure that some spy from Bhithor would not track her down and kill her; but she could at least be sure that no Bhithori would ever dream of venturing over the Border into tribal territory. She already knew that her husband had found a home in Kabul under the roof of a friend of Awal Shah's, Sirdar Bahadur Nakshband Khan, so she knew where to go, and they could not stop her.

They had tried to do so, but without success. The Begum, shedding tears, had locked her in her room and set Gul Baz on guard in the garden below in case she should attempt to escape via the window (though even if she had been able to lower herself to the ground, the surrounding walls were far too high to climb). Anjuli had retaliated by refusing all food and drink, and after two days of this, realizing that she was faced with a determination even greater than her own, the Begum capitulated.

'Forgive me, Begum-Sahiba—dearest aunt—you have been so good to me, so kind, and I have repaid you by causing all this anxiety. But if I do not go I shall die of fear, for I know that he carries his life in his hands, and that if he is betrayed he will die a slow and terrible death . . . and I not there. Not even knowing for months, perhaps for years, if he is alive or dead—or held prisoner in some dreadful place, cold and starving and in torment . . . as I myself once was. I cannot endure it. Help me to go to him, and do not blame me too much. Would you not have done as much for your husband?'

'Yes,' admitted the Begum. 'Yes, I would have done the same. It is not an easy thing to be a woman and love with the whole heart:

which men do not understand—they having many loves, and delighting in danger and war . . . I will help you.'

Deprived of the Begum's support, Gul Baz had been forced to capitulate to what amounted to blackmail, since he could not possibly allow Anjuli-Begum to travel alone. She would not even wait until Ash's views could be obtained; which admittedly might have taken many weeks, for though it had been possible for Zarin to risk smuggling that letter out of Afghanistan, it was not nearly as easy for anyone in Attock to send one the other way, and even Zarin in Jalalabad would have found it difficult to get in touch with 'Syed Akbar'. In consequence, they set out for Kabul on the following day, taking little with them beyond food and a small sum of money—and the jewels that had been part of Juli's dowry and which Ash had brought away from the *chattri* by the burning-ground in Bhithor.

The Begum had provided Afghan dress, a sheepskin poshteen and Gilgit boots for Anjuli, and charged Gul Baz with procuring two broken-down nags in the bazaar, capable of bearing them, but unlikely to attract the attention or envy of even the most acquisitive tribesman. She had herself stayed up to see them depart unobtrusively and by night, as Ash had done; and as she bolted the little side gate behind them, she sighed, remembering her own youth and the handsome young man who had brought her to this house as a bride so many years ago, and whom she had loved so greatly. 'Yes, I too would have done the same,' mused the Begum. 'I will pray that she will be permitted to reach Kabul in safety and find her man there. But it is ill weather for travelling, and I fear the journey will be a hard one.'

It had been even harder than the Begum feared, and in the course of it they had lost one of the horses, the animal having slipped while being led along a narrow track that was barely more than a ledge of rock, and fallen to its death in a gully some three hundred feet below. Gul Baz had risked his neck climbing down that treacherous, icy slope in the teeth of a gale in order to rescue the saddle-bags, because they could not afford to lose the provisions they contained, and he had had a hard time crawling back with them to safety. Later they had twice been snowbound for several days, but the Begum's prayer had been answered: after more than a fortnight on the road they had reached Kabul safely, and knocking at the door of a house in a quiet street in the shadow of the Bala Hissar, found Ash there.

54

On the twenty-first day of February 1879, Shere Ali died in Mazar-i-Sharif in Afghan Turkestan, and his son Yakoub Khan became Amir in his stead. But the new Amir, far from making overtures to the British, was already hard at work building up and re-organizing the Afghan army.

Cavagnari's spies reported that the fighting-men in Kabul and Ghazi were determined to avenge the capture of Ali Masjid and the Peiwar Kotal, and that they already numbered seven thousand cavalry and twelve thousand infantry, together with sixty guns; though this and similar items of information had been treated with a certain amount of scepticism, as it came from native informers who had a tendency to embroider a good story. But Wigram Battye had received private confirmation of this from someone signing himself 'Akbar', the writer also asserting that even those tribes who were regarded as friendly were becoming restless and hostile, and Afridis everywhere were demanding to know why, now that Shere Ali was dead, the Indian Government should continue to keep an army in Afghanistan and to build forts and barracks in their country? Did this mean that the English did not intend to keep the promises made to the people of Afghanistan at the beginning of the war?

'. . . and I would strongly advise,' wrote 'Akbar', 'that you do what you can to persuade those fatheads in authority that this is no time to allow the Survey Department to send out endless small parties to draw maps of the country; it only serves to stir up ill-feeling and confirm a widespread suspicion that the English are plotting to take over the whole of Afghanistan, for as you know, the Pathans have an inveterate hatred of the Surveyor and believe that where the Government sends one, an army will follow. So for God's sake try and get them to stop it.'

Wigram had done his best; but without success.

Mr Scott and his assistants had been savagely attacked while out sketching in the hills, four of their escort being killed and another two wounded; and three weeks later Wally had been involved in a similar incident when he and a troop of the Guides Cavalry, together with a company of the 45th Sikhs, had been ordered to escort yet another survey party. Once again infuriated villagers had attacked the map-makers, and the Sikhs' Company Commander had been mortally wounded.

'Pity about Barclay,' said Wigram. 'He was a good chap.'

'One of the best,' agreed Wally. 'It seems such a waste, somehow. If it had happened in a pukka battle, I suppose one wouldn't have felt so bad about it. But this—!' He kicked an inoffensive boot-tree across the tent, and after a moment or two added bitterly: 'You'd have thought that things were tricky enough in these parts without our deliberately antagonizing the locals by turning up in out-of-the-way places armed with drawing-boards, compasses and theodolites, and letting 'em see that we were making detailed maps of their home villages. Ash was right: it's a lunatic thing to do just now. I suppose you haven't heard from him again?'

'Not since then. I imagine it can't be all that easy for him to send letters. Besides, he must know that each time he does, he runs the risk of being betrayed to the Afghans or blackmailed into paying everything he has in exchange for silence. And anyway, he can have no guarantee that a letter has been delivered.'

'No, I suppose not. I wish I could see him. It's been such a long time, and I miss him like the devil . . . I worry about him, too. I keep thinking what it must be like to be alone and on the run in this damnable country, week after week for months on end, knowing that if you put a foot wrong you won't live to repeat the mistake. I don't understand how he can do it. Faith, I know I couldn't!'

'Nor I,' said Wigram soberly. 'God knows I'm no glutton for fighting, but given the choice, I'd rather take part in half-a-dozen full-scale battles than take on the job of spying behind the enemy lines. One can be scared rigid before a battle—I always am—but the other business calls for a different kind of courage: the lonely, cold-blooded kind that most of us don't have. On the other hand, one has to remember that most of us don't happen to be human chameleons, and that Ashton is a freak in that he can think in Pushtu. Or in Hindi, when the occasion arises—it merely seems to depend on where he happens to be at the time. I've sometimes wondered if he ever thinks or dreams in English. Not very often, I imagine.'

Wally turned away to jerk back the tent-flap and stand gazing up at the hills that surrounded Jalalabad, dark now against the darkening sky, while the boisterous March wind tossed his hair into disorder and swirled about the tent, setting the canvas flapping and sending files and papers fluttering to the ground: 'I wonder if he's somewhere around here, watching us from those hills up there?'

'I shouldn't think so,' said Wigram. 'He's probably in Kabul. Ah!—this sounds like my bath arriving—first I've had in days. The horrors of active service. Well, see you at dinner.'

But Wally's surmise had been nearer the mark than Wigram's, for in fact Ash was at that moment in a little village called Fatehabad, less than twenty miles away.

Ever since the outbreak of war, a certain Ghilzai chief, one Azmatulla Khan, had been actively at work fomenting a rising against the British invaders by the inhabitants of the Lagman Valley; and late in February Colonel Jenkins and a small column had dispersed Azmatulla's forces in the valley, but failed to capture him. Now he was known to be back again, and with an even larger following, and on the last day of March Ash had dispatched a further piece of ill news to Jalalabad. The Khugiani tribesmen, whose territory lay barely seventeen miles distant to the south of Fatehabad, were also gathering in great numbers at one of their border fortresses.

On receipt of this information, the Divisional Commander had given orders that certain units were to set out with all speed to stamp out this new unrest before it gathered strength. They would march that very night, taking no tents or heavy baggage with them, and the force would be divided into three columns: one of infantry, another to consist of two squadrons of cavalry (drawn respectively from the Bengal Lancers and the 10th Hussars), and the third of infantry and cavalry combined. This last, which was under the command of General Gough and included two squadrons of Guides, would march on Fatehabad and disperse the Khugianis. Of the other two columns, one would move against Azmatulla Khan and his bravos, while the other crossed the heights of the Siah Koh to cut off the enemy's retreat.

The speed with which the operation was planned and put into execution, and the fact that the columns would move off after dark, would, the General hoped, result in Azmatulla Khan and the Khugianis being taken by surprise; though he should have known better, for Jalalabad was full of Afghan spies—there were probably scores of them in the town and as many others keeping watch by the Kabul River, and not a sabre could have stirred without it being known within the hour. Then, too, following the occupation of the town, Colonel Jenkins—now Brigadier-General Jenkins—had inspected the ford by which the 10th Hussars and the Bengal Lancers would have to cross the river *en route* to the Lagman Valley, and not only condemned it as unsafe, but advised that it should never be attempted by night even at a time when the river was low. But his report had either been pigeonholed or lost, for though the river was at present in spate, the plan was not altered . . .

The moon was still up when the two squadrons of Hussars and Lancers left camp, but it was sinking fast, and by the time the ford was reached it had been lost to sight behind the near hills, and the valley lay deep in shadow. The river here ran a full three quarters of a mile wide, divided into two channels by a stony island in midstream, and as the trestle bridge had suffered its annual removal some weeks earlier, in order to prevent its being washed away and lost (a major disaster in an area where timber was not easily come by), the only way to cross was by the ford: a wide bar of boulder-strewn gravel that spanned the river between dangerous rapids.

The valley reverberated with the voice of the swollen river, and as the squadrons formed up in half sections, four abreast on the stony bank, even the clash and jingle of accoutrements and the clatter of the chargers' hooves could barely be heard above the roar of the rapids. But the local guide stepped confidently into the water and waded across, followed by the Bengal Lancers whose men, accustomed from childhood to the treacherous Indian rivers had reached the far side in safety. But inevitably, the pull of the current had forced the long column to give ground before it, so that by the time the ammunition mules and their drivers entered the river on the Lancers' heels they found themselves stepping off into deep water, and missing the ford, were snatched away into the rapids.

Their cries were lost in the roar of the river, and the darkness prevented the 10th Hussars—pressing too closely behind them—from seeing what had happened. Captain Spottiswood of the Hussars, at their head, urged his horse forward, felt it lose its footing, recover, and then lose it again. And within minutes the river was full of desperate men and frenzied horses, fighting for dear life as they rolled over and over in the icy grip of the foaming, furious rapids.

Some, including the Captain, survived. But many did not. Numbed by the bitter cold and hampered by sodden uniforms and cumbersome boots, those who escaped being kicked to death by their struggling chargers were dragged under by the weight of sabres, belts and ammunition pouches, and carried downward, battered and helpless among the unseen boulders, to drown in the deep water.

Forty-two troopers, an officer and three non-commissioned officers died that night—out of a squadron that barely half-an-hour earlier had ridden out from camp seventy-five strong. The news of the disaster had been brought by dripping, riderless horses careering through the lines of the Horse Artillery, making for their own lines beyond; and all that night, by the light of bonfires and torches, men searched and called along the banks of the river.

When dawn broke, the bodies of the officer and eighteen of the rank and file were found wedged among the rocks or drifting face-downward in the eddies under the banks. The rest had been swept down on the flood and were never seen again. As for Azmatulla Khan, his spies having warned him of what was in the wind, he had promptly removed from the Lagman Valley, and the two columns that had been sent to take him had returned empty-handed.

The Khugianis, also forewarned, had shown less caution.

The mixed column whose task was to deal with that tribe had, as planned, been the last to move off. But their departure having been further delayed by the disaster at the ford, midnight had come and gone before they left, and it was close on one o'clock by the time they marched—seeing as they went the distant gleam of bonfires and flares along the river, where the frantic search for survivors continued.

'I said this was an ill-omened year,' muttered Zarin to Risaldar Mahmud Khan of the Guides as the squadrons moved off in the darkness, and Mahmud Khan had replied grimly: 'And it is not yet old. Let us hope that for many of these Khugianis it will grow no older after tomorrow—and that we ourselves will live to see Mardan again and draw our pensions and watch our children's children become Jemadars and Risaldars in their turn.'

'*Ameen!*' murmured Zarin devoutly.

Despite the darkness and the difficulty of keeping to a track that even by daylight was barely distinguishable from the rough and stony ground that stretched away on either hand, the long column of infantry, cavalry and artillery had made good progress, and it was still dark when the cavalry, riding ahead, were halted within a mile of the village of Fatehabad and ordered to wait there until the rest of the column caught up with them. By then there was not much of the night left, but Wigram and his two squadrons, old hands at this sort of campaigning, selected a spot under some trees and made themselves tolerably comfortable for what little remained of it.

The village was reported to be friendly, but when the dawn broke it was seen that no smoke rose from it, and a scouting party sent to investigate found that it was deserted. The villagers had taken all their foodstuffs and livestock with them, and except for a few pariah dogs and a gaunt cat who spat at the sowars from the doorway of an empty house, nothing moved. 'So much for our intelligence,' observed Wigram, eating breakfast in the shade of a tree. ' "Friendly", they said. About as friendly as a nest of hornets! It's obvious that the whole blasted jing-bang have run off to join the enemy.'

He had sent out patrols under Risaldar Mahmud Khan to report on the movements of the Khugianis, but though the patrols had not returned by the time the guns and the infantry appeared at ten o'clock in the morning, he had by then received news from another source:

'Ashton seems to think that they will stand and fight,' said Wigram, tossing over a crumpled scrap of paper that Zarin had just brought him. The brief, scrawled message had come by way of a grass-cutter who said he had been given it by an elderly and unknown village woman, with instructions to take it at once to Risaldar Zarin Khan of the Guides *rissala,* who would reward him. He had supposed it to be a love-letter. But Zarin had known better, for it was written in *Angrezi.* And as only one person could have sent it, he had wasted no time in taking it to his Commanding Officer.

'Enemy entrenched in great strength on plateau overlooking Gandamak road,' read Wally. 'Estimate 5,000. No guns, but position, defences and morale tip-top. Any attempt to dislodge by frontal attack will mean heavy losses. Shelling might do it. If not, they will have to be lured out into the open, which should not be difficult as discipline nil, but warn you they mean business and will fight like demons. A.'

'Good for Ash! I wonder if he is up there with them?—I wouldn't put it past him. Jove, I wish he was here with us. If only— Are you going to pass this on to the General?'

'Yes, for what it's worth,' said Wigram, writing hastily in a small loose-leaf notebook. He ripped out the page, folded it, and calling up his orderly, sent him galloping off with it to General Gough. 'Not that it'll be needed, because his pickets will have told him as much already. But it won't do any harm to have it confirmed.'

'Did you tell him that Ash thinks we should—'

'No, I did not. I don't believe in teaching my grandmother to suck eggs. Believe me, Gough is no fool, and he doesn't need Ashton or anyone else to teach him his business. He'll have worked that out for himself.'

General Gough had indeed done so. He had sent out a number of patrols, and later that day he had talked with as many of the local chiefs and Maliks as could be persuaded to meet him, in an endeavour to sound out the temper of the people, and discover, if he could, which tribes were likely to fight and which could be relied on to remain neutral—or to vanish into the hills like Azmatulla and his men.

But as the day wore on it became increasingly clear to him that the whole countryside was hostile, and when patrol after patrol reported further reinforcements hurrying to the help of the Khugianis, he began to work on his plans for the coming battle. There was nothing much that could be done that day as his baggage-animals had still not arrived, and did not do so until well after sunset—plodding wearily into camp as darkness fell and the cooking-fires filled the air with the scent of wood-smoke and a heartening smell of food.

The whole column now knew that there would be a battle on the morrow, and made their preparations accordingly. Wigram had slept soundly that night, and so too had Zarin. They had, to the best of their ability, done all those things that had to be done, and could rest with quiet minds. But Wally had lain awake for a long time, staring up at the stars and thinking.

He had been seven years old when he had seen in the window of a Dublin shop a hand-tinted engraving that depicted a cavalry regiment charging at Waterloo, sabres in hand and plumes flying, and had then and there decided that when he grew up he would be a cavalry officer and ride like that at the head of his men, fighting his country's foes. Now at last—tomorrow if Wigram was right—that old schoolboy dream would come true. For though he had been in action before, he had never yet been in a major engagement, and until now his only experience of a cavalry charge had been practice ones during squadron training. Would the reality turn out to be very different from anything he had imagined? not wildly exciting, but ugly and terrifying—and not glorious at all?

He had heard countless stories of the Afghans' methods of dealing with cavalry. They would lie on the ground, their long razor-sharp knives at the ready, and slash upwards at the legs and bellies of the horses to bring the riders down. A trick, he was given to understand, that could be remarkably successful, particularly in a scrimmage: and he could well believe it. Wigram said that sabres and lances were little use against it, and that a carbine or revolver were one's best hope, since faced with the prospect of being shot on the ground, most Afghans preferred to fight and die on their feet. It was this sort of thing that no amount of practice charges could teach one. But after tomorrow he would know . . .

He wondered where Ash was, and what he was doing. Would he be watching the battle from somewhere up on the hills? If only the two of them could have ridden together tomorrow! Wally gazed into the darkness, and remembering the past, dropped suddenly into sleep —to be awakened in the first faint light of dawn to find the camp stirring to life and his Commanding Officer shaking his shoulder.

'Awake, O Sleeping Beauty,' exhorted Wigram. ' "Night's candles are burned out and jocund day stands tip-toe on the misty mountain tops"—jostling for standing-room with a few thousand belligerent tribesmen, I gather. The General suggests you reconnoitre the Khugiani country, so up with you, my young dreamer. "Go to the ant, thou sluggard." Breakfast will be along in about ten minutes.'

Wally could not remember having seen Wigram in such tearing spirits before. He was by nature a quiet man, and except on rare occasions, such as the annual Guest Night in celebration of Delhi Day, was anything but boisterous. Yesterday, preoccupied by the cares of command and sobered by the tragedy at the ford, he had been even quieter than usual. But now he seemed to have shed ten years and put care behind him, and Wally, struggling to his feet in horror at finding that he had slept through all the stir and noise of the waking camp, caught the infection of those high spirits and found himself laughing instead of apologizing.

'I believe the old fellow is every bit as excited as I am,' decided Wally, remembering, as he shaved and dressed in haste, that Wigram had once confessed to him that the sum of his ambition was to get command of the Guides Cavalry, and that anything that came after that, however exalted, would be an anti-climax. 'You may think it's not much of an ambition,' Wigram had said, 'but it's all I've ever wanted. And if I get it I shall say *"nunc dimittis"*, and not care too much if I end up retiring as a crusty old has-been who never even rose to be a Colonel—because I shall have had my moment of glory.'

'Well, he's got what he wanted,' thought Wally, 'and I suppose today will be just as much of a red-letter day for him as it is for me, because if there really is a battle, it will be a "first time" for both of us. My first cavalry charge and the first time Wigram has led his beloved Command into action in a full-scale engagement.'

55

The sky above the deserted village of Fatehabad was brightening with the dawn as the two officers sat down to eat a hasty breakfast. And as they ate, Wigram explained between mouthfuls that the General wished to send two members of his staff south towards Khujah, the principal village of the Khugianis, to test the reactions of the tribe, and that Lieutenant Hamilton and thirty sabres of the Guides Cavalry had been detailed to accompany them and see that they got there—and back again.

A second party, with a similar escort of 10th Hussars, would be reconnoitring the road leading to Gandamak to report on its condition, and it was hoped that both parties would avoid getting involved in a premature exchange of hostilities, and report back to General Gough as soon as possible: 'In other words,' said Wigram, kindly translating, 'don't try jumping the gun and starting any private battles of your own. And if the local citizenry start shooting at you, "wait not upon the order of your going", but run like hell. What His Nibs needs at the moment is information, and not a clutch of dead heroes. So keep your eyes peeled. I should imagine you'll be all right —always provided you don't walk into an ambush.'

'Don't worry, we shan't do that,' said Wally cheerfully. 'Zarin says that Ash will see that we don't.'

Wigram helped himself to chuppatti and said with a smile: 'Of course. I'd forgotten he'd be there. Well, that's something off my mind. Hullo—here comes the gilded Staff. Time you were off, Walter.'

It was half past seven and the sun was drying the dew from the near hillside by the time Wally mounted his waler Mushki—'the brown one'—and rode away with the two Staff Officers, the thirty men of the escort cantering sedately behind them. An hour later, from high ground, they came suddenly within sight of a great *lashkar* of tribesmen, barely a mile or so distant across the hills. It was no peaceful gathering, for Wally could see the flutter of standards and the glint and flash of metal as the morning sunlight shone on curved swords and brassbound matchlocks, and studying the vast concourse through his field-glasses, he came to the conclusion that there must be at least three thousand Khugianis there; and possibly many more who were hidden by the folds in the ground.

A single shot, fired from no great distance, struck a shower of splinters from a rock a few yards ahead, and as he hastily put away his field-glasses and gathered up the reins, the stillness of the morning was further broken by a vicious spatter of musket balls. The enemy had not only seen them, but had obviously taken the precaution of posting pickets; and one of these, cunningly concealed behind a tumble of stones and rock barely five hundred yards away, had opened fire on the intruders. Mindful of his instructions Wally had not lingered. His small force turned tail and galloped out of range, and by ten o'clock they were safely back in camp.

The General, after listening to the report of his Staff Officers, had ordered that a certain hill-top, from where the enemy's movements could be seen and signalled back to the camp, should be seized immediately, and Wally had gone forward with this party and remained with them for a short time, ostensibly to study the movements of the Khugianis, though in reality in the hope of locating Ash, whom he suspected of firing that first warning shot this morning, as it had certainly not come from the barrel of a Border musket. But even with the aid of field-glasses it was not possible to make out individual faces in the vast, shifting mass of tribesmen who had gathered on a stretch of high ground over a mile ahead; while a careful inspection of the nearer slopes and ridges showed no signs of life—though Wally did not doubt that at least half-a-dozen outposts were concealed among the rocks in the country between this hill-top and the insurgents.

He put away his field-glasses with a sigh and returned to camp to tell Wigram that Ash was right about the Khugianis—anyone could see that they meant business. 'There must be thousands of them out there, four or five thousand at least, and they've got a whacking great red standard and a few white ones, and judging from some of their shooting this morning I'd say they've got quite a few carbines as well. What on earth do you suppose we're waiting for? Why don't we get started, instead of sitting around as though we'd only come out to look at the view and have a picnic lunch?'

'My dear Walter, Patience, we are told, is a virtue. You should cultivate it,' retorted Wigram. 'We—or rather the General—are waiting to hear what those fellows who went out this morning to reconnoitre the Gandamak road have to say, and as soon as they have made their report I expect we'll get our orders to move. But they haven't come back yet.'

'Not come *back?*' exclaimed Wally, startled. 'But it's half past twelve. I thought they were only going about five miles up the valley? Do you suppose—you don't think they've walked into an ambush, do you?'

'No I don't. If they had, there would have been a lot of firing, and at least some of them would have been able to get back and fetch help. Besides, Ashton would have known and done something about it. No, they're merely doing what they were told to: spying out the land. They'll probably turn up in time for their *tiffin,* so we can enjoy ours with a clear conscience.'

The mid-day meal was already being served, but Wally was impatient for action and far too keyed-up to feel hungry. Having swallowed a mouthful or two standing up, he strode off to see that his men had been fed and that everything was in readiness for the order to march, and Wigram, by now as familiar as Ash with Wally's habit of singing hymns when in high spirits, noticed with amusement that he was crooning 'Onward Christian Soldiers'—and thought that in the circumstances it was a bizarre choice of battle song, considering that the sowars were mostly Mussulmans or Sikhs with a sprinkling of Hindus, and that all of them, in the eyes of the singer's Church, were 'idol-worshipping heathens'.

The Guides had not been kept waiting long. When by one o'clock the missing men had still not returned, General Gough had ordered the camp under arms and despatched Major Battye with three troops of the Guides Cavalry to search for them. He himself following with seven hundred Sikh, Punjab and British infantry, four guns of the Royal Horse Artillery and three troops of the 10th Hussars.

'This is it!' cried Wally joyously, swinging himself into the saddle, and Zarin, to whom the words had been addressed, caught the import though he did not understand the language, and grinned in acknowledgement as the squadrons formed up four abreast and spurred forward into the shimmering heat of the stone-strewn valley.

They came up with the missing Staff Officers and their escort at a point where the road crossed the sloping ground below a plateau on which the Khugianis were gathering, and the two parties turned back together to join the General, who, hearing what they had to say, halted his infantry where they could not be seen by the enemy, and went forward to assess the position for himself. A brief survey had been enough; for as Wigram had said, Gough needed no one to teach him his business or advise him on how to deal with the situation.

The Khugianis had chosen a perfect defensive position. Their line spanned the rim of the plateau, and the hillside immediately below fell away steeply for a short distance before merging into the long, gentle slope that met the Gandamak road and the comparatively level ground on the far side. Both flanks of their line were protected by steep cliffs, while their front had been further reinforced by massive stone breastworks. Had they been able to mount guns, their position would have been virtually impregnable, and as it was, to attack it head-on would be suicidal, while to detach troops in an attempt to turn it would mean seriously weakening the small British force that was already out-numbered by five to one. The only hope, as Ash had said and the General now saw, was to lure the Khugianis out into the open.

'We shall have to take a leaf out of William's book,' observed the General thoughtfully. 'Nothing else for it . . .'

'William, sir?' inquired a puzzled aide-de-camp blankly.

'The Conqueror—see Battle of Hastings, 1066. By rights Harold and his Saxons should have come off the victors, and would have done, if William hadn't tempted them to leave their position on the higher ground in order to pursue his supposedly fleeing soldiery. We must do the same and try luring those fellows down. They won't have heard of that battle, and though they don't know the meaning of fear, they don't know the meaning of discipline either, and I think we can safely trade on that.'

Trading on it, he had sent the Guides, the 10th Hussars and the artillery forward with orders to advance to within three quarters of a mile of the enemy, where the cavalry would halt while the gunners would gallop ahead for a further five hundred yards or so, fire a few rounds, and at the first sign of an advance, fall back a short distance before stopping to open fire again.

In the General's opinion, no tribesman would be able to resist the sight of British troops in apparent retreat—any more than Harold's militia had been able to resist the sight of Norman infantry running away in feigned disorder—and it was his hope that the Khugianis would leave the protection of their breastworks and rush out to try to capture the guns of the retiring artillery. Then, if the same manoeuvre was repeated, it should be possible to entice the enemy far enough down the slope to enable the cavalry to charge them: catching them out in the open and with little chance of being able to scramble back into their entrenchments. In the meantime, while their attention was concentrated upon the pusillanimous antics of the artillery below their front, the infantry would be advancing swiftly up a nullah from where, with any luck, they would emerge, unseen and unsuspected, on the enemy's right flank.

'Told you he wouldn't need any advice,' grinned Wigram as the Guides moved off. 'There are no flies on the General.' He brushed the sweat out of his eyes with the back of his hand and said: *'Phew!* but it's hot. Aren't you grateful you're not in the infantry?'

'By jove yes!' agreed Wally in heartfelt tones. 'Faith, will you just think of having to sweat up that divil of a nullah with the sun scorching your back and every blessed rock and stone red hot. It's lucky we are.'

His spirits rose as he spurred away to take up his station at the head of his troop, singing as he went, and wholly oblivious to the fact that the sun was blazing down just as fiercely on the open slope below the plateau as it was on the steep, rocky nullah and the toiling infantry; or that the tunic of his own uniform was already wet through with sweat. He was conscious only of an exhilarating chill compounded of excitement and tense anticipation, as the line of mounted men formed up and galloped forward to face the enemy position.

A trumpet blared, and obeying the signal the cavalry halted in a cloud of dust. As it settled there was a moment or two of complete silence in which Wally found himself sharply aware of innumerable small details. The way the sun gleamed along the barrels of the limbered guns; the small sharp-edged shadows under every stone, and the way the wide sweep of barren ground that sloped up ahead seemed to reflect the light like snow; the smell of horses and leather and harness oil, of dust, sweat and sunbaked earth; the tiny far-off figures of thousands of tribesmen, clustered thick as swarming bees along the rim of the plateau above, and very high overhead a single watchful lammergeyer gliding in lazy spirals—a lone dark speck in an enormous cloudless arch of blue.

The uniforms of the artillery on the right were a strong note of colour in the sun-bleached desolation of that harsh landscape, and beyond them, almost hidden by the tensely poised gun teams, he could see the khaki helmets of the 10th Hussars who, if the Khugianis could be lured down from those fortified heights, would attack their left flank while the Guides charged their centre.

'Two hundred jawans—' thought Wally '—and we shall be riding uphill to meet more than ten times that number of fanatical tribesmen who hate our guts and can't wait to get at us.'

The odds were so tremendous that they should have been frightening, but instead he was aware of a curious dreamlike feeling of unreality and no real fear, or any trace of animosity towards those tiny puppet-figures up there, who in a little while would be fighting with him face to face and doing their best to kill him—as he would do his best to kill them. It seemed a little foolish and he knew a fleeting moment of regret, but it was drowned almost instantly in a heady surge of elation in which he could hear the blood begin to sing softly in his ears. He felt light-headed and joyous, and no longer impatient. Time, for the moment, seemed to have stopped still—as once the sun had stopped for Joshua. There was no hurry . . .

A breath of wind blew down the valley and dispersed the dust, and the brief spell of silence was broken by a curt command from Major Stewart of the Horse Artillery. On the word his waiting gunners sprang to life, and plying whip and spur, swept forward at a gallop, the gun wheels bounding over the stony ground and the dust whirling up behind them.

They raced on for five hundred yards, and then, pulling up, unlimbered the guns and opened fire at extreme range on the serried masses of the enemy on the heights.

The brilliance of the afternoon sunlight dimmed the flash of the explosions to no more than a fractional glitter, but in that hot stillness the smoke formed a wall that looked as white and as solid as cotton wool, and the bare hillsides threw back the sudden crash of sound and sent it reverberating round the valley until the very air seemed to shudder to it. Wally's charger, Mushki, threw up her head and backed a little, snorting. But the tribesmen on the heights jeered as the shells fell short, and fired their muskets in reply, while some, on the right, advanced boldly under cover of a ridge, bearing the red standard with them.

Seeing them move, the gunners instantly limbered up and galloped back to their original position, and the whole line, cavalry and artillery together, retreated a few hundred yards down the slope. It was enough. As the General had surmised, the sight of the small British force in apparent retreat proved too tempting for the undisciplined tribesmen.

Convinced that the sight of their own immensely superior numbers had struck terror into the hearts of this foolhardy handful of *Kafirs,* and seeing both gun-teams and cavalry running away, they threw all caution to the winds, and shouting exultantly, poured out from behind their entrenchments to race down the slope in an enormous, savage tidal wave of yelling humanity, brandishing banners, muskets and tulwars as they came.

Below them a second trumpet-call cut shrilly through the thunder of retreating hoofbeats and the triumphant shouts of the racing thousands, and hearing it, the cavalry pulled up and wheeled to face the enemy, while the guns unlimbered again and sprayed the converging hordes with grape-shot.

A moment later a distant rattle of musketry on the far left told that the toiling infantry had reached their objective unseen, and were attacking the enemy's flank. But the yelling Khugianis did not hear it; nor did they slow their pace, though by now they were within range of the guns. Crazed with the lust for battle—or the prospect of Paradise, which is assured to all those who slay an infidel—they paid no heed to grape-shot or carbine bullets, but came on as though each man ran a race with his neighbour for the honour of getting first at the foe.

'Whoa, girl!' exhorted Wally softly, steadying the mare and breathing short as he peered ahead through the dust and smoke, eyes narrowed against the glare, at that awe-inspiring torrent of fierce, eager fighting-men rushing towards the guns. He found himself mentally counting the distance: six hundred yards . . . five hundred . . . four . . .

The sun was fire-hot on his shoulders and he could feel the sweat crawling down his face from under his pith helmet, but an ice-cold shiver tingled down his spine, and the joy of a born fighter burned in his eyes as he began to sing under his breath. 'Forward into battle, see our banners go!' crooned Wally joyously.

He glanced away from the on-coming multitude and saw the officer in command of the artillery turn and cup his hands about his mouth to shout to the waiting cavalry: 'This is my last round at them,' yelled Major Stewart, 'and then it's your turn.'

Wigram Battye, who had been sitting relaxed and motionless in the saddle, out in front of his command, transferred the reins to his left hand and laid his right upon the hilt of his sabre. He did so with-out haste, and his Guides smiled grimly as they followed their Com-manding Officer's example, and braced themselves, waiting.

The guns fired again. This time with deadly effect as the shrapnel tore great swathes through the close-packed masses of the enemy. And as the sound died, Wigram's right arm jerked upward, and from the waiting lines behind him came the answering rasp and glitter of steel as his two hundred men drew their sabres. He barked a com-mand, and with a deafening cheer the cavalry charged . . .

They came at the enemy with the impetus of a four-hundred-yard gallop. Knee to knee, the sunlight flashing on their sabres. And now at last the triumphant Khugianis checked and looked back over their shoulders at the entrenchments behind and above them, realizing too late that it had been a fatal mistake to leave their defences on the plateau and allow themselves to be caught out in the open, since being on foot they had no hope of regaining the safety of their en-trenchments before the cavalry overtook them. There was nothing for it but to stay and fight. And they did so: standing fast and firing again and again into the charging phalanx of horsemen.

In every battle the chances are that those most closely involved see only a small part of the whole; and as far as Wally was con-cerned, this one was no exception.

He knew that somewhere ahead and out of sight the infantry must be in action, for he had heard them firing; and also that the 10th Hussars would have charged at the same moment as the Guides. But the Hussars were on the right of the line, beyond the Horse Artillery; and as he had neither the time nor the attention to spare for anything beyond his own squadron and the enemy ahead, for him the battle, from first to last, was confined to what he himself saw—which in turn was restricted by the dust and the confusion of fighting, struggling, yelling men.

The charge had carried the Guides to within a hundred and fifty yards of the enemy when he heard the vicious crackle of muskets and felt the wind of bullets that sang past him like a swarm of angry bees: and saw his Commanding Officer's charger, stretched at full gallop, come crashing down, shot through the heart.

Wigram pitched over its head, rolled clear and was on his feet in an instant. Only to stumble and fall again as a second musket ball smashed into his thigh.

Instinctively, seeing their leader fall, the Sikhs gave the wailing cry of their race and pulled up, and Wally too reined in savagely, his face suddenly white.

'What the hell are you stopping for?' blazed Wigram furiously, struggling to rise. 'I'm all right. I'll come on directly. Take 'em on, Walter!—don't mind me. *Take 'em on, boy!*'

Wally did not pause to argue. He turned in the saddle, and shouting to the squadrons to follow him, flourished his sabre about his head, and with a wild Irish yell spurred forward up the slope towards the waiting enemy, the Guides thundering at his heels and shouting as they rode. The next minute, with the shock of wave meeting wave in a tide-race, the two forces crashed together in a pandemonium of dust and din, and Wally found himself in the thick of the smother, hacking left and right with his sabre as wild-eyed men rushed at him howling war-cries and curses and swinging great curved swords.

He sent one down with half his face cut away, and as the mare stumbled over the fallen body, heard the man's skull crack like an egg-shell; and wrenching Mushki to her feet, urged her forward, singing at the top of his voice and laying about him the while in the manner of a huntsman whipping off hounds. All around him men were shouting and cursing in a fog of dust and smoke that stank of sulphur and sweat and black powder and the cloying scent of fresh blood. Knives and sabres flashed and fell and men fell with them, while wounded horses reared up with flailing hooves, neighing with rage and terror, or bolted riderless through the mêlée, trampling down all who stood in their way.

The solid mass of the enemy had been shattered into fragments by the impact of the cavalry charging headlong into it, and now the Khugianis were fighting in small groups, clinging tenaciously to the grassy, stone-strewn slope and standing their ground with fanatical courage. Wally caught a brief glimpse of Zarin, teeth clenched in a ferocious grin as he drove the point of his sabre into the throat of a shrieking *ghazi,* and of Risaldar Mahmud Khan—his right arm hanging useless and his sabre gone, holding his carbine left-handed and wielding it like a club.

Here and there in the press small whirlpools formed about an unhorsed sowar, defending himself with all the ferocity of a wounded boar against the tribesmen who circled about him, waiting for an opportunity to slash at him with knife or tulwar. One such, Sowar Dowlat Ram, had become entangled with his fallen charger, and the three Khugianis who had brought the horse down rushed in to kill its rider as he struggled to free himself from the dying animal. But Wally had seen him fall and now he charged to the rescue, whirling his blood-stained sabre and shouting 'Daro mut, Dowlat Ram! *Tagra ho jao,* jawan! *Shabash!'*

The three Khugianis turned as one to meet the yelling thunderbolt that fell upon them. But Wally had the advantage of being mounted, and he was the better swordsman. His sabre took one man across the eyes and swept on and down to shear through the sword arm of the second; and as the first fell backward, blind and screaming, Dowlat Ram, still trapped by one foot, reached out and caught him by the throat, while Wally parried a wild blow from the third, and with a swift backhand cut, sliced through the man's neck, all but severing it from the crouching body.

'Shabash, Sahib!' applauded Dowlat Ram, freeing himself with a last frantic kick and scrambling to his feet. 'That was well done indeed. But for you I would now be a dead man.' He lifted his hand in salute and Wally said breathlessly: 'You will be yet, if you aren't careful. Get back to the rear.'

He jerked his revolver from its holster and put a bullet through the head of the thrashing horse, and wheeling Mushki, plunged back into the fray, using the maddened waler as a battering ram and shouting encouragement to his jawans, calling on them to avenge the wounding of Battye-Sahib and dispatch these sons of noseless mothers to Jehanum (hell).

The Khugianis were still holding their ground and fighting fiercely, but there was little shooting now; after the first volley few found time to reload, and in the frenzy and turmoil of battle, firearms had become a liability as it was not possible to ensure that a bullet intended for an enemy would not bring down a friend. Many were using their muskets as clubs, but one man at least, a Khugiani Chief, had taken time to reload.

Wally saw the musket aimed at him and flung himself to one side: and as the bullet whipped past him, he put spurs to Mushki and rode at the man with his dripping sabre. But this time he had met his match. The Khugiani Chief was a skilled fighter and far quicker on his feet than the three tribesmen who had brought down Dowlat Ram. Unable to reload, he stood his ground, ducked the sabre stroke by

---

* Fear not. Be strong. Bravo!

dropping to his knees, and as the mare plunged past, struck upwards with a long Afghan knife.

The razor-sharp blade sliced through Wally's riding boot, but barely scratched his skin, and he dragged the mare back on her haunches and wheeled to attack again; the same fierce joy of battle in his young face as on the eager bearded one of the hardened fighter who crouched, white teeth showing in a tigerish grin, waiting for him. Once again the Chief dropped to avoid the blow, and as it missed him he sprang to his feet like a coiled spring released and ran in, the knife in one hand and a wicked curved tulwar in the other.

Wally only just managed to swing the mare round in time to parry the attack, and the Chief leapt back and stood ready, poised on his toes, his knees a little bent and his sinewy body swaying as a king cobra sways before it strikes, alert to duck again, and holding his weapons low so that when his adversary spurred forward he could strike at the easier target of the waler's legs or belly and bring down horse and rider both.

By now the duel had drawn a circle of watching tribesmen who, momentarily forgetting the larger issues, stood back, knives in hand, waiting to see their champion slay the *feringhi*. But the Chief made the mistake of repeating a successful manoeuvre once too often, and this time when Wally attacked he made allowance for it: he too aimed lower, striking at the body instead of the head. And when once again the Chief dropped to his knees to avoid the blow, the edge of the heavy cavalry sabre sheared through his left temple and he fell sideways, his bearded face a mask of blood. His tulwar scratched the mare's flank as he fell, and when Mushki reared up, screaming, the tribesmen who had rushed in as they saw him fall— and who would not have given way before that dripping sabre—scattered in the face of those murderous hooves and let horse and rider through.

Minutes later, and without warning, the tide turned.

The massed ranks of the enemy broke and scores of Khugianis turned and ran, racing desperately for the safety of their entrenchments on the plateau. And as the cavalry plunged forward, cutting and slashing as they went, the scores became hundreds, and then thousands: and the battle turned into a rout . . .

'Gone away—!' yelled Wally, hatless and triumphant: '*Shabash, jawans! Maro! Maro! Khalsa-ji ki jai!*' And gathering the scattered squadrons together, he stood up in his stirrups and gave the order: 'Gallop!— *Hamla Karo!*'

The Guides obeyed, spurring recklessly forward up the long sweep of broken ground, until suddenly Wally saw for the first time something that had been hidden from him by the rise of the ground. And seeing it his heart seemed to stop.

Between the base of the steeper ground that fell sharply away below the rim of the plateau and the spot where the slope began to level out lay a natural obstacle that presented a far worse hazard than the man-made breastworks of loose rock and stone above: a deep gash in the hillside, running parallel to the rim, cut long ago by some mountain torrent that had dried up and left behind a welter of stones at the bottom of a sheer drop of eight or nine feet. On its far side the hill rose steeply, and along the crest stood the entrenchments —now filling again with wild-eyed tribesmen who turned to howl defiance and fire down into the pursuing cavalry.

It was a sight calculated to daunt many a better and more experienced soldier than young Lieutenant Hamilton. But Wally was drunk with the intoxicating frenzy of battle and he did not hesitate. He used his spur on Mushki, who leapt down into the gulf and bounded across the stones. And behind him, in a wild, slithering, shouting confusion, poured the Guides.

Once down they scattered to left and right searching for a possible way up and out, and when they found one, scrambled up in twos and threes and charged straight into the attack: Wally, with his trumpeter a close second, the first to reach the summit where the long line of breastworks barred the way to the level ground of the plateau. Here the many tribesmen who had managed to scramble back behind these defences turned at bay, firing their muskets as fast as they could load. But the breast-high wall had not checked Mushki. She rose to it with all the ease and grace of a thoroughbred hunter taking a stone wall in Kerry, and by a miracle, and her rider's skill with a sabre, came through the desperate hand-to-hand fighting that followed as she had come through the battle on the slopes below, with no more than a scratch.

There had been no co-ordination in that fight, or any time to wait for the infantry to come up on the flank, or the guns to follow and get into position. The Guides had attacked singly or in small groups, and with a ferocity that drove the undisciplined tribesmen from their entrenchments and back onto the open stretch of the plateau. For though the Khugianis fought stubbornly, most of their Chiefs and all their standard-bearers were dead. And without leaders to rally them, they failed to regroup.

Their entrenchments had been carried in a matter of minutes, and once again they broke and ran, dispersing across the level plateau like fallen leaves in an autumn gale as they fled with bursting lungs and straining muscles for the uncertain refuge of the forts and villages that nestled in the cultivated valleys beyond.

But they were not permitted to go freely. The guns of the artillery were ordered to open fire on any concentration of the tribesmen and the cavalry ordered to pursue; and Guides and Hussars together swept off in the wake of the retreating enemy, cutting down scores of fugitives as they went, and only drawing rein when they were almost under the walls of the Khugiani stronghold of Koja Khel.

The Battle of Fatehabad was over and won, and the weary victors turned and rode back across the blood-soaked plateau, past the tragic debris of war: the mutilated bodies of dead and dying men, the discarded weapons, broken standards, *chupplis,* turbans and empty cartridge-belts . . .

General Gough's column had left Jalalabad with orders to 'disperse the Khugianis'; and they had done so. But it had been a terrible slaughter, for the Khugianis were brave men, and as Ash had warned, they had fought like tigers. Even when they broke and ran, groups of them had turned to fire on their pursuers, or attack them, sword in hand. Over three hundred of them had been killed, and more than three times that number wounded; but they had taken a grim toll. Gough's small force had lost nine men killed and forty wounded, and of the latter—one of whom died later of his wounds—twenty-seven were Guides: as also were seven of the dead—among them Wigram Battye and Risaldar Mahmud Khan . . .

Wally, having seen Wigram fall, had supposed that he had been carried back to the rear and out of danger. But his Destiny had been waiting for Wigram that day and he had not been permitted to escape it. He had ordered Wally, the only other British officer, to take the squadrons forward; and the boy had obeyed him—charging into the thick of the fight and coming through unscathed, with no mark on him except for a faint scratch and a slashed riding boot. But Wigram, following slowly and painfully on foot with the aid of one of his sowars, had been hit again in the hip.

As he fell for the third time a group of tribesmen, rushing in for the kill, had been beaten off, for the sowar carried a carbine as well as a cavalry sabre, and Wigram had his revolver. Five of the attackers fell and the rest drew back, but Wigram was losing blood fast. He reloaded the revolver and with an enormous effort of will managed to raise himself on one knee. But as he did so, a stray bullet fired by someone in the mêlée further up the slope struck him full in the chest and he fell forward and died without a word.

An exultant shout went up from his surviving assailants, and they rushed forward again to hack at his body, for to an Afghan the corpse of a dead enemy merits mutilation—and never more so than when the enemy is a *feringhi* and an Infidel. But they had reckoned without Jiwan Singh, Sowar.

Jiwan Singh had snatched up the revolver, and standing astride his dead Commander, fought them off with bullet and sabre. He had stood there for more than an hour, protecting Wigram's body against all comers, and when the battle was over and the surviving Guides came back from the plateau to count their dead and wounded, they found him still on guard; and around him in a circle the bodies of no less than eleven dead Khugianis.

Later, when all the official reports had been sent in, the praise and blame apportioned and decorations awarded—and when the critics who had not been present had pointed out errors of judgement and explained how much better they themselves would have handled the affair—Sowar Jiwan Singh was awarded the Order of Merit. But to Wigram Battye there fell a greater honour . . .

When the wounded had been taken away and the stretcher-bearers came for his body to carry it back to Jalalabad (as any grave near the battle-field would certainly be dug up and desecrated as soon as the column had gone) his sowars had refused to let the ambulance men touch it. 'It is not fitting that such a one as Battye-Sahib should be borne by strangers,' said their Sikh spokesman. 'We ourselves will carry him.' And they had done so.

Most of them had been in the saddle since dawn, and all, in the heat of the day, had ridden in two charges and fought a desperate hour-long battle against tremendous odds. They were weary to the verge of exhaustion and Jalalabad was more than twenty long miles away over a road that was little more than a track over stony ground. But all through that warm April night, relays of his men plodded forward, carrying Wigram's body shoulder high. Not upon a hospital litter, but laid upon cavalry lances.

Zarin had taken his turn at that sad task, and so for a mile or two had Wally. And once a man who was not a sowar, but from his dress appeared to be a Shinwari, came out of the darkness and took the place of one of the pallbearers. Strangely enough, no one had made any move to prevent him or questioned his right to be there, and it almost seemed as though he was known to them and had been expected; though he spoke only once, very briefly and in an undertone to Zarin, whose reply was equally brief and inaudible. Only Wally, stumbling tiredly in the rear, his mind blurred by fatigue and grief and the sour aftermath of battle, did not notice the presence of a stranger in the cortège. And at the next stop the man vanished as swiftly and unobtrusively as he had come.

56

They reached Jalalabad in the dawn, and a few hours later they buried Wigram Battye in the same stretch of ground where, forty-six years ago, the British had buried their dead at the time of the First Afghan War. And where nineteen new-made graves marked the last resting-place of the eighteen troopers and an officer of the 10th Hussars whose bodies, alone of the forty-six drowned below the ford, had been recovered from the Kabul River only two short days before.

Near him were laid a Lieutenant and a Private of the 70th Foot who had died in the flank attack by the infantry. But Risaldar Mahmud Khan and the five sowars who had also died in the battle of Fatehabad were men of different faiths; and according to their several religions, their bodies were carried to the Mohammedan burial ground to be laid in the earth with the proper ritual and prayers of the Faithful, or else cremated, and their ashes gathered up and cast into the Kabul River so that they might be carried down to the plains of India and from there, by the kindness of the gods, to the sea.

Not only the regiments concerned had watched these ceremonies. The army had turned out in force, and so too had the citizens of Jalalabad and its adjacent villages, and any travellers who happened to be passing through. Among the latter, unnoticed in the peering crowds, was a gaunt, baggy-trousered Shinwari who besides watching the Christian burials from a discreet distance, had also been among the spectators at the Moslem cemetery and at the burning-ground.

When all was over and the crowds and the mourners had dispersed, the Shinwari had made his way to a small house in a backwater of the city where he was presently joined by a Risaldar of the Guides Cavalry, wearing civilian dress. The two had talked together for an hour, speaking in Pushtu and sharing a hookah, and when the Risaldar returned to the camp and his duties there he took with him a letter written on coarse paper of local manufacture with a quill pen, but addressed in English to Lieut. W. R. P. Hamilton, Queen's Own Corps of Guides.

'There was no need to write down the name; I will give it into Hamilton-Sahib's own hand,' said Zarin, storing it carefully away among the folds of his clothing. 'But it would be unwise for you to come into the camp to see him, or for him to be seen speaking to you. If you will wait among the walnut trees behind the tomb of Mohammed Ishaq, I will bring his reply there sometime after the moon is down. Or it may be a little earlier. I cannot tell.'

'No matter. I shall be there,' said Ash.

He had been there, and Zarin had handed him a letter that he read later that night by the light of an oil lamp in a room he had hired that same morning. Unlike Wally's usual letters it was very short, and mostly concerned with his grief at Wigram's death and the loss of Mahmud Khan and the others who had died in the battle. He was, he wrote, delighted to hear that Anjuli was now in Kabul, asked to be remembered to her, and ended by urging Ash to take care of himself and expressing the hope that they would be meeting again soon in Mardan . . .

It was a measure of his grief for Wigram that he had not even thought to mention something that only a short time ago would have taken precedence over almost anything else: the fact that he had just achieved his greatest ambition and the realization of a long-held and most secret dream.

General Gough, who had watched the whole battle from a vantage point on a hill-top, had sent for him to express the greatest admiration for the dash and gallantry of the Guides, and to commiserate over the heavy casualties they had suffered, in particular the death of their Commanding Officer, Major Battye, whose loss would be felt not only by his own Corps, but by everyone who had known him. But that had not been all; the General had gone on to speak warmly of Wally's own exploits, ending by informing him that in view of his taking over Wigram's command and leading it in a charge against vastly superior numbers of the enemy, together with his conduct throughout the battle and his gallant rescue of Sowar Dowlat Ram, he, General Gough, was personally recommending in dispatches that Lieutenant Walter Richard Pollock Hamilton be awarded the Victoria Cross.

It would be untrue to say that Wally had been unmoved by this news, or that he had heard it without a lift of the heart and a sudden quickening of the pulses. That would have been a physical impossibility. But even as he listened to the unbelievable words that told him his name was to be put forward for the highest honour that can be bestowed for gallantry, the blood that rushed to his face drained away again, and he realized that he would gladly exchange that coveted cross for Wigram's life—or for Mahmud Khan's, or any of those other men of his squadron who would never ride back to Mardan again—

Seven dead, twenty-seven wounded (one of whom the doctor said would not pull through), and any number of horses killed or maimed—he could not remember how many. Yet he, who had come through without a scratch, was to be rewarded with a little bronze cross made out of cannon captured at Sebastopol, and bearing the proud inscription *For Valour*. It did not seem fair . . .

That last thought had brought Ash to mind, and Wally had smiled a little ruefully as he thanked the General, and afterwards gone back to his own tent to scribble that brief note to Ash before writing a letter to his parents giving an account of the battle and telling them that he was safe and well.

So it was from Zarin that Ash learned that Wally had been put in for the Victoria Cross. 'It will be a great honour for all in the Guides if the Kaiser-i-Hind should bestow this most coveted of awards on one of our Officer-Sahibs,' said Zarin. But that had not been until late on the following night when the two met once more among the walnut trees; and Ash's delight at the news had been tinged with regret because he had not been able to hear about it at first hand.

'You may do so before long,' consoled Zarin, 'for it is said in the camp that the new Amir, Yakoub Khan, will shortly sue for peace, and that all our *pultons* will be back in their own cantonments before mid-summer. I do not know if this is true, but any fool can see that we cannot stay here much longer when there is not enough food to feed our army, unless we let the Afghans starve. So I can only pray it is true, and if it is, we shall meet in a few months time in Mardan.'

'Let us hope so. But I have had a message from the General-Sahib telling me to return to Kabul, and from what he says it may be that I shall have to stay there for some little time; which will not displease my wife, who being hill-bred has no love for the plains.'

Zarin shrugged and spreading out his hands in acceptance of the inevitable, said: 'Then this is goodbye. Have a care for yourself Ashok, and give my respects to Anjuli-Begum, your wife, and remember me to Gul Baz. *Salaam aleikoum, bhai.*'

'*Wa'aleikoum salaam.*'

The two embraced, and when Zarin had gone Ash wrapped himself in his blanket and lay down on the dusty ground between the walnut trees to snatch an hour or two of sleep before setting out on the road that led past Fatehabad and the Lataband Pass to Kabul.

Little more than six weeks later a Treaty of Peace had been signed in Gandamak by His Highness Mohammed Yakoub Khan, Amir of Afghanistan and its dependencies, and Major Pierre Louis Napoleon Cavagnari, c.s.i., Political Officer on Special Duty, the latter signing 'in virtue of full powers vested in him by the Right Honourable Edward Robert Lytton, Baron Lytton of Knebworth, Viceroy and Governor-General of India'.

By its terms, the new Amir renounced all authority over the Khyber and Michni Passes and the various tribes in that area, agreed to a continued British presence in the Kurram, declared himself willing to accept the advice of the British Government in all his relations with other countries, and, among other things, surrendered at last to the demand that his father had so strenuously resisted—the establishment of a British Mission in Kabul.

In return he had been promised a subsidy and given an unconditional guarantee against foreign aggression, while Major Cavagnari, who had been solely responsible for obtaining his signature to this document, was rewarded by being appointed to head the Mission as British Envoy to his Court at Kabul.

With a view to allaying Afghan suspicions and hostility, it had been decided that the new Envoy's suite should be a comparatively modest one. But though (apart from Major Cavagnari's) no names had yet been mentioned, camp rumour had no doubts as to one other. And as news flies fast in the East, within a day of the Amir's return to Kabul a member of his household guard had informed a personal friend—once a Risaldar-Major in the Guides and now a pensioner of that Corps—that his old Regiment had been selected for the honour of providing an escort for the *Angrezi* Mission, and that a certain officer-Sahib who had distinguished himself in the battle against the Khugianis would command it.

Sirdar Bahadur Nakshband Khan had in turn carried this information to a guest in his house: one Syed Akbar, to whom, with his wife and a Pathan servant, the kindly Sirdar had offered the hospitality of his home . . .

Following his dismissal by Cavagnari, Ash had given up his post in the Bala Hissar, though in obedience to the General's wishes he had continued to make Kabul his base. Yet because the type of information required by the Peshawar Valley Field Force was not so readily available in Kabul as in the countryside surrounding the headquarters of the invading army, he was often away, and Anjuli saw little of him. But from her point of view even that little compensated a thousand times for the hardships of the journey through the snowbound passes, since it was immeasurably better than not seeing him at all and getting no news of him other than an occasional oblique verbal message sent by Zarin to his aunt in Attock.

These days, when Ash left her he could never tell her with any certainty how long he would be away, or send her word of his return; but at least it meant that each day when she awoke she could think— 'Perhaps he will come today.' So that she lived always in hope, and when that hope was realized, was happy beyond expression—far more so than those who take happiness for granted because they feel their hold on it to be secure, and do not visualize it ending. In addition to which, as she had told the Begum, she felt safe in Kabul, safe from the Rana's people, whose spies would never track her here, so that she could forget the fears that had haunted her in India. And after the glaring sun-burned landscape of Bhithor, and the rocks and the barren salt-ranges around Attock, the air of Kabul and the sight of snow and high mountains was a perpetual source of refreshment.

Her host, who was a wise and cautious man, had taken pains to ensure that no one in his house, neither his family nor his servants, should suspect that Syed Akbar was anything other than he seemed. And when Anjuli had arrived in mid-winter and Ash had declared that they must move elsewhere, the Sirdar had insisted that they both stay, but suggested that in case Anjuli's command of Pushtu should prove inadequate when subjected to the strain of daily conversation with the women-folk of the household, it might be as well to say that she was a Turkish lady, which would account for any mistakes she might make.

The household had seen no reason to query this, and accepted her as such. They had also taken a great liking to her, as the Begum had done, and Anjuli soon became one of them, learning their ways and helping with the numerous household tasks—cooking, weaving, embroidering, grinding spices and preserving, pickling or drying fruit and vegetables. And in her spare time, studying the Koran and commiting as much as possible to memory, for she could not afford to show ignorance in religious matters. The children adored her because she was never too busy to fashion toys for them, fly kites or invent enthralling stories as she had been used to do for Shushila; and here, in a land of tall, fair-skinned women, she was no longer considered raw-boned and over-large, but accounted beautiful.

Had she been able to see more of Ash she would have been completely happy, and the times when they were together were as idyllic as the honeymoon days of that long, enchanted voyage up the Indus. Nakshband Khan had rented them a small suite of rooms on the topmost floor of his house, and here they could retreat into a private world of their own, high above the hubbub of the busy, bustling life below.

Yet even when Ash was in Kabul, there was still work for him to do, and he must tear himself away from those peaceful upper rooms and go into the city to listen to the talk in the great bazaar, and discover what was being said in the coffee shops and serais, and in the outer courtyards of the Bala Hissar where an army of petty officials, place-seekers and idle servants whiled away the days in intrigue and gossip, and where he would talk with acquaintances and listen to the opinions of the citizens and men who were passing through Kabul. Merchants with caravans from Balkh, Herat and Bokhara, peasants from outlying villages bringing goods to market, Russian agents and other foreign spies, soldiers drifting back from the fighting in the Kurram or the Khyber, slant-eyed Turkomans from the north, strolling-players, horse-dealers, fakirs and men on pilgrimage to one of the city's mosques.

In this way he learned of the signing of the Peace Treaty, and after that he looked hourly for a message recalling him to Mardan: but none came. Instead, he heard one day from the Sirdar that a British Mission headed by Cavagnari would be coming to Kabul, and that its Escort would almost certainly be drawn from his own Corps and commanded by his best friend. And within an hour of hearing this, he set off hot-foot for Jalalabad to see the Commandant of the Guides.

Ash had confidently expected to be back within a week. But when he reached Jalalabad it was to find that Colonel Jenkins, who now that hostilities were ended was once again in command of the Corps, had already left; as had Cavagnari and General Sam Browne, and Wally too—for when the Peace Treaty had been ratified in early June, the invading army began to pull out of Afghanistan. Jalalabad was to be evacuated, and those regiments still encamped there were preparing to leave.

'You are too late,' said Zarin. 'Hamilton-Sahib left with the advance party, and the Commandant-Sahib some days before them. If all went well, they should be back in Mardan by now.'

'Then I too must go to Mardan,' said Ash. 'Because if it is true that Cavagnari-Sahib is to take a British Mission with an Escort of Guides to Kabul, then I must see the Commandant-Sahib at once.'

'It is true,' confirmed Zarin. 'But if you will be advised by me you will turn back, since to go forward is to take your life in your hands, and there is your wife to be thought of. It was all very well when she was in Attock where my aunt would have cared for her, but what will become of her now if you die on the road and she is left alone in Kabul?'

'But the war is over,' said Ash impatiently.

'So they say. Though as to that I have my doubts. But there are worse things than war, and cholera is one of them. Living in Kabul, you will not have heard that the black cholera is raging in Peshawar so fiercely that when it reached the garrison, the *Angrezi* troops were moved in haste to a camp six miles outside the cantonments; but to no purpose, for this time it is the *Angrezi-log* whom it is striking the hardest, and few who take it recover. They are dying like flies in a frost, and now it is sweeping up the passes to meet our army as it returns to Hind, so that it seems we shall lose more lives in quitting this country than ever we lost in taking it. I am told that so many have already died of the cholera that the roadside is lined with graves.'

'This I had not heard,' said Ash slowly.

'You are hearing it now! June has always been an ill month for marching; but here, where there is little shade or water and the heat and dust are worse than in the deserts of Sind, it is a foretaste of Jehanum. So take my advice, Ashok, and return to your wife. For I tell you that the road through the Khyber is so choked with troops and guns and transport, and so full of the sick and the dying, that even if you escaped the cholera you would not get through to Jamrud for several days. It would be quicker to go on foot across the mountains than to try and force a way for yourself through the press and tumult that prevails between here and the mouth of the Khyber. If your business with the Commandant-Sahib is so urgent, write it down and I will undertake to deliver it.'

'No. A letter would not serve. I must speak to him myself face to face if I hope to convince him that what I say is true. Besides, you yourself will be travelling on that same road and are just as likely to be struck down by the cholera as I am.'

'If I were, my chances of recovery would be greater than yours, for I am not an *Angrezi*,' said Zarin dryly. 'And if I died, my wife would not be left alone and friendless in a strange land. But there is little fear of my taking the cholera because I shall not be travelling by that road.'

'You mean you are staying here? But I understood that Jalalabad was to be evacuated—horse, foot and guns. That everyone would be leaving.'

'That is so. And I too will be going, but by way of the river.'

'Then I will go with you,' said Ash.

'As yourself? Or as Syed Akbar?'

'As Syed Akbar; for as I shall be returning to Kabul, it would be too dangerous to do anything else.'

'That is true,' said Zarin. 'I will see what can be done about it.'

It was a tradition with the Guides that an officer who died while serving with the Corps should, if humanly possible, be buried at Mardan. So that when his men urged that Battye-Sahib's body should not be left behind, it was agreed that the coffin should be exhumed. But because of the difficulties of taking it with them in the heat of June, it was decided to try sending it by raft down the Kabul River through the gorges north of the Khyber, and that *terra incognita* the Mallagori country, to Nowshera.

Risaldar Zarin Khan and three sowars had been assigned to escort the coffin. And at the last moment Zarin had asked permission to take a fifth man: an Afridi who had arrived in Jalalabad the previous evening, and who, said Zarin mendaciously, was a distant connection of his and would be an invaluable addition to the escort, as he had made this journey before and was familiar with every turn and twist and hazard of the river.

Permission had been granted, and in the dark hour before dawn, the raft that was to carry Wigram's remains back to their last resting place in Mardan set out on the long and hazardous voyage to the plains.

57

Daylight was beginning to fade when the look-out, who had lain all day on a ledge of cliff above the river, lifted his head and whistled in imitation of a kite. Sixty yards away a second man, concealed by a crevice in the rock face, passed on the signal, and heard it repeated by a third.

There were more than a dozen watchers lying in wait along the left bank of the gorge, but even a man with binoculars would not have suspected it; and the men on the raft had no such aids. Moreover, they needed to concentrate the greater part of their attention on keeping their unwieldy craft clear of rocks and whirlpools, for the snows were melting in the mountains to the north, and the Kabul River ran high and swiftly.

There were six men on the raft, four of whom—a tall Pathan, two black-bearded Sikhs and a burly Punjabi Mussulman—wore the dust-coloured uniform of the Corps of Guides. The fifth, a lean Afridi with a ragged red-tinged beard, was less formally clad, it being his task to wield the heavy ten-foot pole that served as a rudder; and in deference to the heat and the exertions of his office he wore only a thin shirt above the wide cotton trousers of his race. The sixth was a British officer, but he was dead. He had, in fact, been dead for close on two months—a circumstance that was all too apparent to the five who were escorting his body back to India by raft through the gorges where the Kabul River carves its way through the wild mountain country north of the Khyber, past Dakka and Lalpura and the whirlpools of the unknown Mallagori country—for the coffin had been made from unseasoned wood, and though it had been wrapped in a tarpaulin for extra protection, even the evening breeze that blew through the gorge was not sufficient to disperse the sickly odour of corruption.

The voice of the river was a rustling, hissing murmur that filled the gorge with sound but failed to drown the shill cry of a kite, and the tall Pathan turned sharply—for the sun had already set and that call is not normally heard at dusk: 'Down! there are men among those rocks,' said Zarin Khan, reaching for his carbine. 'Mohmands—may they fry in hell. Keep down: we are too good a target. But the light is poor and by Allah's grace we may win through.'

'They may mean us no harm,' said a Sikh, checking the loading of his rifle. 'They cannot know who we are, and may take us for men from one of their own villages.'

The Punjabi laughed shortly. 'Do not deceive yourself, Dayal Singh. If there are men on the cliffs they know very well who we are and will have been waiting for us. Perhaps it was fortunate after all that Sher Afzal should have fallen from the raft and been drowned in those rapids, for had that not delayed us we should have reached this spot two hours earlier and been an easier mark. As it is—' He did not finish the sentence, for the first shot took him in the throat and he leapt up as though jerked by a string, his arms flailing, and fell backwards into the river.

The splash and the sound of the shot echoed together through the gorge, and for a brief moment a dark smear stained the colourless water and was whirled away on the current; but the Punjabi's body did not surface again. The raft swept forward into the gut of the gorge, the steersman flinging his weight on the great pole and grunting with the effort as he struggled to keep the unwieldy platform on a straight course, since he knew only too well what their fate would be if they were to run aground.

A vicious spatter of shots whipped the water about them, and the three remaining men of the escort lay flat on the logs and returned the fire with the unhurried precision of long practice, aiming for the puff and flash of the old fashioned muzzle-loaders that thrust out from a dozen crevices on the cliff. But it was an unequal contest, for the enemy lay concealed on ledges and crevices high overhead and could take their time sighting for a shot, while the men of the Guides were handicapped by lack of cover and the uneasy motion of the raft, and had only the speed of their passage and the swiftly gathering dusk in their favour. The coffin provided a narrow margin of protection; but it had been lashed dead centre, and if all three took shelter on the far side of it the raft would overturn.

'Move the stores,' gasped the steersman, thrusting off from dimpled water that betrayed an unseen shoal. 'Over to the left—quick! That will balance one of you.'

Zarin laid aside his carbine, and crawling to the pile of tin boxes that contained the stores and ammunition for their journey, began to stack them on one side of the raft, while Sowar Dayal Singh continued to load and fire. His fellow Sikh shifted his position, and lying down beside him, rested the muzzle of his carbine on the coffin and taking careful aim, pressed the trigger.

Something that looked like a bundle of clothing fell screaming from a ledge of rock to crash down into the boulder-strewn shallows, and Zarin laughed and said: '*Shabash*, Suba Singh. That was good shooting. Almost good enough for a Pathan.'

Suba Singh grinned and retorted with a crude country joke that was uncomplimentary to the prowess of Pathans, and Dayal Singh smiled. They had run into a trap in which one of their number had already lost his life, and their chances of escaping from it alive were not high; but all three were men whose trade was war. They loved a fight for its own sake, and their eyes glittered in the dusk as they laughed and re-loaded and fired at the flashes, and made grim jokes as the bullets pattered onto the raft.

A shot smashed into the coffin and the ugly stench of death was suddenly strong on the evening air, blotting out the reek of black powder and the scents of the river.

'*Apka mehrbani,** Battye-Sahib,' said Suba Singh quietly, sketching a salute to the thing in the coffin. 'You always had a care for your men, and but for you that would have been my head. Let me see if I cannot avenge their discourtesy towards you.'

He lifted his head and sighted carefully, allowing for the jerk and sway of the raft. The rifle cracked, and a man near the cliff top flung up his arms and toppled forward to lie still, while the jezail he had held slid from his grasp and clattered down the cliff face in a shower of stones. Suba Singh might not be a Frontiersman, but he was known to be the finest marksman in his squadron.

'Two to us. Now let us see you do better, Pathan,' said the Sikh.

Zarin grinned appreciatively, and ignoring the bullets that hummed about him like a swarm of angry bees, took aim at a mark that would have been invisible to anyone not bred in a country where every stone may conceal an enemy: a narrow crevice between two rocks, where the muzzle of a long-barrelled jezail protruded a few inches. The shot went cleanly home above the small circle of metal, and the muzzle dropped with an abruptness that told its own tale.

'There,' said Zarin. 'Are you satisfied?'

There was no reply, and turning his head he met a blind fixed stare above the coffin. The Sikh had not moved: his chin was still

* Thank you

propped on the stiff folds of tarpaulin and his mouth was agape as though he were about to speak, but there was a bullet hole through his temple, and Dayal Singh, lying beside him, had not even known that his compatriot had been hit . . .

'*Mara gaya?*' (Is he dead?) asked Zarin harshly, knowing the foolishness of the question even as he asked it.

'Who? The misbegotten dog you fired at? Let us hope so,' said Dayal Singh. He reached for more ammunition, and as he did so the body of Suba Singh fell sideways and lay sprawled across the raft with one arm trailing in the water.

Dayal Singh stared down at it, his outstretched hand rigid and his breath coming short. Then suddenly he began to shiver as though he had a fever. His fingers came to life again and he loaded his carbine with furious haste, cursing the while in a harsh unsteady whisper, and leaping to his feet, began to fire at the cliff, re-loading from a handful of bullets he had stuffed into his pocket.

The raft lurched dangerously, riding the full flood of the treacherous current, and the steersman flung his weight over to balance it and yelled to the Sikh to get down. But Dayal Singh was temporarily beyond the reach of reason. A red blaze of rage had swept away caution and he stood squarely astride the body of his dead comrade, facing the cliff and cursing as he fired. A bullet clipped his jaw and blood streamed into his dark beard, and presently his puttees turned red where a second shot had struck his leg. He must have been hit half a dozen times, but he neither flinched nor ceased his steady, furious swearing, until at last a bullet smashed into his chest and he staggered and dropped his carbine and fell back across the body of his fellow Sikh.

His fall tilted the raft violently to one side, and a flood of water raced across it, foaming about the coffin and sweeping away a clutter of tins and equipment; and before Zarin or the steersman could right it, the bodies of the two dead men slid down the wet logs and vanished into the river.

Relieved of their weight, the clumsy craft righted itself and Zarin rose to his knees, and wringing the water from his uniform said bitterly: 'There go two good men; and in these times we cannot afford to lose even one such. This has indeed been a costly campaign for the Guides. Too many have died or been sorely wounded already, and now four more of us are gone—and if it does not get dark soon, you and I may well die too. A plague on these sons of warlocks. Would that I . . .' He broke off and his eyes narrowed: 'You are hit!' he said sharply.

'A scratch only. And you?'

'I have taken no hurt—as yet.'

But there had been no more shots from the cliff, perhaps because the light was now too poor and the raft no longer presented a possible mark to the watchers among the rocks. The river was a grey ribbon in the dusk and the raft no more than a bobbing shadow, as elusive as a moth or a bat flitting down the gorges. An hour later the two men and their burden were clear of the cliffs with the worst of the rapids behind them, and being swept forward in the starlight through a country less well adapted to ambush.

The day had been very hot, for the monsoon had not yet reached these northern latitudes, and among the parched and treeless hills the ground gave off the stored heat of the sun in almost visible waves, as though the doors of a furnace had been thrown open. But the Kabul River was fed by the snowfields and glaciers of the Hindu Kush, and as the night wind blew coolly off the water the steersman shivered and huddled above his pole.

The coffin had been lashed to the raft with a length of stout country-made rope, but the hemp had become sodden with the night dews and the spray from the rapids, and as the weight that it held shifted to the motion of the current, the rope stretched and sagged so that the coffin moved uneasily, as though it imprisoned someone who was alive and restless.

'Lie still, Sahib, or we lose you at the next bend,' grunted Zarin, addressing the dead. 'Is there a knot on your side, Ashok?'

'Two,' said the steersman. 'But I dare not tighten them in the dark. If we were to strike a rock or rough water while retying them, the whole thing would pull free and throw us into the river. You must wait until dawn. Besides, after steering all day my hands are too stiff for tying knots.'

'And you a hillman,' jeered Zarin. 'Why, the night is as hot as Jehanum.'

'And the river as cold as charity,' retorted Ash. 'It is snow water, and I have been in it twice, so I know. Had I realized that the current ran so swiftly and that the Mohmands would lie in wait for us, I would have thought twice before I asked to come with you on such a journey. It is a mad one, anyway, for what difference does it make where a man's body lies? Will Battye-Sahib care if he rests in the earth by Jalalabad or in the cemetery at Mardan? Not he! Nor would he have cared if after we had gone the Afridis dug him up to spit on him or scatter his bones.'

'It is we of the Guides who would care,' said Zarin shortly. 'We do not permit our enemies to insult the bodies of our dead.'

'Of our *Angrezi* dead,' corrected Ash with an edge to his voice. 'This war cost us the lives of others. Yet we left their bodies among the Afghan hills and brought away only this one.'

Zarin shrugged his shoulders and made no answer. He had discovered long ago the uselessness of arguing with Ashok who, it seemed, did not see things as most other men did. But presently he said: 'Yet you *would* come—and not for my sake, either!'

Ash grinned in the darkness: 'No, brother. You have always proved fairly capable of looking after yourself. I came, as you know, because I wish to speak with the Commandant-Sahib before it is too late. If I can only see him in time, I may be able to persuade him that this mission that they talk of is doomed to disaster and must be abandoned; or at the very least, postponed. Besides, they say that the Government will send an escort of the Guides with the new Envoy to Kabul, and offer the command of it to Hamilton-Sahib.'

'So I have heard,' said Zarin. 'And why not? It will be a further honour for him: and a great honour for us of the Guides.'

'To die like rats in a trap? Not if I can help it! I shall do my best to see that he does not accept.'

'You will not succeed. There is no officer in all the armies of the Raj who would refuse such an honour. And no regiment, either.'

'Perhaps. But I must try. I have made very few friends in my life— which I suppose is a fault in me. Out of those few, two have meant a great deal to me: you and Hamilton-Sahib; and I can't face losing you both . . . I *cannot*.'

'You will not,' said Zarin reassuringly. 'For one thing, they may not send me to Kabul. And if—when—we win back to Mardan, you will see things in a better light. It is only because you are over-tired, and because life has been hard for you of late, that you talk like this.'

'Oh no I don't. I talk like this because I have spoken to too many men who do not know or talk to the Sahib-log or to soldiers of the Sirkar—and also to very many others who have never even seen either—and from them I have heard things that have made me afraid.'

Zarin was silent for a space, then he said slowly: 'I think, myself, that this has been your great misfortune: that you can talk to such people. Years ago when you were a child, my brother Awal Shah said to Browne-Sahib, who was then our Commandant, that it was a pity that you should forget to speak and think as one of us; there being few Sahibs who could do so, and such a one might be of great service to our Regiment. Therefore, because of his words, it was arranged that you should *not* forget. That was perhaps a mistake; for it has been your fate to belong to neither East nor West, yet to have one foot in both—like a trick rider at a *Pagal*-Gymkhana who stands astride between two galloping horses.'

'That is so,' agreed Ash with a short laugh. 'And I fell between them long ago, and was torn in two. It is time I tried belonging to myself only—if it is not already too late for that. Yet if I had it all to do again—'

'You would do the same as you have done; that you know,' said Zarin, '—seeing that each man's fate is tied about his neck and he cannot escape it. Give me the pole: by the sound, there are rapids ahead; and if you do not have some rest that wound in your arm will give you trouble before morning. We shall not be attacked in the dark, and I will wake you before moonrise. See if you can get some sleep, for we may need all our wits tomorrow. You had better tie one of those rope-ends about your waist before you lie down, or else you will slide off into the water if the raft should tilt.'

Ash complied with the suggestion and Zarin grunted approval. 'Good. Now take these. It may help you to sleep, and serve to lessen the pain in your arm.' He handed over several small pellets of opium which Ash swallowed obediently. '*Faugh!* how the Sahib stinks. Have we anything with which to plug that bullet hole?'

Ash tore a piece of cloth from his turban and Zarin stuffed it into the hole. They had nothing to eat, the stores they had brought with them having been lost when the raft tilted and threw the bodies of the Sikhs into the river, but both men were too tired to feel hungry; and at least they were assured of a plentiful supply of water. Ash surrendered the pole to Zarin, and having washed his arm and bound up the wound, lay down alongside the coffin. But as the raft drifted onward down the Kabul River he found that he could not sleep. His arm throbbed painfully and he lay awake and tried to think out what he should say to Colonel Jenkins when—if—they reached Mardan.

He would have to present the information he had acquired in such a way that the Commandant would not only believe him, but be able to convince all those senior officers and officials whom he himself could not hope to make any impression on that this was the truth. But the arguments he needed eluded him, and as the opium took effect, he fell asleep.

The current swept the raft forward out of the shadow of the Malla-gori hills and began to lose force as the river widened.

The slower pace aroused Ash, and he saw that the dawn had come and that the land ahead was level plain. They had won through. Though for an appreciable time that meant nothing to him, because he could not remember where he was . . . Then, as the dawn light broadened over the wide river and the wider land, his brain cleared; and realizing that it was morning, he found it hard to believe that so much time could have elapsed since Zarin had taken the pole from him and told him to rest. It seemed only a moment ago: yet the night was over—

In a little while, fifteen or twenty minutes at most if their luck held, they would be across the invisible border that divided Afghanistan from the North-West Frontier Province; and after that it would only be a matter of floating with the current that would carry them past Michni and Mian Khel to Abazai, and southward, below Charsadda, to Nowshera. They would be back in British India and Zarin could afford to tie up to the bank and sleep for an hour or two; there could have been no sleep for him during the past night, that was certain.

A breath of wind ruffled the glassy smoothness of the river and Ash shivered as it blew on him, and discovered with a vague sense of surprise that his clothes were soaking wet and that the whole raft ran with water. It looked as though they must have had a rough passage through rapids, and fairly recently, for no dew could have been heavy enough to account for it; which presumably meant that he must have slept for at least part of the night, though he could have sworn that he had not closed his eyes. He heard a rush and a fluster of wings and water as a group of paddy-birds took off in startled haste and flew down river, and realized that the raft was no longer in midstream but drifting in towards the left-hand bank.

A minute or two later sand and pebbles crunched beneath it as it drove in on a shallow ledge below a bank fringed with tussocks of grass and a few thorn bushes and jolted to a stop, and he knew that they must be back in British India again. Zarin would not have risked tying up while they were still in tribal territory—or even within gun-shot of it.

Ash stirred at last and made the discovery that he was tied to the coffin beside him by a length of rope. He had forgotten that. He sat up, feeling dazed and stupid, and began to untie it, fumbling with numbed fingers at the sodden knot. As he did so, a voice that he barely recognized said hoarsely: 'Allah be praised! You are not dead then,' and turning to look across the dripping canvas he saw that Zarin's face was grey and drawn with exhaustion, that he had lost turban and *kulla,* and his uniform was dripping wet as though he had been swimming in the river.

He made an effort to reply, but the words clogged on his tongue and he could not speak, and Zarin said huskily: 'When you did not stir as we were flung like a leaf in a millstream through a mile-long canyon little wider than a city gate, or when the whirlpools caught us and spun us round and round like a top, I was sure that you were dead, because you rolled to and fro at the end of that rope like a corpse and did not lift head or hand even when the waves washed over you.'

'I . . . I was not asleep,' said Ash haltingly. 'I can't have been. I didn't close my eyes . . . at least, I don't think so—'

'Ah; that was the opium,' said Zarin. 'I ought not to have given you so much. But at least it must have rested you a little. I myself am an old man before my time, and I hope never to endure such a night again. I am stiff in every limb.'

He drove the pole into the wet sand so as to hold the raft against the bank, and straightened himself wearily. He had fought the river all night, single-handed and without being able to relax for a moment —not even long enough to discover whether Ash had been more severely wounded than he had thought, and was either dead or bleeding to death. His hands were raw and blistered from working the heavy pole that was their only means of steering, and every muscle in his body was so cramped from strain that he could barely move. He was also hungry, thirsty and drenched to the skin. But where a European would have slaked his thirst from the river and then set about finding something to eat, Zarin first washed himself ritually and then turned to face towards Mecca and began the prayers that the Faithful say at dawn.

Ash had learned those prayers long ago. It had been necessary that he should know them (and be seen to say them), during the years when he had helped to track down Dilasah Khan through Afghanistan—and more recently, when he had gone back there at Wigram Battye's instigation in the guise of an Afridi. He had said them daily at the proper times, since they were as much a part of his disguise as the clothes he wore or the language he spoke, and to neglect them would have invited remark; so that now, instinctively, seeing Zarin begin the ritual, he too rose to face Mecca and automatically began to murmur the familiar prayers. But he did not finish them. Zarin broke off, and turning his head said angrily: '*Chup!* You are safe here. There is no need for play-acting!'

Ash stopped, open-mouthed, startled into attention by the look on Zarin's face rather than the anger in the harshly spoken words. It was a look he had never seen there before, and had never thought to see, a mixture of revulsion and animosity that was as shocking as it was unexpected, and that made him feel curiously breathless, as though he had walked into a solid object in the dark and winded himself. He was aware that his heart had begun to beat heavily, thudding like a drum in his chest.

Zarin turned abruptly back to his prayers, and Ash stared at him, frowning and intent, as if he were seeing something he recognized but had never conceived of finding here . . .

Because he had always known that to Hindus, whose gods were legion, caste was all-important, and that the only way to become a Hindu was to be born one, he had accepted the fact that as far as they were concerned he would always remain on the far side of an invisible line drawn by religion and impossible to cross. But with Koda Dad and Zarin and others of their faith (who worshipped one god only, were prepared to accept converts and had no inhibitions about eating and drinking with anyone, irrespective of creed, nationality or class) there had seemed to be no similar barrier; and even though their Koran taught them that the slaying of Unbelievers was a meritorious act rewarded by entry into Paradise, he had never felt less than at home with them. Until now . . .

That look on Zarin's face explained many things: the Mogul conquest of India and the Arab conquest of Spain, and all the many Holy Wars—the Jehads waged in the name of Allah—that have drenched the long centuries with blood. It had thrown a white light on something else too: something he had always been dimly aware of but had not troubled to think about. The fact that religion has not brought love and brotherhood and peace to mankind, but, as was promised, a sword.

The bond between Zarin and himself had been strong enough to withstand almost any strain that could be put upon it—except the stroke of that sword. For though on one level they were friends and brothers, on another, deeper one, they were traditional enemies: the 'Faithful'—the followers of the Prophet—and the 'Infidels', the Unbelievers to whose destruction the Faithful are dedicated. For it is written *'kill those who join other gods to God wherever ye shall find them, besiege them, lay in wait for them with every kind of ambush'*.

Zarin must have known that he, Ash, would for his life's sake have had to observe every ritual of the Mohammedan religion as part of his disguise, even though he had never actually seen him doing so. Yet now, seeing it for the first time—and when the necessity for it had passed—he saw it only as sacrilege; and Ash as an Infidel making a mockery of the True God.

It was strange, thought Ash, that he should never have realized before that between himself and Zarin there yawned a gulf as wide as the one that separated him from all caste Hindus, and that this too was one that he would never be able to cross.

He turned away, feeling strangely bereft, and more shaken by that sudden revelation than he would have believed possible. It was as though the very ground under his feet had disintegrated without warning, and all at once the pearly morning was full of an aching sense of loss and sadness, because something of great value had gone out of his life and would never be regained.

In that moment of crisis his mind turned to Juli as gratefully as a man turns to a glowing fire in a cold room, holding out his hands to its comforting warmth. And as the first flush of the morning lit the snows on the Safed Koh, he said his own prayers, the same that he had said facing towards the Dur Khaima when Zarin Khan was a magnificent youth in Gulkote and he himself an insignificant little Hindu boy in the service of the Yuveraj: 'Thou art everywhere, yet I worship thee here . . . Thou needest no praise, yet I offer thee these prayers . . .'

He prayed too for Juli, that she might be shielded from all harm and that he might be permitted to return to her in safety. And for Wally and Zarin, and the repose of the soul of Wigram Battye and all those who had died in the hills near Fatehabad and in the ambush last night. There was no food on the raft, so he could make no offerings: which was, he reflected wryly, just as well, for Zarin would certainly have recognized it as a Hindu rite and been even more displeased.

Zarin finished his prayers, and after they had rested awhile, Ash took over the pole and thrust off from the bank. As the sun rose and the morning mists smoked off the river, they saw ahead of them the mud walls of Michini glow gold as the bright rays caught them, and presently they landed and bought food, and arranged for a man to ride to Mardan with a message warning of their arrival and asking that arrangements should be made to meet the raft at Nowshera and escort the body of Major Battye by road to the cantonment.

They saw the messenger leave, and having eaten, went on themselves by river: Ash poling their cumbersome craft and its grim burden forward through the pitiless, shadeless heat of June, while Zarin slept the sleep of utter exhaustion.

It had been an appalling day, even though the river now ran smooth and swiftly between low sandbanks and through quiet country. The sun beat down on his head and shoulders like a red-hot hammer, and with each hour the stench from the coffin became more pervasive and intolerable. But all things come to an end, and as twilight fell they reached the bridge of boats at Nowshera, and saw Wally with an escort of Guides Cavalry drawn up on the road, waiting to take Wigram home to Mardan.

58

Not having known that Ash was on the raft, Wally failed to recognize him in the dusk, and there had been no opportunity for speech until much later, for as the condition of the body made it necessary to re-bury it immediately, the coffin had been hurried to the outskirts of Mardan in a brake, where it had been transferred to a gun-carriage, and the funeral had taken place that night by torchlight.

Only when the prayers for the dead had been recited, the Last Post sounded and the volleys fired above the mound of raw earth that marked Wigram's final resting place, and when the mourners had gone back to their quarters leaving the little cemetery to the moonlit silence and the black shadows, had Ash been able to see Wally alone.

He had hoped to see the Commandant first, but as Colonel Jenkins was playing host to two senior Frontier Force officers, friends of Wigram's who had ridden over from Risalpur for the funeral and were staying the night, that interview would have to be postponed until sometime next day; so Zarin had smuggled him into Wally's rooms in the fort instead.

Wally had been delighted to see Ash, but the emotional strain of Wigram's second funeral had subdued his normally good spirits and he was in no mood to listen to any criticism of the proposed British Mission to Afghanistan, let alone consider refusing command of the Escort—supposing he were offered it, which he had not been; or at least, not officially. At the moment it was only a rumour, though everyone, according to Wally, was agreed that Cavagnari would be the best possible choice for Envoy, if and when a Mission were sent to Kabul. 'I fancy he must have received a pretty broad hint to that effect from the Viceroy, because he was good enough to tell me that if he got the job he would ask for me as Military Attaché, in command of an Escort of Guides. And I don't believe he'd have said that unless he was fairly certain of getting the appointment. All the same, I don't mean to count my chickens before they're hatched.'

'If you've any sense,' said Ash, 'you'll put up a prayer that this particular clutch turns out to be addled.'

'*Addled*? What on earth do you mean by that?' demanded Wally blankly.

'I mean that when the late Amir, Shere Ali, was trying to get it into the heads of our Lords and Masters that his people would never take kindly to the establishment of a British presence—or, for that matter, any foreign presence—in his country, he pointed out that no Amir of Afghanistan could possibly guarantee the safety of such foreigners *"even in his own capital"*. Wally, don't you ever read anything but poetry?'

'Don't be an ass. You know I do.'

'Then you must have read Kaye's history of the First Afghan War, and ought to remember his conclusions—which should have been written up in letters a foot high over the entrance to the War Office, *and* over Viceregal Lodge and Army Headquarters in Simla as well! Kaye wrote that after an enormous waste of blood and treasure we left every part of Afghanistan bristling with our enemies, though before the British Army crossed the Indus the name of England had been honoured in Afghanistan, because the people associated it with vague traditions of the splendour of Mr Elphinstone's mission; but that all they remembered now were "galling memories of the invasion of a desolating army". That is still true today, Wally. And that is why this Mission has simply got to be called off. It *must* be stopped.'

'It won't be. It's too late for that. Besides—'

'Well, postponed then—delayed for as long as possible, to allow time for every effort to be made to build up confidence and establish really friendly relations with the Amir and his people. Above all to allay their fears that the British mean to take over their country as we took over this one. Even at this late date that might still be done if only men like Lytton and Colley and Cavagnari could be persuaded to try a different approach—to lay aside the big stick and see what moderation and good-will can do instead. But I promise you, Wally, that if Cavagnari really means to take this disastrous Mission to Kabul, he'll never come back alive. Nor will you or anyone else who goes with him—you've got to believe that.'

Wally, who had been listening with ill-concealed impatience, said: 'Ah, blather!' and pointed out that the Amir himself had agreed to accept the Mission.

'Only under duress,' corrected Ash sharply. 'And if you think his subjects have accepted it, you're a long way out. They are as much against it as they ever were: more, if anything, after this war. And it's *their* wishes that count and not the Amir's—a fact that he is so well aware of that he came to the Gandamak Conference prepared to fight against it every inch of the way, and nothing that the Generals or the Politicals could say could make him budge. He stuck out against them all, and it was only when Cavagnari demanded that he be allowed to talk to him alone, without anyone else being present, that he—'

'I know. You don't have to be telling me. Dammit, I was there!' interrupted Wally irritably. 'And what's more, Cavagnari talked him round.'

'Did he? I take leave to doubt it. I imagine he threatened him, and pretty strongly. All that anyone knows for certain is that he forced the Amir to give in—and boasted afterwards that he had "rated him as though he had been a mere Kohat Malik". It's no use shaking your head at me, for it's true. If you don't believe me, ask him yourself—he won't deny it. But he would have done better to have kept quiet about it, because it got about, and I cannot believe that it will have helped him to make a friend of the Amir. Or of his people either, who are not ready to accept a British presence in Afghanistan because in their eyes it means only one thing: a prelude to the annexation of their homeland in the same way that the first small trading posts of the East India Company led to the annexation of India.'

Wally observed coldly that they would have to lump it, and that, though he realized that the Mission would not be popular at first, once it was there it would be up to its members to see that they got on good terms with the Afghans and showed them that they had nothing to fear. 'We shall all do our damnedest, I promise you. And if anyone can bring them round his thumb it's Cavagnari. That's something I *do* know!'

'Then you're wrong. I agree that he might have done it once, but riding rough-shod over the Amir has lost him a vital ally. Yakoub Khan is not one to forgive an insult, and now he will give him as little help as possible, and probably intrigue against him behind his back. Wally, I know what I'm talking about. I've lived in that damned country for months on end, and I know what is being said there—and in places like Herat and Kandahar and Mazar-i-Sharif too. The Afghans do not want this Mission, and they are in no mood to have it forced down their throats.'

'Then that is their misfortune,' said Wally, brusquely. 'Because they are going to have it whether they want it or not. Besides, we gave them such a hell of a thrashing in the Khyber and the Kurram that they had to sue for peace, and I think you'll be finding that troops who have just been as soundly defeated in battle as these fellows have will have learnt their lesson by now and not be over-eager to get another dose of the same medicine.'

Ash came to a stop, and gripping the back of a chair with both hands until his knuckles showed white, explained in a strictly controlled voice that the whole point was that they hadn't learned anything—because they didn't even know that they were defeated. 'That's one of the things I came here to tell the Commandant: there have been insurrections in Turkestan and Badakshan, and as the defeated regiments have all been hurried off to deal with the situation there, the Amir is having to raise fresh ones to take their place, and the new troops are nothing but an undisciplined rabble who have never been in action against the British Army, and know nothing about the defeats. They have, on the contrary, swallowed whole a score of fairy-tales about "Glorious Afghan Victories", and worse still they have received no pay for months, because the Amir insists that there is no money in the exchequer to pay them. So they are preying on the wretched villagers instead, and by and large I'd say they were a far greater menace to him than having no troops at all. It's obvious that they are already pretty well out of control, and in my opinion they're likely to prove a serious threat to any British Mission foolish enough to set up shop in Kabul and trust to them to keep order; because they can't do so, and what's more they won't!'

Wally retorted crossly that Cavagnari was bound to have heard all about this already as he had scores of spies collecting information for him. To which Ash agreed: 'But the trouble is that they come and go, and only someone who has actually lived in Kabul during these past months can have any inkling of the situation there. It's unstable as water and potentially dangerous as a wagon-load of gunpowder, for you can't expect reason from an undisciplined, unpaid rabble that having played no part in the recent hostilities thinks the present withdrawal of our army is a retreat, and is therefore firmly convinced that the invading British were soundly defeated and are scuttling out of Afghanistan with their tails between their legs. Because that is how it looks to them, and so they can see no reason why their new Amir should permit a handful of the defeated, despised and hated "*Angrezi-log*" to establish a permanent Mission in Kabul. If he does, they will merely regard that as weakness, and think the less of him: and that isn't going to help matters, either.'

Wally turned away to sit on the edge of the table, swinging a booted foot and gazing out of the window at the moonlight that filled the interior of the little fort; and presently he said slowly: 'Wigram used to say that he wouldn't be in your shoes for anything in the world—because you didn't know where you belonged. But I don't think he was quite right about that. I think myself that you've made up your mind and taken sides: and that it isn't our side you've chosen.'

Ash did not reply, and after a brief pause Wally said: 'Somehow I always thought that when it came down to brass tacks, you'd choose us. I didn't dream . . . Ah well, there it is; no use talking about it. We shall never agree as long as you apparently have adopted the Afghan view of this business, while I can't avoid seeing it from ours.'

'By which you mean Cavagnari's and Lytton's, and all that lot,' said Ash with something of a snap.

Wally gave a small shrug. 'If you like.'

'I don't. But how do you yourself see it, Wally?'

'Me? Faith, I should have thought that was obvious. I may not know these people like you do—the tribesmen I mean—but I do know that they despise weakness, as you yourself have just pointed out! Well then, whatever your views are as to the rights and wrongs of it, we went to war with them and we won. We defeated them. We made their Amir come to Gandamak to discuss peace terms and sign a treaty with us, and the most important of those terms was that we should be allowed to establish a British Mission in Kabul. Now I'm not going to argue the pros and cons with you, because, praise be, I'm not a politician, but if we back down now, they'll think us a backboneless lot who haven't even the guts to insist on our rights as victors, and despise us accordingly—which you of all people must know is true. We should earn neither friendship nor respect, but only scorn, and even the men of our own Corps would despise us for it and begin to wonder if we'd lost our nerve. Ask Zarin and Awal Shah, or Kamar Din or any of them, what they think, and see what they say. It'll surprise you.'

'No it wouldn't,' said Ash tiredly. 'They'll think the same as you. It's all this fatuous business of "saving face". We all suffer from that: and pay for it—in blood. We daren't risk "losing face" even if it means throwing justice and reason and common-sense to the winds, and doing something that we know is not only foolhardy, but appallingly dangerous: and in this case, completely unnecessary.'

Wally heaved a resigned sigh and said with a grin: ' "It isn't fair", in fact. God be helping us if he isn't at it again! It's no good, Ash: it's wasting your time you are.'

'I suppose so,' admitted Ash ruefully. 'But as Wigram once said, "One has to try". Let's hope the Commandant can be brought to see how serious the situation is, and try his hand at persuading Cavagnari and his Forward Policy cronies to have second thoughts on the subject of this Mission. Though I admit I haven't a spark of confidence in our Simla-based decision-makers. Or in Homo-sapiens in general, if it comes to that!'

Wally laughed, and for the first time that night looked as he had done in the old days in Rawalpindi: young and gay and carefree. 'Wisha, but it's a gloomy devil you are an' all, an' all. 'Tis ashamed of you I am. Ah, come now, Ash, don't be such a Jeremiah. We really aren't such a hopeless lot as you make out. I know you didn't see eye to eye with Cavagnari, but for all that I'll lay you any odds you like that he brings the Afghans round his thumb and has them eating out of his hand inside a month of our arrival in Kabul. He'll win them over just as Sir Henry Lawrence won over the defeated Sikhs in the days before the Mutiny—you'll see.'

'Yes . . . Yes, I shall see,' said Ash slowly.

'Of course—I forgot you'd be in Kabul yourself. When do you go back?'

'As soon as I've seen the Old Man, which I hope will be sometime tomorrow. There's no point in my staying here any longer, is there?'

'If you mean you won't be able to persuade me into turning down command of the Escort if I have the luck to be offered it, no there isn't.'

'When do you think you'll know?'

'I suppose when Cavagnari gets back from Simla.'

'Simla! I might have known he'd be there.'

'Faith, I think you might. He came out through the Khyber with General Sam and went straight up there to report to the Viceroy.'

'And to be rewarded for having bullied Yakoub Khan into accepting the terms of that wretched Peace Treaty, no doubt,' said Ash with an edge to his voice. 'A knighthood at the least—Sir Louis Cavagnari, K.C.S.I., etc., etc.'

'Why not?' demanded Wally, beginning to bristle. 'He's earned it.'

'No doubt. But unless he can persuade his fellow fire-eater, Lytton, to hold up this Mission until Yakoub Khan has had a chance to re-establish some sort of law and order in Kabul, it's likely to prove his death-warrant. And yours too, Wally! Not to mention the jawans, and everyone else he'll be taking with him. Have the members of the escort been selected yet?'

'Not officially, though it's more or less settled. Why?'

'I wanted to know if Zarin would be going.'

'Not as far as I know. Nor is Awal Shah. In fact none of your particular cronies.'

'Except yourself.'

'Oh, I shall be all right,' said Wally buoyantly. 'You don't have to worry about me—I was born under a lucky star. It's yourself's the one you should be worrying about, ye scutt. You can't go hanging around indefinitely in a trouble-spot like Afghanistan merely in order to keep a weather-eye out for your friends, so it's I who'll be giving you a piece of advice for a change. When you see the Old Man, get him to let you come back to us. Go on your knees if necessary. Tell him we need you—which is God's truth so it is.'

Ash looked at him a little oddly and started to say something, but changed his mind and inquired instead when this Mission was supposed to leave—if it did leave.

'It'll leave all right, make no mistake about that. We expect to set off as soon as Cavagnari returns from Simla. But as I told you, nothing has been decided yet, and for all I know the Viceroy may have other ideas.'

'Let's hope so. They couldn't be worse than this one,' observed Ash dryly. 'Well, goodbye, Wally. I don't know when I shall be seeing you again, but I hope for your sake it won't be in Kabul.'

He held out his hand and Wally gripped it and said warmly: 'Wherever it is, it can't be too soon: you know that. And if it's Kabul, at least you'll know that I wouldn't have missed being there for anything in the world. Why, it'll be the chance of a lifetime, and if all goes well it's bound to mean promotion for Hamilton, and another long step towards getting my hands on that Field Marshal's baton. Sure now, you wouldn't want to do me out of that, would you? Sorra-a-bit! So don't say "goodbye", say "I'll see you in Kabul".'

Zarin had taken much the same view as Wally, when Ash related their conversation the following morning. And once again, as on the previous one, there had been that in his voice that sounded an ominous note of change and warning. A hint of impatience that verged on irritation, and an indefinable suggestion of withdrawal, as though he had retreated to the far side of some invisible barrier. He might almost, thought Ash, appalled by the reflection, have been speaking to a stranger.

Zarin had stopped short of telling him in so many words that his warnings were unwelcome, but that was made clear by his tone. 'We your friends are no longer boys,' said Zarin. 'We are all grown men and can look to our affairs. Awal Shah tells me that he has spoken with the Commandant-Sahib who will see you during the afternoon, when everyone if not asleep is at least within doors.'

He would not meet Ash's eyes, but rose and went out about his duties, saying that he would be back before two o'clock to take Ash to the Commandant's bungalow, and advising him to get some sleep, because he would need to be rested if he meant to set out for Kabul that night—it being too hot to travel by day.

But Ash had not slept, for apart from the fact that Zarin's small, brick-built quarter behind the Cavalry Lines was intolerably hot, he had too many things to think of; and a vital decision to make.

The years that had once seemed to drift by so slowly were now passing with ever-increasing swiftness, like a sluggish train that pants and jerks and puffs as it draws away from a station platform, and then, gathering speed, rattles forward faster and ever faster on the iron rails, eating up the miles as time eats up the years. And Ash, sitting cross-legged on the mud floor and gazing unseeingly at a whitewashed wall, looked back down the long corridor of those years and saw many Zarins. The Zarin he had first seen in Koda Dad's quarters in the Hawa Mahal: a tall, handsome youth who could ride and shoot as well as a man, and who had seemed—then and always—to be everything that was brave, splendid and admirable. A dashing, confident Zarin, riding away from Gulkote to join the Guides Cavalry. Zarin at Mardan, wearing the uniform of a sowar; consoling him for the death of Sita and mapping out his future with the aid of Awal Shah. An older Zarin, waiting to greet him on the dock at Bombay, still unchanged, still the same staunch friend and elder brother . . .

He had been afraid once that their relationship might not survive his return to Mardan as an officer in the Corps, and their sudden reversal in status. But it had done so, thanks in a large part, reflected Ash, to the astringent common-sense and level-headedness of Koda Dad's youngest son rather than to any qualities that he himself possessed. After that it had seemed to him that it would survive anything, short of death, and he had never visualized it ending like this.

Yet it was the end. He realized that quite clearly. They could not continue to see each other and talk together as they used to do, because their paths had already diverged, and the time had come when he must step to the music that he had heard.

That was something that Wigram had once quoted to him, and the words had stayed in his mind: 'If a man does not keep pace with his companions, perhaps it is because he hears a different drummer: let him step to the music that he hears.' It was good advice, and high time he acted upon it, for he knew now that he had never yet succeeded in keeping in step with his companions, whether European or Asiatic, because he himself was neither one nor the other.

The time had come to close the Book of Ashok and Akbar and Ashton Pelham-Martyn of the Guides; to put it away on a shelf and begin a new volume—'The Book of Juli': of Ash and Juli, their future and their children. Perhaps one day, when he was old, he would take down that first volume, and blowing the dust from it, leaf through its pages and re-live the past in memory—fondly, and with no regrets. But for the moment it was better to put all that away and forget it. *Ab kutum hogia.**

By the time Zarin returned, the decision had been made: and though Ash did not say so, Zarin was instantly aware of it. Not because of any tension between them, for they spoke together as easily as they had always done, and as though nothing had changed. Yet in some indefinable way, Zarin was aware that Ashok had withdrawn from him; and he knew without being told that in all probability they would not meet again . . .

'Perhaps when we are old,' thought Zarin, as Ash had done. He put the thought away from him and talked cheerfully of the present, speaking of such things as a projected visit to Attock to see his Aunt Fatima and the necessity of purchasing new chargers to replace those lost in the recent campaign, until it was time to take Ash to see the Commandant.

This interview had lasted much longer than the one with Wally on the previous night, for in the hope of persuading Colonel Jenkins to pull any available strings that could possibly help to postpone the sending of a British Mission to Afghanistan (or better still, cause the whole project to be abandoned), Ash had gone into considerable de-

* Now it is finished

tail as to the situation prevailing in Kabul, and the Commandant, who was well aware that his own Corps were more than likely to be involved, had listened with absorbed attention, and after asking a number of pertinent questions, had promised to do what he could to help; though he admitted that he held out no great hopes of success.

Ash thanked him, and went on to talk of more personal matters. He had a request to make, one that he had given a great deal of thought to during the past few months but had only finally decided upon that same morning, during the hours that he had spent in Zarin's quarters. He asked to be relieved of his present duties, and also to be allowed to resign his Commission and leave not only the Guides, but the army.

He had not, he explained, come to this decision in haste, as the conviction that he could never settle down to becoming an army officer had been growing on him for some time. He presumed that Wigram, when Adjutant, must have told the Commandant something about Anjuli? The Commandant nodded without speaking, and Ash looked relieved and said that in that case he would understand the difficulties that had to be faced. If he had been able to return to Mardan and live openly with his wife it might have been possible for him to come to terms with army life in British India; but as there were several reasons why that could not be considered, he felt that the time had come to try and make a new life for his wife and himself . . .

Those long months on the journey to Bhithor, the weeks he had spent there and the years in Afghanistan had spoiled him for the narrow existence of an army officer—even an officer in such a Corps as the Guides—and made him realize that he would never be able to fit into any groove formed by nationality or creed. Therefore the only thing for him to do was to cut his ties with the past and start again, begin afresh as an individual who was neither British nor Indian, but merely a member of the human race.

The Commandant had been kind and sympathetic; and secretly relieved. For bearing in mind that peculiar story of the Hindu widow whom Ashton (according to poor Wigram) claimed to have married, and the scandal such a tale could cause if it were to become generally known, it seemed to him that the best thing for the Corps, as well as for Ashton, was for the young man to resign his commission and retire into civil life, where he could do what he liked.

They had discussed the matter rationally and without animosity;

and as the war was now over and the British Army in the process of withdrawing from Afghanistan, and General Browne had already left that country, the Commandant had no hesitation in saying that Ash could consider that his term of duty as intelligence officer to the Peshawar Valley Field Force had ended. He had also accepted Ash's resignation from the Guides and promised to arrange that there would be no difficulties over his resigning his commission. All that could be left to him, but in return he would like to ask a favour.

Would Ashton consent to remain in Kabul for a little longer (it might even be as much as a year) and act as an intelligence agent for the Escort of Guides?—always supposing the proposed British Mission became a reality.

'I will certainly see that all the information you have just given me is sent to Simla, and do anything else I can do to discourage the Mission being sent—though as I have said before, I am afraid that will be very little. But if it goes, young Hamilton will almost certainly go with it as Military Attaché in command of an Escort of Guides; and after what you have just told me, I would like to know that you were at hand to give him any information he may need about the state of affairs in Kabul, and the attitude of the local population, and so forth. If the Mission is abandoned or the Guides are not, after all, called on to supply an Escort, I would let you know immediately, and you can take it that you would be a civilian from that moment, and need not even return here unless you wish.'

'And if it is not abandoned, sir?'

'Then I would ask you to remain in Kabul as long as the Guides are there. As soon as their term of duty expires and they are relieved by some other regiment, you are free to go. Will you do that?'

'Yes, sir,' said Ash. 'Yes, of course.'

It would have been difficult, in the circumstances, to refuse such a request—even if it had occurred to him to do so, which it did not. In fact, it suited him very well. Juli was happy in Kabul—and besides, it would give him more time to decide what he meant to do and where they would go, for if the Corps sent an Escort to Kabul, their tour of duty would not be less than a year. Which would also mean that he would be seeing a good deal of Wally, who need not be told until the year was almost up that he, Ash, had sent in his papers and would never be returning to the Guides . . .

*   *   *

Ash left Mardan for the last time as the moon rose, and Zarin accompanied him past the sentries and watched him stride away across the milky plain towards the Border hills.

They had embraced at parting and exchanged the formal sentences of farewell as they had done so often before: *'Pa makhe da kha'*—may your future be bright . . . *'Amin sara'*—and yours also. But both knew in their hearts that they were saying them to each other for the last time, and that this was a final farewell. They had reached the parting of the ways, and from now on their paths would lead in different directions and would not cross again, no matter how bright their separate futures might be.

Ash turned once to look back, and saw that Zarin had not moved but was still standing there, a small dark shape against the moon-washed spaces. Lifting an arm in a brief salute he turned and went on; and did not stop again until he was beyond Khan Mai. By which time Mardan had long been hidden from him by distance and the folds of the plain.

'That leaves only Wally,' thought Ash. '. . . *my brother Jonathan: very pleasant hast thou been unto me . . .*'

The four pillars of his imaginary house were falling one by one. First Mahdoo and then Koda Dad; and now Zarin. Only Wally left; and even he was no longer the staunch support that he had once been, for he had grown away and acquired other interests and different values, and Ash wondered how long it would be before he too must be left behind—as Zarin had been. Not yet, at least; for they would probably be meeting in Kabul in the near future. Besides, there was no reason to fear that he would lose Wally as he had lost Zarin. And even if he did, would it matter so much, now that he had Juli?

Thinking of his wife, he saw her face as clearly as though it had actually materialized out of the moonlight before him: her grave eyes and sweet, tender mouth, her serene brow and the lovely, shadowy hollows below her cheek bones. Juli, who was his quietness and peace and refreshment: his dear delight. It seemed to him that her gaze held a faint trace of reproach, and he said aloud: 'Is it selfish of me to want you both?'

The sound of his own voice startled him. The hot night was so still that although he had spoken very softly, the moonlit silence magnified the sound out of all proportion and served to remind him that he might not be the only traveller abroad that night. The reflection successfully changed the direction of his thoughts, for he knew that the people of this region had no love for strangers and a habit of shooting first and asking questions afterwards; and quickening his pace he strode on with his mind alert to danger rather than preoccupied with unprofitable hopes and regrets.

Shortly before dawn he found a safe cleft among the rocks, where he was able to sleep for the best part of the day. And when he dreamed it was not of Zarin or Wally, or anyone in the life he had left behind him, but of Anjuli.

He returned to Kabul by way of the Malakand Pass, and found the city and the plain simmering in an unaccustomed cauldron of heat and dust that made him think more kindly of the temperatures that he had left behind in Mardan, because although Kabul stood six thousand feet above sea-level, the rainfall was scanty and the earth was parched for lack of moisture. But the breeze that blew off the snowfields of the Hindu Kush at evening cooled the upper rooms of the Sirdar's house and made the nights pleasant. And Anjuli had been waiting for him.

They had not talked much that first night, and Ash had touched only briefly on his abortive trip to Mardan and his parting with Zarin. But next day, and on many of the long June days that followed, they talked of the future, though in a desultory manner and with no sense of urgency, for Nakshband Khan pressed them to stay, saying that even if a British Mission did not after all come to Kabul, there was no point in their leaving until the hot weather was over and autumn brought in cooler days. There was no hurry. The whole summer lay before them, and there was plenty of time in which to decide where they would go when they left Afghanistan—if they left at all this year, and did not decide to spend the winter there and leave in the spring, after the almond trees had bloomed, which might be the best plan.

As June gave place to July, summer lightning flickered among the hills and clouds drove across the mountain ranges, but though little rain fell, that little was enough to turn the withered grass green again, and Anjuli rejoiced in the grey days because sun-glare and dust and blazing skies reminded her of Bhithor, while Ash, watching her, would forget to make plans for the future because he found the present so deeply satisfying.

But July was barely half over when the future broke in upon them in the form of disturbing stories concerning the ruthless pillaging of lonely hamlets by bands of unpaid and undisciplined soldiers, who ever since the signing of the Peace Treaty had been converging on Kabul from all parts of Afghanistan.

Each day brought more of these masterless men to the valley, until even the Sirdar became alarmed and reinforced the bars on his doors and windows: 'For if even half the tales we hear are true,' said the Sirdar, 'we are none of us safe. These men may call themselves soldiers, but having received no payment for many weeks they have become a disorderly rabble and no better than bandits. They are preying on the people of this valley, snatching anything they desire from the villagers and shooting down all who resist.'

'I know,' said Ash. 'I have been among the villages.'

He had indeed; and in doing so had both seen and heard more than enough to show him that the Sirdar's fears were far from groundless, for the situation in the valley had deteriorated sharply during the past weeks. There were far too many armed and aimless men in the villages and on the road leading to the city, and on several occasions he had passed through sizeable crowds who were being exhorted by some fakir to wage a Jehad against all Infidels. As for the capital itself, it was overfull of truculent, hungry-looking soldiers who swaggered through the streets, shouldering aside the more peaceful citizens and openly helping themselves, without paying, to fruit and cooked food from shops and stalls in the bazaars.

The very air felt heavy with the threat of violence and unrest, and there were times when Ash was tempted to desert his post and take Juli away, because it seemed to him that Afghanistan was becoming too dangerous a country for her to linger in. But he had given his word to the Commandant, and he could not break it: for by now there was no one who had not heard that a British Mission, headed by Cavagnari-Sahib and accompanied by an Escort of the 'Guide Corps', had already set out for Kabul.

Book Eight

The Land of Cain

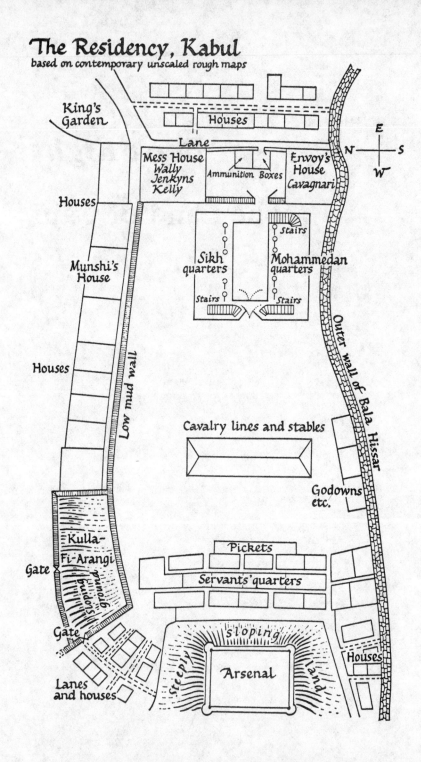

The Residency, Kabul
based on contemporary unscaled rough maps

King's Garden

Houses

Houses

Munshi's House

Houses

Low mud wall

Lane

Houses

Mess House
Wally
Jenkyns
Kelly

Ammunition Boxes

Envoy's House
Cavagnari

E
N — S
W

Sikh quarters

Mohammedan quarters

stairs

Stairs

Stairs

Cavalry lines and stables

Outer wall of Bala Hissar

Godowns etc.

Kulla-Fi-Arangi

Gate

Sloping ground

Gate

Lanes and houses

Pickets

Servants' quarters

steep

sloping land

Arsenal

Houses

59

The solitary bird, its beak agape in the simmering heat, had been dozing on the branch of a stunted pine tree near the crest of the pass when it heard the first sounds from below, and opened a wary eye.

As yet the voices and the clop and clatter of horses' hooves were too far off to be alarming, but they were coming nearer, and as the sounds grew in volume and the creak of saddles and the jingle of harness were added to the noise of hoof-beats and voices, the bird flattened its ruffled feathers and cocked its head, listening to the racket caused by a large body of horsemen riding up the hill path. There must have been close on three hundred of them, of which less than a third were Englishmen—the others being Indian troops and Afghan soldiery—and as the two leading riders came into view the bird took fright, and abandoning its siesta, flew away with an angry chattering cry.

The General was aware that the distinguished civilian who rode beside him had put up his hand as though in salute and muttered something under his breath, and supposing himself to be addressed he said: 'I'm sorry; what did you say?'

'That bird: look—'

The General glanced in the direction of the pointing finger and said: 'Oh yes. A magpie. One doesn't often see them at this height. Is that what you were saying?'

'No. I was counting ten backwards.'

'Counting—?' Major General Sir Frederick Roberts, known to his command as 'Bobs', appeared bewildered.

Cavagnari laughed and looked a little shamefaced. 'Oh, it's just a foolish superstition. It's supposed to ward off bad luck if you count ten backwards when you see a magpie. Don't you do that in England, or is it only an Irish superstition?'

'I don't know. I certainly haven't heard of it in my part of England. Though I believe we salute them. Magpies, I mean.'

'You didn't salute that one.'

'Nor I did. Well, it's too late now. It's gone. Anyway, I'm not a particularly superstitious chap.'

'I wonder if I am?' mused Cavagnari. 'I wouldn't have said so. But I suppose I must be, for I admit I would rather not have seen that bird. You won't tell my wife we saw a magpie, will you? She wouldn't like it. She's always been superstitious about such things, and she'd think it was a bad omen and worry about it.'

'No, of course I won't,' returned the General lightly. But the request surprised him, and it occurred to him that poor Louis must be feeling less confident about this Mission to Kabul than one had supposed, if a trivial incident like seeing a magpie could upset him—which it obviously had, because he was looking gloomy and thoughtful; and all at once, much older . . .

Major Cavagnari had arrived in Simla in early June to discuss the implementation of the Treaty of Gandamak with his friend the Viceroy, and to receive his reward for having induced the new Amir, Yakoub Khan, to sign it. When he left again in July it was as Major Sir Louis Cavagnari, K.C.S.I., Her Majesty's Envoy Designate and Minister Plenipotentiary to the Court of Kabul.

Never one to allow grass to grow beneath his feet, the one-time Deputy Commissioner of Peshawar had completed his arrangements within a few days of his return, and as soon as all was ready the British Mission had set out for Kabul.

Considering that a war had been fought in order to establish it, the Mission was a surprisingly modest one. But Pierre Louis Napoleon was no fool, and though the Viceroy, Lord Lytton (who regarded it as the first step toward establishing a permanent British presence in Afghanistan, and, as such, a triumph for the Forward Policy), might be blithely confident of its success, the newly appointed Envoy was not so sanguine.

Unlike Lord Lytton, Louis Cavagnari's work had given him considerable experience of the Amir's subjects, and whatever Ash might think to the contrary, he was well aware of the risks involved in forcing such a presence upon a reluctant population, and equally aware that nothing short of an army could guarantee the safety of any British Mission. Consequently he saw no reason to hazard more lives than necessary, and had therefore kept the numbers down to a minimum, restricting his suite to only three men: William Jenkyns, secretary and political assistant; a medical officer, Surgeon-Major Ambrose Kelly, and a military attaché, Lieutenant Walter Hamilton, v.c., both of the Guides, the latter in command of a picked Escort of twenty-five cavalry and fifty-two infantry of the same Corps.

Apart from a single hospital assistant and the indispensible camp-followers—servants, syces and others who accompanied the Mission—

that had been all. For though the Envoy designate had been careful not to damp the Viceroy's enthusiasm, he had admitted to certain close friends in Simla that he reckoned the chances were four to one that he would never return from his mission, adding that if his death were to lead to 'the red line being placed on the Hindu Kush', he would not complain.

The size of the Mission had been a disappointment to Wally, who had visualized a far larger and more imposing cavalcade: one that would impress the Afghans and do credit to the British Empire. The meagreness of the Envoy's party struck him as a depressing example of Government cheese-paring, but he had consoled himself with the thought that it was an indication of the power and prestige of the Raj that where lesser nations would have found it necessary to bolster their Envoy's consequence with a horde of minor officials and an outsize Escort, a mere handful of men was sufficient for the British. Besides, the smaller the numbers the greater the glory.

It did not strike him as odd that Cavagnari proposed to travel to Kabul by way of the Kurram Valley and the Shutergardan Pass rather than by the far shorter and easier route through the Khyber, as he himself had already marched through the charnel-house that heat and drought and cholera had made of that road when the army had withdrawn from Afghanistan after the signing of the Peace Treaty, and men and baggage animals had dropped and died in their thousands on the line of march. The bodies of the former had been buried in shallow graves hurriedly scraped out of the scanty earth by the roadside, but it had not been possible to do the same for the corpses of mules and camels; and knowing that the Khyber would still be foul with the sight and stench of corruption, Wally had no desire to pass that way again until time, weather and the eaters of carrion had cleansed the road and hidden the evidence under a merciful pall of dust and grass.

By comparison the Kurram Valley, even at that season of the year, must be a paradise. And as it was no longer a part of Afghanistan (having been ceded to the British under the terms of the treaty) the victorious troops that garrisoned it had not been withdrawn; which Wally confidently supposed would ensure a peaceful passage as far as the Afghan frontier. But in this he was mistaken.

The tribes were indifferent to such things as treaties or agreements between rival governments and they continued to harass the garrisons, murdering soldiers and camp-followers and stealing rifles, ammunition and baggage animals. Deserters carried off camels under the very noses of the sentries, caravans carrying fruit from Afghanistan to India were stopped on the Shutergardan Pass and plundered by marauding bands of Gilzais, and in July alone, a British surgeon had been stabbed to death and an Indian officer of the 21st Punjabis, together with his orderly, had been attacked and killed within sight of their escort who had been riding a short distance behind. Even General Roberts himself had narrowly escaped being captured by men of the Ahmed Khel . . .

'They will all be killed. Every one of them!' exclaimed that onetime Viceroy of India, John Lawrence—brother of Sir Henry of Punjab fame—when the news reached London that the British Mission had set out for Kabul. And if conditions in the Kurram were anything to go by, the outlook was murky enough to justify that pessimistic remark.

There was certainly little sign of peace in the valley, and in order to ensure the Mission's safety a mountain battery, a squadron of Bengal Lancers and three companies of Highlanders and Gurkhas had been detailed to protect them. In addition to which General Roberts, and no less than fifty of his officers who wished to honour the new Envoy, had joined his party to set it on its way.

Thus royally escorted, Sir Louis Cavagnari and the members of his Mission had arrived at Kasim Khel, five miles from the crest of the Shutergardan Pass and barely three from the Afghan border—the cliffs known as Karatiga, the White Rock. Here, having camped for the night, they entertained the General and his staff to a farewell dinner: a function that proved to be remarkably noisy and convivial in spite of the fact that tomorrow they would be parting company, and no one could be certain as to what lay ahead.

The party broke up late, and on the following morning the Amir's representative, Sirdar Khushdil Khan, escorted by a squadron of the 9th Afghan Cavalry, rode into the camp to conduct the Mission on the last leg of its journey towards the frontier.

The Amir's representative was accompanied by the head of the Ghilzai tribe, a gaunt, hatchet-faced greybeard by the name of Padshah Khan, whom Wally, for one, distrusted on sight. Not that he thought much better of Khushdil Khan, whose sinister countenance and sly, evasive eyes struck him as even more unpleasant than the wolf-like face of the robber chief. 'Wouldn't trust either of 'em as far as I could throw the mess piano,' confided Wally in a whispered aside to Surgeon-Major Kelly, who smiled a tight-lipped smile and replied in an undertone that from now on they would have no alternative but to trust them, as until they reached Kabul that unprepossessing pair and the motley crew of ruffians they had brought with them were officially responsible for their safety. 'Which I have to admit, I do not find particularly comforting,' added the doctor thoughtfully.

The motley crew referred to were mounted on small, wiry-looking horses and decked out in what appeared to be the cast-off uniforms of British Dragoons, topped by long-discarded helmets acquired from the Bengal Horse Artillery. They were armed with smooth-bore carbines and tulwars, and Wally, eyeing them with professional interest, decided that his Guides ought to be able to handle them with ease. Apart from village hall amateur dramatics, he could not remember having seen such an outlandish assortment of warriors, and had it not been for their fierce, bearded faces and the hard gleam in their eyes, the effect would have been laughable.

But Wally's gaze held no amusement, for he was well aware that despite their ridiculous appearance and straggling, undisciplined lines, they did not know the meaning of fear—or of mercy, either. And like Major Kelly, he did not find it a reassuring thought that to such men as these the Amir of Afghanistan must look to preserve peace in Kabul and protect the lives of the British Envoy and his entourage.

'We can deal with this lot if they try anything on the road,' thought Wally, 'but there will always be others to replace them. Hundreds of others—thousands. And there are less than eighty of us to protect the Mission . . .'

Riding towards Karatiga, it occurred to him that Ash might not, after all, have been taking such an alarmist view of the situation in Kabul and the new Amir's uncertain grip on authority as he had liked to think. For if a sullen, shifty-eyed Sirdar, a wolf-like Ghilzai chief and this ramshackle squadron of cavalry was the best that the Amir could send to greet the British Mission and take over responsibility for its safe arrival in Kabul, then it looked as though conditions might be almost as chaotic as Ash had made out. If so, he had misjudged him. Not that he himself could have behaved any differently if he had believed every word of it—as Ash should have known.

However great the danger might be, he would still not have

changed places with anyone, and as he watched the detachments that had accompanied them to the frontier turn back and ride away, he felt sincerely sorry for them, because they were having to return tamely to the Kurram and garrison duty, while he, Walter Hamilton, would be riding forward towards Adventure and the fabulous city of Kabul . . .

The Afghan delegation had pitched a tent on a stretch of level ground near the foot of the Shutergardan Pass, and here the Amir's representative and the head of the Ghilzais gave a banquet for Sir Louis and his suite and General Roberts and his fifty British officers, before hosts and guests remounted and rode together to the summit, where carpets had been spread on the ground and glasses of tea were served. The air on the crest of the pass had been cool and bracing, and the view of the surrounding peaks and the peaceful Loger Valley far below enough to raise the spirits of any but the most dedicated of pessimists. But the sun was already moving down the sky, and Khushdil Khan hurried his guests on and downward to the Afghan camp, where after compliments had been exchanged and the last farewells said, Roberts and his officers took their leave of the Mission.

An uninstructed bystander listening to that light-hearted leave-taking would never have suspected either of the principals of harbouring any fears, for Cavagnari had long since regained the equanimity that had briefly deserted him when he saw the magpie, and both men were in the best of spirits as they renewed a promise to meet again in the cold weather, shook hands, and wishing each other God-speed, turned to go their separate ways.

But they had ridden no more than fifty yards when some impulse made them stop and turn simultaneously to look back at each other.

Wally, instinctively checking his own horse, saw them exchange a long look and then move quickly forward and, without speaking, grip hands once more before parting again. It was a curious incident, and to Wally, an oddly disturbing one. It seemed to take much of the brightness from that exhilarating day, and when the party camped for the night at the western foot of the Pass, he lay down with his carbine at his side and his service revolver under his pillow, and did not sleep any too soundly.

Five days later the British Mission was received in Kabul with the same honours that had been accorded to General Stolietoff and his

Russians, the two state entries into the capital differing only in size (Stolietoff's retinue having been far more numerous and imposing) and the fact that a different National Anthem was played.

Neither entry had been regarded with favour by the population. But a show is always a show, and as before, the citizens of Kabul turned out *en masse* to enjoy a free *tamarsha* and watch the state elephants sway past, carrying another foreign Envoy and his political assistant in their gilded howdahs, and closely followed by another military escort—a mere handful this time: only two Sahibs and a detachment of twenty-five cavalrymen.

But whatever the crowds might think, Sir Louis had no criticism to make. The men of the Afghan regiments who lined the route and held back the jostling staring crowds saluted, albeit raggedly, as he passed, and as he entered the Bala Hissar the din of military bands blaring out 'God Save the Queen' was almost drowned by the thunder of guns firing a Royal Salute. It was an eminently satisfactory welcome: the triumphal vindication of his policy, and the crowning moment of his life . . .

The guns and the bands, the good-tempered crowds, the capering, shouting children and the affability of the officials who had been sent out with the bedizened elephants to welcome him and escort him into the Afghan capital had all served to convince him how right he had been to insist that the Amir kept to the letter of the Gandamak treaty and accepted a British presence in Kabul without further delay. Well, that presence was now here, and establishing it was clearly going to be easier than he had thought. The moment he and his party had settled into their quarters he would set about making a personal friend of Yakoub Khan and getting on good terms with his ministers, as a first step towards forging strong and lasting ties between Great Britain and Afghanistan. Everything was going to be all right.

The Envoy was not the only one to be pleased at the reception accorded to the Mission, and heartened by the good humour of the vast crowds that had turned out to see its arrival.

The members of his suite had been equally impressed, and Wally, searching the sea of faces as he rode by in the hope of seeing Ash, had noted the expressions on those faces and thought: 'What an old scare-monger the dear fellow is. Won't I just pull his leg about this when I see him! All that blather about the whole place boiling with unrest and the Afghans hating our guts and loathing the very idea of any foreigners setting up house in their capital city. Why, you only have to look at these chaps to see it isn't true. They're more like a bunch of children at a school treat, crowding up for a slice of cake.' The simile was apter than he knew.

The population of Kabul was indeed, metaphorically speaking, expecting cake, and had it occurred to Wally to turn round and look back along the route, he might have noticed that the eager expressions of the onlookers had changed to disbelief and bewilderment as they took in the fact that the British Mission consisted of no more than this handful of men. They had expected a far more lavish and formidable display of power from the British Raj, and felt cheated. But Wally did not think to look back; nor did he find the face he had hoped to see.

Ash had not been among the crowds that flocked to watch the arrival of Her Britannic Majesty's Envoy and Minister Plenipotentiary at the Court of Kabul. Having no desire to catch the eye of anyone among the visitors who might recognize him (and, by showing it too obviously, draw unwelcome attention to him) he had purposely stayed away, contenting himself instead with listening from the rooftop of Sirdar Nakshband Khan's house to the crash of bands and the boom of guns that heralded the Envoy's arrival at the Shah Shahie Gate of Kabul's great citadel, the Bala Hissar.

The sounds had been borne clearly on the still air, for the Sirdar's house was no great distance from the citadel, and like Wally, Ash was agreeably surprised by the mood of the crowds that streamed past on their way to watch the procession. But the Sirdar, who with other members of his household had gone out to see the Mission arrive, reported that its size and lack of grandeur had disappointed the Kabulis, who had expected something far more flamboyant. True, there had been elephants, but only two of them, and as they had come from the Amir's elephant lines they could be seen on all state occasions.

'Also only three Sahibs besides Cavagnari-Sahib, and not even four-score men from my old regiment. What manner of Embassy is this? The Russ-log numbered many more. Moreover they wore rich furs and great boots of leather, and tall hats fashioned from the pelts of young lambs, and the fronts of their coats were bright with silver cartridges, row on row of them. Ah, that was indeed a great *tamarsha*. But this,'—The Sirdar spread out a lean hand and wagged it to and fro, palm downwards, to indicate something small and near the ground, 'this was a poor show. The Sirkar should have arranged a better one, for many of those who watched were asking how it was possible that a Government who could not afford to send a larger embassy would be able to pay the Amir's soldiers all they are owed; and if not—'

'What is that?' interrupted Ash sharply. 'Where did you hear this?'

'I have told you: from those I stood among in the press near the Shah Shahie Gate, where I went to watch Cavagnari-Sahib and those with him enter the Bala Hissar.'

'No, I mean this tale that the Mission is expected to give the army its arrears of pay. There was no mention of that in the Treaty.'

'Was there not? Then I can only tell you that many here believe it to be so. They say also that Cavagnari-Sahib will not only pay the army in full, but that he will put an end to compulsory military service and abate the excessive taxation that has long been a cause of great hardship to our people. Are these things also untrue?'

'They must be. Unless there was some secret agreement, which I think is unlikely. The terms of the Peace Treaty were made public, and the only mention of financial aid was a promise on the part of the Government of India to pay the Amir a year's subsidy of six *lakhs* of rupees.'

The Sirdar said dryly: 'Then perchance the Amir will spend those rupees, when he gets them, on paying his soldiers. But you must not forget that few here have even heard of that Treaty, and fewer still will have read it. Also, as you and I both know, half Afghanistan believes that their countrymen won great victories in the war and forced the armies of the Raj to retreat back to India, leaving many thousands dead behind them, and if they believe that, why should they not believe these other things? It may even be that the Amir himself has caused such tales to be spread abroad in the hope of persuading the people to allow Cavagnari-Sahib and his following to come here without hindrance, and to refrain from harming them, since only a fool kills the man who pays. Myself, I can only tell you that half Kabul believes that Cavagnari-Sahib is here to purchase all they need from the Amir, whether it be exemption of taxes and military service or peace from the depredations of their unpaid army; and for this reason they were dismayed when they saw how small a train he had brought with him, and at once began to doubt if it were true that he came laden with riches.'

The Sirdar's disclosures came as an unpleasant surprise to Ash, who, not having come across this particular story before, went out at once into the city to see for himself how much truth there was in these statements. Half an hour had been enough to confirm them all: and if he needed further discouragement he received it on his return, when his host met him with the news that Munshi Bakhtiar Khan, the acting representative of the British Government in Kabul, had died on the previous day.

'It was given out that he died of the cholera,' said the Sirdar, 'but I have heard otherwise. I have been told in secret by—by someone well known to me that he was poisoned in order that he should not speak to Cavagnari-Sahib of certain things that he knew. This I think very likely, because there is no doubt that he could have told the Sahib much. But now his knowledge is buried with him in the grave. He was no friend of the late Amir's, and his appointment caused great offence in the Bala Hissar. But he was both clever and cunning and he made other friends here, several of whom are whispering behind their hands that his death was contrived by enemies—though I doubt if any word of that will reach the ears of the Sahibs.'

It was enough that it had reached Ash's, and on the following day he deliberately broke a promise he had made to Anjuli, and applied for the post he had held once before in that city: as scribe in the service of Munshi Naim Shah, one of the many officials attached to the court, who lived in the Bala Hissar itself.

'It will only be for a few hours each day, Larla,' he explained to Anjuli when she protested, white-faced, that he was putting his head into the tiger's mouth to no purpose; 'and I shall be in no more danger there than I am here—perhaps even less, since half Kabul knows that the Sirdar-Sahib is a pensioner of the Guides, so it is always possible that his guests may be suspect. But having worked for Munshi Naim Shah before, I am known to a number of people in the Bala Hissar, and none will question my right to be there. Besides, the citadel is like a great ants' nest, and I doubt if anyone can say how many people live within its walls and how many come there daily to work or ask for favours, or to visit relatives or sell goods. I shall be no more than one ant among many.'

But Anjuli, who throughout the spring and early summer had been so happy in Kabul, had recently fallen a prey to terror, and the city and its surroundings that she had once thought so friendly and beautiful had suddenly become sinister and threatening. She knew that the entire valley was subject to earth tremors, and though the first of these that she had experienced had been barely noticeable, of late there had been one or two that were far more daunting. The tall house had swayed alarmingly, and though the Kabulis accepted the frequent earthquakes as a matter of course, to Anjuli the tremors had always been eerie and frightening. Nor, in these days, did she find anything reassuring when she looked out of any window that faced the street, and saw the men who passed below.

These lean hawk-faced Afghans with their long ragged locks and unkempt beards, their cartridge-belts, muskets and tulwars, were a very different breed of men from the gentle, friendly, unarmed hill-folk she remembered from her childhood days in Gulkote, and even bearing in mind the viciousness and cruelty that had existed in Bhithor and been practiced by Janoo-Rani and Nandu in Karidkote, it seemed to her now that compared with Kabul both had been places where the majority of people lived safe and very ordinary lives, undisturbed by blood-feuds, armed revolt against their rulers or the sudden outbreak of fratricidal strife between one tribe and the next, such as bedevilled this violent land. The very name of the great range of mountains that bounded the Land of Cain to the north had become a threat to her, for 'Hindu Kush' meant 'Killer of Hindus', and she was—she had once been—a Hindu.

She knew that the Sirdar's house had stout walls and strong doors, and that the few windows that looked out on to the narrow street were protected by carved shutters and iron bars, but the feeling of tension and danger from the streets outside seemed to seep into the house through every chink and crack, as insidiously as the pervasive dust and the evil smells of the city. And she had only to look up from the flat mud roof, or the windows of the rooms that had been allotted to Ashok and herself, to see the menacing bulk of the Bala Hissar.

The great citadel appeared to loom over the Sirdar's house, its ancient towers and endless battlements blocking out the morning sun and preventing any wind from the south or east cooling the close-packed buildings below, and lately, living in its shadow, Anjuli had become aware of a recurrence of those terrors that had afflicted her during the flight from Bhithor and for so many days afterwards. But this time the source and the focus of that terror was the Bala Hissar, though she could not have explained even to herself why this should be. It was as though some evil emanated from it, and the thought of her husband entering such an ill-omened place was not to be borne.

'But why go there at all?' implored Anjuli, her eyes dark with dread. 'Where is the need, when you can learn all you wish in the city? You say you will come back each evening, but what if these people should rise in revolt? If that happens, those who live in the Bala Hissar will close the gates, and it will become a trap from which you may not be able to escape. Oh my love, I am afraid . . . afraid!'

'There is no need, Heart's-dearest. I promise you I shall be in no danger,' said Ash, holding her tightly and rocking her in his arms. 'But if I am to help my friends, it is not enough to hear only the wild tales that rumour-mongers spread in the city, because half of them are untrue. I must also hear what is said in the palace itself by those who see the Amir or his ministers daily, and so know what they say and think and how they mean to act. The four Sahibs in the Mission will not learn this, for no one will tell it to them—unless I do. That is what I am here for. But I promise you that I will be careful and take no risks.'

'How can you say that when you must know that every time you enter its gates, you walk into danger?' protested Anjuli. 'My love, I beg of you—'

But Ash only shook his head and stifled her words with kisses, and when he tore himself away it was to go to the Bala Hissar, where, as he well knew, the room in which he would work overlooked the Residency and the compound in which the British Mission had been housed.

60

The ancient citadel of the Amirs of Afghanistan was built upon the steep slopes of a fortified hill, the Shere Dawaza, that dominated the city and a large part of the valley of Kabul.

It was surrounded by a long, rambling outer wall, some thirty feet high and pierced by four main gateways that were flanked by towers and topped with crumbling battlements. Within this were other walls, one of which enclosed the Amir's palace in the upper Bala Hissar. Higher still stood the fort, while above it the whole Shere Dawaza hill was ringed by a wall that climbed the steep flanks and followed the line of the rocky heights, so that sentries manning the block-houses here could look out at the enormous circle of mountain ranges, and down on palace and city, the entire sweep of the valley and the wide, winding ribbon of silver that was the Kabul River.

The lower Bala Hissar was a town in itself, crammed with the houses of courtiers and officials and all those who worked for them, and possessing its own shops and bazaars. It was in this part of the citadel that the Residency stood, and from his window Ash could see the whole stretch of the compound—the clutter of servants' quarters and store rooms, the cavalry pickets and the stables at the far end, lying almost in the towering shadow of the Amir's great Arsenal, and directly below him the barracks, an oblong, fort-like structure that enclosed a line of covered quarters on either side, and was bisected by a long open courtyard entered through a deep archway at one end and a stout door at the other.

Behind that far door a narrow lane divided the barrack block from the Residency proper, which consisted of two separate houses facing each other across a walled courtyard some ninety feet square, in the nearer and taller of which Wally, Secretary Jenkyns and Surgeon Kelly had their rooms, while the Envoy himself occupied the other: a two-storey building that on the southern side was part of the outer wall of the citadel, so that the windows there had a sheer drop below them to the moat, and a magnificent view of the valley and the far snows.

Ash too shared that view, since not only the Envoy's house but the far side of the entire compound stopped at the thirty-foot drop of the wall, beyond which stretched the open country, the river and the hills and the vast panorama of the Hindu Kush. But the beauty of the view held no interest for him—his attention being reserved for the compound below, where he could catch an occasional glimpse of the Envoy and his suite, watch their servants and the men of the Escort busy about their duties, and keep a check on callers at the Residency —and an eye on Wally's comings and goings.

Wally, like Anjuli, had formed an unfavourable impression of the Bala Hissar, though for different reasons. He did not find it sinister: he thought it deplorably shoddy. Having expected the famous citadel to be a magnificent and impressive place (something along the lines of Shah Jehan's Red Fort at Delhi, only better, as it was built on a hill), he had been disgusted to find it a rabbit-warren of dilapidated buildings and fetid alleyways, huddled behind a series of irregular and often half-ruined walls and interspersed by what appeared to be waste ground on which little or nothing grew.

The grandly styled 'Residency' had proved equally disappointing, being no more than a number of mud-brick buildings in a large compound that was hemmed about, on three sides, by houses built on rising ground, and on the fourth by the south wall of the citadel.

There was not even a proper entrance gate, and the sole barrier between the compound and the surrounding houses was a crumbling mud wall that a child of three could scramble over without difficulty; which augured a complete lack of privacy, as any member of the public who wished to do so could stroll in without let or hindrance to gaze at the Escort, hang around the stables watching the horses being groomed and fed, or even (if the doors of the barrack block were open) stare through the long central courtyard at the Residency itself.

'Faith, it's a combination of a gold-fish bowl and a rat-trap, so it is,' pronounced Wally that first afternoon in the Bala Hissar, as he and the surgeon surveyed the place that was to be the home of the British Mission. His critical gaze travelled to the towering bulk of the Arsenal, and from there to the tiers of tall, flat-roofed Afghan houses that overlooked the compound. Behind and above these rose the walls and windows of the palace; and above again, the fortified heights of the Shere Dawaza . . .

'Glory be, will you look at that now!' exclaimed Wally, appalled. 'We might just as well be living on the floor of a bull-ring or the Circus Maximus, with every seat filled with spectators staring down on us, watching every move we make and hoping to see us bite the dust.

What's more, they can get in here as easy as winking, while we can't get out if they choose to stop us—bad cess to them. *Brrr!* it's enough to give one the creeps. We shall have to do something about this.'

'What? If that is not a leading question?' inquired Dr Kelly absently, surveying the surroundings from a professional viewpoint that took account of drains, smells, sanitation (or lack of it), the direction of the prevailing wind and the source of water, while Wally was interested only in the military angle.

'Well, put the place into a state of defence, to begin with,' said Wally promptly. 'Build a good stout wall across the entrance of the compound, with a door we can bar from this side: an iron one for choice. And get another one put up on this side of that archway bit that leads into the barracks, and close both ends of the lane that runs behind it, so that if there should be a shindy we could stop anyone getting at the Residency itself except through the barracks; or into the compound, once we'd closed the gate. As things are now, we'd be sitting ducks if anyone wanted to attack us.'

'Ah, come now, no one's going to attack us,' returned the doctor comfortably. 'The Amir won't be wanting another war on his hands, and as he'll know that's the quickest way to get one, he'll take good care to see there's no trouble. Besides, the Bala Hissar is his own particular stamping-ground, which means that while we are here he is our host; and I'll have you know that Afghans are very punctilious on the subject of hospitality and the treatment of guests, so you can stop worrying and relax. In any case, there isn't much you can do about it, for if all those spectators you mentioned—the boyos up there in the dress-circle and the gallery—decided to turn their thumbs down, they could pick us off one by one as easy as wink your eye.'

'That's just what I said,' returned Wally forcefully. 'I said we'd be sitting ducks, and it's not a role that appeals to me. Nor do I think it's a good idea to put temptation into the heads of the ungodly. Remember the C.O. of that Yeomanry regiment that was stationed in Peshawar a couple of years ago?'

'If you mean old "Bloater" Brumby, yes—vaguely. I thought he was dead.'

'He is. He died during a period of piping peace while the Brigade were on autumn manoeuvres near the Frontier. Took a stroll on his own one evening all dressed up in his scarlet-coated best because some big-wig had come out from Peshawar that day, and was standing around admiring the view when a tribesman picked him off. The tribal elders were most apologetic, but they insisted that it was the Colonel-Sahib's own fault for providing such a beautiful target that the temptation had been too great for poor Somebody-or-other Khan, who had not been able to resist taking a shot at him. They were sure the Sahibs would understand that there was no malice about it. *Verb. sap.!*'

'*Hmm.*' The doctor glanced up at the rooftops and the small barred or latticed windows that looked down on the British Mission's compound, and said: 'Yes, I see what you mean. But we're in a cleft stick, Wally. You'll just have to grin and bear it, and trust to the luck of the Irish that no marksman finds us an equally tempting target. Because there's nothing to be done about it at all, at all.'

'We'll see about that,' retorted Wally vigorously. And that same evening, when the Envoy and his suite returned from paying their first official visit at the palace, he had spoken about it to William Jenkyns, and later to Sir Louis himself; only to receive a dusty answer from both. Nothing, as Ambrose Kelly had predicted, could or would be done. For the simple reason that refusal to occupy the accommodation that had been placed at their disposal would be grossly discourteous, while to demand that it be made secure against attack would be regarded as an insult not only to the Amir, but to the Commander-in-Chief of the Afghan Army, General Daud Shah, together with practically every high-ranking official in Kabul.

Nor was it possible for the members of the Mission to take matters into their own hands and set about closing off the compound or improvising defences, for to be seen doing anything of the kind could only suggest that they distrusted their host and were afraid of being attacked—which could not fail to offend the Amir and Daud Shah, and might well put ideas into the heads of many citizens who would otherwise have remained peaceably inclined.

'In any case,' said Sir Louis, 'it is no bad thing that the Residency should be easily accessible to anyone who wishes to walk in. The more visitors we have the better. Our first duty is to establish friendly relations with the Afghans, and I want no one turned away, or anything done that might suggest that the public are unwelcome and that we wish to keep them at arm's length. In fact, as I have just been saying to the Amir . . .'

The Amir had received the British Envoy and his suite with flattering cordiality and every sign of friendship, and appeared only too willing to accede to any demand. Sir Louis' request that members of his Mission should be free to receive visits from Afghan officials and Sirdars had been instantly granted, and Sir Louis had returned to the Residency in high feather and dictated a telegram to the Viceroy that read: 'All well. Had interview with Amir and delivered presents.' After which he had sat down to write his first dispatches from Kabul, and been able to retire to bed that night feeling elated and confident: everything was going smoothly and his mission to Afghanistan was going to be a triumphant success.

Wally, lying awake in the house on the opposite side of the Residency courtyard, was feeling less pleased with life, having discovered that his bed contained lodgers. It had been bad enough to be reminded of the fact that another and rival Mission had also been official guests in the Residency (and not so long ago either) by finding Russian names scribbled on the walls of his room. But bedbugs as well were beyond the line. He hoped fervently that his Russian predecessor had suffered equally badly from their attentions, and decided that if these were the best quarters that the Amir of Afghanistan could offer to high-ranking foreign guests, then the rest of the Bala Hissar must be a slum.

The house in which he lay, and the one opposite to it, were both gimcrack structures of lath and plaster supported by wooden pillars, the Envoy's house being a mere two storeys high, while the newly christened 'Mess House', in which the three members of the suite were quartered, was a storey higher. Both houses, after the Afghan pattern, had flat roofs that were reached by a flight of stairs, but unlike the single-storey barrack block, neither roof possessed anything that could be called a parapet, and Wally decided that he had seen considerably better buildings in many an Indian bazaar.

He was soon to discover that large, stone-built buildings, tall towers and marble minarets are unsuitable for an area that is subject to earth tremors, and though mud-bricks, wood and plaster may not make for magnificence, they can be safer. Almost the only stonework in the compound was to be found in the large, single-storeyed barrack block, where a line of stone pillars supported a sloping verandah roof and formed an arcade on either side of the long, open courtyard that divided the quarters allotted to the Mohammedans from those of the Sikhs. Here, despite Cavagnari's orders, Wally had eventually managed to get a second door made to close the front of the open archway that led into it, on the pretext that it would 'help to keep the place warmer in the winter'.

This archway ran back a full ten feet, like a miniature tunnel, to form a portico from which two flights of steps, one on either side of the entrance, led up in the thickness of the wall to the roof above. The inner end of this tunnel already boasted a massive iron-barred door, and now Wally had had another put in the outer one: admittedly a regrettably flimsy affair, as it was made from unseasoned planks. But in an emergency it would allow his men to use those stairways unseen.

There was a third stairway at the opposite end of the long courtyard near the door that opened on to the Residency lane. But as any attack would come from the front, the stairs in the thickness of the archway would be as vital to the defence of the barracks as the barracks were to the defence of the Residency. Not that Wally believed that there was the least likelihood of an attack, yet as this was his first solo command it behoved him to take what precautions he could —though they were few enough, in all conscience. But at least he had made a gesture in that line.

He was to make others. 'Once we are there, it'll be up to us to see that we get on good terms with the people,' he had told Ash on that night in Mardan. And now he set about doing so with enthusiasm, organizing Mounted Sports, that because they called for skilled horsemanship would appeal to the Afghans, whom he invited to compete with the Guides at tent-pegging, lemon-cutting, spearing a ring with a lance and similar contests. Nor were the others behindhand in the task of fostering good relations; Ambrose Kelly laid plans to start a dispensary, while the Envoy and his Secretary filled their days with informal talks with the Amir, discussions with Ministers, and endless visits of ceremony from nobles and officials.

Sir Louis also made a point of being seen daily riding through the streets, though at the same time he issued an edict forbidding all members of the Mission access to the roofs of any of the Residency buildings, and ordered canvas awnings to be stretched across the barrack courtyard; the aim of both these measures being to protect the susceptibilities of neighbours in the Bala Hissar from the possibility of being affronted by the sight of the 'foreigners' taking their ease.

'This is an amazing country,' wrote Wally, replying to a cousin serving in India who had written to congratulate him on winning the Victoria Cross and inquire what Afghanistan was like. 'But you wouldn't think much of Kabul. It's a seedy-looking place . . .'

The letter had included a light-hearted account of a well-attended 'Pagal-Gymkhana' he had organized on the previous day, and contained no suggestion that the Herati regiments in the city were a continuing source of trouble. But the dâk-rider who carried that particular letter to the British-held outpost of Ali Khel, where all the Mission's telegrams and letters were either forwarded or received, had already carried a telegram from Sir Louis Cavagnari to the Viceroy that read: 'Alarming reports personally reached me today from several sources of the mutinous behaviour of the Herat Regiments lately arrived here, some of the men having been seen going about the city with drawn swords and using inflammatory language against the Amir and his English visitors, and I was strongly advised not to go out for a day or two. I sent for the Foreign Minister and, as he was confident that the reports were exaggerated, we went out as usual. I do not doubt that there is disaffection among troops on account of arrears of pay, and especially about compulsory service, but the Amir and his ministers are confident that they can manage them.'

A further telegram, sent on the following day, was considerably shorter: 'State of affairs reported yesterday continues in a milder degree. Amir professing complete confidence to maintain discipline.' Yet in the diary that Sir Louis wrote up every evening and sent off at the end of each week to the Viceroy, he described the arrival of the mutinous Heratis in Kabul, clamorous for pay and completely out of hand.

It was all very well, thought Sir Louis, for the Amir's Foreign Minister to assert that these men would be given their arrears of pay in full within a day or two, after which they would return to their homes; or to insist (as he did) that the reports of their lawlessness and looting were greatly exaggerated and due solely to the behaviour of a 'few wild spirits'. But Sir Louis had his own sources of information and he had been given several well-authenticated accounts of the conduct of the malcontents that implicated far more than a 'few wild spirits'. He had also heard that the troops had flatly refused to disperse to their homes until each man had had every anna of his back pay counted out into his hand, but that there was not enough money in the Treasury to pay them. None of which squared with the optimistic statements of the Foreign Minister and his master the Amir.

Yet in one way Ash had been right in thinking that Sir Louis did not fully appreciate the danger in which he and his Mission stood.

The Envoy was by no means ignorant of what was going on in Kabul, but he refused to take it too seriously. He preferred to accept the Minister's assurance that the situation was under control, and to immerse himself instead in schemes for reforming the administration of Afghanistan, together with plans for an autumn tour with the Amir, rather than concentrate on a far more urgent and immediate problem—the devising of ways and means of bolstering up the Amir's shaky authority in the face of the rising tide of lawlessness and violence that had flooded into the valley of Kabul, and was now threatening to engulf the city, and even the citadel itself.

'He cannot know what is going on,' said Ash. 'They are keeping it from him. He must be told, and you are the one who must tell him, Sirdar-Sahib. He will listen to you because you were a Risaldar-Major of the Guides. For their sakes, I beg you to go to the Residency and warn him.'

The Sirdar had gone and Sir Louis had listened attentively to everything he had to say, and when he had finished, smiled and said lightly: 'They can only kill the three or four of us here, and our deaths will be avenged,' an observation that enraged Ash when he heard it, as he felt certain that in the event of trouble not only 'us', but the entire Escort, together with the numerous servants and camp-followers who had accompanied the Mission to Kabul, would also be killed.

Ash had not heard of the remark that Cavagnari was reported to have made before leaving Simla, to the effect that he would not mind dying if his death led to the annexation of Afghanistan, but nevertheless he began to wonder if the Envoy had not become a little unhinged of late and perhaps saw himself as a willing sacrifice on the altar of Imperial expansion. It was a crazy suspicion, and instantly dismissed. Yet it returned again and again in the days that followed, for there were times when it seemed to Ash that there could be no other explanation for the Envoy's lofty attitude towards all warnings.

The Sirdar, disturbed by the swaggering insolence of the Herati troops and worried about the safety of-the Guides, had paid a second visit to the Residency in order to tell Sir Louis of certain things that he himself had seen and heard:

'I do not speak from hearsay, Your Honour,' said the Sirdar, 'but only of what I have seen with my own eyes and heard with my own ears. These regiments march through the streets with their bands playing and their officers at their head, and as they march they shout threats and vile abuse at the Amir, and revile the Kazilbashi regiments—who being loyal to him they accuse of cowardice and subservience to the infidels, jeering at them that they, the Heratis, will show the Kazilbashi slaves how to deal with foreigners. You too, Excellency-Sahib, they abuse—naming you by name. I have heard them. This you should know, for it bodes ill and should be stopped while there is yet time.'

'But I do know,' said Cavagnari. 'And so does His Highness the Amir, who has been before you in this, having already warned me to keep away from the city until the trouble dies down, which it will surely do. As for the Heratis, you need have no fear, Risaldar-Sahib. Dogs who bark do not bite.'

'Sahib,' said the ex-Risaldar-Major gravely, 'these dogs *do* bite. And I, who know my people, tell you that there is great danger.'

Sir Louis frowned at the implied criticism, then his face cleared and he laughed and said: 'And I tell you again, Sirdar-Sahib, that they can only kill us; and if they do, we shall be terribly avenged.'

The Sirdar shrugged and gave up.

'It was profitless to say more,' he told Ash. 'Nevertheless, after I had left his presence I saw Jenkyns-Sahib leaving the courtyard, and I followed him and asked permission to speak to him apart. We walked together by the stables in the cavalry lines while I disclosed the same matters to him, and when I had done, he spoke sharply, saying "Have you told Cavagnari-Sahib this?" When I told him that I had just done so, and of the reply I had received, he was silent for a space, and then he said: "What the Envoy-Sahib says is true. The British Government will not be harmed by losing three or four of us here." Now I ask you, what can one do with men like that? I have wasted my time and theirs, for it is clear that they will not be warned.'

Ash had fared little better with Wally, whom he had managed to meet on several occasions and with comparative ease, as Sir Louis' policy of encouraging visitors and keeping open house meant that the Residency was always full of Afghans, who left their attendants in the compound where they fell into conversation with the Residency servants and the men of the Escort. This had made it a simple matter for Ash to mingle with them and get a message passed to Wally making an assignation to meet at some spot where they could talk together without attracting attention, and after that first meeting they had also devised a simple code.

But though Wally was always unfeignedly glad to see him and took a deep interest in all he had to say, there was never any question of his attempting to pass on anything Ash told him to Sir Louis. The Commandant, with whom Ash had discussed this point in Mardan, had recognized the trouble this could lead to, and in briefing

Wally before he left, had impressed it upon him that the Envoy would have his own sources of information and that it was no part of Lieutenant Hamilton's duties to supplement them. If at any time he had reason to believe that Sir Louis was ignorant of some vital matter that he himself had learned from Ashton, then he should mention it to the Envoy's Secretary and Political Assistant, William Jenkyns, who would decide whether to pass it on or not.

'I did that the other day,' confessed Wally ruefully, 'and never again. Will bit my head off. Told me that Sir Louis knew a damn sight more than I did about what went on in Kabul, and suggested that I run away and play with my soldiers—or words to that effect. And he's right of course.'

Ash shrugged and remarked ungraciously that he sincerely hoped so. He was feeling worried and apprehensive, not only on account of the many disturbing things that were being said and done in the city, or his fears for the safety of Wally and the Guides, but because he was afraid for Juli. For there was cholera in the city. There had as yet been no cases of it in the Bala Hissar or near the quiet street in which Nakshband Khan's house stood, but the disease was rampant in the poorer and more congested quarters of Kabul; and there came a day when Ash heard from a friend of the Sirdar's, a well-known Hindu whose son was in the service of the Amir's brother Ibrahim Khan, that it had broken out among the disaffected troops.

Had it not been for the fact that half India, to his certain knowledge, was also suffering from a raging cholera epidemic that year, he would almost certainly have taken Anjuli away that same day and abandoned Wally and the Guides without a second thought. But there being nowhere he could take her with any certainty of escaping it, he had decided that it was probably safer for her to stay where she was, as with luck the cholera would not reach their quarter of the city; and in any case it was bound to diminish drastically with the onset of autumn. But it was an anxious time, and he grew thin from strain and found it increasingly difficult to talk to Wally of the dangers that threatened the Mission. Or, with his mind filled with fears for Juli, to sit around discussing that indefatigable poet's latest composition.

A visit to the village of Bemaru, scene of the outbreak of the Kabul disaster of 1841, had inspired a particularly tedious epic, and Ash had wasted a precious afternoon listening in growing frustration while Wally strode to and fro reciting lines that only the author him-

self or his doting family could possibly have regarded as serious
poetry—

> *'Though all is changed,' declaimed Wally, 'yet*
> *   remnants of the past*
> *Point to the scenes of bloodshed, and, alas!*
> *Of murder foul; and ruined houses cast*
> *Their mournful shadow o'er the graves of grass*
> *Of England's soldiery, who faced a lot*
> *That few, thank Heaven! before or since have shared;—*
> *Slain by the hand of Treachery, and not*
> *In open Combat . . .'*

There had been more to the same effect, and the poet (who had
put in a lot of hard work on it and was not displeased with the result) was disconcerted when Ash had merely remarked thoughtfully
that it was curious that the four Europeans in the Residency should
think and speak of themselves as 'Englishmen' when one was a Scot,
two were Irish, and the fourth was half Irish and half French. A
comment that showed he had been thinking of something else and
missed the finer points of the poem.

All the same, Wally drew more comfort than he would have cared
to admit from the knowledge that his friend spent a large part of
each day in a house that backed on the Residency compound. It was
consoling to know that he need only glance up at a certain window
to confirm whether he was there or not, for each morning, when Ash
came to work, he would place a cheap blue and white pottery jar
with a spray of flowers or greenery in it between the two centre bars
of his window, as a sign that he was still there and had not left Kabul.

Yet even without the information he received from Ash, Wally
could hardly have avoided being aware that the situation in Kabul
was deteriorating daily. He knew—he could hardly fail to know—that
neither the servants nor the men of the Escort any longer went singly, or even in pairs, to bathe or wash their clothes in the river, but
preferred to go in groups—and armed; that even the Mussulmans did
not care to venture alone into the city now, while as for the Sikhs
and Hindus, it was as much as their lives were worth to be seen in
the streets at all, so that except when on duty they stayed within the
compound. What he did not know was that Ash had already taken
action in one small sphere to defuse some of the ill-feeling that was
being generated against the foreigners.

It was a minor matter, and one that invited more risk than Ash had a right to take. But it had had its effect. He had taken part in the mounted sports, riding a borrowed horse and disguised as a Gilzai tribesman, and had won several events—to the delight of the Kabulis, who had been resentful of the prowess shown by the Guides, and had become convinced that the contests were designed to demonstrate the superiority of the 'Sahibs' Army' over their own.

Ash's skill at this particular type of sport had helped redress the balance a little. But he had not dared to repeat the experiment, even though the muttered comments of the spectators continued to worry him—as did the talk in the bazaars. The latter to such an extent that eventually he approached the Sirdar's Hindu friend (who, as the Sirdar said, 'knows the ins and outs of what goes on in the houses of great men') to beg him to call at the Residency and speak to Sir Louis Cavagnari of the increasingly virulent attitude of the citizens towards the presence of the foreign Mission in their midst.

'For His Excellency,' explained Ash, 'has so far spoken only with Afghans. And who can say how much truth they have told him, or whether it is to their advantage to make him believe that all will be well? But you, being a Hindu, and one whose son is in the service of His Highness the Amir's own brother, he may listen to with attention; and believing what you say, take measures to protect himself and his followers.'

'What measures?' inquired the Hindu sceptically. 'There is only one which might serve: to dissolve this Mission and return with it to India without delay. Though I would not care to vouch for it reaching there in safety, as the tribes might well fall upon it on the way.'

'That he would never do,' said Ash.

'No. Yet there is little else that he can do, for he must know that the quarters in which he and his Mission live cannot be defended against attack. Therefore if he treats all warnings lightly and replies to them with brave words, this may well be because he is wise, and not, as you suppose, because he is either blind or foolish. He will know that his words will be repeated, and the very fact that they are bold and fearless may well give the hot-heads pause; and placed as he is that is wisdom, not foolishness. I have called on him before, but if you and the Sirdar-Sahib wish, I will certainly do so again and see if I cannot enlighten him as to the ill-will against the Mission that prevails in the city. Though I think you will find that he already knows this.'

The promised visit had been made that very day. But this time the caller had not succeeded in seeing the British Envoy, for the Afghan sentries who by the Amir's orders stood guard by the entrance to the compound (ostensibly for the greater safety and protection of the British Mission) had not only turned him away, but had abused and stoned him as he left. 'I was struck several times,' reported the Hindu, 'and when they saw me stagger they laughed. This is no longer a safe place for men such as myself, or for foreigners of any persuasion. I think it is time I left Kabul for a while and went south to visit my relations.'

He had refused categorically to make any further attempt to see Sir Louis, and true to his word had left Kabul a few days later. But the tale of his friend's treatment at the hands of the Afghan sentries had disturbed Sirdar Nakshband Khan almost as much as it had shaken Ash, and though after his previous visit to the Residency the Sirdar too had sworn that he would not go there again, he had done so.

Sir Louis had greeted him graciously enough, but made it clear from the outset that he was already fully informed as to the situation in Kabul and needed no further information on that head, and though pleased to see the ex-Risaldar-Major, was unfortunately too busy to spare as much time as he would wish to on purely social calls.

'Indeed so. That is understood,' agreed the Sirdar politely. 'As is also the fact that your Honour has many sources of information and therefore knows much of what goes on in the city. Though not all, I think,' and he had told Sir Louis how a well-known and much-respected Hindu who had called at the Residency desiring to speak with him, had been refused admittance and driven away with stones and abuse by the Afghan sentries.

Sir Louis' eyes blazed as he listened and even his luxuriant black beard seemed to bristle with anger. 'That is untrue,' rasped Sir Louis. 'The man lies!'

But the Sirdar was not to be intimidated by the Envoy's wrath. 'If the Huzoor does not believe me,' he replied calmly, 'let him ask his own servants, several of whom witnessed the stoning of the Hindu, as did many of the Guides also. The Huzoor has only to ask; and when he does so he will learn that he is little better than a prisoner. For what profit is there in remaining here if he is not permitted to see men who only desire to talk truth to him?'

The suggestion that he was not a free agent touched the Envoy on the raw, for Pierre Louis Cavagnari was an intensely proud man, so much so that he had frequently been accused by those who did not share his views, or had been treated to the rough side of his tongue, of being insufferably arrogant. It is certain that he had a high opinion of his own capabilities and did not take kindly to criticism.

Sirdar Nakshband Khan's story struck at his personal pride as well as his official dignity as the representative of Her Britannic Majesty the Empress of India, and he would have liked to disbelieve it. Instead he replied coldly that he would inquire into the matter, and having dismissed his visitor, sent for William Jenkyns and ordered the secretary to find out at once if anyone in the Residency compound had in fact witnessed such an incident as Nakshband Khan described.

William was back within fifteen minutes. The story, he reported, was unfortunately true. It had not only been vouched for by several of the Residency servants, but by two grass-cutters and a dozen men of the escort, including Jemadar Jiwand Singh of the Guides Cavalry and Havildar Hassan of the infantry.

'Why was I not informed of this before?' demanded Cavagnari, white with rage. 'By God, I'll have those men disciplined! They should have reported it at once, if not to me, then to Hamilton or Kelly, or to you. And if young Hamilton knew, and did not tell me— Tell him I wish to speak to him immediately.'

'I don't think he's here at the moment, sir. I believe he went out about an hour ago.'

'Then send him to me the minute he comes back. He has no right to slip off without letting me know. Where the devil has he gone?'

'I'm afraid I've no idea, sir,' said William woodenly.

'Then you should have. I will not have my officers leaving the Residency whenever they think fit. They ought to have more sense than to go jaunting about the city at a time like this. Not that I believe . . .'

He left the sentence unfinished and dismissing William with a curt gesture, sat scowling into the middle-distance and jerking at his beard with lean, angry fingers.

But Wally was not jaunting about the city. He had ridden out to see Ash, whom he had arranged to meet on the hillside to the south of Kabul where the Emperor Barbur lies buried. For it was the eighteenth of August and his birthday: he was twenty-three.

61

The last resting place of Barbur—'Barbur the Tiger', who had seized the Land of Cain only a few years after Columbus discovered America, and gone on to conquer India and establish an imperial dynasty that had lasted into Ash's own life-time—was in a walled garden on the slope of a hill to the south-west of the Shere Dawaza.

The spot had been known in Barbur's day as 'The Place of Footsteps', and it had been a favourite haunt of his, so much so that though he had died far away in India, at Agra, he had left instructions that his body was to be brought back there for burial. This his widow, Bibi Mubarika, had done, travelling to Agra to claim her husband's body and take it back through the passes to Kabul.

Nowadays the garden was known as 'The Place of Barbur's Grave', and few people visited it at this season, for Ramadan, the month of fasting, had begun. But as it was regarded as a pleasure park, no one would think it odd that the young Sahib who commanded the foreign Envoy's Indian escort should choose to visit such a historic spot, or that once there he should fall into conversation with one of the local sight-seers. In fact, Ash and Wally had the garden to themselves, for though the day had been sultry and overcast, no rain had fallen as yet, and the hot wind that herded the sluggish clouds across the valley was stirring up enough dust to keep all sensible Kabulis indoors.

A little stream in a formal channel flowed past the worn slab of marble and the ruined fragments of a pavilion that marked the great man's grave, and the wind strewed the water with fallen leaves and sent eddies of dust whirling between the trees and flowering shrubs, and through the carved wooden arches of a small memorial mosque— an open-sided, unpretentious building that like Barbur's tomb was sadly in need of repair. There had been only one devotee there that day, and it was not until he rose and came out that Wally realized it was Ash.

'What were you doing in there?' he inquired when they had greeted each other.

'Saying a prayer for the Tiger. May he rest in peace,' said Ash. 'He was a great man. I've been reading his memoirs again, and I like to think that his bones are lying here under the grass and that I can sit beside them and remember the tremendous life he lived, the things he saw and did, the chances he took . . . Let's get out of the wind.'

There were other humbler graves in the garden. A number of conventional Moslem stelae in weathered marble or stone rose out of the parched grass, some still standing upright, but the majority canted to left or right by the hand of time, or lying half hidden on the ground. Ash by-passed these and having paused a moment by Barbur's grave, led the way to a level piece of ground that was sheltered from the wind by a clump of shrubs, and sat down cross-legged on the dusty grass.

'Many happy returns of the day, Wally.'

'So you remembered,' said Wally, flushing with pleasure.

'Of course I did. I've even got a present for you.' Ash groped among his robes and produced a little bronze horse: a piece of ancient Chinese craftsmanship that he had bought in the bazaar at Kabul, knowing that it would delight Wally. It had done so; but the donor had not been pleased to discover that Lieutenant Hamilton had ridden out to meet him without an escort.

'For God's sake, Wally! Are you mad? Didn't you even bring your syce?'

'If you mean Hosein, no. But you can keep your hair on, because I gave him the day off so that I could bring one of our troopers instead: Sowar Taimus. You wouldn't know him—well after your time. He's a first-rate fellow with guts enough for six. The Kote-Daffadar says that he's a Shahzada in his own right and a Prince of the Sadozai dynasty, which is probably true. What he doesn't know about Kabul and the Kabulis isn't worth knowing, and it's due to him that we managed to sneak out without trouble, and without having a couple of Afghan troopers trotting along behind us. He's waiting outside with the horses, and if he doesn't like the look of anyone approaching this place you can be sure he'll let me know. So will you be calm now, and stop fussing like an old hen.'

'I still say you should have brought at least three of your sowars with you. *And* your syce,' said Ash angrily. 'I would never have agreed to meet you here if I'd dreamt that you'd be such a chucklehead as to ride out without a proper escort. For God's sake, don't *any* of you realize what is going on around here?'

'Faith, and that's a foine way to talk to a feller on his birthday, so it is,' grinned Wally, unabashed. 'Yes, you old ass, of course we do.

I'll have you know we're not nearly as stupid as you think. In fact that's precisely why I came here on the sly with only Taimus, instead of attracting a lot of attention to myself and stirring up the angry passions of the locals by clattering out with an armed escort at my heels.'

'That's as may be,' retorted Ash, still shaken. 'But I understand the Amir himself has advised your Chief to avoid riding through the streets for a time.'

'Through the streets, yes. His Nibs seems to think it would be better if we weren't seen going about his city just now. But there are no streets here and it's a long way from the city—and where did you hear that, anyway? I thought that particular bit of advice had been given to Sir Louis on the quiet. It's not at all the sort of thing he'd like every Tom, Dick and Harry to know.'

'I don't suppose they do know,' said Ash. 'I heard it from that pensioner of ours, Risaldar-Major Nakshband Khan. Who incidentally got it from the horse's mouth—Sir Louis himself.'

'Did he now,' murmured Wally, lying back on the grass and firmly shutting his eyes. 'And I suppose it was yourself put that old spalpeen up to calling at the Residency to warn us that the city was full of rude, rough boys from Herat, and that if we didn't hide indoors until they went away, some of them might call us naughty names or even thumb their noses at us? Sure I might have known it. No, don't be telling me that it's all in the line of duty, because I know it is. But dammit, today's my birthday, so can't we just for once forget the political situation and all this Intelligence business and talk about other things for a change? Pleasant things . . .'

There was nothing that Ash would have liked better, but he hardened his heart and said: 'No, Wally: I'm afraid we can't, because there are several things I have to say to you. To begin with, you're going to have to stop these mounted sports you've been arranging between your fellows and the Afghans.'

Wally abandoned his restful pose and sat bolt upright, staring and indignant. 'Stop them? What the blazes for? Why, the Afghans love 'em!—they're damned good horsemen and they thoroughly enjoy competing against my chaps. We always have a huge turn-out, and there couldn't be a better way of getting on friendly terms with them.'

'I can see why you think so. But then you don't understand how these people think. They see it quite differently, and far from encouraging friendly feelings it has caused great offence. The truth is, Wally, that your sowars are too damn good at this type of sport, and the Kabulis have been saying that you hold them solely in order to show how easily you can defeat them, and that when your men ride at a dangling lemon and slash it in half with a sabre, or spear a tent-peg out of the ground on the point of a lance, they are merely demonstrating how they would cut down or spear their enemies—in other words, the Afghans. If you'd been able to stand among the spectators and listen, as I've done, and hear what they say among themselves as they watch, you wouldn't talk so glibly about "establishing friendly relations with the Afghans", when in point of fact all you are doing is helping to make them a deal sourer than they are already; which God knows is sour enough.'

'Well if that isn't the outside of enough!' exploded Wally. 'So *that's* why you were dressed up like a scarecrow and carrying off the prizes for the opposition that day. I couldn't think what you were playing at, and for two pins I'd have—' Words appeared to fail him and Ash had the grace to look ashamed of himself and say defensively: 'I didn't do it for fun, whatever you may think. I hoped it might even up the balance a bit and take some of the heat out of the situation. But I didn't think you'd recognize me.'

'Not recognize you? When I know every trick of riding you possess and the way you always— Holy smoke! It's yourself who's mad, so it is. Have any idea of the risks you were running? It's all very well for me to spot you, but I'm willing to lay you a year's pay to a rotten orange that there isn't a single jawan in the Escort who doesn't know by now who you are.'

'I wouldn't take you,' said Ash with a crooked smile. 'I imagine they know a lot more than you think. But they also know how to keep their mouths shut. Have any of them, for instance, reported to you that whenever they show their faces outside the citadel, the Kabulis don't just insult them, but make the worst kind of abusive remarks about you and Kelly and Jenkyns, and particularly about Cavagnari? No, I can see they haven't! And you can't blame them. They'd be ashamed to let any of you know the sort of things that are being said about you in the bazaars; which is your bad luck, because if they spoke out you might learn a thing or two.'

'God, what a people,' said Wally disgustedly. 'That Sikh obviously knew what he was talking about after all.'

'What Sikh?'

'Oh, just a Havildar of the 3rd Sikhs I was talking to one day when we were in Gandamak. He was scandalized by the Peace Treaty and the fact that we were pulling the army out of Afghanistan, and seemed to think we were all mad. He wanted to know what kind of warfare this was, and said, "Sahib, these people hate you and you have beaten them. There is only one treatment for such *shaitans* (devils)—grind them to powder." Perhaps that is what we should have done.'

'Perhaps. But it's no good talking about that now, because the main thing I came here to tell you about is a deal more important than your mounted sports. I know I've brought this up before, but this time, whether you like it or not, you're going to have to talk to Jenkyns about it. As I've already told you, the Amir has allowed a rumour to get around that the Mission is only here to act as paymaster and general benefactor: in other words, to be milked of rupees like an obliging cow. Almost everyone believes this to be true, so the sooner Sir Louis persuades the Viceroy to let him act the part, and sends him enough money to pay off the arrears owed to the troops, the better. It's the only thing that may stop the pot from boiling over and scalding everyone within sight, because the minute that starving rabble from Herat have been given their just dues, they'll leave Kabul; and once they are out of the way the disaffected elements in the city can simmer down a bit and give the Amir a chance to get a firmer grip on his country and restore some respect for authority. I'm not saying that a large injection of cash will solve all that wretched chap's problems, but at least it'll help to shore him up and delay the roof falling in on him—and on your precious Mission as well.'

Wally was silent for a moment or two, and then he said irritably: 'It would take a deuce of a lot of money, and I don't see why we should be expected to stump up the arrears of pay that are owed to the armed forces of a country that we have been at war with—an enemy country! Do you realize that a large part of what these fellows claim they are owed seems to be back pay, so that if we were fools enough to foot the bill we'd actually be paying those men for fighting us? Paying them for killing Wigram?—and a whole lot more of our fellows too? No, it's obscene! It's a monstrous suggestion and you can't possibly mean it.'

'But I do mean it, Wally.' Ash's voice was as grim as his face, and there was a note in it that Wally recognized with a curious sense of shock as fear: real fear. 'It may sound like a monstrous suggestion to you, and I'm not even sure that it would work, except as a temporary measure. But it would at least remove the immediate threat and give your Mission a breathing space. It would be worth it for that alone. What Cavagnari needs most is time, and it doesn't look to me as though he's going to get it unless he buys it.'

'Then you're really suggesting that he sends for these mutinous divils and hands them out—'

'No I am not. I am not suggesting that he, personally, pays anything directly to the Herati regiments (who, by the way, were never in action against us and don't believe we won a single battle). But I'm willing to bet that he could galvanize the Viceroy into sending the Amir, *immediately,* a sum sufficient to cover what his troops are owed. It wouldn't even need to be a gift, because it could be counted as part of the yearly subsidy that was promised him by the terms of the Peace Treaty, which amounts to six crores a year. Damn it, Wally, that's six million rupees. Even a small part of that would wipe out the Amir's debt to his troops. But if the money isn't forthcoming soon, it won't be long before the whole Afghan Army is faced with the choice of starving or stealing; and believe me, they'll choose the latter, as the Heratis have done. And as you yourself would do, if you were in their shoes!'

'That's all very well, but—'

'There's no "but" about it. Hunger can do a lot of strange things to people as I've learned at first hand, and I only wish I could talk to Cavagnari myself. But I promised the Commandant I wouldn't, because . . . Well, anyway, it seems young Jenkyns is our only hope; and after all he is supposed to be the Political Assistant. You'll have to pass it on to him—tell him you had it from old Nakshband Khan—tell him anything. But for God's sake get it into his head that it's deadly serious, and that if Cavagnari hasn't realized this already, which he may well have done, he has got to realize it now. As for you, Wally, if you've any sense at all, you'll stop these sports of yours and warn the Rosebud' (this was a reference to Ambrose Kelly, who for obvious reasons was known in the Guides and to his friends as 'Rosie') 'to write off his equally well-meaning scheme for starting a free dispensary, because it is already being said in the city that the Sahibs are planning to use this as a means of poisoning anyone who is foolish enough to attend.'

'The Black Curse of Shielygh on them,' sighed Wally with feeling. 'May the divil fly away with the spalpeens: he's welcome to them.

When I think of all we meant to do—and dammit, will do—to help these ungrateful bastards to have a better life and fairer laws, I could spit, so I could.'

Ash frowned and observed with an edge to his voice that possibly they did not want to be helped by foreigners—except financially. Money was the one and only thing that could help the Amir and his people, and save the foreigners in the Residency from disaster. 'If the troops get paid you may all still have a chance of scraping through with nothing worse than a bloody nose and a few bruises. But if it doesn't, I wouldn't bet a brass farthing on the safety of the Mission, or the future prospects of the Amir either.'

'Faith, what a cheerful little ray of sunshine you are,' observed Wally with a wry smile. 'I suppose you'll tell me next that every mullah in the place is calling for a Holy War?'

'Oddly enough, they aren't. Or only a very few. There is a fiery gentleman down Herat way who is being very vocal, and an equally vocal fakir here in the city. But by and large the majority of mullahs have been remarkably pacific and seem to be doing their best to keep things on an even keel. It's a pity they haven't got a better Amir; one can't help feeling sorry for the poor fellow, but he's not half the man his father was—and he, Heaven knows, wasn't anything to write home about. What the Afghans need now is a strong man: another Dost Mohammed.'

'Or a fellow like that one over there,' suggested Wally, nodding his head in the direction of Barbur's tomb.

'The Tiger? God forbid!' said Ash fervently. 'If *he'd* been in command here, we would never have got further than Ali Masjid. Now there's someone you should write an epic poem about: Ode to a Dead Emperor. *Hic jacet ecce Barbur, magnus Imperator. Fama semper vivat** . . . "Lie lightly on him, gentle earth."'

Wally laughed and said that he would try his hand at Barbur when he had finished with 'The Village of Bemaru', which was still giving him trouble. The political situation was not mentioned again and the talk turned to pleasanter subjects: to books and horses, mutual friends and the prospects of *shikar* in the cold weather. 'Do you remember that Christmas we spent at Morala,' said Wally, 'and the evening we brought down eight teal between us at one go, and seven

---

* Here lies Barbur the great Emperor. May his fame live for ever.

of them fell into the river and we had to go in after them because the *shikari* couldn't swim? Do you remember—'

A sudden and stronger gust of wind whined through the bushes and raised a cloud of dust that set him coughing. Mingled with the dust were a few rain drops, and he scrambled to his feet, exclaiming: 'Glory be! I believe it's going to rain. That's something to be thankful for. We could do with a good downpour provided it doesn't wash the whole place away in a river of mud. Well, I must be off. Time I got back to my neglected duties if I don't want to get a rap over the knuckles from my respected Chief. See you sometime next week. And in the meantime I'll have a talk with William, and think about discontinuing the sports—though I suspect you're exaggerating, you old Job's Comforter. No, don't see me to the gate: Taimus is out there. *Salaam aleikoum!*'

'And the same to you, you poor purblind blinkered off-scouring of an Irish bog. And for God's sake don't go trailing your coat riding around the countryside without an escort again. It's too damned unhealthy.'

' "Too rash, too unadvised, too sudden," ' declaimed Wally soulfully. 'Ah, away with you! It's a pessimist ye'are and I don't know how I put up with you at all, at all.' He laughed again, and gripped Ash's hand: 'Be easy now; I'll watch out for myself, I promise. Next time I'll bring a posse with me, all armed to the teeth. Will that satisfy you?'

'I shan't be satisfied until you and Kelly and the rest of our fellows are safe back in Mardan again,' replied Ash with a worn smile, 'But for the present I suppose I shall have to settle for an armed posse. Mind now that you don't move without it, you benighted bog-trotter.'

'Cross-me-heart,' said Wally cheerfully, suiting the action to the word. 'Not that I shall get the chance if your depressing view of the future turns out to be correct. Ah well, as Gul Baz would say "All things are with God". *Ave*, Ashton, *morituri te salutant!*' He flung up an arm in the Roman salute and strode off singing 'Kathleen Mavourneen' in a loud, tuneful voice and as though he had not a care in the world.

62

Apart from an occasional spatter of drops, the threatened storm did not break until close on sunset, and Wally arrived back at the Residency only lightly bespeckled by raindrops and in excellent spirits. But once there he had been brought sharply back to earth, for he was met with a message that ordered him to report to Sir Louis Cavagnari the instant he returned.

As the order had been given more than two hours earlier, the reception he received from his Chief was not cordial. Sir Louis had suffered a severe blow to his self-esteem and he was still fuming with anger and inclined to blame all those who had witnessed the mistreatment of the Hindu by the Afghan sentries, but failed to inform him of it. In particular the officer in command of the escort, whose business it was to have known of the incident and reported it at once, either to him or to his secretary, Jenkyns.

If young Walter knew about it and had said nothing, by God he'd give the boy a piece of his mind. And if he did not know, then he should have known. His Indian officers ought to have told him about the disgraceful treatment that had been meted out to a Hindu gentleman who had merely called to pay his respects to the British Envoy. How many others had also been refused admittance by the Afghans? Was this the only would-be caller who had been turned away, or merely the latest?

Sir Louis required an answer to these questions at once, and the fact that Lieutenant Hamilton, when sent for, could not be found, had done nothing to soothe his ill-humour, and Wally, who had never seen his hero really angry before and thought of him as a man whom nothing and no one could ruffle, discovered his error within minutes of his return.

The Envoy had found relief for his pent-up rage in giving his military attaché not the 'rap over the knuckles' so recently and lightly referred to, but a coldly furious dressing-down of major proportions. A hail of questions had rattled about Wally's ears, and when at last he was given the opportunity to speak, he had disclaimed any knowledge of the incident involving the Hindu, promised to speak severely to all those under his command who had seen it and not reported it, and suggested that they had only kept silent out of consideration for

Sir Louis, as it reflected great *shurram* (dishonour) on the Envoy and every member of the Mission that such things should be done by the Afghans, and even greater *shurram* to speak of it and thereby put the Sahibs to shame. But he would certainly talk to them and make them understand that any further incidents of this kind should be reported at once.

'That will be unnecessary,' said Sir Louis icily. 'I intend to ensure that there shall be no more. You will go at once to the Afghan guard and tell them that I do not desire their services any longer, and that they are dismissed and will leave immediately. See to it please. And mount a double guard of your own men. Now send Jenkyns to me.'

A curt nod dismissed Wally, who saluted smartly and withdrew, conscious of an odd feeling that his knees were made of india-rubber and that he had recently been run over by a railway train. The sweat that was running down his face and neck was not solely due to the heat, and he mopped it dry with his handkerchief and having drawn a deep breath and let it out again slowly, shook himself like a dog coming out of water and went off to fetch William and dismiss the Afghan guard.

The guard commander had questioned his authority to do so, insisting that his men were there by order of the Amir and for the protection of the 'foreigners'. But Wally's command of Pushtu was excellent (Ash had seen to that) and smarting from the effects of that tongue-lashing from his Chief, he was in no mood to put up with what he regarded as Afghan shennanigans. Just as Cavagnari had vented his pent-up wrath on Wally's head, so Wally in turn found relief for his own feelings in telling the Afghans what they could do with themselves and why. They had not lingered.

That done, he had turned his attention to speaking strongly to his jawans on the unwisdom of keeping silence when they saw dishonour being put upon them themselves and the entire British Mission. But the replies he had received had shaken him, for they confirmed everything Ash had said about the insults that were hurled at any soldier or servant from the Residency who had the temerity to appear in the city, and the reason why this had been kept from the Sahibs.

'We were ashamed to repeat such things to you,' explained Jemadar Jiwand Singh, speaking for the Guides; and later Wally's own bearer, fat Pir Baksh, had used the self-same words on behalf of the many servants who had accompanied the British Mission to Kabul.

'I suppose the Chief *does* know what's going on?' said Wally uneasily, talking the matter over later that evening with Dr Kelly while the storm that had been threatening since late afternoon raged above Kabul. 'I mean about . . . Well, things like the ill-feeling there is against us—the Mission—among the Afghans; and all that row and rumpus they are kicking up in and around Kabul.'

The doctor's eyebrows rose and he said placidly: 'Of course he does. He's got spies all over the shop. Don't be a young ass.'

'He didn't know about the Afghan guard turning people away,' said Wally, troubled. 'None of us knew until today. None of us four, that is, though apparently all the rest knew what was going on inside our gates and under our very noses. Did *you* know that any of our fellows who go into the city get insulted by the Kabulis? I didn't, and it makes me wonder just how much our lot have been keeping from us, and how many of the rumours we hear are true. Or if the Chief even hears half of them. Do you suppose he knows?'

'You can be sure he does,' insisted Rosie loyally. 'He's always been up to every rig and row, and there have never been any flies on him. So don't be worrying your head about him. He's a great man, so he is.'

'Damn you, Rosie, I'm not worrying,' said Wally indignantly, flushing up to the roots of his hair. 'Nor have I got the wind up. But —but I only learned today that the local population have decided that those mounted sports I've been putting on are solely designed to show 'em that the regiments of the Raj can beat the stuffing out of them with one hand tied behind our backs; and that they resent them accordingly.'

'Poor silly bastards,' observed Rosie dispassionately. 'Who told you that?'

'Oh . . . just a fellow I know.'

'Well it don't do to believe every blatherumshkite you hear, for it's more than likely that your fine friend merely overheard some disgruntled competitor who'd made a fool of himself by missing the target altogether, excusing his failure by taking a swipe at the Guides and enjoying a good old green-eyed grumble.'

'To tell you the truth,' confessed Wally, 'I was inclined to think along those lines myself at first. But then this business—all the things I learned this evening from our fellows—has made me think differently, because . . . Well he, this same chap, told me about these other things too, and he was right. And there was something else he said that is quite likely to be true. He said that you ought to give up your idea of opening a free clinic to treat the Kabulis, because it's already being said that it's only a plot to get rid of as many people as possible by giving them poison instead of medicines.'

'Well of all the—!' began the doctor explosively; and then broke into laughter. 'Bunkum, my dear boy—bunkum! Faith, I never heard such twaddle in me life, and you can tell your friend I said so and advise him from me to be putting his head in a horse bucket. It's as plain as the nose on your face that the feller was just pulling your leg, or as likely as not trying to put the wind up you. Even the most bigoted infidel-hating barbarian couldn't be so woollen-witted as to imagine that we'd try anything as childishly silly as that. They must have *some* sense, so they must.'

But Wally's brow remained furrowed, and when he spoke again it was in an undertone that was barely audible above the noise of the wind and the rain, and as though he was speaking a thought aloud: 'But he was right about . . . other things. And—and they *are* bigoted and barbaric. And they do hate us: they really hate us . . .'

'Whisht now! it's making a mountain out of a mole-hill you are.' Ambrose Kelly wagged an admonitory finger at the youthful Commander of the Escort and by way of showing that the subject was now closed, reached for a battered tin of tobacco and turned his attention to knocking out and refilling his pipe. Wally laughed a little shamefacedly and leaning back in the creaking cane chair, felt the accumulated tensions of the last few hours seep away as his mind and his muscles relaxed under the peaceful influence of Rosie's optimism and the soothing sight of tobacco smoke weaving back and forth in the draught.

Outside the closed and shuttered windows the lightning flared and thunder rolled among the hills, while the rain and wind shook the fabric of the flimsy lathe-and-plaster house, and from the next room came the *plink, plink* of water dripping into a tin basin that one of the doctor's servants had positioned below a leak in the ceiling. The flames of the two oil lamps bent and flickered in the draught that blew in under the ill-fitting doors and window frames, and Wally sat watching them with half-shut eyes as he listened gratefully to the noise of the rain and thought of what William Jenkyns had had to say earlier that evening on the subject of the unpaid troops and the advisability of paying them immediately, or at least promising that the Government of India would see to it that they were paid in full in the near future.

William had agreed that this would probably have to be done, and had told him in strict confidence that the Viceroy had already in-

timated his willingness to do so. 'Everything will be all right, laddie.
You'll see. There's precious little that goes on in Kabul that the
Chief don't know about, and he'll have laid his plans and decided
just how he means to deal with this particular problem long ago, I
can tell you that.'

But though William's conviction that His Excellency the Envoy
was aware of all that went on in Kabul was in the main justified, his
confidence in his Chief was less well-founded.

Sir Louis was certainly very well informed, and the diary that he
dispatched to Simla at the end of each week would have been an eye-
opener for those who thought that his confident bearing indicated ignorance of the unrest in the Amir's capital city. Both he, and via him
Lord Lytton, knew what was going on, but both treated the knowledge lightly, Lord Lytton for his part being so little troubled by it
that he had allowed a full ten days to drift by before forwarding,
without comment, Sir Louis' account of the behaviour of the mutinous Heratis to the Secretary of State, as though it was no more than
another trivial piece of information to be filed and forgotten.

As for Sir Louis, despite the fact that he had learned early—and
immediately informed the Viceroy—that the Kabulis appeared to expect him, among other things, to pay the arrears owed to the Afghan
army, he made no move to deal with this particular problem; not
even when he received a telegram from the Viceroy offering to provide financial assistance to the Amir if the money would help His
Highness out of his present difficulties.

The offer had not been entirely altruistic (Lord Lytton having
pointed out that if it was accepted, it would eventually provide the
Government with a useful lever for obtaining certain administrative
reforms that the Amir might be reluctant to concede), but at least it
had been made. The money that Ash had seen as the only solution to
the problem of the mutinous Heratis and the hatred and unrest that
they were creating in Kabul was there for the asking. Yet Sir Louis
did not take advantage of it—perhaps because he too, like Wally,
recoiled in distaste from paying the wages of an army that had so
recently been involved in a war against the British Empire.

But not even to William, who decoded all the Envoy's confidential
messages, did he give his reasons. An omission that troubled his
loyal secretary not a little, since to William the Viceroy's offer had
seemed a godsend: a quick and easy way out of an exceedingly
tricky situation, and an admirable solution to the most pressing of

the problems that were bedevilling the harassed Amir, not to mention his equally harassed capital.

It had never occurred to William that his Chief would not see the offer in this light. But August wore on and Sir Louis made no move to accept it, or even to discuss the possibility of doing so, though every day brought fresh evidence that passions in the city were rapidly building up to flash-point, and that disaffection was now rife among the regiments on duty in the Bala Hissar itself.

This last was no more than a rumour that had only recently reached William at secondhand, via Walter Hamilton; yet he could not help wondering if were true. Was it possible that the regiments at present quartered inside the Bala Hissar were in fact any more reliable than the Heratis, and if so, was the Amir playing a double game? There was no doubt that he had been exceedingly angry over the affair of the sentries who had stoned the Hindu: but not with the sentries. His wrath had been directed against Sir Louis for daring to dismiss them and refusing to allow them to be replaced—and with Lieutenant Hamilton, who had carried out Sir Louis' order.

Did the Amir, mused William, really intend to go on an autumn tour of his northern borders with Sir Louis, leaving his capital to the mercy of a mutinous gaggle of unpaid regiments and scheming ministers? Sir Louis certainly seemed to think so, and spoke of it as though it was an accepted fact.

No one could possibly have wished for a more loyal or admiring supporter than William Jenkyns. But as the summer drew to a close there were times, particularly if he happened to lie awake too long in the small hours of the night, when small pin-pricks of doubt nagged at William's mind and he caught himself wondering uneasily if Louis Cavagnari's sudden elevation in rank had not impaired his judgement and made him blind to much that would never have escaped his attention in the old days.

Wild horses could not have dragged the verbal expression of such a suspicion from the Envoy's loyal Secretary, but he was increasingly baffled by his Chief's determination to ignore what was becoming clear to others in the Mission (and glaringly obvious to many outside it, if the warning words of such visitors as the Sirdar Nakshband Khan were anything to go by). Yet as day succeeded day without any sign that the tension in the city was decreasing, Sir Louis still continued to occupy himself with ideas for reforming the administration, plans for the forthcoming tour and the prospects of partridge shooting on the *charman*—the uncultivated grazing grounds in the valley—and, despite the Amir's warnings, to ride out daily with a guard of Afghans to see and be seen by the citizens of Kabul.

William could not understand it. He was well aware that his Chief was a man who did not suffer fools gladly and was inclined to be a little too scornful of lesser men. It was part of his character, and William had once heard someone at a dinner-party in Simla saying of Cavagnari that one could easily visualize him behaving as the Comte d'Auteroches had done at the Battle of Fontenoy, when he called out to the opposing British line that the 'French Guards never fired first'.

At the time, William had laughed and agreed—and thought the more of Pierre Louis Napoleon in consequence. But now he recalled how that famous incident had ended, and no longer felt like laughing; for in response to those flamboyant words the British had fired first, and their murderous volley had mown down the immobile French guards, decimating their ranks and killing or wounding every one of their officers, so that the survivors, left without leaders, had broken and run.

That fellow in Simla had been right, thought William . . . Louis Cavagnari was perfectly capable of making a similar gesture . . . he was that sort of man. Brave, proud and fanatical; supremely self-confident, and contemptuous of lesser men . . .

Only last week there had been an ugly incident in the city that had arisen out of a quarrel involving a woman and four sowars of the Guides. The sowars had been attacked and only rescued with difficulty, and afterwards Sir Louis had told young Hamilton to see that his men kept clear of the city until tempers had cooled. But a few days later his own orderly, an Afridi, Amal Din, who had been with him for many years, had also been involved in a brawl, this time with a group of Afghan soldiers. Amal Din feared no one, and having taken exception to some derogatory remarks about his Sahib, he had attacked the speakers and done a good deal of damage before the fight was broken up. A formal complaint on behalf of the injured soldiers had been made to Sir Louis, who, having expressed regret in the coldest possible terms, had followed this up by rewarding Amal Din—and letting it be known that he had done so.

'That can't have done anything towards making him popular with the Afghans,' brooded William in the intervals of dealing with official correspondence in the Envoy's office on the evening following this affair, 'but does he care? Not him!' William gazed at the opposite wall with unseeing eyes and thought about the local women whom the men kept smuggling into the compound, though they had been warned often enough against doing so. That too was bound to lead to trouble one day, but it was difficult to know how to stop it. He began to write again, found that the ink had dried on his nib and, dipping it in the standish again, went on with his work . . .

In the Mess House on the opposite side of the courtyard, Wally too was busy writing, for the dâk-rider was due to leave at dawn for Ali Khel with the Residency post-bag, and anyone anxious to catch the next Home mail knew that their letters must be handed to the head chupprassi tonight.

Wally finished the last of his letters and reached for the fair copy of his poem on 'The Village of Bemaru', which he intended to enclose in the letter to his parents. It was, he considered, one of his best, and though he had spent half the afternoon polishing it, he could not resist reading the final copy again before sending it off. Yes, not a bad effort at all, he decided with some complacency: . . . *'Yet to die Game to the last as they did, well upheld Their English name . . . E'en now their former foe Frankly avers . . .'*

Ash was going to be rude about that 'E'en' . . . But then Ash was no poet and did not realize how impossible it was to make one's lines scan without resorting to such perfectly legitimate short-cuts as 'e'en' and 't'were' and 'were't' . . . *'Regret were uppermost, were't not for pride'*. Wally frowned over the line, chewing the end of his pen, but could think of no other way of putting it. Anyway, even Ash must agree that the ending was not half bad. He read it aloud, pleased with the sound of his own lines—

> *'How England's fame shone brighter as she fought*
> *And wrenched lost laurels from their funeral pile*
> *And rose at last from out misfortunes tide*
> *Supreme—for God and Right were on her side.'*

That was the stuff to give them! He repeated the last few lines again, beating time with his pen in the manner of a conductor, and had got as far as 'supreme' when his baton wavered and he stopped in mid-flight, it having suddenly occurred to him that Ash would certainly not approve of that final sentiment.

Ash had never made any secret of his views on the subject of England's dealings with Afghanistan, and had expressed them pretty freely to Wally, denouncing them as unjust and indefensible. He was therefore the last person to agree that 'God and Right were on her side'. In Ash's opinion, England had never had any right to interfere with Afghanistan, let alone attack her, and he would undoubtedly say that God—or Allah—ought by rights to be on the side of the Afghans. Ash would say . . .

'Ah, to hell with Ash,' thought Wally irritably. He stuffed the poem in with the letter, and having sealed and addressed the envelope, added it to the pile in the 'out' tray and went off to dress for dinner.

Sir Louis Cavagnari was another who had spent the latter part of the afternoon and most of the evening at his desk, bringing his diary up-to-date and writing letters and telegrams for dispatch to Ali Khel. He had been feeling considerably easier of late, for the sudden death from cholera in the course of a single night of a hundred and fifty of the Herati soldiers in the city, though a shocking piece of news, had proved to be a blessing in disguise.

The regiments concerned, panic-stricken by the sudden loss of so great a number of their comrades, had settled for part of the pay they were owed plus forty days furlough to return to their homes, and rushing to the Bala Hissar to hand in their arms, had not even waited to obtain their certificates of leave before marching away from the city, hurling threats and abuse as they went at the Commander-in-Chief, General Daud Shah, who had come to see them leave.

From Sir Louis's point of view, this could not have been better. They had caused a great deal of trouble, and the effort of preserving a bold front, and keeping up the pretence that the undisciplined behaviour of a rabble of mutinous troops was a matter of complete indifference to him instead of a constant source of anxiety, was becoming increasingly tedious. Not that he had at any time been in the least afraid of the disgruntled troops from Herat, whom he regarded as no more than hooligans.

All the same, it was a relief to know that a considerable number of them had at last been paid off (he had always known that the money would be forthcoming as soon as the Amir and his ministers realized that there was no other way of ridding themselves of a dangerous nuisance), and had handed in their arms and left the city. He fully realized that fear of the cholera had probably played a greater part than money in bringing about that welcome exodus; and also that not all the Herati regiments had left—some were still encamped in cantonments outside the city, and a number of men drawn from these were actually helping to guard the Arsenal, which on the face of it seemed a little unwise. But then the Amir had assured him that they had been carefully selected and were well disposed towards him, which Sir Louis took to mean that they had probably been paid something on account.

There remained the Ardal Regiment from Turkestan and three Orderly Regiments, whose pay was also many months in arrears. They too were pressing for their money, but had shown no signs of emulating the deplorable behaviour of the Heratis. And as General Daud Shah had apparently promised them that if they would only have a little patience they would all be paid at the beginning of September, Sir Louis felt justified in taking a more rosy view of the future.

It was unfortunate that this year the start of Ramadan, the Mohammedan Month of Fasting, should have fallen in mid-August, since during Ramadan the Faithful may not eat or drink except between sunset and the first streak of dawn, and men who have fasted all day and gone without water in the heat and dust of August are apt to be short-tempered. But then August would soon be over, and with it that long, eventful summer that had seen the metamorphosis of plain Major Cavagnari into His Excellency Sir Louis Cavagnari, K.C.S.I., Envoy and Minister Plenipotentiary. Only another week, and then it would be September.

Sir Louis looked forward to the autumn. He had heard that it was almost the best time of year in Kabul: not as beautiful as spring, when the almond trees were in bloom and the valley was white with fruit blossom, but with a spectacular beauty of its own as the leaves of poplars and fruit trees, vines, walnuts and willows flamed gold and orange and scarlet, the snow-line crept down the mountain-sides, and thousands of wild fowl on their way south flew in from the tundras beyond the great ranges of the Hindu Kush. The stalls in the bazaars of Kabul would be piled high with apples, grapes, corncobs, walnuts and chillies, and there would be snipe and quail and chikor in the uncultivated grasslands and on the lower slopes of the hills. And tempers would cool with the coming of the cooler days.

The Envoy smiled as he contemplated the day's entry in his diary, and putting down his pen he rose and went to stand by one of the windows that faced south across the darkening plain, gazing out at the far snow peaks that a short while ago had glowed bright pink in the last of the sunset, and now showed silver in the light of a sky that blazed with stars.

The storm of the previous week had been followed by several days of hot sunshine and a blustery wind that had dried up the puddles and filled the valley with a haze of dust. But yesterday rain had fallen again, not in a deluge as before but gently—the last dying tears of the monsoon—and now the new-washed air was fresh and cool.

The night was full of sounds, for after the abstinence of the day all Kabul, released from fasting by the setting of the sun, was relaxing over the *Iftari*, the evening meal of Ramadan, and the darkness hummed like a hive. A contented hive, thought Cavagnari, listening to the cheerful medley of noises that came from the Residency compound, and sniffing the scent of wood-smoke and cooked food and the pungent smell of horses. He could hear someone in the King's Garden that lay near by, behind the Residency, playing a flute; and from further up the hill came the faint sound of drums and sitars and a woman's voice singing a song of Barbur's day—*'Drink wine in this hold of Kabul—send the cup around . . .'*

Beneath his window-sill the wall of the citadel fell away into darkness, its shadow blotting out the road below. Yet here too there were sounds—the clip-clop of unseen hoof-beats on the hard earth and the sound of footsteps and voices as a party of travellers hurried towards the Shah Shahie Gate. Only the shadowy plain and the vast wall of mountains lay still and silent.

Cavagnari sniffed the night breeze, and presently, hearing feet on the stair, said without turning: 'Come in, William. I've finished the letters for the dâk, so you can put the code book away; we shall not need it tonight. No point in sending another telegram to Simla when there is nothing new to report. They'll find anything they need to know when they get the next diary. What day does that go off?'

'Morning of the 29th, sir.'

'Well, if anything of interest comes up before then we can always send a *tar*. But with a bit of luck, the worst is over and things should settle down a bit now that most of those pestilential nuisances from Herat have dispersed to their homes. You can take the letters. I must change for dinner.'

Half-a-mile away, on the rooftop of Nakshband Khan's house, Ash too had been looking at the mountains and thinking, as Cavagnari had been, that the worst was over. After last week's downpour and the rain of yesterday there was more snow on the high hills, and tonight there was a distinct hint of autumn in the cool air, so it was more than likely that the worst of the cholera was over—or soon would be. And like Sir Louis, Ash had been encouraged by the departure of the mutinous regiments.

Now if only the Amir would pay the rest of his troops what they were owed, or the cholera scare them away—or the British Envoy buy time for himself and the Amir by insisting that the Government of India lend the Afghan treasury enough money to pay the soldiers —there was a reasonable chance that the Mission might yet succeed in turning the present hostility and distrust of a resentful people into something approaching tolerance, or even, with luck, a certain degree of respect if not liking. Time was what both Cavagnari and the Amir needed, and Ash was still of the opinion that money could buy it; and only money.

'Yet if the Amir was able to find the money to pay the Heratis,' reasoned Ash, 'he can probably find enough to pay off the others. He must have realized by now that he can't afford not to, and that the money must be raised somehow, even if he has to squeeze it out of his rich nobles and merchants, or from the money-lenders.'

He must have spoken the last words aloud without realizing it, because Anjuli, sitting beside him in the curve of his arm with her head resting on his shoulder, stirred and said softly: 'But such people do not give willingly. And if it is taken from them by force they will extort it in their turn, by one means or another, from the poor. This we know. So how shall it profit the Amir if in order to appease his soldiers he angers his nobles and rich men, and incurs the hatred of the poor? That way the unrest will not only remain, but grow greater.'

'True, my wise little heart. It's a hard knot, but until it is untied or cut there will be no peace in Kabul—least of all for those in the Residency compound or in the Palace of the Bala Hissar.'

Anjuli shivered at the name, and instinctively his arm tightened about her; but he did not speak, because he was thinking of Wally . . .

He had not spoken to Wally since the afternoon they had spent in the garden of Barbur's tomb, though he had seen him often enough from the window of the Munshi's house—fleeting glimpses of him going about his duties in the Residency compound. He must arrange another meeting soon, which might not be so easy now; it had been tolerably simple until the day that Cavagnari had angered the Amir by insisting on the removal of the Afghan sentries, but since then none of the four European members of the Mission had been able to move a yard beyond the compound without a double guard of Afghan cavalry clattering at their heels, in addition to their own escort.

In these circumstances it had been impossible for Wally to go anywhere on his own, let alone stop and fall into conversation with some apparently chance-met Afridi. But working in the Bala Hissar had its uses, for Ash had recently learned something that was not yet known to the Residency: that from the first of September the British Mission would be required to collect the fodder needed for their horses themselves.

Hitherto, the grass and *bhoosa* for this purpose had been supplied by the Amir, but now this practice was to be discontinued. In future the Guides' own grass-cutters would have to go out to forage for what they required, and as it was certain that for their own safety the foragers would be accompanied by an escort of sowars, it would not be thought in the least odd if Wally were to ride out with them.

The inevitable Afghan guard would of course be there to keep an eye on him, but the chances were that after the first day or two they would relax their vigilance and make it possible for Ash to have speech with him without arousing anyone's suspicions. In that way the two of them ought to be able to meet at least once or twice before the end of Ramadan, by which time, if fate were kind, it was possible that the ominous tide of hate and unrest that had been washing through the streets of Kabul for the past few weeks would have turned at last and begun to ebb.

One person at least appeared to harbour no doubts as to the ebbing of that tide. Sir Louis Cavagnari was convinced that it had already turned, and on the twenty-eighth of the month he instructed William to dispatch another telegram to Simla to say that all was well with the Kabul Embassy, and two days later wrote in a private letter to his friend, the Viceroy, that he had nothing whatever to complain of as regards the Amir and his ministers: 'His authority is weak throughout Afghanistan,' wrote Sir Louis, 'but, notwithstanding all that people say against him, *I* personally believe he will prove a very good ally, and that we shall be able to keep him to his agreements.'

The only other contribution to the out-going dâk that day had been a light-hearted post-card from Wally to his cousin in India, signed only with an initial. It had clearly been written in high spirits, but William, whose duties included sealing the mail bag, had caught sight of the concluding words and been startled by them. For Wally had ended: *'Scribe a votre Cousin in exilis vale,* and now farewell till . . .'

63

'Faith, that's a fine way to begin the autumn, I must say!' exclaimed Wally indignantly. 'You'd think those scutts could have given us a bit more notice, wouldn't you now? It's a shabby lot they are and no mistake.'

'Oh, come now, babe,' protested William. 'They know very well that we have our own grass-cutters and that they are under no obligation to provide us with fodder for our horses, yet they've been giving us the stuff free, gratis and for nothing ever since we arrived. It's only fair that now we've settled down and found our feet, we should start to fend for ourselves.'

'I suppose you're right,' conceded Wally. 'But it wouldn't have hurt His Imperial Afghan Highness to let us know beforehand that he meant to cut off supplies at the end of August, instead of waiting until the first of September to break the news that from now on we can get out and forage for ourselves. Because it's not something we can do straight off the bat, you know. At least, not in this particular country. Unless we want to find ourselves up to our eyebrows in trouble, we're going to have to make dashed certain where we are allowed to go, and even more important, where we are not—which isn't something we can sort out in five minutes.'

'You mean that *I* can sort out. It'll be on my tray, not yours,' retorted William wryly. 'But we must have a good two days' supply in hand, surely? That last consignment ought to tide us over at least until the day after tomorrow, so I don't know what you're complaining about. I'll have a talk with the Chief about fixing up where our grass-cutters can go, and they can trot off and start earning an honest living again on the morning of the third. I suppose you will have to send a guard with them?'

'There's no "suppose" about it,' said Wally bitterly. 'They wouldn't budge a yard without one.'

'Bad as that, is it?'

'You know it is. It's been weeks since any of the camp-followers would risk putting a nose outside the compound unless they went in a group, and preferably accompanied by one or two jawans—Mussulmans for choice. Even my Sikhs and Hindus haven't been going about much either. Do you mean to say you didn't know that?'

'Of course I did, my wee laddie. What on earth do you take me for? I may be a few years older than you, but I'm not actually doddering yet; or deaf or short-sighted either. But I'd rather hoped that the situation would have eased a trifle after half those noisy bastards from Herat grabbed their pay and bolted.'

'I daresay it has. But it's too soon for the effects to be felt, and I wouldn't dream of sending out a flock of grass-cutters without someone to play sheep-dog and keep an eye on them. In fact I shall probably go along myself at first, just to make sure that everything is all right. We don't want 'em rushing back to barracks empty-handed and in a panic because some sturdy local patriot has called them naughty names and heaved a brick at them.'

'We don't indeed,' agreed William, and went away to discuss a number of questions that had been raised by the abrupt announcement that in future the Residency would be responsible for feeding its own horses.

The decision had come as a surprise, but apart from the lack of notice it was not one that could be cavilled at, because as William had pointed out, there was no earthly reason why the Afghan Government should supply fodder for the British Mission's horses—particularly when the Guides had their own grass-cutters, who were perfectly capable of getting it for them. Wally had not been blind to that, and his annoyance had been solely on account of the suddenness of the announcement, which struck him as unnecessarily discourteous.

He could see no reason why the Residency should not have been informed at the outset that this particular amenity was strictly temporary and would be withdrawn at the end of August; but apart from that, the change was not unwelcome. In fact the more he thought about it the better it pleased him, for it would give him an excuse to ride out to parts of the valley and the lower slopes of the hills that he had not yet visited, besides providing him with many more opportunities of meeting Ash.

He had been on his way back to the Mess House following his morning inspection of Stables and Lines when William met him with the news about the new arrangement for fodder, and now, turning back to pass it on to his cavalry officers, he recrossed the Residency courtyard and went out again past the sentry on the gate into the narrow lane that separated the Residency from the barrack block.

The door leading into the barracks stood open, but he did not walk through the jawans' courtyard, but turned right down the lane, and then left again to skirt the northern wall of the barracks and stroll out across the dusty sun-flooded compound towards the stables that stood at the far end under the shadow of the Arsenal. As he went he glanced up casually, eyes narrowed against the sun-glare, at the barred windows of the tall houses that stood on the higher ground beyond the compound wall: small, secretive windows like watchful eyes peering down from the high mud walls at the doings of the strangers in their midst.

No one seeing him glance up would have said that his gaze had rested on any particular window, or that he was in the least interested in the houses. But that brief survey had shown him that a blue and white pottery jar containing a spray of leaves stood on the sill of a certain window, and walking on he wondered if Ash already knew that in future the Guides would be sending out their own grass-cutters, or (which was more to the point) where they would be permitted to go; and if he too had seen this as an excellent opportunity for further meetings?

The final consignment of fodder sent by the Amir had been a generous one, and Jemadar Jiwand Singh, the senior Indian officer of the cavalry, was of the opinion that it would last for another two to three days and that the grass-cutters need not go out until the third. 'But there is the winter to be thought of,' said Jiwand Singh, 'and if, as they say, the snow lies four feet deep in the valley, we shall need to lay in a great store of fodder. And for that we shall need more space.'

' "Sufficient unto the day is the evil thereof", Jemadar-Sahib,' quoted Wally lightly. 'This is still only the first day of autumn and snow will not fall until late in November. But I will speak to the Burra-Sahib tonight and tell him that we shall need another store house, and space on which to build one.'

'Over there,' said Jiwand Singh grimly, jerking his head towards an enclosed slope of waste ground, known as the Kulla-Fi-Arangi, that lay just beyond the perimeter of the compound and separated from it only by a low mud wall. 'It would be no bad thing to gain permission to build on that ground, since by doing so we could close it against the many idlers and thieves and *budmarshes* who now use it as an approach to this compound, which they enter at will. Moreover if ever the need should arise to defend ourselves, we would find that of great service.'

Wally swung round to stare at the waste ground with an arrested look in his eyes. He had always been worried by the ease with which the compound could be entered, and now he muttered half under his breath, and in English: 'By Jove, that's not a bad idea . . . Now why didn't I think of that before? Not walls: store houses. Good, strongly built sheds; and perhaps a few more servants' quarters. I wonder . . .'

He pondered the matter and at tea-time that day discussed it with Rosie, who agreed that it would certainly make the compound more secure if access to it could be reduced to a single entrance—preferably a narrow one that could be closed by a stout gate, instead of half-a-dozen alleyways and a slope of waste ground wide enough to drive a herd of cattle down.

'And no one,' said Wally slowly, 'could accuse us of insulting our hosts by building defensive walls and barricades if we asked to put up a shed to store our fodder in for the winter, and perhaps a couple of extra servants' quarters to—to ease the overcrowding.'

'Not servants' quarters,' said Rosie thoughtfully. 'A large dispensary. I could do with one. Yes, it's not a bad scheme, and provided the Chief approves—'

'Of course he'll approve. Why shouldn't he? He can't feel any happier than we do about living in such a hopelessly vulnerable spot as this. He merely didn't want to upset the Amir by demanding defensive walls all round the shop, and I see his point. But this idea is quite different, and if anyone can bring the Amir round to it, he can. They get on together like a house on fire and hardly a day goes by without their having a long friendly blarney together—in fact they're having one now. So as we're obviously going to need extra storage space anyway, the whole thing should be plain sailing. I'll see if I can have a word with the Chief when he gets back from the palace. He's always in a good mood after a chat with the Amir.'

But as William's favourite poet and fellow-countryman had so truly said, 'the best laid schemes o' mice an' men gang aft a-gley'. Sir Louis had returned unexpectedly late from the palace, and in such a noticeably bad temper that Wally had decided that this was definitely one of those times when junior officers should be seen and not heard.

Normally when Sir Louis paid a social call at the palace, he stayed for about an hour and returned in the best of spirits, particularly on those occasions when, as today, the subject under discussion was the projected tour of the northern provinces, which the Amir had been as enthusiastic about as he himself was. This evening they were to have settled the final details; yet now, with the date of their departure set and endless arrangements already in train, the Amir had suddenly chosen to announce that he could not possibly go—

It was, declared Yakoub Khan, out of the question that he should leave his capital at a time of grave unrest: how could he possibly do so when his regiments in Kabul could not be trusted to behave in an orderly manner? When a number of his provinces were in open revolt, his cousin Abdur Rahman (a protégé of the Russians and living under their protection) plotting to invade Kandahar and take his throne, and his brother, Ibrahim Khan, intriguing against him with the same object in view? He had no money and little authority, and were he to leave Kabul for so much as a week he was very certain that he would never be able to return again. In the circumstances he was sure that his good friend Sir Louis would fully appreciate the difficulties of his situation, and agree with him that any idea of a tour at this juncture must be abandoned.

One would have thought that Sir Louis (who was equally well aware of those difficulties and had himself reported on them in a number of official telegrams and dispatches during the past few weeks) would have been the first to agree that the tour must be called off: but this was not so. He was seriously upset, for he had visualized this tour as a combination of a Royal Progress under his personal aegis—a public demonstration of the friendship and trust that now existed between Great Britain and Afghanistan—and a subtle reminder that it was the British who had won the recent war. Also, having lavished a great deal of time and thought on plans and arrangements for it, his anger at the Amir's sudden *volte face* was aggravated by an uncomfortable suspicion that he would be made to look foolish when the various officials he had written to, or to whom William had written on his behalf, learned that the tour would not take place after all.

As a result, he had argued with the Amir and done his best to make him change his mind. But nothing he could say had served to make Yakoub Khan budge an inch, and eventually, realizing that if he were not very careful he would lose his temper, he had brought the interview to a close and returned to the Residency in anything but a good mood.

Wally took note of the fact, and wisely recognizing that this was not the moment to start any new hares, decided to say nothing about

the possibility of improving the defences of the compound by building storage sheds or a dispensary, and confined himself instead to
asking William if he had found out where they could go for fodder.

William had: they could take all that was needed from the *charman,* the uncultivated grazing land that formed a large part of the
plain of Kabul, and it had been suggested that a start could be made
in the vicinity of the village of Ben-i-Hissar, which was no great distance from the citadel.

'I said we'd be sending our grass-cutters out on the morning of the
third. That's the day after tomorrow,' said William. 'They wanted to
know because of sending a guard with them, though they must know
we'll be sending one of our own. However, just as well to have them
around. We don't want any trouble from villagers claiming afterwards that our chaps trespassed on their fields and damaged their
crops, and as long as a squad of Afghan cavalry are keeping an eye
on proceedings, that isn't likely to happen.'

Wally was in agreement with him, for much as he disliked being
followed around by Afghan troopers, their presence on this sort of
occasion would ensure that even the most truculent villagers would
think twice before flinging a stone at the strangers. All the same he
intended to accompany the grass-cutters himself to make certain that
they kept well away from any cultivated land; and also to spy out the
surrounding country and study the behaviour of the Afghan guard
with a view to seeing how easy—or how difficult—it would be to meet
and talk to Ash in the course of these forays.

He was inclined to think that it would prove a simple matter once
the novelty had worn off and foraging on the *charman* became a routine affair. 'No point in his coming out the first day though,' decided
Wally. 'But as our grass-cutters will be out every alternate day the
Afghans are going to get bored in next to no time, and after that it
will be as easy as falling off a log.'

It was only on the following day that it occurred to Wally that
there could be no harm if Ash happened to ride past Ben-i-Hissar,
say on the morning of the fifth, just to get some idea of the situation
and assess the possibilities it offered.

A brief glance at the Munshi's house had already shown him that
Ash was at work there, so he strolled across to an itinerant fruit-
seller who had set up a stall on the edge of the compound, and
bought half-a-dozen oranges, five of which he later placed in a neat
row on the window-ledge of his dressing-room before carefully clos-

ing the shutters behind them. The room looked out across the roof of the Sikh quarters in the barrack-block towards the stables and the far end of the compound, and the oranges, standing out vividly against the white-painted shutters, could be clearly seen from a considerable distance away.

There was no need to give Ash any directions, for if he did not know already, he would have no difficulty in finding out where Hamilton-Sahib was bound; and if he could manage to get away he would be there. If not, he would certainly come the next time—and as that would be the seventh, there was a reasonable chance that the Afghan guard would not be in attendance. The seventh being a Friday and the Moslem sabbath, with any luck they might be at their devotions in one of the city mosques.

Sir Louis had still been noticeably short-tempered at breakfast, and as the usual succession of callers hoping for preferment or bringing complaints against the Amir or one or other of the ministers had kept him fully occupied until late in the day (after which he had gone off to shoot partridges with one of the local landowners), Wally had no opportunity of bringing up the subject of the sheds: for which he was not altogether sorry. He still considered it a capital scheme, but instinct warned him that his brain-child was likely to receive short shrift from Sir Louis in his present mood, so instead he mentioned it to William, who being a civilian, and at present an exceedingly busy one, was not all that interested in matters that from the viewpoint of a professional soldier appeared vitally important.

William was well aware of the precarious position of the British Mission, and recognized as clearly as Wally did the alarming insecurity of the accommodation provided for them by the Amir. But then he, like Cavagnari, was convinced that, situated as they were, any defence from a military standpoint was out of the question, and that they must therefore trust to other methods. To diplomacy and the careful and cautious building up of good-will. To the patient breaking-down of suspicion and hostility, and the fostering of friendly relations. Above all, to the preservation of a bold front and a show of complete confidence.

These things might pull them through where tangible defences of brick and plaster could only serve to hold off an armed assault for an hour or two—if that. He was therefore not as enthusiastic about the shed idea as Wally had hoped, though he promised to sound out Sir Louis on the subject and seemed to think there was a good chance that his reaction would be favourable, because after all, defence or no, they would certainly need to lay in extra fodder against the months when Kabul would be deep in snow. But then there was still plenty of time before that.

William's tepid reception of his 'capital scheme' had depressed Wally, but he consoled himself with the reflection that if Sir Louis could be brought to agree and the Amir give his permission, the sheds would not take long to build. And once they were up, he was going to feel a lot easier about the men under his command, whose safety and welfare were his personal responsibility, and who in turn were responsible for the protection of every single person in the Residency compound, from the Envoy down to the humblest sweeper.

Later, strolling back to the Mess House after discussing arrangements for the foraging party with Jemadar Jiwand Singh, he glanced up at the Munshi's house and was pleased to see that the pottery jar with its spray of green leaves was no longer standing dead centre, but had been moved to the right-hand end of the window; which could be translated briefly as 'can do'—the left hand signifying the reverse.

Wally returned to the Residency whistling 'The Minstrel Boy', and having regained his rooms, removed the five oranges that he had placed on his dressing-room window-sill earlier in the day.

That evening the Envoy had taken his secretary with him when he went off to shoot partridge, and Lieutenant Hamilton and Surgeon-Major Kelly, who had not been invited to the shoot, rode out with an escort of two sowars and the inevitable guard of Afghans along the banks of the Kabul River to the site of the old British cantonments near Sherpur.

The day had been warm and cloudless, and though there had been barely more than a breath of wind, it had been enough to stir up the dust so that the air was faintly hazy, and the sunset, even with that clear sky, was one of the most spectacular that Wally had ever seen.

Having only known Kabul in high summer, he had never been able to understand why Ash though it such a beautiful place, and could only suppose that because Ash was in love and had been living there with Juli, he saw it through rose-coloured glasses, as thousands of lovers, honeymooning in cheap boarding-houses, see wet seaside towns or foggy industrial cities as gardens of Eden.

The snow peaks were fine enough, but none of them, to Wally's eyes, could rival the heart-stopping loveliness of Nanga Parbat, the 'Naked Goddess', as he had first seen her in the dawn from a hillside above Barramulla. Nor would he have dreamed of comparing the flat lands around Kabul with the enchanting valley of Kashmir with its lotus-strewn lakes and winding, willow-shaded streams, its wealth of flowers and trees and Mogul gardens. But now of a sudden it was as though his eyes had been opened and he saw Kabul and its setting for the first time: not as stark and desolate and dun-coloured, but beautiful with a wild, spectacular beauty that took his breath away.

A combination of sunset and dust and the smoke of cooking fires had transformed the valley to a sea of gold, out of which the near hills and the jagged snow-capped ranges behind them rose up in layer after layer of glittering splendour, caught in the bonfire blaze of the dying day and flaming like Sheba's jewels against an opal sky. The soaring pinnacles of the mountains might have been the spires and towers of some fabulous city—Valhalla, perhaps; or the outer ramparts of Paradise . . .

' "And the city was pure gold, like unto clear glass, and the foundations of the wall of the city were garnished with all manner of precious stones",' murmured Wally under his breath.

'What did you say?' asked Rosie, turning to look at him.

Wally coloured and said confusedly, 'Nothing . . . I mean—it looks like that description of the Holy City, doesn't it. The one in Revelations. The mountains, I mean. All that bit about jasper and topaz and chrysolyte and amethyst . . . and the gates of pearl . . .'

His companion turned back to study the view, and being of a more prosaic turn of mind than Walter, observed that it reminded him more of a transformation scene in a pantomime. 'Pretty,' approved Rosie, and added that he wouldn't have believed that this god-forsaken corner of the world could ever have looked anything but forbidding.

'Ash used to talk about a mountain called the Dur Khaima,' mused Wally, his gaze still on the jewelled glory of the snow peaks. 'The Far Pavilions . . . I never realized . . .' his voice slowed and stopped and Rosie said curiously: 'Are you talking about Pandy Martyn, by any chance? He was a friend of yours, wasn't he?'

'Is,' corrected Wally briefly. He had not meant to mention Ash's name and was annoyed with himself for having done so, because although Rosie had never actually served with Ash, he must have learned quite a lot from those who had, and might be sufficiently interested to ask awkward questions about Ash's present whereabouts.

'Remarkable fellow, by all accounts,' observed Rosie. 'The only time I ever met him was in '74, when he turned up in Mardan with a nasty head-wound and I had the job of patching him up. That was the year after I first came to the Guides, I remember. He didn't talk much. But then he wasn't in very good shape at the time, and as soon as he was fit enough he was hustled off to Rawalpindi. But I did hear that he had been to Kabul, so I suppose the mountain he told you about was one of these. Magnificent, aren't they.'

Wally nodded agreement and did not contradict the statement about the Dur Khaima, but fell silent, gazing at the enormous panorama of the Hindu Kush and seeing it in astonishing detail so that every last, least fold and spur and gully, and every soaring peak, looked as clear and distinct as though he were seeing it through a powerful telescope—or with the eye of God. And all at once he knew that this was one of those moments that for no particular reason one remembers for ever, and that remain indelibly printed on the mind when many more important ones fade and are lost.

As the light ebbed the valley filled with shadow and the high snow-crests took fire, and it occurred to Wally that he had never realized before what a beautiful place the world was: how full of wonder. Man might be doing his best to mar it, but every bush—and every stone and stick too—was still 'afire with God'. 'Ah, it's good to be alive!' thought Wally with a sudden surge of exultation and a lifting of the heart that made him feel that he would live for ever and ever . . .

A discreet cough from one of the sowars brought him back to earth and reminded him that there were other persons present besides Ambrose Kelly—and also that it was Ramadan and the escort and the Afghan guard must be impatient to be back in their quarters in time to say the customary evening prayers before the setting of the sun allowed them to break the day's fast.

'Come on, Rosie, race you to the river!' He turned away from the ruins of the old cantonment and urging his horse into a gallop, rode back laughing towards the Bala Hissar that stood out blackly against the bright gold of the evening sky.

Ash, leaving the citadel somewhat later than usual, passed him as the small party of Guides rode in through the Shah Shahie Gate. But Wally had not seen him. The sun was still above the horizon, but the Bala Hissar was in shadow, and the air under the dark arch of the gate was so thick with dust and smoke that Ash had walked by unnoticed. He heard Kelly say: 'That's a bottle of hock you owe me, young Walter; and faith, it'll be welcome, for it's parched I am.' And then they were out of sight.

Ash too was parched, for as 'Syed Akbar' he must keep the fast. Besides the day had been a long and tiring one for everyone in the Munshi's employ: one of the regiments stationed within the Bala Hissar, the Ardal Regiment, only recently arrived from Turkestan, had demanded three months' pay, and surprisingly been told that they would receive this on the following morning. The Munshi, among others, had been told to see to this, and Ash and his fellow *likhni wallahs* (writing fellows) had been hard at work all day compiling lists of names and ranks, together with the varying sums due to be paid in cash to each man, and the total sum that would have to be drawn from the Treasury.

Given reasonable notice the task would not have been arduous, but the shortness of time and the fact that it must be done fasting— and for the most part in a small, hot and airless room—made it an exhausting one. The normal mid-day rest had had to be dispensed with, and Ash was both tired and parched with thirst by the time the work was done and he was able to remove the blue and white jar from the window and return to the Sirdar's house and Anjuli. But despite his weariness he was conscious of an enormous sense of relief and a sudden flowering of hope and optimism.

The fact that the Ardal Regiment was to be paid showed that the Amir and his ministers had at last realized that a starving and mutinous army was far more dangerous to them than no army at all, and despite their protestations of penury, had decided to find the money before another regiment was driven to mutiny. It was a giant stride in the right direction and, to Ash, an excellent omen for the future.

He was pleased too about Wally, whose signal to him proved that their minds had been working on identical lines, which alone was almost as heartening as this Ardal business. It was good to know that they would be meeting soon, and that with the threat of insurrection that had menaced the foreigners in the citadel about to be removed, they would be able to talk of 'pleasant things' again.

The news that the regiments were to be paid had blown through Kabul like a fresh breeze, dispersing the tension and the sullen and barely restrained fury that had brooded there for so long, and Ash could sense the difference with every nerve in his body. As he drew back in the shadows under the Shah Shahie Gate to let Wally and Dr Kelly ride past, and heard Wally laugh in reply to the doctor's words, he caught the infection of the boy's high spirits and his own rose headily. Tiredness and thirst were suddenly forgotten, and walking on with a lighter step along the mud road below the outer wall of the citadel and through the narrow streets of the city, it seemed to him that for the first time in many months the evening air breathed of peace and quiet.

The Envoy and his secretary had returned from the partridge shoot in equally good spirits, the evening's sport having banished Sir Louis' ill-temper and made him forget for the time being his annoyance at the Amir's sudden cancellation of the autumn tour. He was an excellent shot, and the landowner who had organized the shoot had assured him that there would be many more game birds as soon as the weather became cooler. 'If that is so,' said Sir Louis at dinner that night, 'we ought to be able to keep ourselves in duck and teal and roast goose for much of the cold weather.'

Turning to Wally, he asked about the foraging party that would be going out on the following morning; and on hearing that Lieutenant Hamilton proposed to accompany them in order to see that they did not go anywhere they shouldn't, was pleased to approve, and suggested that Surgeon-Major Kelly went with him for good measure.

Rosie said that he would be delighted to do so and Wally had no option but to agree, though the suggestion was not a welcome one, because if Rosie were to fall into the habit of accompanying him it was going to be difficult to meet Ash. However he would deal with that later, for at the moment he intended to broach the more important question of winter fodder and the extra sheds that would be needed for storing it. But Sir Louis had begun to talk to Dr Kelly about the prospects of duck shooting later on in the year, and from there they had passed to discussing hunting in County Down and mutual acquaintances in Ballynahinch. After which the conversation became general, and as Sir Louis retired to his own quarters in the Envoy's House to write his diary as soon as the meal was over, Wally had no further chance to speak of sheds that night.

Even if he had been able to do so, it is doubtful if Sir Louis would have accorded the scheme much sympathy. The good temper engendered by a pleasant evening's sport had been considerably improved by the welcome news, conveyed to him by a trusted agent shortly before dinner, that the Ardal Regiment would parade on the morrow to receive their arrears of pay in full: a piece of information that had much the same effect on Sir Louis' spirits as it had had on Ash's, as it confirmed his belief that the money would and could be found, and that now the rest of the army would shortly be paid its wages and law and order would reign in Kabul. He had immediately instructed William to see that the usual telegram confirming that all was well with the Kabul Residency went off first thing in the morning, and in the circumstances he would not have been particularly interested in a scheme for improving the military defences of the Residency compound by devious and complicated means.

'I'll ask Ash about it, and see what he thinks,' decided Wally later that night as he prepared to go to bed. 'Ash'll know if it would be any use, and if he thinks it wouldn't and I'm crazy, I'll hold my tongue.' On which thought he said his prayers and turned out the lamp, though he did not immediately retire to bed.

The talk at dinner had reminded him of home, and he went to the window, and leaning his arms on the sill, looked out across the dark courtyard below and the flat roof of the Envoy's House towards the horizon, and thought of Inistioge.

Beyond the sheer drop of the outer wall lay the valley, with the pale ribbon of the Kabul River winding across it, and behind and beyond the wrinkled hills, grey in the starlight, rose the immense, shadowy rampart of the Hindu Kush. But the river he saw was the Nore, for he was back in Inistioge . . . There were the dear familiar fields and woods and the blue hills of Kilkenny, and that was not Shah Shahie's tomb, but the little church at Donaghadee, while the far shimmer in the sky was not snow, but white clouds floating high and serenely above the Blackstairs mountains in Carlow . . .

'I wonder,' mused Lieutenant Walter Hamilton, v.c., *aetat* twenty-three, 'why Generals always seem to choose the name of one of their battles when they are made peers? I shan't—I shall choose Inistioge . . . Field Marshal Lord Hamilton of Inistioge, v.c., k.g., g.c.b., g.c.s.i.—I wonder if I shall be allowed to go Home to get my medal from the Queen? or if I shall have to wait my turn for Home Leave? . . . I wonder if I shall ever get married . . .'

Somehow he did not think that he would: or not unless he found someone exactly like Ash's Juli, which seemed to him unlikely. Ash ought to send her away from Kabul, for by all accounts there was a deal too much cholera in the city. He must speak to him about that on Wednesday. It would be grand to see Ash again, and with any luck . . .

A cavernous yawn interrupted his train of thought and he laughed at himself and went to bed feeling enormously happy.

64

The sun was still well below the horizon when Sir Louis Cavagnari, always an early riser, left for his customary ride on the following morning, attended by his Afridi orderly Amal Din, his syce, four sowars of the Guides and half-a-dozen troopers of the Amir's cavalry.

The dâk-rider had left even earlier, carrying a telegram that would be transmitted from Ali Khel to Simla. And not long afterwards a procession of twenty-five grass-cutters, carrying ropes and sickles, had also left the citadel, shepherded by Kote-Daffadar Fatteh Mohammed and Sowars Akbar Shah and Narain Singh of the Guides, and accompanied by four Afghan troopers.

Wally and Ambrose Kelly had followed some twenty minutes later, just as Ash, who had arrived early that day because of the pay parade, was placing the pottery jar in position on his window-sill. He watched them ride away and wished that he could have gone with them. The air would be sharp and fresh in the open country, whereas it was already stale and warm in here, and would be even warmer in the large open space near the palace where the Ardal Regiment would soon be gathering to receive their pay, as that was not only a sun-trap, but an insalubrious one into the bargain, since all kinds of rubbish was thrown out there, and there were no trees to provide shade.

Ash sighed, envying Wally and his companions riding out to meet the sunrise through the dewy croplands along the river and among the groves of poplars, chenars and walnut trees that hid Ben-i-Hissar and the grassy sweep of the *charman* beyond. The cloudless sky was still pale with the opalescent paleness of dawn, and the land an indeterminate colour between dove-grey and sand, unmarked by shadows. But high above the neutral tinted ridges the hidden sun had already turned the snows to apricot. It was going to be a wonderful day: 'a day for singing hymns', as Wally would have said.

Remembering those tuneful mornings in Rawalpindi, Ash smiled to himself and began to hum 'All things bright and beautiful', only to check abruptly as he realized, with a queer stab of fear, that he was doing something that was so completely alien to the character of

Syed Akbar, scribe, that if anyone had overheard it he would certainly have been betrayed.

For over a year now he had been careful—deadly careful—never to say or do anything that might arouse suspicion, until by now he had imagined that any chance of his doing so was too remote to be worth considering, and that to all intents and purposes he had become Syed Akbar. Yet now he realized that he had not; and suddenly, with that knowledge, came an intense longing to be rid of pretence and be himself—only himself. But which self? Who was he? Ashton . . . ? Ashok . . . ? Akbar . . . ? Which? Which two could he discard? Or must he always be an amalgam of all three, joined together like . . . 'like Siamese triplets,' thought Ash wryly.

If so, was there anywhere in the world where he and Juli could live without having to remember and pretend? Where they need not act a part, as both were doing now; forced to be for ever on their guard for fear of making some trivial slip that, by exposing them as impostors, could endanger their very lives? The sort of slip he had made just now, when he began to hum an English hymn. It was frightening to realize that he would have done so even if there had been someone else in the room, and that it was only sheer luck that had saved him from being overheard. The knowledge left him profoundly shaken, and when he turned from the window to collect the ledgers that the Munshi would need, he found that his hands were cold and not entirely steady.

The sun was up by the time Wally and his party reached the outskirts of Ben-i-Hissar, and avoiding the village and the croplands surrounding it, selected an area of the uncultivated *charman* where the grass-cutters could collect all they needed without infringing on the rights of the local peasantry.

'By gum, what a day!' breathed Wally, awed by the dazzle of the morning. There had been a heavy dew during the night, and now every leaf and twig and blade of grass was hung with diamonds that flashed and glittered in the early sunlight, while the Bala Hissar, basking in the bright rays, might have been Kubla Khan's palace built on a hill of gold. 'Will you look at that now, Rosie. Who would ever believe, seeing it from here, that the place is no more than a rat's nest of tumble-down mud-and-plaster houses and half-ruined walls?'

'Not to mention dirt and smells and sewage,' grunted Rosie. 'Don't be forgetting that. It's a wonder to me so it is that we aren't all dead from typhoid and cholera. But I grant you it looks very fine from here, and as I'm as empty as a drum and breakfast is calling, I suggest we leave these fellows to their own devices and get back there as soon as possible. Unless you feel we should stay around a bit longer, of course?'

'Good Lord, no. They'll be all right now. Besides, the Chief said he wanted breakfast an hour early this morning—quarter-to-seven at the latest. He has to see some local big-wig at eight, I believe.'

Wally turned to the Kote-Daffadar and instructed him to see that the grass-cutters came back before the sun became too hot, and having saluted the escort and the Amir's men, rode off at a gallop, singing 'Get thee, watchman, to the ramparts! Gird thee warrior with the sword!'

Ash was usually right about Wally.

'Slow down, you young madman,' exhorted Rosie as they raced across the *charman* and their horses, reaching a bank that concealed an irrigation ditch, rose to it as though it had been a bullfinch in distant Kildare and came down on cultivated land once more. Wally reined in reluctantly, and they approached the citadel at a sedate canter and entered the Shah Shahie Gate at a walk; pausing under the arch to exchange salutes with the Afghan sentries and speak to a passing sepoy of the Guides Infantry, one Mohammed Dost, who explained that he was on his way to the Kabul bazaar to arrange for the purchase of flour for the Escort . . .

The fact that he was going there unaccompanied, and plainly had no qualms about doing so, was an indication of how greatly the feeling in the city had changed for the better of late, and both officers realized it, and in consequence returned to the compound buoyed up by a conviction that from now on life in Kabul was going to be far more enjoyable than they had supposed.

Sir Louis, who had returned from his morning ride some time before them, had already bathed and changed and was strolling in the courtyard, and though not normally loquacious before breakfast, today he was full of plans for the cold weather, and in such good spirits that Wally, taking his courage in both hands, at last broached the subject of fodder for the winter months and the extra storage space that would be needed for it; pointing out that the slope of waste ground known as the Kulla-Fi-Arangi would provide ample space for a few sheds, but being careful not to mention the question of defence. Sir Louis agreed that something would have to be done about it, and turned the matter over to William, who made a face at Wally and said blandly that he was sure that the Guides would be able to find room for a haystack or two near the stables.

A few hundred yards away, in a building that overlooked the open ground where the pay parade was due to take place, General Daud Shah, Commander-in-Chief of the Afghan Army, was already seated by an open window from where he could oversee the proceedings, while below him on the ground floor, on a narrow recessed verandah that ran the length of the building, Ash squatted among a number of underlings and watched the Munshi and a number of minor officials fussing with ledgers as the dusty space before them filled up with men.

The prevailing mood was a holiday one, and there was nothing suggestive of smartness or military discipline about the men of the Ardal Regiment as they sauntered up by twos and threes, talking and laughing and making no attempt to form up in ranks. They might have been a crowd of ordinary citizens attending a fair, for they were not in uniform and such weapons as they carried were no more than any subject of the Amir took with him when he walked abroad, a tulwar and an Afghan knife, Daud Shah having prudently ordered that all firearms and ammunition must be handed in and stored in the Arsenal for safe keeping, and even the Herati Regiment on guard there obeying this edict.

By now the sun was well up, but though the time was barely seven o'clock, the day was already warm enough to make Ash grateful for the shade provided by the painted roof and carved wooden arches of the verandah. And even more so for the fact that the matting-covered floor stood a full six feet above the level of the ground, which enabled those who sat there to look down on the crowd and avoid being stifled by that shifting sea of bearded, ill-washed humanity.

It also gave them the opportunity to study the faces of the men who stood below them, and Ash was conscious of a sudden prickle of unease as he recognized one of them: a thin, wizened little man with a hook nose and the eyes of a fanatic, who had no business to be there at all, since he was neither a soldier nor a resident in the Bala Hissar, but a holy man, the Fakir Buzurg Shah, whom Ash knew to be an agitator who hated all 'Kafirs' (unbelievers) with a burning hatred, and worked tirelessly for a Jehad. He wondered what had brought the man here this morning, and whether he hoped to sow the good seed among the soldiers of the Ardal Regiment as he had sowed it among the Heratis? Ash could only hope that this soil would prove less fertile.

He had begun to wonder how long the pay parade would take and if the Munshi would allow him to have the rest of the day off as soon as it was over, when a portly official from the Treasury rose to his feet and took his stand at the top of the central flight of steps that led up to the verandah. Raising a podgy hand he called for silence, and having achieved it, announced that if the men would line up and advance one by one to the foot of the stairs, they would receive their pay; but—here he paused and flapped both hands angrily to quiet the babble of approval—*but* . . . they would have to be content with one month's pay instead of the three that had been promised them, as there was not enough money in the Treasury to cover the sum demanded.

The news had been received with a stunned silence that lasted for what seemed like minutes, but was probably less than twenty seconds. And then pandemonium broke loose as the men of the Ardal Regiment surged forward, pushing and shouting, screaming at the portly gentleman and his companions on the verandah, who screamed back at them that they would be well advised to take what they were offered while they had the chance—the Treasury had already been drained to give them even that one month's pay and there was no more to be had, not so much as one pice. Could they not understand that? The money was not there—they were welcome to come and see for themselves if they did not believe it.

The explosion of rage that greeted this last announcement resembled nothing so much as the snarling roar of a gigantic tiger, hungry, furious and thirsting for prey. And hearing it Ash felt his nerves tighten, and for a brief moment was tempted to run to the Residency and warn them of what had happened. But the narrow verandah was so crowded that it would not be easy to leave without attracting notice; and besides, this was a dispute between the Afghan Government and its soldiers, and no affair of the British Mission—which would in any case have already been warned by the noise that trouble was afoot, since the uproar must be loud enough to be heard in the city.

It was soon to grow louder.

A bull-voiced man in the forefront of the crowd bellowed *'Dam-i-charya!'*—'pay and food'—and those about him took up the cry.

Within seconds half the men were shouting the words in unison, and the thunderous beat of that slogan boomed under arches of the verandah until the whole fabric of the building seemed to vibrate to the sound. *'Dam-i-charya! Dam-i-charya . . . ! Dam-i-charya . . . !'*

Then suddenly stones began to fly as the hungry, cheated troops stooped to snatch up this handy and time-honoured ammunition and hurl it at the upper windows where their Commander-in-Chief sat. One of his Generals and some of the Ardal's officers, who had been standing in a group by the central steps, began to move among the men in an effort to calm them, shouting for silence and exhorting them to remember that they were soldiers and not children or hooligans. But it proved impossible to make themselves heard above the din, and presently one of them fought his way back, and thrusting aside the dismayed officials on the verandah ran into the house to beg the Commander-in-Chief to come down and talk to them himself, as that might quieten them.

Daud Shah had not hesitated. He had suffered many insults of late from the soldiers of the Afghan Army, and only a handful of days ago the departing Herati regiments had booed and jeered him as they marched out. But he was a fearless man, and it was not in his nature to seek safety in inaction. He descended at once and strode to the top of the steps, lifting his arms for silence.

The men of the Ardal Regiment made a concerted rush, and the next moment he was down and fighting for his life as they dragged him from the verandah and fell on him like a pack of wolves on a buck.

In an instant everyone on the verandah leapt to their feet, Ash among them. He was too far to one side to see what was happening, nor could he move forward, for he found himself hemmed in by horror-struck civilians: clerks, chupprassis and minor officials, who pushed and jostled each other as some strove to get a better view and others struggled to make their escape from the verandah and take refuge in the rooms behind.

Ash himself was in two minds whether to go or stay. But with the troops in their present mood, any civilian intent on escape and trying to force his way through them would probably be beaten up as savagely as they were beating Daud Shah, so it seemed better to stand fast and wait upon events. But for the first time in several days he was glad that he carried a pistol and a knife with him, and regretted that he had not brought his revolver as well, instead of deciding at the last moment that in view of the slackening of tension and the return of a more relaxed and peaceful atmosphere throughout Kabul there was no longer any need to carry such a bulky weapon with him and that it could be safely left in his office, hidden in one of the locked boxes in which he kept the Munshi's files.

That had been a mistake. But then no one had anticipated the present situation—certainly not Daud Shah, who seemed likely to pay for this error of judgement with his life. That he did not do so was due to luck more than anything else, for when the furious Ardalis had beaten and kicked him until he could barely see or speak, one of them plunged a bayonet into the fallen man. The savage act served to sober them, and they drew back and fell silent, staring down at their handiwork and making no attempt to prevent his entourage—who to give them their due had tried to go to his assistance—from carrying him away to his own house.

Ash caught a glimpse of him as they went past, and would have found it hard to believe that this battered object, turbanless and clad now in no more than a few torn and bloodstained rags, could possibly be alive, had it not been for the vigorous stream of profanity that issued from those split and bleeding lips. The indomitable Commander-in-Chief, having recovered his breath, was using it to express his opinion of his assailants: 'Filth! Offal! Sons of diseased swine! Spawn of reputationless mothers! Sweepings of hell!' snarled Daud Shah between gasps of pain as he was borne away, dripping blood that left a vivid scarlet trail on the white dust below the verandah.

The Ardal Regiment, deprived of this focus for its rage and realizing that there was nothing to be gained by attacking the hapless array of underlings on the verandah, remembered the Amir, and with shouts and oaths turned to make instead for the palace. But the rulers of Afghanistan had taken good care to fortify the royal residence against just such an eventuality as this, and the palace gates were far too stout to be easily forced, while its battlemented walls were high and massive and well loop-holed against attack. Moreover the two regiments on guard were the Kazilbashi Horse and the Artillery Regiment, both loyal to the Amir.

The yelling mutineers found the gates closed against them and the gun-crews standing to their guns, and there was nothing they could do except hurl stones and insults at the Kazilbashis and those who looked down on them from the walls, and renew their demands for pay and food. But after some minutes of this, the shouting gradually began to die down; and taking advantage of the lull, a man on the wall—some say a General of the Afghan Army—shouted at them angrily that if they wanted more money they should go to Cavagnari-Sahib for it—there was plenty of money there.

It is possible that the speaker intended no mischief but was merely exasperated and had put the suggestion sarcastically. But the Ardal Regiment received it with acclaim. Of course!—Cavagnari-Sahib. The very man. Why had they not thought of that before? Everyone knew that the English Raj was rich beyond the dreams of avarice, and was not Cavagnari-Sahib the mouth-piece and representative of that Raj? Why was he here in Kabul, uninvited and far from welcome, if not to buy justice for all and help the Amir out of his difficulties by paying off the arrears due to his troops? Cavagnari-Sahib would right their wrongs. To the Residency, brothers—!

The crowd turned as one, and cheering wildly began to race back the way they had come. And Ash, still on the verandah, saw them coming and heard the shouts of 'Cavagnari-Sahib!' and knew where they were headed.

He was not conscious of the process of connected thought. There had been no time for that and his reaction had been purely automatic. There were steps at each end of that long verandah, yet he had not attempted to reach the flight nearest him, but thrusting aside the man in front of him, leapt down from the edge a split second before their panic rush began, to be caught up and swept forward in the van of a tumultuous wave of shouting, cheering men.

It was only then that he knew why he must at all costs reach the Residency compound ahead or at least among the first of the throng.

He had to warn the Mission that this vociferous and apparently menacing crowd was not as yet activated by any hostility towards them, but that their anger was all for their own Government, for Daud Shah and the Amir, who having promised them three months' pay had gone back on their word and tried to fob them off with one. Also that they firmly believed that the *Angrezi* Government was not only fabulously rich and well able to pay them, but that its Envoy would be able to obtain justice for them . . .

Running with them, Ash could sense the mood of the crowd as clearly as though he had been one of them. But he knew that the least little thing could change that mood and turn them into a mob, and as he ran he found himself praying that Wally would not let the Guides open fire. They *must* not fire. Provided they kept calm and gave Cavagnari time to talk to the ring-leaders of this shouting horde, all would be well . . . Cavagnari understood these people and could speak their language fluently. He would realize that this was no moment for quibbling and that his only hope was to give them a firm promise to pay them what they were owed, then and there if the money was available, and if it was not, to pledge his word that it would be forthcoming as soon as his Government had time to send it . . .

'Dear God, don't let them open fire!' prayed Ash. 'Let me get there first . . . If only I can get there first I can warn the sentries that this isn't an attack and that whatever happens they must not lose their heads and do anything silly.'

He might even have succeeded, for some of the Guides had known him and would have recognized and obeyed him; but any chance of that was swept away by another and entirely unexpected influx of men from the left. The regiments on duty at the Arsenal had heard the uproar and seen the mutinous Ardalis come pouring down towards the Residency compound, and had raced to join them, and as the two separate streams of excited men, coming from different directions, cannoned into each other, Ash, among others, was sent sprawling.

By the time he was able to roll clear and struggle to his feet, bruised, dazed and choked by dust, the rout had gone past and he was at the back of the crowd; and there was no longer any hope of his being able to get into the compound in time—if at all—for the noisy throng that milled to and fro ahead of him now numbered close on a thousand, and there was no question of his being able to force his way through it.

But he had under-estimated Wally. The youthful commander of the Escort might be an indifferent poet and hold an over-romantic view of life, but he possessed the extreme military virtue of keeping his head in a crisis.

The first inkling that something had gone wrong with the pay parade had dawned on the denizens of the Residency compound when they heard the roar of rage that greeted the disclosure that the Amir's Government was defaulting on its promise. And though that sound and the tumult that followed had been muffled by the houses in between, there were few in the compound who did not hear it, and stop whatever they were doing to stand stock still, listening . . .

They did not hear the suggestion that Cavagnari-Sahib would pay, for that had been a single voice only. But the uproar that had preceded it and the applause with which it was received, above all the cry of *Dam-i-charya* chanted in unison by several hundred voices, had been clearly audible. And when presently they realized that the volume of sound was not only increasing but coming steadily nearer, they knew before they saw the first of the running soldiers where the shouting crowd was heading.

Except for Wally, the Guides were not yet in uniform: the infantry and those who were not on guard duty had been taking their ease in the barracks, and Wally himself had been down at the cavalry pickets beyond the stables, inspecting the horses and talking to the cavalrymen and the syces. A sepoy of the Guides Infantry, Hassan Gul, ran past without seeing him, making for the barracks where the Havildar of B Company stood by the open archway, picking his teeth with a splinter and listening with detached interest to the hullabaloo being raised by those undisciplined *shaitans* of the Ardal Regiment.

'They are coming here,' panted Hassan Gul as he reached the barracks. 'I was outside and saw them. Quick, shut the gate!'

It was the makeshift one that Wally had had made and put up only a short while ago, and would not have stood up to any determined battering. But the Havildar closed it while Hassan Gul ran on past the inner door of the deep archway and through the long courtyard, to shut and bolt the far door that faced the entrance to the Residency.

Wally too had been listening to the din of that abortive pay parade as he strolled along the line of picketed horses, pausing to fondle his own charger, Mushki, while he discussed cavalry matters with the sowars. He turned, frowning, to watch the running sepoy, and seeing the door into the barracks being closed, reacted to the situation as swiftly and instinctively as Ash had done:

'You—Miru—go and tell the Havildar to open that gate and keep them open. All three, if they have shut the others. And tell him that whatever happens, no one is to fire unless I give the order. No one!'

Sowar Miru left at a run and Wally turned to the others and snapped: '*No one*—that is an order,' and went swiftly back to the Residency by way of the barrack courtyard, where the doors now stood open, to report to Sir Louis.

'You heard what the Sahib said: there will be no firing,' said Jemadar Jiwand Singh to his troopers. 'Moreover—' But he had no time to say more, for in the next instant a cataract of yelling, leaping

Afghans poured into the peaceful compound, shouting for Cavagnari, demanding money, threatening and rollicking, pushing and jostling the Guides with howls of laughter, like a drunken gang of hooligans at a country fair.

A humorist among them called out that if there was no money to be had here either, they could always help themselves to the equipment in the stables, and the suggestion was received and acted upon with enthusiasm, the invaders rushing to get their hands on saddles, bridles, sabres and lances, horse-blankets, buckets and anything else that was movable.

Within minutes the stables were stripped bare and fights had broken out between the looters over the possession of the more highly prized items, such as English saddles. A panting sowar, his clothing torn and his turban awry, fought his way clear of the boisterous mass of looters and managed to get to the Residency to report to his Commanding Officer that the Afghans had stolen everything from the stables and were now stoning and stealing the horses.

'*Mushki!*' thought Wally with a contraction of the heart, visualizing his beloved charger gashed by stones or in the hands of some Ardali lout. 'Oh no, not Mushki . . .'

He would have given anything at that moment to have been able to run to the stables himself, but he knew very well that he would be unable to stand by and see Mushki stolen, and also that even if he did not lift a hand to prevent it, the mood of the crowd could change in a moment and the sight of one of the hated *feringhis* might act on it as a red rag to a bull. There was nothing for it but to order the breathless sowar to return and tell the Guides that they must leave the Cavalry lines and get back into the barracks.

'Tell the Jemadar-Sahib that we need not fear for our horses, because tomorrow the Amir will recover them from these thieves and restore them to us,' said Wally. 'But we must get our men back into the barracks before one of them starts a fight.'

The man saluted and ran back to plunge into the frightening mêlée in the lines where the terrified horses squealed and reared, lashing out at the Afghans, who snatched at them, pulling them this way and that as they quarrelled among themselves for the possession of each animal or cut at them for sheer sport while sowars and syces struggled to save them. But the message was delivered, and because the Afghans were pre-occupied with looting, all but one of the

Guides had been able to obey that order and retreat in safety to the barrack block, angry, bitter and dishevelled, but unharmed.

Wally came out to them and ordered twenty-four sepoys of the infantry to take their rifles and go up to the roof to stand behind the high parapet that surrounded it, but to keep their rifles out of sight, and on no account open fire unless they received an order to do so. 'Not even when those reputationless ones come this way, as they will do as soon as they find nothing left to steal in the lines or the stables. See that they find no weapon here. Now up with you—and the rest of you bring your arms and come into the Residency. Quickly.'

He had not been a moment too soon. As the last of the twenty-four sepoys disappeared up the steep flight of steps that led to the roof, and the door in the wall of the Residency courtyard closed behind the rest of the Escort, the riotous crowd that had been milling around at the far end of the compound in search of plunder began to break up.

Those who had been lucky enough to gain possession of a horse, or (less enviably) a saddle or a sabre or some such desirable piece of loot, were hastening to leave with their spoils before their less successful comrades succeeded in robbing them of these ill-gotten gains. But the empty-handed, who numbered several hundred, abandoned the deserted lines and ransacked stables, and suddenly recalling the purpose for which they had come, surged in a body across the compound and through and around the barracks, to gather before the Residency and shout once more for money—and for Cavagnari.

A year and more ago Wally, writing to Ash of his latest hero, had said that he did not believe that Cavagnari knew the meaning of fear: an extravagant statement that has been made about many men, and is usually untrue. But in this instance it was no exaggeration. The Envoy had already received a garbled warning from the Amir, who hearing that all was not going well with the pay parade, had hurriedly dispatched a message to Sir Louis urging him not to allow anyone to enter the Mission compound that day. But the message had arrived only minutes before the mob, and far too late to be acted upon, even if there had been any adequate way of keeping them out, which there was not.

The Envoy's first reaction to the tumult in the compound had been anger. It was, he considered, a disgrace that the Afghan authorities should permit the precincts of the British Mission to be invaded in this manner by a horde of undisciplined savages, and he would have to speak sharply about it both to the Amir and Daud Shah. When the looting stopped and the rabble turned their attention to the Residency and began to shout his name, demanding money with uncouth threats and flinging stones at his windows, his anger merely turned to disgust, and as the chupprassis hurried to close the shutters, he withdrew to his bedroom, where William, running up from his office on the ground floor below, found him donning his Political uniform: not the white of the hot weather, but the blue-black frock-coat usually worn in the cold months, complete with gilt buttons, medals, gold braid and narrow gold sword-belt.

Sir Louis appeared to be completely oblivious of the racket below, and seeing the look of cold and disdainful detachment on his face, William was torn between admiration and an odd feeling of panic that had nothing to do with the howling horde outside or the sound of stones rattling like hail against the wooden shutters. He was not normally given to imaginative flights, but as he watched the Envoy shrug himself into his coat it struck him that so might a noble of Louis XVI's day—an 'Aristo'—have looked when hearing the screeching of the *canaille* outside the walls of his château . . .

William cleared his throat, and raising his voice in order to be heard above the din said hesitantly: 'Do you mean to . . . are you going to speak to them, sir?'

'Certainly. They are not likely to leave until I do, and we really cannot be expected to put up with this ridiculous form of disturbance any longer.'

'But . . . Well, there seem to be an awful lot of them, sir, and—'

'What has that got to do with it?' inquired Sir Louis chillingly.

'Only that we don't know how much they want, and I—I wondered if we'd got enough. Because our own fellows have only just been . . .'

'What on earth are you talking about?' inquired the Envoy, busy adjusting the fastening of his ceremonial sword so that the tassels showed to advantage.

'Money, sir, rupees. It seems to be what they want, and I presume this means that when it came down to brass tacks there wasn't enough to go round this morning, and that is why—'

He was interrupted again. *'Money?'* Sir Louis' head came up with a jerk and he glared at his secretary for a moment and then spoke in tones of ice: 'My dear Jenkyns, if you imagine for one moment that I would even consider allowing myself and the Government I have the honour to represent to be blackmailed—yes, that is the word I mean

—blackmailed, by a mob of uncivilized hooligans, I can only say that you are very much mistaken. And so are those stone-throwing yahoos outside. My topi, Amal Din—'

His Afridi orderly stepped smartly forward and handed him the white pith helmet topped by a gilt spike that a Political Officer wore with his official uniform, and as he clapped it firmly on his head, adjusted the gilded strap across his chin and moved to the door, William sprang forward saying desperately: 'Sir—if you go down there—'

'My dear boy,' said Sir Louis impatiently, pausing in the doorway, 'I am not really in my dotage. I too realize that if I were to go down to them only those in the forefront of the crowd would see me, while those who could not would continue to shout and make it impossible for me to be heard. I shall of course speak to them from the roof. No, William, I do not require you to come with me. I will take my orderly, and it will be better if the rest of you keep out of sight.'

He crooked a finger at Amal Din and the two tall men left the room, Sir Louis striding ahead and the Afridi following a pace behind, hand on sword hilt. William heard their scabbards clash against the side of the narrow stairway to the roof and thought with a mixture of admiration, affection and despair: 'He's magnificent. But we aren't in a position to refuse them, even if it does mean giving in to blackmail. Can't he see that? That fellow in Simla was right about him—he's going up there to do just the same sort of thing that French Guards' officer did at Fontenoy . . . and the Light Brigade at Balaclava . . . "C'est magnifique, mais ce n'est pas la guerre!" It's suicide—'

Unlike the barracks, there was no parapet surrounding the flat roofs of the two Residency houses, though both were screened from the view of the maze of buildings directly behind them by a man-high wall. The other three sides had a rim of brick no more than a few inches high, and Sir Louis walked to the edge, where all below could see him, and held up a commanding hand for silence.

He did not attempt to make himself heard above the din but stood waiting, erect and scornful: a tall, black-bearded, imposing figure in the trappings of his official uniform, with the gilt spike on his helmet adding inches to his height. Medals glittered on his coat and the broad gilt stripe that adorned each trouser-leg shone bright in the early sunlight of that brilliant morning, but the cold eyes under the brim of the white pith helmet were hard and unwavering as they stared down contemptuously on the clamouring mob below.

The Envoy's appearance on the roof had been greeted with an ear-splitting yell that might well have made even the bravest man flinch and draw back, but for all the response it drew from Sir Louis it might have been a whisper. He stood there like a rock, waiting until it pleased the crowd to stop shouting, and as they gazed up at him, man after man fell silent, until at last he lowered that imperious hand —it had not even quivered—and demanded in stentorian tones what they had come for and what did they want with him?

Several hundred voices answered him, and once again he raised his hand and waited, and when they fell quiet, asked them to choose a spokesman: 'You—you with the scarred cheek'—his lean forefinger pointed unerringly at one of the ring-leaders—'stand forward and speak for your fellows. What is the meaning of this shameful *gurrh-burrh,* and why have you come battering at the doors of one who is the guest of your Amir and under His Highness's protection?'

'The Amir—*ppth!*' The man with the scar spat on the ground, and related how his regiment had been cheated at the pay parade, and that having failed to get any satisfaction from their own Government they had bethought them of Cavagnari-Sahib and come here seeking justice from him. They asked only that he would pay them the money that was their due. 'For we know that your Raj is rich and so it will mean little to you. But we here have starved for too long. All we ask for is what we are owed. No more and no less. Give us justice, Sahib!'

Despite the looting and the rowdy, hooligan behaviour of the re-bellious troops, it was plain from the speaker's tone that he and his fellows genuinely believed that the British Envoy had it in his power to right their wrongs and give them what their own authorities re-fused: their arrears of pay. But the expression on the strong, black-bearded face that looked down on them did not change, and the stern, carrying voice that spoke their own language with such admirable fluency remained inflexible:

'I am grieved for you,' said Sir Louis Cavagnari. 'But what you ask is impossible. I cannot interfere between you and your ruler, or meddle in a matter that is the sole concern of the Amir and his army. I have no power to do so, and it would not become me to attempt it. I am sorry.'

And he had stuck to that in the face of howls and shrieks of rage and a growing chorus of threats; repeating again, in pauses in the uproar, that this was a question that they must settle with the Amir or their Commander-in-Chief, and though he sympathized with them he could not interfere. Only when Amal Din, standing behind him, warned him through shut teeth that certain *shaitans* below were gathering stones did he turn and leave the roof. And then only because he realized that to wait any longer left him with the choice of becoming an easy target for the stone-throwers, or else allowing them to suppose that they had driven him to retreat from the roof and take cover below.

'Barbarians,' commented Sir Louis unemotionally, divesting himself of his uniform in the safety of his bedroom and replacing it with cooler and more comfortable garb. 'I think, William, that I had better send a message to the Amir. It is high time he sent some responsible person to control this rabble. I cannot imagine what Daud Shah is up to. No discipline, that is their trouble.'

He strode into his office next door, and was about to sit at his desk to write when a voice that did not come from the lane below, but from the roof of the barrack block on the opposite side where the twenty-four men of the Guides Infantry stood to their arms behind the parapet, bellowed across the narrow gap that fighting had broken out by the stables and that the mutineers had killed a syce and were attacking Sowar Mal Singh . . . That Mal Singh was down . . . That he was wounded . . .

The mob in front of the Residency heard and roared its approval, and while some broke away and began to run back towards the stables, others began to batter on the door leading into the Residency, where Wally, waiting with the Guides in the courtyard behind it, moved among his men, reiterating that no one must fire until ordered to do so, and urging restraint. When the flimsy wood began to splinter and the rusty iron hinges bent and cracked they rushed to put their shoulders to the door, pushing against the weight of the rioters outside; but it was a losing game. As the last hinge snapped the door fell in on them and the crowd burst into the courtyard, and simultaneously, from somewhere outside, a shot rang out.

65

The sharp, staccato sound sliced through the din, silencing it as swiftly and effectively as a slap across the face will silence a fit of hysterics; and Wally thought automatically, 'Jezail'—for a modern imported rifle does not make the same noise as the long-barrelled muzzle-loading jezail of India.

The silence lasted less than ten seconds. Then once again pandemonium exploded as the mob, momentarily halted by the sound of the shot, began to fight its way forward into the Residency courtyard, yelling 'Kill the *Kafirs!* Kill them!—Kill! Kill!' Yet still Wally would not give the order to fire.

Even had he done so it is doubtful if he would have been heard above that frenzied clamour. But suddenly, somewhere in the mêlée, a carbine cracked, and then another—and another . . . And all at once the attackers turned and fled, stumbling and trampling over the bodies of fallen men and the wreckage of the broken door, and shouting now for firearms—for muskets and rifles with which to slay the infidels. *'Topak rawakhlah. Pah makhe! Makhe!'** screamed the mutineers as they ran from the Residency and streamed back across the compound, some making for the Arsenal and the rest for their own cantonments outside the city limits.

Once again the brilliant morning was calm and still . . . and in that stillness the men of the British Mission, left alone, breathed deep and counted the dead. Nine mutineers and one of their own syces; and Sowar Mal Singh, who was still alive when they found him by the stables, but died as they carried him into the Residency—and whose sabre had accounted for three of the enemy dead, for he had gone to the assistance of the unarmed syce and defended him valiantly against impossible odds. Of the other six, four had been shot and two killed in hand-to-hand fighting, tulwar against sabre. And seven of the escort had been wounded. The Guides looked at each other and knew that this was not the end but only the beginning, and that it would not be long before the enemy returned. And that this time the Afghans would carry more than side-arms.

'Fifteen minutes,' thought Wally, 'if that. Fifteen minutes at most.' And aloud: 'Close the gates and give out the ammunition. Block the

* Go back and get your muskets. On! On!

ends of the lane—no, not with bales of straw, that will burn too easily. Use yakdans, feed bins, anything—take the bars from the stables. And we will need to cut loopholes in the parapets . . .'

They worked desperately. Officers, servants, syces; soldiers and civilians, toiling together literally for dear life; dragging up baggage-wagons and empty ammunition boxes, flour barrels, firewood, saddle-bags, tents and ground-sheets and anything else that could possibly be pressed into service to reinforce the entrance to the compound and barricade the lane. They piled bales of fodder to form a flimsy wall across the open ground behind the gutted stables, pierced loopholes in the walls of the Residency and the parapet surrounding the barrack roof, and pitched the bodies of the enemy dead into a go-down at the far end of the compound, laying their own two on *char-poys* in Amal Din's vacated quarter.

Cavagnari sent an urgent message to the Amir informing him that his troops had made an unprovoked attack upon the Residency, and claiming the protection he owed to his guests; and while awaiting his messenger's return from the palace, turned his hand to helping construct a makeshift parapet out of scratched-up earth, furniture and carpets on the roofs of the two Residency houses. But his messenger did not return.

The man had arrived at the palace only to be put in a side room and told to wait, and an answer had been sent back instead by the hand of a palace servant. 'As God wills, I am making preparations,' wrote His Highness the Amir Yakoub Khan. But he sent no guards, not even a handful of his loyal Kazilbashis.

Others were also making preparations.

Aided by his lone hospital assistant and a motley group of bearers, *khidmatgars,* cooks and *masalchis* (scullions), Ambrose Kelly was preparing rooms on the lower floor of the Mess House to accommodate casualties and provide an operating theatre, while William Jenkyns and half-a-dozen sepoys raced to and fro removing the contents of the ammunition tent—which, together with a second tent containing an assortment of baggage, had been pitched for greater safety in the Residency courtyard. This they divided between the barracks and an ante-room on the ground floor of the Envoy's House, where it would be less vulnerable to rifle-fire from the roof-tops and windows of the many houses that overlooked both the Residency and the Mission's compound—from the nearest of which, though they did not know it, another officer of the Guides was even then looking down on them and watching them as they toiled.

Ash had recognized the futility of forcing his way into the compound in the wake of several hundred disgruntled and undisciplined soldiers, when it was too late to warn or advise. And when no shots greeted the invaders he realized that neither advice nor warning was needed. Wally must already have instructed the Guides not to fire and was in no danger of losing his head and precipitating a battle by reacting too strongly. The boy clearly had his men well in hand, and with a modicum of luck the situation would not get out of control before Cavagnari was able to speak to the Afghan soldiery.

Once let the Envoy talk to them, and their fears would subside. He had only to promise them that he himself would see to it that their grievances were righted and that they would receive the pay they were owed—if not from the Amir then from the British Government—and because to the tribes his name was one to conjure with, they would believe him. They would accept Cavagnari-Sahib's word where they would have accepted no one else's and everything might yet be well.

Ash had turned and gone back to his office in the Munshi's house, and looking down from his window, had witnessed the looting of the stables, the theft of the horses from the cavalry pickets and the subsequent rush to the Residency. He had seen, too, the tall, frock-coated figure in the white helmet come out upon the roof of the Envoy's house and walk calmly to the edge to quell the vociferous crowd below, and had thought, like William, 'By God, he's a wonder.'

He had never had any great liking for Louis Cavagnari, and had come to detest his policy. But seeing him now he was filled with admiration for the coolness and courage of a man who could walk out, unarmed and alone except for a solitary Afghan orderly, and stand calmly looking down on that threatening, stone-throwing mob without showing the least sign of alarm.

'I'm damned if I could have done that,' thought Ash. 'Wally is right: he's a great man and he'll get them all out of this jam. He'll pull them through . . . it's going to be all right. It's going to be all right . . .'

The acoustics of that part of the Bala Hissar were peculiar (a fact not fully realized by the dwellers in the Residency compound, though Ash had once warned Wally about it), the reason for this being that the site of the compound made it a natural theatre, in the manner of ancient Greece where the stone seats swept upward in a semi-circle of steeply rising tiers from the stage below, to form a sounding-board that enabled even those in the topmost tiers to hear every word spoken by the actors.

Here, in place of seats there were the solid walls of houses built on rising ground, and therefore producing much the same effect. And though it would be an exaggeration to say that every word spoken in the compound could be heard by the occupants of those houses, shouted orders, raised voices, laughter and snatches of conversation were clearly audible to anyone in the nearer buildings who cared to stand at a window, as Ash was doing, and listen. Particularly when the breeze was blowing from the south, as it was today.

Ash caught every word that the spokesman for the mutineers shouted up to Sir Louis, and every syllable of Sir Louis' reply. And for a full half minute he could not believe that he had heard aright. There must be some mistake . . . he must have heard wrong. Cavagnari could not possibly . . .

But there was no mistaking the full-throated howl of rage that burst from the mob when the Envoy ceased speaking. Or the cries of 'Kill the Kafirs!' 'Kill! Kill!' that succeeded it. His ears had not deceived him. Cavagnari had gone mad and now there was no knowing what the mob would do.

He saw the Envoy turn and leave the roof, but his view of the Residency courtyard was restricted by the west wall of the three-storeyed Mess House in which Wally, Jenkyns and Kelly had their quarters, and he could only see the further half by the Envoy's House, and the turbaned heads of the escort who waited there; indistinguishable at that range from the servants, as they were still in undress, having not yet changed into uniform when the compound was invaded. But he could pick out Wally easily enough, for he was hatless.

Ash saw him moving among the Guides and realized from his gestures that he was urging them to remain calm and not on any account to fire. Then suddenly his attention was drawn from the courtyard to the stables by frantic shouts from the sepoys who were stationed on the roof of the barracks . . .

The sepoys were yelling and pointing, and looking in the direction of the outflung arms Ash saw a single man—presumably a sowar, for he was wielding a cavalry sabre—standing astride the huddled body of a syce and surrounded by a ring of Afghans who were attacking him from every side, slashing at him with knives and tulwars and leaping back as he whirled his sabre about him, fighting like a cornered leopard. He had already brought down two of his assailants and wounded others, but he himself had taken terrible punishment: his clothing was ripped in a dozen places and stained with his own blood, and it was only a question of time before he tired sufficiently to allow his attackers to close in. The end came when three men engaged him simultaneously, and as he fought them off, a fourth leapt at him from behind and drove a knife into his back. As he fell the pack closed in, stabbing and hacking, and a yell of rage went up from the watching sepoys on the barrack roof.

Ash saw one of them turn from the parapet and run back along the roof of the Mohammedan quarters to cup his hands about his mouth and bellow the news to the Residency, and heard the mob in the lane below howl their approval as they rushed to attack the door into the Residency courtyard, flinging themselves against it again and again, like a human battering-ram.

He did not see who had fired that first shot, though he too realized that it had been fired from an old-fashioned muzzle-loader and not a rifle, and presumed that one of the men from the Arsenal must have carried a jezail as well as a tulwar, and discharged it to discourage any camp-followers from coming to the rescue of the wounded Sikh. But the momentary silence that followed that shot made the concerted yell that ended it ten times more shocking, and the murderous cries of 'Kill! Kill!' told him that any chance there may have been of persuading the mob to leave by peaceful means had been lost.

The pendulum had swung over to violence, and should the mutineers succeed in breaking into the Residency they would loot it as thoroughly as they had looted the stables: only this time there would be no jostling and horseplay. The time for that had gone. The swords and knives were out, and now the Afghans would kill.

The din outside was so great that it was surprising that Ash should have heard the door of his little office creak open. But he had lived too long with danger to be unmindful of small sounds, and he whirled round—to see ex-Risaldar-Major Nakshband Khan, of all people, standing in the doorway.

The Sirdar had never, to his knowledge, visited the Munshi's house before, yet it was not the unexpectedness of his arrival that startled Ash, but the fact that his clothing was torn and dusty and that he was shoeless and breathing heavily, as though he had been running.

'What is it?' demanded Ash sharply. 'What are you doing here?'

The Sirdar came in and closed the door behind him, and leaning against it, said jerkily: 'I heard that the Ardal Regiment had mutinied and attacked General Daud Shah, and that they were besieging the palace in the hope of getting money from the Amir. But knowing that the Amir has none to give, I ran quickly to warn Cavagnari-Sahib and the young Sahib who commands the Guides to beware of the Ardalis, and to let none of them enter the compound today. But I was too late . . . And when I followed these mutinous dogs and tried to reason with them, they set upon me, calling me traitor, spy and *feringhi*-lover. I was hard put to it to escape them, but having done so I came here to warn you not to leave this room until this *gurrh-burrh* is over, since too many here will know that you dwell as a guest under my roof—and half Kabul knows that I am a pensioner of the Guides, who are now being attacked down there; for which reason I do not dare return to my own house while this trouble lasts. I could be torn to pieces in the streets, so I mean to take refuge with a friend of mine who lives here in the Bala Hissar, close by, and return later when it is safe to do so—which may not be until after dark. Stay you here also until then, and do not venture out until— *Allah! What is that?'*

It was the crack of a carbine, and he ran to join Ash at the window.

The two stood side by side, glaring down at the turmoil below where the Guides in the Residency courtyard, driven back by the sheer weight of numbers, were giving ground before the tulwars and knives of the yelling mob, fighting them off with drawn sabres. But it was clear that the shot had taken effect in more ways than one.

Apart from the fact that fired into the scrimmage it had almost certainly killed or wounded several of the invaders, the impact of the sound in that enclosed space was a sharp reminder that tulwars were useless against bullets. The lesson was driven home by the three shots that followed, and the courtyard cleared like magic; but Ash and the Sirdar, watching the mutineers break and run, knew that they were not seeing a rabble in retreat, but men racing to fetch muskets and rifles—and that it would not be long before they were back.

'May Allah have mercy on them,' whispered the Sirdar. 'This is the end . . .' And then sharply: 'Where are you going?'

'To the palace,' said Ash curtly. 'The Amir must be told—'

The Sirdar caught his arm and jerked him back. 'True. But you are not the man to do it. Not now. You would be set on even as I was—and you they would kill. Besides, Cavagnari-Sahib will send a message at once, if he has not done so already. There is nothing you can do.'

'I can go down there and fight with them. They will obey my orders because they know me. They are my own men—it is my own Corps, and if the Amir does not send help they will have no chance. They will die like rats in a trap—'

'And you with them!' snapped Nakshband Khan, grappling with him.

'Better that than stay here and watch them die. Take your hands off me, Sirdar-Sahib. Let me go.'

'And what of your wife?' demanded the Sirdar furiously. 'Have you no thought for her? Or of what will become of her if you die?'

'*Juli*—' thought Ash in horror; and was suddenly still.

He had actually forgotten about her. Unbelievably, in all the turmoil and panic of the last half hour, he had not spared a single thought for her. His mind had been wholly taken up with Wally and the Guides and the terrible danger that menaced them, and he had had no time to think of anyone else. Not even of Anjuli . . .

'She has no kin here, and this is not her own country,' said the Sirdar sternly, relieved at having hit upon an argument that appeared to weigh with Ash. 'But if you die and your wife, being widowed, wishes to return to her own people, she might find it hard to do so: and harder still to remain here among strangers. Have you made arrangements for her future? Have you thought—?'

Ash pulled the restraining hand from his arm and turning away from the door said harshly: 'No, I have thought too much and too long of my friends and my Regiment, and not enough of her. But I am a soldier, Sirdar-Sahib. And she is the wife of a soldier—and the granddaughter of another. She would not have me put my love for her above my duty to my Regiment. Of that I am sure, for her father was a Rajput. If—if I should not return, tell her that I said so . . . and that you and Gul Baz and the Guides will look after her and see that she comes to no harm.'

'I will do so,' said the Sirdar—and as he spoke reached stealthily for the door, and before Ash had time to turn, snatched it open, whisked through and slammed it shut behind him. The heavy iron key had been on the outside, and even as Ash swung round and leapt forward he heard it turn in the lock.

He was caught and he knew it. The door was far too stout to be broken down and the window-bars were of iron and would not bend. Nevertheless he tugged frantically at the heavy latch and shouted to Nakshband Khan to let him out. But the only answer was the rasp of metal as the key was withdrawn, and then the Sirdar's voice speaking softly through the empty keyhole: 'It is better this way, Sahib. I go now to Wali Mohammed's house, where I shall be safe. It is only a stone's throw from here, so I shall reach it long before those *shaitans* return; and when all is quiet again I will come back and release you.'

'And what of the Guides?' demanded Ash furiously. 'How many of them do you think will be alive by then?'

'That is in God's hands,' replied the Sirdar, his voice almost inaudible, '—and there is neither hem nor border nor fringe to the mercy of Allah.'

Ash abandoned his assault on the door and fell to pleading, but there was no answer, and presently he realized that Nakshband Khan had gone—taking the key with him.

The room was a narrow oblong with the door at one end, the window at the other, and the entire building, like those on either side of it, was very different from the flimsy Residency houses, for it was of a much earlier date and had once been part of the inner defences. Its outer walls were solidly constructed, and the small square windowframes were of stone in which the bars had been set before the frames were built into the house front. Had Ash possessed a file it might have been possible for him, after hours of labour, to remove two of these (one would not have been enough), but the office equipment did not include that kind of file, and an examination of the lock showed him that nothing short of a considerable charge of gunpowder could blow it in, for it was of a pattern only seen in Europe in a few medieval dungeons; the bolt being formed from a thick rod of iron that when the key was turned, slid home into a deep iron socket embedded in the stone door frame. There was no point in attempting to use his pistol on the thing; the lock was far too strong and too simple for that, and the most that a bullet could do was to damage it so that when Nakshband Khan returned with the key he would be unable to open the door . . .

There was no longer any question of attempting to fetch help from the palace or to join Wally and the Guides in defending the Residency, or of getting back to Juli and the house in the city either. He was as securely trapped as the members of the British Mission to Afghanistan who were making frantic efforts to prepare for the attack that they knew must come at any moment; an attack that they would have to fend off alone unless the Amir sent troops to prevent the return of the mutineers, and closed the gates of the Bala Hissar to the Heratis and others who had made for their cantonments to fetch their rifles.

But the Amir had done nothing.

Yakoub Khan was a weakling, possessing none of the fire and steel of his grandfather the great Dost Mohammed, and few if any of the good qualities (and they were many) of his unfortunate father the late Shere Ali, who might have made an excellent ruler if he had been left to himself instead of being hounded unmercifully by an ambitious Viceroy. Yakoub Khan had ample military resources at his disposal: his Arsenal was crammed with rifles, ammunition and kegs of gunpowder, and quite apart from the mutinous regiments he had close on two thousand loyal troops in the Bala Hissar: the Kazilbashis and the Artillery, and the guard on the Treasury. These, had he given the order, would have closed the citadel against the troops from the cantonments and moved against the men of the Ardal Regiment, who were breaking into the Arsenal to seize rifles and ammunition for themselves, and passing out firearms to the riff-raff from the bazaar and any infidel-hater who would join them.

A mere hundred or so Kazilbashis, or two guns and their crews, sent posthaste to bar the way to the Mission's compound, could have halted the mob and almost certainly have dissuaded them from attacking. But Yakoub Khan was far more concerned for his own safety than that of the guests whom he had sworn to protect, and he would only weep and wring his hands, and bewail his fate.

'My Kismet is bad,' wept the Amir to the mullahs and syeds of Kabul, who had hurried to the palace to urge him to take immediate steps to save his guests.

'Your tears will not help them,' retorted the head Mullah sternly. 'You must send soldiers to guard the approaches to their compound and turn back the mutineers. If you do not, they will all be murdered.'

'That will not be *my* fault . . . I never wished it. As God is my witness, it will not be my fault, because I can do nothing—nothing.'

'You can close the gates,' said the head Mullah.

'Of what use, when there are so many of these evil men already within the citadel?'

'Then give orders for these guns here to be moved where they can fire on the troops when they return from their cantonments, and thus prevent them re-entering.'

'How can I do that, when I know that if I did so, the whole city would rise against me and the *budmarshes* would force their way in and eat us all up? No, no, there is nothing I can do . . . I tell you, my Kismet is bad. I cannot fight against my fate.'

'Then it is better that you should die rather than disgrace Islam,' said the Mullah harshly.

But the weeping Amir was lost to all shame, and no argument or pleading—no appeals to him for the sake of honour and in the name of hospitality to protect those who were his guests—could galvanize him into taking any action whatsoever. The wild rioting, and the attack on Daud Shah that had resulted from the pay parade, had so terrified him that he did not dare give any order for fear that it would not be obeyed. For if it were not . . . ? No, no, better anything than that. Oblivious of the scornful eyes of the mullahs, ministers and nobles who stood watching him, he tore his hair and rent his clothes, and bursting into renewed tears, turned from them to stumble away and shut himself up in his private rooms in the palace.

Yet weakling or no, he was still the Amir, and therefore, in name at least, head of the Government and lord and ruler of all Afghanistan. No one else dared give the orders that he himself would not give, and avoiding each others' eyes they followed him into the palace. When the British Envoy's messenger arrived with a letter asking for help and claiming his protection, a senior minister took it in to him, and the reply that was sent back consisted of that single procrastinating sentence: *As God wills, I am making preparations,* which was not even true—unless, of course, he was referring to preparations for the saving of his own skin.

Sir Louis had stared in stunned incredulity at this puerile answer to his urgent appeal for help. ' "Making preparations . . ." Good God! is *that* all he can say?' breathed Sir Louis.

His hand clenched on the scrap of paper, crumpling it up, and lifting his head he gazed blindly out at the far snows, realizing in that moment that the man of whom he had written only a day or two ago 'I personally believe he will prove a very good ally' was weak, worthless and a coward, a broken reed who should never have been trusted or relied upon; seeing at last and very clearly the futility of his Mission and the deadly nature of the trap into which he had led his entourage so proudly. 'Her Britannic Majesty's Mission to the Court of Kabul' had lasted exactly six weeks—that was all; only forty-two days . . .

It had all seemed so feasible once—those brave schemes for establishing a British presence in Afghanistan as a first step towards planting the Union Jack on the far side of the Hindu Kush. But now, suddenly, he was not so sure that that strange fellow Pelham-Martyn —'Akbar', who had been a friend of poor Wigram Battye's—had been so wrong-headed after all when he had argued so vehemently against the Forward Policy, insisting that the Afghans were a fiercely proud and courageous people who would never accept government by any foreign nation for more than a limited time, a year or two at most— and had quoted precedence to prove it.

'But we shall be avenged,' thought Sir Louis grimly. 'Lytton will send an army to occupy Kabul and depose the Amir. But how long will they be able to stay here? . . . and how many lives will be lost before . . . before they have to retreat again? I must write again to the Amir. I must make him see that it is as much in his interests as ours to save us, because if we go down he will go down with us. I must write at once—'

But there was no time. The mutineers who had broken into the Arsenal were racing back armed with rifles, muskets and cartridge-belts, the majority heading for the compound, firing as they ran, while others took up positions on the rooftops of the surrounding houses, from where they would be able to fire directly down on to the beleaguered garrison. And as the first musket ball whipped across the compound, Sir Louis sloughed off the politician and the diplomat and became a soldier again. Flinging away the useless scrap of crumpled paper that bore a coward's reply to his appeal for help, he snatched up a rifle and made for the top of the Mess House where he had lately been helping to erect a make-shift parapet, and lying flat on the sun-baked roof took careful aim at a group of men who had begun to fire at the Residency.

The roof of the Mess House was the highest point in the Mission compound, and from it he had a clear view of the great Arsenal that looked down on the compound from the rising ground beyond the cavalry lines. The range was barely two hundred yards; and there was a man standing in the doorway handing out muskets . . .

Sir Louis fired and saw him throw up his hands and fall, and re-loading swiftly, fired again: taking deliberate aim and paying no attention to the hail of bullets that pattered about him as men on the surrounding house-tops began to fire in reply at the roof of the barracks and the Residency. Below him several women of the town, who had been hiding in the servants' quarters where they had no business to be, ran screeching like pea-hens across the compound, herded by a sepoy and one of the *khidmatgars* to the *hammam,* the bath-house, that was built partly underground and where the majority of the servants had already taken refuge. But though Sir Louis heard them, he did not look down.

Had the compound been on higher ground it would have made an excellent defensive position, since it contained a series of courts, each separated from the next by low mud walls that could have been easily loopholed, and the defenders could have held off any number of attackers, inflicting enormous casualties for as long as their ammunition lasted. But its position was precisely that of the arena of a bull-ring to which Wally had compared it on the day of the Mission's arrival, so that the walls that would have provided cover against a frontal attack were useless against an enemy that was able to fire down from above: and by now, on house-tops ahead and along one entire side of the Residency and its compound—in high windows and on the battlements of the Arsenal and even on the roofs of many buildings in the upper Bala Hissar—men clustered thick as flies on a sweetmeat stall, firing as fast as they could load and yelling in triumph whenever a shot told.

Yet for all the notice he took of them, Sir Louis Cavagnari might have been lying peacefully on a rifle-range, engaged in target-practice and intent on marking up a high score. He fired and re-loaded swiftly, calmly, methodically, aiming at the men who swarmed down from the Arsenal, and selecting those in the forefront so that the ones who pressed behind tripped over the bodies as they fell.

He was a superb marksman, and his first nine shots had accounted for nine of the enemy when a spent bullet, ricocheting off the low brick rim of the roof a few inches from his head, struck him on the forehead. His head dropped and his long body jerked once and lay still, while the rifle slid from his nerveless hands and toppled into the lane below.

An exultant yell burst from the enemy on the nearer house-tops, and Ash, who had been watching from the window of his room, drew a harsh breath between his teeth and thought: 'Oh God, they've got him'—and in the next moment, 'No they haven't!' For the wounded man began to raise himself slowly and painfully, first to his knees and then with an enormous effort to his feet.

Blood was pouring down from the gash in his forehead, blotting out one side of his face and staining his shoulder scarlet, and as he stood there, swaying, a score of muskets cracked and as many puffs of dust exploded all around him from the mud-plastered surface of the roof. But it was as though he bore a charmed life, because not one struck him, and after a moment or two he turned and walked unsteadily to the stairs that led down from the roof and groped his way down and out of sight.

The Mess House was full of servants who had run in from their quarters to take refuge in the Residency, and of Guides who were firing steadily through loopholes cut in the walls and through the wooden shutters, and who did not look round when the wounded Envoy reached the turn of the stairs. Walking unaided into the nearest bedroom, which happened to be Wally's, he told a trembling *masalchi,* whom he found hiding there, to go and fetch the Doctor-Sahib immediately. The youth fled, and a few minutes later Rosie arrived at the double, expecting, from the *masalchi*'s description, to find his Chief dying or dead.

'Only a scratch,' said Sir Louis impatiently. 'But it's made my head swim like the very devil. Tie it up like a good fellow and send one of those idiots for William. We've got to get another letter through to the Amir. He's our only hope, and— Oh, there you are, William. No, I'm all right. It's only a flesh wound. Get a pen and paper and write while Kelly patches me up—hurry. Are you ready?'

He began to dictate while William, having snatched pen and paper off the desk in the next room, wrote rapidly, and Rosie cleaned him up and bandaged his head, and stripping off the stained shirt replaced it with one of Wally's.

'Who are we going to get to take it, sir?' asked William, hastily sealing the folded sheet of paper with a wafer. 'It isn't going to be easy to send anyone out, now that we're surrounded.'

'Ghulam Nabi will take it,' said Sir Louis. 'Send him up here and I'll talk to him. We shall have to smuggle him out by the back door of the courtyard and pray to God that there is no one out there as yet.'

Ghulam Nabi was a native of Kabul and an ex-Guide whose

brother was at that time Wordi-Major of the Guides Cavalry in Mardan. He had taken service with the British Mission on their arrival as a chupprassi, and he agreed at once to take Cavagnari-Sahib's letter to the palace. William had accompanied him down to the courtyard and stood by with a revolver while the bolts were withdrawn from a small, unobtrusive and seldom-used door in the back wall of the courtyard, near the tent that housed the baggage.

The wall itself was no thicker than a single mud brick, and behind it lay a narrow street that was part of a network of alleyways and houses, the roofs of the latter already packed with excited spectators, many of whom had armed themselves with ancient jezails and opened fire on the Infidels in the spirit of Jehad. In consequence the street itself was almost deserted, and Ghulam Nabi had slipped through the little door, and crossing to the opposite side where any marksman immediately overhead would find him a difficult target, took to his heels and ran in the direction of the palace in the Upper Bala Hissar.

But even as he vanished round the corner into a connecting alleyway, shouts from behind him and a spatter of shots from above showed that he had been spotted. Feet raced in pursuit, and the door had barely been closed and bolted when fists beat upon it.

Within minutes a crowd had gathered on the far side and were pounding on it with staves and musket butts, and though it was stouter than the main door into the courtyard, there was no knowing how long it would stand up to that sort of treatment. 'We shall have to block it off,' panted William; and they had done so with everything they could lay their hands on—tables, yakdans, tin-lined boxes full of winter clothing, a sofa and an imported mahogany sideboard, while Ghulam Nabi, having shaken off his pursuers in the maze of alleyways, reached the palace in safety by way of the Shah Bagh, the King's Garden.

But though he had been permitted to deliver Sir Louis' letter, he had not been allowed to return with a reply. Instead, like the previous messenger, he had been ordered to wait in one of the small anterooms while the Amir considered what answer he would send. And there he had waited all day.

Out on the plain near Ben-i-Hissar, the grass-cutters and their escort heard the sound of firing, and Kote-Daffadar Fatteh Mohammed, realizing where it came from and well aware of the hatred with which the Herati regiments and the city regarded the foreigners in the Bala Hissar, was uneasily certain that it spelled danger for the British Mission. Hastily rounding up the scattered foragers, he placed all but two of them in the charge of the four Afghan troopers, with instructions to take them at once to the care of the Commander of an Afghan regiment of horse, one Ibrahim Khan who had previously served with the Bengal Cavalry and whose present command was stationed near Ben-i-Hissar. The remaining two, with sowars Akbar Shah and Narain Singh, would return with him to the citadel immediately.

Riding at full gallop it did not take the five men long to come within sight of the south wall of the city and the roofs of the Residency, and the instant they did so any hopes they may have cherished died; for the roof-tops they had been forbidden to appear on for fear of offending the sensibilities of their neighbours were now alive with men, and that sight told them everything. They knew then that it was their own compound that was under attack, and they spurred towards it hoping to force a passage through the Shah Shahie Gate. But they were too late—the rabble was before them.

Half the city had heard the firing and seen the mutinous regiments running to their cantonments to fetch arms, and the rabble, grasping the situation, had wasted no time. Snatching up any available weapon they had rushed to join the attack on the hated interlopers, and their vanguard were already on the road ahead—racing for the same gate and led by a fakir who waved a green banner and urged them forward with frenzied screams. On their heels came others, many others: the scum of that ancient city, swarming out of every foul-smelling hovel, lane and alleyway, spurred on by the hope of loot and the lust for slaughter, and hastening to be in at the kill.

The Kote-Daffadar reined in savagely, realizing that any attempt to reach the gate first or to cut a path through that murderous horde would be tantamount to committing suicide, and that to seek refuge in the city would be equally fatal. Their best chance—if not their only one—would be to make for the fort commanded by the Amir's father-in-law, Yayhiha Khan; and snapping out a curt order he wrenched his horse round and rode off at a tangent across the plain, his four companions following behind him. But with their goal in sight they were overtaken by the four Afghan troopers, who having placed the grass-cutters in the care of Ibrahim Khan, had followed them with the intention of killing the Sikh sowar, Narain Singh, in which laudable task (for are not the Faithful instructed to slay Unbelievers?) they appeared to think that his four Mussulman comrades would be only too pleased to join. Disillusionment came swiftly . . .

The two grass-cutters were unarmed except for sickles—which can be wicked weapons in a fight—but the three Guides carried cavalry carbines that can be whipped in an instant from the leather buckets that hang from the saddle and levelled with one hand. 'Come then, and take him,' invited the Kote-Daffadar, the barrel of his weapon aimed at point-blank range at the breast of the spokesman, his finger taut on the trigger.

The Afghans looked at the three carbines and the two knife-edged sickles, and drew back, cursing and scowling, but unwilling to face such daunting odds. They had expected that their fellow-Mussulmans would at least stand aside even if they would not assist in killing the Sikh, and with the odds four to one in their favour would have had no hesitation in attacking a single man armed with a carbine, since he could only fire once and they would have been on him before he could reload. But now they were four against five, and the chances were that if they attempted to rush that group of determined men only one of them would live to get within striking distance, and what chance would that one, armed with a tulwar, have against three sabres and two sickles?

With a final burst of profanity they turned and made for the citadel and the eager hordes that were hurrying to join in the attack upon the Residency, leaving the Kote-Daffadar and his companions to ride on to the fort, where luck had been with them; for a sizable proportion of the garrison were Kazilbashis, men of the Kote-Daffadar and Akbar Shah's own tribe, who had escorted all five to safety in the Murad Khana—their own walled quarter of the city.

Ash, watching from his window, had glimpsed the five tiny figures, dwarfed by distance and trailing a white cloud of dust as they rode back at a gallop from Ben-i-Hissar, and guessed who they were. But he did not know why they had turned aside until he saw the first of the riff-raff from the city come pouring in from beyond the stables to his right, because the window-bars were set too close to allow him to lean out, so he could not see the Arsenal—or the Kulla-Fi-Arangi either: that empty enclosure on which Wally had hoped to build forage-sheds and servants' quarters so that he could prevent it being used as a way of entering the compound or, in the event of hostilities, occupied by an enemy.

66

Wally had been speaking to the sepoys on the barrack roof when the city *budmarshes* arrived to join the insurgents, and he had seen a number of mutineers, encouraged by these reinforcements, begin to run forward under cover of the fire from the Arsenal towards the Kulla-Fi-Arangi, from where—if they were allowed to occupy it—they would soon be able to make two thirds of the compound untenable. They would have to be dislodged and there was only one way to do it.

Making for the steps that led down in the thickness of the outer wall he pelted down them, raced across the lane into the Residency courtyard, and up to the Envoy's office where he found Cavagnari and William: the Envoy, with his head bandaged, firing through a slit made by breaking out a slat of the shutter, while his orderly acted as loader, taking the empty rifle and handing him a loaded one as fast as he fired, as methodically as though they had been on a duck shoot.

William was kneeling at one of the windows that faced inwards across the courtyard and returning the fire of a group of men on the roof of a house overlooking the barracks, and the room itself was littered with spent shells and full of the reek of black powder.

'Sir,' said Wally breathlessly, 'they are trying to occupy that Kulla enclosure up on the left, and if they get a foothold there we're done. I believe we could drive them out if we made a charge, only we'll have to do it quickly. If William—'

But Cavagnari had tossed aside the rifle and was already half-way across the room. 'Come on, William.' He snatched up his sword and revolver and was down the stairs and shouting for Rosie, who was tending a wounded man. 'Come on, Kelly, leave that fellow. We've got to chase those bastards out. No, not a rifle, your revolver. And a sword, man—a sword.'

Wally, racing ahead of him, collected Jemadar Mehtab Singh and twenty-five men, and explaining the position briefly, watched the sowars stack their carbines and draw their sabres while the sepoys fixed bayonets and two men ran to open the doors in the archway at the far end of the barrack courtyard. 'Now we will show those sons of perdition how the Guides fight,' said Wally joyously. *'Argi, bhaian. Pah Makhe—*Guides *ki-jai!'**

Ash saw them stream across the lane and into the barracks, where the canvas awnings hid them from his view until they burst out through the archway and into the open, the four Englishmen, Wally leading, running ahead with the Guides racing behind them—the sepoys charging with the bayonet and the sowars with sabre and pistol.

They tore cheering across the bullet-swept compound, the sunlight flashing on their blades; and through all the din and tumult of shouting and rifle fire he could hear Wally singing at the top of his voice: '. . . "And hearts are brave again and arms are strong, Alleluia!— All-e-lu-ia!"'

'A day for singing hymns,' thought Ash, remembering. 'Oh God—a day for singing hymns . . .'

Two of the Guides fell before they reached the Cavalry lines, one of them pitching forward on his face as he ran, and recovering almost instantly, rolling aside to avoid being trodden on and limping painfully away to the shelter of the stables; the other checking, to sink slowly to his knees and topple sideways and lie still. The rest swerved to avoid his body and ran on out of Ash's range of view, and he heard the firing stop abruptly and realized that both the enemy and the sepoys on the barracks had been forced to hold their fire for fear of killing their own men.

He did not see the attacking party reach their objective. But Nakshband Khan had done so, for the waste ground of the Kulla-Fi-Arangi lay directly in view of the house where he had taken refuge, and the Sirdar, peering from an upper window of that house, saw them vault over the low mud wall that enclosed it, and charging up the slope, drive the enemy before them: 'The Afghans running like sheep before wolves,' said the Sirdar, describing it later.

But Ash had seen them come back, walking now, for they brought three wounded men with them, but moving swiftly and confidently like soldiers who have acquitted themselves well and won a victory, though all of them must have known that it could only be a temporary one.

The sowar who had been the first to fall had managed to drag himself back to the barracks with a broken leg, but the second man

* Forward, brothers. On—Victory to the Guides.

was dead, and two of his comrades stopped to retrieve his weapon and carry the body into a near-by godown before following the others into the barracks where Wally waited under the arch, his stained sabre in his hand, to see them all safely in before the doors were closed behind them and they returned to the Residency.

The firing that had ceased during the attack on the Kulla-Fi-Arangi broke out again with renewed fury as Kelly hurried back to the wounded, while Cavagnari reeled into the dining-room and called for a glass of water: and when it came remembered that, war or no war, the Mohammedans who had fought with him were keeping the Ramadan fast, and put it down untouched. Jenkyns, the civilian, who had no such scruples, drank thirstily, and wiping his mouth with the back of his hand said hoarsely: 'What were our losses, Wally?'

'One dead and four wounded—two of them not too badly. Paras Ram's leg is smashed, but he says that if the Doctor-Sahib will put a splint on it and prop him up at a window, he can still shoot.'

'That's the spirit,' approved William. 'We got off pretty lightly when you think of the damage we must have done. We must have killed at least a dozen, and wounded twice as many more when they were scrambling to get back through the entrance or over the far wall. It was like shooting at a row of haystacks. That ought to hold them for a time.'

'With luck, about fifteen minutes,' observed Wally.

'Fif—? But good Lord, can't you post a few of your sepoys there to hold it?'

'With around five hundred rifles and muskets able to draw a bead on them from three different directions, and not a shred of cover? Not a chance, I'm afraid.'

'Then for God's sake what are we going to do? We can't afford to let them get dug in there.'

'As soon as they try it we make another sortie and chase them out again. And when they come back, we do so again—and if necessary, again. It's our only hope, and who knows, if we make it expensive enough for them they may get tired of it before we do.'

Wally grinned at him and hurried away, and William said bitterly: 'You'd almost think he was enjoying it. Do you suppose he doesn't realize—?'

'He realizes all right,' said Cavagnari sombrely, 'probably better than any of us. England will lose a first-rate soldier in that boy. Listen to him now—he's cracking jokes with those men out there. Amal

Din tells me that the Guides would do anything that Hamilton-Sahib asked of them, because they know that he would never ask them to do anything that he would not do himself. A good boy and a born leader of men. It's a pity . . . Ah well, I'd better get back to my loophole.'

He dragged himself from the chair he had slumped into on his return, and stood clutching the back of it, and William said anxiously: 'Are you sure you are all right, sir? Oughtn't you to lie down?'

Cavagnari gave a crack of laughter. 'My dear boy! At a time like this? If a jawan with a smashed leg is prepared to sit at a window to take pot shots at the enemy provided someone props him up first, I can surely do the same when all I have suffered is a slight crease in my head.' He turned away, and followed by William went back up the stairs to take over the positions that had been occupied during their absence by two of the Escort who had been keeping up a steady fire on the mutineers around the Arsenal, and who now moved up to the roof to join a group of the Guides who were firing at the enemy-held house-tops to the north of the compound.

Another and larger group on the roof of the Mess House opposite had turned their attention to the buildings that lay immediately behind the Residency, and Wally, running up to see how they were getting on and to take stock of the situation, saw from that vantage point that his recent estimate of fifteen minutes had erred on the side of generosity. The mutineers were already creeping back again into the Kulla-Fi-Arangi, and there was nothing for it but to launch a second sortie and clear them out again.

Pelting back down the stairs he collected a fresh party of Guides, snatched Rosie away from setting Paras Ram's shattered leg—apologizing in the same breath to the wounded man and assuring him that he would not keep the Doctor-Sahib long—and turned and ran across the courtyard and up the Envoy's staircase to fetch William and Cavagnari. But the sight of the older man's face made him change his mind.

Wally had lost none of his old admiration for his Chief, but he was a soldier first and foremost, and he had no intention of jeopardizing his men unnecessarily. He needed William, but he refused point-blank to allow Cavagnari to accompany them: 'No, I'm sorry, sir, but any fool can see you ain't fit and I can't take the risk,' said Wally brutally. 'If you collapsed we'd only have to stop and pick you up, and that could mean throwing away the lives of several valuable men. Besides, it wouldn't do 'em any good to see you fall. Come on, William, we haven't got all day . . .'

Ash and Nakshband Khan, together with several hundred of the enemy, witnessed that second sortie, and seeing that only three of the four Sahibs took part in it, drew their own conclusions. The enemy, being convinced that one of the Sahibs had been slain, were greatly heartened, while Ash and the Sirdar (who had noted the bandage about Cavagnari's head and realized that he had been wounded) were correspondingly dismayed, because they knew that if he were to die it could have a serious effect on the spirits of the beleaguered garrison.

Once again the firing had of necessity slackened off, and once again the waste ground had been cleared. But this time at the cost of two lives and another four men wounded, two of them severely.

'We can't go on like this, Wally,' gasped Rosie, wiping the sweat out of his eyes as he directed the stretcher-bearers to carry the injured men into the rooms that he had set aside as hospital wards. 'Do you realize that as well as these we've already had over a dozen men killed and God knows how many wounded?'

'I know. But then we've accounted for at least ten of their men to every one of ours—if that's any comfort to you.'

'It's none at all—when I'm knowing that those divils out there outnumber us by twenty to one, and that as soon as the lot that left for their cantonments get back here, it'll be nearer fifty or a hundred to one . . . *Accha,* Rahman Baksh, *mai aunga* (all right, I'm coming)— Look, Wally, isn't it time we tried another letter to that scutt of an Amir? . . . *Accha, accha. Abbi arter* (I'm coming now).'

The doctor hurried away, and Wally handed his sabre to his bearer Pir Buksh, and taking the Havildar with him went over to the barracks to see how things were with the sepoys who were firing from the shelter of the parapets, and if anything could be done to improve the defences of that building against the mass attack that would surely come if the Amir failed to send help. There had still been no reply to the letter that had been taken out by the chuprrassi Ghulam Nabi, and now Sir Louis wrote another and sent it by the hand of one of the Mohammedan servants, who volunteered to see if he could not get through by way of the temporarily cleared Kulla-Fi-Arangi, and from there through the King's Garden.

'Keep to the south side of the barracks and seek what cover you can between there and the stables,' instructed Sir Louis. 'The jawans will distract the enemy with rapid fire until you reach the wall. God be with you.'

William sent an orderly to find Wally and tell him what was planned, and to ask for covering fire. And presently the messenger slipped away to the accompaniment of a barrage of shots, and having run the gauntlet of the open stretch of compound between the barracks and the near wall of the Kulla-Fi-Arangi, scrambled over it . . . to be seen no more.

Somewhere between that low mud wall and the palace, the fate that Allah is believed to tie about the neck of all His creatures may have lain in wait for him; or perhaps he had friends or relatives in Kabul or elsewhere in Afghanistan, and decided to take refuge with them in preference to carrying out an appallingly hazardous mission. All that is certain is that his message never reached the palace, and that he himself vanished as completely as though he had been no more than a grain of sand on the autumn wind.

In the barracks Wally and Havildar Hassan, assisted by half-a-dozen sepoys, several syces and some of the Residency servants, had been barricading the doorless stairways that led up in the thickness of the wall on either side of the archway to the long strips of roof that surrounded the canvas-covered central courtyard. This would leave them with only a single staircase—the one at the far end near the door that gave on the Residency lane—but at least, in the event of a mass attack from the front, the men on the roof would not have to worry about the enemy storming up from below when or if Wally's makeshift outer door went down.

Their position was already precarious enough without that, and Rosie had erred in imagining that Wally did not realize the extent of the casualties that the garrison had suffered. Wally not only knew, but had been mentally crossing them off one by one and re-arranging the disposition of his little force, carefully husbanding his resources and doing everything he could to avoid risking the life of a single man unnecessarily, or allowing their morale to sink. His own was still high, for the sight of a familiar blue and white jar had told him that Ash was somewhere around, and he felt confident that Ash would not be idle.

Ash could be relied on to see that the Amir was informed of the parlous plight of the British Mission, even if every minister and high official in the entire Afghan Government was bent on concealing it. He would manage it somehow, and help would come. It was only a question of holding out long enough and not allowing themselves to be overrun . . . 'Shabash, Hamzulla! Ab mazbut hai . . . That should fox the hosts of Midian,' said Wally. 'Now if we can—'

He stopped, listening to a new sound: a deep, slowly gathering roar that he had been aware of for the past few minutes as a distant background to the tumult raging beyond the north-western limits of the compound, but that now, unmistakably, was coming nearer. Not 'Dam-i-charya' this time, but 'Ya-charya'—the war-cry of the Suni sect of Moslems, rolling towards him with ever-increasing speed and growing louder, nearer and fiercer until even the solid barrack walls seemed to shake to the rhythmic thunder of that rabble-rousing battle cry—

'It is the troops from the cantonments,' said Wally. 'Bar the doors and get back into the Residency, all of you. Tell Jemadar Jiwand Singh to choose his men and be ready for another sortie. We may have to clear them out of that waste ground again.' He turned and made for the stair at the far end of the barrack courtyard, and leaping up it ran forward along the roof above the Mohammedan quarters to the shorter strip of roof above the archway.

Looking over the loopholed parapet and the kneeling sepoys who were firing from behind it, he saw that the high ground by the Arsenal was a solid mass of frenzied humanity that was surging forward, thrust on by the pressure of thousands more behind, towards the flimsy barricades that separated the Mission's compound from the surrounding lanes and houses. The mutinous troops who had run back to their cantonments to fetch arms were back again in force, and not alone—they had brought others with them, the remaining Herati regiments who had been cantoned there, and thousands more budmarshes from the city. Even as he watched, they reached the barricades, and trampling them down, overran the cavalry lines and occupied the gutted stables.

In front of them, leading them, ran a wizened figure who waved a green banner and screamed to those behind him to kill the Infidels and show no mercy. Wally did not recognize him, but even at that range Ash did. It was the fakir whom he had seen earlier that day at the pay parade: Buzurg Shah, whom he had also seen on other occasions, calling for a Jehad in the more inflammable sections of the city.

'Destroy them! Root out the Unbelievers. Kill. Kill!' shrieked

Fakir Buzurg Shah. 'In the name of the Prophet smite and spare not! For the Faith. For the Faith. *Maro! Maro**—!'

'*Ya-charya! Ya-charya!*' yelled his supporters as they fanned out over the compound and began to fire at the heads of the sepoys behind the parapet on the barracks.

Wally saw one of his men fall backwards, shot between the eyes, and a second slump sideways with a bullet through his shoulder, and did not wait for more. It was no longer a question of clearing the waste ground, but of driving the mob out of the compound; and three minutes later Ash saw him lead a third sortie, racing out through the arch of the barracks with William at his side. But this time neither Kelly nor Cavagnari had been with them: Cavagnari because Wally still would not hear of his coming, and Rosie because by now his hands were too full with the care of the wounded to allow him to take part in another charge.

The fight had been a fiercer one than the two previous sorties into the waste ground, for though once more the marksmen on the roof-tops, both inside and outside the compound, were forced to hold their fire for fear of killing their own men, the odds against the garri-son had lengthened considerably. The Guides were now outnum-bered by fifty to one, and would have been outnumbered by even more if space had permitted, since the forces opposing them included a full three regiments of armed and mutinous soldiers as well as every disaffected, hostile or bloodthirsty citizen in Kabul. But their very numbers proved a handicap to the Afghans, for they not only hampered each other, but in the fury and stress of battle no man could be sure that he was not attacking one of his own side, as with the exception of Wally their opponents were not in uniform.

The Guides, on the other hand, knew each other too well to make any such mistake. Moreover, their sepoys carried rifles with fixed bayonets while the two Englishmen and both the Indian officers were armed with service revolvers as well as sabres; and in the murderous hand-to-hand fighting that followed, every revolver shot told, for knowing that there would be no chance to reload, the men of the Es-cort held their fire until the last possible moment. But the mob had not followed their example, and in the initial rush to reach the Mis-sion compound every Afghan had discharged his musket—many of

* strike; kill

them into the air—so that now they could only oppose steel to the rifle and revolver bullets of their adversaries.

The Guides had made the best possible use of that tactical error, and followed it up so fiercely with bayonet and sabre that the Afghans gave ground before the fury of their attack. Unable to flee because of the pressure of those at the back, who could not see and urged them forward, hampered by the bodies of the dead and wounded on whom they trod as the fight swayed to and fro, they turned at last and began to attack those behind them; and suddenly panic flared like a fire through dry grass and the mob were turning and clawing at each other in an attempt to escape. Retreat became a rout, and within seconds the compound was clear except for the dead and wounded.

Between them, the little band of Guides had fired exactly thirty-seven shots in the course of that brief engagement, of which no less than four—all heavy bullets fired from Lee-Enfield rifles at a distance of six yards—had smashed straight through the chest of an enemy soldier to kill a second behind him. The remainder had accounted for one man apiece, while a dozen more had been bayonetted and eight cut down by sabres.

The resulting carnage was not pleasant to look upon, for scores of men lay dead on the dusty, blood-spattered ground, while here and there a wounded one strove to drag himself to his knees and crawl like an injured animal towards the kindly shade and out of the glare of the sunlight.

The Guides had exacted a terrible toll and almost evened the odds. But they had paid a high price for that brief victory, one that with their dwindling numbers they could ill afford. Out of the twenty men who had taken part in that third sortie, only fourteen came back; and of these, half-a-dozen were barely able to walk, while none came through entirely unscathed, even though many wounds were no more than superficial.

The sepoys on the barrack roof had covered their return with rifle fire, and others of the Escort waited for them under the archway to bar the doors behind them before following them into the Residency. But this time the victors walked tiredly and there was no elation in their faces, only grimness. The grimness of men who know that the fruits of their hard-won fight cannot be retained, but will have to be fought for again and again—and with ever dwindling resources—or else abandoned to the enemy, which must spell disaster.

They had not been away very long, yet during that brief interval five of the men who had been posted on the roofs of the two Residency houses had been killed and another six wounded; for the makeshift parapets gave them little protection from the marksmen stationed on the higher rooftops of the near-by houses, and the skies seemed to be raining lead. They helped the wounded down to where the desperate Kelly and his solitary Hospital Assistant, Rahman Baksh, were working like men possessed—coatless, and splashed with blood from head to foot like butchers in an abattoir as they tirelessly swabbed, cut and stitched, bandaged, applied tourniquets and administered anaesthetics and opiates in the hopelessly overcrowded rooms where the wounded sat or lay or stood leaning against the walls, their powder-grimed faces drawn with weariness and pain, but making no complaint.

The dead had been treated more cavalierly; there was no time to spare for carrying away corpses, and they had been used instead to reinforce those inadequate parapets. For the Guides were realists. In a crisis such as this they saw no reason why their comrades should not continue to serve their Corps to the end; and the end did not look to be far off, because there were now less than ten men on the two roofs not counting the dead. And the enemy had no shortage of men or ammunition . . .

'Has there been an answer from the Amir yet, sir?' asked William, stripping off his stained coat as he limped into the office and found his Chief grey-faced from pain, but still firing methodically through the broken shutter.

'No. We must send again. Are you wounded?'

'Only a hack on the shin, sir. Nothing to worry about.' William sat down and began to tear his handkerchief into strips and knot them together. 'But I'm afraid we lost six men, and several of the others were badly mauled.'

'Is young Hamilton all right?' inquired Sir Louis sharply.

'Yes, bar a scratch or two. He's a bonnie fighter, yon laddie. He fought like ten men and sang the whole time. Hymns, of all things. The men seem to like it—I wonder if they've any idea what he's singing about? They probably think it's a war-song . . . which I suppose it is, when you come to think of it: "The Son of God goes forth to war" and all that—'

'Was that what he was singing?' asked Cavagnari, sighting carefully. He pulled the trigger and gave a grunt of satisfaction: 'Got him!'

'No,' said William, winding his home-made bandage about a shallow cut on his left hand. 'It was something about "charging for the God of Battle and putting the foe to rout"—' He used his teeth to help him pull the knot tight, and resuming his coat said: 'Do you want me to write another letter, sir?'

'Yes. Make it short. And tell that damned scoundrel that if he lets us die he's done for, as the Sirkar will send an army to take over his country and— No, better not say that. Just urge the fellow in the name of hospitality and honour to come to our assistance before we are all murdered. Tell him our case is desperate.'

William sat down to write again to the Amir, while Cavagnari sent a servant to inquire if there was anyone with a reasonable knowledge of the Bala Hissar who was prepared to run the risk of trying to take a letter to the palace—other than a soldier, who could not be spared. The risk was a grave one, for, with the back door barricaded, every rooftop within sight occupied by enemy sharpshooters, and the approaches to the compound held by the mob, the chances of anyone being able to win through were negligible. Yet William had barely finished writing when the servant returned with one of the office clerks, an elderly quiet-voiced Hindu with relatives in Kabul, who knew his way about the Bala Hissar, and possessing the Hindu indifference to death, had volunteered to make the attempt.

William went down with him to the courtyard while Wally sent a man over to the barracks and two more up to the roofs of the Residency, to tell the jawans there to do what they could to draw the fire of the enemy while the messenger made his attempt.

The Hindu had been helped over the barricade that blocked the southern end of the lane between the Residency and the barracks, and turning right, hurried forward, hugging the windowless back wall of the Mohammedan quarters, where he was temporarily protected from the enemy on the house-tops to the north. But once past the barrack block he had to run the gauntlet of the open ground; and already a number of the enemy had crept back into the compound to take cover in the cavalry lines and behind the low mud walls that enclosed the pickets. A score of these, led by the fakir, rushed out to intercept him before he could reach the Kulla-Fi-Arangi, while others cut off his retreat. And though he held up the letter, calling out to them that he was unarmed and bore a message to their Amir, they fell upon him with knives and tulwars, slashing, stabbing and literally hacking the defenceless man to pieces in full view of the garrison.

The brutal murder did not go unavenged, for the sepoys on the barrack roof leapt to their feet and fired volley after volley at the killers, and Wally, who had watched from the roof of the Mess House, sent Jemadar Jiwand Singh and twenty Guides to drive them out of the compound. It was the fourth sortie that the Guides had launched that morning, and once again they drove the Afghans back and took a terrible revenge for the mangled thing that still clutched in one severed hand a blood-soaked piece of paper that implored the help of the useless craven who sat upon the throne of Afghanistan.

Wally had seen many ugly sights during the past year, and thought himself immune from them. But the savage and barbaric dismembering of the unfortunate Hindu—who as an unarmed messenger carrying a letter to the ruler of Afghanistan should have been protected by his office—had turned his stomach, and he had run down from the roof with the intention of leading that charge himself. But on reaching the courtyard he had been greeted by the news that the enemy in the rear, having failed to break down the small door in the back wall of the Residency courtyard, were now sapping the wall itself and had already broken through in two places.

The threat was too grave to be ignored, so sending the Jemadar to lead the sortie instead, he turned to deal with this new threat. It had been bad enough to have to fend off attacks from their front and their right flank while being harassed by fire from the surrounding house-tops; but if the enemy were to break through from the rear and pour in troops at ground level, the garrison might find themselves forced to abandon the Residency, together with their wounded, and retreat to the barracks as the only position left to them. An untenable position at that, as the barracks would be impossible to hold once the Residency was lost, because the enemy would then be able to concentrate their fire on it from a range of a few yards; and once penned inside it there would be no way of seeing across the compound or gaining any idea of what the Afghans were doing.

The rear wall was only too easy to breach as it was woefully thin, and the men who filled the narrow street behind it were hacking at it in perfect safety, for they could not be fired on except from the roofs of the Residency houses—which entailed standing up on the curtain wall of the Envoy's House or the extreme edge of the Mess House, and aiming directly downwards: and since the first three jawans to attempt this were killed instantly by enemy marksmen crouching behind the parapets of rooftops on the opposite side of the street, it was not tried again.

The sappers below had been at work for some time before the danger was spotted, for the continuous crackle of firing, allied to the roar of a mob whose rage against the Infidel and inbred lust for fighting had been inflamed by the long fast of Ramadan, had masked the sounds of pick-axes from the men inside the Residency. The existence of this new and deadly threat had only been realized when a group of servants, crouching in a ground-floor room of the Envoy's House, saw a hole appear near the skirting. One of them had rushed upstairs to give the alarm, and implored the Envoy to leave his office and go over to the other house.

'*Huzoor,* if these *shaitans* break through below, you will be trapped. And then what shall become of us? You are our father and our mother, and if we lose you, we are lost—we are all lost!' yammered the terrified man, beating his head against the floor.

'*Be-wakufi!*' snapped Cavagnari angrily. 'Stand up, thou. Weeping will not save your lives, but work may do so. Come on, William—and you others too—they'll need help down there.'

He made for the stairs, followed by William and the two jawans who had been firing through loopholes in the shutters, the wailing servant bringing up the rear. But Wally, appraising his Chief's grey face and unfocused eyes and realizing that this time he could not refuse his help, managed to persuade him that he would be far better employed as a sniper on the top floor of the Mess House, firing through a loophole at the mob surrounding the Arsenal to discourage them from invading the compound again.

Cavagnari had not demurred. He was beginning to suffer from the effects of concussion, and he did not suspect that Lieutenant Hamilton's real reason for asking him to man that particular position was that the top floor of the Mess House seemed to Wally a far safer place than the crowded courtyard, and he meant to ensure that his wounded Chief ran no unnecessary risks.

As though to prove that his caution was justified, he had no sooner escorted Sir Louis from the courtyard than a musket ball was fired into it from close range and at knee level. The shot had wounded two men, and created considerable confusion among the remainder as it appeared to have come from inside the tent that had contained the ammunition; and it was only when a second and third shot followed that the garrison realized that the enemy's sappers must have broken through the wall behind the empty tent, and were firing at them blindly from the street behind the Residency. The courtyard cleared with magical swiftness, and William detailed Naik Mehr Dil and sepoys Hassan Gul and Udin Singh to block the hole, which could not be reached until the tent came down.

The three jawans had managed to dismantle it and push the heavy folds of canvas into the breach with the aid of tent poles, after which they had reinforced this inadequate barricade with a large tin-lined box containing their Commanding Officer's winter underwear and sheepskin poshteen, and a massive wood and leather screen from the dining-room. But in the process the Naik was shot in the arm, so as soon as the work was finished Hassan Gul took the wounded man into the Mess House to find the Doctor-Sahib, for Mehr Dil's arm hung useless, and blood was pouring from under the waist-cloth that he had tied above the wound as a tourniquet in the hope of checking the flow.

They found the ground-floor rooms full of dead, wounded and dying men, but there was no sign of the Doctor-Sahib, and his exhausted hospital assistant, Rahman Baksh, looking up briefly from tying a pad made from a towel over a hole in a sepoy's thigh, said that the Sahib had been called upstairs and that Hassan Gul had better take the Naik up there—there was no room down here for any more wounded.

The two jawans climbed the stairs in search of the doctor, and peering in through an open doorway saw him leaning over Sir Louis, who was lying on a bed with his knees drawn up and one hand to his head. The sight did not dismay them, since everyone knew that the 'Burra-Sahib' had been wounded in the head early on in the siege; and supposing him to be suffering from the after-effects of that wound (and being unwilling to call the doctor away from such an exalted patient) they turned back and went below again to wait until he should come down.

But Sir Louis had not collapsed from concussion. He had been hit again: this time in the stomach and by a bullet that had smashed through the wooden shutter into the room in which he had been standing, a bullet fired from one of the English-made rifles that a previous Viceroy, Lord Mayo, had presented to Yakoub Khan's father, Shere Ali, as a good-will gift from the British Government . . .

Sir Louis had managed to reach the bed, and the sowar who had been firing through a loophole to one side of the window had run down to fetch Surgeon-Major Kelly. But there was nothing that Rosie could do beyond giving him water to drink—for he was very thirsty—and something to deaden the pain. And hoping that the end would come quickly.

He could not even stay with him, for there were too many others who needed his help, some of whom could be patched up sufficiently to continue fighting. Nor was there any point in letting it be known that Cavagnari-Sahib was mortally wounded, since such news could only serve to take the heart out of everyone in the garrison, and the assault upon their spirits was already severe enough without that, the rabble in the street and on the house-tops immediately behind it having begun to call upon their fellow-Mussulmans to join them, exhorting them to slay the four Sahibs and help themselves to the treasure in the Residency . . .

'Kill the Unbelievers and join us!' urged the stentorian voices of unseen men who were sapping the flimsy, mud-brick wall. 'We have no quarrel with you. You are our brothers and we wish you no harm. Only give up the *Angrezis* to us and you will all go free. Join us—join us!'

'Thank God for young Wally,' thought Rosie, listening to that continual stream of exhortations. 'If it wasn't for him, some of our fellows might be tempted to do just that and save their own skins.' But Wally seemed to know just how to counter those shouted lures and keep up the spirits of the garrison, not only of his own jawans but of the countless non-combatants who had taken refuge in the Residency, both servants and clerical staff. He also appeared to have mastered the art of being in half-a-dozen places at once—one moment on the roof of one or other of the two houses, the next over at the barracks or in the courtyard, and the third in the rooms in which the wounded and dying lay—praising, encouraging, comforting; rallying the faint-hearted, cracking jokes, singing as he raced up the stairs to hearten the dwindling band of Guides who held out on the roof, or over to the barracks to encourage those who knelt firing at the insurgents from behind the inadequate shelter of the parapets.

Rosie looked down at the dying Envoy on the bed, and thought: 'When he is gone, the whole responsibility for the defence of this rat-trap is going to fall on young Wally's shoulders . . . it's there now.

Well, it couldn't be on better ones.' He turned and went out, shutting the door behind him and calling one of the servants to sit in front of it and allow no one in to the room, as the Burra-Sahib's head was paining him and he must be allowed to rest.

The room was an inner one and comparatively cool, but as Rosie left it the heat and stench outside met him like a blow, for by now the sun was overhead and there was little shade to be found in the enclosed courtyard . . . and none at all for the Guides on the roof-tops. The freshness of the early morning had vanished long ago, and now the hot air reeked of sulphur and black powder, while from the ground-floor rooms of both houses rose the sickening, all-pervading stench of spilt blood and iodoform—and other, uglier smells that Rosie knew would get worse as the day advanced.

'We shall be out of drugs soon,' he thought, 'and bandages and lint. And men . . .' He glanced back over his shoulder at the closed door behind him and lifting his hand in a half-unconscious gesture of salute, turned and went back down the stairs to the stifling heat and stench of the rooms below, where buzzing clouds of flies added to the torments of the uncomplaining wounded.

Many of the mutineers had already crept back to the compound to take cover again in the stables, and behind the numerous mud walls in which they were now hacking loopholes so that they could fire at the barracks and the Residency, but Wally no longer had enough men to attempt another sortie against them. Between the enemy in the compound and the ever-increasing numbers on the surrounding house-tops, his inadequate defences were subjected to such a blizzard of fire that it was a wonder to him that anyone in the garrison still survived. Yet survive they did, though their numbers were shrinking rapidly. The fact that the enemy had suffered even more severely gave him no consolation, knowing as he did that they had inexhaustible reserves to draw on, and that however many times the Guides drove them back and however many they killed, a hundred others would spring up like the dragon's teeth to replace them. But there was no replacement for the dead and wounded in the Residency. And still no word from the palace, or any sign of help . . .

He had been organizing counter-measures against the sappers on the far side of the courtyard wall, when a breathless sowar ran down the three flights of stairs from the Mess House roof and panted out that the mob in the street had fetched ladders and were thrusting them out laterally from the houses on the far side, to form bridges across which they were clambering like monkeys. Some had already reached the roof and what were the defenders to do? They could not hold out against the numbers that were getting across.

'Tell them to retreat down the stairs,' directed Wally urgently—'but slowly, so that the Afghans will follow.' The man fled back, and Wally sent a similar message to the Guides on the roof of the Envoy's House, and calling to Jemadar Mehtab Singh to follow him with every jawan who could be spared, ran for the roof.

The Guides had managed to thrust off the first two ladders and send them hurtling down on the heads of the crowd below. But there had been others—half-a-dozen at least—and though the first Afghans to reach the roof had fallen, shot at point blank range, it had been impossible to stem the tide of those who scrambled across behind them, and the survivors of the little band of Guides retreated to the stairwell and descended, a step at a time.

Wally met them on the top landing with reinforcements at his back, and though he held a loaded revolver he did not fire it, but waved them on downward, issuing terse instructions that were barely audible above the yells of the Afghans, who, seeing them in retreat, tore after them and came leaping down the stairs brandishing their tulwars and jostling each other in their haste. And still the Guides retreated, stumbling ahead of them in apparent disorder and looking back over their shoulders as they went . . .

'Now!' yelled Wally, leaping onto a cane stool that stood outside his bedroom door. '*Maro!*' And as the Guides turned in the narrow hallway and fell upon the leading Afghans, he fired over their heads at those who were crowding down behind them and who could not turn because of the pressure of others treading on their heels.

Even a poor shot would have found it difficult to miss his mark at that range, and Wally was anything but a poor shot. Within six seconds half-a-dozen Afghans on the steep flight of stairs dropped forward with a bullet in their brains, and as many fell headlong over the bodies and came cascading down like a flock of sheep at a bank, to be cut down by the sabres and bayonets of the Guides.

Ambrose Kelly had heard the noise of the fighting, and realizing that the enemy must have broken into the Mess House, he abandoned his scalpel in favour of a revolver and dashed upstairs—only to be swept backwards by a mass of struggling men who stabbed and hacked and wrestled with each other (there was little room for sword-play) or used their carbines and rifles as clubs, there being no time to reload or, for that matter, for anyone in Rosie's position to use a revolver. But Wally, standing head and shoulders above the scrum, caught sight of him, and realizing that he dare not risk a shot into the demented mêlée, took a flying leap from the stool, snatched the weapon from him, and regaining his vantage point, used it himself to excellent effect.

The fusillade of shots, the shambles on the stair and the uproar and confusion of the fight below made the rear ranks of the invaders suddenly aware that disaster had overtaken their leaders. They checked at the top of the stairs and some of them, losing their heads, fired wildly down at the murderous scrimmage below while others scrambled back and made no further attempt to invade the Residency from above. But of their comrades who had rushed so boldly down the steep stairway, not one came back.

'Come on, Rosie,' shouted Wally breathlessly, tossing back the empty revolver and hurriedly re-loading his own: 'they're bolting. Now's our chance to clear 'em off the roof.'

He turned to Hassan Gul, who leant against the wall of the landing panting from his exertions, and told him to call the others together and they would charge up the stairs and clear the roof. But the sepoy only shook his head and said hoarsely: 'We cannot do it, Sahib. There are too few of us . . . Jemadar Mehtab Singh is dead, and Havildar Karak Singh also . . . they were killed in the fighting on the stairs . . . And of those who were on the roof, only two remain. I do not know how many there may still be in the other house, but here there are only seven left . . .'

Seven. Only seven left to hold the three floors of that tall, mud and plaster rat-trap that was pock-marked with bullet holes and crammed with wounded men.

'Then we must block off the staircase,' said Wally.

'With what?' asked Rosie tiredly. 'We've already used almost everything we could lay our hands on to make barricades. Even the doors.'

'There's this one—' Wally turned towards it, but the doctor caught his arm and said sharply: 'No! Leave it, Wally. Let him be.'

'Who? Who is in there? Oh, you mean the Chief. He won't mind. He's only—' He stopped abruptly, staring at Rosie with a sudden horrified comprehension. 'Do you mean, it's serious? But—but it was only a head wound. It couldn't . . .'

'He was shot in the stomach not long ago. There wasn't anything I could do except give him as much opium as I could spare and let him die in peace.'

'*Peace,*' said Wally savagely. 'What sort of peace could he possibly die in, unless . . .'

He stopped and his face changed. Then, jerking his arm free, he turned the handle and went into the shadowed room where the only light came through the bullet-splintered slats of the shutters and the rough loopholes that had been hacked through those lath and plaster walls that still bore the scrawled names of the Russians who had been the last—and luckier—guests of an Amir of Afghanistan.

The closed door had kept out the heat that filled the courtyard and beat down upon the whole compound, but it could not keep out the flies that circled and settled in buzzing droves, or the sounds of battle. And here too there was the same choking smell of blood and black powder.

The man on the bed still lay in the same position and, incredibly, he was still alive. He did not move his head, but Rosie, following Wally into the room and shutting the door behind him, saw his eyes turn slowly towards them and thought, 'He won't know us. He's too far gone: and too drugged.'

The dying man's gaze was blank and it seemed that the movement of those clouded eyes was no more than a reflex action. Then of a sudden intelligence returned to them as with a gigantic effort of will, Louis Cavagnari forced his conscious mind to drag itself back from the darkness that was closing in on it, and summoning the last shred of his strength, spoke in a harsh croak:

'Hullo, Walter. Are we . . . ?'

His breath failed him, but Wally answered the unspoken question:

'Fine, sir. I came to tell you that the Amir has sent two Kazilbashi regiments to our assistance, and the mob are already on the run. I'm thinking it won't be any time now before the place is cleared of them, so you don't have to worry, sir. You can have a rest now, for we've got them licked.'

'Good boy,' said Sir Louis in a clear, strong voice. A trace of colour returned to his ash-white face and he tried to smile, but a sharp spasm of pain caught him unaware and turned it to a grimace. Once again he fought for breath, and Wally leaned down to catch the words he was struggling to say:

'The . . . Amir,' whispered Sir Louis: '. . . glad to know . . .

not wrong about him . . . after all. We shall be . . . all right now. Tell William . . . send thanks and . . . telegraph Viceroy. Tell . . . tell my—wife—'

The hunched figure jerked convulsively and was still.

After a moment or two Wally straightened up slowly and became aware once more of the maddening drone of flies and the ceaseless surf-life roar of the mob, which together formed a background for the sharp crackle of musketry and rifle fire and the thwack of bullets striking the walls outside.

'He was a great man,' said Rosie quietly.

'A wonderful one. That's why I—we couldn't let him die thinking that he . . .'

'No,' said Rosie. 'Be easy, Wally, the Lord will forgive you the lie.'

'Yes. But *he'll* know by now that it was a lie.'

'Where he is, that won't matter.'

'No, that's true. I wish—'

A musket ball smashed into one of the shutters and sent a shower of splinters across the floor, and Wally turned and walked quickly out of the room, not seeing where he was going because his eyes were full of tears.

Rosie paused for a moment to cover the quiet face, and following more slowly, found him already at work arranging to block the way to the roof with the only material available: the bodies and the broken weapons—tulwars, muskets and jezails—of the Afghans who had been killed on the stairs.

'We may as well make them useful,' said Wally grimly as he helped to pile the corpses one upon the other, wedging them into place with cross-bars made from the long-barrelled jezails, and constructing an effective *chevaux-de-frise* from the razor-sharp blades of tulwars and Afghan knives from which the hilts had first been removed. 'I don't suppose it will hold them up for long, but it's the best we can do; there isn't anything else. I must see William and find out how many of our fellows are over in the other house. Now *suno* (listen), Khairulla'—he turned to one of the sowars—'do you and one other remain here and prevent the enemy from removing those bodies. But do not expend more ammunition than you need. A shot or two should be enough.'

He left them and went down the stairs to run the gauntlet of the open courtyard and break the news to William that Sir Louis was dead.

'He was always lucky,' observed William quietly.

The Secretary's face, like Wally's—like all their faces—was a sweat-streaked mask of blood and dust and black powder. But his eyes were as quiet as his voice, and though he had been firing or fighting without intermission for hours now, he still looked what he was: a civilian and a man of peace. He said: 'How much longer do you suppose we can hold out, Wally? They keep tunnelling through like moles, you know. As fast as we block up one hole they make another. It's been fairly easy to deal with, because now we know what they're at, whenever we see a bit of plaster fall out we stand clear and then empty a shot-gun into the hole the minute it gets big enough. They don't fancy that. But it needs a lot of men to watch the whole length of the wall in the courtyard as well as inside both houses. I don't know how many you've got, but there are less than a dozen of your chaps left over here. And not so many more than that in the courtyard, I imagine.'

'Fourteen,' confirmed Wally briefly. 'I've just checked. Abdulla, my bugler, says he thinks there are still between fifteen and twenty over in the barracks, and with seven in the Mess House—'

'Seven!' gasped William. 'But I thought— What's happened?'

'Ladders. Didn't you notice? Those bastards behind us got hold of ladders and managed to get onto the roof and drive our fellows off it. They got into the house and gave us a bad few minutes, but we got rid of them. For the time being, anyway.'

'I didn't know,' said William numbly. 'But if they're on the roof that means we're surrounded.'

'I'm afraid so. What we've got to do now is to immobilize that gang on the Mess House, by stationing a couple of chaps with shotguns by the inner windows of the Chief's office to blaze off the moment any scutt up there shows the tip of his nose. They may have chased us off it, but it won't do them any good if they have to huddle on their stomachs in the furthest corner of it. You'd better stay down here and deal with the lot who are trying to dig through the wall, while I—' he stopped, and tilting his chin, sniffed the tainted air and said uneasily: 'Can you smell smoke?'

'Yes, it's coming from the street at the back. We've been getting a whiff of it through the holes those rats have been making. I imagine there must be a fire in one of their houses. Not surprising when you think of the number of archaic muzzle-loaders that are being loosed off in every direction.'

'As long as it stays on the other side of the wall,' said Wally, and was turning to leave when William stopped him.

'Look, Wally, I think we ought to try again to see if we can't get a message through to the Amir. He can't have got any of the others. I won't believe that if he knew how serious things were with us he wouldn't do something to help. We've got to find someone to take another letter.'

They had found someone, and this time the messenger had won through, posing as one of the enemy. Dressed in blood-stained garments, with an artistic bandage about his head, he had actually succeeded in delivering William's letter. But the confusion that he found at the palace was far worse than when Ghulam Nabi (who still waited anxiously in an ante-room) had brought that second letter from Sir Louis, hours ago. This latest messenger was also told to wait for a reply: but no reply was ever given him, for by now the Amir had become convinced that when the mobs from the city had dealt with the British Mission, they would turn on him for having permitted the Infidels to come to Kabul, and make him and his family pay for it with their lives:

'They will kill me,' wailed the Amir to the persistent mullahs, who had finally been granted another audience. 'They will kill us all.'

Once again the head Mullah had pleaded with him to save his guests and urged him to order his artillery to fire on the mob. And once again the Amir had refused, insisting hysterically that if he should do so the mob would instantly attack the palace and murder him.

At long last, shamed into action by their reproaches, he summoned his eight-year-old son, Yahya Khan, and setting the little boy on a horse, sent him out accompanied only by a handful of Sirdars and his tutor—the latter carrying a copy of the Koran held high above his head where all could see it—to implore that maddened mob, in the name of God and His Prophet, to sheathe their weapons and return to their homes.

But the mob that had howled so fervently for the blood of the Unbelievers was not to be turned from its savage sport by the mere sight of the Holy Book—or the scared face of a child, heir to Afghanistan or no. The trembling tutor was pulled from his saddle and the Koran wrenched from his hands to be flung on the ground and kicked and trampled upon, while the mob shrieked insults and threats at the hapless ambassadors, jostling and clawing at them until they turned tail and fled back to the palace in fear of their lives.

But there was still one Afghan who did not fear the mob.

The indomitable Commander-in-Chief, Daud Shah, wounded as he was, left his bed, and summoning a few of his faithful troopers, rode out to face the scum of the city with as much courage as he had faced the mutineers of the Ardal Regiment earlier that same day. But the mob cared as little for the authority of the army as it had for the sacred Book of its loudly proclaimed faith. Its interest was concentrated on killing and loot, and it turned on the valiant General like a pack of snarling pariah-dogs attacking a cat; and like a wild cat he fought back with teeth and claws.

For a brief space he and his troopers managed to hold them off, but the odds were too great. He was dragged from his horse, and once on the ground, the mob closed in, kicking and stoning him. Only the intervention of a handful of his soldiers, who had seen him ride out and who now charged to the rescue, laying about them with such fury that they drove the mob back, saved the battered man and his hopelessly outnumbered troopers from death. But they had had no option but to withdraw, and supporting their wounded Commander-in-Chief they limped back to safety.

'We can do no more,' said the watching mullahs, and recognizing at last the fruitlessness of human intervention, they left the palace and returned to their mosques to pray instead for Allah's.

67

It seemed to Ash, as he raged to and fro racking his brains for a way of escape, that he had been trapped in this small, stifling cell for a lifetime . . . Could time have moved so slowly for the Guides who had been fighting all through that hot, interminable morning and on into the afternoon without a moment's respite, or were they too hard pressed to take account of it, unaware of its passing because they knew that for them each breath they drew could be the last one, and knowing it lived only for the moment, and that by the grace of God?

There must be *some* way of getting out . . . there *must* be.

Hours ago he had considered the possibility of hacking his way out through the mud ceiling between the joists, until the thud of feet on the hard *mutti* roof overhead warned him that there were men up there, a great many of them judging by the clamour of voices and the vicious crackle of muskets—as many as there were on every house-top and at every window within his range of vision, not to mention those that he could not see.

After that he had turned his attention to the floor. It should be comparatively easy to break through it, since like all the floors in the building it consisted of pine-wood planks supported on heavy cross-beams and plastered over with a mixture of mud and straw; and had it not been only too evident that the room below was already occupied by the enemy, who were firing out of the window immediately under his own, the long Afghan knife he carried with him would have made short work of the dried mud, and enabled him to pry loose a plank so that he could wrench up one or more neighbouring ones. But where the window was concerned the knife was useless.

Ash had spent some time on the window, and had actually made a rope so that he would be able to lower himself from it, using knotted strips torn from the cotton sheeting that covered the platform on which a scribe sat cross-legged at work. But the bars had defeated him. And though the inner walls on either side of him were reasonably thin (in contrast to the one with the door in it) even if he were to break a hole through one or other it would not help him, because the room on his right was a windowless store room crammed to the roof with old files, while the one on the left contained the Munshi's library, and both were always kept locked.

Despite this knowledge, he had wasted a considerable amount of time and energy on burrowing through into the latter, in the hope that either the window-bars or the lock in the library might prove to be flimsier than his own. But when at last he managed to kick and hack and scrape a hole large enough to squeeze through, it was only to discover that the lock was of the same pattern, while the window (besides being as stoutly barred) was even smaller than the one in his own room.

Ash wriggled back again and resumed his vigil, watching and listening, hoping against hope, and praying for a miracle.

He had seen each of the four sorties, and though unlike the Sirdar he had not been able to see the first of the two charges that drove the mutineers out of the waste ground of the Kulla-Fi-Arangi, he had seen the whole of the third engagement. And it was while watching it that he had remembered belatedly that he not only carried a pistol, but had a service revolver and fifty rounds of ammunition hidden away in one of the numerous tin boxes that were stacked against the walls.

If he could not go down and fight with the Guides in the compound below, at least he could still do something to help them, and hastily removing the revolver from its hiding place, he levelled it from the window only to realize afresh why both sides had ceased firing. While the fight lasted and the protagonists were embroiled in a hand-to-hand struggle, no one could be certain whom a bullet or a musket ball might strike, and he too must hold his fire. Even when the enemy broke and ran, he resisted the temptation to speed them on their way because the range was too great to allow him to be certain of hitting his mark and his supply of ammunition was limited and too valuable to be wasted.

The twenty-three rounds he had subsequently expended during the course of that morning had certainly not been wasted, nor had there been any risk of the shots being traced to his window. There being too much lead flying round for anyone to be certain of such a thing. Five had accounted for as many enemy snipers, who had been firing from other and less closely barred windows lower down and further to the right and been incautious enough to lean well out in order to fire at the sepoys holding the barrack roof. A further fourteen had caused several deaths and considerable damage among the mob who had murdered the Hindu clerk, while the last four had disposed of four mutineers who during the sortie led by Jemadar Jiwand Singh had attempted, under cover of the fighting, to crawl towards the barracks in the lee of the low boundary wall that divided the Munshi's house from the British Mission's compound.

Koda Dad Khan would have approved his pupil's performance, for it had been good shooting. But as the range of a revolver is small, Ash's field of fire was very limited, and he knew that against the enormous numbers that the enemy were throwing against the Residency, any assistance that he could give was at best derisory.

The compound lay stretched out below him like a brightly lit stage seen from the royal box of a theatre, and had he been able to exchange the service revolver for a rifle, or even a shot-gun, he could have helped to reduce the fire that was being directed at the barracks and the Residency from every house-top within a radius of three or four hundred yards. But as it was he could do almost nothing. He could only watch in an agony of fear and frustration as the enemy bored loopholes in the compound wall that enabled them to fire at the garrison in complete security, while members of the mob that had been routed and driven from the compound by that last furious charge began to steal back again, at first by twos and threes, and then, getting bolder, by tens and twenties until at length several hundred had taken cover in the gutted stables and deserted servants' quarters, and behind the maze of crumbling walls.

It was, thought Ash, like watching a spring tide crawling in across mud flats on a windless day, creeping inexorably forward to drown the land; except that the rising of that human tide was not silent, but accompanied by shots and screams and yelling voices that together fused into a continuous roar of sound: a roar that rose and fell as monotonously as storm waves crashing on a pebble beach. *Ya-charya! Ya-charya!* Slay the Infidels. Kill! Kill!—*Maro! Maro!*

Yet gradually, as the day wore on and throats became hoarse from continual shouting and parched with dust and smoke and the choking fumes of black powder, the war cries and the yelling began to die down, and with the voice of the mob reduced to a menacing growl, the sharp crackle of fire-arms became magnified—as did the shrill exhortations of the Fakir Buzurg Shah, who continued to harangue his followers with unflagging zeal; calling upon the Faithful to smite and spare not, and reminding them that Paradise awaited all who died that day.

Ash would have given much to assist the Fakir to achieve this goal himself, and he waited hopefully for the man to come within range. But that fanatical rabble-rouser appeared to be in no hurry to enter Paradise, for he stood well back among the mob on the far side of the stables, safely out of sight of the Guides who manned the parapets of the barracks and the windows of the Residency—and far beyond the reach of Ash's revolver; though not, unfortunately, out of hearing. His high-pitched litany of Hate had the carrying quality of a hunting horn, and his repetitive shrieks of 'Kill! Kill! Kill!' rasped at Ash's taut nerves and almost drove him to close the heavy wooden shutters in order to escape from that sound.

He had actually been on the verge of doing so—despite the fact that it meant shutting out the daylight and his view of the compound —when another sound stopped him: one that he was first aware of only as a distant murmur, but that as he listened grew in volume until it was identifiable as cheering . . . The mob were acclaiming someone or something, and as the vociferous applause came steadily nearer and louder until it drowned both the ravings of the Fakir and the din of firing, Ash's heart leapt, for the thought flashed into his mind that the Amir had sent the Kazilbashi Regiments to the relief of the beleaguered British Mission after all.

But the hope was no sooner born than he saw the Fakir and the rabble surrounding him begin to leap and yell and throw up their arms in frenzied welcome, and knew that this was no relieving force that was being hailed, but some form of enemy reinforcements, probably a fresh contingent of mutinous troops from the cantonments, thought Ash.

He did not see the guns that were being man-handled by scores of men through the narrow approaches by the Arsenal until both were well clear of the surrounding buildings and almost level with the cavalry lines. But the Guides on the barrack roof had seen them as they were manoeuvred through a breach in the mud wall and into the compound, and while a sepoy ran to tell Hamilton-Sahib of this new danger, the rest turned their fire on the scores of Afghans who were dragging and pushing the two guns towards the barracks.

The sepoy's news had spread through the Residency with lightning swiftness. But it is one of the advantages of military life that in times of crisis the issues are apt to be clearly defined, and a soldier is often faced with a simple choice: fight or die. No one had needed to wait for orders, and by the time Wally and the men who had been with him on the upper floor of the Envoy's House reached the courtyard, William and every active sepoy and sowar in the Residency had already assembled there.

All that was necessary was to tell the jawan who had brought the news to warn his companions to concentrate their fire on the enemy beyond the perimeter, and to send two men ahead to unbar the far doors that closed off the archway from the barrack courtyard. But even as they ran across the lane, both guns fired almost simultaneously. The men staggered as the ground rocked to the deafening crash of the double explosion, but reeled on, coughing and choking, through an inferno of smoke and flying debris and the reek of saltpetre.

The echoes of that thunderous sound reverberated around the compound and beat against the furthest walls of the Bala Hissar, sending flocks of crows flapping and cawing above the roofs of the palace, and drawing a howl of triumph from the mob as they saw the shells explode against the corner of the barrack block. But unlike the two buildings in the Residency, the outer walls of the barracks were not lath and plaster but built of mud bricks to a thickness of more than six feet, while the two corners at the western end were further protected by the fact that each contained a stone stairway to the roof.

The shells had therefore done little damage to the men behind the parapets, who, though momentarily blinded by smoke and debris and deafened by the noise, obeyed their orders, and lifting their sights continued to fire at the enemy as Wally and William, with twenty-one Guides, emerged from the archway below them and raced towards the guns.

The fight was a brief one, for the mutineers who had dragged the guns into position and fired them were exhausted by their efforts, while the rabble from the city had no taste for facing trained soldiers at close quarters, and fled at the sight of them. After a fierce ten minutes the mutineers had followed their example, abandoning the guns and leaving behind them more than a score of dead and wounded.

The cost to the Guides had been two men killed and four wounded, yet that by comparison was a far higher figure for a force whose numbers were being whittled down with frightening speed, and though they had captured the guns—and with them the shells that had been brought down from the Arsenal and abandoned when the amateur gunners fled—that too proved to be a hollow victory. For the guns were too heavy and the distance to the barracks too great; and now scores of enemy rifles and muskets were opening fire again . . .

Despite that storm of bullets the Guides had struggled desperately to pull their booty back, harnessing themselves to the ropes and straining to drag the unwieldy things over the dusty, stony ground. But it was soon clear that the task was beyond them: it would take too long, and to persist could only result in the entire party being killed.

They took the shells, though that was small comfort as it was obvious that further supplies would soon be hurried down from the Arsenal; but they could not even put the guns out of action, for in the heat and urgency of the moment one small but vital thing had slipped Wally's mind—the fact that though he alone among his men had been in uniform when the mutineers from the pay parade had invaded the compound, he had not been wearing his cross-belt, and had not thought to put it on since, or had time to do so. But a cross-belt carries two small items that are not intended for ornament but strictly for use: the 'pickers' that can be used, among other things, for spiking guns.

'It's my own fault,' said Wally bitterly. 'I ought to have thought. If we'd even had a *nail*—anything. I'd clean forgotten we weren't properly dressed. Well, the only thing for it is to concentrate all our fire on those bloody guns and see that no one is able to re-load them again.'

The doors inside the archway had been closed and barred again behind them, and the survivors slaked their thirst from chattis of cold water that had been brought up from the *hammam:* Mussulmans as well as Unbelievers, for the regimental Mulvi had declared this to be a time of war, and at such times it is permissible for soldiers engaged in battle to break the fast of Ramadan.

Having drunk they had returned to the Residency which they had left barely a quarter of an hour ago—only to find it full of smoke, for the enemy behind the wall had not been idle while they were gone. More ladders had been pushed out from house-tops on the far side of the street, and while the Afghans, crawling along these perilous bridges, had reinforced the survivors of the fight on the stairway, their friends in the street below had hacked their way through the flimsy walls and thrust live coals and oil-soaked rags through holes they had made in the foundation.

The Residency and the compound, already hemmed in on three sides, was now being assailed from above and below as well, since besides possessing themselves of the stables and cavalry lines and every house-top in sight, the enemy had established themselves in force on the roof of the Mess House and had broken through its foundations.

The courtyard, the ground-floor rooms and the barrack-block were full of dead and dying men, and of the seventy-seven Guides who had seen the sun rise that morning, only thirty were left. Thirty . . . and the 'troops of Midian' who 'prowled and howled around' numbered—how many thousands? Four? . . . six? . . . eight thousand men?

For the first time that day Wally's heart sank, and facing the future squarely and clear-eyed he deliberately abandoned hope. But this was something that William, as a member of the Foreign and Political Department and an apostle of Peace by Negotiation and Compromise, was still not prepared to do.

William had returned from that abortive attack on the guns to exchange the unfamiliar sabre and service revolver for his shot-gun, and hastily filling his pockets with cartridges, he hurried up to the roof of the Envoy's House to fire at the Afghans who were massing on the roof of the higher house on the opposite side of the courtyard. It was only then that he became aware of the volume of smoke that was billowing out from the ground-floor rooms of the Mess House, and realized that if the fire took hold they were lost.

Yet even then he did not give up hope, but once again, lying on the roof among five jawans who were also engaged in discouraging the opposition entrenched on top of the Mess House, scribbled another desperate appeal to the Amir, using a blank page ripped from a small notebook he carried in his pocket. They could not hold out much longer, wrote William, and if His Highness did not come to their aid, their fate—and his own—was sealed. They could not believe that His Highness was prepared to stand aside and do nothing while his guests were murdered . . .

'Take that to Hamilton-Sahib,' said William, ripping out the page and handing it to one of the jawans. 'Tell him he must find someone among the servants who will deliver it to the Amir.'

'They will not go, Sahib,' said the man, shaking his head. 'They know that four Mussulmans have gone with letters and none have returned, and that the Hindu who went was hacked to pieces in full sight. Nevertheless—'

He tucked it in his belt, and wriggling away in the direction of the stairs, vanished down them in search of his Commanding Officer, whom he found over at the Mess House, firing from a window on the first floor at a group of mutineers who were attempting to reload the guns. Wally took the scrap of paper and dismissing the messenger with a brief nod read it through and wondered with a detached feeling of curiosity why William should think it was worth sending another appeal to the Amir, when the only tangible result of previous appeals had been one evasive reply that could hardly be matched for weakness and hypocrisy. In any case none of the messengers had returned, so it was always possible that all of them had met the same fate as the unfortunate Hindu, and it seemed pointless to Wally to send yet another to his death. But though the entire responsibility for the defence of the Residency had fallen on his shoulders, young Mr Jenkyns, as the Envoy's Secretary and Political Assistant, still represented the civil authority, and so if William wanted this letter sent, then it must be sent.

'Taimus,' called Wally.

'Sahib?' The sowar who had been firing from the other window lowered his carbine and turned to look at his Commanding Officer.

Wally said: 'Jenkyns-Sahib has just written another letter to the Amir, asking for help. Do you think that you could reach the palace?'

'I can try,' said Taimus. He put his carbine down and came across to take the paper, and folding it small, hid it among his clothing.

Wally smiled and said quietly: *'Shukria, Shahzada* (Prince). *Khuda hafiz!'*

The man grinned at the title, saluted and went out to cross the lane into the barracks and survey the situation from the barrack roof, but a bare half-minute was enough to show him the impossibility of attempting to leave by the compound, for by now the mob were everywhere and not even a lizard could have got through. There was nothing for it but to go back to the Residency and see if he could not find some other way of escape. The back door had been blocked long ago, and since to have opened it again would have been to invite a flood of armed Afghans into the courtyard, he turned in desperation to the Envoy's House and went up to the roof, where one of the jawans who was still holding out there helped him up on to the curtain wall that shielded the roof from the view of the houses behind the Residency.

Standing there, he had been in full sight of the enemy on the roof of the Mess House and in the street below; and as he gazed down on the close-packed crowd of yelling, hate-distorted faces, he was suddenly filled with the same contempt for the mob that Cavagnari had felt much earlier that day. For Sowar Taimus, though serving as a trooper of the Guides, was also a prince of a royal line: a Shahzada—and an Afghan. His lip curled in disdain as he surveyed those contorted faces, and drawing a deep breath, he deliberately leapt into space, launching himself feet-first into the thick of the press below and landing on heads and shoulders that broke his fall.

The mob, momentarily stunned by shock, recovered itself and set on him with a howl of fury, but he fought his way through them, shouting that he was a prince and an Afghan and that he bore a message to the Amir; which would not have saved him had he not been recognized by a close friend, who rushing to the rescue had managed by dint of blows, high-words and cajolery to extract him from the clutches of the mob—battered and bleeding but alive—and helped him to reach the palace. But once there he had fared no better than anyone else.

The Amir was locked away, weeping, among his women; and though he had eventually agreed to see the Shahzada Taimus and to read the message he carried, he would only bewail his fate and reiterate that his Kismet was bad and that he was not to blame for this and could do nothing—nothing.

He had given orders that the Shahzada was to be detained, and this had been done. But though the Amir's Kismet was undoubtedly bad, Taimus's had proved to be far otherwise, because in the room into which he had been hurriedly thrust by the palace guards lay an Afghan who had been shot in the back during the first attack on the compound. The wounded man had been left to look after himself, and though by now he was in considerable pain, no one had done anything to help him because of the panic that prevailed in the palace. But Taimus had learned something of the treatment of wounds during his service in the Guides, and he had extracted the bullet with his knife, and having washed the wound and managed to staunch the bleeding, had bound it up with the sufferer's waist-cloth.

His grateful patient, who had proved to be a man of some standing, had repaid the debt by smuggling him out of the palace and arranging for his escape from Kabul. And Fate had been doubly kind to him that day, for not five minutes after he had leapt from the roof of the Envoy's House, and while he was still fighting his way forward through the frenzied crowd with his life hanging in the balance, behind him in the Residency the garrison who had been battling equally frantically to dowse the burning foundations of the Mess House were driven back by a sudden uprush of flame that burst through the blinding clouds of smoke, and seconds later the whole lower storey was ablaze.

There had been no question of saving the wounded; the fire had taken hold far too suddenly and violently to allow anyone to attempt it. Those who could do so had run for their lives, and scorched, choked and half blind, had stumbled across the smoke-filled courtyard to take refuge in the Envoy's House.

The Afghans on the roof of the burning building, realizing with what swiftness the flames would destroy that ramshackle wood and plaster structure, had scrambled back across their ladders in haste, and instantly transferred their attentions to the opposite house. Thrusting out other ladders onto the high parapet that Taimus had jumped from, they clambered across and leapt down among the half-dozen men who still held out there: and though their leaders died as they came, falling sideways into the street or pitching head-first on to the roof, those behind them pressed forward, and as William and the jawans reloaded they sprang down to the attack . . .

There had been no hope of holding the roof, even though Wally and every Guide who remained in the Residency had rushed up to try and stem the horde of invaders who came leaping down from the parapet like a band of monkeys swarming on to a melon patch. Their very numbers had made the task impossible and the end a foregone conclusion.

The garrison, closing ranks and using their useless firearms as clubs, retreated towards the stairwell and were driven down it step by step, until the last man down slammed shut the door at the foot of the stairway and dropped the bars into place. But that door, like all the rest in that ancient and dilapidated building, was incapable of withstanding a determined attack, and there was no time—and no materials—to reinforce it.

The house itself would soon be on fire, for if the Afghans sapping from below failed to set it alight, it seemed only too likely that the flames and sparks that were now pouring from every doorway and window of the Mess House would do the job for them; and even if it did not, the garrison could no longer hold out in the Residency, because the enemy, taking advantage of the fighting on the roof and under cover of the smoke, had smashed another breach in the back wall of the courtyard, and widening it unhindered, were streaming in from below.

Wally caught a nightmare glimpse of them through the acrid clouds of smoke, shooting and slashing at a panic-stricken handful of servants who had been driven out of the Mess House by the fire and taken refuge in the lee of a pile of baggage that had been used to barricade the back door, Sir Louis' bearer and his own fat Pir Baksh among them—Pir Baksh defending himself with a knife in one hand and a boot-tree in the other. But there was nothing he could do for them, and he turned away, sickened, and striding to the nearest of the two windows that faced the compound, wrenched back the shutters and sprang up on to the sill.

'Come on!' yelled Wally, waving his companions forward, and in the same breath, leapt out and down across the narrow lane and onto the roof of the barracks.

They had not waited for any further urging, but followed unhesitatingly, leaping as he had done down across the gap to land on the barracks; Jenkyns, Kelly and the jawans who had survived the fight on the roof, and half-a-dozen non-combatants who had been helping to fight the fire and had run up from the floor below.

Even as the last man jumped and landed, the roof of the Mess House fell in with a roar that equalled that of the guns, and they turned and saw a brilliant fountain of sparks, vivid even in the afternoon sunlight, shoot up from the pyre that was consuming the body of Louis Cavagnari—and with it a great number of the soldiers and servants who had accompanied him to Kabul.

'Like a Viking Chieftain going to Valhalla with his warriors and servingmen around him,' thought Wally.

He turned from the sight to order his little force off the roof and down into the barracks. For now that the Residency had fallen and the enemy were in possession of the Envoy's House, the Afghans would be able to fire from the windows that he and the other survivors of the garrison had just leapt from—and from an angle that made the scanty cover of the parapets of no account. But down below, the original doors of the block were as stoutly built as its outer walls, while the canvas awnings that shaded the long central courtyard, though no protection against bullets, at least prevented the enemy from seeing what went on there.

'We ought to be able to hold out here for a fair time,' said William breathlessly, glancing about him at the solid stone pillars and brick archways that gave on to the cool, windowless cells of the troops' quarters. 'Nothing much to set on fire. Except the doors, of course. I don't know why we didn't come here before.'

'Because we can't see out of it or shoot out of it, or do a damn thing but stay put and try to prevent those divils breaking the doors down. That's why,' snapped Rosie, who had worked like a demon to try and get the wounded into the Residency courtyard, only to desert them in order to defend the Envoy's House: and who now felt that he had abandoned them to be murdered by the Afghans or burned alive in the Mess House.

'Yes. I suppose you're right. I hadn't thought about that. But at least we should be able to stop them breaking in, and providing they don't burn the doors down—'

'Or blow a hole in the wall,' said Rosie, 'or . . .' He reeled as the guns roared again, and the pillars shuddered to the impact of the force and sound of the shells that struck the front wall of the barracks, missing the archway and burying the stairway to the east of it under a pile of rubble.

It did not need a professional gunner to tell that this second salvo had been fired from a much closer range than the first one, and it was clear to everyone in the barracks that the mob, freed from the sniping of the sepoys who had been harassing them from behind the parapets, had lost no time in reloading the guns and running them forward. And also that the next salvo would probably be fired from directly opposite the archway, which would smash both doors to matchwood and leave the way clear for the enemy to rush in.

Once again the sky rained debris, and the exhausted doctor, who had clutched a pillar and then sat down abruptly, leaning against it, saw Walter Hamilton and Daffadar Hira Singh racing towards the inner door of the archway and pulling it open; and thought dazedly that the shock of the explosions must have unhinged them both, and that they intended to go out and attack the mob before the guns could be reloaded. But they did not touch the new outer door that by now was so spattered with bullet-holes that it had the appearance of a colander. Instead they turned back to confer briefly with Havildar

Hassan and Lance-Naik Janki, and presently Wally nodded briefly, and returning to William and Rosie, said tersely:

'Look, we've got to get those guns. *We've got to!* I don't mean spike them. I mean capture them. If we can only get 'em back here we can blow the Arsenal sky high—and with it most of that mob out there and half the Bala Hissar as well. We've only got to land one shell fair and square on it, and all that ammunition and gunpowder inside is going to go up with a bang that will wreck everything within a radius of several hundred yards.'

'Including us,' said William wryly.

'What the divil does that matter?' demanded Wally impatiently. 'Not that it will, for we're much lower down here, and these walls are far too thick. Ah, I know it sounds a crazy idea, but it's worth a try—anything's worth a try now. If we can get our hands on those guns we've got a fighting chance, but if we don't—well, we can say our prayers now.'

William's eyelids flickered and his youthful face whitened under its mask of blood and dust. He said tiredly: 'We can't do it, Wally. We've proved that already.'

'We hadn't got enough rope last time. Besides, the guns were too far away then. But they aren't now, and I'll bet you anything you like that they are being dragged nearer this minute, because those bastards out there are certain that they've got us beat and we can't do anything about it. My Havildar says that there's a fakir out there who's been egging them on all afternoon, screeching to them to blow in the door so that they can fire straight through the barracks and smash down the back wall to allow their friends in the Residency to rush us from the rear. That's why I had the inner door opened: so that if they smash in the front one, we've still got that to fall back on.'

Rosie said shortly: 'It's mad you are. What would we be using for ammunition even if we did get a gun? Bullets?'

'The shells we brought back with us last time, of course. We left them here in one of the quarters—twelve of 'em. That's six for each gun. Just think what we could do with that!'

But William remained unconvinced.

'I've no objection to charging the damn things again,' said William, 'but if we get our hands on them, for God's sake let's spike them this time and be done with it, instead of trying to bring them back with us.'

'*No!*' insisted Wally passionately. 'If we do that it's all up with us, because they'll have other guns. And they've already got all the ammunition they need, while we're running out of ours; and when we do, and they realize we aren't firing any more, they'll rush this place in force and it will fall inside five minutes. No, there's only one thing for it: we've got to cut off their source of supply, and the only way we can do that is by shelling the Arsenal—and killing as many of them as we can in the process. I tell you we've *got* to get those guns! One of them, anyway. We'll spike the second—I'll get Thakur Singh to do that while the rest of us concentrate on getting the other back. We ought to be able to manage that. Ah sure now, I know it sounds crazy, but it's better than cowering here until they realize that we've run out of ammunition and that all they have to do is get a few ladders and pour in on us over the roof, as they did in the Residency. Is *that* the way you want to die?'

Surgeon-Major Kelly gave a harsh croak of laughter, and coming wearily to his feet, said: 'Be easy boy, we're with you. Faith, it's a mad gamble, so it is. But there's no saying it couldn't come off. And if we don't take it we're dead men anyway. Well, if we're going to try it you'd best be telling us what to do and getting us started.'

Wally had been right about the guns. While they talked, the mob had been dragging them nearer and nearer until now both were less than seventy yards distant, loaded and facing the wall to the left of the archway; and ready to be fired—

Once again the crash of the double explosion was followed by a wild outburst of cheering. But as the echoes died away the dry-throated mob fell silent, and from his prison high above the compound Ash could hear, cutting through the unceasing rattle of musketry, the muted roar and crackle of burning timber, the hoarse cawing of startled crows and the shrill voice of the Fakir encouraging the mutineers who were pushing the guns towards the barrack archway.

He did not see the barrack doors swing open. But suddenly Wally came in sight, running with William and Rosie and a dozen Guides at his heels to charge straight into that blizzard of bullets and across the dusty open ground towards the guns.

For the second time that day they drove the crews back, and having done so eight of them swung one of the guns round so that it faced the mob, and with six of them harnessed to the ropes and another two putting their shoulders to the wheels, they began to drag it back towards the barracks while the rest held off the enemy with revolvers and swords, and a solitary jawan flung himself at the other gun with the intention of spiking it. But once again the task had proved beyond them.

The hail of bullets killed two of the men who were harnessed to the gun and the sowar who was attempting to spike the other, and who dropped the spike as he died, letting it fall to be lost in the blood-stained dust below the wheels. Another four were wounded, and Wally shouted to the others to run for it, and sheathing his sabre, hastily reloaded his revolver. William and Rosie followed his example, and as the men freed themselves from the ropes and ran for the barracks, taking their wounded with them, the three Englishmen covered their retreat, walking backwards and firing steadily and with such deadly effect that the Afghans wavered and held back, allowing the little party to reach the shelter of the archway in safety.

At the last moment Wally turned, and looking up at Ash's window, flung up his arm in a Roman salute. But the gesture of farewell went unanswered, for Ash was not there. The despair that had stabbed through him when he saw the guns had served to goad his brain into searching yet again, and for at least the hundredth time that day, for a way of escape; and this time, suddenly, he had remembered something. Something that it had not occurred to him to consider before—the geography of the storey below . . .

He knew which room lay below his own, but he had not thought to visualize those that lay on either side of it; and doing so now he realized that under the Munshi's library lay a small disused room that had once possessed a balcony window. The balcony itself had fallen long ago and the window had subsequently been boarded up; but by now those boards were probably rotten, and once he had broken through the library floor and dropped down through the cavity, it would not be difficult to wrench them off. After which it would merely be a matter of using the sheet rope to negotiate the twenty-foot drop to the ground below.

Any Afghan seeing him slide down from the window would suppose him to be an ally eager to get to grips with the enemy, and the only danger was that one of the jawans on the barrack roof would spot him, and taking the same view, shoot him before he could reach the ground and the cover of the low wall that separated the line of tall houses from the Residency compound. But that was a risk that would have to be taken, and Ash did not trouble his head over it, but within a matter of seconds was back in the Munshi's library and attacking the floorboards.

William, who had seen that valedictory gesture and jumped to a wrong conclusion, clutched at Wally's arm and said breathlessly: 'Who were you waving at? Was someone trying to signal us? Is the Amir . . . are they . . . ?'

'No,' gasped Wally, flinging his weight against the door to help close it. 'It's—only—Ash . . .'

William stared at him blankly: the name meant nothing to him and the sudden flare of hope that had sprung to life at the sight of that gesture died again. He turned away and sank down to the ground, but Ambrose Kelly looked up from the wounded sepoy he was tending and said sharply: '*Ash?* You can't mean—do you mean Pelham-Martyn?'

'Yes,' panted Wally, still busy with the bars of the outer door. 'He's up there . . . in one of those . . . houses.'

'In—? For Christ's sake! Then why isn't he doing something for us?'

'If he could do anything, he'll have done it. He'll have tried, anyway. And God knows he warned us often enough, but no one would listen—not even the Chief. Get that fellow into one of the quarters, Rosie. We're too near the door and they're bound to blast off again. Get back—all of you.'

The mob had only waited until the door was closed before rushing forward to take possession of the guns once more and drag them round and into position in front of the archway, while from every housetop their allies directed a storm of musket-balls onto the stout, windowless walls of the barracks, the unmanned roof and the tattered, bullet-torn canvas awnings.

There was very little light inside the barracks, for the sun had sunk behind the heights of the Shere Dawaza, and by now the whole compound was in shadow. But as the day waned the flames from the burning Residency gathered brightness, and when the guns fired again the flash was no longer dimmed by sunlight, but a vivid glare that dazzled the eyes and gave a fractional warning of the deafening crash that followed.

This time there had been no attempt to fire both guns simultaneously. The first shell had been intended to break in both doors of the archway, and as far as the mutineers were concerned it had done so, for they were unaware that the second one had been left open. They saw the woodwork of the outer one disintegrate in a haze of flying splinters, and when the smoke cleared, the archway gaped on a view of the long central courtyard and the far wall.

Cheering wildly, they touched off the second gun, and the shell streaked through the centre of the barracks to smash a ragged hole that gave access to the lane. Behind that breach lay the courtyard of the Residency—full now of their victorious brothers, who had only to cross the lane and fall upon the infidels from the rear while their exultant allies in the compound rushed them from the front. But though the scheme was an excellent one, it contained two serious flaws, only one of which was immediately apparent: the fact that the inner and far stouter door of the archway had not been destroyed and was now slammed shut.

The other and more serious one, which was known to the garrison but still not realized by the mutineers, was that in setting fire to the Residency the Afghans had made the place untenable for themselves, so that instead of massing there in strength they had looted what they could find and hastily withdrawn out of reach of the flames. The likelihood of an attack from that direction was therefore minimal, and Wally could afford to disregard it and concentrate on one front only since by now there would be no snipers firing on them from the Residency, and the smoke from the burning building would confuse the aim of many of the marksmen on the nearby rooftops.

Secure in this knowledge, his first act after retreating to the barracks and closing that flimsy outer door had been to order four of his men up the stairway at the far end with instructions to keep down out of sight until the guns fired, and then run forward under cover of the smoke and take up their former positions behind the front parapet above the arch, from where they would open fire on the guncrews to prevent them reloading.

The rest of his small force had scattered to left and right; neither he nor they having any illusions as to what would happen next. Nor had it been long in happening. The outer door duly went, and the shell that demolished it also damaged one of the stone pillars and brought down a shower of bricks; though without injuring anyone.

They waited tensely for the second, and the instant it came, raced forward to close and bar the heavy inner door, while the four jawans who had been crouching at the top of the far stairs leapt to their feet, and concealed by the smoke, ran forward to take cover behind the parapet overhead and open fire on the cheering gun-crews.

Now the loading and firing of a piece of heavy artillery is no easy task for inexperienced men; and the mutineers were not gunners. Not only should the gun be swabbed out between shots, but the live shell must be thrust into the muzzle and rammed down the barrel, the touch-hole primed with gunpowder and lit with a port-fire—or, if necessary, a match. All this takes time, and can be an exceedingly difficult and dangerous task when the crews are being fired on at close range.

Had the walls of the barrack-block possessed proper loopholes that offered protection and a reasonable field of fire, the garrison would have found it a simple matter to prevent the guns being used against them. But as the only place from which they could fire was from behind parapets surrounding a roof that was overlooked by enemy snipers, the guns were strong cards that could not be trumped, and Wally knew it.

He knew too that it was only a matter of time before the four on the roof ran out of ammunition—and that the rest of them had very little left. When that was gone the guns would be loaded without interference and the door would be blown in.

The end was a foregone conclusion, and he realized now that he must have recognized that long ago, and unconsciously based all his actions upon it.

If they must die, then at least let them die in a manner that would redound to the credit of the Guides and the traditions they upheld. Let them go down fighting, and by doing so add lustre to their Corps and become a legend and an inspiration to future generations of Guides. That was the only thing they could do.

He knew that there was very little time left, and that little was running out fast; but for a brief space he stood silent, staring into space and thinking of many things . . . Of Inistioge and his parents and brothers; of his mother's face as she kissed him goodbye; of Ash and Wigram and all the splendid fellows in the Guides . . . He had had a good life—a wonderful life. Even now he would not have exchanged it for anyone else's.

A host of foolish memories passed in procession before his mind's eye, all of them clear-cut and bright. Birds'-nesting with his brothers on Wimbledon Common. A ball at the Military Academy. The long voyage to Bombay and his first sight of India. The happy days in the bungalow in Rawalpindi and later on in Mardan, and those carefree holidays that he and Ash had spent together . . . The work and the play, the talk and the laughter and the fun. All the pretty girls he had fallen in love with—gay ones, demure ones, shy ones, flirtatious ones . . . their faces merged into one face—Anjuli's, and he smiled at it and thought how lucky he was to have known her.

He would never marry now, and perhaps that was no bad thing; it would have been hard to find anyone who could live up to the ideal she had set: and he would also be spared the sadness of discovering that love does not last and that time, which destroys beauty and youth and strength, can also corrode many things of far greater value. He would never know disillusionment, or failure either, or live to see the gods of his idolatry brought down and shown to have feet of clay . . .

This was the end of the road for him, yet he had no regrets—not even for the loss of that imaginary figure, Field Marshal Lord Hamilton of Inistioge, for had he not won the most coveted award of all, the Victoria Cross? That alone was enough glory to make up for anything: and besides, the Guides would remember him. Perhaps one day, if he could leave an unsullied name, his sword would hang in the Mess at Mardan and men of the Corps yet unborn would finger it and listen to an old story from by-gone history. The story of how once, long ago, seventy-seven men of the Guides under the command of one Walter Hamilton, v.c., had been besieged in the British Residency at Kabul and held it against overwhelming odds for the best part of a day—and died to the last man . . .

'Stat sua cuique dies, breve tempus— Omnibus est vitae; sed famam extendere factis— Hoc virtutis opus,' murmured Wally under his breath. It was an odd time to remember a Latin tag from the *Aeneid,* and he thought how Ash would laugh if he knew. But it fitted the occasion: 'Everyone has his allotted day. Short and irrecoverable is the lifetime of all; but to extend our fame by deeds, this is the task of greatness.'

Today it had been his task to help extend the fame of the Guides, and Ash would understand that. It was good to know that Ash was close by and would see and approve—would realize that he had done his best, and be with him in spirit. He could not have asked for a better friend, and he knew that it was not Ash's fault that help had not come. If he could . . .

The boy collected his wandering thoughts with an effort and

looked about him at the tattered, blood-stained, smoke-begrimed scarecrows who were all that were now left of the more than three score and ten whom he could have mustered that morning. He had no idea how long he had been standing there silent and thinking of other things, or what the hour was, for now that the sun had left the compound the barracks were full of shadows. The daylight seemed to be fading, and there was no time to be lost.

Lieutenant Walter Hamilton, v.c., straightened up and drawing a deep breath addressed his men, speaking in Hindustani, which was the lingua-franca of a corps that contained Sikhs, Hindus and Punjabis as well as the Pushtu-speaking Pathans.

They had fought, he said, like heroes, and most splendidly upheld the honour of the Guides. No men could have done more. Now all that remained for them was to die in a like manner, fighting the foe. The alternative was to be killed like rats in a trap. There was no other choice, and he did not need to ask which they would choose. He therefore proposed that they should make one last effort to capture a gun. But this time they would all harness themselves to it while he alone would hold off the enemy and cover their retreat:

'We will charge the left-hand gun only,' said Wally. 'And when we reach it you will not look aside even for a moment, but rope yourselves to it and put your shoulders to the wheels, and get it back here. Do not stop for anything—do you understand? You must not turn to look behind you and I will do all I can to cover you. If you get it back, turn it on the Arsenal. If not, no matter if I fall, or how many of us fall, remember that those who are left will still hold the honour of the Guides in their hands. Do not sell it lightly. It is told of a great warrior who conquered this land and half the world many hundreds of years ago—none other than Sikandar Dulkhan (Alexander the Great) of whom all men have heard—that he said "It is a lovely thing to live with courage and to die leaving behind everlasting renown." You have all lived with courage and what you have done this day will bring you everlasting renown; for your deeds will not be forgotten as long as the Guides are remembered. Your children's children will tell their grandchildren the tale and boast of what you have done. Never give in, brothers—never give in. Guides, *ki-jai!*'

The cry was greeted with a shout that echoed under the arches and among the shadowy quarters until it sounded as though the ghosts of all the Guides who had died that day were cheering in unison with the few who still lived. And as the echoes died away, William called out, 'Scotland for Ever!—Political Department *ki-jai!*' and the men laughed and took up the sabres and ropes that they had laid down.

Ambrose Kelly came stiffly to his feet and stretched tiredly. He was the oldest of the group by a number of years and, like Gobind, his talents and training had been devoted to saving life and not taking it. But now he loaded and checked his revolver, and buckling on the sword that he had never learned to use, said: 'Ah well now, I'm not saying it won't be a relief to get it over with, for it's been a long day and it's dog-tired I am—and as some poet fellow has said, "how can man die better than facing fearful odds?" Hakim *ki-jai!*'

The Guides laughed again; and their laughter made Wally's heart lift with pride and brought a lump to his throat as he grinned back at them with an admiration and affection that was too deep for words. Yes, life would have been worth living if only to have served and fought with men like these. It had been a privilege to command them —an enormous privilege: and it would be an even greater one to die with them. They were the salt of the earth. They were the Guides. His throat tightened as he looked at them, and he was aware again of a hard lump in it, but his eyes were very bright as he reached for his sabre, and swallowing painfully to clear that constriction, he said almost gaily: 'Are we ready? Good. Then open the doors—'

A sepoy sprang forward to lift the heavy iron bar, and as it fell clear, two others swung back the massive wooden leaves. And with a yell of 'Guides *ki-jai!*' the little band charged out through the archway and raced towards the left-hand gun, Wally leading, a full six paces ahead.

The sight of them had a curious effect upon the mob: after the failure of the last attack every member of it had been confident that the 'foreigners' had shot their bolt and would never be able to mount another, yet here they were, rushing out again and with undiminished ferocity. It was unbelievable—it was uncanny . . . For a moment the mob stared at the ragged scarecrows in almost superstitious awe, and in the next second scattered like dry leaves before the whirlwind force of the attack as Wally fell upon them, his sabre flashing and his revolver spitting death.

As he did so a solitary turbanless Afghan whose hair and clothes were white with plaster and brick dust, raced from the left to join him, and was recognized by two sowars with a yell of 'Pelham-Dulkhan! Pelham-Sahib-Bahadur!'

Wally heard that greeting above the clash of battle, and glancing swiftly aside saw Ash fighting beside him—a knife in one hand and a tulwar snatched from a dead Herati in the other: and he laughed triumphantly and cried, 'Ash! I knew you'd come. *Now* we'll show 'em—!'

Ash laughed back at him, drunk with the terrible intoxication of battle and the relief of fast, violent action after the frustrations of that long nerve-wracking day of helpless watching . . . of seeing his comrades die one by one without being able to lift hand or arm to help them. His wild exhilaration communicated itself to Wally, who suddenly lifted out of himself was fighting like one inspired.

Afghans are not small men, but the boy seemed to tower above them, wielding his sabre like a master—or one of Charlemagne's Paladins. And as he fought he sang. It was, as usual, a hymn: the same that Ash himself had sung as he galloped Dagobaz across the plain of Bhithor on the morning of the Rana's funeral. But hearing it now he felt his heart jerk roughly, for this was not a verse that Wally had ever sung before, and listening to it he realized that the boy cherished no false hopes. This was his last fight and he knew it, and his choice of that particular verse was deliberate, a valediction. For calm and rest had never held any appeal for Wally, yet now he sang of both—loudly and joyously so that the words were clearly audible above the clamour of the fight . . .

'*The golden evening brightens in the West,*' sang Wally, plying that deadly sabre: '*Soon, soon, to faithful warriors comes their rest. Sweet is the calm of Paradise the Blest; Alleluia! Al-le-lu—*'

'Look out, Wally!' yelled Ash, and beating aside the blade of an opponent, leapt back to attack an Afghan armed with a long knife who had come up behind them unseen.

But even if Wally had heard, the warning came too late. The knife drove home to the hilt between his shoulder-blades, and as Ash's tulwar slashed through his attacker's neck, he staggered, and firing his last round, flung the useless revolver into a bearded face. The man reeled back, tripped and fell, and Wally transferred his sabre to his left hand: but his arm was weakening and he could not lift it. The point dropped and caught on a roughness in the ground, and as he pitched forward, the blade snapped.

In the same moment the butt of a jezail crashed down on Ash's head with stunning force, and for a split second lights seemed to explode inside his skull before he plunged down into blackness. And then the tulwars flashed and the dust fumed up in a blinding cloud as the mob closed in.

A few paces behind them, William had already fallen with a scimitar half buried in his skull and his right arm shattered below the elbow. And Rosie too was dead, his crumpled body lying barely a yard beyond the barrack archway, where he had been struck down by a musket-ball through the temple as he ran out at Wally's heels.

Of the rest, two, like Surgeon-Major Kelly, had died before they reached the gun, and three more had been wounded. But the survivors had obeyed their commander's orders to the letter: they had not looked aside or attempted to fight, but harnessing themselves to the gun had strained every nerve and muscle to drag it back. Yet even as they panted and struggled, others among them dropped; and now the ground was too littered with bodies, fallen weapons and spent bullets, and the dust too sticky with spilt blood, to make the task a possible one for so few men. Those who were left found that they could move the gun no further, and at last they were forced to abandon it and stumble back to the barracks, gasping and exhausted.

They closed and barred the great door behind them, and as it shut, a howl of triumph went up as the mob became aware that all three *feringhis* were dead.

Hundreds began to stream towards the barracks, led by the Fakir, who, leaving the shelter of the stables, ran at their head capering and waving his banner, while the crowds on the house-tops, realizing what had happened, ceased firing to dance and shout and brandish their muskets. But the three remaining jawans of the four whom Wally had sent up to the roof of the barracks continued to fire, though coldly now, for they had very few rounds left.

The mob had forgotten those four. But it remembered when three of its members fell dead and a further two, immediately behind them, were wounded by the same heavy lead bullets that had killed the men in front. As the Afghans checked, the rifles cracked again and a further three died, for the Guides were firing into a solid mass of men at a range of less than fifty yards, and it was not possible for them to miss. And presently a bullet struck the Fakir full in the face, and he threw up his arms and fell backwards, to be trampled under the feet of his followers, who running behind him, could not check in time.

68

There were several factors that contributed to Ash's survival. For one thing, he was wearing Afghan dress and clutching a tulwar; and for another, only those who had been in the forefront of the fighting were aware that a man who appeared to be a citizen of Kabul had for a while fought side by side with the *Angrezi* officer. Then in the subsequent rush to finish off the mortally wounded Sahib, his unconscious body had been spurned aside, so that by the time the dust had settled he was no longer lying where he had fallen, but was some little distance away; not among the fallen Guides, but among half a dozen enemy corpses, his face unrecognizable under a mask of blood and dirt, and his clothing dyed scarlet from the severed jugular of a Herati soldier whose body lay sprawled above his own.

The blow on his head had been a glancing one, and though sufficiently violent to knock him insensible, it had not been severe enough to keep him so for very long; but when he recovered consciousness it was to discover that not one but two corpses lay above him; the second being a heavily built Afghan who had been shot through the head by one of the jawans on the barrack roof less than a minute earlier, and fallen across his legs.

The two inert bodies effectively pinned him to the ground, and finding that he could not move, he lay still for a while, dazed and uncomprehending, and with no idea where he was or what had happened to him. He had a hazy recollection of crawling through a hole —a hole in a wall. After that there was nothing— But as his mind slowly cleared he remembered Wally and strove futilely to move, only to find that the effort was beyond him.

His head throbbed abominably and his whole body felt as though it was one vast bruise and as weak as wet paper; yet gradually, as his wits returned, he realized that in all probability he had received no wound beyond a blow on the head and rough handling at the hands— or more likely the feet—of the mob. In which case there was nothing to prevent him struggling free of this weight that was pinning him down, and returning to the attack the minute he could collect the strength to do so and rid himself of this appalling dizziness: for to get on his feet merely in order to stagger round like a drunken man would be to invite instant death, and be no help to anyone.

The roar of the mob and the continued crackle of muskets and carbines told him that the battle was by no means over, and though his face was bruised and swollen, and his eyelids clogged with a sticky paste of dust and blood that he was unable to remove because he was still too weak to free his arms, he managed by dint of an enormous effort to force open his eyes.

At first it was impossible to focus anything, but after a minute or two his sight, like his brain, began to clear, and he realized that he was lying a yard or two behind the main bulk of the mob, which was being kept at bay by the determined fire of three sepoys above the entrance to the barrack block. But their shots came at longer and longer intervals, and he became dimly aware that they must be running out of ammunition, and presently, as his gaze wandered, that there was some sort of conference going on among the mutineers who stood behind the abandoned guns.

As he watched, one of them—a member of the Ardal Regiment judging from his dress—climbed up onto one of the guns and standing upright brandished a musket to the barrel of which he had tied a strip of white cloth that he waved to and fro as a flag of truce, shouting: 'Sulh. Sulh . . . Kafi. Bus!'*

The crackle of musketry died and the sepoys kneeling behind the parapet held their fire. And in the silence the man on the gun climbed down, and advancing into the open space before the barracks, called up to the beleaguered garrison that he would have speech with their leaders.

There followed a brief pause in which the sepoys were seen to confer together, and then one of them laid aside his rifle and stood up, and walking to the inner edge of the roof, called down to the survivors in the troops' quarters below.

A few minutes later three more Guides came up to join him, and together they went forward to stand behind the parapet above the archway, erect and unarmed.

'We are here,' said the jawan who had been elected spokesman because he was a Pathan and could speak freely to Afghans in their own tongue—and because no one of higher rank was left alive. 'What is it that you wish to say to us? Speak.'

Ash heard a man who was standing a yard or so away draw in his breath with a hiss and say in an awed whisper: 'Are there no more

* Please. Enough. Stop!

than that? There cannot be only *six* left. Perchance there are others within.'

'Six . . .' thought Ash numbly. But the word carried no meaning.

'Your Sahibs are all dead,' shouted the mutineer with the flag, 'and with you who are left, we have no quarrel. Of what use to continue the fight? If you will throw down your arms we will give you free passage to return to your homes. You have fought honourably. Surrender now, and go free.'

One of the Guides laughed, and the grim, battle-grimed faces of his comrades relaxed and they laughed with him, loudly and scornfully, until their listeners scowled and gritted their teeth and began to finger their muskets.

The jawan who was their spokesman had not drunk for many hours and his mouth was dry. But he gathered his spittle and spat deliberately over the edge of the parapet, and raising his voice, demanded loudly: 'What manner of men are you, that you can ask us to forfeit our honour and shame our dead? Are we dogs that we should betray those whose salt we have eaten? Our Sahib told us to stand and fight to the last. And that we shall do. You have been answered—*dogs!*'

He spat again and turned on his heel, the rest following; and while the mob yelled its fury the six strode back along the roof and down the far stair into the barrack courtyard. Here they wasted no time, but paused only briefly to line up shoulder to shoulder: Mussulmans, Sikhs and a Hindu—sowars and sepoys of the Queen's Own Corps of Guides. They lifted the bar and threw back the doors, and drawing their swords, marched out under the archway to their deaths as steadily as though they had been on parade.

The Afghan who had spoken before sucked in his breath and said as though the words were wrenched from him: '*Wah-illah!* but these are Men!'

'They are the Guides,' thought Ash with a hot surge of pride, and struggled desperately to rise and join them. But even as he fought to free himself, a rush of men from behind trampled him down, driving the breath from his lungs and leaving him writhing helplessly among choking clouds of dust and a forest of *chuppli*-shod feet that trod on him, tripped over him, or spurned him aside as heedlessly as though he had been a bale of straw. He was dimly aware of the clash of steel and the hoarse shouting of men, and, very clearly, of a clarion voice that cried 'Guides *ki-jai!*' Then a shod foot struck his temple and once again the world turned black.

This time it had taken him longer to recover his senses, and when at last he swam slowly up out of darkness it was to find that although he could still hear a clamour of voices from the direction of the Residency the firing had stopped, and except for the dead the part of the compound in which he lay appeared to be deserted.

Nevertheless he made no immediate attempt to move, but lay where he was, conscious only of pain and an enormous weariness, and only after a lapse of many minutes, of the need to think and to act. His brain felt as sluggish and unresponsive as his muscles, and the sheer effort of thinking at all, let alone thinking clearly, seemed too great to make. Yet he knew that he must force himself to it; and presently the cogs of his mind meshed once more and memory returned—and with it the age-old instinct of self-preservation.

At some time during that final massacre the bodies that had lain above him had been displaced, and after a cautious trial he discovered that he could still move, though only just. To stand upright was beyond him but he could crawl, and he did so—as slowly and uncertainly as a wounded beetle: creeping painfully on hands and knees between the sprawled corpses, and making automatically for the nearest shelter, which happened to be the stables.

Others had had the same idea, for the stables were full of dead and wounded Afghans: men from the city and the Bala Hissar as well as soldiers of the Ardal and Herati regiments, huddled together on the reeking straw; and Ash, suffering from a combination of mild concussion, multiple bruises and mental and physical exhaustion, collapsed among them and slept for the best part of an hour, to be aroused at last by a hand that grasped his bruised shoulders and shook him roughly.

The pain of that movement jerked him into consciousness as effectively as though a bucket of snow-water had been dashed onto his face, and he heard a voice say, 'By Allah, here is another who lives. Heart up, friend; you are not dead yet, and soon you will be able to break your fast'—and opening his eyes, he found himself staring up at a burly Afghan whose features seemed vaguely familiar to him, though at the moment he could not place him.

'I am attached to the household of the Chief Minister's first secretary,' supplied the stranger helpfully, 'and you I think are Syed

Akbar in the service of Munshi Naim Shah: I have seen you in his office. Come now, up with you—it grows late. Take my arm . . .' The nameless Samaritan helped Ash to his feet and guided him out of the compound and towards the Shah Shahie Gate, talking the while.

The sky ahead was softening to evening and the far snows were already rose-coloured from the sunset; but even here in the smoke-filled alleyways between the houses the corporate voice of the mob was still clearly audible, and Ash checked and said confusedly: 'I must go back . . . I thank you for your help, but—but I must go back. I cannot leave . . .'

'You are too late, my friend,' said the man softly, 'your friends are all dead. But as the mob are now looting the buildings and will be too busy stealing and destroying to trouble themselves with anything else, if we leave quickly we shall do so without being molested.'

'Who are you?' demanded Ash in a hoarse whisper, pulling back against the arm that would have urged him forward. 'What are you?'

'I am known here as Sobhat Khan, though that is not my name. And like you I am a servant of the Sirkar, who gathers news for the Sahib-log.'

Ash opened his mouth to refute the charge and then shut it again without speaking; and seeing this the man grinned and said: 'No, I would not have believed you, for an hour ago I spoke with the Sir-dar-Bahadur Nakshband Khan in the house of Wali Mohammed. It was he who gave me a certain key and bade me unlock your door as soon as the fighting was over, which I did—only to find that your room was empty and that there was a hole in one wall large enough for a man to creep through. I went through that hole and saw where the floorboards had been torn up, and looking down, saw also by what means you had escaped. Whereupon I came swiftly to the compound to search for you among the dead, and by good fortune found you living. Now let us leave this place while we can, for once the sun has set the looters will remember their stomachs and hurry home to break the day's fast. Hark to them—'

He cocked his head, listening to the distant sound of shouting and laughter that accompanied the work of destruction, and as he urged Ash forward, said scornfully: 'The fools think that because they have slain four *Angrezis* they have rid the land of foreigners. But once the news of this day's doings reaches India the English will come to

Kabul, which will spell disaster for them and their Amir. And also for the English—of that we can be sure!'

'How so?' asked Ash incuriously, stumbling obediently forward and discovering with relief that his strength was returning to him and his brain becoming clearer with every step.

'Because they will depose the Amir,' replied the spy Sobhat; 'and I do not think that they will put his son on the *gadi* in his place. Afghanistan is no country to be ruled by a child. This will leave his brothers, who have no following and would not last long if the English tried to put either on the throne, and his cousin Abdur Rahman; who though a bold man and a good fighter they distrust, because he took refuge with the Russ-log. Therefore I will make you a prophecy. In five years' time, or it may be less, Abdur Rahman will be Amir of Afghanistan, and then this country, upon which the English have twice waged war because (so they said) they feared that it might fall into the hands of the Russ-log and thereby endanger their hold on Hindustan, will be ruled by a man who owes all to those same Russ-log and . . . Ah, it is as I thought; the sentries have left to join in the looting and there is no one to stay us.'

He hurried Ash through the unguarded gate and turned along the dusty road that led past the citadel, in the direction of Nakshband Khan's house. 'Wherefore,' continued the spy, 'all this war and killing will have been in vain, for my countrymen have long memories, and neither Abdur Rahman nor his heirs, or his people who have fought two wars and engaged in countless Border battles with the English, will forget these things. In the years to come they will still remember the English as their enemies—an enemy whom they defeated. But the Russ-log, whom they have neither fought against nor defeated, they will look upon as their friends and allies. This I told Cavagnari-Sahib when I warned him that the time was not ripe for a British Mission in Kabul, but he would not believe me.'

'No,' said Ash slowly. 'I too . . .'

'Ha, so you also were one of Cavagnari-Sahib's men? I thought as much. He was a great Sirdar, and one who spoke every tongue of this country. But for all his cunning and his great knowledge he did not know the true heart or mind of Afghanistan, else he would not have persisted in coming here. Well, he is dead—as are all whom he brought here with him. It has been a great killing: and soon there will be more . . . much more. This has been a black day for Kabul, an evil day. Do not linger here too long my friend. It is not a safe place for such as you and I. Can you walk alone from here? Good. Then I will leave you, since I have much to do. No, no, do not thank me. *Par makhe da kha.*'

He turned and strode away across country in the direction of the river, and Ash went on alone and reached Nakshband Khan's house without incident.

The Sirdar had returned half an hour earlier, his friend Wali Mohammed having smuggled him out of the Bala Hissar in disguise as soon as the firing stopped. But Ash did not wish to see him.

There was only one person he wanted to see or speak to just then —though even to her he could not bear to talk of what he had seen that day. Nor did he go to her at once, for the horrified expression of the servant who opened the door to him showed him too clearly that his battered face and blood-drenched clothing suggested a mortally wounded man, and even though Juli would have learned by now that he had been securely locked up and therefore (as far as the Sirdar knew) could have come to no harm, to appear before her in his present state would only add to the terrors that she must have endured during that tragic, interminable day.

Ash sent instead for Gul Baz; who had spent the greater part of the day on guard outside the door leading into the rooms that Nakshband Khan had set aside for the use of his guests, in order to prevent Anjuli-Begum from running through the streets to the Sahib's place of work in the Bala Hissar—which she had attempted to do once it became clear that the Residency was being besieged. In the end reason had prevailed; but Gul Baz was taking no chances, and after that he had remained at his post until the Sirdar returned with the welcome news that he had taken steps to ensure the Sahib's safety. Not that the Sahib's present appearance justified that claim.

But Gul Baz had asked no questions, and done his work so well that by the time Ash went up to see his wife the worst of the damage had been either repaired or hidden, and he was clean again. Nevertheless Anjuli, who had been sitting on a low rush stool by the window and had leapt up joyfully when she heard his step on the stairs, sank back again when she saw his face, her knees weak from shock and her hands at her throat, because it seemed to her that her husband had aged thirty years since he had left her at dawn that morning, and that he had come back to her an old man. So aged and so altered that he might almost have been a stranger . . .

She gave a little wordless cry and stretched out her arms to him, and Ash came to her, walking like a drunken man, and falling on his knees, hid his face in her lap and wept.

The room darkened about them, and outside it lights began to blossom in the windows of the city and on the steep slopes of the Bala Hissar as throughout Kabul men, women and children finished their evening prayers and sat down to break their fast. For though the Residency still burned and hundreds of men had died that day, the evening meal of Ramadan would still have been prepared; and as the spy Sobhat had predicted, the hungry mob had left the ransacked, blood-soaked shambles that only that morning had been a peaceful compound, to hurry home in droves in order to eat and drink with their families and boast of the deeds they had done that day.

And in the same hour, on the other side of the world, a telegram was being handed in to the Foreign Office in London that read: *All well with the Kabul Embassy.*

At long last Ash sighed and lifted his head, and Anjuli took his ravaged face between her cool palms and bent to kiss him, still without speaking. Only when they were seated side by side on the carpet by the window, her hand in his and her head on his shoulder, did she say quietly: 'He is dead, then.'

'Yes.'

'And the others?'

'They too. They are all dead: and I—I had to stand there and watch them die one by one without being able to do anything to help them. My best friend and close on four score of my own Regiment. And others too—so many others . . .'

Anjuli felt the shudder that racked him and said: 'Do you wish to tell me of it?'

'Not now. Some day perhaps. But not now . . .'

There was a cough outside the door and Gul Baz scratched on the panels requesting permission to enter, and when Anjuli had withdrawn to the inner room he came in bearing lamps and accompanied by two of the household servants. The latter carried trays of cooked food, fruit and glasses of snow-cooled sherbet, and brought a message from their master to say that after the exigencies of the day he thought that his guests would prefer to eat alone that night.

Ash was grateful for the thought, as during Ramadan it was the custom of the house for the men-folk to take the evening meal together, the women doing the same in the Zenana Quarters, and he had not been looking forward to the prospect of being forced to listen to a discussion of the harrowing events of the day; or worse still, having to take part in it. But later on, when the meal was over and Gul Baz came to remove the trays, another servant scratched on the door to ask if Syed Akbar could spare the time to see the Sirdar-Sahib, who greatly desired to speak with him; and though Ash would have excused himself, Gul Baz spoke for him, accepting the invitation and saying that his master would be down shortly.

The servant murmured an acknowledgement and left, and as his footsteps retreated Ash said angrily: 'Who gave you leave to speak for me? You will now go down yourself to the Sirdar-Sahib and make my apologies to him, because I will see no one tonight: no one, do you hear?'

'I hear,' said Gul Baz quietly. 'But you will have to see him, for what he has to say is of great import, so—'

'He can say it tomorrow,' interrupted Ash brusquely. 'Let there be no more talk. You may go.'

'We must all go,' said Gul Baz grimly. 'You and the Memsahib, and myself also. And we must go tonight.'

'We . . . ? What talk is this? I do not understand. Who says so?'

'The whole household,' said Gul Baz, 'the women-folk more loudly than the rest. And because they will put great pressure upon him, the Sirdar-Bahadur may have no remedy but to warn you of it when he sees you tonight. Of that I was sure even before you returned here, for I spoke with certain servants of the Sirdar's friend, Wali Mohammed Khan, with whom he took refuge today when they brought him back to this house. Since then I have listened to much more talk, and learned many things that you as yet do not know. Will you hear them?'

Ash stared at him for a long moment, and then, motioning him to sit, sat down himself on Anjuli's rush stool to listen, while Gul Baz hunkered down on the floor and began to speak. According to Gul Baz, Wali Mohammed Khan had thought along the same lines as the spy Sobhat, and decided that his friend's best chance of leaving the Bala Hissar and reaching his own house in safety lay in going while the mob were engaged in looting the Residency. He had lost no time in arranging it and had, apparently, been only too anxious to get rid of his guest . . .

'Being greatly afraid,' said Gul Baz, 'that once the killing and looting is done, many who took part in that will turn to searching for fugitives, since it is already being said that two sepoys who were caught up in the fighting and unable to get back to their fellows were saved from death by friends among the mob, and are now in hiding in the city—or perchance in the Bala Hissar itself. There is also another sepoy who is known to have gone into the Great Bazaar to buy *atta* before the fight began, and could not return, as well as the three sowars who rode out with the grass-cutters. This the servants of Wali Mohammed Khan told us when they brought our Sirdar back in disguise after the fighting at the Residency Koti was over. And hearing it, the folk in this house also became afraid. They fear that tomorrow the mob will turn to searching for these fugitives and attacking anyone whom they suspect of harbouring them or of being a "Cavagnari-ite". And that the Sirdar-Bahadur's life may be endangered, because he once served with the Guides. Wherefore they have urged him to leave at once for his house in Aoshar, and remain there until this trouble is past. This he has agreed to do, for he was recognized and sorely mishandled this morning.'

'I know. I saw him,' said Ash; 'and I think he does right to go. But why us?'

'His household insist that he must send you and your Memsahib away now—tonight. For they say that if men should come here asking questions and demanding to search the house, they will become suspicious when they find strangers who cannot give a good account of themselves—such as a man who is not of Kabul and who may well be a spy, and a woman who claims to be Turkish. Foreigners . . .'

'Dear God,' whispered Ash. 'Even here!'

Gul Baz shrugged and spread out his hands: 'Sahib, most men and all women can be hard and cruel when their homes and families are threatened. Also the ignorant everywhere are suspicious of strangers or those who in any way differ from themselves.'

'That I have already learned to my cost,' retorted Ash bitterly. 'But I did not think that the Sirdar-Sahib would do this to me.'

'He will not,' said Gul Baz. 'He has said that the laws of hospitality are sacred, and he will not break them. He has shut his ears and refused to listen to the appeals and arguments of his family and his servants.'

'Then why—' began Ash, and stopped. 'Yes. Yes, I see. You did right to tell me. The Sirdar-Sahib has been too good a friend to me and mine to be repaid in this fashion. And his people are right: our presence in this house could endanger them all. I will see him now and tell him that I think it best for us to leave at once . . . for our own safety. No need to let him know that you have told me anything.'

'So I thought,' nodded Gul Baz; and came to his feet: 'I will go now and make arrangements.' He salaamed and withdrew.

Ash heard the door of the inner room open and turned to see Anjuli standing on the threshold.

'You heard,' he said.

It was not a question, but she nodded and came to him, and he rose and took her in his arms, and looking down into her face thought how beautiful she was: more beautiful than ever tonight, for the anxiety and strain that of late he had seen too often in her face had gone, and her candid eyes were serene and unclouded. The lamplight made her skin glow pale gold and the smile on her lovely mouth turned his heart over. He bent his head and kissed it, and after a while he said: 'You are not afraid, Larla?'

'To leave Kabul? How could I be? I shall be with you. It has been Kabul and its citadel that I have been afraid of. And after what has taken place today, you are free to go—and must be happy to do so.'

'Yes,' agreed Ash slowly, '—I had not thought of that . . . I'm free . . . I can go now. But—but what Gul Baz said was true: people everywhere are suspicious of strangers and hostile towards anyone different from themselves, and we two are both strangers, Larla. My people wouldn't accept you because you're both Indian and half-caste, while your people wouldn't accept me because I'm not a Hindu and therefore an outcaste. As for the Mussulmans, to them we are "Unbelievers" . . . Kafirs—'

'I know, my love. Yet many of different faiths have shown us great kindness.'

'Kindness, yes. But they haven't accepted us as one of themselves. Oh dear God, I'm so sick of it all—of intolerance and prejudice and . . . If only there were somewhere we could go where we could just live quietly and be happy, and not be hedged about by rules and trivial, ancient tribal taboos that mustn't be broken. Somewhere where it wouldn't matter who we were or what gods we worshipped or didn't worship, as long as we harmed no one: and were kind, and didn't try to force everyone else into our own mould. There ought to be somewhere like that—somewhere where we can just be ourselves. Where shall we go, Larla?'

'To the valley, where else?' said Anjuli.

'The *valley?*'

'Your mother's valley. The one you used to tell me about, where we were going to build a house and plant fruit trees and keep a goat and a donkey. You cannot have forgotten! I have not.'

'But my Heart, that was only a story. Or . . . or I think it may have been. I used to believe it was true and that my mother knew where it was; but afterwards I wasn't so sure: and now I think it was only a tale . . .'

'What does that matter?' asked Juli. 'We can make it come true. There must be hundreds of lost valleys among the mountains: thousands. Valleys with streams running through them that would grind our corn, and where we could plant fruit trees and keep goats and build a house. We have only to look, that is all—' and for the first time in several weeks she laughed; that rare, enchanting laugh that Ash had not heard since the day the British Mission came to Kabul. But he did not smile in reply. He said slowly: 'That's true, but . . . it would be a hard life. Snow and ice in the winter, and—'

'—and fires of pine-cones and deodar logs, as in all hill villages. Besides, the hill-folk of the Himalayas are a kindly people, soft-spoken, merry, and charitable to all wayfarers. They neither carry arms nor engage in bloodfeuds—or make war upon each other. Nor would we need to live in too much isolation, for what is ten *koss* to a hill-man who can walk twice as much in one day? And none would begrudge us a virgin valley that lay too far beyond their home village for their cattle to graze in or their women to collect fodder from. Our hills are not harsh and barren like these of Afghanistan, or in Bhithor, but green with forests and full of streams.'

'—and wild animals,' said Ash. 'Tiger and leopard—and bears. Do not forget that!'

'At least such animals only kill for food. Not for hate or revenge; or because one bows towards Mecca and another burns incense before the gods. Besides, since when has either of us been safe among men? Your foster-mother fled with you to Gulkote to save you from being slain because you, a child, were an *Angrezi;* and later you both fled again because Janoo-Rani would have killed you—as you and I fled from Bhithor fearing death at the hands of the Diwan's men. And now, though we thought ourselves safe in this house we must leave it in haste because our presence here endangers everyone in it and if we stay we may all be slain—you and I for being "foreigners" and the others for having harboured us. No, Heart's-dearest, I would rather the wild animals. We shall never lack money, for we have the jewels that were part of my *istri-dhan,* and these we can always sell little by little; a stone at a time as need arises. So let us look for that valley and build our own world.'

Ash was silent for a space, and then he said softly: 'Our own Kingdom, where all strangers shall be welcome . . . Why not? We could go north, towards Chitral—which will be safer at this time than trying to cross the Border and get back into British India. And from there through Kashmir and Jummu towards the Dur Khaima . . .'

The leaden weight of despair that had fallen on him since he realized that Wally was dead, and that had grown heavier and colder with every word that Gul Baz had spoken, was suddenly lightened, and a measure of the youth and hope that he had lost that day returned to him. Anjuli saw the colour come back to his haggard face and his eyes brighten, and felt his arms tighten about her. He kissed her hard and fiercely, and sweeping her off her feet, carried her into the inner room and sat down on the low bed, holding her close and speaking with his lips buried in her hair . . .

'Once, many years ago, your father's *Mir Akor,* Koda Dad Khan, said something to me that I have never forgotten. I had been complaining that because I was tied to this land by affection and to *Belait* by blood, I must always be two people in one skin; and he replied that one day I might discover in myself a third person—one who was neither Ashok nor Pelham-Sahib, but someone whole and complete: myself. If he was right, then it is time that I found that third person. For Pelham-Sahib is dead: he died today with his friend and the men of his Regiment whom he could not help. As for Ashok and the spy Syed Akbar, those two died many weeks ago— very early one morning on a raft on the Kabul River, near Michni . . . Let us forget all three, and find in their stead a man with an undivided heart: your husband, Larla.'

'What are names to me?' whispered Anjuli, her arms tight about his neck. 'I will go where you go and live where you live, and pray that the gods will permit me to die before you die, because without you I cannot live. Yet can you be sure that if you turn your back upon your former life you will have no regrets?'

Ash said slowly: 'I don't believe that anyone can have no regrets . . . Perhaps there are times when even God regrets that He created such a thing as man. But one can put them away and not dwell upon them; and I'll have you, Larla . . . that alone is enough happiness for any man.'

He kissed her long and lovingly, and then with increasing passion; and after that they did not say anything for a long time, and when at last he spoke again it was to say that he must go down and see the Sirdar at once.

The news that his guests had decided that they were no longer safe in Kabul, but must leave immediately, was more than welcome to the harassed master of the house. But Nakshband Khan was far too polite to betray the fact, and though he agreed that if the mob were to embark on a house-to-house hunt for fugitives or suspected 'Cavagnari-ites' they might all find themselves in grave danger, he had insisted that as far as he was concerned, if they wished to stay they were welcome to do so and he would do all he could to protect them. Finding them set on leaving, he had offered to give them any help they might need, and had, in addition, given Ash much good advice.

'I too shall leave the city tonight,' confessed the Sirdar. 'For until the temper of the mob has cooled, Kabul is no place for one who is known to have served the Sirkar. But I shall not set out until an hour after midnight, by which time all men are asleep—even thieves and cut-throats, who more than any have been too busy today to stay awake this night. I would advise you to do the same, because the moon will not rise until an hour later, and though my road is a short one and easy to follow even on a dark night, yours will not be; and once you are clear of the city you will have need of the moonlight. Where do you go?'

'We go to find our Kingdom, Sirdar-Sahib. Our own Dur Khaima —our far pavilions.'

'Your . . . ?'

The Sirdar looked so bewildered that Ash's mouth twitched in the shadow of a smile as he said: 'Let me say, rather, that we hope to find it. We go in search of some place where we may live and work in peace, and where men do not kill or persecute each other for sport or at the bidding of Governments—or because others do not think or speak or pray as they do, or have skins of a different colour. I do not know if there is such a place, or, if we find it, whether it will prove too hard to live there, building our own house and growing our own food and raising and teaching our children. Yet others without number have done so in the past. Countless others, since the day that our

First Parents were expelled from Eden. And what others have done, we can do.'

Nakshband Khan expressed neither surprise nor disapproval. Where a European would have expostulated he merely nodded, and on hearing that Ash's goal was a valley in the Himalayas, agreed that his best plan would be to follow the caravan route to Chitral and from there across the passes into Kashmir. 'But you cannot take your own horses,' said the Sirdar. 'They are not bred for hill work. Also they would attract too much notice. I will give you my four Mongolian ponies in their stead—you will need a spare one. They are small, ill-looking beasts compared with yours, but as strong and hardy as yaks and as sure-footed as mountain goats. You will also need poshteens and Gilgit boots, for as you go further north the nights will become cold.'

He had refused to take any payment for his hospitality, saying that the difference in value between Ash's three horses and the sturdy, rough-coated ponies would more than repay him for all. 'And now you must sleep,' said the Sirdar, 'because you have far to ride if you wish to put a safe distance between yourselves and Kabul before the sun rises. I will send a servant to wake you at the half-hour after midnight.'

This advice too seemed good, and Ash returned to Juli and told her to take what rest she could, as they would not be leaving the house until one o'clock. He had also spoken to Gul Baz, explaining what he intended to do and asking him to tell Zarin when he returned to Mardan.

'Our ways part here,' said Ash. 'I have, as you know, made provision for you, and the pension will be paid until you die. That is assured. But no money can repay your care of me and of my wife. For that I can only give you my thanks and my gratitude. I will not forget you.'

'Nor I you, Sahib,' said Gul Baz. 'And were it not that I have a wife and children in Hoti Mardan, and many relatives in the Yusufzai country, I would come with you to look for your kingdom—and maybe live there also. But as it is, I cannot. Nevertheless, we do not part tonight; this is no time for such as the Memsahib to travel through Afghanistan with only one sword to protect her. Two are better and therefore I will go with you as far as Kashmir, and having set you on your way, return from there to Mardan by way of the Murree road to Rawalpindi.'

Ash had not argued with him, for apart from the fact that he knew it would be a waste of breath, Gul Baz would be of invaluable help, particularly on the first part of the journey. They talked together for a little while longer before Ash joined his wife in the small inner room, where presently both had fallen asleep, worn out by the terrible strain of that long, agonizing day, and, on Anjuli's part, relieved beyond measure at the prospect of quitting the violent, blood-stained city of Kabul to set out at last for the familiar scenes of her childhood. Those vast forests of fir and deodar, chestnut and rhododendron, where the air smelled sweetly of pine-needles, wild Himalayan roses and maiden-hair fern, and one could hear the sough of the wind in the tree-tops and the sound of running water, and see, high and far away, the serene rampart of the snows and the white wonder of the Dur Khaima.

Thinking of these things she had fallen asleep, happier than she had been for very many days; and Ash too had slept soundly, and woken refreshed.

He left the house half-an-hour earlier than his wife and Gul Baz, for he had an errand to perform that did not call for the presence of any other person. Not even Juli's. He said goodbye to the Sirdar and went away on foot, armed only with the revolver that he carried carefully hidden from sight.

The streets were empty except for the rats that scurried along the gutters and a few lean, prowling cats, and Ash met no one: not even a night watchman. All Kabul seemed to be asleep—and behind barred shutters, for though the night was warm it was noticeable that few if any citizens had cared to leave a single window open, and every house had the appearance of a fortress. Only the gates of the citadel still stood wide and unguarded, the sentries who had been on duty when the Ardal Regiment mutinied having left their posts to join in the attack on the Residency and not returned, and when later ones had followed their example, no one, in the aftermath of the massacre, had thought to post fresh sentries or order the gates to be closed.

There was a lurid glow in the sky above the Bala Hissar, but the houses there, like those in the city, were barred and shuttered; and in darkness—save only for a few lamps in the palace, where the sleepless Amir consulted with his ministers, and the Residency compound where the Mess House still burned with a red glare that rose and fell and flared up again, giving the staring faces of the dead a curious illusion of being alive and aware.

The compound was as silent and deserted as the streets had been, and here too nothing moved except the night wind and the wavering shadows, while the only sound was the steady purr and crackle of the flames, and from somewhere beyond the wall of the citadel, a night-bird crying.

The victorious Afghans had been so occupied with ransacking the buildings and mutilating the bodies of their enemies, that sunset had come upon them before they were aware of it and they had not had time to remove all their own dead. There were still a large number of these lying around the stables and near the entrance to the compound, and it was not too easy to differentiate between them and those jawans who having been Mohammedans, and in many cases Pathans, wore similar clothing. But Wally had been in uniform, and even by that lurid, flickering light it had been easy to pick him out.

He was lying face downward near the gun that he had hoped to capture, his broken sword still in his hand and his head turned a little sideways as though he were asleep. A tall, coltish, brown-haired young man who had celebrated his twenty-third birthday just over two weeks ago . . .

He had been terribly wounded, but unlike William, whose hacked and almost unrecognizable body lay a few yards away, he had not been mutilated after death, and Ash could only suppose that even his enemies had admired the boy's courage and spared him that customary degradation as a tribute to one who had fought a good fight.

Kneeling beside him, Ash turned him over very gently.

Wally's eyes were closed, and *rigor mortis* had not yet stiffened his long body. His face was begrimed by smoke and black powder and smeared with blood and the furrows of sweat, but apart from a shallow cut on the forehead it was unmarked by wounds. And he was smiling . . .

Ash smoothed back the dusty, ruffled hair with a gentle hand, and laying him down, stood up and walked over to the barracks, picking his way between the huddled dead and through the gaping archway.

There was a cistern in the courtyard, and having found it he removed his waist-cloth, tore a strip from it and soaking it in the water, went back to Wally to wash away the blood and grime as gently and carefully as though he were afraid that a rough touch might disturb him. When the young, smiling face was clean again, he brushed the dust from the crumpled tunic, set the sword belt straight above the swathed crimson of the Guides' waist-cloth, and hooked up the open collar.

There was nothing he could do to disguise the gaping swordcuts or the dark, clotted stains that surrounded them. But then they were honourable wounds. When he had set all straight, he took Wally's cold hand in his, and sitting beside him, talked to him as though he were still alive: telling him that what he had done would not be forgotten as long as men remembered the Guides, and that he could sleep quietly, for he had earned his rest—and gone to it as he wished to go, leading his men in battle. Telling him that he, Ash, would remember him always and that if he had a son he would call him Walter '—though I always said it was a terrible name, didn't I, Wally? Never mind, if he turns out half as well as you, we shall have every reason to be proud of him.'

He talked too of Juli and the new world they were going to build for themselves—the kingdom where strangers would not be regarded with suspicion and no door would ever be locked against them. And of that future that Wally would have no part in, except as an unfading memory of youth and laughter and unquenchable courage. 'We had a lot of good times together, didn't we?' said Ash. 'It's good to remember that . . .'

He had taken no account of the passing time and had no idea of how quickly it had gone. He had come to the Residency with the intention of burning or burying Wally's body so that it would not be left to rot in the sun or be torn and disfigured by kites and carrion crows, but now he realized that he could not do this; the ground was too hard for him to dig a grave in it single-handed and the Residency was still burning far too fiercely to make it feasible for him to carry Wally's body into it without being badly burned himself—or possibly overcome by heat and smoke.

Besides, if the body were to disappear, rumours might spread that the Lieutenant-Sahib had not been killed after all but had recovered sufficiently to escape from the compound during the night, and must be hiding somewhere; which would certainly ensure a house-to-house search, and the possible death of a number of innocent people. Anyway, Wally would not know or care what happened to his body now that he had discarded it.

Ash laid down the quiet hand, and getting to his feet, stooped and lifted Wally from the ground, and carrying him to the gun, laid him on it, placing him carefully so that he should not fall. He had led three charges in an effort to take that gun, so it was only right that it should provide him with a bier on which he could lie in state; and when he was found there, those who came would only think that one of their number had placed him there for the same reason that he had been spared mutilation—in recognition of gallantry.

'Goodbye, old fellow,' said Ash quietly. 'Sleep well!'

He lifted his hand in a gesture of farewell, and it was only as he turned away that he noticed that the stars had begun to pale, and knew that the moon must be rising. He had not realized that so much time had passed since he came into the compound to look for Wally, or that he had stayed far longer than he intended. Juli and Gul Baz would be waiting for him, and wondering if he had come to any harm; and Juli would think—

Ash began to run, and reaching the shadows of the houses around the Arsenal, fled through the network of narrow alleyways and streets to where the Shah Shahie Gate, still unguarded, gaped on a view of the valley and hills of Kabul lying grey in the waning starlight and the first rays of the rising moon.

Anjuli and Gul Baz had been waiting for him in the shelter of a clump of trees by the roadside. But though they had waited there for more than an hour in a growing fever of fear and anxiety, they asked no questions; for which Ash was more grateful than for anything else that either of them could have done for him.

He could not kiss Juli because she was wearing a bourka, but he put his arms about her and held her close for a brief moment, before turning aside to change quickly into the clothes that Gul Baz had ready for him. It would not do to travel as a scribe, and when he mounted one of the ponies a few minutes later he was to all outward appearances an Afridi, complete with rifle, bandolier and tulwar, and the wicked razor-edged knife that is carried by all men of Afghanistan.

'I am ready,' said Ash, 'let us go. We have a long way to travel before dawn, and I can smell the morning.'

They rode out together from the shadows of the trees, leaving the Bala Hissar and the glowing torch of the burning Residency behind them, and spurred away across the flat lands towards the mountains . . .

And it may even be that they found their Kingdom.

Achkan tight-fitting three-quarter-
length coat
'Afsos!' 'Sorrow!'; 'How sad!'
Angrezi English; Englishman
Angrezi-log English people
Ayah child's nurse

Baba baby; young child
Baba-log children
Badshahi royal
Bai brother
Barat friends of the bridegroom
Begum Mohammedan lady
Belait England
Beshak without doubt
Beta son
'Be-wakufi!' 'Stupidity'; 'Nonsense!'
Bheesti water-carrier
Bhoosa straw
Bibi-gurh women's house
Bourka one-piece head-to-heels
cloak, with small square of
coarse net to see through
Boxwallah European trader
Budmarsh rascal; bad man
Burra khana big dinner-party
Burra-Sahib great man; top man

Cha-cha uncle
Charpoy bed (usually string or
webbing)
Chatti large earthenware water-pot
Chik sun-blind made of split cane
Chirag small earthenware oil lamp,
used in festivals
Chokra boy
Chota hazri literally, small break-
fast (early morning tea with
fruit)
Chowkidar night watchman
Chuddah sheet; shawl
Chunam polished plaster; lime

Chuppatti flat cake of unleavened
bread
Chuppli heavy leather sandal with
studs on sole, worn on the
Frontier
Chutti leave

Dacoits robbers
Daffadar sergeant (cavalry)
Dai nurse; midwife
Dâk mail; post
Dâk-bungalow posting-house; rest-
house
Dâk-ghari horse-drawn vehicle
carrying mail
Dal lentils
Dawaza door; gate
'Dekho!' 'Look!'
Dhobi washer of clothes; laundry-
man
Dhooli palanquin
Durbar public audience; levee

Ekka light two-wheeled trap

Fakir religious mendicant
Feringhi foreigner
Fu-fu band village band of Indian
instruments

Gadi throne
Ghari any horse-drawn vehicle
Ghari-wallah driver of the above
Ghazi religious fanatic
Ghee clarified butter
Godown storage room or shed
Gur unrefined cane sugar
Gurral mountain goat
Gurrh-burrh tumult; noise

Hakim doctor
Halwa sweetmeats
Havildar sergeant (infantry)

Hazrat Highness

Hookah water pipe for smoking tobacco

Howdah seat carried on back of elephant

Hukum order

Huzoor Your Honour

Istri-dhan inheritance

Itr scent

Izzat honour

Jawan literally, young man; used for soldier

Jehad holy war

Jehanum hell

Jellabies fried sweets made of honey and batter

Jemadar junior Indian officer promoted from the ranks (cavalry or infantry)

Jezail long-barrelled musket

Jheel shallow, marshy lake

Jung-i-lat Sahib Commander-in-Chief

Kala black

Khansamah cook

Khidmatgar waiter at table

Kila fort

Kismet fate

Koss two miles

Kus-kus tatties thick curtains made of woven roots

Larla darling

Lathi long, heavy stick, usually made from bamboo

Lotah small brass water-pot

Machan platform built in a tree for hunting big game

Mahal palace

Mahout elephant driver

Mali gardener

Malik tribal headman

'Maro!' 'Strike!'; 'Kill!'

'Mubarik!' 'Congratulations!'; 'Well done!'

Mullah Mohammedan priest

Munshi teacher; writer

Narwar coarse webbing

Nauker servant

Nauker-log servants

Nautch-girl dancing girl

Nullah ravine or dry watercourse

Ooloo owl

Padishah Empress

Pan betel-nut rolled in a bay leaf and chewed

Panchayat council of five elders

Patarkar small firework

Piara (-i) dear

Pice small coin

Pujah worship

Pulton infantry regiment

Punkah length of matting or heavy material pulled by a rope to make a breeze

Purdah seclusion of women (literally, curtain)

Pushtu the language of the Pathans

Raja King

Rajkumar Prince

Rajkumari Princess

Rakhri pendant worn on the forehead

Rang colour

Rani Queen

Resai quilt

Resaidar junior Indian officer promoted from the ranks (cavalry)

Risaldar senior Indian officer promoted from the ranks (cavalry)

Risaldar-Major the most senior Indian officer promoted from the ranks (cavalry)
Rissala cavalry (regiment)

Sadhu holy man
Sahiba lady
Sahib-log 'white folk'
Saht-bai 'seven brothers'—small brown birds which go about in groups, usually of seven
Sepoy infantry soldier
Serai caravan hostel
'Shabash!' 'Well done!'
Shadi wedding
Shaitan devil
Shamianah large tent
Shikar hunting and shooting
Shikari hunter, finder of game
Shulwa sleeved tunic
Sikunder Dulkhan Alexander the Great

Sirdar Indian officer of high rank
Sirkar the Indian Government
Sowar cavalry trooper
Syce groom

Tálash inquiry
Tamarsha show; festival
Tar telegram (literally, wire)
Tehsildar village headman
Tiffin lunch
Tonga two-wheeled horse-drawn vehicle
Tulwar curved sword

Yakdan leather trunk, made to be carried on mules
Yuveraj heir to the throne

Zenana women's quarter
Zid resentment
Zulum aggression